THE *NEW* BASEBALL READER

THE *NEW* BASEBALL READER

More Favorites from THE FIRESIDE BOOKS OF BASEBALL

Edited by
Charles Einstein

Viking

VIKING
Published by the Penguin Group
Viking Penguin, a division of Penguin Books USA Inc., 375 Hudson Street, New York, New York 10014, U.S.A.
Penguin Books Ltd, 27 Wrights Lane, London W8 5TZ, England
Penguin Books Australia Ltd, Ringwood, Victoria, Australia
Penguin Books Canada Ltd, 2801 John Street, Markham, Ontario, Canada L3R 1B4
Penguin Books (N.Z.) Ltd, 182–190 Wairau Road, Auckland 10, New Zealand

Penguin Books Ltd, Registered Offices: Harmondsworth, Middlesex, England

First published in 1991 by Viking Penguin, a division of Penguin Books USA Inc.

1 3 5 7 9 10 8 6 4 2

Copyright © Charles Einstein, 1991 All rights reserved

LIBRARY OF CONGRESS CATALOGING IN PUBLICATION DATA
The new baseball reader: more favorites from the Fireside books of
baseball/edited by Charles Einstein.
p. cm.
Collection of articles, essays, and excerpts from works on baseball.
ISBN 0-670-83504-8
1. Baseball. 2. Baseball—Stories. I. Einstein, Charles.
II. Fireside book of baseball.
GV873.N49 1991
796.357—dc20 90-50515

Printed in the United States of America
Set in New Aster Designed by C. Linda Dingler

Grateful acknowledgment is made for permission to reprint the following copyrighted works:

Excerpt from "Baseball and Writing" from *The Collected Poems of Marianne Moore*. Copyright © 1961 by Mari-
anne Moore. Reprinted by permission of Viking Penguin, a division of Penguin Books USA Inc. "The Silver-
Colored Yesterday" by Nelson Algren. Reprinted from *The Saturday Evening Post* © 1951. "A Letter to Mrs.
Gilligan" from *The Hot Stove League* by Lee Allen. Copyright 1951. Reprinted by permission of Oak Tree Publi-
cations, Inc. "A Killing" by Roger Angell. Reprinted by permission; © 1946, 1974 Roger Angell. Originally in *The
New Yorker*. "Casey in the Box" by Meyer Berger, *The New York Times*. Copyright © 1941 by The New York Times
Company. Reprinted by permission. "Pete Rose Breaks Cobb's Record" by Ira Berkow, *The New York Times*.
Copyright © 1985 by The New York Times Company. Reprinted by permission. Excerpt from *Ball Four* by Jim
Bouton edited by Leonard Shecter. Reprinted with permission of Macmillan Publishing Company. Copyright
© 1970, 1981, 1990 by Jim Bouton. "1908: Chicago Cubs 4, New York Giants 2" by Mordecai Brown as told to
Jack Ryan, *The Chicago Daily News*. Reprinted by permission of Knight-Ridder Newspapers. Excerpt from *It's
Good to Be Alive* by Roy Campanella. Copyright © 1959 by Roy Campanella. By permission of Little, Brown and
Company. "Two-Top Gruskin" from *Try and Stop Me* by Bennett Cerf. Copyright 1944 by Bennett Cerf, renewed
© 1971 by Mrs. Bennett Cerf, Christopher Cerf and Jonathan Cerf. Reprinted by permission of Simon & Schus-
ter, Inc. "New York Yankees 4, Kansas City Royals 3 (or 5)" by Murray Chass, *The New York Times*. Copyright ©
1983 by The New York Times Company. Reprinted by permission. From a Letter to E. J. Lanigan by Ty Cobb.
Courtesy Baseball Hall of Fame, Cooperstown, N.Y. "The Left-Handed Genius: Best Pitcher in Baseball" from
Babe: The Legend Comes to Life by Robert W. Creamer. Copyright © 1974 by Robert W. Creamer. Reprinted by
permission of Simon & Schuster, Inc. "Cleveland Indians 8, Brooklyn Dodgers 1" by Harry Cross, *The New York
Times*. Copyright © 1920 by The New York Times Company. Reprinted by permission. "Mr. Dooley on Baseball"
reprinted with permission of Charles Scribner's Sons, an imprint of Macmillan Publishing Company, from *Mr.
Dooley on Making a Will and Other Necessary Evils* by Finley Peter Dunne. Copyright 1919 Charles Scribner's
Sons; copyright renewed 1947 by David Leonard Dunne & Finley Peter Dunne, Jr. From *A Dictionary of Con-
temporary American Usage* by Bergen Evans and Cornelia Evans. By permission of Random House, Inc. "In the
Eye of the Storm" by Ron Fimrite. Reprinted courtesy of *Sports Illustrated* from the January 6, 1986 issue.
Copyright © 1986, Time, Inc. All Rights Reserved. "Cobb Would Have Caught It" from *In the Rose of Time* by
Robert Fitzgerald. Copyright 1943 by Robert Fitzgerald. Reprinted by permission of New Directions Publish-
ing Corporation. "The Base Stealer" by Robert Francis. Copyright ©1948 by Robert Francis. Reprinted from
The Orb Weaver by permission of University Press of New England. Excerpt from *The Redheaded Outfield* by
Zane Grey. Copyright 1920 Grosset & Dunlop. Renewed 1948 Lina Elise Grey. "Couplet" from *Fathers Playing
Catch with Sons* by Donald Hall, copyright © 1985 by Donald Hall. Published by North Point Press and
reprinted by permission. "How to Pitch to Ted Williams" by Pat Harmon. Reprinted with permission of *The*

Page 460 constitutes an extension of this copyright page.

Contents

Introduction

IT WAS ROGER KAHN who said that old baseball writers elevate complaining to a saga. As one of them, I have to suppose he was right. The press box has long been haven to a certain irascibility, and maybe a sample of it can serve a useful purpose here.

The episode foremost in my mind took place on an evening more than a generation ago when Frank Finch, who covered the Dodgers for the *Los Angeles Times* when they first moved west, arrived at the ball park with the game already in progress. Accordingly, he took his seat, opened his scorebook, turned to the colleague beside him, and invoked the time-honored mantra of the Baseball Writers' Association of America: "Catch me up."

The fellow writer nodded and commenced a routine recitation of the play-by-play up to that moment, with Finch recording the appropriate symbols in his book to cover the action he had missed.

The recapitulation was proceeding apace. "Parker struck out swinging," the man was saying. "Fairly flew to right. And put a star next to that one: The guy made a hell of a catch."

Finch fixed him with a cool gaze. "I'll be the judge of that," he said.

Do those words contain a warning? If so, it is one that I think few anthologists, least of all the collector of baseball literature, ought to ignore.

This book is, after all, the lineal descendant of *The Baseball Reader,* which was published in 1980 and which, consisting mainly as it did of some 60 selections from the first three *Fireside Books of Baseball,* whose publishing history dated back to 1956, could thus assert a bloodline of its own.

It wasn't a pedigree that went overlooked. "A book that will surely take its place alongside the great Fireside series," one reviewer declared. "Brings together the best of the three great books," wrote another. "The best of the best," said a third.

In the heady aura of reviews like those, the readiest benison could have been to say what the fellow said to Frank Finch—"Put a star next to that one"—and let it go at that.

But then one remembers Finch's response. What went quite unnoticed here were two things, the first of which may be most aptly summarized by Mike Shannon in his 1989 book *Diamond Classics*, printed by McFarland and Company and subtitled "Essays on 100 of the Best Baseball Books Ever Published."

We'll have the fun of meeting Shannon as a poet here within the pages of *The New Baseball Reader*, but he also functions as the editor of *Spitball*, the literary baseball magazine. And as one of the game's leading bibliophiles, he thinks the golden age of baseball writing is now.

Shannon indeed refers to the 1968 publication of *The Third Fireside Book of Baseball* as "a harbinger of the proliferation of excellent baseball books," which he sees as testimony to what he calls "baseball's apparent inexhaustibility as a source and inspiration for authors and publishers who aspire to create great books."

In this he is hardly alone. Paul Fisher wrote that a passion for statistics was the hallmark of a literate people, and surely of all undertakings baseball has the vastest statistical library (augmented nowadays by databanks and satellite downlinks that vest even the daily won-and-lost standing of the teams with the gravity of the Dead Sea Scrolls).

It sets in early, too. "Baseball," Philip Roth has written, "was the literature of my boyhood," and it was the poet Marianne Moore, of all people, who took Roth to the next step:

> Fanaticism? No. Writing is exciting
> and baseball is like writing.
> You can never tell with either
> how it will go
> or what you will do.

And who, pray, took Marianne to the next step? The late commissioner Bart Giamatti, that's who, in his own book *Take Time for Paradise*, published posthumously in the wake of his untimely death in 1989. "Serendipity is the essence of both games, the writing one and baseball," he wrote. "But is not baseball more than *like* writing? Is not baseball a form of writing? Is that not why so many writers love baseball?"

One response to these questions was furnished by Allen Barra in *The New York Times Book Review*. "No," he wrote, "baseball is *not* a form of writing, and not only is it *not* necessary to understand the Greek concept of sport in order to appreciate baseball, it might be the lack of interest in trying to make such connections that makes baseball so American to begin with."

The battle lines were drawn. Next up was Russell Baker, *The New York Times* columnist, reporting early in 1990 on a conversation he'd had with his small son. "All writers nowadays are supposed to love baseball more than they love Henry James and know more baseball than Casey Stengel," he told the boy.

The youngster's reaction was nothing if not direct: "Who's Casey Stengel?"

"It breaks your heart," Bart Giamatti had written some 13 years earlier, while he was still president of Yale. "It is designed to break your heart. The game begins in the spring, when everything else begins again, and it blossoms in the summer, filling the afternoons and evenings, and then as soon as the chill rains come, it stops and leaves you to face the fall alone."

Interesting: "Baseball is quite good enough without sentimentalizing it," George Will told Larry King in a television interview. Yet in purest refutation of this view, we find not only a Giamatti but, as the last piece in this anthology can only attest, Will himself, reminding us that "the musical 'crack' " of wood on ball "is the sound the cosmos makes each spring when it clears its throat and says, 'We made it.' "

Is there a middle ground? Probably. "Baseball, like good design, is made up of a thousand challenges, decisions and minute strategies," Roger Angell has written. "A little sentiment is not amiss, either, as long as it doesn't rule the enterprise."

What does rule the enterprise, for whatever reason, has been great writing by great writers, and, as Shannon notes, a good deal of it is recent stuff. A generation has passed since publication of *The Third Fireside Book of Baseball* (which, with its two predecessors, has long since gone out of print), but in that time a panoply of baseball literature, none of whose authors had appeared in any of the first three Fireside books—among them Roth, Donald Hall, Garrison Keillor, William Kennedy, James Michener, Chaim Potok, Mordecai Richler—had surfaced. A fourth book in the Fireside series, published in the mid-1980s, included these and brought the aggregate for the four books, published over a span of 31 years, to more than 400 text pieces totaling well in excess of a million words.

So much for the vitality and pure pleasure of today's baseball writing and the part a book like this can play in wanting to preserve it. But there was another silent factor at work here, because baseball is no respecter of time. Just as there is no clock on the game, there is no statute of limitations on its literature, and it needs to be said here that when *The Baseball Reader* appeared in 1980, its roster of 60 text pieces from the first three Fireside books was actually culled from an original list nearly twice as large.

Talk about Frank Finch and his "I'll be the judge of that": the reaction I got, beneath the sheen of the glowing reviews, was something else. Here I was in quixotic possession of a stockpile of some 50 leftover selections from the first three books, any of which could have made it into *The Baseball Reader* but didn't. I found myself looking down the barrel of half a hundred accusatory fingers: "What about Bernard Malamud and *The Natural*?" . . . "John Lardner on Bobo Newsom?" . . . "The day George Plimpton tried to pitch?" . . . "The unassisted triple play in the 1920 World Series?" . . . "The girl who shot the first baseman?" . . . "The *Baseball Joe* chapter?" . . . "That first box score?" . . .

To all such inquiries, my answer was purest Finch. I would be the judge of that, I said. What else could I say?

If that is the question—*What else could I say?*—then I hope *The New Baseball Reader* can be an answer. For within the covers of this book are all of those pieces that all of those people kept asking about from those first three *Fireside* books, together with more recent entries from the fourth volume, so that, taken as a whole, the contents bridge more than 120 years of baseball writing, from Henry Chadwick in 1869 to Fay Vincent in 1990.

The reader will find Chadwick toward the beginning of the book, Vincent toward the end, in accordance with the traditional Fireside format of presenting authors, regardless of category, in alphabetical order. The Vincent piece, incidentally, is the only one in the book that did not appear in one or another of the Fireside books, for the simplest reason that it is too recent to have done so. But I thought it belonged, and—Finch again—I'll be the judge of that.

Or will I? In the end, only the reader will judge the larger idea at work here. More than anything, I guess it has to deal with continuity. Maybe I can personify it in terms of my immigrant grandfather, who took my father to his first baseball game in 1910 and chose a point late in the action to announce that he was a magician. In 1932 my father took me to my first game and made the same announcement. "When I say stand up," he told me, "everybody here will stand up." In a quiet voice he told the people to stand up, and they did. Then in an even softer voice, he told them to sit down, and they did that too. In 1957 I took my oldest son to his first game and executed that same small miracle for him. In 1986 he took his first son to his first game and did the same.

So this book is for anyone with a memory and a field of dreams. Is it the recent, woven of George Brett's "game-losing" home run or Pete Rose beating Cobb's record or Bill Buckner's immemorial flub of Mookie's grounder? Is it the unexpected, as seen in the celebrated writing talent of the vice president of Nicaragua? Or is it most of all for the small boy who says "Who's Casey Stengel?" Because you can turn to Damon Runyon's story, and together—father and son, grandfather and grandson—recreate the legend, which of course is nothing other than truth itself, that this is how old Casey ran, running his home run home. . . .

Charles Einstein

THE *NEW* BASEBALL READER

THERE ARE many viewpoints that deal with the infamous Chicago Black Sox scandal. Here is one. There can be none more vivid. Mr. Algren's piece was done in 1951.

The Silver-Colored Yesterday

NELSON ALGREN

ALL THAT LONG AGO August day the sun lay like shellac on the streets, but toward evening a weary small breeze wandered out of some saloon or other, toured Cottage Grove idly awhile, then turned, aimlessly as ever, west down Seventy-first.

The year was 1919, Shoeless Joe Jackson was outhitting Ty Cobb, God was in his Heaven, Carl Wanderer was still a war hero, John Dillinger was an Indiana farm boy and the cops were looking cautiously, in all the wrong corners, for Terrible Tommy O'Connor.

And every Saturday evening the kid called Nephew and I hauled a little red wagon load of something called the *Saturday Evening Blade,* a rag if there ever was one, down Cottage Grove to the wrought-iron Oakwoods Cemetery gate. There to hawk it past the long-moldering graves of Confederate prisoners who had died at Camp Douglas in some long-ago wrought-iron war.

When we sold out we'd just hang around the gate waiting for Nephew's Uncle Johnson to break out of the saloon directly across the way. The bartender ran us off if we came near the doors without the ironclad alibi of having a fight to watch, and Uncle J. was the white hope of that corner.

If no brawl developed of itself the barflies were certain to arrange something for poor Johnson, an oversized spastic with a puss like a forsaken moose, whose sole idea in battle was to keep his hands in front of his eyes. Some white hope.

Uncle's whole trouble, Nephew confided in me as half-owner of the little red wagon, was that he had gone to work too young.

Some uncle. We used to hear him hymning at the bar—

> Oh he walks wit' me
> 'N he talks wit' me—

and the barflies encouraging him mockingly.

He was deeply religious, and the barflies encouraged him in everything—drinking, hymning or fighting, fornication or prayer. As though there were something wondrously comical about everything Uncle attempted.

I remember that poor hatless holy Johnson yet, lurching upon some unsaved little tough with a face shadowed by a cap and a lit cigarette on his lip—the cigarette bobbles and Uncle reels back, blood from his nose coming into his mouth. The Cap yanks him forward, feints his hands down off his eyes and raps him a smashing banneger in the teeth. "It's a case of a good little man whippin' a good big man, that's all," Nephew advised me confidentially, holding our little red wagon behind him. Then the soft shuffle-shuffle of The Cap's shoes imitating the White City professionals.

"Finish the clown off," Nephew encourages The Cap softly. That's the kind of family it was.

Uncle had never learned to fall down. He'd reel, lurch, bleed, bellow and bawl until the bartender would break the thing up at last, wiping Uncle's ashen face with a bar towel in the arc lamp's ashen light. Till the others came crowding with congratulations right out of the bottle, pouring both into Uncle right there on the street. Then a spot of color would touch his cheeks and he'd break out into that terrible lament—" 'N he tells me I am his own"—to show us all he'd won again. Uncle had some such spiritual triumph every Saturday night.

I used to hang openmouthed around that sort of thing, coming away at last feeling nothing save some sort of citywide sorrow. Like something had finally gone terribly wrong between the cross atop St. Columbanus and that wrought-iron gate, out of an old wrought-iron war, forever guarding the doubly-dead behind us.

No one could tell me just what.

The wisest thing to do was simply to go beer-cork hunting behind the saloon. With the city spreading all about. Like some great diseased toadstool under a sheltering, widespread sky. Then to haul our little red wagon slowly home, with Nephew humming all to himself, "Be my little bay-bee bum-bul bee, buzz buzz buzz."

Maybe the whole town went to work too young.

For it's still a Godforsaken spastic, a cerebral-palsy natural among cities, clutching at the unbalanced air: top-heavy, bleeding and blind. Under a toadstool-colored sky.

Maybe we all went to work too young.

• • •

Yet that was a time of several treasures: one sun-bright-yellow beer cork with a blood-red owl engraved upon it, a Louisville slugger bat autographed by Swede Risberg, and a Comiskey Park program from one hot and magic Sunday afternoon when Nephew and I hid under the cool bleachers for three hours before game time. To come out blinking at last into the roaring stands, with the striped sun on them. And Eddie Cicotte shutting out Carl Mays.

The morning we moved from the far Southside to North Troy Street I had all three treasures on me. And Troy Street led, like all Northside streets—and alleys too—directly to the alien bleachers of Wrigley Field.

"Who's yer fayvrut player?" the sports in baseball caps waiting in front of the house had to know before I could pass. I put the horn of the Edison victrola I was carrying down on the sidewalk at my feet before replying. It didn't sound like something asked lightly.

But the suddenly far-distant White Sox had had a competent sort of athlete at short and I considered myself something of a prospect in that position too. "Swede Risberg," I answered confidently, leaning on the Louisville slugger with the autograph turned too casually toward the local loyalty board.

I didn't look like such a hot prospect to North Troy Street, I could tell that much right there and then. "It got to be a National Leaguer," the chairman advised me quietly. So that's how the wind was blowing.

I spent three days leaning on that autograph, watching the other sprouts play ball. They didn't even use American League bats. "Charley Hollocher then," I finally capitulated, naming the finest fielding shortstop in the National League, "account I t'row righty too."

"Hollocher belongs to Knifey," I was informed—but I could fight Knifey for him. I had the right.

I wouldn't have fought Knifey's baby sister for Grover Cleveland Alexander and Bill Killefer thrown in. And could only think nostalgically of the good simple life of the far Southside, where kids had names like "Nephew" and "Cousin," and where a man's place among men could be established by the number of *Saturday Evening Blades* he sold. I went through the entire roster of National League shortshops before finding one unclaimed by anyone else on Troy Street—

Ivan Olson, an ex-American Leaguer coming to the end of his career with the team then known as the Brooklyn Robins.

But Olson was taking a lot of booing from the Flatbush crowd that season because he had a habit of protesting a called third strike by throwing his bat in the air—and every time he did it an umpire would pick it up and toss it higher. No eleven-year-old wants to be on the side of any player who isn't a hero to the stands. "If I *got* to pick a Swede—" I stood up to The Committee at last—"I'll stick to Risberg—I seen him play once is why."

Well, you could say your old man was a millionaire if that was your mood and nobody would bother to make you take it back. You might even hint that you knew more about girls than you were telling and still get by. But there wasn't one of those Troy Street wonders who'd yet seen his "fayvrut player" actually play. You had to back that sort of statement up. I pulled out the Comiskey Park program hurriedly.

They handed it around in a circle, hand to grubby hand, examining the penciled score for fraud. When it came back to my own hand I was in.

In without selling out: I'd kept the faith with The Swede.

The reason I never got to play anything but right field the rest of that summer I attribute to National League politics pure and simple.

Right field was a coal-shed roof with an American League sun suspended directly overhead. A height from which I regarded with quiet scorn the worshipers of false gods hitting scratchy little National League bloopers far below. There wasn't one honest-to-God American League line drive all summer.

It wasn't till a single sunless morning of early Indian summer that all my own gods proved me false: Risberg, Cicotte, Jackson, Weaver, Felsch, Gandil, Lefty Williams and a utility infielder whose name escapes me—wasn't it McMillen? The Black Sox were the Reds of that October and mine was the guilt of association.

And the charge was conspiracy.

Benedict Arnolds! Betrayers of American boyhood, not to mention American Girlhood and American Womanhood and American Hoodhood. Every bleacher has-been, newspaper mediocrity and pulpit inanity seized the chance to regain his lost pride at the expense of seven of the finest athletes who ever hit into a double play. And now stood stripped to the bleacher winds in the very sight of Comiskey and God.

I was the eighth. I climbed down from right field to find The Committee waiting.

"Let's see that score card again."

I brought it forth, yellow now with a summer of sun and honest sweat, but still legible. When it came back this time I was only allowed to touch one corner, where a grubby finger indicated the date in July of 1920. Risberg had sold out in the preceding September and I was coming around Troy Street almost a year later pretending I believed Risberg to be an honest man. I'd gone out to the ball park, seen him play in person and was now insisting I'd seen nothing wrong, nothing wrong at all. The moving finger stopped on Risberg's sorrowful name: four times at bat without a hit, caught sleeping off second, and a wild peg to first. And I still pretended I hadn't suspected a *thing!*

"I wasn't there when he *really* thrun the game," I tried to hedge. "It was a different day when he played bum on purpose."

The Tobey of *that* committee was a sprout who had a paying thing going, for weekdays, in the resale of colored paper-picture strips of major-league players. He bought them ten for a penny and resold them to us for two, making himself as high as a dollar a week, of which fifty cents went to his Sunday-school collection plate. I'd once seen his lips moving at the plate, praying for a hit. "What do *you* think he was doin' tossin' wild to first?" this one wanted to know now.

"I figure he was excited. It was a real close play."

"You mean for your all-time All-American fayvrut player you pick a guy who gets excited on close ones?"

"I didn't know it was for all time" was all I could think to reply. "I thought it was just for this year."

"What kind of American *are* you anyhow?" he wanted to know. He had me. I didn't know what kind I was.

"No wonder you're always in right field where nothin' ever comes—nobody could trust you in center." He was really cutting me up, this crusader.

"Well, I asked for Hollocher in the first place," I recalled.

"You could still fight Knifey for him."

"I'll just take Ivan Olson."

"That's not the question."

"What *is* the question?"

"The question is who was the guy, he knock down two perfec' pegs to the plate in a World Series game, one wit' the hand 'n one wit' the glove?"

"Cicotte done *that.*"

" 'N who was Cicotte's roommate?"

Too late I saw where the trap lay: Risberg. I was dead.

"We all make mistakes, fellas," I broke at last. "We all goof off, we're all human—it's what *I* done. I goofed off too—it just goes to show you guys I'm human too. I ain't mad at you guys, you're all good guys, don't be mad at *me.*" Choked with guilt and penitence, crawling on all fours like a Hollywood matinee idol, I pleaded to be allowed, with all my grievous faults, to go along with the gang. "Can I still have Olson, fellas? Can I keep my job if I bum-rap some people for you?"

Out of the welter of accusations, half-denials and sudden silences a single fact drifted down: that Shoeless Joe Jackson couldn't play bad baseball even if he were trying to. He hit .375 that series and played errorless ball, doing everything a major-leaguer could to win. Nearing sixty today, he could probably still outhit anything now wearing a National League uniform.

Only, I hadn't picked Shoeless Joe. I'd picked the man who, with Eddie Cicotte, bore the heaviest burden of all our dirty Southside guilt. The Black Sox had played scapegoat for Rothstein and I'd played the goat for The Swede.

So I wound up that melancholy season grateful to own the fast-fading Olson. When he went back to Rochester or somewhere they started calling me "Olson" too. Meaning I ought to go back to Rochester too. I took that. But when they began calling me "Svenska" that was too much. I fought.

And got the prettiest trimming you'd ever care to see. Senator Tobey himself administered it, to ringing applause, his Sunday-school change jingling righteously with his footwork. Leaving me at last with two chipped teeth, an orchid-colored shiner and no heart left, even for right field, for days.

However do senators get so close to God? How is it that front-office men never conspire? That matinee idols feel such guilt? Or that winners never pitch in a bill toward the price of their victory?

I traded off the Risberg bat, so languid had I become, for a softball model autographed only by Klee Brothers, who were giving such bats away with every suit of boy's clothing bought on the second floor. And flipped the program from that hot and magic Sunday when Cicotte was shutting out everybody forever, and a triumphant righthander's wind had blown all the score cards across home plate, into the Troy Street gutter.

I guess that was one way of learning what Hustlertown, sooner or later, teaches all its sandlot sprouts. "Everybody's out for The Buck. Even big-leaguers."

Even Swede Risberg.

HISTORY

THE LATE Lee Allen may have been without peer when it came to collecting and cataloguing the minutiae of the national pastime. Here's a sample, from his book *The Hot Stove League*. It was published in the 1950s, a bit too early for Allen to have collected the wit and wisdom of Yogi Berra. But how about the pitching poet, or the Hotel Episode in Rockford, Ill.?

A Letter to Mrs. Gilligan

LEE ALLEN

ALTHOUGH BRANCH RICKEY, the learned chief executive of the Pittsburgh Pirates, has a deserved reputation for manipulating the English language to suit his purposes, it is doubtful that he will ever achieve the heights of rhetoric reached by James (Orator Jim) O'Rourke, the player who caught an entire game for the New York Giants at the age of fifty-two in 1904. O'Rourke was one of the first clubhouse lawyers, and his command of the English tongue was astonishing and bizarre.

When an outfielder named Louis Sockalexis, a Penobscot Indian, signed a contract containing a clause that forbade drinking, O'Rourke read about it, then turned to a friend and said, "I see that Sockalexis must forgo frescoing his tonsils with the cardinal brush; it is so nominated in the contract of the aborigine."

On another occasion, when Orator Jim was a manager, one of his players, John Peters, asked for a ten-dollar advance. "I am sorry," O'Rourke replied sympathetically, "but the exigencies of the occasion and the condition of our exchequer will not permit anything of the sort at this period of our existence. Subsequent developments in the field of finance may remove the present gloom and we may emerge into a condition where we may see fit to reply in the affirmative to your exceedingly modest request." Understandably, Peters did not try again.

The most remarkable document attesting to O'Rourke's powers appeared in the New York *Sporting Times*, a short-lived journal of the trade, in its issue of November 23, 1890. It seems that a widow named Gilligan who lived in Bridgeport, the Orator's home town, heard a disturbance in the barn where she kept a calf. Not knowing that the intruder was a lion which had just escaped from Barnum's winter headquarters, she rushed into the fray with a pitchfork, routing the beast. The newspapers then made her a sensation. O'Rourke, reading about her feat and overcome with admiration, wrote her as follows:

DEAR MRS. GILLIGAN:

The unparalleled bravery shown by you, and the unwavering fidelity extended by you to your calf during your precarious environment in the cowshed, when a ferocious, carnivorous beast threatened your total destruction, has suddenly exalted your fair name to an altitude much higher than the Egyptian pyramids, where hieroglyphics and other undecipherable mementos of the past are now lying in a state of innocuous desuetude, with no enlightened modern scholar able to exemplify their disentangled pronunciation. The exuberance of my verbosity is as natural as the chrysanthemums exhibited at the late horticultural exhibition, so in reality it cannot be called ostentation, even though the sesquipedalian passages may seen unintelligible to an untutored personality. The lion—or it may have been a lioness—but you, of course, in the impending predicament could only make a cursory and rather unsatisfactory investigation—must have discerned your courageous eye (a trait so characteristic of the Celtic Micks and Biddys), which shows, beyond peradventure, that you are possessed of undeniable hypnotical mesmerization qualities, as well as the diabolical intricacies of legerdemain and therapeutics. We should arise, Phoenix-like, and show our appreciation of your unswerving loyalty. We should extol your bravery to the coming generation in words more lofty than my unprepared efforts can faithfully depict, for your name hereafter will be synonymous with fearlessness in all that the word can unconsciously imply. Standing before a wild, unrestrained pitcher with a mellifluous and unconquerable courageousness is as of nothing compared with the indomitable fortitude exhibited by you when destruction seemed inevitable—when pandemonium rent the oxygenic atmosphere asunder with the tragic vociferation of Barnum's untamed and inhospitable intruder. A thousand blessings to you!

Yours admiringly,
James O'Rourke

Take it away, Mr. Rickey!

Ballplayers differ widely in temperament but are more apt to be laconic than verbose, and there are few O'Rourkes in the profession. Two of the quietest performers of all time were Clyde Barnhart, an outfielder, and Charles (Whitey) Glazner, a pitcher, who roomed together at Pittsburgh from 1920 to 1923. Barnhart never talked at all and Glazner was hard of hearing. One night Johnny Morrison, a pitcher whose name still bobs up in Hot Stove League circles because of his amazing curve ball, visited their room. Only once during his stay was there any attempt at conversation at all. Barnhart opened his mouth to ask the time, but the question was never answered because Whitey failed to hear him.

Charlie Gehringer, the great second baseman of the Tigers, and Elon Hogsett, an Indian pitcher at Detroit, formed another taciturn pair. Like Barnhart and Glazner they roomed together. One morning Hal Walker, a writer for the Toronto *Globe* and *Mail,* had breakfast with them. Hogsett turned to Gehringer and said, "Pass the salt, please." Gehringer obliged, but said in reproach, "You might have pointed."

The stupidity of certain players was acknowledged long before Ring Lardner painted his classic pictures of bushers, alibi artists, boneheads and bores. Pete Browning, a favorite in Louisville and one of the greatest hitters of the 1880s, is supposed to have said, upon hearing of the assassination of James A. Garfield, "Yeah? What league was he in?"

Lardner's creations, by the way, were not at all exaggerated. He is believed to have received the inspiration for one of his more pleasant characters, the busher, after watching Butcher Boy Joe Benz pitch an exhibition game for the White Sox while wearing hip boots. But just as the automobile has helped destroy baseball interest in some sections of the country it has helped destroy provincialism, and the rookie that Lardner knew so well, the kid with his badger haircut and straw suitcase, has disappeared from the scene. The cultural level of players has been raised greatly in the past thirty years. Today's businessman-ballplayer is at ease before the television cameras and in the dining rooms of the snootiest hotels. He buys stocks and bonds and sends his children to private schools. There are still a few who confine their reading to comic books and box scores but their number is decreasing, and it will be a sad day for the game when they disappear entirely because they supply the few splotches of color in the fabric of a game that sometimes approaches the monotony of near-perfection.

Almost every anecdote about the illiteracy of players dates back to the period before World War I when Lardner was using his genius to describe the genus. Shoeless Joe Jackson, greatest of natural hitters and one of the unfortunates who became involved in the Black Sox scandal of 1919, had little or no education and the fact that he could not spell was known to the galleries. Once, after Joe had delivered a resounding triple and was perched on third base, a fan shouted from the grandstand, "Heh, Joe. Spell 'cat.'" Jackson glared at him, squirted a stream of tobacco juice out the side of his mouth and retorted, "Spell 'hit.'"

But long before Jackson certain players were celebrated for their lack of formal learning. William (Blondie) Purcell, a pitcher and outfielder, was a popular member of the first Phillies team in the National League in 1883. One night he was invited to a party at the home of an affluent admirer and arrived late. "Why, hello there, Blondie," his hostess greeted him. "Do come right in; we're having tableaux." "I know," Blondie replied. "I smelt 'em when I come in."

Connie Mack, who witnessed players of every variety in his unparalleled career, once conducted a clubhouse meeting in which he carefully went over the batting weaknesses of every opposing player. After he finished, a rookie rose to his feet and said, "Mr. Mack, there's one fellow you forgot; this man Totals. I looked at the box score and seen that he got four hits yesterday."

Quite similar is the story, probably apocryphal, about the National League outfielder who could neither read nor write. Each morning he used to sit in the hotel lobby and have other players read the box score to him. One morning he listened patiently while a mate read the box score of one game in its entirety, even the summary, and concluded by saying, "Time of game, one fifty-three. Umpires, Messrs. Klem and Emslie." Hearing this, the rookie jumped to his feet, shouting, "Don't tell me that Messrs. is in this league! He umpired in the Southern League last year and he was terrible!"

But perhaps the most ridiculous of all these stories is the one involving Heinie Zimmerman, who played second and third for the Cubs and Giants from 1907 through 1919. Zim, so the story goes, was limbering up at third one day in Chicago during batting practice. A boy who worked on the pass gate approached him and said, "Heinie, there's a guy out there from Rockford, Illinois, named Kelly who wants you to leave a pass for him."

"Never heard of him," Heinie grunted. "The hell with him."

But in a few minutes the boy was back. "Heinie, this guy says you will remember him all right. Name's Kelly, from Rockford."

"Look," Heinie insisted. "I don't know any Kelly from Rockford. Now, go away."

When the boy returned the third time, he was almost in tears. "Please, Heinie," he begged. "Help me out. This guy swears he knows you. He said for me to ask you about that hotel episode in Rockford."

"Now I know he's a four-flusher," Zim sneered. "I know Rockford like a book and there ain't no Hotel Episode there."

There is apparently no connection between formal education and success on the diamond, although native intelligence is a great asset. But Moe Berg, the most erudite player the game has ever seen, had a batting average that persisted at the .250 level. Berg is a graduate of Princeton, the Columbia Law School and Sorbonne. He speaks English, Latin, Greek, French, Italian, German, Spanish, some Russian, Japanese, Hebrew and Sanskrit. His thesis on Sanskrit is a valuable work of reference at the Library of Congress.

But when Moe was catching for Washington, the player on the team he most admired was Dave Harris, a hard-hitting outfielder whose schooling had stopped somewhere in the vicinity of the seventh grade. "There's a fellow who really had the pitchers licked," Berg once told Shirley Povich of *The Washington Post*. "He wasn't burdened with too much imagination; he'd just step up there and take a beautiful cut. He used to rib me about my own batting average and say

I was too smart to be a good hitter. He may have been right because I liked to try to guess with the pitcher. Once Harris hit a home run and I followed him to the plate. 'Moe, you go on and try your best,' he told me, 'but don't forget, none of them seven languages you know is gonna help you.' "

The best players, educated or otherwise, seem to be those who concentrate completely on the job at hand and who believe absolutely that they can control the outcome of the game. They take baseball seriously and do not exhibit such indifference as was shown by Frank Woodward, a pitcher on the Phillies in 1918. A writer once stopped in the Phillies' clubhouse and asked Woodward, "Who's going to work today?" Frank, who was scheduled to pitch that day, replied, "Who's gonna work? Me and the outfielders."

Woodward may have been an irresponsible kid but he was not lacking in imagination. Two years after leaving the Phillies he found himself a member of the Cardinals in training at Brownsville, Texas. One evening he wanted to go to the movies but did not have the price of admission. After thinking over his problem at some length, he finally strolled down to the theater, sought out the manager and said, "I was sent here by Branch Rickey. Mr. Rickey has called a meeting of the players and he wants all those who are here at the movies to go back to the hotel right away."

This information was immediately flashed on the screen, and the players filed out. Watching the proceedings from under a tree across the street, Woodward waited until a decent interval had passed, then walked back to the theater and said to the ticket-taker, "Meeting's over. Now to watch the rest of the picture."

There is no way you can safely generalize about the personalities of players. They can be as verbose as Jim O'Rourke, as quiet as Charlie Gehringer, as ignorant as the Lardner prototype or as erudite as Moe Berg. There are players from the mountains of Tennessee and West Virginia who are as suspicious as moonshiners. There are the college boys with the crew haircuts who collect swing records. There are the Oklahomans, bronzed by the sun, who look older than their years. Club owners have long claimed that baseball, absorbing all these men, is a great social leveler, that it is democracy in action. The claim is not without merit. Charlie Devens was a pitcher who joined the Yankees in 1932. He had attended Groton and Harvard, where he had been a member of the Hasty Pudding Club. His mother was a Vanderbilt. But when he reported to the big stadium across the Harlem, he found that his new team's greatest star, Babe Ruth, was an alumnus of a different institution, a graduate of the St. Mary's Industrial School, a semireform school at Baltimore, Class of '14.

Rookies are supposed to be brash and confident. When Billy Gleason, a young second baseman on the 1921 Browns, was asked the distance between home plate and second base, he quipped, "I don't know. I never ran that way." Such answers are given to cover up any insecurity the player might feel.

Ernie Sulik certainly did not indicate that he felt insecure when he reported to the Phillies as a young outfielder in 1936. In his first game he was called upon to face Dizzy Dean, who was then at the height of his pitching fame with the Cardinals. In his first time at bat Sulik looked at three blistering strikes, tossed his bat away and muttered, "That guy ain't shown me much." When his fellows on the bench looked at him in amazement, he confided, "Just watch me when I go to bat again; I'll hit that ball between the outfielders." Strange to say, that is exactly what he did, splashing a triple into right center. "How is it you looked at those three strikes the first time up?" Ernie was asked after the game. "I wanted to see what Dean had," he explained. "That's how I knew he didn't have anything."

One of the few players who ever achieved more than average success despite the lack of confidence was Emerson (Pink) Hawley, a pitcher from Beaver Dam, Wisconsin, who won 182 major league games in a decade starting in 1892. Hawley was in constant need of reassurance. One day, when he was pitching for St. Louis, he called time and motioned to his catcher, Heinie Peitz, to join him in a conference. "Heinie," he said. "Do you like to catch me?" Peitz was so astonished he had to grope for words, and when he was finally able to mumble that there was nothing he would rather do than catch Pink Hawley, the pitcher seemed reassured and went back to the job of throwing at the hitters.

Charles (Chief) Zimmer was a National League catcher who owned a cigar store and one day, in the dead of winter, Hawley strolled in, walked up to Zimmer and said, "Chief, will you forgive me?" "Certainly," replied the Chief, not having the slightest notion of what Pink was talking about, as the two players, in years of acquaintance, had never had cross words.

Early during the following season Zimmer came up to bat in a game against Hawley, who was leading in the late innings, 12 to 0, and just toying with the opposition. "Chief, what's your batting average?" Hawley asked.

"Oh, about .214 I guess," Zimmer admitted.

"Well, boost it a little," Pink said, and when the next pitch was down the middle Zimmer connected for a home run and his team's only score.

Ballplayers simply do not follow any pattern of personality. It is even possible to find some who are genuinely modest. Eddie Moore, for instance. Eddie was an infielder with the Pirates, and during the season of 1924 a Pittsburgh paper hired him to write his daily impressions of the games. He refused to use a ghost. One day, after winning a 3 to 2 contest by delivering a late-inning home run, Moore did not refer to the feat or even mention his name in the copy. On the other hand, shortly after the Phillies had released a pitcher named Pete Sivess to Milwaukee, a Philadelphia baseball writer received a wire that read, "Please send Milwaukee papers full sketch of Pete Sivess and send pictures." The message was signed by Pete Sivess.

There are even players with a romantic streak. Ed Kenna was a pitcher with the Athletics in 1902. The son of John E. Kenna, a United States Senator from Virginia, he attended West Virginia University and became a hero of sorts when he kicked three field goals in a football game against Grove City. He was a fair pitcher, but his heart really was not in the game, for his principal interest in life was in poetry. They called him the "Pitching Poet" and he could be found scribbling verses in the clubhouse before and after games. Here is a sample of his wares taken from his published book of verse, *Lyrics of the Hills,* written while he was employed to pitch at Wheeling, West Virginia:

> Fall time in the country, when the
>   Sunshine filters down
> The tangled maze of cloudland
>   And through the beeches brown;
> In the golden rays it scatters
>   On the dear, old dirty sod
> I can trace in wondrous letters
>   The mystic word of God
> And the goodness of the master,
>   Who willed that it should be—

Oh, the olden, golden autumn
    Is the best of times for me.

Play ball!

FICTION

ROGER ANGELL's baseball reporting for *The New Yorker,* collected and published in book form every five years beginning with *The Summer Game* in 1972, brought a fresh touch of grace and imagery to the literature of the game. But fully a quarter of a century earlier, Angell was already writing about baseball, in a way that had nothing—and everything—to do with what goes on inside the foul lines. Here is a short story of his from the 1940s.

A Killing

ROGER ANGELL

THE YOUNG MAN with steel-rimmed glasses walked into the dark hall of the apartment house and let the door close behind him. In a moment the clicking of the lock release stopped and he heard a door being opened two flights above him. A shrill feminine voice called down, "Who's that?" He stood still and said nothing. "Who's down there?" the voice cried, more insistently. Let her call, he thought. It was what Mr. Penney had said was one of the First Points of Approach. In a walkup you rang an upstairs bell but you didn't go up. No housewife would listen to you if you made her wait while you climbed two or three flights and her expecting God knows who—the ice-man, perhaps, or the delicatessen or maybe even a boy friend. A salesman would just make her sore. Silently he put down his big case and listened to his breathing in the hall until he heard the upstairs door close. When his eyes became accustomed to the darkness, he carried his case over to a door on his right. He took off his hat and smoothed down his pale hair. He felt in his right overcoat pocket for the box containing the matched English military hairbrushes ("Our quickest seller and a fine opening line," Mr. Penney had said), but he didn't take it out. You didn't show what you had to sell at the door, but you had it handy. First establish your personality, then your merchandise. He felt for his discharge button on his overcoat lapel and made sure it was right side up. That was his own best First Point of Approach. He bent over and read the smudged typewritten card beside the door: "Foltz." Mrs. Foltz. All set. He pressed the doorbell.

Smiling, not touching the door frame, he waited for almost thirty seconds. He was about to press the bell again when the door was thrown open by a woman. She wore a faded pink housecoat that bulged at the seams, and her plump face was powdered dead white. Her bleached hair was pinned in tight curls against her head. Without curiosity she leaned against the door jamb and looked at him with pale little eyes.

"Mrs. Foltz," he began hastily, "Mrs. Foltz, I trust I'm not disturbing you. I would consider myself an intruder if I were not convinced that I am here to help you. I am here because I know that you, like every American housewife, are interested in the latest and the best in modern accessories to ease work and strain in your home. My concern also is anxious to get your reaction to our line of personal accessories for the entire household. We have hairbrushes for your husband and children as well as the finest in hair and nail brushes for feminine allure." He paused for a moment. The woman hadn't moved or spoken; she was still staring at him dully, or rather at the top of his head. Damn! It was all wrong. He should have mentioned brushes right away. Maybe she was a dummy or something.

"What is it?" she said abruptly. "What have you got?"

"Brushes," he said loudly. "Brushes, Madam." He fingered the box in his pocket and wondered whether he should begin again.

Just then there was a hoarse cry from inside the apartment. "Who's 'at? Who's you pal out there?"

Mrs. Foltz suddenly bent from the waist in a loud giggle of laughter. She straightened up, her hand over her mouth, and giggled louder. "My God!" she gasped. "My good, sweet God!" She turned from the open door and walked back into the apartment. She was still laughing. "It's the brush man," she whispered loudly. "The Fuller Brush man."

"Well, go ahead," the voice inside the apartment said. "Don't just stand there. Ask him in, give 'm a drink. I gotta see a Fuller Brush man. Don't let him stand out there in the cold hall with his brushes. Bring him in here."

Mrs. Foltz came back to the door, dabbing at her eyes with a tiny handkerchief. "C'mon in," she said, still giggling faintly. "Come in and sit down."

The young man picked up his case hastily and followed her into the apartment. This was a break, he thought, after a bad start. All the good sales were made inside; in the hall you didn't have a chance. He put his hat down on a chair inside the door and carried his case into the room. The place was small, and the air was thick with smoke and the smell of whisky. Although it was still afternoon, the shades on the two windows had been drawn and a bridge lamp in the corner was lit. A woman was sitting on a small, flowered couch between the windows, and before her was a small table crowded with two whisky bottles, a pitcher of water, an overflowing ash tray, and a huge glass bowl, almost an urn, half-filled with potato chips. There were ashes and bits of potato chips on the floor. The woman was sitting carefully erect in one corner of the couch, a glass in her hand. Her wrinkled purple dress was pulled up over her knees and she wore a black velvet hat slightly askew. She looked about forty.

"This is Mrs. Kernochan," said Mrs. Foltz. "We were having a little drink here. Honey, this is the brush man."

"Sit down," said Mrs. Kernochan hoarsely. "Sit down there where I can see you. Take off your coat, Mr. Fuller."

"No, thank you," he said, smiling. He put his case down and sat uncomfortably in a little wooden chair under the bridge lamp. "I'll just keep it on, thanks."

"Lily, give Mr. Fuller a drink," said Mrs. Kernochan, squinting her eyes at him across the room.

"I am," said Mrs. Foltz. She poured some whisky into a glass. "You like it neat or with water?"

"I don't think—"

"Oh, go ahead, go ahead," Mrs. Kernochan said. "We won't snitch on you, Mr. Fuller."

"All right, then," he said. "A small one with water."

"We haven't got no ice," said Mrs. Foltz. She walked over and handed him his drink. "We just ran out."

"So you're Mr. Fuller," Mrs. Kernochan said. "The original one and only. My God! Imagine you right here in the same room with me. How's business, Mr. Fuller?"

The young man smiled and glanced at Mrs. Foltz. "Well, you see, Madam," he said quickly, "I don't represent the Fuller people. They have their line and we have *ours*. Now, I don't like to knock a competitor, so I'll just say that we think we have about as fine an assortment of merchandise as you can find in the field. Now, if you'll let me show you . . ." He put his drink on the floor and knelt down to open his case.

"The original one and only," repeated Mrs. Kernochan, peering at him.

"Honey, didn't you hear him?" asked Mrs. Foltz as she sat down on the other end of the couch. "He's not Mr. Fuller. He don't even work for them. He's Mr. . . ."

"Mr. Schumacher," the young man said, from the floor. He had his case open and was arranging brushes on the floor. "Mr. Linwood P. Schumacher." He looked up and smiled at Mrs. Foltz. "Now, Madam," he began, "here you see our complete line. A brush for every imaginable need. You will notice that they are ornamental as well as useful. The modern plastic bristles are—"

"Prince Hal!" cried Mrs. Kernochan from the couch. "My Prince Hal!" Mr. Schumacher started and almost upset his drink.

"Old Prince Hal," she repeated loudly. "Ah, you were the boy. Always in trouble. Always men on the bases. But how you could bear down! Prince Hal and King Carl! What a pair! You two and Fat Freddie. Those were the days, huh, Hal?"

Mr. Schumacher looked around wildly. For a moment he seemed ready to bolt from the room. Then he saw that Mrs. Foltz was shaking with laughter.

"Ballplayers!" she gasped. "She always talks ballplayers when she gets like this. Ballplayers or babies. Today it's ballplayers. She thinks you're Hal Schumacher now. My God! Prince Hal!" She rocked back and forth on the couch, dabbing at her eyes.

"Hubbell, Schumacher, and Fitzsimmons," Mrs. Kernochan intoned, looking now at her glass. "Fitz on Saturday and you and Carl on the double-headers. Those were the days, huh? Remember 1933? Remember 1936, Schumie?"

"I'm afraid there's a misunderstanding," said Mr. Schumacher nervously. Still on his knees, he rummaged in his pocket for a card. "I'm Linwood P. Schumacher. No relation to the ballplayer, I'm afraid." He smiled up at Mrs. Foltz, but she was still laughing too hard to see him. "Prince Hal!" she repeated, almost speechless. "Always in trouble."

"You look different, Hal," said Mrs. Kernochan anxiously. She was squinting across the room at him again. "You look thinner. How's the soupbone, Schumie?"

"Well," he said slowly, "I did lose some weight in the army, but it's coming back now."

"We've missed you, Hal," Mrs. Kernochan said, nodding her head. She downed her drink and unsteadily set the glass on the table. "We've all missed you. I remember when they said you were washed up. And what happened to the Giants then, Hal? What happened then? Who did they get? I'll tell you who. Mungo, that's who." She almost spat the name out. "Van Lingle Mungo. Just a refugee from Brooklyn."

She was silent, vaguely watching him as he began to put the brushes back in his case. Suddenly she groped on the couch beside her and found a pocketbook. Clutching it, she stood up, showering more pieces of potato chips on the floor.

"I'll take them," she said, looking into her purse. He could see the tears squeezing out of her eyes. "I'll take your dear, sweet brushes, Hal—every last one of them. You don't have to get on your knees, Schumie." She found some wadded bills and held them out to him blindly.

He had risen to his feet and stood in the middle of the room, looking from the money to Mrs. Foltz. Mrs. Foltz had stopped laughing. Now she laboriously stood up and walked over to the weeping Mrs. Kernochan.

"Now, wait a minute, Gloria," she said warningly. "This isn't Hal Schumacher and you know it. Hal Schumacher's up at the Polo Grounds with the Giants right now. And you don't need no brushes. Hal Schumacher isn't selling no brushes."

"Don't you do it!" cried Mrs. Kernochan. "Don't you stop me! Schumie was nothing in your life, Lily Foltz, but he'll always be my Prince Hal. And now look at him, with his brushes, the poor lamb!" She burst into a flood of tears, got up, pushed past Mrs. Foltz, and pressed the money into Mr. Schumacher's hand. "Take it, Hal," she sobbed. "Take it and have that chipped elbow operated on."

Mr. Schumacher looked over her shoulder at Mrs. Foltz. She looked at the weeping woman for a minute, then shrugged and turned back to the couch. "O.K.," she said. "Maybe it'll shut her up."

Hastily, Mr. Shumacher sat down on the chair and pulled out his account book. On the printed slip he checked off the names of the brushes and added the figures up. He looked at the money in his hand and felt in his pocket for change. "There you are," he said, cheerfully.

"Exactly twenty-seven fifty for the entire line." Then he ripped the receipt off, carried the case to the couch, and took out the brushes in handfuls. They made quite a pile beside Mrs. Foltz. He handed her the receipt and the change. "I'll just give it to you to hold, Mrs. Foltz," he said, talking fast. "Two dollars and a half makes thirty. And thank *you!*"

"O.K.," said Mrs. Foltz. She stood up and walked out behind him. At the door he stopped and looked back, but Mrs. Kernochan had collapsed onto the little wooden chair and was sobbing quietly.

"I'm sure she'll find it useful," he said to Mrs. Foltz as he put on his hat. "We don't often sell the complete line to one person, but I'm sure she'll be satisfied. Of course, I don't usually sell my samples, but with a big order like this at the end of the day I made an exception, just for your friend. Now with—"

"O.K., O.K.," said Mrs. Foltz quickly. "Just beat it now, Prince Hal, that's a good boy."

He went out and slammed the door behind him.

• • •

In the hall he put down his empty ornament case—without the brushes it was very light—and lit a cigarette. Twenty-seven fifty! It was a killing, nothing less. Already he knew that Mr. Penney would mention it at the next sales meeting. Perhaps he might even be called on to give a little talk about it. As he picked up his case and started down the hall, he decided that it wouldn't do to tell about the liquor and the ballplayers. They might not understand. But no matter how you looked at it, it was a killing. "The initial resistance was high," he would say, "but once I got admittance and set up the display . . ." He began to whistle as he opened the outside door.

LITIGATION

BEGINNING with the 1976 season, certain established major leaguers could play out that year without signing a contract, then deal elsewhere for their services for the next year. It was a part of the revolution in free agency, and twenty-four players—five of them with the Oakland A's—opted for that course. Figuring that so long as he was going to lose them he might as well get something for them, A's owner Charles O. Finley traded two of them—Reggie Jackson and Ken Holtzman—to Baltimore just before the 1976 season started. Then in mid-June he sold three more stars—outfielder Joe Rudi and pitcher Rollie Fingers to the Boston Red Sox for $2 million and pitcher Vida Blue to the New York Yankees for $1.5 million.

That's what he thought. However, no player sale in baseball can be final until the commissioner says so. Commissioner Bowie Kuhn decided the Rudi/Fingers/Blue transactions would be bad for the game, and that was that.

That's what he thought. Finley sued him, claiming among other things that Kuhn had acted in restraint of trade. Legal sales had taken place between consenting parties, each of whom was to receive something of value, in the greatest tradition of this nation and the free enterprise system. By and large, the public, loudly led by the sporting press, agreed with Finley and forecast his victory in the trial that lay ahead.

That's what they thought. There was no trial—not on the main issues, anyway. Having read all the documents, including the one you are about to read, which was the crusher, Federal Judge Frank McGarr in Chicago simply threw the case out, concurring that among other things Finley was one of the club owners who specifically had hired Kuhn to do exactly what he did here in the exercise of his authority as commissioner.

Some months later, Judge McGarr did hold a trial, this one limited to seeing whether Kuhn had properly exercised the cosmetics of that authority—given all parties a chance to be heard, served due notice, that sort of thing. Kuhn, of course, won that one too.

As you read this, incidentally, you will get as good—and as enjoyable—an account of baseball's historical exemption from the antitrust laws as can be found anywhere. And you may find yourself shaking your head and wondering how anybody could have supposed Finley had a chance of winning.

Motion to Dismiss

BAKER, McTURNAN, BLEAKLEY, NATHAN ET AL.

IN THE UNITED STATES DISTRICT COURT

FOR THE NORTHERN DISTRICT OF ILLINOIS,

EASTERN DIVISION

CHARLES O. FINLEY & CO. INC., an Illinois Corporation *Plaintiff*, v. BOWIE K. KUHN, *et al.*, *Defendants*.	No. 76 C 2358

MEMORANDUM IN SUPPORT OF
MOTION OF DEFENDANT
BOWIE K. KUHN FOR SUMMARY JUDGMENT

BY THIS LAWSUIT, plaintiff, owner of the Oakland A's major league baseball club, seeks to have this Court reverse the discretionary decision of the Commissioner of Baseball disapproving plaintiff's proposed transfer of three ball players in mid-season to competing teams. Notwithstanding a blunderbuss 38 page complaint—raising charges ranging from the Commissioner's alleged violations of the United States Constitution to purported antitrust conspiracy against plaintiff involving the Commissioner and every other major league club—the critical material facts underlying this suit are undisputed and, we submit, entitle the Commissioner to summary judgment as a matter of law.

Plaintiff's complaint should be dismissed in its entirety with prejudice as a matter of law for the following reasons:

1. Plaintiff, as well as each of the other major league club owners, has entered into a lawful agreement "to be bound by the decisions of the Commissioner" as to all baseball disputes and controversies, including such matters as player transfers, and to "waive such rights of recourse to the courts as would otherwise have existed. . . ." Recognizing that the national pastime of baseball could not function if internal disputes and their resolution by the Commissioner were to become embroiled in protracted litigation—no more than if every ball and strike call by an umpire were appealable to higher authorities—the major league club owners have voluntarily, knowingly and with good reason agreed that the decisions of the Commissioner shall be final and unreviewable in a court of law, and have lawfully deprived themselves of recourse to this forum. Accordingly, this suit must be summarily dismissed for lack of subject matter jurisdiction.
2. Even if this Court were to assume jurisdiction, it would be required, based on the indisputable facts of record and the law of this jurisdiction for almost half a century,* to uphold the Commissioner's decision because:
   (a) The Commissioner's authority to approve or disapprove player transfers in accordance with the best interests of baseball is clearly delegated to him by the Major League Agreement and the Major League Rules promulgated thereunder;
   (b) The Commissioner acted after providing all interested parties with a fair and transcribed hearing, in which plaintiff participated without protest or objection; and
   (c) The Commissioner's written decision articulates the reasonable basis for his conclusion that the proposed $3.5 million sale of three mainstays of plaintiff's championship team in mid-season to plaintiff's wealthy competitors would not be in the best interests of baseball, thereby negating any possible claim that the decision is arbitrary or capricious.
3. Plaintiff's antitrust claim is untenable since the United States Su-

* *Milwaukee American Association* v. *Landis,* 49 F. 2d 298 (N.D. Ill. 1931).

preme Court has ruled in an unbroken line of precedents—reaffirmed as recently as 1972—that professional baseball is not subject to the antitrust laws. *Flood* v. *Kuhn*, 407 U.S. 258 (1972); *Toolson* v. *New York Yankees, Inc.*, 346 U.S. 356 (1953); and *Federal Baseball Club of Baltimore* v. *National League*, 259 U.S. 200 (1922).

4. And finally, plaintiff's claim that the Commissioner of Baseball, a private citizen responsible for overseeing the internal affairs of a private association, violated the due process and equal protection clauses of the Fifth and Fourteenth Amendments to the United States Constitution is patently without merit since the decision by the Commissioner to disapprove player transfers does not in any conceivable fashion constitute "state action."

In light of these fully dispositive legal grounds, the Commissioner of Baseball respectfully urges this Court to dismiss this action forthwith. Despite the multiple counts and theories in which plaintiff purports to cast its complaint, this case comes down to no more than a disagreement by one major league club owner with a judgmental decision rendered by the Commissioner in a matter expressly and exclusively delegated by plaintiff and all of the other major league club owners to the Commissioner's discretion. Put simply, the plaintiff disputes the "call" and improperly seeks to have this Court review and substitute its judgment for that of the Commissioner as to whether these proposed player transfers would be in the "best interests of baseball."

In addition to the standard reasons supporting the efficacy of summary judgment—including the conservation of judicial time and energy and the savings of substantial litigation costs by all parties—there is an overriding public interest in this case which justifies prompt dismissal. As plaintiff knew full well, both when it became a party to the Major League Agreement and agreed to be bound by the Commissioner's decisions, and when it participated without protest in the hearing before the Commissioner to determine whether to approve the player transfers in issue here, the public's continued confidence in the integrity of baseball requires that the decisions of the Commissioner be final and unreviewable by the courts.

The millions of baseball fans around the country must be assured that internal baseball disputes will be resolved expeditiously and authoritatively by the Commissioner, who is knowledgeable about and dedicated to protecting the best interests of the game, and not in complex, protracted judicial trials and appeals. In particular, the fans must be promptly assured that the three players in question here owe their full allegiance to plaintiff's team and have no reason to aid the teams to which plaintiff proposed to transfer them. The prolongation of this litigation—with protracted pretrial discovery, multiple evidentiary hearings and all of the attendant publicity—would totally frustrate these objectives and, in so doing, have a definite adverse impact on the public's confidence in and support for the national pastime.

In the following sections of this memorandum, defendant Commissioner Kuhn shall set forth in detail the undisputed material facts and governing legal precedents which, we submit, require the Court to dismiss the complaint with prejudice.

STATEMENT OF MATERIAL, UNCONTESTED FACTS*

The operative facts underlying this controversy can be simply stated: After conducting a full hearing,** the Commissioner of Baseball, acting under the Major League Agreement and the Major League Rules, issued a written decision disapproving plaintiff's proposed assignment in mid-season of the contracts of players Joe Rudi and Rollie Fingers to the Boston Red Sox for $2 million, and player Vida Blue to the New York Yankees for $1.5 million on the ground that the sales were not "consistent with baseball's best interests, the integrity of the game, and the maintenance of public confidence in it." (Kuhn Aff. ¶ 19.) The authority for and propriety of the Commissioner's action and its immunity from review in this forum are established by the following undisputed material facts.

* This statement of undisputed facts is drawn exclusively from the affidavit of Commissioner Bowie Kuhn attached hereto as Exhibit A, and the documents annexed thereto. While plaintiff can have no possible disagreement with the facts set forth in the affidavit or the contents of the documents, the complaint raises additional allegations, which defendant vigorously denies. However, defendant submits that for the reasons set forth below, the additional allegations, even if true, are legally irrelevant and immaterial and that the undisputed facts warrant dismissal.

** A copy of the transcript of the hearing is attached as Exhibit D to Commissioner Kuhn's Affidavit. Citations to the transcript are as follows, "Tr. p. –."

A. Organization of Baseball

Defendant Bowie K. Kuhn is the Commissioner of Baseball. (Kuhn Aff. ¶ 1.) The office of the Commissioner was created by the Major League Agreement, which is a contract among the American and National Leagues and each of their 24 constituent ball clubs, including the Oakland A's Baseball Club, which is owned and operated by the plaintiff. (Kuhn Aff. ¶ 5.) (A copy of the Agreement is attached as Exhibit A to Kuhn Affidavit.) The Agreement, which establishes the organization and governmental structure of major league baseball, empowers the Commissioner, *inter alia:*

"TO INVESTIGATE, either upon complaint or upon his own initiative, any act, transaction or practice charged, alleged or suspected to be not in the best interests of the national game of Baseball . . . [and]

"TO DETERMINE, after investigation, what preventive, remedial or punitive action is appropriate in the premises, and to take such action either against Major Leagues, Major League Clubs or individuals, as the case may be." (Article I, Sections 2(a) and (b)) (Kuhn Aff. ¶ 8)

The most recently amended version of the Major League Agreement was adopted by all 24 major league club owners, including plaintiff, on January 1, 1975. (Kuhn Aff. ¶ 5.)

Articles II, IV and V of the Major League Agreement further provide for the promulgation of the Major League Rules. These rules are made "binding upon the Major Leagues and their constituent clubs." (Kuhn Aff. ¶ 9.) Rule 12(a) provides that no assignment of a player contract "shall be recognized as valid *unless* within fifteen (15) days after execution a counterpart original of the document shall be filed . . . *and approved by the Commissioner*." (Kuhn Aff. ¶ 10) (emphasis added). (A copy of Rule 12 is attached as Exhibit B to the Kuhn Affidavit.)

The Major League Agreement expressly provides that each of the parties, including plaintiff, agreed to be bound by the decisions of the Commissioner and to waive any rights they might otherwise have to seek judicial review of the Commissioner's decisions. Thus, Article VII, Section 2, of the Agreement reads as follows:

"The Major Leagues and their constituent clubs, severally agree to be bound by the decisions of the Commissioner, and the discipline imposed by him under the provisions of this Agreement, *and severally waive such right of recourse to the courts as would otherwise have existed in their favor.*" (Emphasis added.) (Kuhn Aff. ¶ 11.)

In explaining the reasons for the original incorporation of this provision in the Major League Agreement, the owners stated in a unanimous resolution attached to the Agreement:

"We, the undersigned, earnestly desirous of insuring to the public wholesome and high-class baseball, and believing that we ourselves should set for the players an example of sportsmanship which accepts the umpires' decisions without complaint, hereby pledge ourselves loyally to support the Commissioner in his important and difficult tasks; and we assure him that each of us will acquiesce in his decisions, even when we believe them mistaken, and that we will not discredit the sport by public criticism of him or of one another." (Kuhn Aff. ¶ 12.)

The language of Article VII was first incorporated in the Major League Agreement in 1921. In 1945, Article VII of the Major League Agreement was amended by deleting the clause in which the clubs explicitly waived their rights of recourse to the courts; the Agreement continued to provide that the clubs would be bound by the decisions and discipline imposed by the Commissioner. (Kuhn Aff. ¶ 13.) Effective January 1, 1965, Article VII of the Major League Agreement was amended, expressly restoring the provision that the clubs "severally waive such rights of recourse to the courts as otherwise would have existed in their favor." (Kuhn Aff. ¶ 13.) This language from the 1965 Agreement was readopted in the 1975 Agreement, which became effective approximately 18 months ago.

B. Plaintiff's Proposed Transactions

On June 15, 1976—the final day of the baseball season in which interclub player transactions are permitted under the Major League Rules—plaintiff negotiated tentative and unapproved agreements to assign the contracts of outfielder Joe Rudi and relief pitcher Rollie Fingers to the Boston Red Sox for a total of $2 million and the contract of starting pitcher Vida Blue to the New York Yankees for $1.5 million. (Complaint ¶ 11.) The A's, Red Sox and Yankees are all members of the American League and regularly compete against each other.

In the past five years, the Oakland A's baseball team has won five divisional titles, three American League pennants, and three world championships. (Tr. p. 10.) Throughout this period, the leading players for the A's have included Blue, Rudi, Fingers, as well as Reggie Jackson and Ken Holtzman. Earlier in the season, plaintiff traded Jackson and Holtzman to a competing team. (Tr. p. 10.)

Concerned about the large sums of cash involved, the impact on the competitive balance among teams in the American League, the absence of any players to be received by the A's in return for the sale of its stars and the substantial depletion of talent of a championship team, the Commissioner, pursuant to the authority vested in him by the Major League Agreement to initiate investigations into transactions which may not be in the best interests of baseball, invited all parties to a hearing on June 17, 1976, and his New York office. (Kuhn Aff. ¶ 15.) In a telegram sent to all of the parties, the Commissioner explained that the purpose of the hearing was "to provide a prompt means of establishing the full facts regarding these transactions and to afford all parties the opportunity to present their views and contentions as to their propriety." The telegram added, "All concerned are of course entitled to be represented by counsel if they desire." A copy of the telegram is attached as Exhibit C to Commissioner Kuhn's Affidavit.

C. *The Hearing Before the Commissioner*

Appearing at the hearing before the Commissioner were Charles O. Finley, president of plaintiff, and his son, Paul Finley; the general partner, the president and counsel for the New York Yankees; the executive vice president and general manager, the treasurer and counsel for the Boston Red Sox; the president of the American League; and the executive director and counsel for the Major League Baseball Players Association. (Kuhn Aff. ¶ 17, Tr. p. 2.) A copy of the transcript of the hearing is attached as Exhibit D to the Kuhn Affidavit.

At the outset of the hearing, the Commissioner explained that the question presented was "whether these transactions are consistent with the best interests of baseball's integrity and maintenance of public confidence in the game." (Tr. p. 5.) The Commissioner invited the participants to set forth all "details or facts that you believe are relevant to the inquiry which I have described," reminding all of the participants that "it is at least possible that I might determine that the assignments here involved should not be approved." (Tr. pp. 5, 6.)

At no time before or during the hearing did plaintiff's representative challenge or even intimate any reservation about the authority of the Commissioner to approve or disapprove player transfers, nor did plaintiff's representative lodge any protest or objection to the procedures at the hearing. (Kuhn Aff. ¶ 18.) Instead, Mr. Charles Finley volunteered to begin the proceedings and made a vigorous presentation of all of the factors which, in his view, justified the Commissioner in approving the proposed transactions. (Tr. pp. 9–34.) Similarly, all of the other participants availed themselves of the opportunity to present the factors which they believed relevant to the Commissioner's decision to approve or disapprove the proposed player transfers. (Kuhn Aff. ¶ 18.)

D. The Commissioner's Decision

On June 18, 1976, after considering the presentations made at the hearing, the Commissioner issued a written decision disapproving the proposed transfers of the player contracts in exchange for $3.5 million as "inconsistent with the best interests of Baseball, the integrity of the game and the maintenance of public confidence in it." (Kuhn Aff. ¶ 19.) A copy of the decision is attached as Exhibit E to the Kuhn Affidavit.

The decision does not contest the good faith of the club owners involved in negotiating the proposed player transfers. However, the decision reasons that, if the Commissioner approved the sales for enormous sums of cash of three stars of one team to wealthy competitors,

> "[T]he door would be opened wide to the buying of success by the more affluent clubs, public suspicion would be aroused, traditional and sound methods of player development and acquisition would be undermined and our efforts to preserve competitive balance would be greatly impaired."

In accordance with the responsibility expressly vested in him by the Major League Agreement to protect the best interests of baseball, the Commissioner's decision reflects his concern that both for the present season and for all future seasons baseball fans must be assured that each of the teams, not only those with large cash reserves, will be able "to compete effectively" in their respective pennant races.

In part, the decision was based on the Commissioner's concern that the Oakland A's "shorn of much of its finest talent in exchange for cash" would not be able to play competitively this season against the other teams in its league, thereby depriving the A's' fans of the team and caliber of play which they have supported in the past. More importantly, for the long run, the decision states the Commissioner's concern that baseball fans may not support a sport where all of the best talent is purchased by one or two of the wealthiest clubs and when all the remaining teams, consisting of inferior players, will not be able to mount serious competition to the wealthy few.

Finding that "public confidence in the integrity of club operations and in baseball would be gravely undermined should such assignments not be restrained," the Commissioner disapproved the proposed transfers and directed the three players to remain on the active roster of the Oakland A's and to be available to play in their games.

E. The Complaint

Without seeking reconsideration by the Commissioner, plaintiff filed this suit on June 25, 1976, in the Northern District of Illinois. The suit seeks, in addition to monetary damages and other relief, an injunction from this Court "ordering defendant Kuhn to approve the assignments" of Rudi, Fingers and Blue and "ordering defendant Kuhn to rescind, reverse, nullify and withdraw his order of June 18, 1976, disapproving said assignments." (Complaint, p. 35.)

Neither of the other major league baseball clubs involved in the proposed transfer joined the A's in filing the suit, and the Yankees and Red Sox have been named as defendants along with the Commissioner, the American and National Leagues and the Executive Council of major league baseball.*

While the complaint contains seven counts, each of them is premised upon the Commissioner's disapproval of the proposed transfers.

* The Executive Council, consisting of four major league club owners (two from each major league), the presidents of the two major leagues, and the Commissioner, was established by the owners in the Major League Agreement. Article II, Section 2(a) of the Agreement provides that it shall be the function of the Executive Council:

> "To COOPERATE, advise and confer with the Commissioner and other offices, agencies and individuals in an effort to perpetuate Baseball as the national game of America, and to surround it with such safeguards as may warrant absolute public confidence in its integrity, operations and methods." (Kuhn Aff. ¶ 4.)

Counts 1 and 5 charge that the Commissioner's disapproval of the proposed assignments constitutes a breach of his employment contract with the major league baseball clubs and an inducement to the Yankees and Red Sox to breach their contracts to purchase the players. Count 2 alleges that the Commissioner's disapproval was part of a conspiracy in restraint of trade in violation of the Sherman Act, 15 U.S.C. § 1. Counts 3 and 4 charge that the Commissioner's disapproval constitutes a violation of the due process and equal protection clauses of the U.S. Constitution. Count 6 seeks a declaratory judgment that the Commissioner lacked the authority to disapprove the transfers, and Count 7 seeks to compel the Yankees and Red Sox to consummate the transfers, notwithstanding the Commissioner's disapproval.

ARGUMENT

• I. Plaintiff's lawful agreement to waive judicial review of the Commissioner's resolution of internal baseball disputes bars this action

Section 2 of Article VII of the Major League Agreement, the most recent version of which was adopted by plaintiff and every other major league club owner in 1975, provides:

"The Major Leagues and their constituent clubs, severally agree to be bound by the decisions of the Commissioner, and the discipline imposed by him under the provisions of this Agreement, and *severally waive such right of recourse to the courts as would otherwise have existed in their favor.*" (Emphasis added)

The underscored portion of this fundamental provision was deliberately reinstated in the Major League Agreement in 1965 and reaffirmed by the major league owners in 1975 because they recognized that the Commissioner of Baseball would be unable to perform his "important and difficult tasks" unless all of the owners "assure him that each of us will acquiesce in his decisions" and that he will not be threatened by a lawsuit every time he makes a decision which displeases one of the 24 major league club owners. (Unanimous Resolution attached to original Major League Agreement.) (Kuhn Aff. ¶ 12.)

In order to preserve public confidence in the integrity of baseball—thereby insuring the public's continued patronage—the owners established, through the Major League Agreement, the Office of the

Commissioner of Baseball, and granted him broad powers to prevent actions which might undermine public confidence in the integrity of the sport. The owners recognized that decisions made in the exercise of such powers by the Commissioner could be difficult and might displease one or more of the owners. For this reason, the owners adopted Article VII, Section 2 as a manifestation of their intent to shield the Commissioner from the risk that any of his decisions could subject him to protracted, expensive litigation (including, as in this case, a $10 million damage suit against him personally as well as in his capacity as Commissioner).

If the Commissioner of Baseball were forced to consider the cost of a possible lawsuit every time he made a decision which one or more club owners might consider adverse to their interests, he would not be able to perform the tasks assigned to him under the Major League Agreement. In certain cases, he might be discouraged from taking any appropriate action. In any event, the public would have reason to question whether the Commissioner's decisions were made "in the best interests of baseball" or in an effort to appease particular club owners and avoid litigation. Recognizing that public confidence in the integrity of baseball depends on the public's trust in the ability of the Commissioner to prevent conduct "not in the best interests of baseball," the club owners agreed that decisions made by the Commissioner were to be final and binding, and they agreed to waive such right of recourse to the courts as might otherwise have been available to them.

It has long been the rule that voluntary agreements to be bound by the decisions of nonjudicial tribunals and to waive judicial review are valid and binding. *See, e.g., Bower* v. *Eastern Airlines,* 214 F.2d 623 (3d Cir.), *cert. denied,* 348 U.S. 871 (1954); *Rossi* v. *TWA,* 350 F. Supp. 1263, 1269–70 (C.D. Cal. 1972), *aff'd,* 507 F.2d 404 (9th Cir. 1974); *Rood* v. *Railway Passenger & Freight Conductors' Mutual Benefit Ass'n,* 31 F. 62 (N.D. Ill. 1887); *Pacaud* v. *Waite,* 218 Ill. 138, 75 N.E. 779 (1905). Thus, in *Berlin* v. *Eureka Lodge,* 64 P. 254 (Cal., 1901), the court described as "settled law" that:

> "[A] member of a lodge, by his subscribing to the by-laws, may waive his right to sue in the courts of law for the redress of his grievances; and, if such member brings an action in a court of law, it is a defense thereto if he has agreed within the order to look solely to its tribunals for the redress of those grievances, and those tribunals have decided against him upon the merits of his case." *Id.*

Similarly, the Illinois Supreme Court recognized in *Railway Passenger & Freight Conductors' Mutual Aid & Benefit Ass'n* v. *Robinson*, 147 Ill. 138, 35 N.E. 168, 176 (1893), that:

". . . [I]t is competent for members of societies of this character to so contract that their rights as members shall depend upon the determination of some tribunal of their own choice, and that such determination shall be conclusive, . . ."*

Particularly where, as here, the parties agree not only to be bound by the decision of a nonjudicial tribunal, but further expressly and unequivocally convenant to forego any recourse to the courts, complaints filed in breach of such agreements have been summarily dismissed. *See, e.g., Railway Passenger & Freight Conductors' Mutual Aid & Benefit Ass'n* v. *Robinson, supra; Supreme Lodge of Order of Select Friends* v. *Raymond,* 57 Kan. 647, 47 P. 533 (1897); *Wuerthner* v. *Workingmen's Benev. Soc.,* 121 Mich. 90, 79 N.W. 921 (1899).

Like agreements to compromise litigation prior to trial, agreements to waive judicial review are favored because they spare the caseload of overburdened courts and permit the parties to resolve their differences without the enormous cost and inconvenience of litigation. As one court emphasized in upholding the waiver of judicial review of an arbitrator's award:

"Such a policy of non-review is grounded in the desire to avoid litigation. In fact one must assume that the main reason the parties resorted to arbitration in the first place was to circumvent the identical protracted altercation Plaintiff now invites by coming into the Federal Courts. Both parties knew the arbitration process would be quick and cheap; moreover, the differences would be resolved by people familiar with the practical intricacies of their particular occupation. We hesitate to cancel the advantages that both sides appreciated before and during their dispute." (citation omitted) *Rossi* v. *TWA,* 350 F. Supp. 1263, 1270 (C.D. Cal. 1972).

* The enforceability of agreements by private associations to forego resort to the courts is a corollary to the more general rule, recognized in this Circuit and in the Illinois state courts, that rules and bylaws of private associations governing the rights and obligations of their members shall be judicially enforced. *See, e.g., Talton* v. *Behncke,* 199 F.2d 471, 473 (7th Cir. 1952); *Parsons College* v. *North Central Association of Colleges and Secondary Schools,* 271 F. Supp. 65, 70 (N.D. Ill. 1967); *Engel* v. *Walsh,* 258 Ill. 98, 101 N.E. 222 (1913); *Bostedo* v. *Board of Trade,* 227 Ill. 90, 81 N.E. 42 (1907); *Werner* v. *International Association of Machinists,* 11 Ill. App. 2d 258, 137 N.E. 2d 100 (1956).

In short, plaintiff, like all of the other major league club owners, voluntarily, knowingly and with good reason agreed to be bound by the decisions of the Commissioner and expressly agreed to forego judicial review of the Commissioner's decisions. Because such voluntary, contractual arrangements are valid and enforceable, plaintiff is barred from maintaining this action. Accordingly, we request the Court to enter dismissal of the complaint in its entirety with prejudice.

• II. The Commissioner's rational exercise of the authority vested in him by the Major League Agreement and Rules should be sustained

Even if this Court were to entertain jurisdiction in this suit, under well established precedents in this Circuit its review of the Commissioner's decision is limited to determining whether the Commissioner acted (1) within the scope of his authority; (2) with procedural fairness; and (3) upon a rational basis. *Milwaukee American Association* v. *Landis*, 49 F.2d 298 (N.D. Ill. 1931).*

In this case, the undisputed facts of record—more particularly, the Major League Agreement and Rules, the transcript of the hearing, and the Commissioner's written decision—establish that the Commissioner was authorized to disapprove the proposed player transfers and that his decision to disapprove them "in the best interests of baseball" was procedurally fair and reasonable.

A. *The Commissioner Acted Within the Scope of the Authority Vested in Him by the Major League Agreement and Rules*

As set forth above, the Major League Agreement empowers the Commissioner to initiate investigations into any act or transaction "suspected not to be in the best interests of baseball," and to take such preventive or remedial actions as are appropriate under the circumstances. (Major League Agreement: Article I, Section 2). Without more, these broad powers would authorize the Commissioner to re-

* This is the same standard applied in this Circuit to the review of decisions by all quasi-judicial tribunals of private associations. *See, e.g., Rosee* v. *Board of Trade of City of Chicago*, 311 F.2d 524, 527 (7th Cir.), *cert. denied*, 374 U.S. 806 (1963); *Parsons College* v. *North Central Association, supra*, 271 F. Supp. at 70.

view proposed player assignments and disapprove them when he found that they were not in the best interests of baseball.

But the Commissioner's authority to review proposed player transfers does not rest on these broad powers alone because Major League Rule 12(a) specifically provides that no assignment of a player contract "shall be recognized as valid unless within fifteen (15) days after execution a counterpart original of the document shall be filed . . . *and approved by the Commissioner.*" (Kuhn Aff. ¶ 10.) (Emphasis added.) In disapproving plaintiff's proposed player transfers, the Commissioner expressly relied on the authority vested in him by Rule 12(a) and the Major League Agreement.

In *Milwaukee American Association* v. *Landis,* 49 F.2d 298 (N.D. Ill. 1931), this Court described the broad authority vested in the Commissioner by the Major League Agreement:

"We have observed that, in addition to his jurisdiction over disputes certified to him, the commissioner is empowered to investigate upon his own initiative any act, transaction, or practice charged or alleged to be detrimental to the best interests of baseball, to determine what preventive, remedial or punitive action is appropriate in the premises and to take such action against leagues or clubs as the case may require. Certain acts are specified as detrimental to baseball, but it is expressly provided that nothing contained in the code should be construed as exclusively defining or otherwise limiting acts, practices or conduct detrimental to baseball. It is contended that this phrase should be so construed as to include only such conduct as is similar to that expressly mentioned. *However, the provisions are so unlimited in character that we can conclude only that the parties did not intend so to limit the meaning of conduct detrimental to baseball, but intended to vest in the Commissioner jurisdiction to prevent any conduct destructive of the aims of the code.* Apparently it was the intent of the parties to make the commissioner an arbiter, whose decisions made in good faith, upon evidence, upon all questions relating to the purpose of the organization and all conduct detrimental thereto, should be absolutely binding." (Emphasis added.) 49 F.2d at 302.*

* Remarkably, the complaint avers that the Commissioner's power to remedy conduct deemed not to be in the best interests of baseball is limited to the five specific punishments listed in Article I, Section 3 of the Major League Agreement. (Complaint, ¶ 64.) This contention is patently erroneous and is inconsistent with the plain meaning of the Major League Agreement. Article I, Section 2(a) of the Agreement explicitly authorizes the Commissioner to determine *and take* whatever "preventive, remedial or punitive action is appropriate in the premises. . . ." This clearly encompasses disapproval of proposed transactions found not to be in the best interests of baseball. Moreover, Rule 12(a) specifically authorizes the Commissioner in his discretion to review and approve or disapprove transfers of player contracts.

Other courts which have considered the powers of the Commissioner of Baseball have agreed with this Court's analysis in *Landis* that the Commissioner possesses broad authority in determining what actions are not in the best interests of baseball. In *Livingston v. Shreveport-Texas League Baseball Corp.*, 128 F. Supp. 191 (W.D. La. 1955), *aff'd per curiam*, 228 F.2d 623 (5th Cir. 1956), the *Landis* holding was specifically approved:

"After careful consideration of the number and the technical nature of problems involved in the sport, we are convinced that this is as it should be. Surely the officials designated are best qualified by training, experience and practical judgment to pass upon such matters; and, if it were otherwise—if all the persons and organizations in baseball were required to litigate their many differences—endless delays and undue burdens upon the courts certainly would result. Not unlike a military organization, in baseball there must be a set of governing rules through which these officials speedily may pass upon and finally decide the multitude of disputes inherent in the game." 128 F. Supp. at 197–198.

In short, as plaintiff virtually conceded when it submitted without protest to the hearing before the Commissioner, there can be no question but that Article I of the Major League Agreement and Major League Rule 12(a) authorize the Commissioner to review and, in appropriate cases, disapprove proposed player transfers, such as plaintiff's cash sales of Rudi, Blue and Fingers.

B. *The Commissioner Scrupulously Followed Fair and Reasonable Procedures in Rendering His Decision*

At no time prior to the filing of the complaint did plaintiff or any other party suggest that the procedures followed by the Commissioner in rendering his decision were unfair or improper. A description of the procedures—including notice and a full opportunity to be heard—demonstrates that the Commissioner scrupulously adhered to procedures which were fair and reasonable to plaintiff.

The Commissioner learned of plaintiff's proposed player transfers on June 15, 1976. On June 16, he sent to all parties concerned a notice, advising them of his intention to hold a hearing, stating the time, place and issue to be considered at the hearing, permitting them an opportunity to present all relevant considerations and affording them the opportunity to be represented by counsel at the hearing.*

The hearing was conducted in accordance with the specific Rules of Procedure which the Commissioner had previously promulgated in accordance with Article I, Section 2(d) of the Major League Agreement. These Rules provide, in pertinent part, that:

> "Proceedings before the Commissioner shall be conducted in general like judicial proceedings and with due regard for all of the principles of natural justice and fair play, but the Commissioner may proceed informally when he deems it desirable."

At the hearing, the Commissioner again advised the parties of the issue before him, and the possible options open to him, and asked each party to present all of the pertinent facts and considerations bearing on his decision. All of the parties, many of them represented by counsel, took full advantage of the opportunity to present what they deemed to be the material facts and considerations.

Following the hearing, the Commissioner issued a written decision, articulating his reasons for disapproving the proposed player transfers. Copies of this decision were sent by telegram to all parties on the date the decision was rendered.

In light of these indisputable facts, we submit that, in considering and reaching his decision, the Commissioner followed procedures that were impeccably fair and reasonable to plaintiff and all of the other parties.

C. The Commissioner's Exercise of Discretion Was Reasonable and Should Be Sustained by This Court

As noted, it is well-established in this jurisdiction that the courts will refuse to hear *de novo* appeals from quasi-judicial tribunals of private

* While the complaint alleges that there was inadequate time between the notice and the hearing, plaintiff raised no such objection at any time prior to or during the hearing. Nor does the complaint suggest any prejudice which plaintiff suffered from the alleged shortness, failing to enumerate any additional information which plaintiff might have adduced if there had been more time before the hearing. Further, since the American League championship season is in full progress, time was of the essence and, under these circumstances, the one-day notice was clearly reasonable. Morever, as the Court stated in *Parsons College* v *North Central Association, supra,* "the nature of the hearing, if required by rudimentary due process, may properly be adjusted to the nature of the issue to be decided." 271 F. Supp. at 72.

associations and will limit their review to determining whether, based on the record before him, the administrator's decision was arbitrary and capricious. *See, e.g., Parsons College* v. *North Central Association, supra; Robinson* v. *Illinois High School Association,* 45 Ill. App. 2d 277, 195 N.E.2d, 38 (1963).*

As one court explained, under this applicable standard of limited judicial review a court may not substitute its judgment for that of the Commissioner and "must guard against unduly interfering with the [Commissioner's] autonomy by substituting judicial judgment for that of the [Commissioner] in an area where the competence of the court does not equal that of the [Commissioner]." *Pinsker* v. *Pacific Coast Society of Orthodontists,* 526 P.2d 253, 266 (Cal., 1974). The court added that administrative actions would be set aside only when "contrary to established public policy or . . . 'so patently arbitrary and unreasonable' as to be 'beyond the pale of law'. . . ." *Ibid.*

In determining whether a decision is arbitrary and capricious, the Court must simply determine whether on the basis of the record before the administrator there is any reasonable basis for his decision. *See, e.g., Pauley* v. *United States,* 419 F.2d 1061, 1066 (7th Cir. 1969), in which the Seventh Circuit explained:

> "*Administrative action may be regarded as arbitrary and capricious only where it is not supportable on any rational basis.* . . . The fact that on the same evidence a reviewing court could have reached a decision contrary to that reached by the agency will not support a determination that the administrative action was arbitrary and capricious." (citation omitted) (emphasis added)

Based on the materials of record in this proceeding—including the transcript of the hearing, the charter of the Commissioner set forth in the Major League Agreement, and the Commissioner's written decision—we submit that the Commissioner's exercise of the discre-

* The law in other jurisdictions is also that "courts will not interfere with the internal affairs of a private association so long as its affairs and proceedings are conducted fairly and honestly, and after due notice to anyone involved." *Sanders* v. *Louisiana High School Athletic Association,* 242 So. 2d 19, 26 (La. 1970); *see e.g., Pinsker* v. *Pacific Coast Society of Orthodontists,* 526 P.2d 253 (Cal., 1974); *Tennessee Secondary School Athletic Association* v. *Cox,* 221 Tenn. 164, 425 S.W.2d 597 (1968); *State ex rel. West Virginia Secondary School Activities Commission* v. *Oakley,* 152 W. Va. 533, 164 S.E.2d 775 (1968); *State ex rel. Ohio High School Athletic Association* v. *Judges of the Court of Common Pleas,* 173 Ohio 239, 181 N.E.2d 261 (1962); *Morrison* v. *Roberts,* 183 Okla. 359, 82 P.2d 1023 (1938).

tion vested in him was so clearly reasonable as to negate any possible claim that the decision was arbitrary or capricious.*

Relying on his expertise in this sport and fulfilling his obligation to act in accordance with his best judgment to protect the best interests of baseball, the Commissioner—after hearing testimony from representatives of the plaintiff, the other club owners involved and the players association—concluded that it would be detrimental to the best interests of the game if one team were to sell off in mid-season three of its most talented players for enormous sums of cash to two wealthy competitors. Under these circumstances, the Commissioner's written decision concluded that approval of plaintiff's proposed transactions would lead to, among other things, the loss of competitive balance in major league baseball.

The loss of competitive balance could be devastating to baseball which, as the Commissioner's decision notes, is engaged in a "highly competitive" contest for the public's support with many other sports and entertainments. The Commissioner was clearly reasonable in concluding that unless a number of teams are fairly evenly matched, resulting in close pennant races among a number of competitors, fan interest and support will wane. The Commissioner's decision explained that if a few wealthy clubs were free to buy all of the outstanding talent, the results of the pennant races would be foregone conclusions, competitive balance would be destroyed and the public's support of the game diminished.

Plaintiff challenges the reasonableness of the Commissioner's decision on the ground that it is allegedly "contrary to historical precedent." (Complaint, ¶ 14.) While Commissioner Kuhn denies this allegation, it is entirely irrelevant to this lawsuit whether the Commissioner's decision is or is not unprecedented. In his written deci-

* Apparently recognizing that no valid claim of arbitrariness can be sustained, plaintiff has salted its complaint with numerous derogatory epithets, impugning the good faith of the Commissioner in rendering his decision. While the Commissioner vigorously denies the allegations of "malice," "prejudice," and "bad faith," we submit that they are totally irrelevant because the Commissioner's written decision sets forth a fully rational and sustainable basis for his decision. That should be the end of this Court's inquiry. (*See, e.g., Parsons College* v. *North Central Association, supra; Milwaukee American Association* v. *Landis, supra.*) If, upon a totally conclusionary, unparticularized and unsubstantiated cry of "malice," every decision of an administrator could be subjected to lengthy litigation—including extensive investigation into his state of mind—there would be no finality to an administrative decision and the well-established doctrine of limited judicial review of quasi-judicial decisions by private associations would be rendered meaningless.

sion, the Commissioner expressly determined that the cash sales negotiated by plaintiff were unique and completely distinguishable from "cash sales of player contracts in the past" because "there has been no instance in my judgment which had the potential for harm to our game as do these assignments."

Specifically, the Commissioner determined that plaintiff's transactions were both unique and harmful to baseball because: (1) such transactions involved the simultaneous sale of three of the star players—the "finest talent"—of a championship club; (2) the transactions involved "enormous sums of cash," thereby assuring that the player contracts in question could be sold only to the wealthiest and most successful clubs; (3) the transactions would greatly impair the "competitive balance" among clubs which is essential to the maintenance of public interest in and support for professional baseball; and (4) the transactions were peculiarly harmful to baseball because they were made at a time when the "circumstances of baseball's reserve system" were "unsettled."*

While the Commissioner's decision was manifestly in the best interests of baseball, the correctness of his judgment is not the issue in this Court. The issue is not whether this Court would reach the same conclusion but, assuming *arguendo* the propriety of judicial review at all, the question for the Court is whether the Commissioner's decision was predicated upon a reasonable basis. As the court stated in *Livingston* v. *Shreveport-Texas League Baseball Club, supra,* 128 F. Supp. 197:

"After careful consideration of the number and the technical nature of problems involved in the sport, we are convinced that this is as it should be. Surely the officials designated are best qualified by training, experience and practical judgment to pass upon such matters. . . ."**

* Plaintiff's transactions took place during the brief hiatus between *Kansas City Royals Baseball Corp.* v. *Major League Baseball Players Ass'n,* 532 F.2d 615 (8th Cir. 1976), which upheld an arbitrator's decision restricting baseball's "reserve system" and the consensual establishment of a new "reserve system" via collective bargaining. On July 12, 1976, it was publicly announced that the Major League Baseball Players Association, representing the players, and the Player Relations Committee, representing the club owners, had reached an agreement on a new "reserve system"; the agreement requires ratification by both sides.

** This reasoning was applied by the court to uphold the discretionary judgment of National Football League Commissioner Rozelle in *Rentzel* v. *Rozelle,* No. C-63828 (Cal. Super. Ct. 1973). In that case, Commissioner Rozelle's suspension of player Lance Rentzel for "conduct detrimental to the NFL" was upheld on the basis that a court would not substitute its judgment for that of the Commissioner.

In short, since the Commissioner's disapproval of the proposed player transfers was made in the exercise of his discretion, pursuant to the authority vested in him by the Major League Agreement and Rules, following fair and reasonable procedures and based upon eminently reasonable considerations, we submit that the Commissioner's actions should be sustained by this Court.

• III. The propriety of the Commissioner's actions under the Major League Agreement eliminates any possible claim of breach of contract or inducing breach of contract

The foregoing sections of this memorandum demonstrate that the Commissioner acted properly and reasonably within the scope of his authority under the Major League Agreement to determine whether the proposed player transfers were "in the best interests of baseball." This demonstration summarily disposes of plaintiff's claims for breach of contract and inducing breach of contract.

The complaint alleges that the Commissioner's disapproval of the proposed player transfers constituted (1) a breach of the Commissioner's employment contract with the major league clubs (Count 1) and (2) and inducement to the Yankees and Red Sox to breach their contracts to purchase the service of the three A's players (Count 5). In addition to damages, the complaint seeks a declaratory judgment that the disapprovals were improper (Count 6) and requests specific performance by the Yankees and Red Sox despite the Commissioner's disapproval (Count 7). None of these counts states a valid claim for relief in light of the clear propriety of the Commissioner's actions under the Major League Agreement and Rules.

A. The Commissioner Did Not Breach His Employment Contract

As set forth in the Commissioner's Affidavit, as Commissioner of Baseball he is "obliged to faithfully perform and discharge to the best of [his] ability the duties of the Office of Commissioner of Baseball as provided in the Major League Agreement and the Major League Rules." (Kuhn Aff. ¶ 7.)

Thus, the Commissioner's contractual obligations to the owners are completely coterminous with his responsibilities under the Major

League Agreement and the Major League Rules promulgated thereunder. Since we have established in the preceding section of this memorandum that the Commissioner properly exercised the discretionary authority vested in him by the Major League Agreement and Rules, it inexorably follows that he has not breached his employment contract. Accordingly, we submit that Count I must be summarily dismissed.

B. The Commissioner Did Not Induce a Breach of Contract by the Yankees and Red Sox

Count 5 of the complaint alleges that the Commissioner's disapproval of plaintiff's proposed player contract transfers induced the Yankees and Red Sox to breach their "contracts" with the plaintiff. The short and dispositive answer to this contention is that the Yankees and Red Sox have not breached their agreements; in the absence of the Commissioner's approval of the proposed transfers, these clubs had, and continue to have, no obligation, to plaintiff.

The "contracts" which plaintiff negotiated with the Yankees and Red Sox were conditional agreements which, under the express terms of Major League Rule 12(a), were subject to the approval of the Commissioner. Rule 12(a) specifically provides that no transfer of player contracts "shall be recognized as valid unless" such transfer is "approved by the Commissioner." As the cases uniformly hold, in the absence of such approval, the contracts are neither valid nor binding and do not obligate the transferee club. *See, e.g., Los Angeles Rams Football Club* v. *Cannon,* 185 F. Supp. 717, 721 (S.D. Cal. 1960); *Detroit Football Co.* v. *Robinson,* 186 F. Supp. 933, 935 (E.D. La.), *aff'd.* 283 F.2d 657 (5th Cir. 1960). In *Los Angeles Rams Football Club* v. *Cannon, supra,* in interpreting a virtually identical clause in a National Football League contract, the court held that "approval by the [football] Commissioner is essential to the formation of a contract here . . . because the terms of the document make it so. . . . [T]he agreement shall only become valid and binding if, as and when approved by the Commissioner." 185 F. Supp. at 721, 722.

Since the Yankees and Red Sox were conditionally obligated to pay for the contracts of Rudi, Fingers and Blue only if, as and when the Commissioner of Baseball approved the proposed transfers, and since the Commissioner has not approved them, the Yankees and Red

Sox have no obligation to plaintiff. In the absence of any such contractual obligation, it is clear that the Commissioner cannot be held liable for inducing a non-existent breach of contract. Accordingly, Count 5 should be summarily dismissed.

Count 6 (for declaratory relief) and Count 7 (for specific performance by the Yankees and Red Sox) are wholly dependent upon plaintiff's allegations that the Commissioner's disapproval was unauthorized by the Major League Agreement, and that the Commissioner breached his employment contract and induced a breach by the transferee clubs under their contracts with plaintiff. The foregoing discussion has demonstrated beyond question that the Commissioner acted properly within the scope of his authority under the Major League Agreement and Rules and, accordingly, did not constitute a breach of his employment contract and did not induce the Yankees and Red Sox to breach any agreement with plaintiff. Therefore, Counts 6 and 7 should similarly be dismissed.

• IV. Plaintiff's antitrust claim should be dismissed because professional baseball is exempt from the antitrust laws

Count 2 of the complaint charges that the Commissioner's disapproval of plaintiff's proposed player transfers was part of a conspiracy to restrain trade among all of the major league clubs, the two major leagues and baseball's executive council in alleged violation of the Sherman Antitrust Act, 15 U.S.C. § 1. Even if this were true—which the Commissioner vehemently denies—the allegation fails to state a valid claim for relief.

On three separate occasions—and as recently as 1972—the United States Supreme Court has definitively ruled that professional baseball is exempt from the antitrust laws. *Flood* v. *Kuhn,* 407 U.S. 258 (1972); *Toolson* v. *New York Yankees, Inc.,* 346 U.S., 356 (1953); *Federal Baseball Club of Baltimore* v. *National League,* 259 U.S. 200 (1922). Accordingly, the antitrust allegations contained in plaintiff's complaint fail to state any claim upon which relief may be granted and should be dismissed forthwith.

Federal Baseball Club of Baltimore, supra, was the first case in which the Court ruled that the antitrust laws do not apply to professional baseball. In that case, plaintiff baseball club sued the two major leagues, contending, among other things, that the refusal of the two leagues to permit plaintiff to play games against the leagues' teams constituted a boycott in violation of the Sherman Act which effectively forced plaintiff out of business. In an opinion by Justice Holmes, the Court rejected plaintiff's claims on the ground that professional baseball is not within the scope of the antitrust laws.

In *Toolson, supra,* the Supreme Court again ruled that the antitrust laws were inapplicable to professional baseball. *Toolson* was decided together with two companion cases, *Kowalski* v. *Chandler, Commissioner of Baseball* and *Corbett* v. *Chandler, Commissioner of Baseball.* In *Corbett,* plaintiff alleged that many aspects of professional baseball's structure violated the antitrust laws, including, *inter alia,* the Major League Agreement which, according to plaintiff, deprived the Pacific Coast League of Major League status, and unreasonably restricted the number and location of Major League franchises. After considering all three cases, the Court, in a *per curiam* opinion, explicitly reaffirmed the holding in *Federal Baseball Club of Baltimore* that professional baseball is not within the scope of the antitrust laws.

"In *Federal Baseball Club of Baltimore* v. *National League of Professional Baseball Clubs,* 259 U.S. 200 (1922), this Court held that the business of providing public baseball games for profit between clubs of professional baseball players was not within the scope of the federal antitrust laws. Congress has had the ruling under consideration but has not seen fit to bring such business under these laws by legislation having prospective effect. The business has thus been left for thirty years to develop, on the understanding that it was not subject to existing antitrust legislation. The present cases ask us to overrule the prior decision and, with retrospective effect, hold the legislation applicable. We think that if there are evils in this field which now warrant application to it of the antitrust laws it should be by legislation. Without reexamination of the underlying issues, the judgments below are affirmed on the authority of *Federal Baseball Club of Baltimore* v. *National League of Professional Baseball Clubs, supra,* so far as that decision determines that Congress had no intention of including the business of baseball within the scope of the federal antitrust laws." 346 U.S. at 356–57.

In 1972, in *Flood, supra,* the Supreme Court reiterated for the third time, that professional baseball is exempt from the antitrust laws:

"We repeat for this case what was said in Toolson:

" 'Without re-examination of the underlying issues, the [judgment] below [is] affirmed on the authority of *Federal Baseball Club of Baltimore* v. *National League of Professional Baseball Clubs, supra,* so far as that decision determines that Congress had no intention of including the business of baseball within the scope of the federal antitrust laws.' 346 U.S. at 357.

"And what the Court said in Federal Baseball in 1922 and what it said in Toolson in 1953, we say again here in 1972: the remedy, if any is indicated, is for congressional, and not judicial, action." 407 U.S. at 285.

Despite the clear holdings in these cases that professional baseball as a whole is not subject to the antitrust laws, the complaint repeatedly suggests that only baseball's "reserve system" is exempt from the antitrust laws. This is not the first time that a plaintiff has attempted to effect a narrowing of baseball's antitrust immunity. In each previous case, however, the courts uniformly have sustained motions to dismiss antitrust claims brought against the Commissioner of Baseball, the two Major Leagues, or their member teams. For example, in *Portland Baseball Club, Inc.* v. *Kuhn,* 368 F. Supp. 1004 (D. Ore. 1971), *aff'd per curiam,* 491 F.2d 1101 (9th Cir. 1974), plaintiff, a member of the Pacific Coast League, brought suit against the Commissioner of Baseball, the two Major Leagues, and their member teams, alleging that the expansion of the Major Leagues into Seattle and San Diego (resulting in the displacement of Pacific Coast League franchises in those cities) violated the antitrust laws. Plaintiff there, as here, sought to distinguish *Flood, Toolson* and *Federal Baseball Club of Baltimore* by arguing that these decisions merely held that baseball's "reserve system" was exempt from the antitrust laws. The District Court, which granted defendant's motion to dismiss, specifically rejected this argument and held that, on the authority of the three Supreme Court decisions, professional baseball as a whole is exempt from the antitrust laws:

"On the basis of numerous cases which exempt professional baseball from the application of the federal anti-trust laws, I dismissed the claim of plaintiff based upon alleged violations of these laws by the professional baseball leagues." 368 F. Supp. at 1007.

This holding was explicitly affirmed by the Ninth Circuit. 491 F.2d 1101, 1103 (1974).

Even before the Supreme Court handed down the *Flood* decision, the federal courts, on the authority of *Toolson* and *Federal Baseball Club of Baltimore,* routinely dismissed antitrust claims brought against professional baseball. In *Salerno* v. *American League,* 429 F.2d 1003 (2d Cir. 1970), *cert. denied,* 400 U.S. 1001 (1971), the Second Circuit affirmed the dismissal of a claim brought against the American

League and the Commissioner of Baseball by two discharged umpires who alleged that defendants unlawfully conspired to drive them out of baseball in violation of the Sherman and Clayton Antitrust Acts. The Court of Appeals explained that "professional baseball is not subject to the antitrust laws" because "the ground upon which *Toolson* rested was that Congress had no intention to bring baseball within the antitrust laws." 429 F.2d at 1005. Similarly, in *Portland Baseball Club, Inc.* v. *Baltimore Baseball Club, Inc.*, 282 F.2d 680 (9th Cir. 1960), the Ninth Circuit affirmed the dismissal of an antitrust claim against the Commissioner of Baseball, among others, on grounds that baseball is exempt from the antitrust laws.

In sum, based on the decisions of the Supreme Court in *Flood, Toolson* and *Federal Baseball Club of Baltimore,* the courts have ruled consistently that professional baseball, as a whole, is exempt from the antitrust laws. In light of this clear and unbroken chain of precedents, plaintiff's attempt to subject professional baseball to yet another antitrust challenge can only be regarded as frivolous. Accordingly, the antitrust claim set forth in Count 2 of plaintiff's complaint should be dismissed.

- **V. The due process and equal protection claims must be dismissed because the decision by the Commissioner of Baseball did not constitute "state action"**

In Counts 3 and 4 of its complaint, plaintiff claims that it has been denied its Fourteenth Amendment rights to due process and equal protection by virtue of the Commissioner's decision not to approve the purported player transfers. However, the Fourteenth Amendment prohibits only those denials of due process or equal protection that result from "state action"; and, under well-established standards, the actions taken by the Commissioner of Baseball do not constitute "state action." Plaintiff's attempt to elevate its disagreement with the Commissioner to constitutional magnitude is therefore entirely unsupportable and must be dismissed.

It is indisputable that the Commissioner of Baseball is a private individual and that the Major League Executive Council, the National and American Leagues, and their 24 member teams are wholly private organizations. Moreover, the internal affairs of professional baseball—including the making, interpreting and enforcing of Major-

League Rules and the exercise of authority under the Major League Agreement by the Commissioner of Baseball—are carried on by these private entities free of any regulation by federal, state or local governments. Finally, it is indisputable that the specific action giving rise to this lawsuit—the Commissioner's decision to disapprove plaintiff's attempt to sell certain player contracts—was made without any involvement whatsoever by any organ of government.

Nevertheless, plaintiff alleges that the Commissioner's decision constituted "state action" because: (1) "Seventeen of the twenty-three major league clubs located in the United States make use of stadia owned by municipalities located within various states of these United States"; and (2) "Major League baseball enjoys a judicially created exemption for its reserve clause from the antitrust laws, and a legislatively-created exemption under 15 U.S.C. §§ 1291–1295 for agreements covering interstate telecasts of its contests." Clearly, the "connection" between professional baseball and the state set forth in plaintiff's complaint is so insignificant and, more important, so far removed from the activities which plaintiff has challenged in this lawsuit, that it falls far short of constituting the requisite "state action" necessary to invoke the Fourteenth Amendment.*

The courts have been unanimous in ruling that when an action by a private individual or organization is challenged under the Fourteenth Amendment, the "state action" requirement is satisfied *only if there is a close nexus between the state and the particular action being challenged. Jackson* v. *Metropolitan Edison Co.*, 419 U.S. 345 (1974); *Cohen* v. *Illinois Institute of Technology*, 524 F.2d 818 (7th Cir. 1975); *Doe* v. *Bellin Memorial Hospital*, 479 F.2d 756 (7th Cir. 1973); *Gerrard* v. *Blackman*, 401 F. Supp. 1189 (N.D. Ill. 1975).

In *Jackson, supra*, a privately owned and operated utility (Metropolitan) held a license issued by the State of Pennsylvania and was otherwise subjected to extensive regulation by the state. Metropolitan, without holding a hearing, terminated service to petitioner, who claimed that the termination amounted to a denial of due process in contravention of the Fourteenth Amendment. In holding that the termination did not constitute "state action," the Supreme Court ruled

* Even if there were "state action," the procedures followed by the Commissioner in reaching his decision were so clearly fair and his rationale so clearly reasonable as to rebut any contention that plaintiff was deprived of due process or equal protection of the laws. (See II(B), *supra*.)

that the action of a private business would be considered the action of the state *only when the particular action challenged* is the subject of extensive state regulation and involvement:

"It may well be that acts of a heavily regulated utility with at least something of a governmentally protected monopoly will more readily be found to be 'state' acts than will the acts of an entity lacking these characteristics. But *the inquiry must be whether there is a sufficiently close nexus between the State and the challenged action of the regulated entity so that the action of the latter may be fairly treated as that of the State itself.*" (Emphasis added.) 419 U.S. at 350–351.

The rule that "state action" is present only when there is a close nexus between the state and the challenged activity has been applied consistently in the Seventh Circuit. *See, e.g., Cohen* v. *Illinois Institute of Technology,* 524 F.2d 818 (7th Cir. 1975) (per Judge, now Mr. Justice, Stevens); *Doe* v. *Bellin Memorial Hospital,* 479 F.2d 756 (7th Cir. 1973); *Gerrard* v. *Blackman,* 401 F. Supp. 1189 (N.D. Ill. 1975).

Plaintiff has not alleged that there is any nexus between any agency of government and the activity challenged in this lawsuit—that is, the decision by the Commissioner of Baseball, in the exercise of his authority under the Major League Agreement and the Major League Rules, to disapprove plaintiff's proposed transfers. Certainly the alleged leasing of municipally owned stadia to individual teams and the alleged judicial and legislative activity bearing on the status of baseball's reserve system and telecasting agreements under the antitrust laws have no relationship whatever to the activity challenged here. In these circumstances, it is clear that plaintiff has failed to make a sufficient allegation of "state action" to invoke the Fourteenth Amendment. Accordingly, plaintiff's constitutional claims must be dismissed.

CONCLUSION

For the foregoing reasons, we respectfully urge that summary judgment be granted as to each and every count of the Complaint in favor of defendant Commissioner Bowie K. Kuhn.

Respectfully submitted,
James E. S. Baker
Lee B. McTurnan
One First National Plaza
Chicago, Illinois 60607
Telephone: 312-329-5400

Peter K. Bleakley
Irvin B. Nathan
1229 - 19th Street, N.W.
Washington, D.C. 20036
Telephone: 202-872-6700

Attorneys for Defendant,
Bowie K. Kuhn

OF COUNSEL:

SIDLEY & AUSTIN
One First National Plaza
Chicago, Illinois 60607
Telephone: 312-329-5400

David R. Kentoff
Paul S. Reichler
Scott B. Schreiber
ARNOLD & PORTER
1229 - 19th Street, N.W.
Washington, D.C. 20036
Telephone: 202-872-6700

Dated: July 19, 1976

SPOT REPORTING

IN THE FIRST *Fireside Book of Baseball* there appeared the famous Ernest Thayer poem "Casey at the Bat," and it was classified as poetry, of course. This one here we classify as spot reporting, which it is. Done by a Pultizer Prize winner, too—Mr. Berger of *The New York Times.*

1941: Casey in the Box

MEYER BERGER

The prospects seemed all rosy for the Dodger
nine that day.
Four to three the score stood, with one man
left to play.
And so when Sturm died, and Rolfe the Red
went out,
In the tall weeds of Canarsie you could hear
the Dodgers' shout.

A measly few got up to go as screaming rent
the air. The rest
Were held deep-rooted by Fear's gnaw eternal
at the human breast.
They thought with only Henrich, Hugh Casey
had a cinch.
They could depend on Casey when things stood
at the pinch.

There was ease in Casey's manner as he stood
there in the box.
There was pride in Casey's bearing, from his
cap down to his sox.
And when, responding to the cheers, he took
up his trousers' sag,
No stranger in the crowd could doubt, he had
them in the bag.

Sixty thousand eyes were on him when Casey
toed the dirt.
Thirty thousand tongues applauded as he
rubbed his Dodger shirt.
Then while the writhing Henrich stood asway-
ing at the hip,
Contempt gleamed high in Casey's eye. A sneer
curled Casey's lip.

And now the leather-covered sphere came hurtling through the air,
And Henrich stood awaiting it, with pale and
frightened stare.

Close by the trembling Henrich the ball unheeded sped.
"He don't like my style," said Casey. "Strike One!" the umpire said.

From the benches black with people there went up a muffled roar,
Like the thunder of dark storm waves on the Coney Island shore.
"Get him! Get him, Casey!" shouted someone in the stand.
Hugh Casey smiled with confidence. Hugh Casey raised his hand.

With a smile of kindly charity Great Casey's visage shone.
He stilled the Faithful's screaming. He bade the game go on.
He caught Mickey Owen's signal. Once more the spheroid flew,
But Henrich still ignored it. The umpire bawled, "Strike Two!"

"Yay!" screamed the maddened thousands, and the echo answered, "YAY!"
But another smile from Casey. He held them under sway.
They saw his strong jaws tighten. They saw his muscles strain,
And they knew that Hughie Casey would get his man again.

Pale as the lily Henrich's lips; his teeth were clenched in hate.
He pounded with cruel violence his bat upon the plate.
And now Great Casey held the ball, and now he let it go.
And Brooklyn's air was shattered by the whiff of Henrich's blow.

But Mickey Owen missed this strike. The ball rolled far behind,
And Henrich speeded to first base, like Clipper on the wind.

Upon the stricken multitude grim melancholy
perched.
Dark disbelief bowed Hughie's head. It seemed
as if he lurched.

DiMaggio got a single. Keller sent one to the wall.
Two runs came pounding o'er the dish and oh,
this wasn't all.
For Dickey walked and Gordon a resounding
double smashed.
And Dodger fans were sickened. And Dodger
hopes were hashed.

Oh somewhere North of Harlem the sun is
shining bright.
Bands are playing in The Bronx and up there
hearts are light.
In Hunts Point men are laughing, on the Con-
course children shout.
But there is no joy in Flatbush. Fate had
knocked their Casey out.

SPOT REPORTING

HERE IS Ira Berkow's account of what took place at Riverfront Stadium in Cincinnati the night of September 11, 1985.

Five years later, another reporter, Michael Sokolove, published *Hustle*, a biography of Pete Rose that contained an updated reference to that same game. "He sold the bat and ball involved in his 4,192d hit for $129,000," Sokolove wrote. "He wore nine different uniform jerseys that night, and sold them all."

1985: 4,192

IRA BERKOW

TEN MILES from the sandlots where he began playing baseball as a boy, Pete Rose, now 44 years old and in his 23rd season in the major leagues, stepped to the plate tonight in the first inning at Riverfront

Stadium. He came to bat on this warm, gentle evening with the chance to make baseball history.

The Reds' player-manager, the man who still plays with the joy of a boy, had a chance to break Ty Cobb's major-league career hit record, 4,191, which had stood since Cobb retired in 1928.

The sell-out crowd of 47,237 that packed the stadium hoping to see Rose do it now stood and cheered under a twilight blue sky be-ribboned with orange clouds.

Now he eased into his distinctive crouch from the left side of the plate, wrapping his white-gloved hands around the handle of his black bat. His red batting helmet gleamed in the lights. Everyone in the ball park was standing. The chant "Pete! Pete!" went higher and higher. Flashbulbs popped.

On the mound was the right-hander Eric Show of the San Diego Padres. Rose took the first pitch for a ball, fouled off the next pitch, took another ball. Show wound up and Rose swung and hit a line drive to left-center.

The ball dropped in and the ball park exploded. Fireworks being set off was one reason; the appreciative cries of the fans was another. Streamers and confetti floated onto the field.

Rose stood on first base and was quickly mobbed by everyone on the Reds' bench. The first base coach, Tommy Helms, one of Rose's oldest friends on the team, hugged him first. Tony Perez, Rose's long-time teammate, then lifted him.

Marge Schott, the owner of the Reds, came out and hugged Rose and kissed him on the cheek. A red Corvette was driven in from behind the outfield fence, a present from Mrs. Schott to her record-holder.

Meanwhile, the Padres, some of whom had come over to congratulate Rose, meandered here and there on the field, chatting with the umpires and among themselves, waiting for play to resume. Show took a seat on the rubber.

Rose had removed his batting helmet and waved with his gloves to the crowd. Then he stepped back on first, seemed to take a breath and turned to Helms, threw an arm around him and threw his head on his shoulder, crying.

The tough old ball player, his face as lined and rugged as a longshoreman's, was moved, perhaps even slightly embarrassed, by the tenderness shown him in the ball park.

Then from the dugout came a uniformed young man. This one was wearing the same number as Rose, 14, and had the same name on the back of his white jersey. Petey Rose, a 15-year-old redhead and sometime bat boy for as long as he can remember, fell into his pop's arms at first base, and the pair of Roses embraced. There were tears in their eyes.

Most people in the park were familiar with the Rose story. He had grown up, the son of a bank cashier, in the area in Cincinnati along the Ohio River known as Anderson Ferry. He had gone to Western Hills High School here for five years—repeating the 10th grade. "It gave me a chance to learn more baseball," he said, with a laugh.

He was only about 5-foot-10 and 150 pounds when he graduated, in 1960—he is now a burly 5-11 and 205—and the only scout who seemed to think he had talent enough to make the major leagues was his uncle, Buddy Bloebaum, who worked for the Reds.

Three years later he was starting at second base for the Reds, and got his first major league hit on April 13, 1963, a triple off Bob Friend of the Pittsburgh Pirates.

Rose was at first called, derisively, "Charlie Hustle." Soon, it became a badge of distinction. He made believers out of many who at first had deprecatory thoughts about this brash young rookie who ran to first on walks, who slid headfirst into bases, who sometimes taunted the opposition and barreled into them when they were in the way.

But never was there malicious intent, and he came to be loved and appreciated by teammates and opponents for his intense desire to, as he said, "play the game the way it's supposed to be played."

He began the season needing 95 hits to break Cobb's record, and as he drew closer and closer, the nation seemed to be watching and listening and wondering when "the big knock," as he called it, would come.

Tonight, he finished in a most typical and satisfying fashion. He got two hits—he tripled in the seventh inning—and walked once and flied to left in four times at bat. It wasn't just the personal considerations that he holds dear. He cares about team accomplishments, he says his rings for World Series triumphs are his most cherished baseball possessions. And this night he scored the only two runs of the game, in the third and seventh innings, as the Reds won, 2–0.

After the game, in a celebration at home plate, Rose took a phone call from President Reagan that was relayed on the public address system.

The President congratulated him and said he had set "the most enduring record in sports history." He said Rose's record might be broken, but "your reputation and legacy will live for a long time."

"Thank you, Mr. President, for taking time from your busy schedule," said Rose. "And you missed a good ball game."

AUTOBIOGRAPHY

PUBLISHED IN 1970, *Ball Four* was an instantaneous and overwhelming hit, to the point where many people today remember it as the first of the diary-type sports books. It wasn't that, of course. In football, Jerry Kramer's *Instant Replay* was published during the 1960s; and in baseball, even earlier, Jim Brosnan's *The Long Season.*

But for all the diaries before or since, *Ball Four* retains a quality—call it irreverence, if you will—somehow all its own. In this chapter, author Jim Bouton details his salary history with the New York Yankees—a history that suggests why, come 1969, he found himself pitching for the Seattle Pilots.

From *Ball Four*

JIM BOUTON *edited by* LEONARD SHECTER

I SIGNED my contract today to play for the Seattle Pilots at a salary of $22,000 and it was a letdown because I didn't have to bargain. There was no struggle, none of the give and take that I look forward to every year. Most players don't like to haggle. They just want to get it over with. Not me. With me signing a contract has been a yearly adventure.

The reason for no adventure this year is the way I pitched last year. It ranged from awful to terrible to pretty good. When it was terrible, and I had a record of 0 and 7, or 2 and 7 maybe, I had to do some serious thinking about whether it was all over for me. I was pitching for the Seattle Angels of the Pacific Coast League. The next year, 1969, under expansion, the club would become the Seattle Pilots of the American League. The New York Yankees had sold me to Seattle for $20,000 and were so eager to get rid of me they paid $8,000 of my $22,000 salary. This means I was actually sold for $12,000, less than half the waiver price. Makes a man think.

In the middle of August I went to see Marvin Milkes, the general manager of the Seattle Angels. I told him that I wanted some kind of guarantee from him about next year. There were some businesses with long-range potential I could go into over the winter and I would if I was certain I wasn't going to be playing ball.

"What I would like," I told him, "is an understanding that no matter what kind of contract you give me, major league or minor league, that it will be for a certain minimum amount. Now, I realize you don't know how much value I will be for you since you haven't gone through the expansion draft and don't know the kind of players you'll have. So I'm not asking for a major-league contract, but just a certain minimum amount of money."

"How much money are you talking about?" Milkes said shrewdly.

"I talked it over with my wife and we arrived at a figure of $15 or $16,000. That's the minimum I could afford to play for, majors or minors. Otherwise I got to go to work."

To this Milkes said simply, "No."

I couldn't say I blamed him.

It was right about then, though, that the knuckleball I'd been experimenting with for a couple of months began to do things. I won two games in five days, going all the way, giving up only two or three hits. I was really doing a good job and everyone was kind of shocked. As the season drew to a close I did better and better. The last five days of the season I finished with a flurry, and my earned-run average throwing the knuckleball was 1.90, which is very good.

The last day of the season I was in the clubhouse and Milkes said he wanted to see me for a minute. I went up to his office and he said, "We're going to give you the same contract for next year. We'll guarantee you $22,000." This means if I didn't get released I'd be getting it even if I was sent down to the minors. I felt like kissing him on both cheeks. I also felt like I had a new lease on life. A knuckleball had to be pretty impressive to impress a general manager $7,000 worth. Don't ever think $7,000 isn't a lot of money in baseball. I've had huge arguments over a lot less.

When I started out in 1959 I was ready to love the baseball establishment. In fact I thought big business had all the answers to any question I could ask. As far as I was concerned clubowners were benevolent old men who wanted to hang around the locker room and were willing to pay a price for it, so there would never be any problem about getting paid decently. I suppose I got that way reading Arthur Daley in *The New York Times*. And reading about those big salaries.

I read that Ted Williams was making $125,000 and figured that Billy Goodman made $60,000. That was, of course, a mistake.

I signed my first major-league contract at Yankee Stadium fifteen minutes before they played "The Star-Spangled Banner" on opening day, 1962. That's because my making the team was a surprise. But I'd had a hell of a spring. Just before the game was about to start Roy Hamey, the general manager, came into the clubhouse and shoved a contract under my nose. "Here's your contract," he said. "Sign it. Everybody gets $7,000 their first year."

Hamey had a voice like B. S. Pully's, only louder. I signed. It wasn't a bad contract. I'd gotten $3,000 for playing all summer in Amarillo, Texas, the year before.

I finished the season with a 7–7 record and we won the pennant and the World Series, so I collected another $10,000, which was nice. I was much better toward the end of the season than at the beginning. Like I was 4–7 early but then won three in a row, and Ralph Houk, the manager, listed me as one of his six pitchers for the stretch pennant race and the Series.

All winter I thought about what I should ask for and finally decided to demand $12,000 and settle for $11,000. This seemed to me an eminently reasonable figure. When I reported to spring training in Ft. Lauderdale—a bit late because I'd spent six months in the army—Dan Topping, Jr., son of the owner, and the guy who was supposed to sign all the lower-echelon players like me, handed me a contract and said, "Just sign here, on the bottom line."

I unfolded the contract and it was for $9,000—if I made the team. I'd get $7,000 if I didn't.

If I made the team?

"Don't forget you get a World Series share," Topping said. He had a boarding-school accent that always made me feel like my fly was open or something. "You can always count on that."

"Fine," I said. "I'll sign a contract that guarantees me $10,000 more at the end of the season if we don't win the pennant."

He was shocked. "Oh, we can't do that."

"Then what advantage is it to me to take less money?"

"That's what we're offering."

"I can't sign it."

"Then you'll have to go home."

"All right, I'll go home."

"Well, give me a call in the morning, before you leave."

I called him the next morning and he said to come over and see him. "I'll tell you what we're going to do," he said. "We don't usually do this, but we'll make a big concession. I talked with my dad, with Hamey, and we've decided to eliminate the contingency clause—you get $9,000 whether you make the club or not."

"Wow!" I said. Then I said no.

"That's our final offer, take it or leave it. You know, people don't usually do this. You're the first holdout we've had in I don't know how many years."

I said I was sorry. I hated to mess up Yankee tradition, but I wasn't going to sign for a $2,000 raise. And I got up to go.

"Before you go, let me call Hamey," Topping said. He told Hamey I was going home and Hamey said he wanted to talk to me. I held the phone four inches from my ear. If you were within a mile of him, Hamey really didn't need a telephone. "Lookit, son," he yelled. "You better sign that contract, that's all there's gonna be. That's it. You don't sign that contract you're making the biggest mistake of your life."

I was twenty-four years old. And scared. Also stubborn. I said I wouldn't sign and hung up.

"All right," Topping said, "how much do you want?"

"I was thinking about $12,000," I said, but not with much conviction.

"Out of the question," Topping said. "Tell you what. We'll give you $10,000."

My heart jumped. "Make it ten-five," I said.

"All right," he said. "Ten-five."

The bastards really fight you.

For my ten-five that year I won 21 games and lost only 7. I had a 2.53 earned-run average. I couldn't wait to see my next contract.

By contract time Yogi Berra was the manager and Houk had been promoted to general manager. I decided to let Houk off easy. I'd ask for $25,000 and settle for $20,000, and I'd be worth every nickel of it. Houk offered me $15,500. Houk can look as sincere as hell with those big blue eyes of his and when he calls you "podner" it's hard to argue with him. He said the reason he was willing to give me such a big raise right off was that he didn't want to haggle, he just wanted to give me a top salary, more than any second-year pitcher had ever made with the Yankees, and forget about it.

"How many guys have you had who won 21 games in their second year?" I asked him.

He said he didn't know. And, despite all the "podners," I didn't sign.

This was around January 15. I didn't hear from Houk again until two weeks before spring training, when he came up another thousand, to $16,500. This was definitely final. He'd talked to Topping, called him on his boat, ship to shore. Very definitely final.

I said it wasn't final for me, I wanted $20,000.

"Well, you can't make twenty," Houk said. "We never double contracts. It's a rule."

It's a rule he made up right there, I'd bet. And a silly one anyway, because it wouldn't mean anything to a guy making $40,000, only to somebody like me, who was making very little to start with.

The day before spring training began he went up another two thousand to $18,500. After all-night consultations with Topping, of course. "Ralph," I said, real friendly, "under ordinary circumstances I might have signed this contract. If you had come with it sooner, and if I hadn't had the problem I had last year trying to get $3,000 out of Dan Topping, Jr. But I can't, because it's become a matter of principle."

He has his rules, I have my principles.

Now I'm a holdout again. Two weeks into spring training and I was enjoying every minute of it. The phone never stopped ringing and I was having a good time. Of course, the Yankees weren't too happy. One reason is that they knew they were being unfair and they didn't want anybody to know it. But I was giving out straight figures, telling everybody exactly what I'd made and what they were offering and the trouble I'd had with Dan Topping, Jr.

One time Houk called and said, "Why are you telling everybody what you're making?"

"If I don't tell them, Ralph," I said, "maybe they'll think I'm asking for ridiculous figures. They might even think I asked for $15,000 last year and that I'm asking for thirty now. I just want them to know I'm being reasonable."

And Houk said something that sounded like: *"Roworrowrowrr."* You ever hear a lion grumble?

You know, players are always told that they're not to discuss salaries with each other. They want to keep us dumb. Because if Joe

Pepitone knows what Tom Tresh is making and Tresh knows what Phil Linz is making, then we can all bargain better, based on what we all know. If one of us makes a breakthrough, then we can all take advantage of it. But they want to keep us ignorant, and it works. Most ballplayers in the big leagues do not know what their teammates are making. And they think you're strange if you tell. (Tom Tresh, Joe Pepitone, Phil Linz and I agreed, as rookies, to always tell. After a while only Phil and I told.)

Anyway, on March 8, my birthday, Houk called me and said he was going to deduct $100 a day from his offer for every day I held out beyond March 10. It amounted to a fine for not signing, no matter what Houk said. What he said was, "Oh no, it's not a fine. I don't believe in fining people." And I'm sure it never occurred to him just how unfair a tactic this was. Baseball people are so used to having their own way and not getting any argument that they just don't think they *can* be unfair. When I called Joe Cronin, president of the league, to ask if Houk could, legally, fine me, he said, "Walk around the block, then go back in and talk some more."

After walking around the block and talking it over with my dad, I chickened out. Sorry about that. I called Houk and said. "Okay, you win. I'm on my way down." I salved my wounds with the thought that if I had any kind of a year this time I'd really sock it to him.

Still, if I knew then what I know now, I wouldn't have signed. I'd have called him back and said, "Okay, Ralph, I'm having a press conference of my own to announce that for every day you don't meet my demand of $25,000 it will cost you $500 a day. Think that one over."

Maybe I wouldn't have gotten $25,000, but I bet I would've gotten more than eighteen-five. I could tell from the negative reaction Ralph got in the press. And I got a lot of letters from distinguished citizens and season-ticket holders, all of them expressing outrage at Houk. That's when I realized I should have held out. It was also when Ralph Houk, I think, started to hate me.

The real kicker came the following year. I had won eighteen games and two in the World Series. Call from Houk:

"Well, what do you want?"

"Ordinarily, I'd say winning eighteen and two in the Series would be worth about an $8,000 raise."

"Good, I'll send you a contract calling for twenty-six-five."

"But in view of what's happened, last year and the year before that, it will have to be more."

"How much more?"

"At least thirty."

"We couldn't do that. It's out of the question."

A couple of days later he called again. "Does $28,000 sound fair to you?"

"Yes, it does, very fair. In fact there are a lot of fair figures. Twenty-eight, twenty-nine, thirty, thirty-two. I'd say thirty-three would be too high and twenty-seven on down would be unfair on your part."

"So you're prepared to sign now."

"Not yet. I haven't decided."

A week later he called again and said he'd sent me the contract I wanted—$28,000.

"Now, wait a minute. I didn't say I'd sign for that."

"But you said it was a fair figure."

"I said there were a lot of fair figures in there. I said thirty-two was fair too."

"You going back on your word? You trying to pull a fast one on me?"

"I'm not trying to pull anything on you. I just haven't decided what I'm going to sign for. I just know that twenty-eight isn't it."

By now he's shouting. "Goddammit, you're trying to renege on a deal."

So I shouted back. "Who the hell do you people think you are, trying to bully people around? You have a goddam one-way contract, and you won't let a guy negotiate. You bulldozed me into a contract my first year when I didn't know any better, you tried to fine me for not signing last year, and now you're trying to catch me in a lie. Why don't you just be decent about it? What's an extra thousand or two to the New York Yankees? You wonder why you get bad publicity. Well, here it is. As soon as the people find out the kind of numbers you're talking about they realize how mean and stupid you are."

"All right. Okay. Okay. No use getting all hot about it."

When the contract came it was like he said, $28,000. I called and told him I wouldn't sign it. I told him I wouldn't play unless I got thirty.

"No deal," he said, and hung up.

Moments later the phone rang. Houk: "Okay, you get your thirty. Under one condition. That you don't tell anybody you're getting it."

"Ralph, I can't do that. I've told everybody the numbers before. I can't stop now."

Softly. "Well, I wish you wouldn't."

Just as softly. "Well, maybe I won't."

When the newspaper guys got to me I felt like a jerk. I also felt I owed Ralph a little something. So when they said, "Did you get what you wanted?" I said, "Yeah." And when they said, "What did you want?" I said, "Thirty." But I said it very low.

Now, I think, Ralph really hated my guts. Not so much because I told about the thirty but because he thought I went back on my word.

Four years later Ralph Houk was still angry. By this time I had started up a little real-estate business in New Jersey. A few friends, relatives and I pooled our money, bought some older houses in good neighorhoods, fixed them up and rented them to executives who come to New York on temporary assignment. Houses like that are hard to find and Houk, who lives in Florida, needed one for the '69 season. After a long search he found exactly what he wanted. Then he found out I owned it. He didn't take it. Too bad, it might have been kind of fun to be his landlord.

Of course, I may misunderstand the whole thing. It's easy to misunderstand things around a baseball club. Else how do you explain my friend Elston Howard? We both live in New Jersey and during my salary fights we'd work out a bit together. And he always told me, "Stick to your guns. Don't let them push you around." Then he'd go down to spring training and he'd say to the other guys, "That Bouton is really something. Who does he think he is holding out every year? How are we gonna win a pennant if the guys don't get in shape? He should be down here helping the club."

I didn't help the club much in 1965, which was the year the Yankees stopped winning pennants. I always had a big overhand motion and people said that it looked, on every pitch, as though my arm was going to fall off with my cap. I used to laugh, because I didn't know what they meant. In 1965 I figured it out. It was my first sore arm. It was my only sore arm. And it made me what I am today, an aging knuckleballer.

My record that year was 4–15, and we finished sixth. It wasn't all my fault. I needed lots of help and got it. Nevertheless my spirits were high waiting for my contract because of something Houk had said. He'd been painted into a corner with Roger Maris. There was a story around that after Maris hit the 61 home runs he got a five-year, no-cut contract. But he'd had a series of bad years and should have been cut. So to take himself off the hook with Maris, Houk said that nobody who had a poor year because of injuries would be cut. Fabulous, man, I thought. That's me.

When I got my contract it called for $23,000, a $7,000 cut.

"But, Ralph, I was injured and you said . . ."

"You weren't injured."

"The hell I wasn't."

"Then how come you pitched 150 innings?"

"I was trying to do what I could, build my arm up, trying to help the team."

Somehow he remained unmoved. I guessed it was my turn to be humble. "Look, Ralph, I know that people think you lost the battle with me last year and I know some of the players are upset that I got $30,000. So I know there are reasons you have to cut me. Tell you what. Even though I could stand firm on the injury thing if I wanted to, I'll make a deal with you. Cut me $3,000 and we can both be happy." He said okay.

After that, it was all downhill. Which is how come I was happy to be making $22,000 with the Seattle Pilots.

AUTOBIOGRAPHY

ALL RIGHT, the Merkle incident. In 1908, Fred Merkle was on first base when what should have been the game-winning hit drove in a Giant teammate from third with two out in the ninth. Merkle, seeing the runner score and the crowd pour onto the field, headed directly for the clubhouse without going to second. Johnny Evers, Chicago Cubs' second baseman, called for the ball—folk differ as to whether what he finally ended up with was *the* ball—and stepped on second for the inning-ending force. Run didn't count. Game ended in a 1–1 tie, since the churning crowd on the field made further play impossible. The Giants claimed they should have won, 2–1, since the rule called by Umpire Hank O'Day had never before been enforced. The Cubs claimed *they* should have won, 9–0, the score of a forfeit, since the home team was responsible for keeping the field playable and the onpouring crowd took care of *that.* The game was ruled a tie—this was late September—and it was ruled that it would be played off the day after the season ended if necessary. It was necessary—the Cubs and Giants wound up in a tie for first!

Mordecai (Three Finger) Brown, Chicago pitching immortal, takes up from here.

1908: Chicago Cubs 4, New York Giants 2

MORDECAI BROWN
as told to JACK RYAN

WHEN Manager Frank Chance led the Chicago Cub team into New York the morning of October 8, 1908, to meet the Giants that afternoon to settle a tie for the National League pennant, I had a half-dozen "black hand" letters in my coat pocket. "We'll kill you," these letters said, "if you pitch and beat the Giants."

Those letters and other threats had been reaching me ever since we had closed our regular season two days before in Pittsburgh. We'd beaten the Pirates in that final game for our 98th win of the year and we had waited around for two days to see what the Giants would do in their last two games with Boston. They had to win 'em to tie us for the National League championship.

Well, the Giants did win those two to match our record of 98 wins and 55 losses so a play-off was in order. I always thought that John McGraw used his great influence in National League affairs to dictate that the play-off must be held on the Giants' home field, the Polo Grounds.

I'd shown the "black hand" letters to Manager Chance and to the Cub owner, Charley Murphy. "Let me pitch," I'd asked 'em, "just to show those so-and-sos they can't win with threats."

Chance picked Jack Pfiester instead. Two weeks before, Pfiester had tangled with Christy Mathewson, McGraw's great pitcher, and had beaten him on the play where young Fred Merkle, in failing to touch second on a hit, had made himself immortal for the "boner" play. Since Mathewson had been rested through the series with Boston and would go against us in the play-off, Chance decided to follow the Pfiester-Mathewson pitching pattern of the "boner" game. I had pitched just two days before as we won our final game of the schedule from Pittsburgh.

Matter of fact, I had started or relieved in 11 of our last l4 games. Beyond that I'd been in 14 of the last 19 games as we came roaring down the stretch hot after the championship.

In our clubhouse meeting before the game, when Chance announced that Pfiester would pitch, we each picked out a New York player to work on. "Call 'em everything in the book," Chance told us. We didn't need much encouragement, either.

My pet target, you might say, was McGraw. I'd been clouding up on him ever since I had come across his sly trick of taking rival pitchers aside and sort of softening them up by hinting that he had cooked up a deal to get that fellow with the Giants. He's taken me aside for a little chat to that effect one time, hoping, I suppose, that in a tight spot against the Giants I'd figure I might as well go easy since I'd soon be over on McGraw's side.

Sure, it was a cunning trick he had and I didn't like it. So, the day after he'd given me that line of talk I walked up to him and said, "Skipper, I'm pitching for the Cubs this afternoon and I'm going to show you just what a helluva pitcher you're trying to make a deal for." I beat his Giants good that afternoon.

But that was early in the season and I want to tell you about this play-off game. It was played before the biggest crowd that had ever seen a baseball game. The whole city of New York, it seemed to us, was clear crazy with disappointment because we had taken that "Merkle boner" game from the Giants. The Polo Grounds quit selling tickets about one o'clock, and thousands who held tickets couldn't force their way through the street mobs to the entrances. The umpires were an hour getting into the park. By game time there were thousands on the field in front of the bleachers, the stands were jammed with people standing and sitting in aisles, and there were always little fights going on as ticket-holders tried to get their seats. The bluffs overhanging the Polo Grounds were black with people, as were the housetops and the telegraph poles. The elevated lines couldn't run for people who had climbed up and were sitting on the tracks.

The police couldn't move them, and so the fire department came and tried driving them off with the hose, but they'd come back. Then the fire department had other work to do, for the mob outside the park set fire to the left-field fence, and was all set to come bursting through as soon as the flames weakened the boards enough.

Just before the game started the crowd did break down another part of the fence and the mounted police had to quit trampling the mob out in front of the park and come riding in to turn back this new drive. The crowds fought the police all the time it seemed to us as we sat in our dugout. From the stands there was a steady roar of abuse. I never heard anybody or any set of men called as many foul names as the Giant fans called us that day from the time we showed up till it was over.

We had just come out onto the field and were getting settled when Tom Needham, one of our utility men, came running up with the news that, back in the clubhouse he'd overheard Muggsy McGraw laying a plot to beat us. He said the plot was for McGraw to cut our batting practice to about four minutes instead of the regular ten, and then, if we protested, to send his three toughest players, Turkey Mike Donlin, Iron Man McGinnity and Cy Seymour charging out to pick a fight. The wild-eyed fans would riot and the blame would be put on us for starting it and the game would be forfeited to the Giants.

Chance said to us, "Cross 'em up. No matter when the bell rings to end practice, come right off the field. Don't give any excuse to quarrel."

We followed orders, but McGinnity tried to pick a fight with Chance anyway, and made a pass at him, but Husk stepped back, grinned and wouldn't fall for their little game.

I can still see Christy Mathewson making his lordly entrance. He'd always wait until about ten minutes before game time, then he'd come from the clubhouse across the field in a long linen duster like auto drivers wore in those days, and at every step the crowd would yell louder and louder. This day they split the air. I watched him enter as I went out to the bull pen, where I was to keep ready. Chance still insisted on starting Pfiester.

Mathewson put us down quick in our first time at bat, but when the Giants came up with the sky splitting as the crowd screamed, Pfiester hit Fred Tenney, walked Buck Herzog, fanned Bresnahan, but Kling dropped the third strike and when Herzog broke for second, nailed him. Then Turkey Mike Donlin doubled, scoring Tenney, and out beyond center field a fireman fell off a telegraph pole and broke his neck. Pfiester walked Cy Seymour and then Chance motioned to me to come in. Two on base, two out. Our warmup pen was out in right-center field so I had to push and shove my way through the crowd on the outfield grass.

"Get the hell out of the way," I bawled at 'em as I plowed through. "Here's where you 'black hand' guys get your chance. If I'm going to get killed I sure know that I'll die before a capacity crowd."

Arthur Devlin was up—a low-average hitter, great fielder but tough in the pinches. But I fanned him, and then you should have heard the names that flew around me as I walked to the bench.

I was about as good that day as I ever was in my life. That year I had won 29 and, what with relief work, had been in 43 winning ball games.

But in a way it was Hank Chance's day.

That Chance had a stout heart in him. His first time at bat, it was in the second, the fans met him with a storm of hisses—not boos like you hear in modern baseball—but the old, vicious hiss that comes from real hatred.

Chance choked the hisses back down New York's throat by singling with a loud crack of the bat. The ball came back to Mathewson. He looked at Bresnahan behind the bat, then wheeled and threw to first, catching Chance off guard. Chance slid. Tenney came down with the ball. Umpire Bill Klem threw up his arm. Husk was out!

Chance ripped and raved around, protesting. Most of us Cubs rushed out of the dugout. Solly Hofman called Klem so many names that Bill threw him out of the game.

The stands behind us went into panic, they were so tickled and the roar was the wildest I ever heard when Matty went on to strike out Steinfeldt and Del Howard.

Chance was grim when he came up again in the third. Tinker had led off the inning by tripling over Cy Seymour's head. We heard afterward that McGraw had warned Seymour that Tinker was apt to hit Mathewson hard, and to play away back. Seymour didn't. Kling singled Tinker home. I sacrificed Johnny to second. Sheckard flied out. Evers walked, Schulte doubled. We had Matty wobbling and then up came Chance, with the crowd howling. He answered them again with a double, and made it to second with a great slide that beat a great throw by Mike Donlin.

Four runs.

The Giants made their bid in the seventh. Art Devlin singled off me, so did Moose McCormick. I tried to pitch too carefully to Bidwell and walked him. There was sure bedlam in the air as McGraw took out Mathewson and sent up the kid, Larry Doyle, to hit. Doyle hit a high foul close to the stand and as Kling went to catch it, the fans sailed derby hats to confuse him—and bottles, papers, everything. But Kling had nerve and he caught it.

Every play, as I look back on it, was crucial. In the seventh after Tenney's fly had scored Devlin, Buck Herzog rifled one on the ground to left but Joe Tinker got one hand and one shin in front of it, blocked it, picked it up and just by a flash caught Herzog who made a wicked slide into first.

In the ninth a big fight broke out in the stands and the game was held up until the police could throw in a cordon of bluecoats and stop it. It was as near a lunatic asylum as I ever saw. As a matter of fact the newspapers next day said seven men had been carted away, raving mad, from the park during the day. This was maybe exaggerated, but it doesn't sound impossible to anyone who was there that day.

As the ninth ended with the Giants going out, one-two-three, we all ran for our lives, straight for the clubhouse with the pack at our heels. Some of our boys got caught by the mob and beaten up some. Tinker, Howard and Sheckard were struck. Chance was hurt most of all. A Giant fan hit him in the throat and Husk's voice was gone for a day or two of the World Series that followed. Pfiester got slashed on the shoulder by a knife.

We made it to the dressing room and barricaded the door. Outside wild men were yelling for our blood—really. As the mob got bigger, the police came up and formed a line across the door. We read next day that the cops had to pull their revolvers to hold them back. I couldn't say as to that. We weren't sticking our heads out to see.

As we changed clothes, too excited yet to put on one of those wild clubhouse pennant celebrations, the word came in that the Giants over in their dressing room were pretty low. We heard that old Cy Seymour was lying on the floor, in there, bawling like a baby about Tinker's triple.

When it was safe we rode to our hotel in a patrol wagon, with two cops on the inside and four riding the running boards and the rear step. That night when we left for Detroit and the World Series we slipped out the back door and were escorted down the alley in back of our hotel by a swarm of policemen.

AUTOBIOGRAPHY

THE SIMPLE FOREWORD to Roy Campanella's book says: "This book was written during a period of convalescence, at a time when I was fighting to get well. I needed a helping hand in its preparation. I was fortunate in that I had two—Joe Reichler of the Associated Press and Dave Camerer of the Columbia Broadcasting System. To them, my sincere thanks."

Here are the first two chapters from that book.

From *It's Good to Be Alive*

ROY CAMPANELLA

MY MIND is so full of thoughts as I sit in my wheelchair and get ready to dictate the story of my life . . . a life that has been so eventful, so exciting, so wonderful . . . a life that was almost taken away from me but which God spared . . . a life such as few people have been fortunate enough to live.

Where shall I start? How do I begin? There is so much to tell. Shall I begin with the automobile accident? When I recovered consciousness in the car and discovered I was paralyzed? Shall I start with the time I came out of the anesthesia after they cut a hole in my windpipe to allow me to breathe?

Shall I open with the time I presented a baseball to a little boy in the hospital with me; and, after I had apologized for not being physically able to autograph it for him, he said simply, "That's all right, Mr. Campanella, I can't see."?

Then there was the World Series day in Yankee Stadium when I slumped in my wheelchair and cried unashamedly as the huge crowd stood on its feet and cheered me for five full minutes.

Baseball has been my life ever since I was old enough to throw one, so perhaps I should start from the day I played my first professional game; or when I joined the Brooklyn Dodgers organization; or when I hit the first of my 242 major-league home runs; or when I won the first of my three Most Valuable Player awards.

Perhaps the proper beginning would be the day I left Rusk Institute to begin a new life, my life in a wheelchair as a quadriplegic? There are so many starting points, so many new phases, so many milestones, it's hard to decide just where to begin.

What stands out most in my mind of all that has happened since the fateful morning of January 28, 1958, when the world turned upside down for me, was something that happened at Holman Stadium in Vero Beach, Florida, nearly fourteen months after my accident.

From where I was sitting in my wheelchair, I could see this little crippled old lady struggling up the steep ramp. She wore steel braces on both legs. Slowly she made her way up with the aid of a wooden crutch under her right arm. Her left arm hung loosely at her side, paralyzed. Her snow-white head was tilted slightly to the left.

Her attendant, a middle-aged man, walked slowly alongside, ever on the alert to grab her should she stumble or fall. Once or twice he tried to assist her, but she shrugged him off. She finally made the top of the ramp where I was sitting. She was gasping and out of breath. She opened her mouth to speak; but no words came. She stood there looking at me in the chair. Her eyes, sorrowed by years of suffering, looked down on my paralyzed body. She slowly lifted them to my face. Reaching out an old, thinned right arm, she took my limp hand in hers.

"Mr. Campanella," she finally managed to say, "I came a long, long way to see you. More than a thousand miles. I just had to see you and thank you, for you gave me the courage and the will to go on when everything seemed hopeless." Her voice trailed off. She was all spent from the excitement, the long trip, the steep climb, the deep emotion. She was very old, and she must have weighed all of eighty-five or ninety pounds. Who was she? Why had she made this long trip? Had she really come just to see me? I wanted to say something to her as she stood there looking down at me, barely able to stand up and refusing to support herself on the arm of her attendant. Then I saw she was ready to speak again.

"Oh, I'm so glad I came," she said earnestly. "You see, I was a patient in the same hospital with you in New York. At the same time. I had a stroke and my entire left side became paralyzed. I couldn't even talk. They didn't give me much hope. As for me, I didn't care whether I made it or not. Then you were brought in. The people at the hospital said you had no chance to live. Crushed vertebrae. A broken neck.

"But you did live. The doctors marveled at your courage. They were thrilled with your faith. They set you up as the example, the inspiration. You became a symbol.

"I don't know exactly when I stopped giving up. All I know is that one day I decided that I just didn't want to stop yet. I was determined to get back on my feet. It was you who gave me the courage, the will to live."

I sat there without saying a word. I just couldn't find any. I've never been accused of being the quiet, shy type. I'm a firm believer in free speech. But that was one time when my tongue was stuck in my mouth. It was most embarrassing. I wanted to thank her. I wanted to ask her name; find out where she was from; learn whether she had any children. But all I could think of was that this wonderful little crippled old lady had come down the length of the United States just to say hello to me—me, Roy Campanella, a Negro ballplayer who happened to have an accident that ended his career and maybe put him for the rest of his life in a wheelchair.

I thought about that a long time after she left. I thought about this little old lady. I thought about the hundreds, no, thousands of people, strangers, who had come to see me since I arrived at this Dodgers spring-training camp. Men and women who had come to shake my hand, to encourage me and wish me well; boys and girls who had come just to look at me and ask for my autograph and who turned away, some disappointed, some embarrassed, when I apologized for not being able to hold a pen or pencil. I thought of the hundreds of thousands of letters and telegrams I had received while in the hospital, from people in all walks of life, from people all over the world—from President Eisenhower down.

The Dodgers and Reds were playing an exhibition game. As a rule no one watches a game with more interest and more concentration than I do. But at this moment the game could have been miles away. I was sitting in back of the last row of the grandstand, behind home plate. My two attendants, Jimmy Williamson and Danny Mackey, were standing on each side of me, to protect me from foul balls. I had been flown down from my home in Glen Cove, Long Island, only a week before to begin my duties as special coach of all the pitchers and catchers in the Dodgers organization.

Being there with my old buddies, with Pee Wee and Duke and Gil and Carl and Clem and my protégé Johnny Roseboro, and being back with the game I love so much was a wonderful thing for me both physically and mentally. Only a year before, when I was lying flat on my back in Glen Cove Community Hospital, fighting for my life, I didn't dare dream that I would ever be back on a baseball field where I had made my living for twenty years, where I had grown from a scared boy into a confident man, where I had learned that on a ball field it doesn't matter who you are or what you are, but how you're fielding, or hitting, or pitching. It's what you do on that baseball diamond that counts. Nothing else.

I'm a lucky guy. I've got so much to be thankful for. Don't feel sorry for me. Please. I'm on my way back, and I'm going to make it.

Some people may think the Lord turned His back on me because of the accident. That's not so. I consider myself very lucky that I was able to play ball for twenty years, half of them in the big leagues. And even when I had the accident I was lucky. How many people have similar accidents and are killed? I could have burned up in that automobile, and I could have died in the hospital after I got pneumonia. The car turned over on me and the engine was running for I don't know how long. The gasoline could easily have leaked out and caught fire, and I couldn't have done anything about it. I tried to turn off the ignition with my left hand. I couldn't move my arm. I couldn't move anything. That's when I knew my whole body was paralyzed.

I have made a great deal of progress. I'm going to make more. There was a time when I couldn't move my arms or my head, when I couldn't sit up. For many months after the accident I couldn't use my hands at all. I couldn't eat or drink by myself. Now I can do all those things. Each day I feel stronger and every day I try something new.

It doesn't take too much fight if you have the courage and the faith. All of us want to live and maybe to help some others in the same condition who may have given up just a little.

My last year as a ballplayer was 1957. That was the year Walter O'Malley, owner of the Dodgers, decided to move them out of Brooklyn to Los Angeles. I first began hearing rumors of the switch in February of that year when spring training began at Vero Beach. I remember it was on the eve of Washington's Birthday. The Dodgers' pitchers and catchers had been down early and working out before the others arrived. And it was that evening that Mr. O'Malley made a startling announcement. Ever since baseball has been played there have been player swaps and deals. But this was no player deal. This was a franchise deal! Mr. O'Malley and Phil Wrigley, Jr., owner of the Chicago Cubs, had exchanged minor-league clubs. The Cubs got the Dodgers' Fort Worth club in the Texas League in exchange for Chicago's Los Angeles club of the Pacific Coast League. The deal included the ball parks. That meant that the Dodgers now had Wrigley Field in Los Angeles and a foothold on the Coast if and when.

I should have figured it out right then. Why would Mr. O'Malley make such a deal unless he intended to move? Looking back, it's so obvious. But somehow I didn't see it then. Maybe because I didn't want to see it. I had spent nine of my happiest years in Brooklyn. That's where I wanted to finish my playing career. I got my wish all right, but in a much different way.

Not everybody was as innocent as me, though. The people on the West Coast got the idea pretty quick. The newsprint was hardly dry on those Los Angeles papers when the politicians came swarming in on us at Vero Beach. They arrived in camp like conquerors, looking us over the way a guy does a piece of property knowing he's about to own it. Always looking for an angle, the photographers rigged up a Dodger cap with the letters *LA* on it and asked me to pose with the Los Angeles mayor, Norris Poulson, wearing the cap. I went along with it but to me it was a big joke. The Dodgers leave Ebbets Field? Maybe. But the Dodgers leave Brooklyn? Never.

After we shook hands, Mayor Poulson put one arm around me and said, "Campy, next year you'll no longer be a Brooklyn Bum; you'll be a Los Angeles Bum."

"That'll sure be the day," I grinned.

At the time I wasn't thinking about where I'd be playing "next year." I was more concerned with this year. I was coming off a bad season and was looking to make a good comeback. In '56 I'd played the entire season with two bad hands. The left one had been operated on in '54. Some people thought that after '56 I'd had it.

One big reason why I was looking to a good year was because the pain had left my hands. The numbness was still there but the pain had gone, and I could grip a bat again and had been strengthening my hands by swinging a loaded bat in the cellar of my store. And finally, this was the odd year. This was '57, and I had won the National League's Most Valuable Player award three times, all in odd years—1951, 1953, and 1955. If ballplayers are superstitious, this at least was a happy hunch.

For ballplayers, spring training is a time for tuning up, getting set for the season ahead. Each man has to prepare himself, and of course I was thinking most about my hands and my ability to play as well as I had in my good years. Pee Wee Reese was worried about his legs and his back, being the oldest player on the team. Carl Erskine was trying to come back from arm trouble. Duke Snider had a bad knee and was hoping he could get through the season without undergoing surgery. Don Newcombe had his usual sore arm in the spring. Each of us, especially the veterans, had a personal problem.

But we had a mutual concern: the possibility of this being our last year as the Brooklyn Dodgers. As time wore on, we began to think more and more about moving to Los Angeles, and we talked about it almost every day in the clubhouse and on the bench. Some were for it; some didn't care much either way; and others, like myself, didn't like it. We all had personal reasons for the way we felt.

Gil Hodges was like me. He wanted no part of the West Coast. "I just don't want to move," he said. Gil had lived in Indiana until he got to the big leagues. "I live in Brooklyn," he said. "I'm not just a Dodger ballplayer. Brooklyn is my home. I don't want to have to sell my house, take my kids out of school, leave old friends and all that."

Snider felt the opposite. "I guess it's better for me if we shift. I got an avocado ranch up there in the valley not too far from L. A.," he said.

Reese didn't want to go. He wanted to finish his career in Brooklyn. I guess he played there longer than any other player in history. And nobody was more popular in Brooklyn than Pee Wee. He asked me how I felt about moving.

"Man," I said, "I don't like it nohow. I got my business in New York. I got my home in Glen Cove. Yes, and my youngsters are in good schools. Then there's my boat. Jersey City is as far west as I wanna go."

The Dodgers had played eight games in Jersey City the year before, in '56, because Mr. O'Malley was trying to prove his point to New York City officials that the Dodgers were too big for Ebbets Field. We had simply outgrown the old park. We needed a much bigger field, with bigger and better parking areas. Now, we had another eight games scheduled for Jersey City in '57. I kinda looked forward to those games. Not because I loved hitting in that prairie-sized park. Heck, no. It's just that I would take my boat from the dock near my home in the morning and have an enjoyable cruise down Long Island Sound, into the East River and then on into the Hudson River, and tie up at Jersey City. All our games there were played at night, and so it gave me a day on the water. Oh, how I enjoyed those trips.

The rumored shift to California was only a minor annoyance compared to what was really worrying me. My hands. They weren't right. I knew it in spring training just as soon as I began to bear down. The old breaks and the old and new operations all started hurting at once. At thirty-five, plus, my hands felt more like eighty-five. I wore a kid glove on my mitt hand to help ease the impact on catching a fast ball. Foul tips hurt the bare hand.

As that '57 season wore on, the daily pounding made the hands worse. Occasionally I hit the ball hard, but I knew I wasn't myself at the plate. Manager Walter Alston knew it too. He had to bench me. I was really hurtin'. I didn't like to ride the bench, but the rest did help some. That season I managed to catch a hundred games for the ninth consecutive year. I hit only .242, and the thirteen homers were a very little bit for old Campy. My spirits hit a new low in August, and to make it worse, it was in that month that I found out for sure that we were going to Los Angeles. The only thing that could save us was a miracle—like New York giving us a new ball park, strictly a thousand-to-one shot.

Even though most of us older players were having a bad year, our young pitchers such as Johnny Podres and Don Drysdale were very strong. We managed to stay in the pennant race until August as part of a five-team dogfight. It was strictly dog-eat-dog and the fans loved it. Then everybody but Milwaukee started losing all at once—St. Louis, Cincinnati, Philadelphia and Brooklyn. Just like that, the race cracked wide-open. The Braves won the flag in a breeze and the Cardinals beat us out for second place. Milwaukee clinched on September 23, and we just played out the schedule for those last half-dozen games.

The Giants had announced early in August that they were quitting New York for San Francisco, so we felt pretty sure, that last week of the season, that we were locking up Ebbets Field. Mr. O'Malley hadn't announced our move officially, but the rumors were too strong. When I went behind the bat in the windup game in Ebbets Field, I knew it was goodbye to that cozy park. It was Thursday, September 28, 1957, and the few fans on hand for the wake waved goodbye after the final out.

We finished the season that weekend in Philadelphia. I drove down and took Roy, Jr., then eight, with me. Tony, two years younger, was slated to go too, but at the last minute he stayed home with his mother. Whenever we played in Philadelphia in all my years in the National League, I stayed with my parents rather than with the team at the Warwick Hotel.

With nothing at stake, I ordinarily would not have had to catch any of those last three games. But I needed one more to give me a league record of catching a hundred games nine years in a row. Ballplayers don't usually watch such things too closely. But I was proud of it. The reporters with the club reminded me of it. They told Alston, too.

So the manager had me catch the first game of the Sunday doubleheader. I knew it was my last game as a Brooklyn player, but had no idea it would be my last game ever. I caught three innings and that completed exactly twenty years in organized professional baseball, ten years in Negro ball and ten in the National League. And my son Roy, Jr., sitting in a box seat behind home plate, saw me catch my last game of baseball.

I drove to New York after the game. I didn't return to my parents' house because Roy had to get back home and into bed so as to be fresh for school the next morning.

I saw every game of the World Series at Yankee Stadium. The Braves and Yankees had a day off for travel from Milwaukee to New York after the fifth game. On that day, when there was no game, O'Malley announced he was transferring the club from Brooklyn to Los Angeles. It was finally official. Here it was, the move I kept hoping and hoping wouldn't ever happen to us.

It meant that we now had to decide on the things we had talked about in spring training: whether to move our families west and pull out of New York altogether or to just rent in California and remain Eastern people.

My wife Ruthe and I had talked it over at times during the summer hoping we never would be forced to decide, but being sensible enough to realize it might be forced on us. I had to decide whether to sell the business, the house, real estate I own in Harlem, and the boat.

We were very happy in the house, a large, rambling ranch house on Long Island Sound with our own dock. It was wonderful for the children. We knew what we had here. We didn't know what we would get there. And we didn't feel it was right to uproot the children.

My liquor store was doing well, and I saw no sense in selling it. It was the best investment I ever made. I remember when I first mentioned the liquor business, Branch Rickey was dead set against it. Mr. Rickey is a very religious man. He preaches from the pulpit and is a nondrinker. His only vice is smoking expensive cigars. He didn't think that liquor and baseball were a good mix and felt that people might get the wrong idea if a ballplayer sold whiskey.

"Campy," he said, "why don't you invest your money in a sporting goods store or something else where there will be no taint?"

I told him, "Mr. Rickey, you're a white man. Maybe you don't understand the problem a colored man has going into business. How many businesses do you think are open to colored men, outside of entertainment? My people drink. They'll make better customers for whiskey than for sporting goods."

I convinced Mr. Rickey. It was the only time I ever outtalked him. I had no trouble with Mr. O'Malley. He was all for it, and he loaned me the money to get started. So, like I say, I decided to hold onto the store; but the boat was something else.

"I sure hate to sell the *Princess*, Campy," Ruthe said. "But think of the problems it would create. There's no sense shipping it to California. We don't even know where we're going to live. We'd have no place to keep it there and no chance to use it."

I knew she was right.

I decided to get my last licks in enjoying the boat on a one-week fishing cruise in the Atlantic in the nice weather in October.

In many ways that was the most interesting vacation I ever had. I hired a captain and crew of two plus a guide to smell out the fish and bait up the rods. We were after tuna, sail, and marlin.

We picked up the professionals at Montauk, way down at the tip of Long Island. "We" included some fellas—old friends of mine, who didn't get seasick, liked to fish, eat, laugh, and enjoyed drinking beer and tossing the cans in the Atlantic. Once we pulled the hook at Montauk we didn't stop until we were nearly fifty miles out to sea.

As self-appointed cook, I was in charge of the galley. I'd remembered to bring along some frozen meat—pork chops, steaks, and two pheasants. These provisions were brought along just in case. Actually, we expected to eat fish practically every meal. Fish that we caught and boated.

But as things turned out, it's a good thing I brought along that meat. If we'd had to depend on what we caught, we'd have starved. During those first two days out to sea, we never even raised a tuna or sail, much less a marlin. But we did tie into two blue sharks. Each weighed close to 400 pounds. The one I caught took me nearly one and one-half hours to boat. Man, rasslin' with that fish straightened me up! I thought I was in good shape following a full season and all. But that old shark really dragged me out! When I boated him he snapped at me and just missed my toe. We kicked him overboard and cut the other one loose.

On the third and fourth day, we didn't see even a fin. About sundown, I called our home in Glen Cove on the ship-to-shore phone.

"Ruthe," I said, "we're not too lucky out here. We're comin' home."

And that's what we did. I knew that was about the last time I'd be aboard the *Princess*. She would be put up for sale that winter.

It costs cash to maintain a yacht, plenty of it. But for the pleasure she gave my family and me, it was worth it. Some of the nicest times I've ever known have been aboard that boat. One day maybe, when I'm able to do more and get around even better than now, I'll get another boat. There will probably be a lot less of her, but she'll be all boat and something that maybe I can pilot again.

I didn't sell the boat right away. It wasn't until the following June, while I was still in the hospital, that it was sold at auction for $20,000, which was just enough to pay off the notes. I had paid $36,000 for it in 1955 and must have put in about $12,000 in improvements, so I took a pretty good bath.

I got my first look at L.A. in November of 1957. The city threw a welcoming luncheon to celebrate coming into the major leagues. Reese, Snider, Hodges and I were invited. Hodges and I caught a plane from New York together. Reese flew in from Louisville, Kentucky, and Duke drove up from his ranch. While we were there I spent a few days looking for a house to lease but couldn't find what I wanted.

I didn't run into racial or social problems. It was just that it wasn't easy to find the right place for a large family with small children.

After enjoying Christmas at home, I returned to the Coast in January to resume house-hunting and also to appear on a TV spectacular in a salute to Miss Ethel Barrymore. Bing Crosby, Frank Sinatra, Laraine Day, Lauren Bacall, Orson Welles, Joseph Cotten, Hoagy Carmichael were among the theater people on it. Leo Durocher, Braves manager Fred Haney, and Casey Stengel were there too. I presented Miss Barrymore with a season pass for the Dodgers home games, and to her nephew I presented an autographed ball, signed by the whole team. I had to rehearse for a week and spent the free time looking for a place to live.

I was fortunate to find a family in L.A. who would lease me their home all furnished. It was a lovely place in Lincoln Park. I told them that I had young children, and Mrs. Wood said that was all right as she was sure they wouldn't break anything. I phoned Ruthe in Glen Cove, and she was pleased. But I wanted her to actually see it herself. I wouldn't sign the lease until she saw it, so I arranged to come back with her the first Sunday in February.

I'm glad that I didn't know then what would happen to me before Ruthe and I could keep that date.

I'll never forget January 28, 1958. That was the date the world turned around for me.

On Sunday night, the 26th, I attended the Baseball Writers Dinner at the Waldorf-Astoria in New York. I usually go to this affair, which includes a show that kids people and events in baseball. I was sitting at one of the Dodgers tables, with Gil Hodges, Don Drysdale, and Sandy Koufax, when I was interrupted by Harry Wismer, the radio man.

Harry had a TV show on Monday night after the television of the fights at St. Nicholas Arena. He said the Harlem Branch of the YMCA had told him to call me. They had a fund-raising drive on and felt I could help them by appearing on TV. He asked me to appear the next night.

I had been close to the kids at the "Y" working with them in the winters in the gym, and wanted to help. I told Harry I'd go on with him, and we set up the date.

The show was to go on around 10:45 P.M., depending on the length of the fight. I told Wismer to call me at the store before four in the afternoon to make the final arrangements.

Monday was a raw, wintry day. When I walked out of the house to my car around 9:30 in the morning, the wind was howling off the Sound. I got into my 1958 Chevrolet station wagon after waving goodbye to Ruthe and the kids and telling them to watch me on TV that night.

It had snowed a few days before and the roads were icy and treacherous, particularly Eastland Drive and Dosoris Lane, near where I live. Dosoris Lane leads into Glen Cove Road, which in turn leads to Northern State Parkway and on into New York.

When I got into the city, I didn't go straight to my store, which is at Seventh Avenue and 134th Street. Instead, I headed for the Curry Chevrolet service department at 136th and Broadway, a couple of blocks from the store.

The wagon wasn't running right. The motor needed adjustment and the radio was out of whack. These were minor things, but I figured I might as well take it in early in the week and get them fixed. They were busy and said I couldn't get the car back that day. "I want to do a good job for you, Campy," the service manager said. "No sense rushing it. We couldn't get it done in one day and have it the way I'd like it."

I agreed to leave it and rented a 1957 Chevy sedan so I could get around during the day and get home that night. I got to the store around 11 A.M. Cynthia Mason, my secretary, had been away on a two-week vacation; and there were many points to go over, as I had been filling in for her.

Wismer called me before noon and said everything was all set and that I should be at the studios on 67th Street off Central Park West at 10 P.M. I agreed. I told him I'd go out to dinner and be there afterwards. But at nine o'clock after I returned from dinner, Harry called back.

"Campy," he said, "why don't we call off this thing tonight and do it next Monday? That will give me a chance to publicize your appearance, and we should get a larger audience next week. It will mean more money for the 'Y.' "

"Okay, Harry," I said.

Louis Johnson, my clerk, was alone at the time; so I stayed there with him. I usually left the store at four in the afternoon to beat the traffic leaving the city at night, but I had been delayed so long by now that I stayed on.

Johnson and I shifted some stock, and it got so late that I decided to stay until closing and check out the cash register ribbons. We closed the store at midnight, but there was still work to be done. We set up the burglar traps and cleaned up the store.

I counted the receipts and closed the safe, and by the time we had finished, it was about 1:30 in the morning of January 28th. I always have been careful to clean up the store—no empty boxes, no trash on the floor—and to put the plastic covers on the cash registers. I left before two and walked to the car.

How does a man know when he is taking the last steps of his life? I haven't taken one since.

I was tired and it was cold and late. But I drove carefully, as I usually do. I've always been a careful driver and never have been a fast driver. I had never had an accident. The roads in the city had been cleared up from the snowstorms but those in the suburban areas had not been cleaned fully, and they had slippery patches of ice and snow.

I managed the main highways without any trouble and made a left turn into Dosoris Lane, passing the school my children go to. I went down Dosoris Lane and came to this S curve which is a couple miles from my home.

There were big ice patches on the road. They looked like white spots. I could see them clearly. I wasn't going fast, I don't think more than 30 or 35 miles an hour, though I wasn't looking at the speedometer. I followed the road around the bend in the S and was headed for the right side of the road as I came out of the bend. Then I suddenly lost control. The car wouldn't behave. I tried to steer it away from the side of the road. The brakes didn't hold. The surface was sandy and icy. I fought the wheel. The brakes were useless.

I tried furiously to swerve and felt a chill in my spine when I saw I couldn't. I saw this telephone pole right where I was heading. If this had been my own station wagon, which is three hundred pounds heavier and had snow tires, I might have gotten it out of the skid. I managed to turn it away from hitting the pole dead center, but not enough to miss it altogether.

I just did hit it, the right front fender crashing against it. The car bounced off and turned completely over, landing on its right side. I felt the car turning over and the force of it tore my hands from the wheel. The collision knocked me forward and down onto the floor on the passenger's side of the front seat.

I guess my neck hit the dashboard as I plunged. Anyway, my body jackknifed, and I was wedged in under the dash and on the floor. I never thought I was that small to fit into such a small space.

I've gone through the accident a hundred times in my mind. I can still see that pole. You know, it was just about a year later that we went over the same road when Ruthe was driving and I saw patches of ice in exactly the same place. A shudder shot through me at the memory of that night.

"Please, Ruthe," I cautioned her, "take it easy here. This is where it happened."

I guess I never really blacked out for a while, because I remember thinking that the car might catch fire. I was pinned down there under the dashboard with the car overturned. I could feel no pain. In fact, I couldn't feel a thing. But I knew the motor was running. I tried to reach up to turn off the ignition, but I couldn't reach the key. I couldn't move my arms.

That's when the terrible thought came to me: "I'm paralyzed."

I was terrified. I cried out, "O Lord, have mercy on me."

I couldn't move anything.

I don't know how long I lay there, but it seemed long to me. The next thing I knew, a light was shining through the window of the car.

"Why, it's Campy," the fellow with the searchlight said.

"Yes, it's me," I groaned. "Please help me. Help me, somebody. I can't move."

The man with the light was a police officer. Patrolman Frank Poepplein. I recognized his voice. He used to wave to me in town at times and stop and talk. "Okay, Campy," he said. "Just take it easy. We'll get you out."

"Turn off the ignition," I pleaded. "The car will catch fire."

Moments later I must have blacked out for good. I found out later that the sound of the crash woke up people in houses along the road. I've read since that a doctor crawled into the car and gave me a shot with a needle. But I don't remember that at all. As a matter of fact, I don't even remember being taken out of the car. Ruthe told me later that Poepplein had worked his way into the car and held me rigid while a wrecker got it back on its wheels. It took twenty minutes to free me. They had to use crowbars to get me loose. They laid me face down and rushed me to Glen Cove Community Hospital in a Nassau County police ambulance.

In the meantime, Patrolman Poepplein went to my home. Ruthe was woken up by the bell. It was now nearly four o'clock.

"I hate to come with bad news like this, Mrs. Campanella," he said, nervously. "But your husband has had an auto accident and is on the way to the hospital. I'll be glad to take you there."

They arrived at the hospital about 4:30 A.M. By that time, I already had been wheeled into the X-ray room. There were two doctors there: Dr. Gilbert Taylor and Dr. Charles W. Hayden. Dr. Taylor was holding my head.

"I don't want to alarm you, Mrs. Campanella," Dr. Taylor said. "But your husband is in a state of shock. I'm afraid he's paralyzed. He can't move his legs."

Dr. Robert Sengstaken, chief of neurosurgery at the hospital, had already been called. When he arrived, he examined the X-ray pictures. Interns on duty had read the wet plates which indicated damage to the upper part of my spine. He confirmed this. The X-rays showed that two vertebrae had slipped and overlapped each other.

"He has a fracture and dislocation of vertebrae five and six," Dr. Sengstaken said. "He's paralyzed from just below the shoulders to the toes. He can't push his arms out or grasp, but he can pull his arms in if they're held out for him.

"We've got to operate immediately. We haven't a moment to lose. The quicker it's done, the better. The pressure on his spinal cord must be relieved quickly."

Dr. Sengstaken said he had to have Ruthe's permission before he could operate. She said she was willing to go along with whatever the doctors thought best.

"Perhaps it would be a good idea to call the ball club," Dr. Hayden suggested.

Ruthe thought that Mr. O'Malley was on his way from his home in Amityville, Long Island, to Los Angeles, so she called Buzzy Bavasi, the Dodgers' vice president, at his home in Scarsdale. It turned out that it was Bavasi who had left for Los Angeles, but Mrs. Bavasi gave Ruthe the number for Bavasi in L.A., and Dr. Hayden got on the phone and explained the situation to him.

It was close to seven o'clock when Dr. Sengstaken gathered his operating team of three doctors and six nurses. They took me up to the operating room on the elevator. Ruthe walked along beside me. I was on my stomach, face down, but I knew she was there.

When we reached the door of the operating room, Dr. Sengstaken drew her aside.

"Mrs. Campanella, please go home. There's nothing you can do here now. I assure you that you can help your husband more by getting a few hours' sleep. Your children need you, too. We'll keep in touch with you. I promise that we'll call you as soon as the operation is over."

Ruthe didn't want to leave but she realized the doctor was right. As she turned to go, I said, "Honey, it hurts."

Two-Top Gruskin

BENNETT CERF

THE WONDERFUL SAGA of Two-Top Gruskin, the two-headed pitcher, is the brain child of Ed Gardner, the incomparable Archie of Duffy's Tavern radio program. It goes something like this:

Duffy's Irish Yankees have mechanical perfection, but no color. "This guy, Athos and Porthos McGinnes, may be your dish," says Dugan, the shortstop, to the disconsolate Duffy. "They call him Two-Top Gruskin for short, I guess, on account of him having two heads."

"A pitcher with two heads?" says Duffy dubiously. "You think it'd be a novelty?"

"What if it ain't?" points out Dugan. "Who else could watch first and third base at the same time? Besides, he's a great guy to pitch double-headers."

So Two-Top is summoned from his home (Walla Walla, of course) and arrives to sign his contract in a dress suit. "What are all you guys staring at?" he asks sourly. "Ain't none of you seen a tuxedo before?"

"Two-Top," says Duffy, "I'm a man of few words. Report tomorrow. There's a uniform and two caps waiting for you. Waiter, bring my new pitcher two beers."

Two-Top wins a masquerade that very night by disguising himself as a pair of book ends with a copy of *My Son, My Son* between the two heads. The next afternoon Duffy introduces him to his catcher, Gorilla Hogan, who measures 6 foot 14 inches and squats standing up. "Most people," says Duffy proudly, "calls Gorilla a monstrosity, and I agree with them—a swell guy." Gorilla soon gets into trouble with Two-Top, however. He signals for a high fast one. Two-Top nods "yes" with one head, but shakes the other one "no." Confused and mortified, Gorilla hurls off his mask and yells to Duffy, "Duffy, you such-and-such, I am sick and tired of two-headed pitchers around this place."

"Take it easy," soothes Duffy. "Talk it over with the guy. After all, three heads is better than one."

But the Gorilla says, "It's no use, Duffy. I got a feeling that the guy ain't normal. Besides, you notice how he's always got those two heads together? Maybe he's cooking up a strike around here. No, sir, one of us will have to go, Duffy—and don't forget who owns the baseball."

Well, that's the end of Two-Top Gruskin's baseball career. For a while he watches tennis matches for the News of the Day. Then the Army gets him. The doctor takes his chart to the colonel. "Lemme see," says the colonel "Eyes—blue and brown. Hair, blond and brunette. Mustache: yes and no. This guy sounds as if he's got two heads." "He has," says the doc. "Oh," says the colonel.

Two-Top will be a big success in the Army as soon as he can make up his mind which head to salute.

SPOT REPORTING

HENRY CHADWICK is recognized in the Hall of Fame as "baseball's pioneer writer for half a century" and "inventor of the box score." Here, from the New York *Sunday Mercury* of 1869, are the opening paragraph and box score from a Chadwick report. Included in the summary that followed a box score in those days, by the way, was a category called "Fatal Errors."

You can tell from Chadwick's first sentence that the game was played at New York. You can tell it from the box score too. Otherwise, why did the Red Stockings come to bat in the ninth?

1869: Cincinnati Red Stockings 7, New York Mutuals 1

HENRY CHADWICK

ON OCTOBER 26th the Red Stockings returned to New York from Troy, after defeating the strong nine of the Haymakers of that village by a score of 12 to 7, and on the afternoon of that day played the first game of a new series of contests with the Mutual Club. The Saturday previous they had opened play in the east with a noteworthy triumph over the Athletics in Philadelphia by a score of 15 to 8, and therefore they entered upon this contest flushed with two victories, that at Troy being the most creditable display. The Reds, however, went into this game minus the services of Allison, their famous catcher, Deane taking his place in the nine and McVey playing in his position as catcher. The Mutuals, too, were shorthanded, they not having that useful player, Swandell, in their nine. They had a fair substitute, however, in Higham. The weather was all that could have been desired, the temperature being quite warm, and, as a close contest was anticipated, fully 3,000 persons were in attendance at the Union grounds, though the admission fee was double the usual rate. Mr. Ferguson had been agreed upon as umpire before the game, and no more impartial man could have been chosen for the position.

MUTUAL

	R	1B	PO	A
Hatfield, ss	1	1	4	2
Eggler, cf	0	1	2	0
Patterson, lf	0	1	3	0
Nelson, 3b	0	1	2	1
E. Mills, 1b	0	0	6	0
Martin, rf	0	1	2	0
C. Mills, c	0	0	3	1
Wolters, p	0	0	1	1
Higham, 2b	0	0	4	1
Totals	1	5	27	6

CINCINNATI

	R	1B	PO	A
G. Wright, ss	2	3	3	4
Gould, 1b	0	2	14	1
Waterman, 3b	0	1	2	4
Deane, rf	2	2	3	0
H. Wright, cf	1	1	1	0
Leonard, lf	1	1	1	0
Brainard, p	0	2	0	2
Sweasy, 2b	0	1	2	5
McVey, c	1	1	1	0
Totals	7	14	27	16

INNINGS	1st	2d	3d	4th	5th	6th	7th	8th	9th	
MUTUAL	1	0	0	0	0	0	0	0	0	—1
CINCINNATI	0	3	2	1	0	0	1	0	0	—7

FICTION

HERE is the final chapter from *Baseball Joe of the Silver Stars,* first of the Baseball Joe books, which were quite possibly the longest continuous series of boys' books ever done—in point of time, that is; the first Baseball Joe book came out in 1912, the last in 1926. The reason: popular demand. Why is it they don't write like this any more?

The Winning Throw—Conclusion

LESTER CHADWICK

FOR A MOMENT Tom stood there a bit embarrassed, for he saw that something unusual had happened.

"I—I hope I'm not intruding," he stammered. "I didn't think—I came right in as I always do. Has anything—"

"It's all right!" exclaimed Joe quickly. "We just got word that Dad has lost his patent case."

"Gee! That's too bad!" exclaimed Tom, who knew something of the affair. "What are you going to do?"

"I'm going to pitch against the Resolutes, the first thing I do!" cried Joe. "After that I'll decide what's next. But is my glove mended, Clara? Come on, Tom, we mustn't be late. We're going to wallop them—just as you said."

"I hope you do!" burst out Clara.

"Play a good game and—and—don't worry," whispered Mrs. Matson to her son as he kissed her good-bye.

The team and substitutes were to go to Rocky Ford in two big stages, in time to get in some practice on the grounds that were none too familiar to them. A crowd of Silver Star "rooters" were to follow on the trolley. The captain and managers of the rival teams watched their opponents practice with sharp eyes.

"They're snappier than when they beat us before," was Darrell's conclusion.

"They've got a heap sight better pitcher in Joe than Sam Morton ever was," concluded Captain Hen Littell of the Resolutes, who twirled for his team. "I shouldn't wonder but what we'd have a mighty close game."

The last practice was over. The scattered balls had been collected, the batting list made out and final details arranged. Once more came the thrilling cry of the umpire:

"Play ball!"

The Resolutes were to bat last, and Seth Potter went up to bat first for the Stars.

"Swat it," pleaded the crowd, and Seth smiled. But he fanned the air successively as well as successfully and soon went back to the bench. Then came Fred Newton's turn and he knocked a little pop fly that was easily caught before he reached first. Captain Rankin himself was up next and managed to get to first on a swift grounder that got past the shortstop. But he died on second, for the next man up fanned. No runs for the Stars.

The Resolutes were jubilant, thinking this argued well for them, but they looked a little blank when Joe retired their first two men hitless. For Joe had started off in good form. With the first ball he delivered he knew that he was master of the horsehide—at least for a time.

"But oh! I hope I don't slump!" and he almost found himself praying that such a thing would not happen.

He was in an agony of fear when he heard the crack of the bat on the ball when the third man came up. The spheroid went shooting off in center field, but by a magnificent stop Percy Parnell gathered it in and the side was retired runless. Things were not so bad for the Stars.

For the next two innings neither side got a run, though there were some scattered hits. Again was there talk of a pitchers' battle, though in the strict sense of the word this was not so, as both Joe and Hen Littell were hit occasionally, and for what would have been runs only for the efficient fielding on both sides.

"See if we can't do something this inning!" pleaded Rankin when his side came up in their half of the fourth. The lads all tried hard and Joe knocked a pretty one that was muffed by the second baseman. However, he quicky picked it up and hurled it to first. Joe got there about the same time as the ball did, and to many he seemed safe, but he was called out.

"Aw, that's rotten!" cried Tom Davis.

"Let it go!" said Darrell sharply, and Tom subsided.

The Stars got another goose egg—four straight—and in their half of the fourth the Resolutes got their first run. The crowd went wild and Joe found himself clenching his hands, for the run came in because he had given a man his base on balls. The runner had successively stolen second and third, and went home on a nice fly.

"I hope I'm not going to slump!" thought Joe and there was a lump in his throat. For an instant he found himself thinking of his father's troubles, and then he firmly dismissed them from his mind. "I've got to pitch!" he told himself fiercely.

"We've got him going!" chanted the Resolute "rooters." Joe shut his teeth grimly and struck out the next man. Then he nipped the runner stealing second and threw him out with lightning speed. That somewhat silenced the jubilant cries and when Joe managed to retire one of the Resolutes' heaviest hitters without even a bunt a big crowd rose up and cheered him.

"They're only one ahead," said Rankin as his lads came in to bat. "Let's double it now."

And double it they did, the Star boys playing like mad and getting enough hits off Littell to make two runs.

"That's the way to wallop 'em!" sang someone in the crowd and the song composed for the occasion was rendered with vim.

Desperately as the Resolutes tried in their half of the fifth to catch up to their rivals, they could not do it. Joe was at his best and in that half inning did not allow a hit. He had almost perfect control, and his speed was good. Only once or twice did he pitch at all wild and then it did no harm as there was no one on base.

The sixth inning saw a run chalked up for each team, making the score three to two in favor of the Stars.

"Oh, if we can only keep this up!" exclaimed Darrell, "we'll have them. Can you do it, Joe?"

"I guess so—yes, I can!" he said with conviction.

Then came the lucky seventh, in which the Stars pounded out three runs, setting the big crowd wild with joy, and casting corresponding gloom over the cohorts of the Resolutes. The Stars now had six runs and their rivals were desperate. They even adopted unfair tactics, and several decisions of the umpire were manifestly in their favor. The crowd hooted and yelled, but the young fellow who was calling strikes and balls held to his opinion, and the Resolutes closed their half of the seventh with two runs.

"Six to four in our favor," murmured the Stars' manager. "If we can only keep this lead the game is ours."

"That word 'if' is a big one for only two letters," spoke Captain Rankin grimly. "But maybe we can."

Neither side scored in the eighth and then came the final trial of the Stars unless there should be a tie, which would necessitate ten innings.

Joe was to the bat in this inning, and oh! how hard he tried for a run! He knocked a two-bagger and stole third. There was one out when Bart Ferguson came up, and Bart was a heavy hitter. But somehow he did not make good this time. He managed to connect with the ball, however, and as soon as Joe heard the crack he started for home.

But there was brilliant playing on the part of the Resolutes. With a quick throw to home the shortstop nipped Joe at the plate, and then the catcher, hurling the ball to first, got the horsehide into the baseman's hands before Bart arrived. It was a pretty double play and retired the Stars with a goose egg.

Still they had a lead of two runs and they might be able to hold their rivals down. It was a critical point in the game. As Joe took his place and faced the batter he felt his heart wildly throbbing. He knew he must hold himself well in hand or he would go to pieces. The crowd of Resolute sympathizers was hooting and yelling at him. Darrell saw how things might go and ran out to the pitcher.

"Hold hard!" he whispered. "Just take it easy. Pitch a few balls to Bart and your nerve will come back. We've *got* to win."

"And we will!" exclaimed Joe. The delivery of a few balls, while the batter stepped away from the plate, showed Joe that he still had his speed and control. He was going to be wary what kind of curves he delivered.

He struck out the first man up with an ease that at first caused him wild elation, and then he calmed himself.

"There are two more," he reasoned. "I've got to get two more—two more."

He was almost in despair when he was hit for a two-bagger by the next player, and he was in a nervous perspiration about the man stealing to third. Then Darrell signaled him to play for the batter, and Joe did, getting him out with an easy fly.

Then there was a mix-up when the next man hit, and by an error of the left fielder the man on second, who had stolen to third, went home with a run, while the man who had brought him in got to the last bag.

"That's the stuff!" yelled the crowd. "Now one more to make it a tie and another to win!"

"Steady, boys! Steady!" called Darrell, as he saw his team on the verge of a breakdown. "We can't beat 'em!"

There were now two out, one run was in, a man was on third and a heavy batter was up—one of the best of the Resolutes.

"Swat it, Armstrong! Swat it!" cried the crowd, and the big left fielder smiled confidently.

"Ball one!" cried the umpire, after Joe's first delivery.

There was a gasp of protest from Bart behind the plate, for the sphere had come over cleanly. Darrell signaled to the catcher to make no protest. Joe felt a wave of anger, but he endeavored to keep cool. But when the second ball was called on him he wanted to run up and thrash the umpire. The latter was grinning derisively.

"Here's a strike!" cried Joe in desperation and he was gratified when Armstrong struck at it and missed.

"Why didn't you call that a ball?" asked Bart of the umpire. The latter did not answer.

Another ball was called and then a strike. Now came the supreme moment. Two men out, a man on third waiting to rush in with the tying run, a heavy hitter at bat and three balls and two strikes called on him. No wonder Joe's hand trembled a little.

"Easy, old man!" called Darrell to him. "You can make him fan."

Joe thought rapidly. He had studied the batter and he thought that by delivering a swift inshoot he could fool Armstrong. It was his last chance, for another ball meant that the batter would walk, and there was even a better stickman to follow.

Joe wound up, and sent in a swift one. His heart was fluttering, he could hardly see, there was a roaring in his ears. And then he dimly saw Armstrong strike at the ball desperately. Almost at the same moment Joe knew he would miss it.

The ball landed in the center of Bart's big glove with a resounding whack. He held it exactly where he had caught it. Joe had delivered the winning throw.

"Strike three—batter's out!" howled the umpire, and then his voice was drowned in a yell of joy from the sympathizers of the Stars.

For their team had won! The Resolutes were retired with but one run in the ninth and the final score was five to six in favor of our friends. They had beaten their old rivals on their own grounds and they had won the county championship!

"Great work, old man! Great!" yelled Darrell in Joe's ear. "You saved the day for us."

"Nonsense!" exclaimed Joe modestly.

"Three cheers for Baseball Joe!" yelled Tom Davis, and how those cheers did ring out.

"Three cheers for the Stars—they beat us fair and square!" called Captain Littell, and this was quite a different ending than that which had marked the previous game.

Some wanted to carry Joe around on their shoulders but he slipped away, and got off his uniform. Soon the team was on its way back to Riverside.

"You ought to be in a bigger team," Darrell told Joe. "You've got the making of a great pitcher in you."

"Well, I guess I'll have to stick around here for a while yet," replied our hero, as he thought of the fallen finances of his father. Never in all his life had he so longed for the chance to go to boarding school, and thence to college. But he knew it could not be, chiefly through the treachery of Benjamin and Holdney. Joe felt a wave of resentment against them sweep over him, and his thoughts were black and bitter.

Tom walked as far as Joe's street with him. He had a silent sympathy that spoke more than mere words could have done.

"So long," he said softly as they parted. "It was a great game, Joe, and I'm almost glad you've got to stay with the Stars."

"Well, did you win?" asked his mother, as Joe entered the house—entered it more listless than winning a big game would seem to warrant. "Did you beat the Resolutes, Joe?"

"Yes, we did—why, Mother, what's the matter?" cried the young pitcher, for there was a look of joy and happiness on her face, a look entirely different than when he had left her after the bad news. "Has anything—anything good happened?" he asked.

"Yes!" she exclaimed, "there has. I just had another telegram from your father. Everything is all right. He gets back his patents."

"No!" cried Joe, as if unable to believe the news.

"But I tell you yes!" repeated Mrs. Matson, and there was joy in her voice. "At first your father believed that all was lost, just as he wired us. Then, most unexpectedly he tells me, they were able to obtain some evidence from outside parties which they had long tried for in vain.

"It seems that a witness for Mr. Benjamin and his side, on whom they very much depended, deserted them, and went over to your father and his lawyer, and—"

"Hurray for that witness, whoever he was!" cried Joe.

"Be quiet," begged Clara, "and let Mother tell."

"There isn't much to tell," went on Mrs. Matson. "With the unexpected evidence of this witness your father's lawyer won the case, almost at the last moment. In fact your father had given up, and was about ready to leave the court when the man sent in word that he would testify for them. That was after your father sent the telegram that came just before you went off to the game, Joe."

"Oh, I'm so glad!" cried Clara.

"Now it's your turn to be quiet and listen," admonished Joe, with a smile at his sister.

"I have just about finished," went on their mother. "The judge decided in your father's favor, and he doesn't even have to share the profits of the invention with the harvester company or with Mr. Rufus Holdney, as he at one time thought he would, for they have violated their contract. So we won't be poor, after all, children. Aren't you glad?"

"You bet!" exploded Joe, throwing his arms around his mother's neck.

"And we won't have to leave this nice house," added Clara, looking around the comfortable abode.

"Then I can go to boarding school—and pitch on the school nine; can't I, Mother?" cried Joe, throwing his arms around her.

"Oh, yes; I suppose so," she answered, with half a sigh. "But I do wish you'd do something else besides play baseball."

"Something else besides baseball, Mother! Why, there's nothing to be compared to it. Hurray! I'm going to boarding school! I'm going to boarding school!" and Joe, catching Clara around the waist, waltzed her around the room. Then he caught his mother on his other arm—the arm that won the victory for the Stars that day—and her, too, he whirled about until she cried for mercy.

"Oh, but this is great!" Joe cried when he stopped for breath. "Simply great! I must go and tell Tom. Maybe he can go to boarding school with me."

And whether Tom did or not, and what were our hero's further fortunes on the diamond, will be related in the next volume, to be called: "Baseball Joe on the School Nine; or, Pitching for the Blue Banner."

There was an impromptu feast that night for the victorious Silver Stars and Joe was the hero of the occasion. He was toasted again and again, and called upon to make some remarks, which he did in great confusion. But his chums thought it the best speech they had ever heard.

"Three cheers for Baseball Joe!" called Tom Davis, and the room rang with them, while Joe tried to hide his blushes by drinking glass after glass of lemonade.

And now, for a time, we will take leave of him, crying as his chums did after the great victory on the diamond: "Hurray for Baseball Joe!"

SPOT REPORTING

THIS STORY is actually just one-third of the mind-boggling pine tar incident. The second part came a couple of days later, when Lee MacPhail, then president of the American League, reversed the umpires, and the third some time afterward when, taking up where they had left off in the ninth, the two teams, performing in an all-but-empty Yankee Stadium, played out the rest of the game, this time with Brett's homer counting and giving the Royals a 5–4 victory.

This first part made page one of *The New York Times.* So did the second part. So did the third part.

1983: New York Yankees 4, Kansas City Royals 3 (or 5)

MURRAY CHASS

BASEBALL GAMES often end with home runs, but until yesterday the team that hit the home run always won. At Yankee Stadium yesterday, the team that hit the home run lost.

If that unusual development produced a sticky situation, blame it on pine tar.

With two out in the ninth inning, George Brett of the Kansas City

Royals hit a two-run home run against Rich Gossage that for several minutes gave the Royals a 5–4 lead over the Yankees. But Brett was called out by the umpires for using an illegal bat—one with an excessive amount of pine tar. The ruling, after a protest by Billy Martin, the Yankees' manager, enabled the Yankees to wind up with a 4–3 victory.

"I can sympathize with George," Gossage remarked after the game, "but not that much."

The outcome, which the Royals immediately protested, is certain to be talked about for years to come, because it was one of the most bizarre finishes any game has ever had.

"I couldn't believe it," Brett said, infinitely more calm than when he charged at the umpires after their controversial call.

"It knocks you to your knees," added Dick Howser, the Kansas City manager. "I'm sick about it. I don't like it. I don't like it at all. I don't expect my players to accept it."

What the Royals refused to believe or accept was that the umpires ruled the home run did not count because Brett's bat had too much pine tar on it.

Pine tar is a sticky brown substance batters apply to their bats to give them a better grip. Baseball rule 1.10 (b) says a bat may not be covered by such a substance more than 18 inches from the tip of the handle. Joe Brinkman, the chief of the crew that umpired the game, said Brett's bat had "heavy pine tar" 19 or 20 inches from the tip of the handle and lighter pine tar for another three or four inches.

The umpires did not use a ruler to measure the pine tar on Brett's 34½-inch bat; they didn't have one. So they placed it across home plate, which measures 17 inches across.

When they did, they saw that the pine tar exceeded the legal limit. The four umpires conferred again, and then Tim McClelland, the home plate umpire, thrust his right arm in the air, signaling that Brett was out. His call prompted two reactions:

Brett, enraged, raced out of the dugout and looked as if he would run over McClelland. Brinkman, however, intercepted him, grabbing him around the neck. "In that situation," Brinkman said later, "you know something's going to happen. It was quite traumatic. He was upset."

Gaylord Perry of the Royals, who has been long accused of doing things illegal with a baseball, tried to swipe the evidence, according to Brinkman.

"Gaylord got the bat and passed it back and tried to get it to the clubhouse," Brinkman said. "The security people went after it, but I got in there and got it. Steve Renko, another Kansas City pitcher, had it. He was the last in line. He didn't have anyone to hand it to."

Why the stadium security men went after the bat was not clear.

"I didn't know what was going on," Howser said. "I saw guys in sport coats and ties trying to intercept the bat. It was like a Brink's robbery. Who's got the gold? Our players had it, the umpires had it. I don't know who has it—the C.I.A., a think tank at the Pentagon."

Brinkman, when asked about the stadium security's bat force, said, "Maybe if it had been reversed, the bat might be gone."

The umpires declined to show the bat, which they said was on its way to the American League office. Presumably, Lee MacPhail, the league president, will study the bat and measure the pine tar today, then rule on the Royals' protest.

Martin, who has had a few violent encounters with umpires himself, was as peaceful and as smug as he could be about the whole incident.

"We noticed the pine tar on his bat in Kansas City," he said, alluding to the team's visit there two weeks ago. "You don't call him on it if he makes an out. After he hit the home run, I went out and said he's using an illegal bat.

"It's a terrible rule, but if it had happened to me I would have accepted it," Martin said. "It turned out to be a lovely Sunday afternoon."

It was also a bizarre Sunday afternoon—so bizarre, in fact, that the Yankees' computer couldn't digest it. When the operator of the computer tried to expunge Brett's home run, which he had already fed into the computer, it balked and refused to spit out the box score of the game and updated Yankee statistics.

As Brett, by now in the dugout after his triumphant trot around the bases, watched the discussion on the field, he laughed. "They didn't have a case," the Royals' leading hitter said.

But the umpires obviously thought Martin did have a case, although Brinkman acknowledged that pine tar, unlike cork or nails, has no effect on the distance a ball will travel.

"I was aware of the rule," Brett said, "but I thought it couldn't go past the label. Some umpires, when they see the pine tar too high, will say, 'Hey, George, clean up your bat.' "

Why was the pine tar that high on Brett's bat?

"I don't wear batting gloves," Brett explained, showing his calloused hands. "I like the feel of raw skin on raw wood. But you also don't want to hold the bat where pine tar is, so you put it up higher on the bat, get some on your hands when you need it, and then go back to the bottom of the bat. Where I hit that ball, it was on the meat part of the bat, about five inches from the end. There's no pine tar 29 inches from the handle. That ball wasn't even close enough to the pine tar to smell it."

Brett said he especially liked the bat, not for the pine tar but for the kind of wood with which it was made. He called it a seven-grainer ("the fewer grains a bat has, the better it is") and said it is the best bat he has ever had.

"I want my bat back," he said.

What the Royals really want back is their 5–4 lead. But only MacPhail can give it to them. If the league president should uphold their protest, the game would be resumed from Brett's home run, with two out in the Kansas City ninth. If MacPhail denies the protest, the Yankees' 4–3 victory will stand.

"It's unfortunate for them, but it's fortunate for us, of course," said Gossage, who gave up a memorable home run to Brett that clinched the 1980 league championship series for the Royals. "That's what he gets for hitting it."

The Yankees scored their runs presumably with legal bats. Dave Winfield hit a home run about 450 feet into the monuments in left-center field in the second inning, then singled home the third run of the Yankees' three-run rally in the sixth inning that overcame a 3–1 Kansas City lead. Don Baylor, who scored on the single, had tripled home the first two runs.

GENERAL

THE FOLLOWING existed as a letter that had hung in the Hall of Fame at Cooperstown, written at the request of Mr. E. J. Lanigan, the Hall's historian at the time. One of my own private delights in this letter is the fact that Cobb goes around the infield first-second-short-third, which makes sense. Baseball writers, in scoring, do it first-second-third-short. For what?

From a Letter to E. J. Lanigan

TY COBB

MENLO PARK, CALIF.
APRIL 21, 1945

DEAR MR. LANIGAN:

. . . Enclosed find selection of all-star team. Note that I do not select anyone that I have not played with or against, or seen much of.

PITCHERS: Walsh, Johnson, Alexander, Mathewson and Plank.
CATCHERS: Cochrane and Dickey.
FIRST BASE: Sisler.
SECOND BASE: Collins.
SHORTSTOP: Wagner.
THIRD BASE: Weaver.
LEFT FIELD: Joe Jackson.
CENTER: Tris Speaker.
RIGHT: Babe Ruth.

Note I have placed Weaver and Jackson, am only judging them on their ability.* I saw Jimmy Collins after he was through. I never saw Traynor . . . To my way of thinking no contest at second base, Hornsby couldn't catch a pop fly, much less go in the outfield after them, could not come in on a slow hit, Lajoie could not go out, nor come in, and did not cover too much ground to his right or left. Collins could do it all, besides being a great base stealer and base runner. Career average of .330-odd, I think. Also another manager on the field . . .

Sincerely
TY COBB

* Black Sox whose records have been stricken from the books . . . ED.

HISTORY

HERE is a chapter from *Babe,* which has been called the best baseball biography ever done. There have been other pieces about Babe Ruth in the *Fireside* volumes, of course, but none that zeroed in on what a punster might call his flip side. The title to this chapter says it all.

The Left-handed Genius: Best Pitcher in Baseball

ROBERT W. CREAMER

THE FEDERAL LEAGUE died at the end of 1915, and with its death the major league owners reverted to type and began to slash their player salaries. During the two-year war, salaries had soared, particularly for star players. Now, with no place to jump to, or threaten to jump to, the players lost their only effective weapon and were more or less helpless. The demise of the Federal League meant there was a horde of ballplayers scrambling for places on the rosters of the legitimate big league teams. It was a buyer's market, and the owners wasted no time in letting the players understand that. The hitherto generous Lannin was no exception.

Ruth was not affected, because he still had a year to go on the three-season contract he signed in the summer of 1914, but Joe Wood, whose 34 victories in 1912 moved him well up in the salary scale even before the Federal League came into being, was cut so drastically that he refused to report to the Hot Springs training camp in 1916. His friend Speaker agreed to report and work out, but he too refused to sign the contract Lannin offered him. In 1914, when the Federals were throwing money like rose petals at the feet of major league stars, Lannin paid Speaker a $5,000 bonus to stick with the Red Sox and gave him a two-year contract at $15,000 a year, which was very close to being the highest salary in the majors. Now, in 1916, Speaker accepted the reality that he would have to take a salary cut, which was remarkably understanding when you consider that he was the star of the World Champions, the only .300 hitter in the Boston lineup in both 1914 and 1915 and by all standards the best fielding outfielder in baseball. When he found out what the Red Sox were planning to pay him, Speaker stopped being so understanding. Lannin was offering $9,000, a 60 per cent cut. Speaker said he might accept $12,000, but that was the lowest figure he could even consider. All through spring training he and the Red Sox owner sparred. Lannin, adamant, said $9,000 was his top price; if Speaker wanted to play with the Red Sox, that is what he would have to sign for. Speaker continued to train but would not sign.

Despite the salary disputes the Red Sox looked very strong that spring. Even though Wood was not there and Ray Collins had gone the way of all failing ballplayers, Carrigan had a wealth of superior starting pitchers. Ruth, the erstwhile erratic rookie, was still clowning around off the field, and his gargantuan appetite had ballooned his weight to 212 pounds, but on the mound he showed every sign of maturity. Mays too looked impressive. And in Shore, Foster and Leonard he had three of the best pitchers in baseball. The rest of the lineup was solid and set. The Lewis-Speaker-Hooper outfield had been playing as a unit since 1910, and all three were in their prime. Hoblitzell at first base and Gardner at third were fixtures. Scott, a rookie at shortstop in 1914, was good enough in 1915 to make the nonpareil Barry shift to second, and behind that pair was the graceful Janvrin. Thomas and Cady were fine catchers. It was a very solid team, a little weak at bat, of course, but nonetheless the class of the league. It was a big favorite to retain the pennant.

The Speaker thing was still unsettled as the Red Sox made their way toward Boston for the opening of the season, but the players—notably Ruth—were bubbling with enthusiasm and optimism. A week before the season began they played Jack Dunn's Orioles in Baltimore, and Ruth appeared before the home folks for the first time as a major leaguer. The next day Lannin announced, almost incidentally, that he had bought an outfielder named Clarence (Tilly) Walker from the Philadelphia Athletics. That was not startling news, since hardly a day went by without someone buying a player from Connie Mack. Walker, who hit the ball hard, had been around the league for five years with Washington and St. Louis and had ended up with Mack that winter as an offshoot of the Federal League settlement. A couple of Federal League owners had been allowed to buy legitimate big league franchises. One of these was Phil Ball of St. Louis, who bought the Browns. Among his Federal League stars was Eddie Plank, who jumped from the Athletics after the 1914 season. It was agreed that Ball could keep Plank with him in St. Louis, but in return he had to give Walker to Philadelphia. Mack, who needed money, decided to sell him. Lannin's decision to buy Walker made sense, everyone agreed, because Duffy Lewis had been slightly injured that spring and it never hurt to have a little insurance. No one thought about the new outfielder as a possible replacement for Speaker—except Lannin, who had been doing some maneuvering behind the scenes.

The day after Walker's purchase the Red Sox lost to Brooklyn, 3–2, in an exhibition game; Speaker, still unsigned but in top form, got Boston its two runs with a pair of homers. Opening day was only five days away, but Bostonians were sure the disagreement between Lannin and his star outfielder would be settled by then. They were right. On the Saturday before the season opened, Lannin stunned players, fans, sportswriters and half the country by announcing he had sold Speaker to the second-division Cleveland Indians. The price was $50,000, the largest amount ever paid for one player up to that time. Two unimportant young Cleveland players also came to Boston in the deal. One of them, Sam Jones, eventually became one of the best pitchers in the American League, but no one knew anything about that in April 1916. It was Speaker for cash, and it was almost unbelievable. It was impossible for Boston to accept the news at first. The Red Sox sell Speaker! He was the big man, the hero of the team. More practically, he was the only really good hitter on a weak offensive club. The Red Sox players walked around shaking their heads. Ruth said he felt as though a rug had been pulled out from under him. What did this do to their pennant chances? Speaker was gone. Wood was gone. (Joe, who held out all season, ultimately was sent to Cleveland, where he rejoined Speaker, gave up pitching and became an outfielder; he hit .366 one season as a part-time player.) Downcast, the players muttered and grumbled.

Carrigan, as hurt as any of them by the deal, which was completely Lannin's idea, reacted the way a leader should. He gathered his team together and chewed them out in his tough no-nonsense way. "All right," he said. "We've lost Speaker. That means we're not going to score as many runs. But we're still a good team. We have the pitching. We have the fielding. And we'll hit well enough. We'll win the pennant again if you guys will just stop your goddamned moaning and get down to business." Fired up, the Red Sox opened the season by winning their first four games and six of their first eight. Ruth, now a major factor in Carrigan's strategy, pitched the opening game and won it, 2–1. In his second start he was sent against Walter Johnson, the best pitcher in American League history. Babe had pitched against Johnson once in 1915 and beat him, 4–3; now he defeated the great Walter again, 5–1.

Babe won his first four starts, the club was in first place and everything seemed to be going swimmingly. But it was not so, not really. The team was not hitting at all. It was shut out in New York and shut out again in Washington; in its first 15 games it was able to score as many as three runs only six times. Inevitably, the defeats began to come. The team slid out of the league lead as April ended. Ruth lost his first game on the first of May and the club began to stumble badly. Carrigan was most disturbed by his unsettled outfield, hitherto the team's pride. Walker was late in reporting and Carrigan put Lewis, who had recovered from his injury, in center and Chick Shorten, a rookie, in left. When Walker was ready, Carrigan put him in left. But Lewis was uncomfortable in center, so Carrigan shifted him back to left and put Shorten, a weak hitter but a capable fielder, in center. Finally he stuck Walker in center and left him there, even though the newcomer was a hitter more than he was a fielder.

For almost two months, through May and most of June, the Red Sox played sluggish .500 ball in a league that had turned upside down because of the infusion of Federal League players. The big teams—the Red Sox, Tigers and White Sox—were far behind, while the perennially weak Yankees, Indians and Senators were taking turns in first place. Speaker, playing like a man possessed, was leading the league in hitting and had lifted drab Cleveland into contention. In May, when the Indians played in Boston for the first time, a delegation of Boston fans gave Speaker a silver loving cup, partly as a gesture to their departed hero, partly as a slap at owner Lannin. The next afternoon, with Tris starting, the Indians walloped Ruth, and the Red Sox fans didn't know whether to cheer or cry. It was an unhappy spring for Boston.

The hitting picked up a little with Walker in the lineup, but then the pitching began to go bad. Something was wrong with Shore. Foster was not right. Mays pitched very little. There were fits and starts of brightness. Leonard's first three starts were shutouts, and Ruth was generally superb. Late in May he pitched a shutout against Detroit. On June 1 he beat Walter Johnson again, this time 1–0. Four days later he pitched another shutout, stopping Cleveland after the Indians had beaten Boston two days running by big scores. Speaker went 0 for 4 against him this time, which made the victory that much more satisfying, and the Babe, who was beginning to hit after a slow start, had two singles and scored a run.

He lost to Detroit a few days later, after holding a 4–1 lead in the eighth inning, but he had a perfect day at bat and even hit a home run, his first since the previous July. Three days later, in St. Louis, Carrigan had him pinch-hit with two men on base and the Red Sox behind 3–0. Ruth hit a three-run homer over the bleachers in right field to tie the score. He pitched against the Browns the next afternoon, won 5–3, had another perfect day at bat and hit another home run, his third in three games, which created a sensation. (Oddly, these three were the only home runs he hit all season.) His batting average jumped to .300, and people were remembering all over again what a powerful batter he was. The Red Sox scored fewer runs than any team in the league except the last-place Athletics, and Carrigan, talking about Ruth's home runs, wondered out loud if he ought not put the Babe in the outfield to fill some of the hitting void that Speaker had left. Carrigan was only speculating. He was essentially conservative when it came to baseball. He always put Ruth in the ninth spot in the batting order, the traditional place for a pitcher, despite Babe's obvious hitting ability, and he was not going to gamble with the man who was now his best pitcher. Indeed, Ruth was not only Boston's best, he was the best pitcher in the league that year, including Walter Johnson.

He was beginning to be something of a character, too. Everyone was aware of his amazing appetite and his love of night life (though he really was not much of a drinker yet, except for beer). Now his trait of not remembering names was becoming part of the growing legend. One evening in Philadelphia he was in the hotel lobby after defeating the Athletics that afternoon, when Stuffy McInnis, the Philadelphia first baseman, came in. McInnis was from Massachusetts and he had stopped by to visit some of his old Boston friends. When he saw Ruth he walked over and said, "Babe, that was a hell of a fine game you pitched this afternoon." It was a significant compliment. McInnis had been in the league since 1909, had played on four pennant-winning teams, was, like Barry, a widely publicized member of the famous $100,000 infield and had played against Ruth frequently since Babe's debut against the Athletics in North Carolina in the spring of 1914. Ruth looked at him blandly and said. "Thanks, keed, that's very nice of you. Glad you were able to come out and watch us play." McInnis nodded dumbly and more or less staggered away. "He didn't know me," he would say in awe to people to whom he would tell the story. "He didn't even know I was a ballplayer."

Late in June things began to swing Boston's way. Foster pitched a no-hitter, Ruth and Shore followed with shutouts and Mays and Leonard won a doubleheader to make it five straight. The beautiful pitching staff was in top form again, and with improved hitting the Red Sox began to move steadily upward. The last three months of the season were much more fun than the first three. There was a lovely fight in Washington one day after a Mays pitch hit George McBride, the Senator's veteran shortstop. McBride threw his bat, à la Cobb, and Sam Agnew, a third-string catcher Boston recently acquired, raged at McBride. Carrigan came off his bench, Clark Griffith, the Washington manager, came off his, Agnew punched Griffith, the police arrested Agnew (he had to pay $50 bail at a police station) and Ban Johnson suspended Carrigan for five days.

Cleveland and the Yankees were still wrestling for first place, but the Red Sox were coming on, winning two games for every one they lost, getting closer and closer to the top. By late July Boston was only half a game off the lead, and after they won three straight in Detroit, including a 6–0 shutout by Ruth, they moved into first place. They fell back again when they lost three games in St. Louis, but in Chicago they took three of four and regained the lead. They were a strong road club, and after this trip they had a commanding lead.

Ruth's pitching sloughed off briefly, but by mid-August he was riding high again. He beat Washington, 2–1, came back three days later to beat Johnson, 1–0, in thirteen innings, beat Cleveland, 2–1, four days after that and shut out Detroit, 3–0, in his next start. The Red Sox lead widened to six and a half games and it seemed as though they would win the pennant easily. But as September began they slumped, and Detroit and Chicago closed in for the long anticipated pennant battle among the three best teams in the league. On September 9 Ruth beat Johnson, 2–1, for his fifth in a row over the Washington star, but Detroit was only one game behind and Chicago two. On September 12 Carrigan sent Ruth against Johnson again, and Walter finally won one, 4–3, in ten innings, although Ruth, who was taken out in the ninth after losing a 2–0 lead, was not charged with the defeat.

That same day, just as the club was about to leave on its last western trip of the season, Lannin revealed that Carrigan was planning to retire at the end of the season. Whether this news upset the players is conjectural, but they lost two of their first three games in the west and fell from first to third place. Then, in that curious way baseball has, the next two days abruptly settled the pennant race. On Sunday, September 17, the Red Sox met the White Sox before more than 40,000 people, the largest crowd in the history of Chicago baseball to that time. Ruth won the game, 6–2, for his 20th victory of the season and lifted the Red Sox past Chicago into second place behind Detroit. The next day Shore defeated the White Sox again and Boston found itself back in the lead, because that afternoon the Tigers suffered an astonishing 2–0 defeat at the hands of the Athletics. To appreciate the impact of Detroit's defeat you must know that the Tigers had won 35 of their previous 50 games, a vigorous .700 pace, and had charged up from the second division into first place. The Athletics, on the other hand, were at the absolute nadir of the worst season any team has had in the modern history of major league baseball. The Mets in their abysmal 1962 season won 40 games and lost 120 for a .250 winning percentage. The 1916 Athletics won 38 games and lost 117 for a .238 percentage, which was bad enough, but on that Monday in September when they beat the Tigers their record was 30 won and 108 lost, a percentage of .217. When the Mets finished last in 1962, they were 18 games behind the next worst team, a staggering margin when you consider that a team is said to have run away with a pennant when it wins by 12 games. But the Athletics—stand back, now—finished 40½ games behind the team next above them in the standings. They had one pitcher who lost 23 games, another who lost 22, a third with a record of one and 19 and a fourth who was one and 16. And yet in the midst of a pennant race this majestically inept team beat Ty Cobb and the Tigers, the hardest-hitting team in baseball, shut them out and knocked them out of first place.

The next day the Red Sox arrived in Detroit for a three-game series, swept all three (Ruth won the final game, 10–2), and that was the end of the season, practically speaking. Boston finished its triumphant road trip by beating Speaker and the Indians three out of four. Ruth shut out Cleveland in the last game there and four days later in Boston blanked the Yankees for his ninth shutout of the season, which a half century later was still the American League record for a lefthanded pitcher. It was also his 23rd and final victory of the season.

It was a year of singular achievement for Ruth—23 wins, nine shutouts, league-leading earned-run average, the three home runs in three games, the 20th victory before the huge crowd in Chicago that started Boston on its final drive to the pennant, the thirteen-inning 1–0 defeat of Walter Johnson—but his biggest moment of the season was still to come.

The 1916 World Series matched the Red Sox with the Brooklyn Dodgers, and Ruth pitched the second game. Carrigan had passed over him for the opener, had used Ernie Shore instead and had won. That first game was played on a Saturday in Boston, and Ruth's game was to be the following Monday, since Sunday was always an off-day in staid Boston. Hugh Fullerton, the old sportswriter, wrote that the players "spent a Boston sabbath, which is considerable sabbath," and things were indeed quiet everywhere in the city except at the Brunswick Hotel, which was World Series headquarters. There, Joe Lannin saw Charlie Ebbets, the Dodgers' owner, and asked him casually if he had arranged for tickets at Ebbets Field for Boston's Royal Rooters, a considerable segment of whom were planning to travel to Brooklyn for the third and fourth games. Ebbets looked at Lannin angrily and said, "No, but I'll do it right now." He picked up a telephone and put in a long distance call to Brooklyn. When he was connected with his Ebbets Field ticket office he said loudly, "I want you to hold out some of the best reserved seats for Tuesday's game. And while you're at it, save 250 of the worst seats in the grandstand for the Boston Rooters." He hung up the phone and glared at Lannin, who stared back in stunned silence for a moment before turning and walking out of the hotel. Ebbets, who was ill (he was suffering from dizzy spells and had disobeyed doctors' orders in order to come to Boston for the Series), was obviously upset. Asked for an explanation of his behavior, he said, "We received very bad treatment in the first game here. The seats the Brooklyn Boosters got were the worst in the ballpark. I am only retaliating." Ah, the good old days.

Boston's Royal Rooters were much in evidence the next afternoon, sitting in a group, complete with red-coated band, near the Red Sox dugout. Over and over the band played and the Rooters sang a tune called "Tessie," which for some inane reason had become their fight song. "Tessie," they sang, "you make me feel so bahadly. Why don't you turn around? Tessie, you know I love you sadly, babe. My heart weighs about a pound." Tessie might have been popular with the Royal Rooters, but followers of rival teams found her an agonizing bore. "That measly, monotonous melody," one newspaperman called it, but the Rooters, from politicians like James Michael Curley and Honey Fitzgerald down, sang it gleefully, soulfully and repeatedly.

When Ruth took the mound to start what was to become one of the most memorable of all World Series games, dark clouds were hanging low over Boston and rain was threatening. Ruth got rid of the first two Brooklyn batters with dispatch but the third man, Hy Myers, a stocky righthanded-hitting outfielder, hit Babe's second pitch on a line to right center field. Speaker might have caught the ball if he had still been playing center for the Red Sox, but Walker tripped as he started after it and fell. Hooper, coming over from right field, also stumbled, and the ball bounded through for extra bases. Hooper retrieved the ball near the fence and threw it in. The relay was bobbled and Myers, who never stopped running, beat the throw easily with a colorful but totally unnecessary head-first slide into home plate. It was an inside-the-park home run, and it put Brooklyn ahead, 1–0. It was also the only run the Dodgers were to score in the game, which lasted fourteen innings, although they came very close a couple of times.

In the third inning Ruth's rival pitcher, the lefthanded Sherry Smith, hit a clean double down the right field line but was out at third when he tried to stretch it into a triple; if he had stopped at second he most likely would have scored a moment later, because the next batter singled. The Dodgers went out without scoring, but the Red Sox picked up a run in their half of the inning when Ruth grounded out with a man on third. The base runner scored and Babe was credited with batting in a run.

The score was now tied, and it remained tied for eleven more innings, through a succession of melodramatic events. In the fifth, Thomas of the Red Sox hit a double and was tripped by Ivy Olson, the Dodger shortstop, as he tried for third. He was awarded the extra base by the umpires, who then had to break up a fight that erupted between Olson and Heinie Wagner, the Boston third base coach. After all that, Ruth struck out to end the inning.

The Red Sox might have scored in the sixth, except for a diving, rolling catch of a line drive by Myers in center field. In the seventh a Dodger rally was aborted and a furious argument begun when Myers—who seemed to be in the middle of everything—was called out at first base on an obviously bad decision by the umpire. In the eighth the Dodgers should have scored. Mike Mowrey, the third baseman, singled and was sacrificed to second. Otto Miller, the catcher, followed with a clean single to left, but the cautious Mowrey stopped at third. The throw from the outfield to the plate was wide, and Mowrey would have scored easily had he tried. The next batter hit a grounder to Scott at shortstop, and on this one Mowrey started for the plate. Scott threw home. Mowrey stopped halfway, backtracked and was immediately caught in a rundown: catcher to the third baseman to Ruth, who made the tag on the baseline.

When the Red Sox came to bat in the last of the ninth, it was becoming dark, the gloom of the heavy overcast aggravated by the early October dusk. Janvrin opened the inning with a line-drive double off Zach Wheat's glove in left field. Walker tried to sacrifice but hit a little foul ball off to one side of the plate. Carrigan, who wanted the runner moved over to third base, immediately took Walker out of the game and sent a substitute outfielder named Jimmy Walsh to bat in his place. Walsh bunted directly to the pitcher, and Smith pounced on it and threw to Mowrey at third in time to catch Janvrin. The umpire had lifted his arm to call Janvrin out when the ball trickled from Mowrey's glove. The decision was reversed, and there were the Red Sox with men on first and third and no one out in the last half of the ninth inning of a tie ball game. Hoblitzell, the dependable, was up, and sure enough he lifted a fly ball into center field. Janvrin tagged up at third and the crowd began moving toward the exits. But Myers—who else?—took the fly ball on the run, threw perfectly to the plate and Janvrin was out by a foot.

The game went into extra innings. Boston almost scored in the eleventh when Scott singled and went to second on a sacrifice. After Ruth struck out, Hooper hit a ground ball off Mowrey's glove and Scott, moving as the ball was hit, went safely into third. The third baseman chased the ball to his left, picked it up and started to throw to first in an apparently hopeless attempt to get Hooper. It was a fake, but Scott fell for it. He took a couple of strides toward home plate and was tagged out when Mowrey turned and threw to Olson, the shortstop, who had come up behind the base.

Smith was in trouble each inning now, but Ruth, who had difficulty earlier, looked stronger than ever. He had given up six hits and three walks in the first seven innings, but from the eighth inning on he allowed no hits at all and only one walk. Boston was oozing confidence. When the popular Lewis came to bat in the eleventh with a man on first and two out, the Royal Rooters came to life. "Tessie!" they sang, and the band blared its accompaniment. Wilbert Robinson, the rotund Brooklyn manager, came red-faced and fuming off the Dodger bench and complained bitterly to the umpires, who dutifully ordered the Royal Rooters to knock it off. Nothing happened in the twelfth except that Ruth with two outs tried to bunt for a base hit and was thrown out. In the thirteenth Mowrey reached second for the Dodgers on an error and a sacrifice. Smith, a good hitting pitcher, poked a blooper into left field for what seemed a certain hit and an almost certain run. But Lewis came sprinting in and caught the ball off his shoe tops for the third out. You should have heard the Rooters sing "Tessie" then.

In the last of the fourteenth Smith, very tired, opened the inning by walking Hoblitzell for the fourth time. Lewis sacrificed him to second. It was so dark now that it was hard to see the ball. Carrigan therefore put Del Gainor, a righthander, in to bat for the usually dependable Gardner, who hit lefthanded, against the lefthanded Smith. Carrigan felt a righthanded batter would be better able to follow Smith's pitches in the murky light. And using all his weapons, he sent slim young Mike McNally in to run for the heavy-footed Hoblitzell. The wheels of baseball strategy turned even then, but Carrigan's maneuvers paid off. Gainor took a ball and a strike and then hit a liner over the third baseman's head. Most of the spectators could not tell where the ball went, but they could see Wheat, the left fielder, running desperately toward the foul line. McNally was around third and on his way to the plate before Wheat picked up the ball, and he scored easily with the winning run. Pandemonium. More "Tessie." And Babe Ruth, in his World Series debut, unless you count that pinch-hitting effort against Alexander the year before, had a 2—1, fourteen-inning victory in the longest and one of the most exciting World Series games ever played.

Ruth was roaring and shouting and jumping around the clubhouse afterwards like a high school kid. He grabbed Carrigan and yelled at him, "I told you a year ago I could take care of those National League bums, and you never gave me a chance." Carrigan, easing out of the Ruthian bear hug, laughed and said, "Forget it, Babe. You made monkeys out of them today."

It was Ruth's only appearance in the Series, which the Red Sox won, four games to one. Mays was the only Boston pitcher to lose, dropping the third game to the veteran Jack Coombs, who had previously been a star with the Philadelphia Athletics during their pennant-winning years. Ruth, in his ingenuously boorish way, tried to comfort the bad-tempered Mays by saying, "Well, if we had to lose one I'm glad it was to an old American Leaguer." Mays's reply was not recorded.

SPOT REPORTING

YOU NEVER SEE the fifth game of the 1920 World Series included in anybody's list of the most memorable Series games. Maybe it's because there aren't that many people left to remember it. Or maybe it's because the issue was never in doubt.

And yet, dear friends, this one game had the first grand slam home run in World Series history, the first home run by a pitcher, and—are you ready for this?—the only unassisted triple play!

From the standpoint of the baseball writer doing the game story for the next morning's paper, this one was not exactly a piece of cake. You not only had to deal with these events in sequence as they occurred on the field, but then decide which should come first in your story!

What you are about to read is the way Harry Cross of *The New York Times* handled it. It has to be not only one of the best-written but one of the best-organized spot stories ever done.

(Trivia Quiz: Q: Were the Brooklyns known as the Dodgers or the Robins in those days? A: Both.)

1920: Cleveland Indians 8, Brooklyn Dodgers 1

HARRY CROSS

THE UNROMANTIC name of Smith is on everybody's lips in Cleveland tonight, for Elmer Smith, the right fielder of Speaker's Indians, accomplished something in the fifth World Series clash this afternoon that is the life ambition of every big league ballplayer. Elmer crashed a home run over the right-field fence with the bases full in the first inning and sent the Indians on their merry way to an 8-to-1 victory over Brooklyn. Fate tried to conceal this lucky boy by naming him Smith, but with that tremendous slap Elmer shoved his commonplace identity up alongside the famous Smiths of history, which include Captain John, the Smith Brothers and the Village Smithy.

This home-run punch which shoved over four runs in a cluster is the first of its kind ever made in a World Series game. Cleveland now has won three games to Brooklyn's two, and an overjoyed city this evening has about come to the conclusion that the championship streamer will float over the proud fifth city of the U.S.A.

While the delirious crowd of more than 25,000 was still rejoicing over Smith's sumptuous smash, Bill Wambsganss broke into the celebration to steal some of Smithy's thunder by accomplishing the first unassisted triple play that has ever whisked a World Series populace up to the heights of happiness.

The crowd was already husky-voiced and nerve-wracked with wild excitement when Wamby started to make baseball history. It seemed as if everything that could happen to make Cleveland's joy complete had happened.

Along in the fifth inning, when Bagby, with a commanding lead behind him, was taking it easy, Kilduff and Otto Miller both made singles and were perched on second and first. Clarence Mitchell, who had succeeded the badly wrecked Burleigh Grimes on the pitching mound, was at bat, and for the first time during the afternoon it looked as if the slipping Robins were going to accomplish something.

Uncle Robbie had evidently wigwagged a sign from the bench for a hit and run play, which means that the runners were expected to gallop just as soon as Mitchell swung his bat. Mitchell connected solidly and jammed a tearing liner over second base. Wamby was quite a distance from second, but he leaped over toward the cushion and with a mighty jump speared the ball with one hand. Kilduff was on his way to third base and Miller was almost within reach of second.

Wamby's noodle began to operate faster than it ever did before. He hopped over to second and touched the bag, retired Kilduff. Then Wamby turned and saw Otto Miller standing there like a wooden Indian. Otto was evidently so surprised that he was glued to the ground, and Wamby just waltzed over and touched him for the third out.

The crowd forgot it was hoarse of voice and close to nervous exhaustion and gave Wamby just as great a reception as it had given Elmer Smith.

Those two record-breaking feats were not all that happened in today's game to make Cleveland feel proud of its baseball club and itself. Not by a long shot! Along in the fourth inning when Grimes was still trying to pitch, Jim Bagby, the Indians' big, slow, lazy box-man, became suddenly inspired and, with two fellow Indians on the bases, soaked a home run into the new bleachers which protrude far out into right center field.

No World Series pitcher has ever received such a humiliating cudgeling as Grimes did this afternoon, for the simple reason that no other pitcher has ever been kept in the box so long after he had started to slip. Uncle Robbie kept him on the mound for three and two-thirds innings and in that time he was badly plastered for nine hits, including two home runs and a triple.

With half a dozen able-bodied pitchers basking in the warm sun, Grimes was kept in the box until he was so badly battered that the game became a joke. Instead of being enormously wealthy in pitchers as Robbie was supposed to be, he became a pauper as far as pitching talent is concerned. When the Indians had the score 7 to 0 Grimes limped out of the game and Mitchell, who had been faithfully warming up ever since he hit Cleveland, went out to the mound and one more run was the best that the Indians could do off him.

The first inning is one which will ever linger in baseball memory. The Sunday crowd jammed every inch of the park. Strong-lunged young men went through the grandstands with megaphones and implored the fans to give the Indians their vocal and moral encouragement.

The Indians were on their toes and ran back and forth to their positions like a college baseball team. The roar of the faithful followers was like a tonic and Tris Speaker's men reveled in the wonderful reception they received. The thing that was uppermost in their minds was to show the home folks that they appreciated the loyalty, and they showed 'em. It didn't matter that it was a one-sided game and that the Brooklyn club, minus good pitching, looked woefully weak and, with the absence of the injured Jimmy Johnston at third base, was inclined to be panicky. The only thing that mattered was that the more runs the Indians could make the more fun there was in it for the Cleveland fans.

Jamieson was the first Indian to face Burleigh Grimes in the opening inning. He pounded a roller down through Konetchy which was too warm for the Dodger first baseman to handle. Wamby poked another single off Grimes and Jamieson went to second. The crowd chanted a flattering chorus of cheers to Speaker when he came to the plate. The wee bit of a tap which bounded off Tris's bat dropped in the infield and Grimes ran over to pick up the manager's bunt. Grimes slipped as he was about to pick up the ball and he was reclining on his back when he made a useless throw to first. It was a hit, and the bases were loaded with no one out.

The National Boiler Works laboring overtime never made the racket that was now taking place in the ball park. The noise waves echoed all over the city of Cleveland, finally rumbling far out in Lake Erie.

Elmer Smith is at bat. You'll find Smiths here, there and everywhere, so there was nothing about the name to arouse enthusiasm. Elmer took a fond look at the high screen on top of the right-field fence and Grimes began to pitch to him. The three Indians on the bases jumped up and down on their toes impatiently.

Elmer took two healthy swings at the ball and missed, and the next one was wide and he let it waft by. Grimes looked around the bases and saw that he was entirely surrounded by Indians. He was ambushed by the Redskins. He felt that danger lurked in this Smith boy at the bat.

When Grimes hurled the next pitch over, Smith took a mighty blow at the ball and it rose like a bird, went so far up in the air that it looked like a quinine pill.

Jamieson, Wamby and Speaker all took one good look at that rapidly rising ball, then they bent their heads, dug their spikes into the dirt and started to run. Grimes was knocked dizzy. As he looked about him he could see nothing but Indians chasing themselves around in a circle.

Smith, who only a few seconds before was just plain Elmer Smith, had become Home Run Smith before he trotted as far as second base. When he reached third, he was Hero Smith, and by the time he crossed the plate he was a candidate for a bronze statue in City Square along with General Moses Cleveland, who founded this town, and Tom L. Johnson, who decorated the park just opposite old General Mose.

Manager Speaker, still a young man, yet gray and bald from baseball worries, was waiting at the plate when Smith touched the platter. Around Smith's neck went Tris's arm. Grimes stood out in the pitcher's box stupefied. The other Brooklyn players walked about in a daze and waited for the noise riot to subside.

Grimes was still pitching when the game was resumed. The Cleveland players wondered just what had to be done to a Brooklyn pitcher before he is taken out of the game. However, Grimes became a little better, and the side was retired after Burleigh had been aided by a double play.

Big Ed Konetchy walloped a triple to left center field in the Brooklyn second, with one gone, but when Kilduff hoisted a fly to Jamieson and Koney tried to score after the catch Jamieson chucked him out at the plate with a perfect throw.

This was the first of three double plays which, with Wamby's matchless triple killing, furnished a defense for Bagby's loose flinging that would have prevented any pitcher from losing. The Dodgers got ten hits off Bagby in eight innings and couldn't put over a single run. Peerless defensive work saved him.

Brooklyn's most wasteful inning was the third, when Miller singled and Grimes hit into a double play. Olson and Sheehnan both singled. Griffith hoisted a foul to Gardner, ending the inning. There were three smacking singles without a runner getting beyond second base.

Smith got a tremendous cheer when he came to bat in the third inning. There were two down at the time, and he jarred a terrific triple to left center. The smash went to seed because Kilduff tossed Gardner out at first.

The next citizen to be hailed as a hero is lazy James Bagby. No pitcher ever before was pounded for thirteen hits in a World Series and emerged a hero. Jim Bagby, big Sergeant Jim, did it. He pitched what was really a bad game of ball, but when it was over he was proud of it.

Doc Johnston opened the fourth inning with a hit off Grimes's leg. Yes, Grimes is still pitching for Brooklyn. Doc went to second on a passed ball and to third as Sheehan was retiring Sewell at first. Grimes walked O'Neill purposely to get Bagby, and that is just where Jim, the barge, has the laugh on Grimes. Bagby slammed a long drive to right center and Johnston and O'Neill both romped home ahead of Jim amid scenes of wild, barbarous disorder.

When the riot was quelled, Grimes was still pitching for Brooklyn. Does this fellow Grimes stand so strongly with Uncle Robbie that he is never taken out of a game, no time, no place, no how?

Jamieson spanked a roller down to first base, and although three Brooklyn fielders, Grimes, Koney and Kilduff, tried to retire the runner at first, Jamieson was too swift and got a hit for himself out of the confusion. It suddenly dawned upon Manager Robinson that the Indians were hitting Grimes, so he took him out and Mitchell went to the box.

Sheehan, at third, was naturally nervous in his first big game and in the fifth, when Speaker hit a roller to him, Sheehan threw the ball right over Konetchy's head, and Speaker went to second. "Home Run" Smith got a single and Speaker went to third. Gardner cracked a single to center and Speaker crossed the plate with the Indians' last run.

Brooklyn's run came in the ninth inning. Bagby fanned Griffith as a starter, and then, as he listlessly chucked the ball over, Wheat singled to right. Jim was still listless when he threw the ball at Myers, who slapped a single to center which sent Wheat to second. Konetchy hit a mean hopper down through Doc Johnston, the ball bounding out into the field as Wheat scampered home and saved the Dodgers from a shutout.

Brooklyn's stock has taken an awful drop.

GIN'RAL

Mr. Dooley on Baseball

FINLEY PETER DUNNE

"D'YE IVER go to a baseball game?" asked Mr. Hennessy.

"Not now," said Mr. Dooley. "I haven't got th'intellick f'r it. Whin I was a young fellow nathin' plazed me betther thin to go out to th' ball grounds, get a good cosy seat in th' sun, take off me collar an' coat an' buy a bottle iv pop, not so much, mind ye, f'r th' refrishment, because I niver was much on pop, as to have something handy to reprove th' empire with whin he give an eeronyous decision. Not only that, me boy, but I was a fine amachure ballplayer mesilf. I was first baseman iv th' Prairie Wolves whin we beat th' nine iv Injine Company Five be a scoor iv four hundherd an' eight to three hundherd an' twinty-five. It was very close. Th' game started just afther low mass on a Sundah mornin' an' was called on account iv darkness at th' end iv th' fourth inning. I knocked th' ball over th' fence into Donovan's coal yard no less thin twelve times. All this talk about this here young fellow Baker makes me smile. Whin I was his age I wudden't count on annything but home-runs. If it wasn't a home-run I'd say: 'Don't mark it down' an' go back an' have another belt at th' ball. Thim were th' days.

"We usen't to think base-ball was a science. No man was very good at it that was good at annything else. A young fellow that had a clear eye in his head an' a sthrong pair iv legs undher him an' that was onaisy in th' close atmosphere iv th' school room, an' didn't like th' profissyon iv plumbing was like as not to join a ball team. He come home in th' fall with a dimon in his shirt front an' a pair iv hands on him that looked like th' boughs iv a three that's been sthruck be lightenin' and he was th' hero in th' neighborhood till his dimon melted an' he took to drivin' a thruck. But 'tis far different nowadays. To be a ball-player a man has to have a joynt intilleck. Inside baseball, th' paapers calls it, is so deep that it'd give brain fever to a profissor iv asthronomy to thry to figure it out. Each wan iv these here mathymatical janiuses has to carry a thousand mysteeryous signals in his head an' they're changed ivry day an' sometimes in the middle iv th' game. I's so sorry f'r th' poor fellows. In th' old days whin they were through with th' game they'd maybe sthray over to th' Dutchman's f'r a pint iv beer. Now they hurry home to their study an' spind th' avnin' poorin' over books iv allgibera an' thrigynomethry.

"How do I know? Hogan was in here last night with an article on th' 'Mysthries iv Baseball.' It's be a larned man. Here it is: Th' ordhinary observer or lunk-head who knows nawthin' about baseball excipt what he learned be playin' it, has no idee that th' game as played to-day is wan iv th' most inthricate sciences known to mankind. In th' first place th' player must have an absolute masthry iv th' theery iv ballistic motion. This is especially true iv th' pitcher. A most exact knowledge in mathymatics is required f'r th' position. What is vulgarly know as th' spit-ball on account iv th' homely way in which th' op'rator procures his effects is in fact a solution iv wan iv th' most inthricate problems in mechanics. Th' purpose iv th' pitcher is to project th' projectyle so that at a pint between his position an' th' batsman th' tindincy to pr-ceed on its way will be countheracted be an impulse to return whence it come. Th' purpose iv th' batsman is, afther judgin' be scientific methods th' probable coorse or thrajecthry iv th' missile, to oppose it with sufficyent foorce at th' proper moment an' at th' most efficient point, first to retard its forward movement, thin to correct th' osseylations an' fin'ly to propel it in a direction approximately opposite fr'm its original progress. This, I am informed, is technically known as 'bustin th' ball on th' nose (or bugle).' In a gr-reat number iv cases which I observed th' experiment iv th' batsman failed an' th' empire was obliged so to declare, th' ball havin' actually crossed th' plate but eluded th' (intended) blow. In other cases where no blow was attimpted or even meditated I noted that th' empire erred an' in gin'ral I must deplore an astonishin' lack in thrained scientific observation on th' part iv this officyal. He made a number iv grievous blundhers an' I was not surprised to larn fr'm a gintleman who set next to me that he (th' empire) had spint th' arly part iv his life as a fish in the Mammoth Cave iv Kentucky. I thried me best to show me disapproval iv his unscientific an' infamous methods be hittin' him over th' head with me umbrella as he left th' grounds. At th' request iv th' iditor iv th' magazine I intherviewed Misther Bugs Mulligan th' pitcher iv th' Kangaroos afther th' game. I found th' cillybrated expert in th' rotundy iv th' Grand Palace Hotel where he was settin' with other players polishin' his finger nails. I r-read him my notes on th' game an' he expressed his approval addin' with a show at laste iv enthusyasm: 'Bo, ye have a head like a dhrum.' I requested him to sign th' foregoin' statement but he declined remarkin' that th' last time he wrote his name he sprained his wrist an' was out iv the game f'r a week.

"What'd I be doin' at th' likes iv a game like that? I'd come away with a narvous headache. No, sir, whin I take a day off, I take a day off. I'm not goin' to a base-ball game. I'm goin' to take a bag iv peanuts an' spind an afthernoon at th' chimical labrytory down at th' colledge where there's something goin' on I can undherstand."

"Oh, sure," said Mr. Hennessy, "if 'twas as mysteryous as all that how cud Tom Donahue's boy Petie larn it that was fired fr'm th' Brothers School because he cuddn't add? . . ."

"Annyhow 'tis a gr-rand game, Hinnissy, whether 'tis played

th' way th' pro-fissor thinks or th' way Petie larned to play it in th' backyard an' I shuddn't wondher if it's th' way he's still playin'. Th' two gr-reat American spoorts are a good deal alike—polyticks an' baseball. They're both played be pro-fissyonals, th' teams ar-re r-run be fellows that cuddn't throw a base-ball or stuff a ballot box to save their lives an' ar-re on'y intherested in countin' up th' gate receipts, an' here ar-re we settin' out in the sun on th' bleachin' boords, payin' our good money f'r th' spoort, hot an' uncomfortable but happy, injying ivry good play, hottin' ivry bad wan, knowin' nathin' about th' inside play an' not carin', but all jinin' in th' cry iv 'Kill th' empire.' They're both grand games."

"Speakin' iv polyticks," said Mr. Hennessy, "who d'ye think'll be ilicted?"

"Afther lookin' th' candydates over," said Mr. Dooley, "an' studyin' their qualifications carefully I can't thruthfully say that I see a prisidintial possibility in sight."

FICTION

The Sleeper

CHARLES EINSTEIN

IN MY TIME, I have roomed with a lot of crazy rookies, a situation that probably was more my fault than theirs. They got thrown in with me because I was kind of the elder statesman on the Barons; and whenever you have a big-league baseball team that has a coach who's been around a long time, you almost always room some wild busher with him. The idea is it is a restraining influence. It calms the kid down.

So I have had Bernhardt, a nineteen-year-old who slept with his catcher's mask on, and Vorhees, who liked to walk on his hands, and Halloway, a young third baseman who used to like to read aloud from the telephone directory.

But those three were nothing. They were a pleasure compared to Groves.

Groves came up to the Barons one season when we didn't have

an eccentric on the club. He had a great record in the Association the season before, and he could hit like crazy. Nottingham, the manager, figured with Groves in left field maybe the Barons had a shot at taking it all, so he roomed Groves with me.

"Just to make sure nothing goes wrong," Nottingham says to me.

"But this one's normal," I said.

"Try to put up with him anyway," Nottingham says.

Well, it's a delight. We're down in Florida at the start of spring training, and this kid Groves is always in bed by nine-thirty P.M. and doesn't shine the light in your eyes or anything. After what I'd been through in other years, in a week's time I wanted to adopt him.

Until the night before our schedule of exhibition games was supposed to begin. Nottingham was going to start Groves in left against the Phillies the next day, and I figured maybe the kid would be nervous. But he goes off to sleep as calm and composed as you ever saw. Me, I read for a while and then I fell off too.

But sometime in the middle of the night—it must have been about four A.M.—something wakes me up. I sit up in bed, and there's Groves, standing in the middle of the room and holding his hands like there's a baseball bat in them.

"Hey, Glen," I said to him—that was his name, Glen Groves—"what's the matter?"

He doesn't say a word. Just stands there, sort of peering into the bathroom like there's a pitcher in there going to throw to him. All of a sudden, he looks behind him, like there's a catcher there, and starts to laugh like crazy.

"Is that all he's got?" he says, and laughs some more.

I said, "Hey, Glen, what's up?"

But he didn't say a thing. Just stood there going through a phantom batting practice for about ten minutes. Then he throws the nonexistent bat away and went and got into bed.

"Listen," I said to him in the morning, "what the hell were you up to in the middle of the night?"

"What do you mean?" he says.

"You were up at bat in the middle of the room."

"In my pajamas?"

"I know it sounds sort of silly," I said, "but . . ."

"It sure does," Groves says. "I'll tell you, though, I had some dream. I dreamed I was batting against the Phillies and I come up twice against Roberts."

"How'd you do?"

"Walked once, flied out to center the next time."

"Yes, sir," I said, and I went down to breakfast without waiting for him.

Sure enough, in the game that afternoon Roberts pitched the first four against us. First time against Groves, he walks him. Next time, Groves flies out to center.

I got Nottingham in a corner and said, "Listen, I think maybe there's some trouble around here. This Groves, he knows what he's going to do before he does it."

"Yeah?" Nottingham said.

"Yeah," I said. "He told me this morning."

"How did he find out?"

"He bats in his sleep."

"You mean he walks in his sleep?"

"He doesn't do a hell of a lot of walking. He just gets up to bat."

"Stay out of the sun," Nottingham says to me.

I had trouble getting to sleep that night. It didn't take much to wake me. And when I did sit up in bed, along around four A.M., there's Groves hitting in the middle of the room again and talking and laughing to beat the band. This time he turned his face toward me, and I could see his eyes were open. What's more, he recognized me.

"Hit or take?" he says.

"Hit away," I said, and watched. He took a good cut, laughed again, and got back in bed.

"Went three for four last night," he told me in the morning. "Brought a man around with a double."

"Okay," I said, and got out of there. At the ball park, before the game, I got ahold of Nottingham and said, "You think I'm crazy, hah?"

"I didn't say that," Nottingham said. "You know how it is."

"Watch Groves," I told him. "He gets three hits."

Groves got three hits. Actually he was up five times, and he didn't bring any runners around, but he gets his three hits, and one of them's a double.

After the game, Nottingham says to me, "What's going on between you two?"

"I'm telling you," I said. "He hits in his sleep. You're the guy that put him in to room with me."

"I don't believe it," Nottingham said. "Don't press me too far or I might see if I can't trade you to Pittsburgh."

"We been friends a long time," I said to him.

"Yeah," Nottingham said.

Next morning, after the same sleep-hitting routine in the middle of the night, Groves awakes, fresh as a flower, and says, "By Hector, I'm finding the range now. Hit two over the wall last night."

He hit a pair of home runs that afternoon, and that convinced Nottingham. "Look," he says to me, "let's make an arrangement. You say he actually talks to you while he's doing this?"

"Hell, yes," I said. "Last night he told me to get a new ball in there because they were throwing a spitter."

"All right," Nottingham said. "Tonight when he's asleep, I'll come in the room to watch. You let me in when I knock. Don't you fall asleep."

"I haven't slept since last Friday," I said.

Well, a little after midnight Nottingham taps on the door and I go and let him in. He sits down in a chair and I get back in bed, and we wait for nearly three hours, and then all of a sudden Glen Groves sits up in bed, goes to the night table, selects a bat, and marches up to the plate in the middle of the room. He stood so that Nottingham was sitting right back of his elbow—about where the catcher would be if Groves was really up at bat. I went and stood behind Nottingham's chair so I could see what was going on.

Well, Groves takes his stance and flexes, and here comes the pitch. He lets it go through. Then he turns and looks at me. "What was it?"

"Ball," I said.

"It looked all right to me," Nottingham says.

"You keep out of this," I said to him. "Play ball."

We went that way for twenty minutes. Then Groves throws away his bat and goes back to bed and begins to snore.

Next day the phone rings at seven A.M. It's Nottingham.

"How'd he do?"

"He had a perfect night," I said. "Three hits and a sacrifice."

"How does he feel?"

"He says he feels great."

"I'm a wreck," Nottingham said.

The manager put up with it for four more days. Two more nights he had to come to our room to see for himself. Then he said to me,

"Listen, there's a Dr. Fleischmann at the Institute in Miami. Let's you and me have a talk with him."

We went to see Dr. Fleischmann. He was a little European guy with a mustache. We told him the story.

"Ah," he said, and his eyes lit up. "I would never have believed it."

"Believe what?" Nottingham says.

"Transcendency in wish fulfillment," Dr. Fleischmann said. "Steckel speaks of it. It is very rare."

"I'll bet," Nottingham said. "What does it mean?"

"We all," Dr. Fleischmann says, "dream of things which in one way or another we wish to come true. Your young friend wishes to hit a baseball."

"Why does he get out of bed to do it?"

"He can't hit lying down," Dr. Fleischmann said. "Can you?"

"No," Nottingham said. "No, I can't. But if it's what you say it is, how come he ever makes out? Why don't he hit safely every time up? The other night Porterfield struck him out twice."

"What is he hitting now?" Dr. Fleischmann said.

".624," Nottingham says.

"Why are you complaining?"

"I ain't complaining."

"Then just leave him alone," Dr. Fleischmann says. "And make sure he doesn't have to take an upper berth when you travel."

"Just tell me one thing," Nottingham says. "You think this . . . this . . ."

"Transcendency in wish fulfillment," the doctor says.

"That's it," Nottingham says. "Hitting in his sleep. You think it gives him confidence?"

"Of course," Dr. Fleischmann says. "That's what makes this such a rare case. Your dreams and mine seldom come true. This young man hits a home run because he dreamed he could. A great rarity. You ought to win the pennant by seven games."

"If I don't die from loss of sleep meanwhile," Nottingham says.

So the club traveled north, and after a while I reached the point where I wouldn't even ask Groves how he did during the night. It was too much fun the other way, trying to guess in advance and then watching him whale the cover off the ball. You never saw such a kid. He got eight hits in the first three games, once the season got under way, and against good pitching, too. By Decoration Day he was hitting .454, and he was the talk of the baseball world.

Then we hit west, and for some reason Groves began to fall off. By the time we got to Chicago, he couldn't buy a base hit.

"Is he still hitting at night?" Nottingham asks me.

"Hell, yes," I said.

"How does he say he's going to do?"

"I'm afraid to ask him."

"Listen," Nottingham said. "We better do something."

That night Nottingham hides out in the room again, and when Groves gets up to do his hitting, Nottingham and I are both sitting there, cheering him on.

"You can do it, boy!" Nottingham calls. "All-away in there, boy! Little base hit, baby! Alla time in the world, boy! Only need one, boy! Straighten it out, baby, let's go!"

In the morning, Nottingham gets me on the house phone.

"How'd he do?"

"Fanned four straight times," I said. "He feels terrible about it."

"What do you suppose is the matter?"

"How the hell do I know?"

"What was the name of that doctor in Miami?"

"Fleischmann," I said.

"Let's get him up here."

We flew Dr. Fleischmann in from Miami and told him the whole story. He twirled his mustache for a while and looked wise. Finally he shrugged his shoulders.

"I know what it is," he said, "but I can't think what to do with it."

"What do you mean?" Nottingham says. "What is it? What's he done?"

"He hasn't done anything," the doctor said. "It's the time of year that's doing it to him." And he nodded gravely and packed his little bag and left.

Long after we benched Groves because of his bad hitting, long after he had been shipped back to the minors, it came to me what he was talking about. It had been June when Glen Groves's slump occurred—the month when the hot weather sets in and the pitchers start to come around.

Like nine rookies out of ten, Groves couldn't hit a curve.

GENERAL

From *A Dictionary of Contemporary American Usage*

BERGEN EVANS *and* CORNELIA EVANS

pinch-hitter, as a term for substitute, is a cliché. Except when used of baseball, the term is often misused. When a manager sends out a pinch-hitter, he assumes that the pinch-hitter will do better than the man at bat. But in other activities, when sickness or some other circumstances makes it impossible for the principal to appear and a substitute or understudy is rushed in to fill the place, he is not expected to do better than the principal would have done. It is a triumph if he or she does what is required in any acceptable fashion.

MEDICAL

FIFTEEN MINUTES before midnight on June 14, 1949, first baseman Eddie Waitkus, then with the Philadelphia Phillies, was shot and critically wounded by a young woman whom he did not know, but who had insisted on seeing him at his Chicago hotel because of "something important." The assailant was arrested and the following is excerpted from the report prepared by the chief of the county behavior clinic pursuant to an order from the felony court. The young woman was adjudged insane and spent three years in a state hospital after which she was found to have recovered her sanity and was freed of a pending charge of assault with intent to kill. Following surgery, Waitkus accomplished a full recovery and went on to play in the 1950 World Series.

From "A Report to Felony Court"

FILE NO. —, THE BEHAVIOR CLINIC

As a child she was gay and happy. As she reached adolescence she changed in many ways. She did not want people to look at her. She became apprehensive and self-conscious when riding in street cars. If in crowds she became fearful that she would be the center of attention. She was overly careful about her personal appearance, especially her hair and nails, but was not concerned about her shoes. She would buy new clothes, but preferred to wear old ones. She was very interested in music, and at one time had a "crush" on Liszt and played his *Hungarian Rhapsodies* over and over. Then she got a craze about Andy Russell and had to have his records. Two years ago she changed to boogy-woogy music and would play these records until the family felt they would go "crazy."

At the age of sixteen she went with a girl friend and this girl's brother to a ball game. Following this she attended the games often. This boy was very interested in her, but she never really cared for him. He was slow and easygoing. At times she would make a date with him and then purposely not be home when he called. She is methodical and exact about many things, especially in relation to money. She is careful about keeping promises. As a child she attended the Lutheran Church. Of late she has attended church with her girl friends. Her parents have been told that during some emotional services she would sit staring and trembling all over.

She was never interested in baseball until she attended with her girl friend and brother. She then attended several times and began to know the different players. She became especially interested in Eddie Waitkus, who was playing first base with the Cubs at the time. She became more and more sentimental in her talk, but no one in the family took her seriously. She started to collect his pictures and press notices. Her friends in turn would send her what they could obtain. As time went on it became more than an ordinary teen-age infatuation. It continued in the winter as well as the summer. She talked constantly about this man. She stated that her father, her boss, other men characters in the movies, etc., reminded her of Eddie. His number was 36 and she became extremely sensitive to that number.

She bought all the records she could obtain that were produced in 1936 and she would play them over and over again. Because he came from Boston she began to eat baked beans and wanted them all the time. The family had a hard time talking about any other subject except Eddie. If they intentionally diverted the subject she would say, "Let's talk about Eddie." If her father became irritated she told him to be quiet, adding, "You just don't care about me." She persuaded her father, who cared nothing about baseball, to attend a game one day, and another time her mother. After the game she would stand with the other "bobby-soxers" who rushed up for autographs and would watch for Waitkus to pass. She would get close to him, but never spoke a word. She would get pale and tremble, and one time almost fainted when he went by.

She became nervous at work and extremely miserable because she thought that her boss looked like Eddie Waitkus. In the middle of November 1948 she suddenly walked out of the office with no explanation. She wandered around town where she thought she might see Eddie, finally coming home at seven o'clock. She told her parents she would not return to work, so they made arrangements for her to have a six-weeks' leave of absence. At this time she was referred to a psychiatrist who saw her for a period of ten days and, as he was leaving town, she was referred to another psychiatrist whom she saw only once. She did not like to appear in crowds, and refused to see another doctor. She stayed home and rested until Christmas time, when she returned to her job in a new department where the work was not so hard. There was less excitement and she got along better. At work she talked constantly of ending her life and stated that she was very miserable. She had mentioned this to her parents, but they did not take it seriously. In January 1949 the work in the office speeded up and she began to have less interest in her affairs at home. She wanted a room of her own, stating that she needed more rest. Because of her continued references to Eddie Waitkus the family agreed to this arrangement.

Because of his nationality she became interested in Lithuanian. She bought books and lessons on that language; she listened to all the Lithuanian programs she could. She secured a room a few blocks away from home and came home almost every night for dinner, which she insisted on paying for. The patient had seen the picture *The Snake Pit.* She liked it and kept going to see it over and over. She said one of the players reminded her of Eddie Waitkus. She felt that it was sure evidence that those considered insane were the normal ones, but the keepers were crazy. She developed a complex about bugs which flew in the house at night, that they must not be killed but should be caught and carried out of the house and released. At night she would spread pictures and press notices of Eddie Waitkus on her bed and make a shrine out of it. She slept with his picture under her pillow at night. In 1948 after his transfer to Philadelphia she cried for a day and a night, stating that she could not live if he went away. She wanted him for her boy friend. When he was in Boston she talked endlessly of going to Boston to have dates with him. When she learned that he would be in town in June she decided she was going to see him and ask him for a date. During that week she cried a great deal and appeared depressed, according to her parents.

Both parents appeared genuinely interested in the patient and are greatly upset over the circumstances.

Her closest girl friend revealed that she and patient had been friends since the fourth grade. She knew all about the "crush" on Eddie and stated that prior to this the patient had a crush on Alan Ladd, and then on "Peanuts" Lowery. At that time they would joke, saying, "You trip him and I will drag him to a cab, take him to Crown Point and marry him." The informant at the same time had crushes on ballplayers, particularly one pitcher named Johnny. When the two attended games each one would discuss the merits of her favorite player. The informant remembers distinctly that the first time the patient noticed Eddie was April 27, 1947. At that time some girl spectators yelled "Hello, funny-face!" and from that time on the patient became very interested in him. They saw every game in which Eddie played, and if, while waiting in the crowd for the players to appear, Eddie should pass close to her, she shrank and hid herself so she would not be seen by him.

She liked movies, especially in regard to prisons and in which psychiatrists were portrayed, liking especially *Parole, Inc.* and *The Snake Pit.* Sex was never discussed. She would tell the informant that Eddie was always near her. She had his picture with her at all times. She would sometimes place his picture against some object and talk to it, saying, "You're so cute. You made such a good play today," etc. She discussed suicide several times with the informant. She was always on time, and furious if she kept people waiting. She never wanted to draw attention to herself and was always shy and self-conscious. The first week in May informant went with patient to buy the gun. At first patient wanted a revolver, but learned that she would have to have a permit, so she looked up pawnshops in the Red Book and finally went to a pawnshop where they bought a .22 rifle for $21. The man showed them how to take it apart and put it together again, and gave her two boxes of shells. She seemed pleased with it and handled it as though it were a new toy. She never said exactly what she wanted it for. On the Monday before the alleged offense the patient and informant got the gun and wrapped it up in heavy paper. She was not suspicious about it at the time, as it appeared to her as just a lark. They called a cab and went to the hotel, where patient had reserved a room. The following day they saw a baseball game and both girls were happy. Nothing unusual occurred. They planned to leave the game together and she was to go to the patient's room because she had stated that she did not like to pass all the wealthy women in the hotel lobby, because they looked at her. Then as the game progressed she appeared nervous and asked what if she should meet Eddie in the lobby. She knew she could not stand it, so she left the game early. The informant did not want to miss seeing Johnny walk out, so did not leave with her. She told the informant she was going to send a note to Eddie that night and ask him to meet her. The informant laughed, because she did not believe she would have nerve enough.

The sister, when interviewed, stated that they got along very well as children. They shared their toys, and the sister added that she was very much surprised when she discovered that when patient moved out she took with her a suitcase full of dolls, Teddy bears, and such toys as she had as a child. They had both objected to the neighborhood. They were reared as gentle, quiet, well-mannered youngsters and did not get along with the rather impolite playmates. They did not know how to fight back.

The sister was extremely bored by ball games, which the patient induced her to attend. She especially hated waiting afterward in the hot sun for as much as an hour for the players to come out. When Eddie would appear the patient would shrink back and never have the courage to ask him for an autograph. For a long time the patient has talked of suicide. When the patient left home they were all glad because they had been getting on each other's nerves. Each Thursday she ate with her sister, who objected if anyone looked at her and would always arrange the chairs so that there was an empty chair facing hers. She stated that Eddie was in this chair. She frequently told her sister that she was sorry for Eddie, because his mother was dead and she wanted to take care of him. Sex was never discussed.

Patient was especially interested in astrology and bought many books on the subject. Informant feels that her sister is enjoying all the publicity and attention she is getting, particularly because she is trying to get revenge for everything that has ever happened to her, all the unhappiness in school, and all the unhappiness she has had because she could not have Eddie.

She was given several psychological tests. On the Bellevue-Wechsler test she had a full-scale I.Q. of 99. She had a brief attention span and it was necessary to call her back to test items. There is a noted lack of social intelligence. On the Rorschach test, a summary reveals that there are indications of a childlike emotional status, incapable of meeting personality conflicts. Her pseudo-solution has been to use reality selectively. It is felt that this investigation indicates an incipient schizophrenic psychosis.

The mental examination was performed in the County Jail. She was seen on numerous occasions. At all times she was cooperative, neat, cheerful, at ease, and volunteered information. She apparently enjoyed talking, and at no time appeared bored with the interview. There were only two occasions in which there were emotional outbursts: One was after an examination by the jail doctor, and the other was when she was discussing what she thought of the people of Philadelphia for buying Waitkus. When discussing the shooting of Waitkus there was no change of emotion whatsoever. At no time were there any tears, but frequently she laughed when discussing the shooting and other serious problems. She gave personal identification and stated that she had eight years of grammar school and four years of high school. She went into detail to tell of difficulties she had with other children while in the grades. At times she would return to difficulties in the first few grades to give minor details such as, "One girl always picked on me. When she said 'Come here' I would do it. I was always afraid of her. . . . Boys used to yell at me." She feels that she was unpopular in high school because she knew very little about sex and for this reason the other students made fun of her.

When she was interviewed for her first position she says she was told that she needed a psychiatric examination. She feels that she is sick mentally, but not insane, adding, "There must be something the matter with me if I go around shooting people . . . My first idea was that I would shoot him because I liked him a great deal and I knew

I never could have him, and if I couldn't have him neither could anybody else. Secondly, I had the idea that if I shot him I would have to shoot myself. In the third place I wanted publicity and attention for once." She has dreamt about killing Waitkus and found herself sitting with him in her arms. She adds, "All my dreams have come true."

She attributes many of her nervous features after first knowing Eddie. First of all, April 27, 1947 was the big day in her life. "The first year I was crazy about him. The second year, when I went out I became self-conscious. I thought people were looking at me. I thought my head was shaking. I pretended he was along with me and talked to me—not out loud—it was in a mental sense, not physical. We walked down the street together. I was not afraid to leave my parents' home. The neighborhood was not so good. I wouldn't take a street car because Eddie was with me. I didn't tell my mother because she would have laughed at me. If I told my dad he would have sent me to a psychiatrist right away . . . I told my girl friends. At no time did I actually feel him—I did mentally, not in body. Mentally I can recall him any time I want to. He has been with me in jail . . . The whole thing sounds so silly. I asked him, 'What are you going to do about me now? You wanted me to do this.' At the present time he evades me. He says, 'Don't you think it would be better if you went to some hospital?' . . . I kept asking him over and over again how he felt about the whole thing, but he keeps evading me, so I got mad and didn't talk to him the rest of the night. . . . One thing I'll say for him, he has always paid a lot of attention to me. Finally I got so far I got this gun. I made plans for going to him. I wanted to get away from here and planned on going to Boston. He got awfully mad about that."

She tells in detail about the registration at the hotel and her infatuation with Eddie Waitkus. "I had my first good look at him on April 27, 1947. I used to go to all the ball games just to watch him. We used to wait for them to come out of the clubhouse after the game, and all the time I was watching him I was building in my mind the idea of killing him. As time went on I just became nuttier and nuttier about the guy and I knew I would never get to know him in a normal way, so I kept thinking I will never get him and if I can't have him nobody else can. And then I decided I would kill him. I didn't know how or when, but I knew I would kill him . . . After a year went by and I was still crazy about him I decided to do something about it.

Then I decided to kill him with a gun, it would be the easiest way. I actually got the gun in May. I didn't think I would have the courage to get a gun, because I am afraid of one. I knew I couldn't get a small gun like I wanted because you have to go through the trouble of getting a permit, so I went to the pawnshop and got this second-hand rifle. My girl friend was with me at the time. After that I looked up the schedule to see when the Phillies would be here. I knew they were staying at this hotel, so I put my reservation in for the time when they would be there. I got the reservation and it was just a question of waiting. During that time I learned how to put it together and take it apart. Then I just waited until it was time to go. . . . The whole thing seemed so funny. After I registered we went back to the house and picked up the gun." She then tells in detail of the events of the next two days, adding, "I had no more than got to sleep when I was awakened by the telephone ringing. It was Waitkus. Well, he wanted to know what the note was all about and why I wanted to see him. He said 'What's so darn important?' and that shocked me. I hadn't figured a guy like him. I didn't expect that from a guy like him. I thought he would ask me what it was all about, but he was so informal. I said, 'I can't discuss it over the 'phone with you.' I said, 'Can you come up tonight for a few minutes?' and he said, 'Yes.' I said, 'Give me half an hour to get dressed . . .' Then I got dressed and waited for him. I remember when he knocked on the door. I was scared stiff, but I thought to myself I will settle this once and for all and really kill him. At that time I had a knife in my skirt pocket and was going to use that on him. When I opened the door he came rushing in right past me. I expected him to stand there and wait until I asked him to come in and during that time I was going to stab him with the knife. I was kind of mad that he came right in and sat down and didn't give me a chance to stab him. He looked at me surprised and said, 'What do you want to see me about?' I said, 'Wait a minute. I have a surprise for you.' I went to the closet and got out the gun. I took it out and pointed it at him and he had such a silly look on his face. He looked so surprised. I was pretty mad at him, so I told him to get out of the chair and move over by the window. He got up right away and said, 'Baby, what's this all about?' That made me mad. He just stood there stuttering and stammering and he asked me again, 'What is this all about? What have I done?' I said, 'For two years you have been bothering me, and now you are going to die'—and then I shot him. For a minute I didn't think I shot him, because he just stood there, and then he crashed against the wall. For a minute I just looked at him. I didn't believe he was shot. He kept saying, 'Baby, why did you do that?' and then I said, 'I don't believe I shot you,' because I was still smiling. Then I knelt down next to him. He had his hand stretched out. I put my hand over his. He said something to the effect, 'You like that, don't you?' I took my hand away from his when he said that. I asked him where he had been shot—I couldn't see a bullet hole or blood or anything. He said I shot him in the guts, and I was convinced he was shot. I don't know why. I thought, well now's the time to shoot myself, and I told him. Then I tried to find the bullets, but I couldn't find them, and I lost my nerve. I was frantic by that time and I called the operator to call the doctor. He kept moaning, 'Oh, baby, why did you do it? Why did you do it?' He was groaning and I didn't like to hear it, so I went out in the hall. The doctor and house detective came. It was so silly. Nobody came out of their rooms. You would think they would all come rushing out. I got mad. I kept telling them I shot Eddie Waitkus, but they didn't know who Eddie Waitkus was. I thought they were just plain dumb if they didn't know who Eddie Waitkus was. After that the police came, but I was burning because nobody was coming out of those other rooms. Nobody seemed to want me much. I could have walked right out of the place and nobody would have come after me."

She denies excessive alcoholism and states that she had three drinks that night in order to bolster her courage. She states she was sober at the time of the shooting. She has read several books on psychiatry. She has had frequent messages from Waitkus, such as seeing his name on a bar of soap, or seeing the number 36 on the screen, etc. She does not feel that she wants to kill anyone else, but should she get out she would want to kill Eddie because he is the only one worth killing. She feels that she should be sent to Dwight, but not to any mental institution. She has read books on American penal and prison systems, so knows what life would be in a prison. She is oriented in all spheres. Questions of general information and calculation are adequately answered.

DIAGNOSIS: Schizophrenia in an immature individual. She is committable to an institution for the mentally ill. At no time does she show concern, nor appear to realize the seriousness of her behavior. She discusses suicide freely and has thought of many methods that she would try. She should be under constant surveillance.

PROFILE

HERE IS an umpire spending the winter in the knowledge that (a) he blew a call and (b) half the country thinks it cost their team the World Series.

In the Eye of the Storm

RON FIMRITE

DON DENKINGER (the name sound familiar?) is, by any accounting, a pillar of Waterloo, Iowa—a native of adjacent Cedar Falls where he was a star athlete in the '50s, a lifelong resident of the area, a popular restaurateur in town and a member of the Shrine, Rotary, Elks Club and Zion Lutheran Church. His wife of 23 years, Gayle, taught at the local high school, was an active Junior Leaguer and worked in the local Red Cross chapter. The Denkingers have three bright and attractive daughters, Darcy, 20, Denise, 18, and Dana, 17, and a perky little schnauzer named Schatzie as well. They live in a fine house. They're a very sociable family, and Don, with his roots so deeply embedded in the community, is a soft touch for any civic endeavor. The Denkingers are well-known, well-liked and definitely respected. But you would never know any of this from the letters and phone calls they've been receiving lately.

The phone calls, though always unnerving, are relatively easy to deal with. After the first burst of profanity, one simply hangs up. Don't even consider collect calls. The mail is a little trickier. One letter, addressed to Gayle, begins, flatteringly enough, "I have always had the greatest respect for your advice and I was wondering if you could help me with this problem." What follows is a recounting of the letter writer's family history, a history so repellent as to make the Snopeses seem wholesome by comparison. And then the kicker: Should the correspondent inform his fiancée, herself a convicted felon, "that my brother is an American League umpire?" This one, though steeped in vulgarity, at least represents some conscious effort at composition. Most of the 200 or more letters the Denkingers have received over the past two months are simple explosions of bile. Most suggest that Denkinger, if not legally blind, should at least seek treatment for advanced myopia. One communication proposes that Don use makeup in all future television appearances because, "You're an ugly bleep." (Not true.) Another, after a full page of billingsgate, closes chummily with, "Give my best to your wife and kids."

There is irony: "Congratulations on changing history." Pathos: "I just wish you could see my tears." Venom: "I wish you the worst." And malapropism: "The mistake you made will go down in the *annuals* of baseball." They are variously signed. "A. Fan," "Louie St. Louis," "Fellow Admirer," "Whitey and Joaquin." Some of the most vicious are, predictably, unsigned. You get the point: Opening the mail has not become a highlight of the Denkingers' day. Even when his equipment bag arrived by air freight from Kansas City, Denkinger found taped to it the unsigned message: YOU BLEW THE CALL.

Denkinger—wearing spectacles, his antagonists will be pleased to learn—reads this scabrous prose in the cozy den of his house in Waterloo with the weary resignation of one long accustomed to abusive language. "I think I've always realized there were those kinds of people out there," he says sadly. Denkinger is, after all, an umpire. More specifically, he is *the* umpire who, in the irrational view of St. Louis baseball fans everywhere (and their number is obviously legion), cost the Cardinals the 1985 World Series. Denkinger's call is, if not yet actually in the "annuals," quickly becoming part of Series lore. As you may remember:

It is the last half of the ninth inning of the sixth game, and the Cardinals, needing only one more win to take the championship, are leading 1–0. The leadoff batter for Kansas City is Jorge Orta, a left-handed hitter. He is facing Todd Worrell, a six-foot-five right-handed reliever. Worrell gets two strikes on Orta right off. His fourth pitch is nubbed softly to the first-base side of the mound. First baseman Jack Clark charges over to field it, and Worrell, who thought about going for it himself, runs to cover first. Clark lobs the ball to him high but on target as Orta rushes down the line. Denkinger is in position to make the call. He is in foul territory about eight feet from the bag. Runner and ball arrive almost, but not quite, at the same time. Denkinger calls the runner safe. Cardinal manager Whitey Herzog explodes from the dugout. There is an argument, but the decision holds. "We can't seem to draw a break," Herzog angrily tells the umpire. He's right. Video replays clearly show that Orta was out. All hell breaks loose after this call: a misjudged pop-up, a hit, a passed ball, a walk and, finally, a bases-loaded single by pinch hitter Dane Iorg that wins the game for the Royals 2–1. The Series is tied. Herzog is fit to be tied. "We're going to win the World Series and that bleeper

[Denkinger] blows the call," he says. "Now we've got the bleeper behind the plate tomorrow. We've got about as much chance as the man in the moon." He's right again.

The Cardinals lose the seventh game 11–0 and the Series and their senses. In the fifth inning, with the score 10–0, St. Louis pitcher Joaquin Andujar complains to Denkinger, the plate umpire, about a ball three call on Jim Sundberg. Herzog rushes out, allegedly to calm his pitcher but really to berate Denkinger again for the Orta call. Denkinger ejects him. When Denkinger calls Andujar's next pitch a ball, the pitcher storms off the mound in a terrible rage. Denkinger ejects him. It is the first time in 50 years both a manager and a player have been kicked out of a World Series game. The Cardinals behave afterward like petulant schoolboys. Their fans are inflamed.

Gayle is in Kansas City for the game while Denkinger's daughters and his mother-in-law, Margaret Price, watch this ugly spectacle on TV in the family home back in Waterloo. Seeing their father assaulted from all sides is such an unsettling experience for the girls that they begin to cry. Denkinger's fellow American League umpires Dave Phillips and Rich Garcia, themselves disturbed by the Game 7 tumult, call the house to offer counsel to the family. Friends in Waterloo and elsewhere call. It's only a game, after all, the girls are told. It will soon be forgotten. And then the other calls start. "A St. Louis disc jockey gave out my address and phone number on the radio," says Denkinger. The girls, still upset by the nasty scene on television, are now exposed to a succession of obscene calls that lasts through the night. And the next night. And the next. Their father's life is threatened. Price calls a friend, who then telephones the local police to ask for protection. The Waterloo police call their counterparts in St. Louis, asking that the inflammatory deejay be ordered to desist.

Denkinger and Gayle drove home from Kansas City on Monday. He had a "sinking feeling" that there might be further trouble. "I could sense there was some frustration." But he thought any trouble resulting from the Series would quickly dissipate. In 26 years as an umpire, 17 in the American League, nine as a crew chief, he had been exposed to any number of cruel stunts. The air had been let out of his car tires. Somebody had put Limburger cheese in the manifold. Young toughs had tailgated him out of town in the minor leagues. Penny-ante stuff. But when he got home to Waterloo, he found his house under the watchful eye of the police and his daughters in a troubled state. "And then," he says, "two or three days later the mail started coming in," so much of it, in fact, that the post office didn't even bother to deliver it at all. "Sometimes," he says, "you can't really know what you're dealing with out there."

Denkinger, who is 49, had never planned to be an umpire. He had been a track man, a wrestler (137 to 157 pounds) and a football player at Cedar Falls High and at Wartburg College in Waverly, Iowa. He was drafted into the Army after 2½ years of college and sent, finally, to a missile base in New Mexico. It was his first prolonged stay away from home. He had planned to return to college after his discharge, but an Army buddy, Master Sergeant Bob Henrion, persuaded him to join him at the Al Somers School for Umpires in Daytona Beach, Fla. Denkinger went on a lark—"I couldn't even fathom what it was an umpire was supposed to do"—but he finished as most likely to succeed among 85 students. He was hooked. "I'm in a unique profession," he says, "one that people don't know a lot about. Oh, yes, I know we have this hateful image, but it's totally untrue that we lead a miserable, lonely life. Why, I've got friends in every city we go to."

Denkinger didn't see the tapes of his historic mistake in the sixth game until the Tuesday following the Series. He had purposely avoided reading the papers, watching television or listening to the radio between games, so as to preserve his objectivity. If he heard actual replays of Herzog's angry denunciations of him, he had feared, his judgment might be colored in some subtle way. Denkinger had already worked two World Series, in 1974 and '80, but the thrill of calling an important game meant fully as much to him as playing in one did to the ballplayers. But with it all over and the dust cleared, he felt it was time to reflect. He was sitting alone in his family room composing his report on the seventh-game mess to commissioner Peter Ueberroth when, to his ultimate dismay, he saw out of the corner of his eye the Orta play being rerun on his television set. He paused in his writing to watch.

"They were calling it the biggest bonehead play of the year," Denkinger recalls. "They must've shown it six times, from every angle. Well, it soon became obvious to me that, let's say, there was a very great possibility the ball beat the runner to the bag. In fact, I was astute enough to recognize that the man was clearly out. The call was wrong. I was in good position, but Worrell is a tall man, the throw was high and I couldn't watch both his glove and his feet at the same time. There was so much crowd noise I couldn't hear the ball hit the glove. Besides, it was a soft throw. My first responsibility is to make sure the ball is caught. Had I been maybe 15 feet back, instead of eight, I might have made the right call.

"I didn't like what I saw. No one wants to be embarrassed like that. My job is predicated on being right all the time, and I like to be right all the time. But [melancholy laughter] we're only human, and now it's history. I can't change anything. Even admitting I was wrong doesn't change anything. But I do know that I didn't cost the Cardinals the World Series, not with all that happened afterward. There were too many 'what ifs' in the game. I think what worries all umpires is the violent reaction to things now. In Yankee Stadium, God save us, there was even a shooting. Please tell me what a man is doing with a gun in the ball park? We have to be concerned about these things, because it's obvious the situation is getting worse. I love baseball and I'm not all that disillusioned by what's happened to me. I'll continue to do what I've always done, which is to take every game very seriously and do my best."

The calls and the letters keep coming in, but there has been no violence to his person, his family or his home. Denkinger is a man with a keenly honed sense of irony, and that has helped him ride over the rough spots. He observes, laughing, that his newfound notoriety has at least given him a certain cachet on the banquet circuit. And he takes special pleasure in one of the neon signs that flash behind the bar of his Silver Fox restaurant in downtown Waterloo. It's the first thing he'll show visitors to the place. "Gussie Busch's company [the *Braumeister* also owns the Cardinals] gave one of these to all the umpires," he says, standing beneath the glittering prize. The sign reads: THIS BUD'S FOR YOU.

POETRY

THE LATE ROBERT FITZGERALD was Professor of Rhetoric and Oratory at Harvard University and a Chancellor of the Academy of American Poets. His works include translations of *The Iliad, The Odyssey,* and, most recently, *The Aeneid. Cobb Would Have Caught It* was first published in 1943.

Cobb Would Have Caught It

ROBERT FITZGERALD

In sunburnt parks where Sundays lie,
Or the wide wastes beyond the cities,
Teams in grey deploy through sunlight.

Talk it up, boys, a little practice,
Coming in stubby and fast, the baseman
Gathers a grounder in fat green grass.
Picks it up stinging and clipped as wit
Into the leather: a swinging step
Wings it deadeye down to first.
Smack. Oh, atta boy, atta old boy.

Catcher reverses his cap, pulls down
Sweaty casque, and squats in the dust;
Pitcher rubs new ball on his pants,
Chewing, puts a jet behind him;
Nods past batter, taking his time.

Batter settles, tugs at his cap:
A spinning ball: step and swing to it,
Caught like a cheek before it ducks
By shivery hickory: socko, baby:
Cleats dig into dust. Outfielder,
On his own way, looking over shoulder,
Makes it a triple; A long peg home.

Innings and afternoons. Fly lost in sunset.
Throwing arm gone bad. There's your ball game.
Cool reek of the field. Reek of companions.

POETRY

The Base Stealer

ROBERT FRANCIS

Poised between going on and back, pulled
Both ways taut like a tightrope-walker,
Fingertips pointing the opposites,
Now bouncing tiptoe like a dropped ball
Or a kid skipping rope, come on, come on,
Running a scattering of steps sidewise,
How he teeters, skitters, tingles, teases,
Taunts them, hovers like an ecstatic bird,
He's only flirting, crowd him, crowd him,
Delicate, delicate, delicate, delicate—now!

FICTION

ZANE GREY wrote more than fifty western novels, as you may well be aware. Are you aware also that he was a college and professional baseball player? Or that his story, "The Redheaded Outfield," is one of the most famous and widely read boys' baseball stories ever done?

The Redheaded Outfield

ZANE GREY

THERE WAS Delaney's red-haired trio—Red Gilbat, left fielder; Reddy Clammer, right fielder, and Reddie Ray, center fielder, composing the most remarkable outfield ever developed in minor league baseball. It was Delaney's pride, as it was also his trouble.

Red Gilbat was nutty—and his batting average was .371. Any

student of baseball could weigh these two facts against each other and understand something of Delaney's trouble. It was not possible to camp on Red Gilbat's trail. The man was a jack-o'-lantern, a will-o'-the-wisp, a weird, long-legged, long-armed, red-haired illusive phantom. When the gong rang at the ball grounds there were ten chances to one that Red would not be present. He had been discovered with small boys peeping through knotholes at the vacant left field he was supposed to inhabit during play.

Of course, what Red did off the ball grounds was not so important as what he did on. And there was absolutely no telling what under the sun he might do then except once out of every three times at bat he could be counted on to knock the cover off the ball.

Reddy Clammer was a grandstand player—the kind all managers hated—and he was hitting .305. He made circus catches, circus stops, circus throws, circus steals—but particularly circus catches. That is to say, he made easy plays appear difficult. He was always strutting, posing, talking, arguing, quarreling—when he was not engaged in making a grandstand play. Reddy Clammer used every possible incident and artifice to bring himself into the limelight.

Reddie Ray had been the intercollegiate champion in the sprints and a famous college ballplayer. After a few months of professional ball he was hitting over .400 and leading the league both at bat and on the bases. It was a beautiful and a thrilling sight to see him run. He was so quick to start, so marvelously swift, so keen of judgment, that neither Delaney nor any player could ever tell the hit that he was not going to get. That was why Reddie Ray was a whole game in himself.

Delaney's Rochester Stars and the Providence Grays were tied for first place. Of the present series each team had won a game. Rivalry had always been keen, and as the teams were about to enter the long homestretch for the pennant there was battle in the New England air.

The September day was perfect. The stands were half full and the bleachers packed with a white-sleeved mass. And the field was beautifully level and green. The Grays were practicing and the Stars were on their bench.

"We're up against it," Delaney was saying. "This new umpire, Fuller, hasn't got it in for us. Oh, no, not at all! Believe me, he's a robber. But Scott is pitchin' well. Won his last three games. He'll bother 'em. And the three Reds have broken loose. They're on the rampage. They'll burn up this place today."

Somebody noticed the absence of Gilbat.

Delaney gave a sudden start. "Why, Gil was here," he said slowly. "Lord!—he's about due for a nutty stunt."

Whereupon Delaney sent boys and player scurrying about to find Gilbat, and Delaney went himself to ask the Providence manager to hold back the gong for a few minutes.

Presently somebody brought Delaney a telephone message that Red Gilbat was playing ball with some boys in a lot four blocks down the street. When at length a couple of players marched up to the bench with Red in tow Delaney uttered an immense sigh of relief and then, after a close scrutiny of Red's face, he whispered, "Lock the gates!"

Then the gong rang. The Grays trooped in. The Stars ran out, except Gilbat, who ambled like a giraffe. The hum of conversation in the grandstand quickened for a moment with the scraping of chairs, and then grew quiet. The bleachers sent up the rollicking cry of expectancy. The umpire threw out a white ball with his stentorian "Play!" and Blake of the Grays strode to the plate.

Hitting safely, he started the game with a rush. With Dorr up, the Star infield played for a bunt. Like clockwork Dorr dumped the first ball as Blake got his flying start for second base. Morrissey tore in for the ball, got it on the run and snapped it underhand to Healy, beating the runner by an inch. The fast Blake, with a long slide, made third base. The stands stamped. The bleachers howled. White, next man up, batted a high fly to left field. This was a sun field and the hardest to play in the league. Red Gilbat was the only man who ever played it well. He judged the fly, waited under it, took a step back, then forward, and deliberately caught the ball in his gloved hand. A throw-in to catch the runner scoring from third base would have been futile, but it was not like Red Gilbat to fail to try. He tossed the ball to O'Brien. And Blake scored amid applause.

"What do you know about that?" ejaculated Delaney, wiping his moist face. "I never before saw our nutty Redhead pull off a play like that."

Some of the players yelled at Red, "This is a two-handed league, you bat!"

The first five players on the list for the Grays were left-handed batters, and against a right-handed pitcher whose most effective ball for them was a high fast one over the outer corner they would naturally hit toward left field. It was no surprise to see Hanley bat a skyscraper out to left. Red had to run to get under it. He braced himself rather unusually for a fielder. He tried to catch the ball in his bare right hand and muffed it. Hanley got to second on the play while the audience roared. When they got through there was some roaring among the Rochester players. Scott and Captain Healy roared at Red, and Red roared back at them.

"It's all off. Red never did that before," cried Delaney in despair. "He's gone clean bughouse now."

Babcock was the next man up and he likewise hit to left. It was a low, twisting ball—half fly, half liner—and a difficult one to field. Gilbat ran with great bounds, and though he might have got two hands on the ball he did not try, but this time caught it in his right, retiring the side.

The Stars trotted in, Scott and Healy and Kane, all veterans, looking like thunderclouds. Red ambled in the last and he seemed very nonchalant.

"By Gosh, I'd 'a' ketched that one I muffed if I'd had time to change hands," he said with a grin, and he exposed a handful of peanuts. He had refused to drop the peanuts to make the catch with two hands. That explained the mystery. It was funny, yet nobody laughed. There was that run chalked up against the Stars, and this game had to be won.

"Red, I—I want to take the team home in the lead," said Delaney, and it was plain that he suppressed strong feeling. "You didn't play the game, you know."

Red appeared mightily ashamed.

"Del, I'll git that run back," he said.

Then he strode to the plate, swinging his wagon-tongue bat. For all his awkward position in the box he looked what he was—a formidable hitter. He seemed to tower over the pitcher—Red was six feet one—and he scowled and shook his bat at Wehying and called, "Put one over—you wienerwurst!" Wehying was anything but redheaded, and he wasted so many balls on Red that it looked as if he might pass him. He would have passed him, too, if Red had not stepped over on the fourth ball and swung on it. White at second base leaped high for the stinging hit, and failed to reach it. The ball struck and bounded for the fence. When Babcock fielded it in, Red was standing on third base, and the bleachers groaned.

Whereupon Chesty Reddy Clammer proceeded to draw attention to himself, and incidentally delay the game, by assorting the bats as if the audience and the game might gladly wait years to see him make a choice.

"Git in the game!" yelled Delaney.

"Aw, take my bat, Duke of the Abrubsky!" sarcastically said Dump Kane. When the grouchy Kane offered to lend his bat matters were critical in the Star camp.

Other retorts followed, which Reddy Clammer deigned not to notice. At last he got a bat that suited him—and then, importantly, dramatically, with his cap jauntily riding his red locks, he marched to the plate.

Some wag in the bleachers yelled into the silence, "Oh, Maggie, your lover has come!"

Not improbably Clammer was thinking first of his presence before the multitude, secondly of his batting average and thirdly of the run to be scored. In this instance he waited and feinted at balls and fouled strikes at length to work his base. When he got to first base suddenly he bolted for second, and in the surprise of the unlooked-for play he made it by a spread-eagle slide. It was a circus steal.

Delaney snorted. Then the look of profound disgust vanished in a flash of light. His huge face beamed.

Reddie Ray was striding to the plate.

There was something about Reddie Ray that pleased all the senses. His lithe form seemed instinct with life; any sudden movement was suggestive of stored lightning. His position at the plate was on the left side, and he stood perfectly motionless, with just a hint of tense waiting alertness. Dorr, Blake and Babcock, the outfielders for the Grays, trotted round to the right of their usual position. Delaney smiled derisively, as if he knew how futile it was to tell what field Reddie Ray might hit into. Wehying, the old fox, warily eyed the youngster, and threw him a high curve, close in. It grazed Reddie's shirt, but he never moved a hair. Then Wehying, after the manner of many veteran pitchers when trying out a new and menacing batter, drove a straight fast ball at Reddie's head. Reddie ducked, neither too slow nor too quick, just right to show what an eye he had, how hard it was to pitch to. The next was a strike. And on the next he appeared to step and swing in one action. There was a ringing rap, and the ball shot toward right, curving down, a vicious, headed hit. Mallory, at first base, snatched at it and found only the air. Babcock had only time to take a few sharp steps, and then he plunged down, blocked the hit and fought the twisting ball. Reddie turned first base, flitted on toward second, went headlong in the dust, and shot to the base before White got the throw-in from Babcock. Then, as White wheeled and lined the ball home to catch the scoring Clammer, Reddie Ray leaped up, got his sprinter's start and, like a rocket, was off for third. This time he dove behind the base, sliding in a half circle, and as Hanley caught Strickland's perfect throw and whirled with the ball, Reddie's hand slid to the bag.

Reddie got to his feet amid a rather breathless silence. Even the coachers were quiet. There was a moment of relaxation, then Wehying received the ball from Hanley and faced the batter.

This was Dump Kane. There was a sign of some kind, almost imperceptible, between Kane and Reddie. As Wehying half turned in his swing to pitch, Reddie Ray bounded homeward. It was not so much the boldness of his action as the amazing swiftness of it that held the audience spellbound. Like a thunderbolt Reddie came down the line, almost beating Wehying's pitch to the plate. But Kane's bat intercepted the ball, laying it down, and Reddie scored without sliding. Dorr, by sharp work, just managed to throw Kane out.

Three runs so quick it was hard to tell how they had come. Not in the major league could there have been faster work. And the ball had been fielded perfectly and thrown perfectly.

"There you are," said Delaney hoarsely. "Can you beat it? If you've been wonderin' how the crippled Stars won so many games just put what you've seen in your pipe and smoke it. Red Gilbat gets on—Reddy Clammer gets on—and then Reddie Ray drives them home or chases them home."

The game went on, and though it did not exactly drag it slowed down considerably. Morrissey and Healy were retired on infield plays. And the sides changed. For the Grays, O'Brien made a scratch hit, went to second on Strickland's sacrifice, stole third and scored on Mallory's infield out. Wehying missed three strikes. In the Stars' turn the three end players on the batting list were easily disposed of. In the third inning the clever Blake, aided by a base on balls and a hit following, tied the score, and once more struck fire and brimstone from the impatient bleachers. Providence was a town that had to have its team win.

"Git at 'em, Reds!" said Delaney gruffly.

"Batter up!" called Umpire Fuller, sharply.

"Where's Red? Where's the bug? Where's the nut? Delaney, did you lock the gates? Look under the bench!" These and other remarks, not exactly elegant, attested to the mental processes of some of the Stars. Red Gilbat did not appear to be forthcoming. There was an anxious delay. Capt. Healy searched for the missing player. Delaney did not say any more.

Suddenly a door under the grandstand opened and Red Gilbat appeared. He hurried for his bat and then up to the plate. And he never offered to hit one of the balls Wehying shot over. When Fuller had called the third strike Red hurried back to the door and disappeared.

"Somethin' doin'," whispered Delaney.

Lord Chesterfield Clammer paraded to the batter's box and, after gradually surveying the field, as if picking out the exact place he meant to drive the ball, he stepped to the plate. Then a roar from the bleachers surprised him.

"Well, I'll be doggoned!" exclaimed Delaney. "Red stole that sure as shootin'."

Red Gilbat was pushing a brand-new baby carriage toward the batter's box. There was a tittering in the grandstand; another roar from the bleachers. Clammer's face turned as red as his hair. Gilbat shoved the baby carriage upon the plate, spread wide his long arms, made a short presentation speech and an elaborate bow, then backed away.

All eyes were centered on Clammer. If he had taken it right the incident might have passed without undue hilarity. But Clammer became absolutely wild with rage. It was well known that he was unmarried. Equally well was it seen that Gilbat had executed one of his famous tricks. Ballplayers were inclined to be dignified about the presentation of gifts upon the field, and Clammer, the dude, the swell, the lady's man, the favorite of the baseball gods—in his own estimation—so far lost control of himself that he threw his bat at his retreating tormentor. Red jumped high and the bat skipped along the ground toward the bench. The players sidestepped and leaped and, of course, the bat cracked one of Delaney's big shins. His eyes popped with pain, but he could not stop laughing. One by one the players lay down and rolled over and yelled. The superior Clammer was not overliked by his co-players.

From the grandstand floated the laughter of ladies and gentlemen. And from the bleachers—that throne of the biting, ironic, scornful fans—pealed up a howl of delight. It lasted for a full minute. Then, as quiet ensued, some boy blew a blast of one of those infernal little instruments of pipe and rubber balloon, and over the field wailed out a shrill, high-keyed cry, an excellent imitation of a baby. Whereupon the whole audience roared, and in discomfiture Reddy Clammer went in search of his bat.

To make his chagrin all the worse he ingloriously struck out. And then he strode away under the lea of the grandstand wall toward right field.

Reddie Ray went to bat and, with the infield playing deep and the outfield swung still farther round to the right, he bunted a little teasing ball down the third-base line. Like a flash of light he had crossed first base before Hanley got his hands on the ball. Then Kane hit into second base, forcing Reddie out.

Again the game assumed less spectacular and more ordinary play. Both Scott and Wehying held the batters safely and allowed no runs. But in the fifth inning, with the Stars at bat and two out, Red Gilbat again electrified the field. He sprang up from somewhere and walked to the plate, his long shape enfolded in a full-length linen duster. The color and style of this garment might not have been especially striking, but upon Red it had a weird and wonderful effect. Evidently Red intended to bat while arrayed in his long coat, for he stepped into the box and faced the pitcher. Capt. Healy yelled for him to take the duster off. Likewise did the Grays yell.

The bleachers shrieked their disapproval. To say the least, Red Gilbat's crazy assurance was dampening to the ardor of the most blindly confident fans. At length Umpire Fuller waved his hand, enjoining silence and calling time.

"Take it off or I'll fine you."

From his lofty height Gilbat gazed down upon the little umpire, and it was plain what he thought.

"What do I care for money!" replied Red.

"That costs you twenty-five," said Fuller.

"Cigarette change!" yelled Red.

"Costs you fifty."

"Bah! Go to an eye doctor," roared Red.

"Seventy-five," added Fuller, imperturbably.

"Make it a hundred!"

"It's two hundred."

"Rob-b-ber!" bawled Red.

Fuller showed willingness to overlook Red's back talk as well as costume, and he called, "Play!"

There was a mounting sensation of prophetic certainty. Old fox Wehying appeared nervous. He wasted two balls on Red; then he put one over the plate, and then he wasted another. Three balls and one strike! That was a bad place for a pitcher, and with Red Gilbat up it was worse. Wehying swung longer and harder to get all his left behind the throw and let drive. Red lunged and cracked the ball. It went up and up and kept going up and farther out, and as the murmuring audience was slowly transfixed into late realization the ball soared to its height and dropped beyond the left-field fence. A home run!

Red Gilbat gathered up the tails of his duster, after the manner of a neat woman crossing a muddy street, and ambled down to first base and on to second, making prodigious jumps upon the bags, and round third, to come down the homestretch wagging his red head. Then he stood on the plate, and, as if to exact revenge from the audience for the fun they made of him, he threw back his shoulders and bellowed: *"Haw! Haw! Haw!"*

Not a handclap greeted him, but some mindless, exceedingly adventurous fan yelled: "Redhead! Redhead! Redhead!"

That was the one thing calculated to rouse Red Gilbat. He seemed to flare, to bristle, and he paced for the bleachers.

Delaney looked as if he might have a stroke. "Grab him! Soak him with a bat! Somebody grab him!"

But none of the Stars was risking so much, and Gilbat, to the howling derision of the gleeful fans, reached the bleachers. He stretched his long arms up to the fence and prepared to vault over. "Where's the guy who called me redhead?" he yelled.

That was heaping fuel on the fire. From all over the bleachers, from everywhere, came the obnoxious word. Red heaved himself over the fence and piled into the fans. Then followed the roar of many voices, the tramping of many feet, the pressing forward of line after line of shirt-sleeved men and boys. That bleacher stand suddenly assumed the maelstrom appearance of a surging mob round an agitated center. In a moment all the players rushed down the field, and confusion reigned.

"Oh! Oh! Oh!" moaned Delaney.

However, the game had to go on. Delaney, no doubt, felt all was over. Nevertheless there were games occasionally that seemed an unending series of unprecedented events. This one had begun admirably to break a record. And the Providence fans, like all other fans, had cultivated an appetite as the game proceeded. They were wild to put the other redheads out of the field or at least out for the inning, wild to tie the score, wild to win and wilder than all for more excitement. Clammer hit safely. But when Reddie Ray lined to the second baseman, Clammer, having taken a lead, was doubled up in the play.

Of course, the sixth inning opened with the Stars playing only eight men. There was another delay. Probably everybody except Delaney and perhaps Healy had forgotten the Stars were short a man. Fuller called time. The impatient bleachers barked for action.

Capt. White came over to Delaney and courteously offered to lend a player for the remaining innings. Then a pompous individual came out of the door leading from the press boxes—he was a director Delaney disliked.

"Guess you'd better let Fuller call the game," he said brusquely.

"If you want to—as the score stands now in our favor," replied Delaney.

"Not on your life! It'll be ours or else we'll play it out and beat you to death."

He departed in high dudgeon.

"Tell Reddie to swing over a little toward left," was Delaney's order to Healy. Fire gleamed in the manager's eye.

Fuller called play then, with Reddy Clammer and Reddie Ray composing the Star outfield. And the Grays evidently prepared to do great execution through the wide lanes thus opened up. At that stage it would not have been like matured ballplayers to try to crop hits down into the infield.

White sent a long fly back of Clammer. Reddy had no time to loaf on this hit. It was all he could do to reach it and he made a splendid catch, for which the crowd roundly applauded him. That applause was wine to Reddy Clammer. He began to prance on his toes and sing out to Scott, "Make 'em hit to me, old man! Make 'em hit to me!" Whether Scott desired that or not was scarcely possible to say; at any rate, Hanley pounded a hit through the infield. And Clammer, prancing high in the air like a check-reined horse, ran to intercept the ball. He could have received it in his hands, but that would never have served Reddy Clammer. He timed the hit to a nicety, went down with his old grandstand play and blocked the ball with his anatomy. Delaney swore. And the bleachers, now warm toward the gallant outfielder, lustily cheered him. Babcock hit down the right-field foul line, giving Clammer a long run. Hanely was scoring and Babcock was sprinting for third base when Reddy got the ball. He had a fine arm and he made a hard and accurate throw, catching his man in a close play.

Perhaps even Delaney could not have found any fault with that play. But the aftermath spoiled the thing. Clammer now rode the air; he soared; he was in the clouds; it was his inning and he had utterly forgotten his teammates, except inasmuch as they were performing mere little automatic movements to direct the great machinery in his direction for his sole achievement and glory.

There is fate in baseball as well as in other walks of life. O'Brien was a strapping fellow and he lifted another ball into Clammer's wide territory. The hit was of the high and far-away variety. Clammer started to run with it, not like a grim outfielder, but like one thinking of himself, his style, his opportunity, his inevitable success. Certain it was that in thinking of himself the outfielder forgot his surroundings. He ran across the foul line, head up, hair flying, unheeding the warning cry from Healy. And, reaching up to make his crowning circus play, he smashed face forward into the bleachers' fence. Then, limp as a rag, he dropped. The audience sent forth a long groan of sympathy.

"That wasn't one of his stage falls," said Delaney. "I'll bet he's dead. . . . Poor Reddy! And I want him to bust his face!"

Clammer was carried off the field into the dressing room and a physician was summoned out of the audience.

"Cap, what'd it—do to him?" asked Delaney.

"Aw, spoiled his pretty mug, that's all," replied Healy, scornfully. "Mebee he'll listen to me now."

Delaney's change was characteristic of the man. "Well, if it didn't kill him, I'm blamed glad he got it. . . . Cap, we can trim 'em yet. Reddie Ray'll play the whole outfield. Give Reddie a chance to run! Tell the boy to cut loose. And all of you git in the game. Win or lose,

I won't forget it. I've got a hunch. Once in a while I can tell what's comin' off. Some queer game this! And we're goin' to win. Gilbat lost the game; Clammer throwed it away again, and now Reddie Ray's due to win it. . . . I'm all in, but I wouldn't miss the finish to save my life."

Delaney's deep presaging sense of baseball events was never put to a greater test. And the seven Stars, with the score tied, exhibited the temper and timber of a championship team in the last ditch. It was so splendid that almost instantly it caught the antagonistic bleachers.

Wherever the tired Scott found renewed strength and speed was a mystery. But he struck out the hard-hitting Providence catcher and that made the third out. The Stars could not score in their half of the inning. Likewise the seventh inning passed without a run for either side; only the infield work of the Stars was something superb. When the eighth inning ended, without a tally for either team, the excitement grew tense. There was Reddie Ray playing outfield alone, and the Grays with all their desperate endeavors had not lifted the ball out of the infield.

But in the ninth, Blake, the first man up, lined low toward right center. The hit was safe and looked good for three bases. No one looking, however, had calculated on Reddie Ray's fleetness. He covered ground and dove for the bounding ball and knocked it down. Blake did not get beyond first base. The crowd cheered the play equally with the prospect of a run. Dorr bunted and beat the throw. White hit one of the high fast balls Scott was serving and sent it close to the left-field foul line. The running Reddie Ray made on that play held White at second base. But two runs had scored with no one out.

Hanley, the fourth left-handed hitter, came up and Scott pitched to him as he had to the others—high fast balls over the inside corner of the plate. Reddie Ray's position was some fifty yards behind deep short, and a little toward center field. He stood sideways, facing two-thirds of that vacant outfield. In spite of Scott's skill, Hanley swung the ball far round into right field, but he hit it high, and almost before he actually hit it the great sprinter was speeding across the green.

The suspense grew almost unbearable as the ball soared in its parabolic flight and the red-haired runner streaked dark across the green. The ball seemed never to be coming down. And when it began to descend and reached a point perhaps fifty feet above the ground there appeared more distance between where it would alight and where Reddie was than anything human could cover. It dropped and dropped, and then dropped into Reddie Ray's outstretched hands. He had made the catch look easy. But the fact that White scored from second base on the play showed what the catch really was.

There was no movement or restlessness of the audience such as usually indicated the beginning of the exodus. Scott struck Babcock out. The game still had fire. The Grays never let up a moment on their coaching. And the hoarse voices of the Stars were grimmer than ever. Reddie Ray was the only one of the seven who kept silent. And he crouched like a tiger.

The teams changed sides with the Grays three runs in the lead. Morrissey, for the Stars, opened with a clean drive to right. Then Healy slashed a ground ball to Hanley and nearly knocked him down. When old Burns, by a hard rap to short, advanced the runners a base and made a desperate, though unsuccessful, effort to reach first the Providence crowd awoke to a strange and inspiring appreciation. They began that most rare feature in baseball audiences—a strong and trenchant call for the visiting team to win.

The play had gone fast and furious. Wehying, sweaty and disheveled, worked violently. All the Grays were on uneasy tiptoes. And the Stars were seven Indians on the warpath. Halloran fouled down the right-field line; then he fouled over the left-field fence. Wehying tried to make him too anxious, but it was in vain. Halloran was implacable. With two strikes and three balls he hit straight down to White, and was out. The ball had been so sharp that neither runner on base had a chance to advance.

Two men out, two on base, Stars wanting three runs to tie, Scott, a weak batter, at the plate! The situation was disheartening. Yet there sat Delaney, shot through and through with some vital compelling force. He saw only victory. And when the very first ball pitched to Scott hit him on the leg, giving him his base, Delaney got to his feet, unsteady and hoarse.

Bases full, Reddie Ray up, three runs to tie.

Delaney looked at Reddie. And Reddie looked at Delaney. The manager's face was pale, intent, with a little smile. The player had eyes of fire, a lean, bulging jaw and the hands he reached for his bat clutched like talons.

"Reddie, I knew it was waitin' for you," said Delaney, his voice ringing. "Break up the game!"

After all this was only a baseball game, and perhaps from the fans' viewpoint a poor game at that. But the moment when that lithe, red-haired athlete toed the plate was a beautiful one. The long crash from the bleachers, the steady cheer from the grandstand, proved that it was not so much the game that mattered.

Wehying had shot his bolt; he was tired. Yet he made ready for a final effort. It seemed that passing Reddie Ray on balls would have been a wise play at that juncture. But no pitcher, probably, would have done it with the bases crowded and chances, of course, against the batter.

Clean and swift, Reddie leaped at the first pitched ball. Ping! For a second no one saw the hit. Then it gleamed, a terrific drive, low along the ground, like a bounding bullet, straight at Babcock in right field. It struck his hands and glanced viciously away to roll toward the fence.

Thunder broke loose from the stands. Reddie Ray was turning first base. Beyond first base he got into his wonderful stride. Some runners run with a consistent speed, the best they can make for a given distance. But this trained sprinter gathered speed as he ran. He was no short-stepping runner. His strides were long. They gave an impression of strength combined with fleetness. He had the speed of a race horse, but the trimness, the raciness, the delicate legs were not characteristic of him. Like the wind he turned second, so powerful that his turn was short. All at once there came a difference in his running. It was no longer beautiful. The grace was gone. It was now fierce, violent. His momentum was running him off his legs. He whirled around third base and came hurtling down the home stretch. His face was convulsed, his eyes were wild. His arms and legs worked in a marvelous muscular velocity. He seemed a demon—a flying streak. He overtook and ran down the laboring Scott, who had almost reached the plate.

The park seemed full of shrill, piercing strife. It swelled, reached a highest pitch, sustained that for a long moment, and then declined.

"My Gawd!" exclaimed Delaney, as he fell back. "Wasn't that a finish? Didn't I tell you to watch them redheads?"

POETRY

Couplet

DONALD HALL

Old-Timers' Day,
Fenway Park, 1 May 1982

When the tall puffy
figure wearing number
nine starts
late for the fly ball,
laboring forward
like a lame truckhorse
startled by a gartersnake,
—this old fellow
whose body we remember
as sleek and nervous
as a filly's—

and barely catches it
in his glove's
tip, we rise
and applaud weeping:
On a green field
we observe the ruin
of even the bravest
body, as Odysseus
wept to glimpse
among shades the shadow
of Achilles.

EXCLUSIVE

How to Pitch to Ted Williams

PAT HARMON

BIRDIE TEBBETTS tells it. "When I was catching with Detroit," recalls the Cincinnati manager, "we were never able to get Ted Williams out. Finally we hit on the idea of letting him call the pitch. Figured he hit whatever we called, so why not let him get in the act?

"His first time up, I explained our new plan to him. He thought it was a gag, but he said, 'Fast ball.'

"So I called for a fast ball, right over the plate. Ted let it go by. He wasn't sure we meant it.

"I asked him what he wanted for the next pitch, and he said 'Fast ball' again.

"So I called for the same thing. This time Ted swung. But he wasn't sure we weren't fooling him this time, so he hesitated, and he swung too late.

"That went on all day. Williams didn't get a hit in five times up. And the reason was he wasn't concentrating on the ball like he usually does. He was concentrating on what we told him, and whether we were kidding him, or were on the level."

GENERAL

Hint from Heloise

HELOISE

Dear Heloise:

I have a lot of baseball caps with different company insignias on them. They seem to get dirty and then I have to throw them away.

Do you have any suggestions on cleaning them? I wear them all the time so I hate to throw them out.

—J. C. Major

Most baseball type caps can be washed in the washing machine with other clothes. You should wash them in cold water on the gentle cycle and hang them outside to dry. If the bill needs stiffening, you can use spray starch and then let it dry.

Another method you can try is washing them in the sink in a mild detergent. Use a soft brush to scrub the cap but don't scrub too hard as it could remove the lettering. Then rinse the cap well and let it dry by placing it on an upside-down two-quart saucepan. Shape the bill and the top of the cap and leave it to dry.

Put the pan and cap on a surface so that when it is drying the water won't harm anything. It usually takes overnight for it to dry.

—Heloise

PROFILE

THIS IS a chapter from Roger Kahn's book *The Boys of Summer,* which was published in 1971 and instantly became a linchpin in where-are-they-now literature. The Boys were, of course, the Brooklyn Dodgers of twenty years earlier. Here is one of them.

The Bishop's Brother

ROGER KAHN

Pozehnaj nas pane a tento pokrym ktory budeme pozivat, aby sme sa zachovali v tvojej svatez sluzbe. Amen.

Bless us, Lord, and this food we are about to take that we may keep ourselves in Your holy service.

SLOVAKIAN MEALTIME PRAYER

GEORGE THOMAS Shuba, the second ball player who ever pinch-hit a World Series home run, had been wholly different from Clem Labine. He was a blunt, stolid athlete, a physical man mixing warmth with suspicion, a bachelor living alone and apart from most of the other players. His abiding love was hitting. All the rest was work. But touching a bat, blunt George became "The Shotgun," spraying line drives with a swing so compact and so fluid that it appeared as natural as a smile.

"Not yet," he said early in 1952, when I suggested a Sunday feature on his batting.

"Why not?"

"I haven't got enough hits."

A month later he approached and said, "Now."

"Now what?"

"I've gotten enough hits. Write the feature." It sounded like an order, but after the story appeared George said thank you for several days.

Joining such disparate people as Labine and Shuba was baseball's persistent encouragement toward self-involvement. "What did *you* throw?" reporters asked. Or, "What did *you* hit?" "How is *your* arm, *your* knee?" And, "*You* pitched a nice game" or "*You* really stroked that double." Even the converse from fans—"*You're* a bum, Clem; hey, George, *you're* bush"—focused a man's thinking on himself. During the prime of Clement Walter Labine and the boyhood of Clement Walter Labine, Jr., baseball was always pulling the father away on road trips and involving the father with his own right arm rather than with his son's cares. It is the nature of the baseball business, and Shuba, through an episodic eight-year career in the major leagues, had decided privately, with no hints at all, to wait for the end of his baseball life before marrying. Now he had written:

> It will be a great pleasure to have you visit our home in Youngstown. The wife and children (3) are waiting to meet you. I'll make a reservation for you at Williams Motel. Leave the Ohio Turnpike at Exit Seven. I put the Postal Inspectors there. As you know, I work for the Post Office.
>
> Went to the last two games of the 1967 World Series at Boston. Saw the 1969 All-Star game at Washington. Drive carefully. See you soon.

On a long day's journey from Manhattan to Youngstown, one follows the appalling new American way west. You escape New York through a reeking tunnel that leads to the New Jersey Turnpike, where refineries pipe stench and smoke into the yellow air above grassless flats. It is three hours to the hills along the Pennsylvania Pike and your first sense or hope that mankind will not choke to death in another fifteen years.

The country levels as Pennsylvania meets Ohio, and the first Midwestern flatlands open toward prairies. Youngstown, 170,000 people strong, produces pig iron, steel, lamps and rubber, in a dozen factories along the Mahoning River, which bisects it. The Williams Motel, on the southern outskirts, turned out to be a brick rectangle, open on one side and comfortable but not lavish. Unlike the nearby Voyager Inn, it offers neither sauna baths nor pool. "We have your reservation," a lady said behind the front desk, a strong-featured woman who wore glasses with colorless plastic rims. "Mr. Shuba made it for you. Are you with the Post Office?"

"No."

"I thought maybe you were with the Post Office. Mr. Shuba puts the postal inspectors here."

"I'm not a postal inspector."

"Twenty-six," she said, losing interest and handing me a key.

I telephoned the main Youngstown post office and George came on, the voice plain, pleasant and tinged with a heaviness from East Europe. I knew then that George's father had been an immigrant. One never thought much about such things when traveling with the team. Black and white, not Slovak or Italian, was the issue.

"Is your room all right?" Shuba said.

"Fine. What are you doing?"

"Just finishing up."

"I mean what do you do at the post office?"

"Clerk-typist," Shuba said. "I knew the room would be good. I put all the inspectors in the Williams Motel. I'll be by soon as I finish. We've got a dinner you'll like."

"I haven't eaten much Slovakian food."

"It's lasagna," George said, sounding very serious. "Didn't you know? I married an Italian girl."

Unpacking, I remembered George on the day he had joined a radio engineer and myself batting a softball in Forest Park, St. Louis, and how, taking turns pitching, we worried about upsetting George's timing. "Just throw," he said, "just throw." He pulled low liners one after another in the park and that night did the same against a Cardinal pitcher called Cloyd Boyer. And then a year later a certain quickness went from his bat, and he was not a fierce hitter, although still dangerous, and outside the Schenley Hotel I saw him carrying a light-weight portable typewriter.

"What's that for, George?"

"Oh," he said, and looked around, as though afraid to be overheard. He winked. He had a plan. "I'm not gonna be through at thirty-five, like some. Maybe I'll be a reporter. Some of those guys go on working till seventy. Look at Roscoe McGowen. So I'm teaching myself how to type."

"George," I wanted to say, "to write, you have to read and know the language and how to organize and, dammit, spell." Thinking that, I said, "Could be a pretty good idea."

At the door leading into Room 26 at the Williams Motel, Shotgun Shuba, now a 46-year-old male clerk-typist in the U. S. Post Office in Youngstown, Ohio, appeared heavier. The face, a study in angles, sloping brow, pointed nose, sharp chin, looked full. The middle was thick. But the sense was of solidity, rather than fat. I hadn't remembered him as so powerful. "You could still go nine," I said.

"Ah."

"Or pinch-hit."

"I got no time for that stuff. Come on. Dinner's waiting. We'll have some red wine. You like red wine? I'll drive."

In the car Shuba mentioned an old book I had written and a recent article. "About student rebels with long hair," he said, "or something like that."

"About the SDS coming apart in Chicago."

"Yeah. That was it. Why do you waste time writing about *them?*" There was no harshness in his voice. He simply did not understand why anyone who was a writer, a craft he respected, would spend time, thought and typing on the New Left.

"I try to write about a lot of things. It keeps you fresh."

George considered and turned into a street called Bent Willow Lane. "Kind of like exercising your mind, isn't it?" he said finally. "Yeah. That must be it. Move around. Do different things. Sure. Keeps up your enthusiasm." We had entered a middle-income neighborhood, of tract homes and roads that twisted, so drivers could not speed, and hyperfertilized lawns of brilliant, competitive green.

"I thought Youngstown had mills, George," I said.

"Over there," he said, indicating the northeast. "You won't see any mills around where *I* live." He pulled up to a gray split-level, saying "This is it," and parked in an attached garage. "I finished this garage myself. I'm a home guy now. Wait till you meet my wife. She's taking courses at Youngstown University."

As we walked into her kitchen, Katherine Shuba, nine years younger than George, said a warm hello and called Marlene, Mary Kay and Michael, nine to four, who greeted me solemnly over giggles. Mrs. Shuba turned off a large color television that dominated the living room and placed the children at a kitchen table. We sat promptly in the dinette. It was six o'clock. Old ball players pursue the pleasures of eating with lupine directness. Suddenly George bowed his head. Katherine clasped her hands. The children fell silent.

"Bless us, Lord," George said, beginning Grace. Then, in almost apologetic explanation he said, "My father said Grace in Slovakian every day of his life. He died when I was pretty young, but I've never forgotten it."

"Well, it's something to remember."

"Ah," George said and we proceeded with an excellent Italian dinner, lasagna and salad, lightened, as George had promised, with red wine.

"So you don't play any more or coach?"

"I watch the kids. Maybe umpire a little. I don't coach small kids. It doesn't make sense to. With small kids, up till about fifteen, let 'em have fun. You know what's damn dumb? A father getting on a small kid, telling him this or that, stuff he can't use much yet. All the father does is spoil the fun."

"Somebody must have coached you."

"It was a different time, and nobody coached me that much anyway. My father, from the old country, what could he teach me about baseball? What did he know?"

"Your swing was natural."

"I worked very hard at it," Shuba said.

Katherine guided the children back to the living room, which was carpeted and comfortably furnished, but showed no sign that Shuba had hit for pennant winners or even that he had played professionally. "Oh, I've got some equipment still," he said. "Maybe after we finish the wine, if you like, we can have a catch."

He fished a half dozen gloves from the trunk of a car and we walked to the back of the house. Shuba's home shares three acres of greensward with other houses, framing a common play area. "If my little guy wants," Shuba said, "he can do some hitting here."

The dusk light held as we started to throw. Shuba did not have an outstanding major league arm. Scouts described it as uncertain, or weak. Now he cocked that arm and fired easily. The ball shot at my Adam's apple and I knew, with a clutch of anxiety, that I was overmatched.

In *Gamesmanship,* Stephen Potter describes that clutch seizing you on a tennis court when an opponent's service turns out to be overwhelming and you return it forty feet beyond the base line. "Cry, 'Where was it?' " Potter recommends.

" 'Where was what?'

" 'My shot, of course.'

" 'Why, it was out. It went over the fence back there.'

" 'Very well. In the future please indicate clearly whether my shots are in or out.' "

The Shubas of Youngstown live removed from English drollery and there was nothing clever or sensible to call at George. Weak or strong, he had a major league arm, and I knew what I would have to do, and hoped I could. Aim at face height and, while appearing to work easily, throw hard by snapping the forearm as I released the ball. That way there could be a rhythm to the catch, a kind of exchange. A good catch is made of sight, sensation, sound, all balancing from one side to the other. The ball is in white flight. Red stitches turning, it whacks a glove; it is back in flight and whacks the other mitt. You can tell quickly from the sound and the speed of the throws and even from the spin what is going on, who has the better arm.

George took my throw and returned it, again hard. My glove felt small. You try to catch a ball in the pocket, so that it strikes the leather at a point slightly lower than the webbing between the thumb and forefinger of the hand within the glove. There is control there without pain. Catch a baseball farther down and it stings. Catch it farther up and you lose control. When you catch a ball in the webbing, you may not realize that you have made a catch. Each point of impact creates a different sound: thin at the webbing, dull toward the heel, resonant and profoundly right in the pocket. Sound tells when you are playing catch, how the other man is grabbing them.

Shuba delivers a heavy ball; it smarts unless caught exactly right. Mostly he throws waist high, moving the ball from one side to the other. I caught mindlessly, ignoring slight stinging to concentrate on my throws. They sailed true, but after ten minutes a twinge raked the inside of my right elbow. We caught in silence, communicating, as it were, with ball and glove. George was studying me and I could feel his eyes and it was a warm evening and I was wondering about my arm and beginning to sweat.

"You've got good body control," Shuba called.

"Hey. You've made my day."

Ebullient, I relaxed. As soon as the next throw left my hand, I knew it was bad. The ball sailed low, but fairly hard to Shuba's backhand. Nimbly, angrily, he charged, scooped the ball on a short hop and fired at my face. The throw thwacked the small glove, low in the pocket, burning my hand.

"What are you trying to do," Shuba said, "make me look bad?"

"No, George," then very slowly: "That's the way I *throw*."

"You're trying to make me look bad," Shuba said, pressing his lips and shaking his head.

"George, George. Believe me." All the years the other writers had made jokes— "Shuba fields with his bat"—had left scars. *They* should have played catch with him, I thought.

Half an hour of light remained. "Come on, George," I said. "Show me the old neighborhood."

"What for?"

"I want to see where you started playing ball."

"I don't know why you'd care about something like that," Shuba said, but led me back to the car.

Fernwood Street was where he lived when Bent Willow Road was part of a forgotten farmer's pasture. Wooden frame houses rise close to one another on Fernwood. Each one is painted white. "This neighborhood hasn't changed in forty years," Shuba said.

"Mostly Slovakians?"

"All Slovakians."

His father, John, or Jan, Shuba, left a farm in eastern Czechoslovakia during 1912 and settled in Youngstown, where other Slovak Catholics had come, and took a job in a mill. George does not know why his father left Europe, but the reason was probably economic. Before 1930 Slovakian emigration was coincident with crop failure. Since then it has been political, to escape Hitler or Soviet Communism. Slovakians have contending symbols. The *drotar* is an itinerant tinker, never anxious to settle down, unable to make use of the resources of the soil. A cry rang through old Slovakia: "*Drotar* is here; have you something to repair?" Slovakians say that *drotari* were the first to emigrate to America. After the long journey, nomadic longings spent, *drotari* settled into jobs in mines and mills. The old itinerants then built fixed, unchanging neighborhoods. The other symbol is based on the historic figure Janosik, who fled a Slovakian seminary in the seventeenth century. Slovakia still was feudal and any lord had power of life and death, but Janosik became a bandit, along the lines of Robin Hood. Caught at length, he was hanged. Disciples of Janosik were called *zbojnici*. When *zbojnici* and their idolators found the relative freedom of the United States, they turned against the romance of roguery and, like Shotgun Shuba, stood strong for law, obedience and the Church.

"We like to keep things the way they were," Shuba said. He parked on Fernwood, in a dead-end block. All the houses rose two stories. "Here's where I first played," he said. "In this street. Day after day. Three on a side, when I was little. That's good baseball, three on a side. Each kid gets a chance." Tall maples made borders at the sidewalks. "We played so hard, when we were kids, you'd have thought we were playing for money.

"It was a big family. My brother John is a steel worker in a mill. Ed is a photographer for the Youngstown *Vindicator*. You know about my brother Joe. He's doing very good in the Church as a monsignor, in Toronto, Canada. I'm proud of him. Counting the ones born in Czechoslovakia there were eleven of us. I was the last. Some died over there. I had one brother died here. He got the flu. They didn't have fancy medicines. My mother gave him a lot of soup. Soup was good for the flu, but that brother died."

We were walking down Fernwood toward ball fields. "This is Borts Park," Shuba said. "Mrs. Borts gave it to the city. When I got older, instead of playing in the street, I played in Borts Park. I was a second baseman."

"Your father must have been proud of you."

We continued under the tall maples. "You don't understand the way it was. My father was forty-five years old when I was born. He never saw me play. Old country people. What did they care for baseball? He thought I should go and work in the mills like him and I didn't want to. I wanted to play."

The nearest diamond at Borts Field was bare; patches of grass had been worn off. "Boy, did I play here," Shuba said. "I had that quick bat. One year there was a Dodger tryout. It was 1943. I was seventeen, not in the mills. I was working in a grocery store. And at the cemetery on Sundays I'd pack black earth to fill around the graves.

They could plant flowers in it. I'd get ten cents a box for the black dirt.

"The Dodgers didn't come to sign me. They wanted a pitcher. Alex Maceyko. They had me playing third. I had the quick bat, but Wid Matthews, who Rickey liked, was the scout and he signed somebody, Alex I guess, who never did much, and I went home, and forgot about it. Then it was February. I remember all the snow. Somebody come to the house on Fernwood and said, 'George, my name is Harold Roettger. I'm with the Brooklyn Dodgers. I want to see you about a contract.'

"I let him in and we sat down and he said he was going to offer me a bonus of $150 to sign. But I'd only collect if I was good enough to stay in baseball through July 1. I thought, hell, wouldn't it be better, a big outfit like the Dodgers to give $150, no strings or nothing? But that was the offer and I took it."

Night had come. Borts Field was quiet. "Well, George," I said, "your mother must have been proud."

"Ah," Shuba said. "You know what she told me. 'Get a job in the mills like Papa. There's lots of better ball players than you up there.' "

The night was warm and very still. "All right. I'll drive you to another part of the neighborhood," George said. It was so dark that all I could see were house lights and a bar with argon and neon signs advertising beer. George angled the car toward a corner grocery. "Dolak's," he said. "Where I worked. I loaded potatoes, fifty pounds to the bag, down in the basement, and carried them up. Years in the minors, they didn't pay me much. I was a ball player, but I still had to come back winters and load bags of potatoes for Dolak."

The signs in the store window were hand-lettered. "SPECIAL," one read, "HALUSKI."

"Like ravioli," Shuba said. "I delivered for Dolak, too, while I was in the bush leagues. Three miles from here is the cemetery where I packed the black dirt. I worked here and I walked to the other work and in the cold it was a long way. A long way a long time ago."

When we returned to the split-level on Bent Willow, Katherine was studying a text on the psychology of preschool children. She is a full-faced woman and she looked up with tired eyes, but cheerful to see people, and closed the book.

"We're going downstairs to talk," George said.

"Can I bring you anything?"

"Bring the V. O."

George loped downstairs. The large cellar was partly finished. A table and two chairs stood in one corner. Files had been pressed against a wall nearby. Farther along the same wall old uniforms hung from a clothing rack. Across the room was a toilet, which George had not yet gotten around to enclosing. The floor was linoleum, patterned in green and white squares.

I walked to the rack; all the uniforms were Dodger blue and white. Across one shirt letters read "BEARS," for the Mobile farm team; across another "ROYALS," for Montreal. The old Brooklyn uniform bore a large blue Number 8 on the back.

"Let me show you some things." Shuba opened a file and took out scrapbooks. He turned the pages slowly without emotion.

"They started me at New Orleans, but I wasn't ready for that, and I came back to Olean and led the league in home runs that first year."

"So you kept the $150."

"Yeah, but they shoulda risked it."

Katherine came with the drinks. "Then to Mobile," George said, "and they moved me to the outfield. They were thinking of me for the major leagues and I didn't have, you know, that major league infielder's glove. But I knew about my bat and one day in Montreal a year or two later, the manager says to me in batting practice, where everyone was supposed to take four swings, 'Hey, Shuba, how come you're taking five?' I told him, 'Look, let somebody else shag flies. I'm a hitter.' "

I laughed, but George was serious. Nothing about hitting amused him. I told him Arthur Daley's story of a catcher chattering at Charlie Gehringer at bat. Finally Gehringer turned and said, "Shut up. I'm working."

"I'm in Mobile," Shuba said. "It's '47. I hit twenty-one homers. Knock in 110 runs. Next spring at Vero Rickey says, 'George, we're sending you back to Mobile. Fine power but not enough average. We can't promote you till you're a .300 hitter.' I shorten up. It's '48. I bat .389. The spring after that he sends me to Mobile *again*. 'Nice batting,' Rickey says, 'but your power fell off. We need someone who can hit them over that short right-field wall in Ebbets Field.'

"What could I say? As long as he could option me, you know, send me down but keep me Dodger property, Rickey would do that so's he could keep some other guy whose option ran out. Property, that's what we were. But how many guys you know ever hit .389 and never got promoted?"

"There's no justice in the baseball business, George," I said.

The high-cheeked, Slavonic face turned hard. "The Saints want justice," he said. "The rest of us want mercy."

"I thought you had some fun," I said.

"It wasn't fun. I was struggling so much I couldn't enjoy it. Snider, Pafko, Furillo, they weren't humpties. I was fighting to stay alive. To play with guys that good was humbling. And I was kidded a lot about my fielding. In 1953 I went out to left field in Yankee Stadium for the second game of the Series. There're bad shadows out there in the fall. You remember I took you out and walked you around to show you the shadows and the haze from cigarette smoke.

"I went out and in the first inning someone hit a line drive and I didn't see it good and kind of grabbed. The ball rolled up my arms, but I held on to it. With two out, somebody else hit a long one into left center and maybe I started a little late, but I just got a glove on it and held it. When I came back to the dugout, Bobby Morgan said, very loud, 'Hey, I think they're going for our weak spot.' "

I laughed again. "Hey," Shuba said. "That's not funny. What he should have said was 'Nice catch.'

"Now something *funny,* that came from an usher. I wasn't going good, and by this time all the bosses, O'Malley, Bavasi and Thompson, are Catholics, and my brother gets promoted to monsignor and word gets around. It's real early and I'm not hitting at all. Some usher hollers down, 'Hey, George. It's a good thing your brother's a bishop.' "

George smiled and sipped.

"When did it really end?" I said.

"All the time Rickey's keeping me in the minors doesn't do me any good and one year in Montreal I rip up my knee ligaments. That's where it started to end. When I made the club to stay in '52 that knee was gone already. It just kept getting worse and worse. Around 1955, I was only thirty-one, but the knee was so bad I couldn't do much. So I quit. That's all there was.

"I tried the sporting goods business. Up and down. So I went to work for the Post Office, steady and safe."

"Does all the excitement and the rest seem real to you now?"

"Oh, yeah. It's real." George was drumming his fingers on the wooden table.

"What do you think of it?"

"Doesn't mean much. When somebody would come up and ask for an autograph, I'd say, 'Is this for a kid?' And if it was, I'd give it to him. But if he said no, if it was for a man, I'd say, 'Ah. Don't be foolish. What does a grown man want something like that for?' I had my laughs. One day against the Cubs, Hank Sauer was on first and Ralph Kiner was on third and neither one could run. I hollered, 'Look for the double steal.' But what does it mean? Ruth died. Gehrig died."

The glasses were empty. He called and Katherine came downstairs and looked hopefully at George, wanting to be invited into the conversation, but Shuba has a European sense of a woman's place. "Why don't you come upstairs and sit with me?" she said.

"Because we're talking," Shuba said. "Men's talk.

"There was this time," he said after fresh drinks had come, "in the World Series when I pinch-hit the home run."

"Sure—1953. Off Allie Reynolds."

"That's not what I'm talking about," Shuba said. "It was the first game of that Series and Reynolds was fast and the fellers were having trouble seeing the ball and he's got a shutout. I come up in the fifth and he throws that first pitch. I never saw it. It was a strike. If it had been inside, it would have killed me. Reynolds was in sun and I was in shadow. I never saw the ball. The next pitch he curved me. I only saw a little better. I was swinging, but I went down on one knee." Shuba was a formful batter, always in control; slipping to a knee was as humiliating as falling flat. "Now the next pitch. I still wasn't seeing the ball good, but I took my swing. My good swing. I hit it and it went to right field and I knew it would be long but maybe the right fielder could jump and as I trotted to first base I was saying, 'Hail Mary, get it up higher. Hail Mary.'

"Only the second time in history anybody pinch-hit a home run in the World Series," Shuba said, his face aglow. "But it wasn't me. There was something else guiding the bat. I couldn't see the ball, and you can think what you want, but another hand was guiding my bat."

"I don't know, George. Birdie Tebbetts was catching once when a batter crossed himself. Birdie called time, and crossed *himself*. And he told the hitter, 'Now it's all even with God. Let's see who's the better man.' "

"I don't care what Tebbetts did. Another hand was guiding my bat."

"Do you remember Ebbets Field, George? Now, if you close your eyes, can you see it?"

"Ah. That don't mean nothing."

"What means something?"

"The Church."

"I mean in this life."

He sprang up, reaching into a top drawer in the nearest file. "Marks in school," he said. "Look at Marlene's." He put one of the girl's report cards in front of me, then opened a notebook in which he had recorded her marks from term to term. "She had some trouble with arithmetic here in the second grade, but my wife talked to the Sister and worked with Marlene at home. Then Mary Kay . . ." He talked for another ten minutes about the way his children fared in school and how he, and his wife, kept notebook entries of their progress. He was still talking about the children when Katherine came downstairs again and without being asked refilled our glasses. "All that baseball was a preparation," Shuba said. "You have certain phases in your life. Baseball prepared me for this. Raising my family."

"Which is more important?"

"This is the real part of my life."

"So all the rest was nothing?"

"Not nothing. Just not important. You do something important. Write. But playing ball." He jerked his head and looked at the beams in the cellar ceiling. "What the hell is that?"

"You might not understand this, or believe me, but I would have given anything to have had your natural swing."

"You could have," George said.

"What?" I said. "What do you mean I could have?" And I saw, again, George standing in to hit as I first saw him, in 1948, when I was twenty and a copyboy and he was twenty-four and trying to become a major leaguer. It was a very clear, bright picture in my mind, and I could not see the pitcher or the crowd or even whether it was day or night. But I still saw Shuba. It was late in the year, when they bring up the good youngsters for a few games. He balanced on the balls of the feet as he waited for the pitch, holding the bat far back, and there was confidence and, more than that, a beauty to his stance. My father said, "What's this Shuba's first name? Franz?" But I was trying to understand how one could stand that beautifully against a pitcher and I did not answer and Shuba hit a long drive to right center field on a rising line. At a point 390 feet from home plate the ball struck the wire screen above the fence. It was still moving fast, thirty feet up. "Pretty good shot for Franz," I said, but now my father, impressed, had fallen serious.

In the basement, Shuba said, "What did you swing?"

"Thirty-one, thirty-two ounces. Depends on the speed and the shape I was in."

"Here's what you do," Shuba said. "Bore a hole in the top of the bat. Pour lead in it. Ten ounces. Now you got a bat forty-one or forty-two ounces. That's what you want, to practice swinging. Builds up your shoulders and your chest and upper arms."

"I couldn't swing a bat that heavy." I sipped the V. O. The cellar had become uncomfortably hot.

George was standing. "You take a ball of string and you make knots in it," he said. "You make a lot of knots and it hangs in a clump." He walked from the table and reached up toward a beam. A string coiled down and suspended, the base multiknotted into a clump. It was waist-high. "That's the ball," George said. His eyes were shining.

A large-thewed arm reached toward a beam. "I got some bats up here." He chose two signed "George 'Shotgun' Shuba." Both had been drilled and filled with lead. He set his feet, balancing as he had when my father joked about Franz Shuba, and he looked at the clumped string and I rose and drew closer, and he swung the bat. It was the old swing yet, right before me in a cellar. He was heavier, to be sure, but still the swing was beautiful, and grunting softly he whipped the bat into the clumped string. Level and swift, the bat parted the air and made a whining sound. Again Shuba swung and again, controlled and terribly hard. It was the hardest swing I ever saw that close.

Sweat burst upon his neck. "Now you," he said, and handed me the bat.

"I've been drinking."

"Come on. Let me see you swing," he said. Cords stood out in Shuba's throat.

I set my feet on green and white linoleum. My palms were wet. "Okay, but I've been drinking. I'm telling you."

"Just swing," Shuba ordered.

I knew as I began. The bat felt odd. It slipped in my hands. My swing was stiff.

"Wrist," George commanded. "Wrist."

I swung again.

"You broke your wrists here." He indicated a point two-thirds through the arc of the swing. "Break 'em here." He held his hand at the center. I swung again. "Better," he said. "Now here." I swung, snapping my wrists almost at the start of the swing. "All right," he said, moving his hand still farther. "Snap 'em here. Snap 'em first thing you do. Think fast ball. Snap those wrists. The fast ball's by you. Come on, snap. That's it. Wrists. Swing flat. You're catching on."

"It's hot as hell, George."

"You're doing all right," he said.

"But you're a natural."

"Ah," Shuba said. "You talk like a sportswriter." He went to the file and pulled out a chart, marked with Xs. "In the winters," he said, "for fifteen years after loading potatoes or anything else, even when I was in the majors, I'd swing at the clump six hundred times. Every night, and after sixty I'd make an X. Ten Xs and I had my six hundred swings. Then I could go to bed.

"You call that natural? I swung a 44-ounce bat 600 times a night, 4,200 times a week, 47,200 swings every winter. Wrists. The fast ball's by you. You gotta wrist it out. Forty-seven thousand two hundred times."

"I wish I'd known this years ago," I said. George's face looked very open. "It would have helped my own hitting."

"Aah," Shuba said, in the stuffy cellar. "Don't let yourself think like that. The fast ball is by the both of us. Leave it to the younger guys."

FICTION

What Did We Do Wrong?

GARRISON KEILLOR

THE FIRST woman to reach the big leagues said she wanted to be treated like any other rookie, but she didn't have to worry about that. The Sparrows nicknamed her Chesty and then Big Numbers the first week of spring training, and loaded her bed at the Ramada with butterscotch pudding. Only the writers made a big thing about her being the First Woman. The Sparrows treated her like dirt.

Annie Szemanski arrived in camp fresh from the Federales League of Bolivia, the fourth second baseman on the Sparrows roster, and when Drayton stepped in a hole and broke his ankle Hemmie put her in the lineup, hoping she would break hers. "This was the front office's bright idea," he told the writers. "Off the record, I think it stinks." But when she got in she looked so good that by the third week of March she was a foregone conclusion. Even Hemmie had to admit it. A .346 average tells no lies. He disliked her purely because she was a woman—there was nothing personal about it. Because she was a woman, she was given the manager's dressing room, and Hemmie had to dress with the team. He was sixty-one, a heavyweight, and he had a possum tattooed on his belly alongside the name "Georgene," so he was shy about taking his shirt off in front of people. He hated her for making it necessary. Other than that, he thought she was a tremendous addition to the team.

Asked how she felt being the first woman to make a major-league team, she said, "Like a pig in mud," or words to that effect, and then turned and released a squirt of tobacco juice from the wad of rum-soaked plug in her right cheek. She chewed a rare brand of plug called Stuff It, which she learned to chew when she was playing Nicaraguan summer ball. She told the writers, "They were so mean to me down there you couldn't write it in your newspaper. I took a gun everywhere I went, even to bed. *Especially* to bed. Guys were after me like you can't believe. That's when I started chewing tobacco—because no matter how bad anybody treats you, it's not as bad as this. This is the worst chew in the world. After this, everything else is peaches and cream." The writers elected Gentleman Jim, the Sparrows' P. R. guy, to bite off a chunk and tell them how it tasted, and as he sat and chewed it tears ran down his old sunburnt cheeks and he couldn't talk for a while. Then he whispered, "You've been chewing this for two years? God, I had no idea it was so hard to be a woman."

When thirty-two thousand fans came to Cold Spring Stadium on April 4th for Opening Day and saw the scrappy little freckle-faced woman with tousled black hair who they'd been reading about for almost two months, they were dizzy with devotion. They chanted her name and waved Annie flags and Annie caps ($8.95 and $4.95) and held up hand-painted bedsheets ("EVERY DAY IS LADIES' DAY," "A

WOMAN'S PLACE—AT SECOND BASE," "E.R.A. & R.B.I." "THE GAME AIN'T OVER TILL THE BIG LADY BATS"), but when they saw No. 18 trot out to second with a load of chew as big as if she had the mumps it was a surprise. Then, bottom of the second, when she leaned over in the on-deck circle and dropped a stream of brown juice in the sod, the stadium experienced a moment of thoughtful silence.

One man in Section 31 said, "Hey, what's the beef? She can chew if she wants to. This is 1987. Grow up."

"I guess you're right," his next-seat neighbor said. "My first reaction was nausea, but I think you're right."

"Absolutely. She's a woman, but, more than that, she's a *person*."

Other folks said, "I'm with you on that. A woman can carry a quarter pound of chew in her cheek and spit in public, same as any man—why should there be any difference?"

And yet. Nobody wanted to say this, but the plain truth was that No. 18 was not handling her chew well at all. Juice ran down her chin and dripped onto her shirt. She's bit off more than she can chew, some people thought to themselves, but they didn't want to say that.

Arnie (the Old Gardener) Brixius mentioned it ever so gently in his "Hot Box" column the next day:

It's only this scribe's opinion, but isn't it about time baseball cleaned up its act and left the tobacco in the locker? Surely big leaguers can go two hours without nicotine. Many a fan has turned away in disgust at the sight of grown men (and now a member of the fair sex) with a faceful, spitting gobs of the stuff in full view of paying customers. Would Frank Sinatra do this onstage? Or Anne Murray? Nuff said.

End of April, Annie was batting .278, with twelve R.B.I.'s, which for the miserable Sparrows was stupendous, and at second base she was surprising a number of people, including base runners who thought she'd be a pushover on the double play. A runner heading for second quickly found out that Annie had knees like ball-peen hammers and if he tried to eliminate her from the play she might eliminate him from the rest of the week. One night, up at bat against the Orioles, she took a step toward the mound after an inside pitch and yelled some things, and when the dugouts emptied she was in the thick of it with men who had never been walloped by a woman before. The home-plate ump hauled her off a guy she was pounding the cookies out of, and a moment later he threw her out of the game for saying things to him, he said, that he had never heard in his nineteen years of umpiring. ("Like what, for example?" writers asked. "Just tell us one thing." But he couldn't; he was too upset.)

The next week, the United Baseball Office Workers local passed a resolution in support of Annie, as did the League of Women Voters and the Women's Softball Caucus, which stated, "Szemanski is a model for all women who are made to suffer guilt for their aggressiveness, and we declare our solidarity with her heads-up approach to the game. While we feel she is holding the bat too high and should bring her hips into her swing more, we're behind her one hundred per cent."

Then, May 4th, at home against Oakland—seventh inning, two outs, bases loaded—she dropped an easy pop-up and three runs came across home plate. The fans sent a few light boos her way to let her know they were paying attention, nothing serious or overtly political, just some folks grumbling, but she took a few steps toward the box seats and yelled something at them that sounded like—well, like something she shouldn't have said, and after the game she said some more things to the writers that Gentleman Jim pleaded with them not to print. One of them was Monica Lamarr, of the *Press*, who just laughed. She said, "Look, I spent two years in the Lifestyles section writing about motherhood vs. career and the biological clock. Sports is my way out of the gynecology ghetto, so don't ask me to eat this story. It's a hanging curve and I'm going for it. I'm never going to write about day care again." And she wrote it:

SZEMANSKI RAPS FANS
AS "SMALL PEOPLE"
AFTER DUMB ERROR GIVES
GAME TO A'S

First Woman Attributes Boos
To Sexual Inadequacy in Stands

Jim made some phone calls and the story was yanked and only one truckload of papers went out with it, but word got around, and the next night, though Annie went three for four, the crowd was depressed, and even when she did great the rest of the home stand, and became the first woman to hit a major-league triple, the atmosphere at the ballpark was one of moodiness and deep hurt. Jim went to the men's room one night and found guys standing in line there, looking thoughtful and sad. One of them said, "She's a helluva ballplayer," and other guys murmured that yes, she was, and they wouldn't take anything away from her, she was great and it was wonderful that she had opened up baseball to women, and then they changed the subject to gardening, books, music, aesthetics, anything but baseball. They looked like men who had been stood up.

Gentleman Jim knocked on her door that night. She wore a blue chenille bathrobe flecked with brown tobacco-juice stains, and her black hair hung down in wet strands over her face. She spat into a Dixie cup she was carrying. "Hey! How the Fritos are you? I haven't seen your Big Mac for a while," she said, sort of. He told her she was a great person and a great ballplayer and that he loved her and wanted only the best for her, and he begged her to apologize to the fans.

"Make a gesture—*anything*. They *want* to like you. Give them a chance to like you."

She blew her nose into a towel. She said that she wasn't there to be liked, she was there to play ball.

It was a good road trip. The Sparrows won five out of ten, lifting their heads off the canvas, and Annie raised her average to .291 and hit the first major-league home run ever by a woman, up into the left-field screen at Fenway. Sox fans stood and cheered for fifteen minutes. They whistled, they stamped, they pleaded, the Sparrows pleaded, umpires pleaded, but she refused to come out and tip her hat until the public-address announcer said, "No. 18, please come out of the dugout and take a bow. No. 18, the applause is for you and is not intended as patronizing in any way," and then she stuck her head out for 1.5 seconds and did not tip but only touched the brim. Later, she told the writers that just because people had expectations didn't mean she had to fulfill them—she used other words to explain this, but her general drift was that she didn't care very much about living up to anyone else's image of her, and if anyone thought she should, they could go watch wrist wrestling.

The forty thousand who packed Cold Spring Stadium June 6th to see the Sparrows play the Yankees didn't come for a look at Ron Guidry banners hung from the second deck: "WHAT DID WE DO WRONG?" and "ANNIE COME HOME" and "WE LOVE YOU, WHY DO YOU TREAT US THIS WAY?" and "IF YOU WOULD LIKE TO DISCUSS THIS IN A NON-CONFRONTATIONAL, MUTUALLY RESPECTFUL WAY, MEET US

After the Game at Gate C." It was Snapshot Day, and all the Sparrows appeared on the field for photos with the fans except you know who. Hemmie begged her to go. "You owe it to them," he said.

"Owe?" she said. *"Owe?"*

"Sorry, wrong word," he said. "What if I put it this way: it's sort of tradition."

"Tradition?" she said. "I'm supposed to worry about *tradition?"*

That day, she became the first woman to hit .300. A double in the fifth inning. The scoreboard flashed the message, and the crowd gave her a nice hand. A few people stood and cheered, but the fans around them told them to sit down. "She's not that kind of person," they said. "Cool it. Back off." The fans were trying to give her plenty of space. After the game, Guidry said, "I really have to respect her. She's got that small strike zone and she protects it well, so she makes you pitch to her." She said, "Guidry? Was that his name? I didn't know. Anyway, he didn't show me much. He throws funny, don't you think? He reminded me a little bit of a southpaw I saw down in Nicaragua, except she threw inside more."

All the writers were there, kneeling around her. One of them asked if Guidry had thrown her a lot of sliders.

She gave him a long, baleful look. "Jeez, you guys are out of shape," she said. "You're wheezing and panting and sucking air, and you just took the elevator *down* from the press box. You guys want to write about sports you ought to go into training. And then you ought to learn how to recognize a slider. Jeez, if you were writing about agriculture, would you have to ask someone if those were Holsteins?"

Tears came to the writer's eyes. "I'm trying to help," he said. "Can't you see that? Don't you know how much we care about you? Sometimes I think you put up this tough exterior to hide your own insecurity."

She laughed and brushed the wet hair back from her forehead. "It's no exterior," she said as she unbuttoned her jersey. "It's who I am." She peeled off her socks and stepped out of her cubicle a moment later, sweaty and stark naked. The towel hung from her hand. She walked slowly around them. "You guys learned all you know about women thirty years ago. That wasn't me back then, that was my mother." The writers bent over their notepads, writing down every word she said and punctuating carefully. Gentleman Jim took off his glasses. "My mother was a nice lady, but she couldn't hit the curve to save her Creamettes," she went on. "And now, gentlemen, if you'll excuse me. I'm going to take a shower." They pored over their notes until she was gone, and then they piled out into the hallway and hurried back to the press elevator.

Arnie stopped at the Shortstop for a load of Martinis before he went to the office to write the "Hot Box," which turned out to be about love:

Baseball is a game but it's more than a game, baseball is people, dammit, and if you are around people you can't help but get involved in their lives and care about them and then you don't know how to talk to them or tell them how much you care and how come we know so much about pitching and we don't know squat about how to communicate? I guess that is the question.

The next afternoon, Arnie leaned against the batting cage before the game, hung over, and watched her hit line drives, fifteen straight, and each one made his head hurt. As she left the cage, he called over to her. "Later," she said. She also declined a pregame interview with Joe Garagiola, who had just told his NBC "Game of the Week" television audience, "This is a city in love with a little girl named Annie Szemanski," when he saw her in the dugout doing deep knee bends. "Annie! Annie!" he yelled over the air. "Let's see if we can't get her up here," he told the home audience. "Annie! Joe Garagiola!" She turned her back to him and went down into the dugout.

That afternoon, she became the first woman to steal two bases in one inning. She reached first on a base on balls, stole second, went to third on a sacrifice fly, and headed for home on the next pitch. The catcher came out to make the tag, she caught him with her elbow under the chin, and when the dust cleared she was grinning at the ump, the catcher was sprawled in the grass trying to inhale, and the ball was halfway to the backstop.

The TV camera zoomed in on her, head down, trotting toward the dugout steps, when suddenly she looked up. Some out-of-town fan had yelled at her from the box seats. ("A profanity which also refers to a female dog," the *News* said.) She smiled and, just before she stepped out of view beneath the dugout roof, millions observed her right hand uplifted in a familiar gesture. In bars around the country, men looked at each other and said, "Did she do what I think I saw her do? She didn't do that, did she?" In the booth, Joe Garagiola was observing that it was a clean play, that the runner has a right to the base path, but when her hand appeared on the screen he stopped. At home, it sounded as if he had been hit in the chest by a rock. The screen went blank, then went to a beer commercial. When the show resumed, it was the middle of the next inning.

On Monday, for "actions detrimental to the best interests of baseball," Annie was fined a thousand dollars by the Commissioner and suspended for two games. He deeply regretted the decision, etc. "I count myself among her most ardent fans. She is good for baseball, good for the cause of equal rights, good for America." He said he would be happy to suspend the suspension if she would make a public apology, which would make him the happiest man in America.

Gentleman Jim went to the bank Monday afternoon and got the money, a thousand dollars, in a cashier's check. All afternoon, he called Annie's number over and over, waiting thirty or forty rings, then trying again. He called from a pay phone at the Stop 'N' Shop, next door to the Cityview Apartments, where she lived, and between calls he sat in his car and watched the entrance, waiting for her to come out. Other men were parked there, too, in front, and some in back—men with Sparrows bumper stickers. After midnight, about eleven of them were left. "Care to share some onion chips and clam dip?" one guy said to another guy. Pretty soon all of them were standing around the trunk of the clam-dip guy's car, where he also had a case of beer.

"Here, let me pay you something for this beer," said a guy who had brought a giant box of pretzels.

"Hey, no. Really. It's just good to have other guys to talk to tonight," said the clam-dip owner.

"She changed a lot of very basic things about the whole way that I look at myself as a man," the pretzel guy said quietly.

"I'm in public relations," said Jim, "but even I don't understand all that she has meant to people."

"How can she do this to us?" said a potato-chip man. "All the love of the fans, how can she throw it away? Why can't she just play ball?"

Annie didn't look at it this way. "Pall Mall! I'm not going to crawl just because some Tootsie Roll says crawl, and if they don't like it, then Ritz, they can go Pepsi their Hostess Twinkies," she told the writers as she cleaned out her locker on Tuesday morning. They had never seen the inside of her locker before. It was stuffed with dirty socks, half unwrapped gifts from admiring fans, a set of ankle weights, and a small silver-plated pistol. "No way I'm going to pay a thousand dollars, and if they expect an apology—well, they better send out for lunch, because it's going to be a long wait. Gentlemen, goodbye and hang on to your valuable coupons." And she smiled her most winning smile and sprinted up the stairs to collect her paycheck. They waited for her outside the Sparrows office, twenty-six men, and then followed her down the ramp and out of Gate C. She broke into a run and disappeared into the lunchtime crowd on West Providence Avenue, and that was the last they saw of her—the woman of their dreams, the love of their lives, carrying a red gym bag, running easily away from them.

FICTION

WINNER of both the Pultizer Prize and the National Book Award, William Kennedy's marvelous novel *Ironweed* has as its central character a haunted ex-ballplayer named Francis Phelan. The author's power is such (said *The Wall Street Journal*) "that the reader will follow him almost anywhere, to the edge of tragedy and back again to redemption."

From *Ironweed*

WILLIAM KENNEDY

ANNIE WAS setting the dining-room table with a white linen tablecloth, with the silver Iron Joe gave them for their wedding, and with china Francis did not recognize, when Daniel Quinn arrived home. The boy tossed his schoolbag in a corner of the dining room, then stopped in midmotion when he saw Francis standing in the doorway to the kitchen.

"Hulooo," Francis said to him.

"Danny, this is your grandfather," Annie said. "He just came to see us and he's staying for dinner." Daniel stared at Francis's face and slowly extended his right hand. Francis shook it.

"Pleased to meet you," Daniel said.

"The feeling's mutual, boy. You're a big lad for ten."

"I'll be eleven in January."

"You comin' from school, are ye?"

"From instructions, religion."

"Oh, religion. I guess I just seen you crossin' the street and didn't even know it. Learn anything, did you?"

"Learned about today. All Saints' Day."

"What about it?"

"It's a holy day. You have to go to church. It's the day we remember the martyrs who died for the faith and nobody knows their names."

"Oh yeah," Francis said. "I remember them fellas."

"What happened to your teeth?"

"Daniel."

"My teeth," Francis said. "Me and them parted company, most of 'em. I got a few left."

"Are you Grampa Phelan or Grampa Quinn?"

"Phelan," Annie said. "His name is Francis Aloysius Phelan."

"Francis Aloysius, right," said Francis with a chuckle. "Long time since I heard that."

"You're the ball player," Danny said. "The big-leaguer. You played with the Washington Senators."

"Used to. Don't play anymore."

"Billy says you taught him how to throw an inshoot."

"He remembers that, does he?"

"Will you teach me?"

"You a pitcher, are ye?"

"Sometimes. I can throw a knuckle ball."

"Change of pace. Hard to hit. You get a baseball, I'll show you how to hold if for an inshoot." And Daniel ran into the kitchen, then the pantry, and emerged with a ball and glove, which he handed to Francis. The glove was much too small for Francis's hand but he put a few fingers inside it and held the ball in his right hand, studied its seams. Then he gripped it with his thumb and one and a half fingers.

"What happened to your finger?" Daniel asked.

"Me and it parted company too. Sort of an accident."

"Does that make any difference throwing an inshoot?"

"Sure does, but not to me. I don't throw no more at all. Never was a pitcher, you know, but talked with plenty of 'em. Walter Johnson was my buddy. You know him? The Big Train?"

The boy shook his head.

"Don't matter. But he taught me how it was done and I ain't forgot. Put your first two fingers right on the seams, like this, and then you snap your wrist out, like this, and if you're a righty—are you a righty?"—and the boy nodded—"then the ball's gonna dance a little turnaround jig and head right inside at the batter's belly button, assumin', acourse, that he's a righty too. You followin' me?" And the boy nodded again. "Now the trick is, you got to throw the opposite of the outcurve, which is like this." And he snapped his wrist clockwise. "You got to do it like this." And he snapped his wrist counterclockwise again. Then he had the boy try it both ways and patted him on the back.

"That's how it's done," he said. "You get so's you can do it, the batter's gonna think you got a little animal inside that ball, flyin' it like an airplane."

"Let's go outside and try it," Daniel said. "I'll get another glove."

"Glove," said Francis, and he turned to Annie. "By some fluke you still got my old glove stuck away somewheres in the house? That possible, Annie?"

"There's a whole trunk of your things in the attic," she said. "It might be there."

"It is," Daniel said. "I know it is. I saw it. I'll get it."

"You will not," Annie said. "That trunk is none of your affair."

"But I've already seen it. There's a pair of spikes too, and clothes and newspapers and old pictures."

"All that," Francis said to Annie. "You saved it."

"You had no business in that trunk," Annie said.

"Billy and I looked at the pictures and the clippings one day," Daniel said. "Billy looked just as much as I did. He's in lots of 'em." And he pointed at his grandfather.

"Maybe you'd want to have a look at what's there," Annie said to Francis.

"Could be. Might find me a new shoelace."

Annie led him up the stairs, Daniel already far ahead of them. They heard the boy saying: "Get up, Billy, Grandpa's here"; and when they reached the second floor Billy was standing in the doorway of his room, in his robe and white socks, disheveled and only half awake.

"Hey, Billy. How you gettin' on?" Francis said.

"Hey," said Billy. "You made it."

"Yep."

"I woulda bet against it happenin'."

"You'da lost. Brought a turkey too, like I said."

"A turkey, yeah?"

"We're having it for dinner," Annie said.

"I'm supposed to be downtown tonight," Billy said. "I just told Martin I'd meet him."

"Call him back," Annie said. "He'll understand."

"Red Tom Fitzsimmons and Martin both called to tell me things are all right again on Broadway. You know, I told you I had trouble with the McCalls," Billy said to his father.

"I 'member."

"I wouldn't do all they wanted and they marked me lousy. Couldn't gamble, couldn't even get a drink on Broadway."

"I read that story Martin wrote," Francis said. "He called you a magician."

"Martin's full of malarkey. I didn't do diddley. I just mentioned Newark to them and it turns out that's where they trapped some of the kidnap gang."

"You did somethin', then," Francis said. "Mentionin' Newark was somethin'. Who'd you mention it to?"

"Bindy. But I didn't know those guys were in Newark or I wouldn't of said anything. I could never rat on anybody."

"Then why'd you mention it?"

"I don't know."

"That's how come you're a magician."

"That's Martin's baloney. But he turned somebody's head around with it, 'cause I'm back in good odor with the pols, is how he put it on the phone. In other words, I don't stink to them no more."

Francis smelled himself and knew he had to wash as soon as possible. The junk wagon's stink and the bummy odor of his old suitcoat was unbearable now that he was among these people. Dirty butchers go out of business.

"You can't go out now, Billy," Annie said. "Not with your father home and staying for dinner. We're going up in the attic to look at his things."

"You like turkey?" Francis asked Billy.

"Who the hell don't like turkey, not to give you a short answer," Billy said. He looked at his father. "Listen, use my razor in the bathroom if you want to shave."

"Don't be telling people what to do," Annie said. "Get dressed and come downstairs."

And then Francis and Annie ascended the stairway to the attic.

When Francis opened the trunk lid the odor of lost time filled the attic air, a cloying reek of imprisoned flowers that unsettled the dust and fluttered the window shades. Francis felt drugged by the scent of the reconstituted past, and then stunned by his first look inside the trunk, for there, staring out from a photo, was his own face at age nineteen. The picture lay among rolled socks and a small American flag, a Washington Senators cap, a pile of newspaper clippings and other photos, all in a scatter on the trunk's tray. Francis stared up at himself from the bleachers in Chadwick Park on a day in 1899, his face unlined, his teeth all there, his collar open, his hair unruly in the afternoon's breeze. He lifted the picture for a closer look and saw himself among a group of men, tossing a baseball from bare right hand to gloved left hand. The flight of the ball had always made this photo mysterious to Francis, for the camera had caught the ball clutched in one hand and also in flight, arcing in a blur toward the glove. What the camera had caught was two instants in one: time separated and unified, the ball in two places at once, an eventuation as inexplicable as the Trinity itself. Francis now took the picture to be a Trinitarian talisman (a hand, a glove, a ball) for achieving the impossible: for he had always believed it impossible for him, ravaged man, failed human, to reenter history under this roof. Yet here he was in this aerie of reconstitutable time, touching untouchable artifacts of a self that did not yet know it was ruined, just as the ball, in its inanimate ignorance, did not know yet that it was going nowhere, was caught.

But the ball is really not yet caught, except by the camera, which has frozen only its situation in space.

And Francis is not yet ruined, except as an apparency in process.

The ball still flies.

Francis still lives to play another day.

Doesn't he?

The boy noticed the teeth. A man can get new teeth, store teeth. Annie got 'em.

Francis lifted the tray out of the trunk, revealing the spikes and the glove, which Daniel immediately grabbed, plus two suits of clothes, a pair of black oxfords and brown high-button shoes, maybe a dozen shirts and two dozen white collars, a stack of undershirts and shorts, a set of keys to long-forgotten locks, a razor strop and a hone, a shaving mug with an inch of soap in it, a shaving brush with bristles intact, seven straight razors in a case, each marked for a day of the week, socks, bow ties, suspenders, and a baseball, which Francis picked up and held out to Daniel.

"See that? See that name?"

The boy looked, shook his head. "I can't read it."

"Get it in the light, you'll read it. That's Ty Cobb. He signed that ball in 1911, the year he hit .420. A fella give it to me once and I always kept it. Mean guy, Cobb was, come in at me spikes up many a time. But you had to hand it to a man who played ball as good as he did. He was the best."

"Better than Babe Ruth?"

"Better and tougher and meaner and faster. Couldn't hit home runs like the Babe, but he did everything else better. You like to have that ball with his name on it?"

"Sure I would, sure! Yeah! Who wouldn't?"

"Then it's yours. But you better look him up, and Walter Johnson too. Find out for yourself how good they were. Still kickin', too, what I hear about Cobb. He ain't dead yet either."

"I remember that suit," Annie said, lifting the sleeve of a gray herringbone coat. "You wore it for dress-up."

"Wonder if it'd still fit me," Francis said, and stood up and held the pants to his waist and found out his legs had not grown any longer in the past twenty-two years.

"Take the suit downstairs," Annie said. "I'll sponge and press it."

"Press it?" Francis said, and he chuckled. "S'pose I could use a new outfit. Get rid of these rags."

He then singled out a full wardrobe, down to the handkerchief, and piled it all on the floor in front of the trunk.

"I'd like to look at these again," Annie said, lifting out the clippings and photos.

"Bring 'em down," Francis said, closing the lid.

"I'll carry the glove," Daniel said.

"And I'd like to borry the use of your bathroom," Francis said. "Take Billy up on that shave offer and try on some of these duds. I got me a shave last night but Billy thinks I oughta do it again."

"Don't pay any attention to Billy," Annie said. "You look fine."

She led him down the stairs and along a hallway where two rooms faced each other. She gestured at a bedroom where a single bed, a dresser, and a child's rolltop desk stood in quiet harmony.

"That's Danny's room," she said. "It's a nice big room and it gets the morning light." She took a towel down from a linen closet shelf and handed it to Francis. "Have a bath if you like."

Francis locked the bathroom door and tried on the trousers, which fit if he didn't button the top button. Wear the suspenders with 'em. The coat was twenty years out of style and offended Francis's residual sense of aptness. But he decided to wear it anyway, for its odor of time was infinitely superior to the stink of bumdom that infested the coat on his back. He stripped and let the bathwater run. He inspected the shirt he took from the trunk, but rejected it in favor of the white-on-white from the junk wagon. He tried the laceless black oxfords, all broken in, and found that even with calluses his feet had not grown in twenty-two years either.

He stepped into the bath and slid slowly beneath its vapors. He trembled with the heat, with astonishment that he was indeed here, as snug in this steaming tub as was the turkey in its roasting pan. He felt blessed. He stared at the bathroom sink, which now had an aura of sanctity about it, its faucets sacred, its drainpipe holy, and he wondered whether everything was blessed at some point in its existence, and he concluded yes. Sweat rolled down his forehead and dripped off his nose into the bath, a confluence of ancient and modern waters. And as it did, a great sunburst entered the darkening skies, a radiance so sudden that it seemed like a bolt of lightning; yet its brilliance remained, as if some angel of beatific lucidity were hovering outside the bathroom window. So enduring was the light, so intense beyond even sundown's final gloryburst, that Francis raised himself up out of the tub and went to the window.

Below, in the yard, Aldo Campione, Fiddler Quain, Harold Allen, and Rowdy Dick Doolan were erecting a wooden structure that Francis was already able to recognize as bleachers.

He stepped back into the tub, soaped the long-handled brush, raised his left foot out of the water, scrubbed it clean, raised the right foot, scrubbed that.

Francis, that 1916 dude, came down the stairs in bow tie, white-on-white shirt, black laceless oxfords with a spit shine on them, the gray herringbone with lapels twenty-two years too narrow, with black silk socks and white silk boxer shorts, with his skin free of dirt everywhere, his hair washed twice, his fingernails cleaned, his leftover teeth brushed and the toothbrush washed with soap and dried and rehung, with no whiskers anymore, none, and his hair combed and rubbed with a dab of Vaseline so it'd stay in place, with a spring in his gait and a smile on his face; this Francis dude came down those stairs, yes, and stunned his family with his resurrectible good looks and stylish potential, and took their stares as applause.

And dance music rose in his brain.

"Holy Christ," said Billy.

"My oh my," said Annie.

"You look different," Daniel said.

"I kinda needed a sprucin'," Francis said. "Funny duds but I guess they'll do."

They all pulled back then, even Daniel, aware they should not dwell on the transformation, for it made Francis's previous condition so lowly, so awful.

"Gotta dump these rags," he said, and he lifted his bundle, tied with the arms of his old coat.

"Danny'll take them," Annie said. "Put them in the cellar," she told the boy.

Francis sat down on a bench in the breakfast nook, across the table from Billy. Annie had spread the clips and photos on the table and he and Billy looked them over. Among the clips Francis found a yellowed envelope postmarked June 2, 1910, and addressed to Mr. Francis Phelan, c/o Toronto Baseball Club, The Palmer House, Toronto, Ont. He opened it and read the letter inside, then pocketed it. Dinner advanced as Daniel and Annie peeled the potatoes at the sink. Billy, his hair combed slick, half a dude himself with open-collared starched white shirt, creased trousers, and pointy black shoes, was drinking from a quart bottle of Dobler beer and reading a clipping.

"I read these once," Billy said. "I never really knew how good you were. I heard stories and then one night downtown I heard a guy talking about you and he was ravin' that you were top-notch and I never knew just how good. I knew this stuff was there. I seen it when we first moved here, so I went up and looked. You were really a hell of a ball player."

"Not bad," Francis said. "Coulda been worse."

"These sportswriters liked you."

"I did crazy things. I was good copy for them. And I had energy. Everybody likes energy."

Billy offered Francis a glass of beer but Francis declined and took, instead, fromBilly's pack, a Camel cigarette: and then he perused the clips that told of him stealing the show with his fielding, or going four-for-four and driving in the winning run, or getting himself in trouble; such as the day he held the runner on third by the belt, an old John McGraw trick, and when a fly ball was hit, the runner got ready to tag and head home after the catch but found he could not move and turned and screamed at Francis in protest, at which point Francis let go of the belt and the runner ran, but the throw arrived first and he was out at home.

Nifty.

But Francis was thrown out of the game.

"Would you like to go out and look at the yard?" Annie said, suddenly beside Francis.

"Sure. See the dog."

"It's too bad the flowers are gone. We had so many flowers this year. Dahlias and snapdragons and pansies and asters. The asters lasted the longest."

"You still got them geraniums right here."

Annie nodded and put on her sweater and the two of them went out onto the back porch. The air was chilly and the light fading. She closed the door behind them and patted the dog, which barked twice at Francis and then accepted his presence. Annie went down the five steps to the yard, Francis and the dog following.

"Do you have a place to stay tonight, Fran?"

"Sure. Always got a place to stay."

"Do you want to come home permanent?" she asked, not looking at him, walking a few steps ahead toward the fence. "Is that why you've come to see us?"

"Nah, not much chance of that. I'd never fit in."

"I thought you might've had that in mind."

"I thought of it, I admit that. But I see it couldn't work, not after all these years."

"It'd take some doing, I know that."

"Take more than that."

"Stranger things have happened."

"Yeah? Name one."

"You going to the cemetery and talking to Gerald. I think maybe that's the strangest thing I ever heard in all my days."

"Wasn't strange. I just went and stood there and told him a bunch of stuff. It's nice where he is. It's pretty."

"That's the family plot."

"I know."

"There's a grave there for you, right at the stone, and one for me, and two for the children next to that if they need them. Peg'll have her own plot with George and the boy, I imagine."

"When did you do all that?" Francis asked.

"Oh years ago. I don't remember."

"You bought me a grave after I run off."

"I bought it for the family. You're part of the family."

"There was long times I didn't think so."

"Peg is very bitter about you staying away. I was too, for years and years, but that's all done with. I don't know why I'm not bitter anymore. I really don't. I called Peg and told her to get the cranberries and that you were here."

"Me and the cranberries. Easin' the shock some."

"I suppose."

"I'll move along, then. I don't want no fights, rile up the family."

"Nonsense. Stop it. You just talk to her. You've got to talk to her."

"I can't say nothin' that means anything. I couldn't say a straight word to you."

"I know what you said and what you didn't say. I know it's hard what you're doing."

"It's a bunch of nothin'. I don't know why I do anything in this goddamn life."

"You did something good coming home. It's something Danny'll always know about. And Billy. He was so glad to be able to help you, even though he'd never say it."

"He got a bum out of jail."

"You're so mean to yourself, Francis."

"Hell, I'm mean to everybody and everything."

The bleachers were all up, and men were filing silently into them and sitting down, right here in Annie's backyard, in front of God and the dog and all: Bill Corbin, who ran for sheriff in the nineties and got beat and turned Republican, and Perry Marsolais, who inherited a fortune from his mother and drank it up and ended up raking leaves for the city, and Iron Joe himself with his big mustache and big belly and big ruby stickpin, and Spiff Dwyer in his nifty pinched fedora, and young George Quinn and young Martin Daugherty, the bat-boys, and Martin's grandfather Emmett Daugherty, the wild Fenian who talked so fierce and splendid and put the radical light in Francis's eye with his stories of how moneymen used workers to get rich and treated the Irish like pigdog paddyniggers, and Patsy McCall, who grew up to run the city and was carrying his ball glove in his left hand, and some men Francis did not know even in 1899, for they were only hangers-on at the saloon, men who followed the doings of Iron Joe's Wheelbarrow Boys, and who came to the beer picnic this day to celebrate the Boys' winning the Albany-Troy League pennant.

They kept coming: forty-three men, four boys, and two mutts, ushered in by the Fiddler and his pals.

And there, between crazy Specky McManus in his derby and Jack Corbett in his vest and no collar, sat the runt, is it?

Is it now?

The runt with the piece out of his neck.

There's one in every crowd.

Francis closed his eyes to retch the vision out of his head, but when he opened them the bleachers still stood, the men seated as before. Only the light had changed, brighter now, and with it grew Francis's hatred of all fantasy, all insubstantiality. I am sick of you all, was his thought. I am sick of imagining what you became, what I might have become if I'd lived among you. I am sick of your melancholy histories, your sentimental pieties, your goddamned unchanging faces. I'd rather be dyin' in the weeds than standin' here lookin' at you pinin' away, like the dyin' Jesus pinin' for an end to it when he knew every stinkin' thing that was gonna happen not only to himself but to everybody around him, and to all those that wasn't even born yet. You ain't nothin' more than a photograph, you goddamn spooks. You ain't real and I ain't gonna be at your beck and call no more.

You're all dead, and if you ain't, you oughta be.

I'm the one is livin'. I'm the one puts you on the map.

You never knew no more about how things was than I did.

You'd never even be here in the damn yard if I didn't open that old trunk.

So get your ass gone!

"Hey Ma," Billy yelled out the window. "Peg's home."

"We'll be right in," Annie said. And when Billy closed the window she turned to Francis: "You want to tell me anything, ask me anything, before we get in front of the others?"

"Annie, I got five million things to ask you, and ten million things to tell. I'd like to eat all the dirt in this yard for you, eat the weeds, eat the dog bones too, if you asked me."

"I think you probably ate all that already," she said.

And then they went up the back stoop together.

When Francis first saw his daughter bent over the stove, already in her flowered apron and basting the turkey, he thought: She is too dressed up to be doing that. She wore a wristwatch on one arm, a bracelet on the other, and two rings on her wedding ring finger. She wore high heels, silk stockings with the seams inside out, and a lavender dress that was never intended as a kitchen costume. Her dark-brown hair, cut short, was waved in a soft marcel, and she wore lipstick and a bit of rouge, and her nails were long and painted dark red. She was a few, maybe even more than a few, pounds overweight, and she was beautiful, and Francis was immeasurably happy at having sired her.

"How ya doin', Margaret?" Francis asked when she straightened up and looked at him.

"I'm doing fine," she said, "no thanks to you."

"Yep," said Francis, and he turned away from her and sat across from Billy in the nook.

"Give him a break," Billy said. "He just got here, for chrissake."

"What break did he ever give me? Or you? Or any of us?"

"Aaahhh, blow it out your ear," Billy said.

"I'm saying what is," Peg said.

"Are you?" Annie asked. "Are you so sure of what is?"

"I surely am. I'm not going to be a hypocrite and welcome him back with open arms after what he did. You don't just pop up one day with a turkey and all is forgiven."

"I ain't expectin' to be forgiven," Francis said. "I'm way past that."

"Oh? And just where are you now?"

"Nowhere."

"Well that's no doubt very true. And if you're nowhere, why are you here? Why've you come back like a ghost we buried years ago to force a scrawny turkey on us? Is that your idea of restitution for letting us fend for ourselves for twenty-two years?"

"That's a twelve-and-a-half-pound turkey," Annie said.

"Why leave your nowhere and come here, is what I want to know. This is somewhere. This is a home you didn't build."

"I built you. Built Billy. Helped to."

"I wish you never did."

"Shut up, Peg," Billy yelled. "Rotten tongue of yours, shut it the hell UP!"

"He came to visit, that's all he did," Annie said softly. "I already asked him if he wanted to stay over and he said no. If he wanted to he surely could."

"Oh?" said Peg. "Then it's all decided?"

"Nothin' to decide," Francis said. "Like your mother says, I ain't stayin'. I'm movin' along." He touched the salt and pepper shaker on the table in front of him, pushed the sugar bowl against the wall.

"You're moving on," Peg said.

"Positively."

"Fine."

"That's it, that's enough!" Billy yelled, standing up from the bench. "You got the feelin's of a goddamn rattlesnake."

"Pardon me for having any feelings at all," Peg said, and she left the kitchen, slamming the swinging door, which had been standing open, slamming it so hard that it swung, and swung, and swung, until it stopped.

"Tough lady," Francis said.

"She's a creampuff," Billy said. "But she knows how to get her back up."

"She'll calm down," Annie said.

"I'm used to people screamin' at me," Francis said. "I got a hide like a hippo."

"You need it in this joint," Billy said.

"Where's the boy?" Francis asked. "He hear all that?"

"He's out playin' with the ball and glove you gave him," Billy said.

"I didn't give him the glove," Francis said. "I give him the ball with the Ty Cobb signature. That glove is yours. You wanna give it to him, it's okay by me. Ain't much of a glove compared to what they got these days. Danny's glove's twice the quality my glove ever was. But I always thought to myself: I'm givin' that old glove to Billy so's he'll have a touch of the big leagues somewhere in the house. That glove caught some mighty people. Line drive from Tris Speaker, taggin' out Cobb, runnin' Eddie Collins outa the baseline. Lotta that."

Billy nodded and turned away from Francis. "Okay," he said, and then he jumped up from the bench and left the kitchen so the old man could not see (though he saw) that he was choked up.

"Grew up nice, Billy did," Francis said. "Couple of tough bozos you raised, Annie."

"I wish they were tougher," Annie said.

The yard, now ablaze with new light against a black sky, caught Francis's attention. Men and boys, and even dogs, were holding lighted candles, the dogs holding them in their mouths sideways. Specky McManus, as usual bein' different, wore his candle on top of his derby. It was a garden of acolytes setting fire to the very air, and then, while Francis watched, the acolytes erupted in song, but a song without sense, a chant to which Francis listened carefully but could make out not a word. It was an antisyllabic lyric they sang, like the sibilance of the wren's softest whistle, or the tree frog's tonsillar wheeze. It was clear to Francis as he watched this performance (watched it with awe, for it was transcending what he expected from dream, from reverie, even from Sneaky Pete hallucinations) that it was happening in an arena of his existence over which he had less control than he first imagined when Aldo Campione boarded the bus. The signals from this time lock were ominous, the spooks utterly without humor. And then, when he saw the runt (who knew he was being watched, who knew he didn't belong in this picture) putting the lighted end of the candle into the hole in the back of his neck, and when Francis recognized the chant of the acolytes at last as the "Dies Irae," he grew fearful. He closed his eyes and buried his head in his hands and he tried to remember the name of his first dog.

It was a collie.

Billy came back, clear-eyed, sat across from Francis, and offered him another smoke, which he took. Billy topped his own beer and drank and then said, "George."

"Oh my God," Annie said. "We forgot all about George." And she went to the living room and called upstairs to Peg: "You should call George and tell him he can come home."

"Let her alone, I'll do it," Billy called to his mother.

"What about George?" Francis asked.

"The cops were here one night lookin' for him," Billy said. "It was Patsy McCall puttin' pressure on the family because of me. George writes numbers and they were probably gonna book him for gamblin' even though he had the okay. So he laid low up in Troy, and the poor bastard's been alone for days. But if I'm clear, then so is he."

"Some power the McCalls put together in this town."

"They got it all. They ever pay you the money they owed you for registerin' all those times?"

"Paid me the fifty I told you about, owe me another fifty-five. I'll never see it."

"You got it comin'."

"Once it got in the papers they wouldn't touch it. Mixin' themselves up with bums. You heard Martin tell me that. They'd also be suspicious that I'd set them up. I wouldn't set nobody up. Nobody."

"Then you got no cash."

"I got a little."

"How much?"

"I got some change. Cigarette money."

"You blew what you had on the turkey."

"That took a bit of it."

Billy handed him a ten, folded in half. "Put it in your pocket. You can't walk around broke."

Francis took it and snorted. "I been broke twenty-two years. But I thank ye, Billy, I'll make it up."

"You already made it up." And he went to the phone in the dining room to call George in Troy.

Annie came back to the kitchen and saw Francis looking at the Chadwick Park photo and looked over his shoulder. "That's a handsome picture of you," she said.

"Yeah," said Francis. "I was a good-lookin' devil."

"Some thought so, some didn't," Annie said. "I forgot about this picture."

"Oughta get it framed," Francis said. "Lot of North Enders in there. George and Martin as kids, and Patsy McCall too. And Iron Joe. Real good shot of Joe."

"It surely is," Annie said. "How fat and healthy he looks."

Billy came back and Annie put the photo on the table so that all three of them could look at it. They sat on the same bench with Francis in the middle and studied it, each singling out the men and boys they knew. Annie even knew one of the dogs.

"Oh that's a prize picture," she said, and stood up. "A prize picture."

"Well, it's yours, so get it framed."

"Mine? No, it's yours. It's baseball."

"Nah, nah, George'd like it too."

"Well I will frame it," Annie said. "I'll take it downtown and get it done up right."

"Sure," said Francis. "Here. Here's ten dollars toward the frame."

"Hey," Billy said.

"No," Francis said. "You let me do it, Billy."

Billy chuckled.

"I will not take any money," Annie said. "You put that back in your pocket."

Billy laughed and hit the table with the palm of his hand. "Now I know why you been broke twenty-two years. I know why we're all broke. It runs in the family."

"We're not all broke," Annie said. "We pay our way. Don't be telling people we're broke. You're broke because you made some crazy horse bet. But *we're* not broke. We've had bad times but we can still pay the rent. And we've never gone hungry."

"Peg's workin'," Francis said.

"A private secretary," Annie said. "To the owner of a tool company. She's very well liked."

"She's beautiful," Francis said. "Kinda nasty when she puts her mind to it, but beautiful."

"She shoulda been a model," Billy said.

"She should not," Annie said.

"Well she shoulda, goddamn it, she shoulda," said Billy. "They wanted her to model for Pepsodent toothpaste, but Mama wouldn't hear of it. Somebody over at church told her models were, you know, loose ladies. Get your picture taken, it turns you into a floozy."

"That had nothing to do with it," Annie said.

"Her teeth," Billy said. "She's got the most gorgeous teeth in North America. Better-lookin' teeth than Joan Crawford. What a smile! You ain't seen her smile yet, but that's a fantastic smile. Like Times Square is what it is. She coulda been on billboards coast to coast. We'd be hip-deep in toothpaste, and cash too. But no." And he jerked a thumb at his mother.

"She had a job," Annie said. "She didn't need that. I never liked that fellow that wanted to sign her up."

"He was all right," Billy said. "I checked him out. He was legitimate."

"How could you know what he was?"

"How could I know anything? I'm a goddamn genius."

"Clean up your mouth, genius. She would've had to go to New York for pictures."

"And she'd of never come back, right?"

"Maybe she would, maybe she wouldn't."

"Now you got it," Billy said to his father. "Mama likes to keep all the birds in the nest."

"Can't say as I blame her," Francis said.

"No," Billy said.

"I never liked that fellow," Annie said. "That's what it really was. I didn't trust him."

Nobody spoke.

"And she brought a paycheck home every week," Annie said. "Even when the tool company closed awhile, the owner put her to work as a cashier in a trading port he owned. Trading port and indoor golf. An enormous place. They almost brought Rudy Vallee there once. Peg got wonderful experience."

Nobody spoke.

"Cigarette?" Billy asked Francis.

"Sure," Francis said.

Annie stood up and went to the refrigerator in the pantry. She came back with the butter dish and put it on the dining-room table. Peg came through the swinging door, into the silence. She poked the potatoes with a fork, looked at the turkey, which was turning deep brown, and closed the oven door without basting it. She rummaged in the utensil drawer and found a can opener and punched it through a can of peas and put them in a pan to boil.

"Turkey smells real good," Francis said to her.

"Uh-huh, I bought a plum pudding," she said to all, showing them the can. She looked at her father. "Mama said you used to like it for dessert on holidays."

"I surely did. With that white sugar sauce. Mighty sweet."

"The sauce recipe's on the label," Annie said. "Give it here and I'll make it."

"I'll make it," Peg said.

"It's nice you remembered that," Francis said.

"It's no trouble," Peg said. "The pudding's already cooked. All you do is heat it up in the can."

Francis studied her and saw the venom was gone from her eyes. This lady goes up and down like a thermometer. When she saw him studying her she smiled slightly, not a billboard smile, not a smile to make anybody rich in toothpaste, but there it was. What the hell, she's got a right. Up and down, up and down. She come by it naturally.

"I got a letter maybe you'd all like to hear while that stuff's cookin' up," he said, and he took the yellowed envelope with a canceled two-cent stamp on it out of his inside coat pocket. On the back, written in his own hand, was: *First letter from Margaret.*

"I got this a few years back, quite a few," he said, and from the envelope he took out three small trifolded sheets of yellowed lined paper. "Come to me up in Canada in nineteen-ten, when I was with Toronto." He unfolded the sheets and moved them into the best possible light at longest possible arm's length, and then he read:

" 'Dear Poppy, I suppose you never think that you have a daughter that is waiting for a letter since you went away. I was so mad because you did not think of me that I was going to join the circus that was here last Friday. I am doing my lesson and there is an arithmetic example here that I cannot get. See if you can get it. I hope your leg is better and that you have good luck with the team. Do not run too much with your legs or you will have to be carried home. Mama and Billy are good. Mama has fourteen new little chickens out and she has two more hens sitting. There is a wild west circus coming the eighth. Won't you come home and see it? I am going to it. Billy is just going to bed and Mama is sitting on the bed watching me. Do not forget to answer this. I suppose you are having a lovely time. Do not let me find you with another girl or I will pull her hair. Yours truly, Peggy.' "

"Isn't that funny," Peg said, the fork still in her hand. "I don't remember writing that."

"Probably lots you don't remember about them days," Francis said. "You was only about eleven."

"Where did you ever find it?"

"Up in the trunk. Been saved all these years up there. Only letter I ever saved."

"Is that a fact?"

"It's a provable fact. All the papers I got in the world was in that trunk, except one other place I got a few more clips. But no letters noplace. It's a good old letter, I'd say."

"I'd say so too," Annie said. She and Billy were both staring at Peg.

"I remember Toronto in nineteen-ten," Francis said. "The game was full of crooks them days. Crooked umpire named Bates, one night it was deep dark but he wouldn't call the game. Folks was throwin' tomatoes and mudballs at him but he wouldn't call it 'cause we was winnin' and he was in with the other team. Pudge Howard was catchin' that night and he walks out and has a three-way confab on the mound with me and old Highpockets Wilson, who was pitchin'. Pudge comes back and squats behind the plate and Highpockets lets go a blazer and the ump calls it a ball, though nobody could see nothin' it was so dark. And Pudge turns to him and says: 'You call that pitch a ball?' 'I did,' says the ump. 'If that was a ball I'll eat it,' says Pudge. 'Then you better get eatin',' says the ump. And Pudge, he holds the ball up and takes a big bite out of it, 'cause it ain't no ball at all, it's a yellow apple I give Highpockets to throw. And of course that won us the game and the ump went down in history as Blindy Bates, who couldn't tell a baseball from a damn apple. Bates turned into a bookie after that. He was crooked at that too."

"That's a great story," Billy said. "Funny stuff in them old days."

"Funny stuff happenin' all the time," Francis said.

Peg was suddenly tearful. She put the fork on the sink and went to her father, whose hands were folded on the table. She sat beside him and put her right hand on top of his.

After a while George Quinn came home from Troy, Annie served the turkey, and then the entire Phelan family sat down to dinner.

PROFILE

THOSE who have read and treasured John Lardner's delightful profile of Babe Herman in the first *Fireside Book of Baseball* or in *The Baseball Reader* will understand that his offering reprinted here from *True* Magazine follows as the night the day.

The One and Only Bobo

JOHN LARDNER

ONCE THERE WAS a ballplayer named Louis Norman Newsom, who called himself and everyone else Bobo. He was born in 1906, 1907, 1908, or 1909, depending on which way he told it. Early in life, he gave out the news that he was the greatest pitcher in baseball. Partly on the strength of this report—but mainly because of certain supporting evidence—he was hired 17 times by big-league ball clubs in the next 20 years. He was fired or sold just as often as he was hired, and seldom with much delay. But, in the end, no one in baseball could have said for sure that Bobo hadn't been right about himself all along.

This doubt—and the legend of Newsom—linger on. They still see him now and then. He casts his portly shadow over baseball gatherings at All-Star Games and World Series, looking like a Dixie senator, or rather, like one Dixie senator standing on another senator's shoulders. And they wonder, was this indeed the most valuable slab of baseball meat in the last quarter-century? Will it turn out that the big fellow's gifts—apart from a nerve of brass, and lungs of leather—were unique in the brittle modern game? Was he a throwback to ancient times? They know what L. N. Newsom would say if they asked him.

"Bobo," Newsom sometimes tells a hard-pressed manager nowadays, in a hotel lobby, backing him up against a potted palm, "you could surely use Bobo now. But where ya gonna find a guy like Bobo? They don't grow in bunches like bananas, son."

Among pitchers, this is an age of sore arms and neuroses. With these boys, the inferiority complex has become as common as freckles. Stalked by fear and insecurity, they rotate between the whirlpool bath and the halls of Johns Hopkins, where they throw their elbow chips into the pot and hear the world's wisest healers say glumly that pitching is fundamentally unnatural. Thanks in part to a ball that takes off from a bat like a skyrocket, the average talented pitcher of today has six or eight years of life as a starter, plus two or three years in the bull pen, living on cunning alone.

Since the birth of the lively, or firecracker, ball, Newsom has been the only pitcher to last 20 years in the major leagues. Twice, he pitched both ends of a double-header. Several times, he started one game of a double-header and relieved in the other.

Once, his knee was broken by a line drive in an early stage of a game. He went on to pitch the distance.

Once, in the third inning of a game, his jaw was broken in two places by an infielder's throw. He finished out the game.

Once, a line drive from the bat of a pitcher named Oscar Judd hit Newsom on the skull and bounced 400 feet into center field. The target remarked later—after completing the game without difficulty—that occasionally, during the later innings, he heard strains of music ringing pleasantly through his brain. After the game, in a hotel, a sports writer introduced Newsom to his wife. Newsom made a courtly bow. "A pleasure, madam," he said gallantly. "Would you like to feel the bump on my head?"

When Bobo retired from baseball for life, in 1953 (after telling Connie Mack, his last manager, "You can't afford my wages, Bobo," which was true), two things had been clearly established about his anatomy (of which there was between 210 and 230 pounds, measuring six feet three in length). You couldn't hurt Newsom in the head. And, while a leg or a jawbone might chip, his right arm was foolproof and painproof. It was a genuine rubber arm—in our time, an anachronism. With it, the owner could work three or four times a week and relieve in between. In the World Series of 1940, he started three games within a week and nearly won all three of them.

That is why present-day managers tend to water at the mouth when they see Newsom at baseball reunions. Then they think it over; and most of them, as one kind of memory leads to another, tremble with relief at the thought that Bobo today, at 50 or so, is too old to tempt them into the kind of trouble that always came to those who tried to harness this erratic natural force.

The late Connie Mack once enlisted a bodyguard, coach Earle Brucker, to keep him from rehiring Newsom, who had worked for Mack and the Philadelphia Athletics once before. Mack was making a trip to Orlando, Florida, near Newsom's home in Winter Park. Newsom was temporarily unemployed. "I know he'll meet me at the train," Connie told Brucker, "and I know that if you don't stick by me every minute, I'll weaken and sign him up." The strategy worked. However—showing the insidious strength of the Newsom habit—Mack did rehire Bobo a year later. In another year, Clark Griffith, owner of Washington, said: "Newsom will never again wear a Washington uniform." He re-employed Bobo the same year.

The explanation of this split or schizoid attitude toward Newsom is that no player in baseball history could fluctuate so swiftly from the sublime to the unspeakable. After winning the pennant and almost winning the World Series for Detroit in 1940, Bobo was rewarded by the highest pitcher's salary in the game, $35,000. The following spring, he drove into training camp in an automobile one block long, which carried a sign that spelled "Bobo" in neon lights, and a horn that played the first four notes of "Tiger Rag." During the season, he kept a table reserved in a Detroit hotel, where quail and champagne were served to Newsom and guests, while the other Tiger players got along on steak and milk. That year, Bobo lost 20 games.

Another thing that upset employers was Newsom's effect on managers. Once, while working for Brooklyn, he inspired a mutiny that drove manager Leo Durocher to tears. As soon as Leo had dried his eyes, Bobo was sold as far out of town as possible (namely, St. Louis). Once, while working for the Boston Red Sox, Bobo got into trouble on the mound, and manager Joe Cronin came in from shortstop with words of advice. "Listen, Bobo," said Bobo. "You play shortstop, and I'll do the pitching." At the end of that season, Newsom was sold as far out of town as possible (namely, St. Louis).

Bobo's crunching impact on managers went back almost as far as his baseball childhood. In 1928, his first season in organized ball, Newsom served a hitch in Greenville, N.C., where Hal Weafer, later a Brooklyn scout, was the manager. Newsom and his young wife lived at Weafer's house when the team was at home. After supper, Bobo and Weafer invariably repaired to the front porch to sit, swat flies, and converse. Invariably, before the evening was over, a fight broke out between them—brought on, perhaps, by the fact that Weafer was charging the Newsoms rent, though the meals were free. Once, Mrs. Weafer and Mrs. Newsom arranged a special reconciliation supper, to make their husbands love each other better. That night, the fight began earlier than usual, at the table.

On the field one day, while pitching for batting practice, Newsom aimed a tangential pitch at the head of Weafer, who was standing on the sidelines. Weafer ducked and chased Bobo twice around the field with a bat in his hand, before peace was restored. They fought again that night after supper.

Temperament was native to Bobo—temperament, a strong imagination, and a tongue that vibrated like a hummingbird. He was born in Hartsville, S.C., the son of a farmer named Henry Quillan Buffkin Newsom. The day was August 11; the year, as noted above, came to depend on Bobo's free-wheeling autobiographical instinct, which never produced the same date twice in a row. The same instinct created three or four stories of how he came by the name Bobo. Once, Bobo said that he had been nicknamed Buck, as a child, by his uncle Jake (J. R. Newsom); he couldn't pronounce Buck, and called himself Bobo instead. Another time, Newsom said that he adopted the name Bobo himself, from a character in a book he'd been reading. These versions of history, and many others, were recited by Bobo tirelessly for the next 40 years, in a high, plaintive voice that came strangely out of his huge body and big, round, blue-jowled face.

Bobo played home-town baseball as a boy. He also developed a gift for preparing food that later won him work as supervisor-of-barbecue in southern eating places, including a café in Hartsville co-managed by his Uncle Jake and himself. This double life became useful to Newsom, when big-league owners hesitated to pay him the princely salaries he thought he deserved. "If you try to starve me up no'th," Bobo would say, "I'll stay home in my kitchen all summer and eat off the fat of the land."

After demoralizing a few minor-league managers like Weafer, and serving a short youthful hitch in Brooklyn, under the late Uncle Wilbert Robinson, who liked big pitchers ("But this fella's head is *too* big," said Uncle Robbie), Newsom signed with the Chicago Cubs early in 1932. He started for training camp in his car and was several miles from home before he drove off the edge of a 200-foot cliff, smashing the car and breaking his leg. Bobo spent the rest of the spring writing bulletins about his health to P. K. Wrigley, Cub owner, and assuring Wrigley that he would win the pennant for him as soon as he got out of bed. When he got out of bed, he went to a mule sale, where a mule kicked him in the same leg and broke it again. What with one thing and another, Newsom played his next baseball for Los Angeles, in 1933. He burned up the Coast League. The record says he won 30 and lost 11. Newsom says he won 32 (if not 33) and lost 10.

"Who ya gonna believe, Bobo," he says, "the record book, or the guy that done it?"

The St. Louis Browns bought the new young star for use in 1934. With this abysmal ball club, Newsom one day pitched a "no-hitter." That is, according to the records, he pitched nine innings of no-hit ball against Boston. In the 10th inning, two bases on balls followed by a bad-hop single beat Bobo 2–1. Records or no records, this feat has always been an official no-hitter in Newsom's book.

"How many no-hit games did you pitch in the big leagues, Bobo?" someone asked him recently.

"Just the one," Bobo said. "They don't grow in bunches like bananas, son."

Newsom had a purpose in pitching well against the Red Sox; he wanted to be sold to Boston, where salaries were big. Instead, the Browns sold him for $45,000 to Washington, where salaries were small. In this way, Bobo found a lifetime home-away-from-home—he was to work for the Senators five different times—and Clark Griffith launched a new career, buying Bobo to get some well-pitched games and selling Bobo to recover expenses (he usually sold him for twice his salary). Between sales, Bobo became Griff's favorite pinochle partner. This alone, some critics have said, was enough to persuade the magnate to buy Newsom again whenever he felt lonely.

In 1937, the rich Red Sox bought Newsom from Griffith in self-defense—twice in the previous season he had beaten the great Lefty Grove in crucial games. As it turned out, wealth did not make Bobo happy, and Bobo did not make Joe Cronin happy. For company's sake, Newsom installed a hutch of rabbits in his hotel room in Boston. Then he forgot them. The rabbits ate their way steadily through the room, missing no bets. They had begun to go to work on the curtains when the hotel management discovered them, dispossessed them, and presented Cronin with a bill for the damages. As noted, Newsom was sold to the Browns soon afterward.

If there was no mistaking Bobo's shortcomings, there was no mistaking his gifts, either. He could work all day, and his arm was as strong and supple as a buggy whip. He threw his vivid fast ball and his sharp curve from all levels, sidearm, overhand, three-quarters. His 1938 season with St. Louis was one of his greatest; the team finished seventh, with a total of 55 wins, and 20 of those wins were Newsom's. Before the season began, the owner, Don Barnes, told Bobo that he would give him a new suit of clothes if he won the opener. Bobo won it. That night, Barnes pressed a roll of money into his hand and told him to buy the suit.

"Keep the sugar, Bobo," Bobo said, handing it back. "Bobo bought the suit before the game. The bill is on your desk."

Big winner though he was that year, Newsom was far from businesslike in all his moves on the mound. Showmanship was vital to him, especially when he worked for losing ball clubs which he felt needed his special sales flair. To the intense distaste of manager Gabby Street of the Browns, Bobo indulged in triple windups. He alternated between right-hand and left-hand batting at the plate. He threw the "ephus" pitch, which sailed high into the air and sometimes—but not often—dropped into the strike zone. After watching an ephus pitch one day, Mr. Barnes decided to entertain a proposition from the Yankees to trade Newsom for Lefty Gomez. Then he thought again. Gomez was getting $20,000 a year. Newsom was getting $10,000. Mr. Barnes canceled the deal.

Newsom, however, did not propose to struggle along forever on $10,000. The Browns were training in San Antonio, Texas, in the spring of 1939. When they refused him a raise in pay, their star pitcher walked out of the hotel in a huff. "Bobo is going home," he said, "to live off the fat of the land." He went as far as a motel on the edge of San Antonio. While living there, he dictated statements and manifestos to the public stenographer at the Browns' hotel, which he then distributed to the press. After several manifestos, Barnes raised Bobo's pay. This move sealed Newsom's fate with the Browns. He had to be sold, to atone for his salary. It also changed his luck, for the better. He was sold in 1940, to Detroit. If Detroit was not the best team in the league, Bobo soon made it so. He also, in his first full season with the Tigers, made pitching history.

In 1940, Newsom had his third straight 20-wins-or-better season, with a record of 21 and 5. He struck out 164 batters. His earned-run average was 2.83. He put together a string of 13 straight wins. While engaged in this streak, he came up against the All-Star Game, in his old home in Washington. Newsom was a member of manager Joe McCarthy's All-Star pitching staff—but when he heard that McCarthy was planning to start Red Ruffing for the American League, he resigned from the squad.

"If I don't start, I don't pitch," Bobo said. "Bobo follows nobody."

It was pointed out to him by friends that McCarthy's plan called for a sequence of Ruffing, Newsom, and Bob Feller. In other words, Bobo would take precedence over Feller, the greatest pitcher in baseball. This thought mollified Bobo, and he rejoined the squad.

"But," he told McCarthy, the smartest man in the game, "if you had the brains of a motherless shoat, Bo, you would pitch Bobo all the way."

It might have been better that way. The National League, in winning the game, 4–0, got three runs off Ruffing, one off Feller, and none at all off Newsom in the three middle innings.

The Tigers had a series with Washington scheduled to follow the All-Star Game. Meeting his old pinochle partner, Griffith, at the ball park, Newsom told him that he was mortally certain to beat Griff's team in his next start, on a Saturday, and that the Washington team stood to make several thousand dollars extra at the box office if it advertised this boast in the newspapers. Griffith said he would think it over.

A day or so before the Saturday game, a Washington sports column carried the news that Bobo had been seen molesting or browbeating a guest in a Washington hotel lobby. The author of the column was Robert Ruark (later a novelist of considerable stamina). His words annoyed Bobo greatly. Newsom and Ruark came face to face at the ball park the same day. Newsom, who was sucking on a bottle of yellow pop, stopped drinking long enough to call the columnist an unchaste name. Ruark drew back his right arm to take a punch at Bobo. Bobo, always nonchalant in action, held Ruark off with one hand while continuing to swill from the pop bottle. In the course of this savage contest, Bobo happened to score a brush knockdown when Ruark fell backward over a bench. The incident created a certain amount of high feeling among Washington fans—and Griffith decided to take Newsom's tip and advertise Bobo's boast that he would infallibly whip the Nats in his next start.

It was a situation made to Bobo's order. Publicity was mother's milk to him. With a splendid crowd in the stands on Saturday, howling now and then, in a brooding way, for his blood, he shut out the Senators with two hits and thumbed his nose grandly at the audience as he walked off the field at the end of the day.

As it happened, this was the 13th win in Newsom's string of winning games. In his next start, in Boston, Bobo jammed and broke his thumb against Ted Williams' ribs in a tag play at first base in an early inning. The thumb went into a cast. When it came out again, a few days later, Newsom pitched and lost a close game in Philadelphia which ended his streak. The thing to be noticed here is that, broken thumb and all, he was out of action no more than a week. With all his childish moods, his bombast and his pettiness, the big man had an oddly heroic quality of mind and body that led him to defy and challenge pain, and to pretend that none of the ills of heaven and earth were a match for a Newsom of South Carolina. Bobo had begun resisting nature long before 1940.

Take the case of a game in 1935, when Newsom was pitching for Washington against Cleveland. He had two strikes on Earl Averill, the fiercest of Cleveland batsmen. He shouted brashly to Averill: "Now, Bobo, I'm gonna whiff you with an outside pitch!" Averill's lips tightened. He clubbed the outside pitch on a low, vicious line that caught Newsom in the knee with a crack that could have been heard in Baltimore. Somehow, Bobo threw his man out at first. Then he stamped around the box in agony for a minute or so. Then he resumed pitching, and kept pitching till the game was over.

"I got a piece of news for you, Mike," he told the trainer in the dressing room afterward. "Bobo thinks his laig is broke." It was. It was in a cast for five weeks.

Take the case of Opening Day, 1936, with President Roosevelt watching from a box seat, and Newsom and Washington facing the Yankees. In the third inning, Ben Chapman, New York's swiftest runner, laid down a bunt toward third. It was a good bunt, and a tough play, and Ossie Bluege, the Nats' third baseman, threw the ball blindly and with all his might toward first. It didn't get to first. Newsom, squarely in the line of fire, was observing the play with detached admiration. The ball hit him in the rear of the jaw, and bounced high into the air. Clasping his face, Bobo reeled in circles like a drunken moose. The players of both teams went to the mound to inspect the victim. "Come on, call it a day," said manager Bucky Harris to Newsom. "We'll put some ice on it." "Naw," mumbled Bobo. "Naw. Ole FDR came out to see me, and he's gonna get me all the way." And that's what the President got—Newsom all the way, and a 1–0 win for Washington.

It turned out later that Bobo's jaw had been broken in two places. For the next few days, he talked only half as much as usual. Which, as manager Harris said at the time, was still more than was strictly necessary.

The 1940 World Series, Detroit against Cincinnati, found Newsom at the height of his glory, clearly—for that year, at least—the most effective pitcher in baseball, and his team's best hope for the Series. What's more, he was behaving like a normal man, as baseball understands normality—no tricks, no ephus balls, no showboating, nothing but efficiency and will to win. And the Goddess of Chance, in her cock-eyed way, chose this time of the great man's utmost sanity to strike him a blow that made his first World Series twice as hard, and twice as memorable.

The entire Newsom family—Bobo's father, H.Q.B. Newsom, his stepmother, his sisters and his wife—had come up to Cincinnati from Hartsville. Bobo, naturally, pitched the opening game. In a strong, steady effort, he beat Paul Derringer and the Reds, 7–2. Early the next morning, his father died of a heart attack in his hotel room. Bobo was broken up. But, when the rest of the family went back to Carolina, to bury the old farmer at home, he elected to stay on and pitch out the Series. He had a thought in mind, a kind and richly sentimental thought that appealed to the depths of his sentimental soul. On the day of the fifth game, in Detroit, with tears streaming down the big, round, dark-bearded face, Bobo announced that he was "dedicating" this one to his dead father. It turned out to be quite a tribute—a three-hit shutout, in which no Red reached third base, and seven of them went down swinging at Bobo's dancing fast ball.

Two days later, Newsom sat in the clubhouse waiting to pitch the seventh and deciding game of the Series on one day's rest. There was a soft, faraway look in his eyes. His thoughts, as he absently oiled his glove, seemed to be a thousand miles from the ball park in space and time. A reporter, touched and curious, stopped in front of him.

"Will you try to win this one for your daddy, too?" the reporter asked.

Bobo looked up. "Why, no," he said, considering the point carefully. "No. I think I'll win this one for Bobo."

If he had won it, he would have been the first pitcher since the dawn of the lively baseball in 1920 (when the Series was the best five games out of nine) to score three wins in one World Series. And Bobo came very close, indeed. He had the Reds blanked, 1–0, in the seventh inning, when Frank McCormick hit to left field for two bases. Jim Ripple, the next Cincinnati hitter, lifted a deep, high fly to right. It was questionable whether the ball would scrape the fence or be caught; so McCormick held up between second and third, waiting to see. The ball struck the top of the fence, dropped onto the field, and was thrown in quickly to the infield; but Dick Bartell, Detroit shortstop, who took the throw, stood with the ball in his hands and his back to the plate for a moment, assuming that the run would score, and so McCormick was able to lope home. When Ripple scored from third a few minutes later, on a fly ball, the score became 2–1. It stayed that way to the end.

Three-game winner or not, Bobo was the greatest man in baseball. He liked to think so, at any rate, and so did his owner, Walter O. Briggs. When the report got out that Feller of Cleveland, at $30,000, would be as highly paid as Newsom in 1941, Briggs decided to raise Bobo an additional $5,000, as a matter of institutional pride. He sent for Newsom to tell him so. Spike Briggs, the late owner's son, had a desk just outside his father's office in those days. He remembers looking up one day and seeing Bobo looming before him, ablaze with great expectations and brand-new haberdashery. "Step aside, Little Bo," said Newsom expansively. "Big Bobo wants to see me." He moved on into the boss's office, and there signed the contract that made him the game's richest and most contented pitcher.

Exactly a year later, as previously noted, contentment, quail, and champagne had set in so deeply that Newsom was a 20-game loser. We find him back in the Tigers' office, prepared to defy to the death a pay cut of about 60 per cent, to $12,500. His opponent was Jack Zeller, the Detroit general manager. Zeller had a surpassingly bald head and recent spiritual flesh wounds, which had been caused when Commissioner Landis liberated 90 Tiger farmhands and declared them free agents. Newsom and Zeller argued Newsom's pay cut with passion. Bobo said he would not stand for it. He screamed that his feelings had been deeply and fatally wounded. "But, listen, Bobo," Zeller expostulated, "you lost 20 games." "Hell, Curly," said Bobo, with a withering glance at Zeller's nude scalp, "you lost 90 of Briggs' ball players last year, and I don't see you taking no cut."

This line of reasoning, cogent though it was, got Newsom nowhere. He continued to hold out and was shortly afterward sold back to his old home-away-from-home on the Potomac River for the season of 1942.

Not that Bobo stayed the whole season in Washington. Griffith, after extracting a certain number of wins and a certain number of pinochle hands from his favorite chattel, scored a most ingenious coup, by selling him to Brooklyn for the sum of about two years' salaries. The purchase was made by Larry MacPhail. Newsom promptly sent manager Durocher of the Dodgers a telegram reading: "Wish to congratulate you on buying pennant insurance."

Things did not quite work out that way. In the following winter, MacPhail was replaced in the front office by Branch Rickey, who liked nearly everything he found in Brooklyn except Bobo. The Dodgers trained in the wartime spring of 1943 in Bear Mountain, N.Y. Newsom, who hated cold weather, held out at home in South Carolina. "B'Judas Priest," said Rickey to Durocher, "this is a wonderful excuse to get rid of the fellow!"

"But I need him," cried Durocher. He was later to eat those words and wash them down with his own tears.

By July of 1943, Newsom was Brooklyn's biggest winner, with nine games in the book. He had also taken full management of himself out of Durocher's hands and, Durocher suspected, was secretly trying to manage the rest of the team as well. One day, in a game against Pittsburgh, Bobo delivered an oddly erratic pitch that got away from Bob Bragan, the young Dodger catcher. Durocher and some of the other Dodgers on the bench thought that it looked like a spitball. A Pittsburgh runner scored from third on the passed ball. Newsom put his hands on his hips, stamped about, and otherwise showed his scorn and disgust with Bragan; when the inning ended, he threw his glove in the air. After the game, which he failed to finish, Bobo heard Durocher and some of the players discussing the so-called "spitter." He broke in on the talk to deny the charge with righteous anger—the pitch had been a good fast ball, Bobo said. Durocher replied by bawling him out for "showing up" Bragan in front of the crowd, and for other shortcomings. Bobo countered with a long, strong oration on managerial incompetence in the National League. Durocher suspended his leading pitcher on the spot, without pay.

The stormy one-day revolution which followed has since taken its place as a milestone in Brooklyn baseball history. It had many dark and twisting ramifications, which we won't follow in detail here, except to claim for Bobo his rightful place at the root of it all. The day after Newsom's suspension, Arkie Vaughan, Dodger infielder, because of a version of the story he had heard, turned in his uniform to Durocher and said he would not play. The mutiny spread quickly, guided by friends of Vaughan's like Dixie Walker. In the end, Durocher, weeping freely as he spoke to the assembled team, won Walker and nearly all the others back. Everyone played that day except Vaughan and Newsom, and Brooklyn beat Pittsburgh by the emotional score of 23–6.

"Do you still want this anarchist on your staff, my dear boy?" said Rickey, speaking of Bobo, to Durocher.

"No, no," said Durocher, almost breaking down again. "How far away can you send him?"

"I can send him to the St. Louis American League club for two competent left-handers," said Rickey complacently, and the deal went more or less as advertised, except that the two left-handers turned out to be worthless, while Bobo, now 35 or more, still had a few volts of genius and 10 years of baseball left in his system. For the moment, after a short stay in St. Louis, he reverted to Washington again, as naturally as a homing squab, and finished out the season as he had begun the previous one, playing pinochle with Griffith.

During the war years, Newsom met and left his mark on the late Connie Mack. Nothing in his seven decades of baseball had prepared this wise and gentle old man for the likes of Bobo. Connie acquired Newsom early in 1944, and Bobo came to Mack's Philadelphia office to discuss salary. He took over Mack's chair, at Mack's desk, while Connie politely sat hugging his knees on a settee.

There was a telephone call for Newsom, which he took outside the office. Mack regained his chair and desk for a few minutes. Then Newsom returned, and Mack went back to the settee. They struck a bargain, and Mack told the press about it, adding the news that, because of wartime restrictions, the team would train that spring in Frederick, Maryland. "Ah, yes," interrupted Newsom. "All the team except me. I will train at home in Hartsville, and will see you all next April. Ain't that right, Bobo?" he said to Mack. "Why—uh—yes, I guess that's right," said Connie, who had never heard of the plan before. Newsom trained at home for the next two springs, on a Philadelphia expense account.

There was not only some baseball left in Newsom's system as he neared 40, there was one more pennant, and one more World Series. In midseason of 1947, Griffith, having briefly repossessed Bobo, sold him at the usual smart profit to the Yankees, who were struggling toward the flag. Newsom won seven games from there on in. He was instrumental in the push that won the pennant. But Bobo, though he often pined from a distance for service with rich teams, was always stifled by the atmosphere of wealth when he reached it. The Yanks were too stuffy for him. He was too gay and uncouth for the Yanks. In one game with Chicago, batting against a pitcher named Joe Haynes, Newsom tapped the ball back to the box. He refused to run to first base. Haynes refused to throw the ball to first. Bobo went back to the dugout, as though to take a drink from the water cooler. From there, he made a sudden, sneaky, elephantine dash toward the base. It was almost successful, because Rudy York, the first baseman, had wandered off the bag, and Haynes had to wait till York got back there to throw Newsom out. The fans giggled. The Yankees looked down their noses. "Fun in the bush, hey?" Bobo heard one of them, who shall be nameless, say to another. The remark mortified him, for he had been pitching in that league when the speaker was, as Bobo pointed out, chin-high to a hog.

He was not surprised when the Yanks voted him only three quarters of a share of the players' World Series pool. At the jeweler's, ordering his Series ring, he said: "Just make it three-quarter size, Bobo. That's my measure in this town." In two Series appearances against Brooklyn, one as a starter, one in relief, Bobo failed to last as much as three quarters of a game. But, by the most likely of the many estimates of his age, he was more than 40 years old by then. He could still win a pennant for a good team, but he could no longer follow it up by dominating the World Series too. Some of the spring was gone from the tall, steamboat-captain's figure and from the buggy-whip arm.

This was the period during which Connie Mack carried a bodyguard to keep him from signing Newsom again. Once, also, around this time, Bobo approached Bucky Harris in spring training for another chance with the Washington team. Harris decided to give him a tryout. In batting practice, Bobo's first pitch broke a finger on the meat hand of Mickey Grasso, the Nats' best catcher. Harris, looking on, reached for a bat. Newsom observed the gesture from a corner of one eye. He dropped his glove where he stood and began to make for a gate in the fence at a fast walk. He was running by the time he reached the gate, and he kept running till he found a cab that took him out of town.

Yet Bobo still had a few big-league wins left in the arm. He won a game here and a game there for the Nats and the Athletics (they could not resist him—and they knew him better than most) in 1952, and a couple for Mr. Mack again in 1953.

There is this to be said. Perhaps there was never a time in his life, old or young, with the kind of arm he had, and the big, loose, easy body, and the whimsical but cunning baseball brain, when Louis Norman Newsom of Hartsville, S.C., could not have pitched and won a ball game at the highest baseball level.

As they used to say, he was a throwback. He was at least 45, probably, when he stopped pitching. And when Bobo stopped pitching, it was by his own choice. Late in the season of 1953, he worked a game for the A's and Mr. Mack against Detroit. He went all the way and won. There was a reason for his stopping right there. It was his 200th victory in the American League. If you add his record with Brooklyn, Bobo won 211 big-league games in all. But the American League was the real big league to him, his home and his favorite stage as an actor, and when he reached the total of 200 there, he was satisfied.

"I guess that's all, Bo," he told Connie. "Besides, you can't afford to pay Bobo no more."

"Maybe not, Newsom," said Mack, who had nearly reached the end of his own span by then. "By the way, you told me you had that Detroit shortstop's weakness figured out, and I noticed he got a couple of two-base hits. What's his weakness?"

"Two-base hits, Bobo," said Newsom.

In the few years since then, Bobo has served as a counselor on barbecue in a Florida eating house, and as a baseball broadcaster in Baltimore. Those were always his specialties: food, baseball, and the human voice.

FICTION

WELL, maybe they didn't have ground-rule doubles in those days, but that's not going to affect your enjoyment any as you read one of the finest and funniest baseball tales ever. There are players just like Speed Parker in baseball today . . . more than three quarters of a century after this story was written!

Horseshoes

RING LARDNER

THE SERIES ENDED Tuesday, but I had stayed in Philadelphia an extra day on the chance of there being some follow-up stuff worth sending. Nothing had broken loose; so I filed some stuff about what the Athletics and Giants were going to do with their dough and then caught the eight o'clock train for Chicago.

Having passed up supper in order to get my story away and grab the train, I went to the buffet car right after I'd planted my grips. I sat down at one of the tables and ordered a sandwich. Four salesmen were playing rum at the other table and all the chairs in the car were occupied; so it didn't surprise me when somebody flopped down in the seat opposite me.

I looked up from my paper and with a little thrill recognized my companion. Now I've been experting round the country with ballplayers so much that it doesn't usually excite me to meet one face to face, even if he's a star. I can talk with Tyrus without getting all fussed up. But this particular player had jumped from obscurity to fame so suddenly and had played such an important though brief part in the recent argument between the Macks and McGraws that I couldn't help being a little awed by his proximity.

It was none other than Grimes, the utility outfielder Connie had been forced to use in the last game because of the injury to Joyce—Grimes, whose miraculous catch in the eleventh inning had robbed Parker of a home run and the Giants of victory, and whose own homer—a fluky one—had given the Athletics another World's Championship.

I had met Grimes one day during the spring he was with the Cubs, but I knew he wouldn't remember me. A ballplayer never recalls a reporter's face on less than six introductions or his name on less than twenty. However, I resolved to speak to him and had just mustered sufficient courage to open a conversation when he saved me the trouble.

"Whose picture have they got there?" he asked, pointing to my paper.

"Speed Parker's," I replied.

"What do they say about him?" asked Grimes.

"I'll read it to you," I said.

" 'Speed Parker, McGraw's great third baseman, is ill in a local hospital with nervous prostration, the result of the strain of the World's Series, in which he played such a stellar role. Parker is in such a dangerous condition that no one is allowed to see him. Members of the New York team and fans from Gotham called at the hospital today, but were unable to gain admittance to his ward. Philadelphians hope he will recover speedily and will suffer no permanent ill effects from his sickness, for he won their admiration by his work in the series, though he was on a rival team. A lucky catch by Grimes, the Athletics' substitute outfielder, was all that prevented Parker from winning the title for New York. According to Manager

Mack, of the champions, the series would have been over in four games but for Parker's wonderful exhibition of nerve and——"

"That'll be a plenty," Grimes interrupted. "And that's just what you might expect from one o' them doughheaded reporters. If all the baseball writers was where they belonged they'd have to build an annex to Matteawan."

I kept my temper with very little effort—it takes more than a peevish ballplayer's remark to insult one of our fraternity; but I didn't exactly understand his peeve.

"Doesn't Parker deserve the bouquet?" I asked.

"Oh, they can boost him all they want to," said Grimes; "but when they call that catch lucky and don't mention the fact that Parker is the luckiest guy in the world, something must be wrong with 'em. Did you see the serious?"

"No," I lied glibly, hoping to draw from him the cause of his grouch.

"Well," he said, "you sure missed somethin'. They never was a serious like it before and they won't never be one again. It went the full seven games and every game was a bear. They was one big innin' every day and Parker was the big cheese in it. Just as Connie says, the Ath-a-letics would of cleaned 'em in four games but for Parker; but it wasn't because he's a great ballplayer—it was because he was born with a knife, fork and spoon in his mouth, and a rabbit's foot hung round his neck.

"You may not know it, but I'm Grimes, the guy that made the lucky catch. I'm the guy that won the serious with a hit—a home-run hit; and I'm here to tell you that if I'd had one tenth o' Parker's luck they'd of heard about me long before yesterday. They say my homer was lucky. Maybe it was; but, believe me, it was time things broke for me. They been breakin' for him all his life."

"Well," I said, "his luck must have gone back on him if he's in a hospital with nervous prostration."

"Nervous prostration nothin'," said Grimes. "He's in a hospital because his face is all out o' shape and he's ashamed to appear on the street. I don't usually do so much talkin' and I'm ravin' a little tonight because I've had a couple o' drinks; but——"

"Have another," said I, ringing for the waiter, "and talk some more."

"I made two hits yesterday," Grimes went on, "but the crowd only seen one. I busted up the game and the serious with the one they seen. The one they didn't see was the one I busted up a guy's map with—and Speed Parker was the guy. That's why he's in a hospital. He may be able to play ball next year; but I'll bet my share o' the dough that McGraw won't reco'nize him when he shows up at Marlin in the spring."

"When did this come off?" I asked. "And why?"

"It come off outside the clubhouse after yesterday's battle," he said; "and I hit him because he called me a name—a name I won't stand for from him."

"What did he call you?" I queried, expecting to hear one of the delicate epithets usually applied by conquered to conqueror on the diamond.

" 'Horseshoes!' " was Grimes' amazing reply.

"But, good Lord!" I remonstrated, "I've heard of ballplayers calling each other that, and Lucky Stiff, and Fourleaf Clover, ever since I was a foot high, and I never knew them to start fights about it."

"Well," said Grimes, "I might as well give you all the dope; and then if you don't think I was justified I'll pay your fare from here to wherever you're goin'. I don't want you to think I'm kickin' about trifles—or that I'm kickin' at all, for that matter. I just want to prove to you that he didn't have no license to pull that Horseshoes stuff on me and that I only give him what was comin' to him."

"Go ahead and shoot," said I.

"Give us some more o' the same," said Grimes to the passing waiter. And then he told me about it.

Maybe you've heard that me and Speed Parker was raised in the same town—Ishpeming, Michigan. We was kids together, and though he done all the devilment I got all the lickin's. When we was about twelve years old Speed throwed a rotten egg at the teacher and I got expelled. That made me sick o' schools and I wouldn't never go to one again, though my ol' man beat me up and the truant officers threatened to have me hung.

Well, while Speed was learnin' what was the principal products o' New Hampshire and Texas I was workin' round the freighthouse and drivin' a dray.

We'd both been playin' ball all our lives; and when the town organized a semipro club we got jobs with it. We was to draw two bucks apiece for each game and they played every Sunday. We played four games before we got our first pay. They was a hole in my pants pocket as big as the home plate, but I forgot about it and put the dough in there. It wasn't there when I got home. Speed didn't have no hole in his pocket—you can bet on that! Afterward the club hired a good outfielder and I was canned. They was huntin' for another third baseman too; but, o' course, they didn't find none and Speed held his job.

The next year they started the Northern Peninsula League. We landed with the home team. The league opened in May and blowed up the third week in June. They paid off all the outsiders first and then had just money enough left to settle with one of us two Ishpeming guys. The night they done the payin' I was out to my uncle's farm, so they settled with Speed and told me I'd have to wait for mine. I'm still waitin'!

Gene Higgins, who was manager o' the Battle Creek Club, lived in Houghton, and that winter we goes over and strikes him for a job. He give it to us and we busted in together two years ago last spring.

I had a good year down there. I hit over .300 and stole all the bases in sight. Speed got along good too, and they was several big-league scouts lookin' us over. The Chicago Cubs bought Speed outright and four clubs put in a draft for me. Three of 'em—Cleveland and the New York Giants and the Boston Nationals—needed outfielders bad, and it would of been a pipe for me to of made good with any of 'em. But who do you think got me? The same Chicago Cubs; and the only outfielders they had at that time was Schulte and Leach and Good and Williams and Stewart, and one or two others.

Well, I didn't figure I was any worse off than Speed. The Cubs had Zimmerman at third base and it didn't look like they was any danger of a busher beatin' him out; but Zimmerman goes and breaks his leg the second day o' the season—that's a year ago last April—and Speed jumps right in as a regular. Do you think anything like that could happen to Schulte or Leach, or any o' them outfielders? No, sir! I wore out my uniform slidin' up and down the bench and wonderin' whether they'd ship me to Fort Worth or Siberia.

Now I want to tell you about the miserable luck Speed had right off the reel. We was playin' at St. Louis. They had a one-run lead in the eighth, when their pitcher walked Speed with one out. Saier hits a high fly to center and Parker starts with the crack o' the bat. Both coachers was yellin' at him to go back, but he thought they was two out and he was clear round to third base when the ball come down. And Oakes muffs it! O' course he scored and the game was tied up.

Parker come in to the bench like he'd did something wonderful.

"Did you think they was two out?" ast Hank.

"No," says Speed, blushin'.

"Then what did you run for?" says Hank.

"I had a hunch he was goin' to drop the ball," says Speed; and Hank pretty near falls off the bench.

The next day he come up with one out and the sacks full, and the score tied in the sixth. He smashes one on the ground straight at Hauser and it looked like a cinch double play; but just as Hauser was goin' to grab it the ball hit a rough spot and hopped a mile over his head. It got between Oakes and Magee and went clear to the fence. Three guys scored and Speed pulled up at third. The papers come out and said the game was won by a three-bagger from the bat o' Parker, the Cubs' sensational kid third baseman. Gosh!

We go home to Chi and are havin' a hot battle with Pittsburgh. This time Speed's turn come when they was two on and two out, and Pittsburgh a run to the good—I think it was the eighth innin'. Cooper gives him a fast one and he hits it straight up in the air. O' course the runners started goin', but it looked hopeless because they wasn't no wind or high sky to bother anybody. Mowrey and Gibson both goes after the ball; and just as Mowrey was set for the catch Gibson bumps into him and they both fall down. Two runs scored and Speed got to second. Then what does he do but try to steal third—with two out too! And Gibson's peg pretty near hits the left field seats on the fly.

When Speed comes to the bench Hank says:

"If I was you I'd quit playin' ball and go to Monte Carlo."

"What for?" says Speed.

"You're so dam' lucky!" says Hank.

"So is Ty Cobb," says Speed. That's how he hated himself!

First trip to Cincy we run into a couple of old Ishpeming boys. They took us out one night, and about twelve o'clock I said we'd have to go back to the hotel or we'd get fined. Speed said I had cold feet and he stuck with the boys. I went back alone and Hank caught me comin' in and put a fifty-dollar plaster on me. Speed stayed out all night long and Hank never knowed it. I says to myself: "Wait till he gets out there and tries to play ball without no sleep!" But the game that day was called off on account o' rain. Can you beat it?

I remember what he got away with the next afternoon the same as though it happened yesterday. In the second innin' they walked him with nobody down, and he took a big lead off first base like he always does. Benton throwed over there three or four times to scare him back, and the last time he throwed, Hobby hid the ball. The coacher seen it and told Speed to hold the bag; but he didn't pay no attention. He started leadin' right off again and Hobby tried to tag him, but the ball slipped out of his hand and rolled about a yard away. Parker had plenty o' time to get back; but, instead o' that, he starts for second. Hobby picked up the ball and shot it down to Groh—and Groh made a square muff.

Parker slides into the bag safe and then gets up and throws out his chest like he'd made the greatest play ever. When the ball's throwed back to Benton, Speed leads off about thirty foot and stands there in a trance. Clarke signs for a pitch-out and pegs down to second to nip him. He was caught flatfooted—that is, he would of been with a decent throw; but Clarke's peg went pretty near to Latonia. Speed scored and strutted over to receive our hearty congratulations. Some o' the boys was laughin' and he thought they was laughin' with him instead of at him.

It was in the ninth, though, that he got by with one o' the worst I ever seen. The Reds was a run behind and Marsans was on third base with two out. Hobby, I think it was, hit one on the ground right at Speed and he picked it up clean. The crowd all got up and started for the exits. Marsans run toward the plate in the faint hope that the peg to first would be wild. All of a sudden the boys on the Cincy bench begun yellin' at him to slide, and he done so. He was way past the plate when Speed's throw got to Archer. The bonehead had shot the ball home instead o' to first base, thinkin' they was only one down. We was all crazy, believin' his nut play had let 'em tie it up; but he comes tearin' in, tellin' Archer to tag Marsans. So Jim walks over and tags the Cuban, who was brushin' off his uniform.

"You're out!" says Klem. "You never touched the plate."

I guess Marsans knowed the umps was right because he didn't make much of a holler. But Speed sure got a pannin' in the clubhouse.

"I suppose you knowed he was goin' to miss the plate?" says Hank sarcastic as he could.

Everybody on the club roasted him, but it didn't do no good.

Well, you know what happened to me. I only got into one game with the Cubs—one afternoon when Leach was sick. We was playin' the Boston bunch and Tyler was workin' against us. I always had trouble with lefthanders and this was one of his good days. I couldn't see what he throwed up there. I got one foul durin' the afternoon's entertainment; and the wind was blowin' a hundred-mile gale, so that the best outfielder in the world couldn't judge a fly ball. That Boston bunch must of hit fifty of 'em and they all come to my field.

If I caught any I've forgot about it. Couple o' days after that I got notice o' my release to Indianapolis.

Parker kept right on all season doin' the blamedest things you ever heard of and gettin' by with 'em. One o' the boys told me about it later. If they was playin' a double-header in St. Louis, with the thermometer at 130 degrees, he'd get put out by the umps in the first innin' o' the first game. If he started to steal the catcher'd drop the pitch or somebody'd muff the throw. If he hit a pop fly the sun'd get in somebody's eyes. If he took a swell third strike with the bases full the umps would call it a ball. If he cut first base by twenty feet the umps would be readin' the mornin' paper.

Zimmerman's leg mended, so that he was all right by June; and then Saier got sick and they tried Speed at first base. He'd never saw the bag before; but things kept on breakin' for him and he played it like a house afire. The Cubs copped the pennant and Speed got in on the big dough, besides playin' a whale of a game through the whole serious.

Speed and me both went back to Ishpeming to spend the winter—though the Lord knows it ain't no winter resort. Our homes was there; and besides, in my case, they was a certain girl livin' in the old burg.

Parker, o' course, was the hero and the swell guy when we got home. He'd been in the World's Serious and had plenty o' dough in his kick. I come home with nothin' but my suitcase and a hard-luck story, which I kept to myself. I hadn't even went good enough in Indianapolis to be sure of a job there again.

That fall—last fall—an uncle o' Speed's died over in the Soo and left him ten thousand bucks. I had an uncle down in the Lower Peninsula who was worth five times that much—but he had good health!

This girl I spoke about was the prettiest thing I ever see. I'd went with her in the old days, and when I blew back I found she was still strong for me. They wasn't a great deal o' variety in Ishpeming for a girl to pick from. Her and I went to the dance every Saturday night and to church Sunday nights. I called on her Wednesday evenin's, besides takin' her to all the shows that come along—rotten as the most o' them was.

I never knowed Speed was makin' a play for this doll till along last Feb'uary. The minute I seen what was up I got busy. I took her out sleigh-ridin' and kept her out in the cold till she'd promised to marry me. We set the date for this fall—I figured I'd know better where I was at by that time.

Well, we didn't make no secret o' bein' engaged; down in the poolroom one night Speed come up and congratulated me. He says:

"You got a swell girl, Dick! I wouldn't mind bein' in your place. You're mighty lucky to cop her out—you old Horseshoes, you!"

"Horseshoes!" I says. "You got a fine license to call anybody Horseshoes! I suppose you ain't never had no luck?"

"Not like you," he says.

I was feelin' too good about grabbin' the girl to get sore at the time, but when I got to thinkin' about it a few minutes afterward it made me mad clear through. What right did that bird have to talk about me bein' lucky?

Speed was playin' freeze-out at a table near the door, and when I started home some o' the boys with him says:

"Good night, Dick."

I said good night and then Speed looked up.

"Good night, Horseshoes!" he says.

That got my nanny this time.

"Shut up, you lucky stiff!" I says. "If you wasn't so dam' lucky you'd be sweepin' the streets." Then I walks on out.

I was too busy with the girl to see much o' Speed after that. He left home about the middle o' the month to go to Tampa with the Cubs. I got notice from Indianapolis that I was sold to Baltimore. I didn't care much about goin' there and I wasn't anxious to leave home under the circumstances, so I didn't report till late.

When I read in the papers along in April that Speed had been traded to Boston for a couple o' pitchers I thought: "Gee! He must of lost his rabbit's foot!" Because, even if the Cubs didn't cop again, they'd have a city serious with the White Sox and get a bunch o' dough that way. And they wasn't no chance in the world for the Boston club to get nothin' but their salaries.

It wasn't another month, though, till Shafer, o' the Giants, quit baseball and McGraw was up against it for a third baseman. Next thing I knowed Speed was traded to New York and was with another winner—for they never was out o' first place all season.

I was gettin' along all right at Baltimore and Dunnie liked me; so I felt like I had somethin' more than just a one-year job—somethin'

I could get married on. It was all framed that the weddin' was comin' off as soon as this season was over; so you can believe I was pullin' for October to hurry up and come.

One day in August, two months ago, Dunnie come in the clubhouse and handed me the news.

"Rube Oldring's busted his leg," he says, "and he's out for the rest o' the season. Connie's got a youngster named Joyce that he can stick in there, but he's got to have an extra outfielder. He's made me a good proposition for you and I'm goin' to let you go. It'll be pretty soft for you, because they got the pennant cinched and they'll cut you in on the big money."

"Yes," I says; "and when they're through with me they'll ship me to Hellangone, and I'll be draggin' down about seventy-five bucks a month next year."

"Nothin' like that," says Dunnie. "If he don't want you next season he's got to ask for waivers; and if you get out o' the big league you come right back here. That's all framed."

So that's how I come to get with the Ath-a-letics. Connie give me a nice, comf'table seat in one corner o' the bench and I had the pleasure o' watchin' a real ball club perform once every afternoon and sometimes twice.

Connie told me that as soon as they had the flag cinched he was goin' to lay off some o' his regulars and I'd get a chance to play.

Well, they cinched it the fourth day o' September and our next engagement was with Washin'ton on Labor Day. We had two games and I was in both of 'em. And I broke in with my usual lovely luck, because the pitchers I was ast to face was Boehling, a nasty left-hander, and this guy Johnson.

The mornin' game was Boehling's and he wasn't no worse than some o' the rest of his kind. I only whiffed once and would of had a triple if Milan hadn't run from here to New Orleans and stole one off me.

I'm not boastin' about my first experience with Johnson though. They can't never tell me he throws them balls with his arm. He's got a gun concealed about his person and he shoots 'em up there. I was leadin' off in Murphy's place and the game was a little delayed in startin', because I'd watched the big guy warm up and wasn't in no hurry to get to that plate. Before I left the bench Connie says:

"Don't try to take no healthy swing. Just meet 'em and you'll get along better."

So I tried to just meet the first one he throwed; but when I stuck out my bat Henry was throwin' the pill back to Johnson. Then I thought: Maybe if I start swingin' now at the second one I'll hit the third one. So I let the second one come over and the ump guessed it was another strike, though I'll bet a thousand bucks he couldn't see it no more'n I could.

While Johnson was still windin' up to pitch again I started to swing—and the big cuss crosses me with a slow one. I lunged at it twice and missed it both times, and the force o' my wallop throwed me clean back to the bench. The Ath-a-letics was all laughin' at me and I laughed too, because I was glad that much of it was over.

McInnes gets a base hit off him in the second innin' and I ast him how he done it.

"He's a friend o' mine," says Jack, "and he lets up when he pitches to me."

I made up my mind right there that if I was goin' to be in the league next year I'd go out and visit Johnson this winter and get acquainted.

I wished before the day was over that I was hittin' in the catcher's place, because the fellers down near the tail-end of the battin' order only had to face him three times. He fanned me on three pitched balls again in the third, and when I come up in the sixth he scared me to death by pretty near beanin' me with the first one.

"Be careful!" says Henry. "He's gettin' pretty wild and he's liable to knock you away from your uniform."

"Don't he never curve one?" I ast.

"Sure!" says Henry. "Do you want to see his curve?"

"Yes," I says, knowin' the hook couldn't be no worse'n the fast one.

So he give me three hooks in succession and I missed 'em all; but I felt more comf'table than when I was duckin' his fast ball. In the ninth he hit my bat with a curve and the ball went on the ground to McBride. He booted it, but throwed me out easy—because I was so surprised at not havin' whiffed that I forgot to run!

Well, I went along like that for the rest o' the season, runnin' up against the best pitchers in the league and not exactly murderin' 'em. Everything I tried went wrong, and I was smart enough to know that if anything had depended on the games I wouldn't of been in there for two minutes. Joyce and Strunk and Murphy wasn't jealous o' me a bit; but they was glad to take turns restin', and I didn't care much how I went so long as I was sure of a job next year.

I'd wrote to the girl a couple o' times askin' her to set the exact date for our weddin'; but she hadn't paid no attention. She said she was glad I was with the Ath-a-letics, but she thought the Giants was goin' to beat us. I might of suspected from that that somethin' was wrong, because not even a girl would pick the Giants to trim that bunch of ourn. Finally, the day before the serious started, I sent her a kind o' sassy letter sayin' I guessed it was up to me to name the day, and askin' whether October twentieth was all right. I told her to wire me yes or no.

I'd been readin' the dope about Speed all season, and I knowed he'd had a whale of a year and that his luck was right with him; but I never dreamed a man could have the Lord on his side as strong as Speed did in that World's Serious! I might as well tell you all the dope, so long as you wasn't there.

The first game was on our grounds and Connie give us a talkin' to in the clubhouse beforehand.

"The shorter this serious is," he says, "the better for us. If it's a long serious we're goin' to have trouble, because McGraw's got five pitchers he can work and we've got about three; so I want you boys to go at 'em from the jump and play 'em off their feet. Don't take things easy, because it ain't goin' to be no snap. Just because we've licked 'em before ain't no sign we'll do it this time."

Then he calls me to one side and ast me what I knowed about Parker.

"You was with the Cubs when he was, wasn't you?" he says.

"Yes," I says; "and he's the luckiest stiff you ever seen! If he got stewed and fell in the gutter he'd catch a fish."

"I don't like to hear a good ballplayer called lucky," says Connie. "He must have a lot of ability or McGraw wouldn't use him regular. And he's been hittin' about .340 and played a bang-up game at third base. That can't be all luck."

"Wait till you see him," I says; "and if you don't say he's the luckiest guy in the world you can sell me to the Boston Bloomer Girls. He's so lucky," I says, "that if they traded him to the St. Louis Browns they'd have the pennant clinched by the Fourth o' July."

And I'll bet Connie was willin' to agree with me before it was over.

Well, the Chief worked against the Big Rube in that game. We beat 'em, but they give us a battle and it was Parker that made it close. We'd gone along nothin' and nothin' till the seventh, and then Rube walks Collins and Baker lifts one over that little old wall. You'd think by this time them New York pitchers would know better than to give that guy anything he can hit.

In their part o' the ninth the Chief still had 'em shut out and two down, and the crowd was goin' home; but Doyle gets hit in the sleeve with a pitched ball and it's Speed's turn. He hits a foul pretty near straight up, but Schang misjudges it. Then he lifts another one and this time McInnes drops it. He'd ought to of been out twice. The Chief tries to make him hit at a bad one then, because he'd got him two strikes and nothin'. He hit at it all right—kissed it for three bases between Strunk and Joyce! And it was a wild pitch that he hit. Doyle scores, o' course, and the bugs suddenly decide not to go home just yet. I fully expected to see him steal home and get away with it, but Murray cut into the first ball and lined out to Barry.

Plank beat Matty two to one the next day in New York, and again Speed and his rabbit's foot give us an awful argument. Matty wasn't so good as usual and we really ought to of beat him bad. Two different times Strunk was on second waitin' for any kind o' wallop, and both times Barry cracked 'em down the third-base line like a shot. Speed stopped the first one with his stomach and extricated the pill just in time to nail Barry at first base and retire the side. The next time he throwed his glove in front of his face in self defense and the ball stuck in it.

In the sixth innin' Schang was on third base and Plank on first, and two down, and Murphy combed an awful one to Speed's left. He didn't have time to stoop over and he just stuck out his foot. The ball hit it and caromed in two hops right into Doyle's hands on second base before Plank got there. Then in the seventh Speed bunts one and Baker trips and falls goin' after it or he'd of threw him out a mile. They was two gone; so Speed steals second, and, o' course, Schang has to make a bad peg right at that time and lets him go to third. Then Collins boots one on Murray and they've got a run. But it didn't do 'em no good, because Collins and Baker and McInnes come up in the ninth and walloped 'em where Parker couldn't reach 'em.

Comin' back to Philly on the train that night, I says to Connie:

"What do you think o' that Parker bird now?"

"He's lucky, all right," says Connie smilin'; "but we won't hold it against him if he don't beat us with it."

"It ain't too late," I says. "He ain't pulled his real stuff yet."

The whole bunch was talkin' about him and his luck, and sayin' it was about time for things to break against him. I warned 'em that they wasn't no chance—that it was permanent with him.

Bush and Tesreau hooked up next day and neither o' them had much stuff. Everybody was hittin' and it looked like anybody's game right up to the ninth. Speed had got on every time he come up—the wind blowin' his fly balls away from the outfielders and the infielders bootin' when he hit 'em on the ground.

When the ninth started the score was seven apiece. Connie and McGraw both had their whole pitchin' staffs warmin' up. The crowd was wild, because they'd been all kinds of action. They wasn't no danger of anybody's leavin' their seats before this game was over.

Well, Bescher is walked to start with and Connie's about ready to give Bush the hook; but Doyle pops out tryin' to bunt. Then Speed gets two strikes and two balls, and it looked to me like the next one was right over the heart; but Connolly calls it a ball and gives him another chance. He whales the groove ball to the fence in left center and gets round to third on it, while Bescher scores. Right then Bush comes out and the Chief goes in. He whiffs Murray and has two strikes on Merkle when Speed makes a break for home—and, o' course, that was the one ball Schang dropped in the whole serious!

They had a two-run lead on us then and it looked like a cinch for them to hold it, because the minute Tesreau showed a sign o' weakenin' McGraw was sure to holler for Matty or the Rube. But you know how quick that bunch of ourn can make a two-run lead look sick. Before McGraw could get Jeff out o' there we had two on the bases.

Then Rube comes in and fills 'em up by walkin' Joyce. It was Eddie's turn to wallop and if he didn't do nothin' we had Baker comin' up next. This time Collins saved Baker the trouble and whanged one clear to the woods. Everybody scored but him—and he could of, too, if it'd been necessary.

In the clubhouse the boys naturally felt pretty good. We'd copped three in a row and it looked like we'd make it four straight, because we had the Chief to send back at 'em the followin' day.

"Your friend Parker is lucky," the boys says to me, "but it don't look like he could stop us now."

I felt the same way and was consultin' the timetables to see whether I could get a train out o' New York for the West next evenin'. But do you think Speed's luck was ready to quit? Not yet! And it's a wonder we didn't all go nuts durin' the next few days. If words could kill, Speed would of died a thousand times. And I wish he had!

They wasn't no record-breakin' crowd out when we got to the Polo Grounds. I guess the New York bugs was pretty well discouraged and the bettin' was eight to five that we'd cop that battle and finish it. The Chief was the only guy that warmed up for us and McGraw didn't have no choice but to use Matty, with the whole thing dependin' on this game.

They went along like the two swell pitchers they was till Speed's innin', which in this battle was the eighth. Nobody scored, and it didn't look like they was ever goin' to till Murphy starts off that round with a perfect bunt and Joyce sacrifices him to second. All Matty had to do then was to get rid o' Collins and Baker—and that's about as easy as sellin' silk socks to an Eskimo.

He didn't give Eddie nothin' he wanted to hit, though; and finally he slaps one on the ground to Doyle. Larry made the play to first base and Murphy moved to third. We all figured Matty'd walk Baker then, and he done it. Connie sends Baker down to second on the first pitch to McInnes, but Meyers don't pay no attention to him—they was playin' for McInnes and wasn't takin' no chances o' throwin' the ball away.

Well, the count goes to three and two on McInnes and Matty comes with a curve—he's got some curve too; but Jack happened to meet it and—Blooie! Down the left foul line where he always hits! I never seen a ball hit so hard in my life. No infielder in the world could of stopped it. But I'll give you a thousand bucks if that ball didn't go kerplunk right into the third bag and stop as dead as George Washington! It was child's play for Speed to pick it up and heave it over to Merkle before Jack got there. If anybody else had been playin' third base the bag would of ducked out o' the way o' that wallop; but even the bases themselves was helpin' him out.

The two runs we ought to of had on Jack's smash would of been just enough to beat 'em, because they got the only run o' the game in their half—or, I should say, the Lord give it to 'em.

Doyle'd been throwed out and up come Parker, smilin'. The minute I seen him smile I felt like somethin' was comin' off and I made the remark on the bench.

Well, the Chief pitched one right at him and he tried to duck. The ball hit his bat and went on a line between Jack and Eddie. Speed didn't know he'd hit it till the guys on the bench wised him up. Then he just had time to get to first base. They tried the hit-and-run on the second ball and Murray lifts a high fly that Murphy didn't have to move for. Collins pulled the old bluff about the ball bein' on the ground and Barry yells, "Go on! Go on!" like he was the coacher. Speed fell for it and didn't know where the ball was no more'n a rabbit; he just run his fool head off and we was gettin' all ready to laugh when the ball come down and Murphy dropped it!

If Parker had stuck near first base, like he ought to of done, he couldn't of got no farther'n second; but with the start he got he was pretty near third when Murphy made the muff, and it was a cinch for him to score. The next two guys was easy outs; so they wouldn't of had a run except for Speed's boner. We couldn't do nothin' in the ninth and we was licked.

Well, that was a tough one to lose; but we figured that Matty was through and we'd wind it up the next day, as we had Plank ready to send back at 'em. We wasn't afraid o' the Rube, because he hadn't never bothered Collins and Baker much.

The two lefthanders come together just like everybody'd doped it and it was about even up to the eighth. Plank had been goin' great and, though the score was two and two, they'd got their two on boots and we'd hit ourn in. We went after Rube in our part o' the eighth and knocked him out. Demaree stopped us after we'd scored two more.

"It's all over but the shoutin'!" says Davis on the bench.

"Yes," I says, "unless that seventh son of a seventh son gets up there again."

He did, and he come up after they'd filled the bases with a boot, a base hit and a walk with two out. I says to Davis:

"If I was Plank I'd pass him and give 'em one run."

"That wouldn't be no baseball," says Davis—"not with Murray comin' up."

Well, it mayn't of been no baseball, but it couldn't of turned out worse if they'd did it that way. Speed took a healthy at the first ball; but it was a hook and he caught it on the handle, right up near his hands. It started outside the first-base line like a foul and then changed its mind and rolled in. Schang run away from the plate, because it looked like it was up to him to make the play. He picked the ball up and had to make the peg in a hurry.

His throw hit Speed right on top o' the head and bounded off like it had struck a cement sidewalk. It went clear over to the seats and before McInnes could get it three guys had scored and Speed was on third base. He was left there, but that didn't make no difference. We was licked again and for the first time the gang really begun to get scared.

We went over to New York Sunday afternoon and we didn't do no singin' on the way. Some o' the fellars tried to laugh, but it hurt 'em. Connie sent us to bed early, but I don't believe none o' the bunch got much sleep—I know I didn't; I was worryin' too much about the serious and also about the girl, who hadn't sent me no telegram like I'd ast her to. Monday mornin' I wired her askin' what was the matter and tellin' her I was gettin' tired of her foolishness. O' course I didn't make it so strong as that—but the telegram cost me a dollar and forty cents.

Connie had the choice o' two pitchers for the sixth game. He could use Bush, who'd been slammed round pretty hard the last time out, or the Chief, who'd only had two days' rest. The rest of 'em—outside o' Plank—had a epidemic o' sore arms. Connie finally picked Bush, so's he could have the Chief in reserve in case we had to play a seventh game. McGraw started Big Jeff and we went at it.

It wasn't like the last time these two guys had hooked up. This time they both had somethin', and for eight innin's runs was as scarce as Chinese policemen. They'd been chances to score on both sides, but the big guy and Bush was both tight in the pinches. The crowd was plumb nuts and yelled like Indians every time a fly ball was caught or a strike called. They'd of got their money's worth if they hadn't been no ninth; but, believe me, that was some round!

They was one out when Barry hit one through the box for a base. Schang walked, and it was Bush's turn. Connie told him to bunt, but he whiffed in the attempt. Then Murphy comes up and walks—and the bases are choked. Young Joyce had been pie for Tesreau all day or else McGraw might of changed pitchers right there. Anyway he left Big Jeff in and he beaned Joyce with a fast one. It sounded like a tire blowin' out. Joyce falls over in a heap and we chase out there, thinkin' he's dead; but he ain't, and pretty soon he gets up and walks down to first base. Tesreau had forced in a run and again we begun to count the winner's end. Matty comes in to prevent further damage and Collins flies the side out.

"Hold 'em now! Work hard!" we says to young Bush, and he walks out there just as cool as though he was goin' to hit fungoes.

McGraw sends up a pinch hitter for Matty and Bush whiffed him.

Then Bescher flied out. I was prayin' that Doyle would end it, because Speed's turn come after his'n; so I pretty near fell dead when Larry hit safe.

Speed had his old smile and even more chest than usual when he come up there, swingin' five or six bats. He didn't wait for Doyle to try and steal, or nothin'. He lit into the first ball, though Bush was tryin' to waste it. I seen the ball go high in the air toward left field, and then I picked up my glove and got ready to beat it for the gate. But when I looked out to see if Joyce was set, what do you think I seen? He was lyin' flat on the ground! That blow on the head had got him just as Bush was pitchin' to Speed. He'd flopped over and didn't no more know what was goin' on than if he'd croaked.

Well, everybody else seen it at the same time, but it was too late. Strunk made a run for the ball, but they wasn't no chance for him to get near it. It hit the ground about ten feet back o' where Joyce was lyin' and bounded way over to the end o' the foul line. You don't have to be told that Doyle and Parker both scored and the serious was tied up.

We carried Joyce to the clubhouse and after a while he come to. He cried when he found out what had happened. We cheered him up all we could, but he was a pretty sick guy. The trainer said he'd be all right, though, for the final game.

They tossed up a coin to see where they'd play the seventh battle and our club won the toss; so we went back to Philly that night and cussed Parker clear across New Jersey. I was so sore I kicked the stuffin' out o' my seat.

You probably heard about the excitement in the burg yesterday mornin'. The demand for tickets was somethin' fierce and some of 'em sold for as high as twenty-five bucks apiece. Our club hadn't been lookin' for no seventh game and they was some tall hustlin' done round that old ball park.

I started out to the grounds early and bought some New York papers to read on the car. They was a big story that Speed Parker, the Giants' hero, was goin' to be married a week after the end o' the serious. It didn't give the name o' the girl, sayin' Speed had refused to tell it. I figured she must be some dame he'd met round the circuit somewheres.

They was another story by one o' them smart baseball reporters sayin' that Parker, on his way up to the plate, had saw that Joyce was about ready to faint and had hit the fly ball to left field on purpose. Can you beat it?

I was goin' to show that to the boys in the clubhouse, but the minute I blowed in there I got some news that made me forget about everything else. Joyce was very sick and they'd took him to a hospital. It was up to me to play!

Connie come over and ast me whether I'd ever hit against Matty. I told him I hadn't, but I'd saw enough of him to know he wasn't no worse'n Johnson. He told me he was goin' to let me hit second—in Joyce's place—because he didn't want to bust up the rest of his combination. He also told me to take my orders from Strunk about where to play for the batters.

"Where shall I play for Parker?" I says, tryin' to joke and pretend I wasn't scared to death.

"I wisht I could tell you," says Connie. "I guess the only thing to do when he comes up is to get down on your knees and pray."

The rest o' the bunch slapped me on the back and give me all the encouragement they could. The place was jammed when we went out on the field. They may of been bigger crowds before, but they never was packed together so tight. I doubt whether they was even room enough left for Falkenberg to sit down.

The afternoon papers had printed the stuff about Joyce bein' out of it, so the bugs was wise that I was goin' to play. They watched me pretty close in battin' practice and give me a hand whenever I managed to hit one hard. When I was out catchin' fungoes the guys in the bleachers cheered me and told me they was with me; but I don't mind tellin' you that I was as nervous as a bride.

They wasn't no need for the announcers to tip the crowd off to the pitchers. Everybody in the United States and Cuba knowed that the Chief'd work for us and Matty for them. The Chief didn't have no trouble with 'em in the first innin'. Even from where I stood I could see that he had a lot o' stuff. Bescher and Doyle popped out and Speed whiffed.

Well, I started out makin' good, with reverse English, in our part. Fletcher booted Murphy's ground ball and I was sent up to sacrifice. I done a complete job of it—sacrificin' not only myself but Murphy with a pop fly that Matty didn't have to move for. That spoiled whatever chance we had o' gettin' the jump on 'em; but the boys didn't bawl me for it.

"That's all right, old boy. You're all right!" they said on the bench—if they'd had a gun they'd of shot me.

I didn't drop no fly balls in the first six innin's—because none was hit out my way. The Chief was so good that they wasn't hittin' nothing out o' the infield. And we wasn't doin' nothin' with Matty, either. I led off in the fourth and fouled the first one. I didn't molest the other two. But if Connie and the gang talked about me they done it internally. I come up again—with Murphy on third base and two gone in the sixth, and done my little whiffin' specialty. And still the only people that panned me was the thirty thousand that had paid for the privilege!

My first fieldin' chance come in the seventh. You'd of thought that I'd of had my nerve back by that time; but I was just as scared as though I'd never saw a crowd before. It was just as well that they was two out when Merkle hit one to me. I staggered under it and finally it hit me on the shoulder. Merkle got to second, but the Chief whiffed the next guy. I was gave some cross looks on the bench and I shouldn't of blamed the fellers if they'd cut loose with some language; but they didn't.

They's no use in me tellin' you about none o' the rest of it—except what happened just before the start o' the eleventh and durin' that innin', which was sure the big one o' yesterday's pastime—both for Speed and yours sincerely.

The scoreboard was still a row o' ciphers and Speed'd had only a fair amount o' luck. He'd made a scratch base hit and robbed our bunch of a couple o' real ones with impossible stops.

When Schang flied out and wound up our tenth I was leanin' against the end of our bench. I heard my name spoke, and I turned round and seen a boy at the door.

"Right here!" I says; and he give me a telegram.

"Better not open it till after the game," says Connie.

"Oh, no; it ain't no bad news," I said, for I figured it was an answer from the girl. So I opened it up and read it on the way to my position. It said:

"Forgive me, Dick—and forgive Speed too. Letter follows."

Well, sir, I ain't no baby, but for a minute I just wanted to sit down and bawl. And then, all of a sudden, I got so mad I couldn't see. I run right into Baker as he was pickin' up his glove. Then I give him a shove and called him some name, and him and Barry both looked at me like I was crazy—and I was. When I got out in left field

I stepped on my own foot and spiked it. I just had to hurt somebody.

As I remember it the Chief fanned the first two of 'em. Then Doyle catches one just right and lams it up against the fence back o' Murphy. The ball caromed round some and Doyle got all the way to third base. Next thing I seen was Speed struttin' up to the plate. I run clear in from my position.

"Kill him!" I says to the Chief. "Hit him in the head and kill him and I'll go to jail for it!"

"Are you off your nut?" says the Chief. "Go out there and play ball—and quit ravin'."

Barry and Baker led me away and give me a shove out toward left. Then I heard the crack o' the bat and I seen the ball comin' a mile a minute. It was headed between Strunk and I and looked like it would go out o' the park. I don't remember runnin' or nothin' about it till I run into the concrete wall head first. They told me afterward and all the papers said that it was the greatest catch ever seen. And I never knowed I'd caught the ball!

Some o' the managers have said my head was pretty hard, but it wasn't as hard as that concrete. I was pretty near out, but they tell me I walked to the bench like I wasn't hurt at all. They also tell me that the crowd was a bunch o' ravin' maniacs and was throwin' money at me. I guess the ground-keeper'll get it.

The boys on the bench was all talkin' at once and slappin' me on the back, but I didn't know what it was about. Somebody told me pretty soon that it was my turn to hit and I picked up the first bat I come to and starts for the plate. McInnes come runnin' after me and ast me whether I didn't want my own bat. I cussed him and told him to mind his own business.

I didn't know it at the time, but I found out afterward that they was two out. The bases was empty. I'll tell you just what I had in my mind: I wasn't thinkin' about the ball game; I was determined that I was goin' to get to third base and give that guy my spikes. If I didn't hit one worth three bases, or if I didn't hit one at all, I was goin' to run till I got round to where Speed was, and then slide into him and cut him to pieces!

Right now I can't tell you whether I hit a fast ball, or a slow ball, or a hook, or a fader—but I hit somethin'. It went over Bescher's head like a shot and then took a crazy bound. It must of struck a rock or a pop bottle, because it hopped clear over the fence and landed in the bleachers.

Mind you, I learned this afterward. At the time I just knowed I'd hit one somewheres and I starts round the bases. I speeded up when I got near third and took a runnin' jump at a guy I thought was Parker. I missed him and sprawled all over the bag. Then, all of a sudden, I come to my senses. All the Ath-a-letics was out there to run home with me and it was one o' them I'd tried to cut. Speed had left the field. The boys picked me up and seen to it that I went on and touched the plate. Then I was carried into the clubhouse by the crazy bugs.

Well, they had a celebration in there and it was a long time before I got a chance to change my clothes. The boys made a big fuss over me. They told me they'd intended to give me five hundred bucks for my divvy, but now I was goin' to get a full share.

"Parker ain't the only lucky guy!" says one of 'em. "But even if that ball hadn't of took that crazy hop you'd of had a triple."

A triple! That's just what I'd wanted; and he called me lucky for not gettin' it!

The Giants was dressin' in the other part o' the clubhouse, and when I finally come out there was Speed, standin' waitin' for some o' the others. He seen me comin' and he smiled. "Hello, Horseshoes!" he says.

He won't smile no more for a while—it'll hurt too much. And if any girl wants him when she sees him now—with his nose over shakin' hands with his ear, and his jaw a couple o' feet foul—she's welcome to him. They won't be no contest!

Grimes leaned over to ring for the waiter.

"Well," he said, "what about it?"

"You won't have to pay my fare," I told him.

"I'll buy a drink anyway," said he. "You've been a good listener—and I had to get it off my chest."

"Maybe they'll have to postpone the wedding," I said.

"No," said Grimes. "The weddin' will take place the day after tomorrow—and I'll bat for Mr. Parker. Did you think I was goin' to let him get away with it?"

"What about next year?" I asked.

"I'm goin' back to the Ath-a-letics," he said. "And I'm goin' to hire somebody to call me 'Horseshoes!' before every game—because I can sure play that old baseball when I'm mad."

AUTOBIOGRAPHY

TOMMY LEACH was an outfielder-third baseman for the great Pittsburgh teams of the early 1900s, including the 1903 Pirates, who played the Red Sox in the first World Series. Here is his salute to that occasion, to "Nuf Sed" McGreevey, and to:

"That Damn 'Tessie' Song"

TOMMY LEACH

THAT WAS probably the wildest World Series ever played. Arguing all the time between the teams, between the players and the umpires, and especially between the players and the fans. That's the truth. The fans were *part* of the game in those days. They'd pour right out onto the field and argue with the players and the umpires. Was sort of hard to keep the game going sometimes, to say the least.

I think those Boston fans actually won that series for the Red Sox. We beat them three out of the first four games, and then they started singing that damn "Tessie" song, the Red Sox fans did. They called themselves the Royal Rooters, and their leader was some Boston character named Mike McGreevey. He was known as "Nuf Sed" McGreevey, because any time there was an argument about baseball he was the ultimate authority. Once McGreevey gave his opinion that ended the argument: nuf sed!

Anyway, in the fifth game of the Series the Royal Rooters started singing "Tessie" for no particular reason at all, and the Red Sox won. They must have figured it was a good-luck charm, because from then on you could hardly play ball they were singing "Tessie" so damn loud.

"Tessie" was a real big song in those days. You remember it, don't you?

> Tessie, you make me feel so badly,
> Why don't you turn around.
> Tessie, you know I love you madly,
> Babe, my heart weighs about a pound.

Yeah, that was a real humdinger in those days. Like "The Music Goes Round and Round" in the '30s. Now you surely remember *that* one?

Only instead of singing, "Tessie, you know I love you madly," they'd sing special lyrics to each of the Red Sox players: like "Jimmy, you know I love you madly." And for us Pirates they'd change it a little. Like when Honus Wagner came up to bat they'd sing:

Honus, why do you hit so badly?
Take a back seat and sit down.
Honus, at bat you look so sadly,
Hey, why don't you get out of town?

Sort of it got on your nerves after a while. And before we knew what happened, we'd lost the World Series.

GENERAL

THE LESS-TRAVELED ROADS of the United States are colored blue on the road map, and that is where William Least Heat Moon got the title *Blue Highways* for his memoir of a journey into Americana on those roads. One of his stopovers was Bagley, Minnesota. And the conversation went as follows.

From *Blue Highways*

WILLIAM LEAST HEAT MOON

WITH A bag of blueberry tarts, I went up Main to a tin-sided, false-front tavern called Michel's, just down the street from the Cease Funeral Home. The interior was log siding and yellowed knotty pine. In the backroom the Junior Chamber of Commerce talked about potatoes, pulpwood, dairy products, and somebody's broken fishing rod. I sat at the bar. Behind me a pronghorn antelope head hung on the wall, and beside it a televised baseball game cast a cool light like a phosphorescent fungus. "Hear that?" a dwindled man asked. He was from the time when boys drew "Kilroy-Was-Here" faces on alley fences. "Did you hear the announcer?"

"I wasn't listening."

"He said 'velocity.' "

"Velocity?"

"He's talking about a fastball. A minute ago he said a runner had 'good acceleration.' This is a baseball game, not a NASA shot. And another thing: I haven't heard anybody mention a 'Texas leaguer' in years."

"It's a 'bloop double' now, I think."

"And the 'banjo hitter'—where's he? And what happened to the 'slow ball'?"

"It's a 'change-up.' "

The man got me interested in the game. We watched and drank Grain Belt. He had taught high-school civics in Minneapolis for thirty-two years, but his dream had been to become a sports announcer. "They put a radar gun on the kid's fastball a few minutes ago," he said. "Ninety-three point four miles per hour. That's how they tell you speed now. They don't try to show it to you: 'smoke,' 'hummer,' 'the high hard one.' I miss the old clichés. They had life. Who wants to hit a fastball with a decimal point when he can tie into somebody's 'heat'? And that's another thing: nobody 'tattoos' or 'blisters' the ball anymore. These TV boys are ruining a good game because they think if you can see it they're free to sit back and psychoanalyze the team. Ask and I'll tell you what I think of it."

"What do you think of it?"

"Beans. And that's another thing too."

"Beans?"

"Names. Used to be players named Butterbean and Big Potato, Little Potato. Big Poison, Little Poison, Dizzy and Daffy. Icehouse, Shoeless Joe, Suitcase, The Lip. Now we've got the likes of Rickie and Richie and Reggie. With names like that, I think I'm watching a third-grade scrub team."

The announcer said the pitcher had "good location."

"Great God in hemock! He means 'nibble the corners.' But which of these throwing clowns nibbles corners? They're obsessed with speed. Satchel Paige—there's a name for you—old Satch could fire the pill a hundred and five miles an hour. He didn't throw it that fast very often because he couldn't make the ball cut up at that speed. And, sure as spitting, his pitching arm lasted just about his whole life."

The man took a long smacking pull on his Grain Belt. "Damn shame," he said. "There's a word for what television's turned this game into."

"What's the word?"

"Beans," he said. "Nothing but beans and hot air."

FICTION

WHEN *The Natural* was published, the *New York Times* called it "a brilliant and unusual book" and Alfred Kazin wrote, "Malamud has raised the whole passion and craziness of baseball . . . to its ordained place. He takes up from where Ring Lardner's stories left off."

In the chapter from *The Natural* that is used here, Roy Hobbs, the hero, makes good in the major leagues—with Wonderboy, the bat he made himself, and under instructions to "knock the cover off the ball." Later, Robert Redford followed the same script in the movie. So did Kirk Gibson in the first game of the 1988 World Series!

From *The Natural*

BERNARD MALAMUD

AT THE CLUBHOUSE the next morning the unshaven Knights were glum and redeyed. They moved around listlessly and cursed each step. Angry fist fights broke out among them. They were sore at themselves and the world, yet when Roy came in and headed for his locker they looked up and watched with interest. He opened the door and found his new uniform knotted up dripping wet on a hook. His sanitary socks and woolen stockings were slashed to shreds and all the other things were smeared black with shoe polish. He located his jock, with two red apples in it, swinging from a cord attached to the light globe, and both his shoes were nailed to the ceiling. The boys let out a bellow of laughter. Bump just about doubled up howling, but Roy yanked the wet pants off the hook and caught him with it smack in the face. The players let out another yowl.

Bump comically dried himself with a bath towel, digging deep into his ears, wiping under the arms, and shimmying as he rubbed it across his fat behind.

"Fast guesswork, buster, and to show you there's no hard feelings, how's about a Camel?"

Roy wanted nothing from the bastard but took the cigarette because everyone was looking on. When he lit it, someone in the rear yelled, "Fire!" and ducked as it burst in Roy's face. Bump had disappeared. The players fell into each other's arms. Tears streamed down their cheeks. Some of them could not unbend and limped around from laughing so.

Roy flipped the ragged butt away and began to mop up his wet locker.

Allie Stubbs, the second baseman, danced around the room in imitation of a naked nature dancer. He pretended to discover a trombone at the foot of a tree and marched around blowing oompah, oompah, oompah.

Roy then realized the bassoon case was missing. It startled him that he hadn't thought of it before.

"Who's got it, boys?"—but no one answered. Allie now made out like he was flinging handfuls of rose petals into the trainer's office.

Going in there, Roy saw that Bump had broken open the bassoon case and was about to attack Wonderboy with a hacksaw.

"Lay off that, you goon."

Bump turned and stepped back with the bat raised. Roy grabbed it and with a quick twist tore it out of his sweaty hands, turning him around as he did and booting him hard with his knee. Bump grunted and swung but Roy ducked. The team crowded into the trainer's office, roaring with delight.

But Doc Casey pushed his way through them and stepped between Roy and Bump. "That'll do, boys. We want no trouble here. Go on outside or Pop will have your hides."

Bump was sweaty and sore. "You're a lousy sport, alfalfa."

"I don't like the scummy tricks you play on people you have asked for a favor," Roy said.

"I hear you had a swell time, wonderboy."

Again they grappled for each other, but Doc, shouting for help, kept them apart until the players pinned Roy's arms and held on to Bump.

"Lemme at him," Bump roared, "and I will skin the skunk."

Held back by the team, they glared at one another over the trainer's head.

"What's going on in there?" Pop's shrill blast came from inside the locker room. Earl Wilson poked his grayhaired, sunburned head in and quickly called, "All out, men, on the double." The players scurried past Pop and through the tunnel. They felt better.

Dizzy hustled up a makeshift rig for Roy. He dressed and polished his bat, a little sorry he had lost his temper, because he had wanted to speak quietly to the guy and find out whether he was expecting the redhead in his room last night.

Thinking about her made him uneasy. He reported to Pop in the dugout.

"What was that trouble in there between Bump and you?" Pop asked.

Roy didn't say and Pop got annoyed. "I won't stand for any ructions between players so cut it out or you will find yourself chopping wood back in the sticks. Now report to Red."

Roy went over to where Red was catching Chet Schultz, today's pitcher, and Red said to wait his turn at the batting cage.

The field was overrun with droopy players. Half a dozen were bunched near the gate of the cage, waiting to be pitched to by Al Fowler, whom Pop had ordered to throw batting practice for not bearing down in the clutches yesterday. Some of the men were at the sidelines, throwing catch. A few were shagging flies in the field, a group was playing pepper. On the line between home and first Earl Wilson was hacking out grounders to Allie Stubbs, Cal Baker at short, Hank Benz, the third baseman, and Emil Lajong, who played first. At the edge of the outfield, Hinkle and Hill, two of the regular starters, and McGee, the reliefer, were doing a weak walk-run-walk routine. No one seemed to be thoroughly awake, but when Roy went into the batting cage they came to life and observed him.

Fowler, a southpaw, was in a nasty mood. He didn't like having his ears burned by Pop, called a showboat in front of the other men, and then shoved into batting practice the day after he had pitched. Fowler was twenty-three but looked thirty. He was built rangy, with very light hair and eyelashes, and small blue eyes. As a pitcher he had the stuff and knew it, but all season long he had been erratic, and did a great amount of griping. He was palsy with Bump, who as a rule had no friends.

When Roy came up with Wonderboy, he hugged the plate too close to suit Fowler, who was in there anyway only to help the batters find their timing. In annoyance Fowler pitched the ball at Roy's head. Roy hit the dirt.

Pop shrieked, "Cut that out, you blasted fool." Fowler mumbled something about the ball slipping. Yet he wanted to make Roy look silly and burned the next one in. Roy swung and the ball sailed over the right-field fence. Red-faced, Fowler tried a hard, sharp-breaking curve. Roy caught it at the end of his bat and pulled it into the left-field stands.

"Try this one, grandpa." Fowler flung a stiff-wrist knuckler that hung in the air without spin before it took a sudden dip, but Roy scooped it up with the stick and lifted it twenty rows up into the center-field stands. Then he quit. Fowler was scowling at his feet. Everybody else stared at Roy.

Pop called out, "Lemme see that bat, son."

Both he and Red examined it, hefting it and rubbing along the grain with their fingers.

"Where'd you get it?" Pop asked.

Roy cleared his throat. He said he had made it himself.

"Did you brand this name Wonderboy on it?"

"That's right."

"What's it mean?"

"I made it long ago," Roy said, "when I was a kid. I wanted it to be a very good bat and that's why I gave it that name."

"A bat's cheap to buy," Red said.

"I know it but this tree near the river where I lived was split by lightning. I liked the wood inside of it so I cut me out a bat. Hadn't used it much until I played semipro ball, but I always kept it oiled with sweet oil and boned it so it wouldn't chip."

"Sure is white. Did you bleach the wood?"

"No, that's the true color."

"How long ago d'you make it?" Pop asked.

"A long time—I don't remember."

"Whyn't you get into the game then?"

Roy couldn't answer for a minute. "I sorta got sidetracked."

But Pop was all smiles. "Red'll measure and weigh it. If there's no filler and it meets specifications you'll be allowed to use it."

"There's nothing in it but wood."

Red clapped him on the back. "I feel it in my bones that you will have luck with it." He said to Pop, "Maybe we can start Roy in the line-up soon?"

Pop said they would see how it worked out.

But he sent Roy out to left field and Earl hit fungos to him all over the lot. Roy ran them down well. He took one shot over his shoulder and two caroming off the wall below the stands. His throwing was quick, strong, and bull's eye.

When Bump got around to his turn in the cage, though he did not as a rule exert himself in practice, he now whammed five of Fowler's fast pitches into the stands. Then he trotted out to his regular spot in the sun field and Earl hit him some long flies, all of which he ran for and caught with gusto, even those that went close to the wall, which was unusual for him because he didn't like to go too near it.

Practice picked up. The men worked faster and harder than they had in a long time. Pop suddenly felt so good, tears came to his eyes and he had to blow his nose.

• • •

In the clubhouse about an hour and a half before game time, the boys were sitting around in their underwear after showers. They were bulling, working crossword puzzles, shaving and writing letters. Two were playing checkers, surrounded by a circle of others, and the rest were drinking soda, looking at the *Sporting News* or just resting their eyes. Though they tried to hide it they were all nervous, always glancing up whenever someone came into the room. Roy couldn't make sense of it.

Red took him around to meet some of the boys and Roy spoke a few words to Dave Olson, the squat catcher, also to the shy Mexican center fielder, Juan Flores, and to Gabby Laslow, who patrolled right field. They sidestepped Bump, sitting in front of his locker with a bath towel around his rump, as he worked a red thread across the yellowed foot of a sanitary sock.

"Changes that thread from sock to sock every day," Red said in a low voice. "Claims it keeps him hitting."

As the players began to get into clean uniforms, Pop, wearing half-moon specs, stepped out of his office. He read aloud the batting order, then flipping through his dog-eared, yellow-paged notebook he read the names of the players opposing them and reminded them how the pitchers were to pitch and the fielders field them. This information was scribbled all over the book and Pop had to thumb around a lot before he had covered everybody. Roy then expected him to lay on with a blistering mustard plaster for all, but he only glanced anxiously at the door and urged them all to be on their toes and for gosh sakes get some runs.

Just as Pop finished his pep talk the door squeaked open and a short and tubby man in a green suit peeked in. Seeing they were ready, he straightened up and entered briskly, carrying a briefcase in his hand. He beamed at the players and without a word from anybody they moved chairs and benches and arranged themselves in rows before him. Roy joined the rest, expecting to hear some kind of talk. Only Pop and the coaches sat behind the man, and Dizzy lounged, half openmouthed, at the door leading to the hall.

"What's the act?" Roy asked Olson.

"It's Doc Knobb." The catcher looked sleepy.

"What's he do?"

"Pacifies us."

The playes were attentive, sitting as if they were going to have their pictures snapped. The nervousness Roy had sensed among them was all but gone. They looked like men whose worries had been lifted, and even Bump gave forth a soft grunt of contentment. The doctor removed his coat and rolled up his shirt sleeves. "Got to hurry today," he told Pop, "got a polo team to cheer up in Brooklyn."

He smiled at the men and then spoke so softly, at first they couldn't hear him. When he raised his voice it exuded calm.

"Now, men," he purred, "all of you relax and let me have your complete attention. Don't think of a thing but me." He laughed, brushed a spot off his pants, and continued. "You know what my purpose is. You're familiar with that. It's to help you get rid of the fears and personal inferiorities that tie you into knots and keep you from being aces in this game. Who are the Pirates? Not supermen, only mortals. What have they got that you haven't got? I can't think of a thing, absolutely not one. It's the attitude that's licking you—your own, not the Pirates'. What do you mean to yourselves? Are you a flock of bats flying around in a coffin, or the sun shining calmly on a blue lake? Are you sardines being swallowed up in the sea, or the whale that does the swallowing? That's why I'm here, to help you answer that question in the affirmative, to help you by mesmerism and autosuggestion, meaning you do the suggesting, not I. I only assist by making you receptive to your own basic thoughts. If you think you are winners, you will be. If you don't, you won't. That's psychology. That's the way the world works. Give me your whole attention and look straight into my eyes. What do you see there? You see sleep. That's right, sleep. So relax, sleep, relax . . ."

His voice was soft, lulling, peaceful. He had raised his pudgy arms and with stubby fingers was making ripples on a vast calm sea. Already Olson was gently snoring. Flores, with the tip of his tongue protruding, Bump, and some of the other players were fast asleep. Pop looked on, absorbed.

Staring at the light gleaming on Pop's bald bean, Roy felt himself going off . . . way way down, drifting through the tides into golden water as he searched for this lady fish, or mermaid, or whatever you called her. His eyes grew big in the seeking, first fish eyes, then bulbous frog eyes. Sailing lower into the pale-green sea, he sought everywhere for the reddish glint of her scales, until the water became dense and dark green and then everything gradually got so black he lost all sight of where he was. When he tried to rise up into the light he couldn't find it. He darted in all directions, and though there were times he saw flashes of her green tail, it was dark everywhere. He threshed up a storm of luminous bubbles but they gave out little light and he did not know where in all the glass to go.

Roy ripped open his lids and sprang up. He shoved his way out from between the benches.

The doctor was startled but made no attempt to stop him. Pop called out, "Hey, where do you think you're going?"

"Out."

"Sit down, dammit, you're on the team."

"I might be on the team but no medicine man is going to hypnotize me."

"You signed a contract to obey orders," Pop snapped shrilly.

"Yes, but not to let anybody monkey around in my mind."

As he headed into the tunnel he heard Pop swear by his eight-foot uncle that nobody by the name of Roy Hobbs would ever play ball for him as long as he lived.

• • •

He had waited before . . . and he waited now, on a spike-scuffed bench in the dugout, hidden from sky, wind and weather, from all but the dust that blew up from Knights Field and lodged dry in the throat, as the grass grew browner. And from time ticking off balls and strikes, batters up and out, halves and full innings, games won and (mostly) lost, days and nights, and the endless train miles from Philly, with in-between stops, along the arc to St. Louis, and circling back by way of Chi, Boston, Brooklyn . . . still waiting.

"C'mon, Roy," Red had urged, "apologize to Pop, then the next time Knobb comes around, join the boys and everything will be okay."

"Nix on that," said Roy. "I don't need a shyster quack to shoot me full of confidence juice. I want to go through on my own steam."

"He only wants everybody to relax and be able to do their best."

Roy shook his head. "I been a long time getting here and now that I am, I want to do it by myself, not with that kind of bunk."

"Do what?" Red asked.

"What I have to do."

Red shrugged and gave him up as too stubborn. Roy sat around, and though it said on his chest he was one of the team, he sat among them alone; at the train window, gazing at the moving trees, in front of his locker, absorbed in an untied shoe lace, in the dugout, squinting at the great glare of the game. He traveled in their company and dressed where they did but he joined them in nothing, except maybe batting practice, entering the cage with the lumber on his shoulder glistening like a leg bone in the sun and taking his chops at the pill. Almost always he hammered the swift, often murderous throws (the practice pitchers dumped their bag of tricks on him) deep into the stands, as the players watched and muttered at the swift flight of the balls, then forgot him when the game started. But there were days when the waiting got him. He could feel the strength draining from his bones, weakening him so he could hardly lift Wonderboy. He was unwilling to move then, for fear he would fall over on his puss and have to crawl away on all fours. Nobody noticed he did not bat when he felt this way except Pop; and Bump, seeing how white his face was, squirted contemptuous tobacco juice in the dust. Then when Roy's strength ebbed back, he would once again go into the batters' cage and do all sorts of marvelous things that made them watch in wonder.

He watched *them* and bad as he felt he had to laugh. They were a nutty bunch to begin with but when they were losing they were impossible. It was like some kind of sickness. They threw to the wrong bases, bumped heads together in the outfield, passed each other on the baselines, sometimes batted out of order, throwing both Pop and the ump into fits, and cussed everybody else for their mistakes. It was not uncommon to see them pile three men on a bag, or behold a catcher on the opposing team, in a single skip and jump, lay the tag on two of them as they came thundering together into home plate. Or watch Gabby Laslow, in a tight spot, freeze onto the ball, or Allie Stubbs get socked with it in the jaw, thrown by Olson on a steal as

Allie admired a lady in the stands. Doc Knobb's hypnotism cut down their jitters but it didn't much help their co-ordination, yet when they were left unhypnotized for a few days, they were afflicted with more than the usual number of hexes and whammies and practiced all sorts of magic to undo them. To a man they crossed their fingers over spilled salt, or coffee or tea, or at the sight of a hearse. Emil Lajong did a backward flip whenever he located a cross-eyed fan in the stands. Olson hated a woman who wore the same drab brown-feathered hat every time she showed up. He spat through two fingers whenever he spotted her in the crowd. Bump went through his ritual with the colored threads in his socks and shorts. Pop sometimes stroked a rabbit's foot. Red Blow never changed his clothes during a "winning streak," and Flores secretly touched his genitals whenever a bird flew over his head.

They were not much different from the fans in the patched and peeling stands. On week days the stadium usually looked like a haunted house but over the weekend crowds developed. The place often resembled a zoo full of oddballs, including gamblers, bums, drunks, and some ugly crackpots. Many of them came just to get a laugh out of the bonehead plays. Some, when the boys were losing, cursed and jeered, showering them—whenever they came close enough—with rotten cabbages, tomatoes, blackened bananas and occasionally an eggplant. Yet let the umpire call a close play against the Knights and he became a target for pop bottles, beer cans, old shoes or anything that happened to be lying around loose. Surprisingly, however, a few players were chosen for affection and even admiration by their fans. Sadie Sutter, a girl of sixty-plus, who wore large flowered hats, bobby sox, and short skirts, showed her undying love for Dave Olson every time he came up to the plate by banging with all her might on a Chinese gong she dragged into the stadium every day. A Hungarian cook, a hearty man with a hard yellow straw hat jammed tight on his skull, hopped up on his seat and crowed like a rooster whenever Emil Lajong originated a double play. And there was a girl named Gloria from Mississippi, a washed-out flower of the vestibules, who between innings when her eyes were not on the game, lined up a customer or two for a quickie later. She gave her heart to Gabby, yelling, "Get a move on, mo-lasses," to set him in motion after a fly ball. Besides these, there had appeared early in the present season a pompous Otto P. Zipp, whose peevish loudspeaker could be heard all over the park, his self-chosen mission to rout the critics of

Bump Baily, most of whom razzed the big boy for short legging on the other fielders. The dwarf honked a loud horn at the end of a two-foot walking stick, and it sounded as if a flock of geese had been let loose at the offenders, driving them—his purple curses ringing in their ears—to seek shelter in some hidden hole in the stands or altogether out of the ball park. Zipp was present at every home game, sitting at the rail in short left field, and Bump made it his much publicized business, as he trotted out to his position at the start of the game, to greet him with a loud kiss on the forehead, leaving Otto in a state of creamy bliss.

Roy got to know them all as he waited, all one if you looked long enough through the haze of cigarette smoke, except one . . . Memo Paris, Pop's redheaded niece, sad, spurned lady, who sat without wifehood in the wives' box behind third base. He could, if she would let him, find her with his eyes shut, with his hands alone as he had in the dark. Always in the act of love she lived in his mind, the only way he knew her, because she would not otherwise suffer his approach. *He* was to blame, she had wept one bitter midnight, so she hated his putrid guts. Since the team's return to the city (the phone banged in his ear and she ripped up his letters when they were delivered) whenever he got up from his seat in the hotel lobby as she stepped out of the elevator, to say how sorry he was for beginning at the wrong end, she tugged at her summer furpiece and breezed past him in green eyed scorn, withering in the process Bump at the cigar stand, who had laughed aloud at Roy's rout. ("Honeybunch," he had explained, "it was out of the pity of my heart that I took that shmo into my room, because they didn't have one for him and I was intending to pass the night at the apartment of my he cousin from Mobile. How'd I know you'd go in there when you said you weren't speaking to me?" He swore it hadn't been a gag—had he ever pulled one on her?—but Memo punished him in silence, punishing herself, and he knew it because she still came every day to see him play.) She walked out of the lobby, with her silver bracelets tinkling, swaying a little on her high heels, as if she had not too long ago learned to walk on them, and went with her beautiful body away, for which Roy everlastingly fried Bump Baily in the deep fat of his abomination.

It was for her he waited.

• • •

On the morning of the twenty-first of June Pop told Roy that as of tomorrow he was being shipped to a Class B team in the Great Lakes Association. Roy said he was quitting baseball anyway, but that same day, in answer to an angry question of Pop's as to why the team continued to flop, Doc Knobb said that the manager's hysterical behavior was undoing all the good he had done, and he offered to hypnotize Pop along with the others without hiking his fee. Pop shrilly told the psychologist he was too old for such bamboozlement, and Knobb retorted that his attitude was not only ridiculous but stupid. Pop got redfaced and told him to go to perdition with his hocus pocus and as of right then the doctor was canned.

That afternoon the Knights began a series with the second-place Phils. Instead of falling into a swoon when they learned there was to be no further hypnosis, the team played its best ball in weeks. Against superior pitching, in the sixth they bunched three singles for a run, and though Schultz had already given up five hits to the Phils, they were scattered and came to nothing. The Phils couldn't score till the top of the eighth, when with two out Schultz weakened, walking one man and handing the next a good enough throw to hit for a sharp single, so that there were now men on first and third. Up came Rogers, the Phils' slugger, and hit a fast curve for what looked like no more than a long fly ball, a routine catch, to left center. Now it happened that Bump was nearer to the ball than Flores, who was shifted to the right, but he was feeling horny in the sun and casting about in his mind for who to invite to his bed tonight, when he looked up and noticed this ball coming. He still had time to get under it but then saw Flores going for it like a galloping horse, and the anguished look on the Mexican's face, his black eyes popping, neck like a thick rope, and mouth haunted, fascinated Bump so, he decided to let him have it if he wanted it that bad. At the last minute he tried to take it away from the Mex, risking a head-on collision, but the wind whipped the ball closer to the wall than he had bargained for, so Bump fell back to cover Flores in case he misplayed it.

The ball fell between them, good for a double, and scoring two of the Phils. Pop tore at what was left of his gray hair but couldn't grip it with his oily, bandaged fingers so he pulled at his ears till they were lit like red lamps. Luckily the next Phil smothered the fire by rolling to first, which kept the score at 2–1. When Bump returned to the dugout Pop cursed him from the cradle to the grave and for once Bump had no sassy answers. When it came his time to go out on deck,

Pop snarled for him to stay where he was. Flores found a ripe one and landed on first but Pop stuck to his guns and looked down the line past Bump. His eye lit on Roy at the far end of the bench, and he called his name to go out there and hit. Bump turned purple. He grabbed a bat and headed for Roy but half the team jumped on him. Roy just sat there without moving and it looked to everyone like he wouldn't get up. The umpire roared in for a batter to come out, and after a while, as the players fidgeted and Pop fumed, Roy sighed and picked up Wonderboy. He slowly walked up the steps.

"Knock the cover off of it," Pop yelled.

"Attention, please," the P.A. man announced. "Roy Hobbs, number forty-five, batting for Baily."

A groan rose from the stands and turned into a roar of protest.

Otto Zipp jumped up and down on his seat, shaking his furious little fist at home plate.

"Throw him to the dogs," he shouted, and filled the air with his piercing curses.

Glancing at the wives' box, Roy saw that Memo had her head turned away. He set his jaw and advanced to the plate. His impulse was to knock the dirt out of his cleats but he refrained because he did not want to harm his bat in any way. Waiting for the pitcher to get set, Roy wiped his palms on his pants and twitched his cap. He lifted Wonderboy and waited rock-like for the throw.

He couldn't tell the color of the pitch that came at him. All he could think of was that he was sick to death of waiting, and tongue-out thirsty to begin. The ball was now a dewdrop staring him in the eye so he stepped back and swung from the toes.

Wonderboy flashed in the sun. It caught the sphere where it was biggest. A noise like a twenty-one gun salute cracked the sky. There was a straining, ripping sound and a few drops of rain spattered to the ground. The ball screamed toward the pitcher and seemed suddenly to dive down at his feet. He grabbed it to throw to first and realized to his horror that he held only the cover. The rest of it, unraveling cotton thread as it rode, was headed into the outfield.

Roy was rounding first when the ball plummeted like a dead bird into center field. Attempting to retrieve and throw, the Philly fielder got tangled in thread. The second baseman rushed up, bit the cord and heaved the ball to the catcher but Roy had passed third and made home, standing. The umpire called him safe and immediately a rhubarb boiled. The Phils' manager and his players charged out of the dugout and were joined by the nine men on the field. At the same time, Pop, shouting in defense of the ump, rushed forth with all the Knights but Bump. The umpire, caught between both teams, had a troublesome time of it and was shoved this way and that. He tossed out two men on each side but by then came to the decision that the hit was a ground-rules double. Flores had scored and the game was tied up. Roy was ordered back to second, and Pop announced he was finishing the game under protest. Somebody then shouted it was raining cats and dogs. The stands emptied like a yawn and the players piled into the dugouts. By the time Roy got in from second he was wading in water ankle deep. Pop sent him into the clubhouse for a change of uniform but he could have saved himself the trouble because it rained steadily for three days. The game was recorded as a 2–2 tie, to be replayed later in the season.

In the locker room Pop asked Roy to explain why he thought the cover had come off the ball.

"That's what you said to do, wasn't it?"

"That's right," said Pop, scratching his bean.

The next day he told Roy he was withdrawing his release and would hereafter use him as a pinch hitter and substitute fielder.

The rain had washed out the Phils' series but the Knights were starting another with the seventh-place Redbirds. In batting practice, Roy, who was exciting some curiosity for his freak hit of yesterday, looked tremendous but so did Bump. For the first time in a long while Roy went out to left field to limber up. Bump was out there too and Earl swatted fungos to both.

As they were changing into clean uniforms before the start of the game, Bump warned Roy in front of everybody, "Stay out of my way, busher, or you will get your head bashed."

Roy squirted spit on the floor.

When Pop later handed the batting order to Stuffy Briggs, the plate umpire, it had Bump's name scribbled on it as usual in the fourth slot, but Pop had already warned him that if he didn't hustle his behind when a ball was hit out to his field, he would rest it a long time on the bench.

Bump made no reply but it was obvious that he took Pop's words to heart, because he was a bang-up fielder that day. He accepted eight chances, twice chasing into center field to take them from Flores. He caught them to his left and right, dove for and came up with a breathtaking shoestringer and, running as if on fire, speared a fantastic catch over his shoulder. Still not satisfied, he pounded like a bull after his ninth try, again in Flores' territory, a smoking ball that sailed up high, headed for the wall. As Bump ran for it he could feel fear leaking through his stomach, and his legs unwillingly slowed down, but then he had this vision of himself as the league's best outfielder, acknowledged so by fans and players alike, even Pop, whom he'd be nothing less than forever respectful to, and in love with and married to Memo. Thinking this way he ran harder, though Zipp's geese honked madly at his back, and, with a magnificent twisting jump, he trapped the ball in his iron fingers. Yet the wall continued to advance, and though the redheaded lady of his choice was on her feet shrieking, Bump bumped it with a skull-breaking bang, and the wall embraced his broken body.

• • •

Though Bump was on the critical list in the hospital, many newspapers continued to speculate about that ball whose cover Roy had knocked off. It was explained as everything from an optical illusion (neither the ball nor the cover was ever found, the remnant caught by the catcher disappeared, and it was thought some fan had snatched the cover) to a feat of prodigious strength. Baseball records and newspaper files were combed but no one could find any evidence that it had happened before, although some of the older scribes swore it had. Then it leaked out that Pop had ordered Roy to skin the ball and Roy had obliged, but no one took that very seriously. One of the sports writers suggested that a hard downward chop could shear off the outer covering. He had tried it in his cellar and had split the horsehide. Another pointed out that such a blow would have produced an infield grounder, therefore maybe a tremendous upward slash? The first man proved that would have uncorked a sure pop fly whereas the ball, as everyone knew, had sailed straight out over the pitcher's head. So it had probably resulted from a very very forceful sock. But many a hitter had plastered the ball forcefully before, still another argued, and his idea was that it was defective to begin with, a fact the company that manufactured the ball vigorously denied. Max Mercy had his own theory. He wrote in his column, "My Eye in the Knot Hole" (the year he'd done the Broadway stint for his paper his eye was in the key hole), that Roy's bat was a suspicious one and hinted it might be filled with something a helluva lot stronger than wood. Red Blow publicly denied this. He said the bat had been examined by league authorities and was found to be less than forty-two inches long, less than two and three-quarter inches thick at its fattest part, and in weight less than two pounds, which made it a legal weapon. Mercy then demanded that the wood be X-rayed but Roy turned thumbs down on that proposition and kept Wonderboy hidden away when the sports columnist was nosing around in the clubhouse.

On the day after the accident Pop soberly gave Roy the nod to play in Bump's place. As Roy trotted out to left, Otto Zipp was in his usual seat but looking worn and aged. His face, tilted to the warming rays of the sun, was like a pancake with a cherry nose, and tears were streaming through slits where the eyes would be. He seemed to be waiting for his pregame kiss on the brow but Roy passed without looking at him.

The long rain had turned the grass green and Roy romped in it like a happy calf in its pasture. The Redbirds, probing his armor, belted the ball to him whenever they could, which was often, because Hill was not too happy on the mound, but Roy took everything they aimed at him. He seemed to know the soft, hard, and bumpy places in the field and just how high a ball would bounce on them. From the flags on the stadium roof he noted the way the wind would blow the ball, and he was quick at fishing it out of the tricky undercurrents on the ground. Not sun, shadow, nor smoke haze bothered him, and when a ball was knocked against the wall he estimated the angle of rebound and speared it as if its course had been plotted on a chart. He was good at gauging slices and knew when to charge the pill to save time on the throw. Once he put his head down and ran ahead of a shot going into the concrete. Though the crowd rose with a thunderous warning, he caught it with his back to the wall and did a little jig to show he was alive. Everyone laughed in relief, and they liked his long-legged loping and that he resembled an acrobat the way he tumbled and came up with the ball in his glove. For his performance that day there was much whistling and applause, except where he would have liked to hear it, an empty seat in the wives' box.

His batting was no less successful. He stood at the plate lean and loose, right-handed with an open stance, knees relaxed and shoulders squared. The bat he held in a curious position, lifted slightly above his head as if prepared to beat a rattlesnake to death, but it didn't harm his smooth stride into the pitch, nor the easy way he met the ball and slashed it out with a flick of the wrists. The pitchers tried something different every time he came up, sliders, sinkers, knucklers, but he swung and connected, spraying them to all fields. He was, Red Blow said to Pop, a natural, though somewhat less than perfect because he sometimes hit at bad ones, which caused Pop to frown.

"I mistrust a bad-ball hitter."

"There are all kinds of hitters," Red answered. "Some are bucket foots, and some go for bad throws but none of them bother me as long as they naturally connect with anything that gets in their way."

Pop spat up over the dugout steps. "They sometimes make some harmful mistakes."

"Who don't?" Red asked.

Pop then muttered something about this bad-ball hitter he knew who had reached for a lemon and cracked his spine.

But the only thing Roy cracked that day was the record for the number of triples hit in a major-league debut and also the one for chances accepted in the outfield. Everybody agreed that in him the Knights had uncovered something special. One reporter wrote, "He can catch everything in creation," and Roy just about proved it. It happened that a woman who lived on the sixth floor of an apartment house overlooking the stadium was cleaning out her bird cage, near the end of the game, which the Knights took handily, when her canary flew out of the window and darted down across the field. Roy, who was waiting for the last out, saw something coming at him in the low rays of the sun, and leaping high, bagged it in his glove.

He got rid of the bloody mess in the clubhouse can.

GENERAL

IN THE MAY 1911 issue of *Pearson's* magazine appeared an article entitled "Outguessing the Batter," and here is an excerpt from it. The author was somewhat of an expert, you'll agree.

From *Outguessing the Batter*

CHRISTY MATHEWSON

MANY THINGS have been said and written about pitchers outguessing batters, and batters outguessing pitchers, and to tell the truth there has always been a question in my mind about the outguessing proposition. I have seen so many instances where guesses went wrong—so many hundreds of instances—that I am about the last human being in the world to pose as an oracle on the subject of pitching psychology. Nevertheless, there certainly is a lot of psychology about pitching a baseball. Joe Tinker, the clever little shortshop of the Chicago club, is a man with whom I have fought many battles of wits, and I am glad to acknowledge that he has come out of the fuss with flying colors on many occasions. There was a time when Tinker was putty in my hands. For two years he was the least dangerous man on the Chicago team. His weakness was a low curve on the outside, and I fed him low curves on the outside so often that I had him looking like an invalid every time he came to the plate. Then Joseph went home one night and did a little deep thinking. He got a nice long bat and took his stand at least a foot farther from the plate, and then he had me. If I kept the ball on the inside edge of the plate, he was in a splendid position to meet it, and if I tried to keep my offerings on the outside, he had plenty of time to "step into 'em." From that day on Tinker became one of the most dangerous batters I ever faced, not because his natural hitting ability had increased, but because he didn't propose to let the pitcher do all the "outguessing."

HISTORY

BASEBALL has had two "miracle" pennant drives. In 1951, the New York Giants, in second place 13½ games off the lead on August 11, caught up to a Brooklyn team which itself was playing better than .500 ball and won the pennant on the last day of a three-day post-season playoff. In 1914, the Boston Braves, in last place 11 games off the lead on July 19, passed not one but all seven other teams in their stretch run. The relative merits of these two finishes make for happy arguments, but few people know that those Braves, starting out in the cellar on July 19, were in first place by September 2! They creamed the mighty A's in the World Series, too. Tom Meany, one of the very best, supplies the details here in a section excerpted from his fine book, *Baseball's Greatest Teams.*

The Miracle Man

TOM MEANY

GEORGE TWEEDY STALLINGS was a man of infinite impatience. One of baseball's greatest legends, Stallings may also have been baseball's first bona fide split personality. Away from the ball park, he was a dignified, fastidious man, meticulous in dress, Chesterfieldian in his manners. Nobody ever would take him for a baseball manager. Swarthy, moon-faced, bright-eyed, he would have been a cinch for today's men-of-distinction ads.

On the bench during a ball game, Stallings was another person. No man, not even John McGraw or Leo Durocher, ever reached the heights of invective stormed by George. He could fly into a schizophrenic rage at the drop of a pop fly. Sputtering with a fury which invited apoplexy, Stallings told off ballplayers as they haven't been told off since.

And, curiously enough, nobody minded the tongue lashings of Stallings. "It was an art with him," Hank Gowdy remarked with awesome reverence over three decades later.

In 1915, a year after his baseball miracle, Stallings walked home from the ball game with Owner Jim Gaffney. All the Braves rode home, for they all had purchased cars out of their series shares, all but Johnny Evers, who had won a Chalmers car as the National League's most valuable player for 1914. Stallings knew the make of every car owned by his players and in that 1915 season, he prefaced his derogatory remarks to his men by inserting the name of the automobile. Thus Rabbit Maranville became an "Aperson Jack-rabbit bonehead," others were "Packard dunces," "Stanley Steamer clowns" and "White simpletons."

Only once did Stallings forget the name of a car owned by one of his players. Seeking to call attention to the mental shortcomings of Gowdy, who missed a sign one day, the Braves' manager turned to the rest of the bench.

"Look at him up there," he sputtered derisively, "the—the—" And there was a pause as Stallings tried in vain to recall the name of the car driven by Gowdy. He was stumped, but not for long.

"Look at him," yelled Stallings, "the bicycle-riding so-and-so."

It was Stallings' habit to sit on the same spot on the bench day after day, his knees and his feet close together. As he grew agitated—and he did so every day, win, lose or draw—he would slide his feet, still close together, back and forth over the floor of the dugout. And sometimes he would slide his body, too. He wore the seat of a pair of trousers clean through during the second game of the 1914 World Series.

Not only was Stallings superstitious but he encouraged his ballplayers in superstition. He couldn't abide scraps of paper anywhere within range of his vision, an idiosyncrasy rival ballplayers exploited to the hilt when they learned of it.

Years after Stallings had left the Braves, when he managed and owned the Rochester Club in the International League, his legend persisted. Even today, two stories of the Stallings repartee are still part of baseball folklore.

One deals of his trials with two collegians, twin brothers who were infielders. Sometimes they're identified as the Shannon twins from Seton Hall, often they're not from Seton Hall at all, neither twins nor brothers and not even infielders. Through all versions of the story, however, they remain collegians.

The story goes that one day the twins were on second and third, with one out. The Rochester batter hit to the shortstop, who threw home to cut off the run. The twin on third was caught in a run-down and eventually tagged out. And the twin on second chose that particular moment to try and make third where he, too, was exterminated and the inning was over.

The enormity of what he had just witnessed left Stallings speechless. But only briefly. The inning over, the twins returned to their defensive positions in the field. George darted off the bench and beckoned the two tyros to him.

Paternally draping an arm on the shoulder of each, Stallings inquired, "You boys are both college graduates, aren't you?"

"Yes, Mr. Stallings," they chorused in assent.

"Well, then," said Stallings briskly and, changing his voice to imitate the staccato bark of a cheer leader, he roared: "Rah, rah, rah! Rah! rah! rah! Rah! rah! rah!"

Perhaps the most hallowed of all the Stallings legends concerns itself with the time when he retired to his plantation at Haddock, Georgia, The Meadows, broken in health and through with baseball. He was suffering from a serious cardiac disturbance.

"Mr. Stallings," said the specialist at the completion of the examination, "you have an unusually bad heart. Is there any way you can account for it?"

"Bases on balls, you so-and-so, bases on balls," cursed Stallings softly, turning his face to the wall.

Stallings managed before it became the baseball style to address managers as "Skipper" but his position with his players may be judged from the fact that they usually called him "Chief." Some of the more intimate called him "George" but none ever took any liberties with him. Baseball, to Stallings, was too serious to permit of any levity.

There were, of course, "meetings" before Stallings' day, as those baseball skull sessions are called, but the Chief intensified these daily conclaves at which strategy was mapped. He was as careful in detail of play as he was in detail of dress, a precise, methodical planner.

Stallings is generally given the credit for being the first to use different outfield combinations for left- and right-handed pitchers. The "percentage" of having a left-hander bat against a right-handed pitcher and vice versa was recognized long before 1914, particularly in the selection of pinch hitters and relief pitchers but Stallings was the first to play the percentage wholesale. He almost was forced into it, because the Braves did not have a strong outfield that season, but Stallings made the best of it, by having Herbie Moran, Larry Gilbert and Joe Connolly as one set of outfielders, against right-handed pitching, and Leslie Mann, Ted Cather and George Whitted against southpaws.

There were others who broke into these combinations, of course—Stallings used nearly a dozen different outfielders during the year—and Connolly, the only member of the team to hit .300 for the season, frequently was used against both right- and left-handed pitchers. It was, nevertheless, the first full outfield switch in history and Stallings stuck to it during the World Series.

One thing Stallings must get credit for introducing into baseball is the "tooth" sign. The Chief would call a certain play by baring his teeth. Dark-complexioned and with teeth of pearly white, Stallings could give his sign from the shadows of the dugout and have it picked up by his coaches or players every time. When the Chief bared his fangs his men knew it was time to run—but literally, since the Braves used it as a steal sign.

• • •

Every story of the Boston Braves of 1914 deals so heavily with the three-man pitching staff of Lefty Tyler, Bill James and Dick Rudolph that latter-day fans may be pardoned for assuming that these three were the only hurlers the Braves had. They were the only ones to appear in the World Series and among them they won sixty-nine of the ninety-four games the Braves won that season. There were other pitchers, droves of them in fact, including Hub Perdue who had been counted on as a regular until he was traded to St. Louis in mid-season for outfielders Whitted and Cather.

Stallings' Big Three had stamina and skill in equal proportions. Tyler was a left-hander who could really wheel the ball in, a big man as was James. Tyler was a power pitcher with a blazing fast ball, while James had one of the most difficult spitters in the league.

While Tyler and James were strong-arm boys, tiny Dick Rudolph was a pitching cutie, gifted with a great curve and superhuman control. He could get a piece of the plate with almost every pitch. Rudolph, for all of his diminutiveness, didn't lag behind the others when it came to staying power. He won twenty-seven games for the Braves that season, had a twelve-game streak going at one time and pitched a half-dozen shutouts right where they did the most good, when the Braves were moving from the cellar to the penthouse.

Rudolph, one of the earliest of the many Fordham graduates to make major league history, also threw a spitball but this was merely to be stylish. His curve and his control were the major weapons of the Bald Eagle. His spitball itself wasn't much but the fact that he faked throwing one most of the time helped throw the batters off.

"As for Dick's spitter," recollects Gowdy, "about the best you could say for it was that it was wet."

Gowdy, who did most of the catching for the Braves that year, still talks with reverence of the Big Three. "They had guts," he says simply, "and they got the ball over in the pinch." Incidentally, Hank once spoke glowingly over the radio of the relief work of a pitcher from Rochester, Tom Hughes, and expressed surprise that he isn't listed among the members of the historic team.

Hank's usually reliable memory tricked him on Hughes. In 1915, Tom did some fine pitching for the Braves but he didn't join the 1914 club until near the close of the season and as a consequence wasn't eligible for the series. He did win one game for the Braves, on September 29, beating the Cubs to clinch the pennant. It undoubtedly was the importance of that game which stuck in Gowdy's mind. Hughes, as a matter of fact, only was in two games for the '14 Braves and Otto Hess had to relieve Tom to win the second one for the Braves.

There were many remarkable things about Rudolph, Tyler and James, over and above their durability. One, and most important, was their talent for winning low-score games. The Braves were not a good hitting team and the pitchers had to make the most of what runs they got. This the Big Three was able to do, particularly from mid-July on, when the chips were down. James won nineteen of his last twenty decisions, Rudolph had his twelve-game winning streak already mentioned and Tyler was untouchable when he had to be, which was most of the time.

No surviving member of the 1914 Braves will consider a report on the pitching staff either complete or authentic unless credit is given to Fred Mitchell, an old catcher who was Stallings' first lieutenant. Fred started in baseball as a pitcher, injured his arm and had become a catcher. He caught for Stallings four years before when George had managed the Yankees.

Mitchell, who also coached at third base, conducted quiet sessions of his own with the pitchers, private confabs superimposed on the general meetings held by Stallings. Not content with this, Fred also used to go over opposing hitters with Gowdy, both before and after a game.

"Fred would ask what sort of pitch So-and-so had hit," recalls Hank, "and suggest that we might have better luck pitching low to some players. He knew pitching as few men ever have known it. Maybe it was because having begun his career as a pitcher and finished it as a catcher, he knew both ends of the business."

• • •

Stallings set a high value on morale. He was away ahead of Bill Roper, Princeton's football coach, with the-team-that-won't-be-beat-can't-be-beat theory. He believed that if his players believed that they could win, they would win. It was as simple as that with the Chief.

It is unlikely that any manager ever had a better team for his own pet theories than Stallings did in 1914. The abuse which the Chief might heap on a player who pulled a boner was equaled by that which the hapless Brave drew from his own mates. Johnny Evers, a veteran of the rowdy-dow Cubs of Frank Chance, was the second baseman and team captain and no captain ever took his duties more seriously. He ran his players ragged and considered it a personal insult when anybody on the squad let him down.

"He'd make you want to punch him," grinned Maranville one day years later, "but you knew Johnny was thinking only of the team."

That remark of Rabbit's explains the 1914 Braves better than an entire book could. Everybody, like Evers, was thinking only of the team. The Rab himself was a source of inspiration to the club, with his amazingly agile scampering around short, his quick, fliplike throws and his happy-go-lucky disposition.

Butch Schmidt, the burly first baseman, was a great jollier. He dealt only in superlatives. When Maranville ran to the outfield to make one of those vest-pocket catches of a pop fly which delighted National League fans for more than a score of years, Schmidt would roar out, "Rab, old boy, you're the best shortstop in the world." When Rudolph cut the plate with a third strike, Butch would yell, "Dick, old man, you're the best pitcher in the world." And so on, down the line.

This penchant of Schmidt's for extravagant praise was so marked that to this day Butch annually receives a Christmas card from Hank Gowdy, addressed to "Butch Schmidt, The Best First Baseman in the World, Baltimore, Md."

Whether it was Stallings or Evers who planted this fire in the 1914 Braves it would be hard to say. Perhaps it was the Chief who kindled it and the peppery Trojan who fanned it. At any rate, the fire was there and any player who came to the 1914 Braves during the season, as many did, caught fire along with them or else he didn't linger long.

No better example of the 1914 Braves' spirit could be offered than the retort of little Herbie Moran to Harry Davis, when the captain of the Athletics visited the Polo Grounds after the Braves had clinched the pennant to congratulate Moran and, incidentally, to look over the club which would meet the A's in the World Series.

"You fellows did a great job, Herbie," said Davis, "and I expect we'll have a great series."

"Harry," answered little Herbie earnestly, "I don't think you fellows will win a single game."

This pride the Braves had in themselves was present even when the club was in last place. Maybe nobody connected with the team, even Stallings, was clairvoyant enough to see a pennant at the end of the trail but they knew they weren't a cellar club. And they never played like one, either, for the Braves had good spirit in the first part of the season as well as in the last. Stallings never abandoned morning practice nor the daily meetings.

Sometime in July, while the Braves were still last, they paused on the eve of a Western trip for an exhibition game in Buffalo. Johnny Evers always claimed it was against "a soap company team" in later years but Gowdy insists it was against the International League club. Both agreed that the Braves had their ears pinned back.

"No matter what the fans think," explained Gowdy, "no big league club likes to lose to a minor league club, even if it is only an exhibition game. Maybe we were last but we were still big leaguers and the pasting we took was galling to our pride. We knew we weren't that bad.

"Western trips in those days were longer than they are now because there were only three such trips a year, instead of four, so you ususally played four days in each city. It was a long trip and it was the one which got us out of the cellar and started us toward the pennant. I'll always believe it was that trouncing we received from the minor leaguers which provided the spark."

• • •

The pennant race in the National League in 1914 was strange in many ways, aside from the rags-to-riches climb of the Braves. On a Sunday morning in Cincinnati, the fateful nineteenth of July, the Braves awoke to find themselves still in the cellar, eleven games behind the first-place Giants and with a double-header scheduled against the Reds that day. The distance from first place to eighth is usually much more than eleven games in mid-July.

Boston, however, had been moving ever since the debacle in Buffalo on the eve of this Western invasion. They had won nine games out of twelve, while the front-running Giants had been able to win only six of fourteen. On the night of July 4, the Braves were fifteen games behind the leaders but on the morning of the nineteenth, they were only eleven games back.

After winning the first game at Redland Field that Sunday, the Braves were trailing 2 to 0 in the ninth inning of the second game but rallied to score three runs and win, moving over Pittsburgh to seventh place. And once having passed the Pirates, the Braves protected their rear by moving in to Pittsburgh and winning four out of five, getting four shutouts from their great staff. Rudolph, Tyler and James each pitched a shutout and Tyler and James pitched in to collaborate on the fourth. The great pitching was beginning to assert itself.

Once started, there was no halting the Braves. Due to the closeness of the pennant race, the Braves were fourth on July 21, two days after they had been in the cellar. Then they reeled a string of nine straight and in three weeks were in second place.

It was a brawling race by now, as tight races always were in those days. Opposing pitchers paid Boston hitters the sincere, if embarrassing, compliment of pitching under their chins and forcing them to hit the dirt. Rabbit Maranville, the midget with the arms and shoulders of a weight-lifter, flattened Heinie Zimmerman during a ruckus with the Cubs but for years afterward der Zim refused to believe that the Rab had cooled him off. He always insisted that the *coup de grâce* had been administered by one of the larger Braves, Butch Schmidt or Moose Whaling, a reserve catcher. He just couldn't see himself kayoed by the little tyke.

Boston went into first place on September 2 by wining a doubleheader in Philadelphia, while the Dodgers were beating the Giants. The next day the Braves tumbled to second when Grover Cleveland Alexander outpitched Tyler. Although the Braves beat the Phils three straight, to make it five out of six for the series, they were tied for the lead with the Giants as they returned to Boston for the big Labor Day series with the men of McGraw.

The present Braves Field had not yet been built but was in the process of construction in 1914 and the team of destiny played its home games at the South End Grounds. Now, however, Joe Lannin, the owner of the Red Sox, offered President Gaffney the use of the more spacious Fenway Park for the remainder of the season and the

Braves took possession on Labor Day to play morning and afternoon games against the Giants.

It is doubtful if any single day of baseball in Boston ever will attract more paid admissions than were collected for the pre- and post-luncheon games with New York that Labor Day, September 7, 1914. The morning game drew more than 35,000 and the afternoon game approached 40,000. Gaffney announced a total of 74,163 paid admissions for the two games.

Cecil B. De Mille couldn't have improved on the script for the morning game, when the Braves, with Rudolph pitching, beat the great Christy Mathewson by scoring twice with one out in the ninth. The final score was 5 to 4.

Josh Devore, a fleet-footed outfielder who was obtained from New York after the season opened, started the ninth inning rally with one out by beating out a "squib" to Merkle. Herbie Moran, who was knocked cold when beaned by Alexander in Philly three days before, hit into the overflow crowd for a ground-rule double, Devore being forced to stop at third.

Up came Johnny Evers, quite possibly the most hated member of the tough, dynamic Braves as far as the opposition was concerned. Matty worked on him but the Trojan laced a low, sinking liner to left. George Burns charged the ball but couldn't get up to it in time and it went for a two-bagger, breaking up the ball game and putting the Braves in first place.

Surrounded by a milling, ecstatic and delirious mob, the Braves had to fight their way from the playing field of Fenway Park. McGraw's club fought back in the afternoon game, behind sturdy pitching by Jeff Tesreau and won 10 to 1 to tie up the pennant race again. As the Giants, no amateurs themselves at the art of invective, taunted the Braves, feelings ran so high that James M. Curley, even then mayor of Boston, came onto the playing field in an effort to have Fred Snodgrass chased on charges of attempting to incite a riot. The Mayor appealed first to Umpire Bob Emslie and then to a police lieutenant but both refused to assist His Honor in ousting Snodgrass.

McGraw, however, did remove Snodgrass, not to placate his fellow Celt, Curley, but to keep Fred intact. The Boston fans treated Snodgrass to a shower of pop bottles, the predecessor to the barrage rained at Joe Medwick by the Detroit fans twenty years later.

Came the morrow, however, and McGraw, Snodgrass and even Mayor Curley were quickly forgotten as the Braves, behind three-hit pitching by James, went into first place to stay. Rube Marquard, who had lost eight straight, was McGraw's choice, quite possibly on a hunch, but he got nowhere, the Braves eventually wining by 8 to 3. From that point on it was a breeze, the Braves turning a dog-fight into a romp, winning the pennant by ten and one-half games.

A sample of what was to come in the closing weeks was offered the next day when George A. Davis, Jr., a student at Harvard Law School, pitched a no-hitter in the night cap as Boston took a double-header from the Phils. Seven Philadelphia players reached first base against Davis, five on passes, two on errors.

The no-hitter pitched by this comparative unknown was typical of the '14 Braves. It was the only no-hit game pitched in the National League that season, despite the great mound feats of Rudolph, Tyler and James. And the reader will remember the previously mentioned Tom Hughes, who joined the Braves just in time to beat the Cubs in his first start on September 29 and clinch the pennant for Boston.

The Braves of 1914 were like that. It was, more than anything else, a team, a unit. If one of the name players wasn't up to it, Stallings always found somebody who was. It was perhaps for this reason that the miracle man wasn't at all upset when J. Carlisle (Red) Smith, his regular third baseman, broke his leg on the last day of the season in Brooklyn.

Smith had started the 1914 season with Brooklyn but was purchased by the Braves when the Dodgers put him on the block. A squatty slugger, Red was one of the few Braves who could be counted on for the long ball and when he was injured it should have been a crushing blow.

Stallings promptly announced that the Braves were no one-man team and that Charley Deal would play third in the World Series. Deal, a good fielder but weak hitter, had opened the season for the Braves at third but it was because of his lightness with the wood that Stallings had grabbed Smith from Brooklyn. Deal batted only .154 in the series, making two two-baggers, but he fielded perfectly and the Braves, as Stallings predicted, never missed the hard-hitting Smith.

It was felt by this time that Stallings and the Braves had run out of miracles. The injury to Smith on the eve of the series was regarded by many as an omen of things to come. The Athletics had won four pennants out of five and the three last World Series in which they had played, beating the Giants four out of five in 1913. Connie Mack's team was a topheavy favorite to cool off the Boston upstarts.

Stallings opened a war of nerves. He accused Mack of closing Shibe Park to the Braves for pre-series practice and he warned his players not to speak to the Athletics, under penalty of a fine, unless it was to insult them. He refused to use the visitors' dressing room in the Shibe Park clubhouse but dressed instead a few blocks away at National League Park, the home of the Phillies. He refused to give the Shibe Park announcer his lineup and chased him from the bench.

Now the A's were no babies at this stuff. They had been in World Series against the Giants and they knew all about bench jockeys because they had been ridden by experts. Or so they thought. But this was different. It was contempt, rather than abuse, and it was puzzling. The series was over before the Athletics ever learned the answer.

A weak hitting team throughout the National League season, the Braves exploded against Chief Bender in the opening game in Philadelphia, knocking him out in the sixth, the first time in all World Series history an Athletics' pitcher had been forced to take cover from enemy bats. And the Braves stole three bases, including a double steal by Hank Gowdy and Butch Schmidt, two of the slowest of the miracle men.

With this sort of batting support, which he rarely enjoyed during the season, Dick Rudolph had no difficulty with the American Leaguers. The only run the A's scored against him was unearned.

Hank Gowdy had a perfect day at bat with a single, double and triple. He was to hit .545 during the series, after batting .243 during the regular season. Gowdy always claimed that he should have hit .300 during the season.

"I hit just as hard during the season as I did during the series," insists Hank, "except that during the season they were going right at somebody while in the series they were going safe."

If the first game was a romp the next three were squeakers but the Braves took them all, just as they had taken the one-sided opener. Bill James had his spitter working for the Braves and the left-handed Eddie Plank was equally untouchable for the Athletics. They came to the top of the ninth locked in a scoreless tie.

It was then that the opportunism of the Braves came to the fore. It was a ball club which might well have had *carpe diem* on its coat of arms, for it never overlooked a bet. Charley Deal, the weak-hitting replacement for Red Smith, got a double with one out when Amos Strunk misjudged his drive to right. As James fanned, Deal was caught off second but, seeing he had no chance to get back, broke for third and just did beat Jack Barry's relay of Wally Schang's throw. It was a close decision and the A's squawked at Umpire Bill Byron but to no avail.

Leslie Mann, leadoff hitter for the Braves, who could pepper southpaws as good as any batter who ever lived, rifled a single to right, just out of Eddie Collins' reach at second, and Deal came in with the only run of the ball game.

Up to this point, James had spitballed his way through a remarkable game. He had held the A's hitless until Wally Schang doubled in the sixth and the second and last Philadelphia hit was a scratch single by Collins in the seventh. Bill had walked only one man, remarkable for a spitballer pitcher.

James's control wavered in the ninth and he passed Barry with one out and then wild-pitched Jack to second. He also walked Jim Walsh, who batted for Plank. Up came Eddie Murphy, the Athletics' leadoff hitter. He smashed one through the box but Maranville was behind second to field the ball almost on the bag, step on the base and flip it to Butch Schmidt at first for a game-ending double play.

As the Braves returned to Boston to resume the series, they were beginning to believe that Stallings was right when he told them they would sweep the series in four straight. And, what's more, there is reason to believe that maybe the A's thought Stallings was right, too.

Identical crowds of 20,562 had seen the first two games at Shibe Park but there were 35,520 at Fenway Park to greet the miracle men and the somewhat bewildered Athletics. Even the repose of an open date on Sunday hadn't allowed the A's to regain their equilibrium.

Stallings trotted out his third ace, Lefty Tyler, and Mack used young Bullet Joe Bush, who already was showing signs of pitching greatness. And Bush three times was given a lead by his mates, the only times in the series in which the A's enjoyed a lead.

Twice the A's were off in front and twice the Braves came back to tie up. All seemed lost in the tenth, however, when Philadelphia scored twice while Evers was kicking Home Run Baker's grounder around with the bases filled. It was one of the few times, perhaps the only time, that the Trojan was guilty of mental aberration in his career.

Hank Gowdy, who continued to plague the Philadelphia pitchers, opened the home half with a home run into the seats in center. Moran walked and raced to third on a single by Evers, scoring on Joe Connolly's fly to tie up the ball game.

Tyler had been removed for a pinch hitter and James, the pitching hero of the second game, took over in the eleventh. He needed to pitch only two innings to gain his second series victory, for in the gathering dusk of the twelfth, the obstreperous Gowdy delivered his third hit and second two-bagger of the day, a shot to the left field bleachers. Leslie Mann ran for him and Larry Gilbert, batting for James, was intentionally passed. With none out, Moran attempted to bunt the runners along and bunted right at Bush. The youngster scooped up the ball to make a play at third but threw wildly and Mann came home with the run which gave the Braves a 5–4 victory and made it three straight.

For the fourth game, Stallings called upon Rudolph, who had become a proud papa since the series had opened. Dick, opposed by Bob Shawkey, another Athletics youngster who was to become a pitching star, won by 3 to 1 and the series was over in four games for the first time in history. During the series, the Chief had called upon no pitchers save his Big Three and Rudolph and James each won two games.

It was a fitting climax to a miraculous season. The Braves of 1914 occupy a unique spot, not merely in baseball, but in American athletic tradition. They have become a symbol for the downtrodden, recorded proof that nothing is ever impossible. One by one, they overcame the seven teams which were ahead of them in the National League race, jsut as they overcame, one by one, the obstacles which cropped up in the course of the season. And then came the glorious sweep of the World Series against the Athletics. It is truly a great chapter in the history of the underdog, a miraculous page in baseball, fashioned by the miracle man himself, George Tweedy Stallings, aided and abetted by as spirited a group of athletes as ever banded together in any sport.

JAMES MICHENER, Pulitzer-prizewinning author and incurable Phillies fan, was Bangkok-bound in an airliner late one night in October of 1980, when the pilot came on the intercom to announce the Phils had just won their first-ever world championship. Michener's reaction? He seized his pen, and—

Lines Composed in Exaltation over the North Atlantic

JAMES MICHENER

Crash the cymbals, blare the trumpets,
Wreathe their noble brows with laurel.
Heap the festive board with crumpets
And with decorations floral.
They deserve the fairest lilies—
Who? The Phillies.

Through the long dark years they stumbled
Scarred with deep humiliations
But our cheering never crumbled
And we kept our expectations.

Yes, we loved them for their sillies—
Who? The Phillies.

Triple plays that did not triple,
Strikeouts with the bases loaded.
Pitchers serving up the cripple,
All our hopes again exploded.
Are they not a bunch of dillies?
Who? The Phillies.

Far behind in early innings,
Doomed to tragedy eternal,
They turn losses into winnings
Through some holy fire internal.
They give enemies the willies—
Who? The Phillies.

Bang the drum and toot the oboes,
Dance until the earth has shaken.

Cheer, for our beloved hoboes
Have at last brought home the bacon.

Garland them with timeless lilies!
Although they are a bunch of dillies
Who give honest men the willies.
We still love them for their sillies—
Hail, The Phillies.

PROFILE

WHEN JIM MURRAY, the syndicated columnist of the *Los Angeles Times*, writes about this shortstop, it is a case of the best describing the best. As of 1990, Murray, too, is a Pulitzer winner.

Ozzie Smith

JIM MURRAY

IT'S POSSIBLE no one ever went after a baseball the way Osborne Earl Smith does, just as it's possible no one ever went after a high C the way a Caruso did or a Bruch concerto the way Heifetz did.

With Ozzie Smith, shortstop isn't a position, it's an art. A yellow-brick road. You watch Ozzie for a while and you figure he came in with a flying dog. You want to ask him where the Tin Man went.

God made Ozzie Smith a shortstop the way he made Tracy an actor or Kelly a dancer. I mean to say, if you had a license to construct a shortstop, when you got through putting all the pieces together, it would come out like Ozzie Smith. The grace, the speed, the leaps, the rhythmical sweeping motions—Baryshnikov in cleats. Tchaikovsky would have set music to him. You get the feeling he's going to turn into a swan any minute.

He propels his body through the air like a rubber band. He used to back-flip his way out to his position. You get the feeling, with Ozzie they shouldn't just let him field ground balls like every other human being, they should make him catch them upside-down while standing on his head and playing Stars and Stripes Forever on a flute. You feel he could field a ground ball while juggling three oranges and get the guy out without dropping a one. Asking Ozzie to make a routine out is like asking Horowitz to play Chopsticks. Or Hillary to climb Bunker Hill.

One of the mysteries of baseball is how come he hasn't won an MVP? On the other hand, it's not such an enigma. It's been 25 years since a shortstop has won an MVP in the National League.

There are 153 players in the Hall of Fame. Of those voted in, only five are shortstops.

Shortstop may be the most overlooked position in the whole fabric of baseball—with the possible exception of groundskeeper. Last year, Ozzie Smith led all National League shortstops in fielding and in chances accepted for the fifth time in his career and the fourth out of the last six seasons. And he finished 18th in the MVP balloting (one guy picked him as the eighth most valuable and another, the ninth).

"Baseball is offense-oriented," says Ozzie Smith. "If you don't do it with the stick, you don't do it."

That may be. But there probably isn't a pitcher in the game who would vote for Babe Ruth over Ozzie Smith as MVP. Pitchers, you see, don't like home runs no matter who hits them. Pitchers like guys who catch or stop three-base hits, not guys who hit them. "When I throw a ground ball," the great Warren Spahn used to say sternly, "I expect it to be an out—maybe two." Tommy John, who never threw anything but ground balls, once jumped one club for another because it had a better third baseman. Geography wasn't as important to Tommy as geometry.

Still, Ozzie Smith is troubled. Once, years ago, a scribe complained to the coach, Bob Zuppke, that all the footballer, Red Grange, could do was run. "Yeah," Zuppke is supposed to have retorted, "and all Galli-Curci could do was sing."

Shortstops are like Grange and Galli-Curci. What they do is supposed to be enough. For years, the only player in the Hall of Fame with a batting average under .300 was a shortstop—Rabbit Maranville (.268). The St. Louis Cardinals cheerfully pay Ozzie Smith millions to win championships with his glove. Since he joined the club they have won two pennants and one world championship.

Shortstop is an error position. The record is 95 in a season. The man held to be the greatest shortstop who ever played, Honus Wagner, made 676 in his career. Ozzie Smith made 12 errors in 1984. He made only 14 the next year. And he almost annually leads the league in chances accepted.

There is a theory that shortstops don't hit because the position demands full concentration. A right fielder has nothing else to think about but his next at-bat. With the shortstop the hitting is an afterthought.

Ozzie has decided to rearrange his priorities. He wants to be a .300 hitter and is programming himself to do just that.

There is a risk involved in muscling up to be a better hitter. Do you lift weights to get stronger at the plate but end up clumsier in the field?

Hall of Fame balloters have been hard to please, anyway. Even a player they nicknamed "Mr. Shortstop" they failed to vote into the Hall. Couldn't hit, they said of Marty Marion (.263). Then, they got a shortstop who could hit (Arky Vaughan, .385 one season, .318 lifetime) and they wouldn't vote *him* in either. Couldn't field, they said. (Probably not true but the evidence was devastating—.385. How could a guy who could do that have time for fielding?)

Jack Clark of the Cardinals hit the most famous home run of 1985. But it would have been less famous if Ozzie Smith hadn't hit a more astonishing one the game before. Ozzie hit the only home run he has ever hit batting left-handed off Tom Niedenfuer in the ninth inning of Game 5 of the playoffs to give the Cardinals a 3–2 edge in the series and set up Clark's homer.

Ozzie is still 701 homers behind Babe Ruth (and 742 behind Henry Aaron) but he did bat .276 last year, about 40 points above his previous average. And, this year, he is batting right around .300. He has become a super contact hitter—he only struck out 27 times last year.

There is danger in this. The wizard who tied a major league record for most seasons over 500 assists and who got his sixth consecutive gold glove for top-fielding shortstop may find he is turning off the Hall of Fame electorate. If he starts to hit .300, when the time comes to vote on him for the Hall of Fame, they may reject him. "Couldn't field," they may explain. "How can a guy who hits .300 be a good shortstop? Besides, didn't he win a pennant with a home run once? Call that a shortstop? Rabbit Maranville would be ashamed."

FROM the fascinating book *A Zen Way of Baseball,* here is the account of the home run that eclipsed Henry Aaron's lifetime total—told by the man who did it.

1977: 756

SADAHARU OH *and* DAVID FALKNER

WHEN NAGASHIMA-SAN took over as manager in 1975, there was big fever over my pursuit of the home-run record. When would I reach 650, 700? When would I finally catch Babe Ruth and overtake Hank Aaron? There was also very big fever over the fate of the Giants. For the first time in ten years we had failed to win the pennant in 1974, finishing a close second to the Chunichi Dragons. Because the Giants had been together successfully for so long, not many people realized that a time of rebuilding was at hand. I think our players may not have realized it either. We did terribly in 1975, worse than anyone expected. We finished last, an almost inconceivable turn of events, given who we were and given the expectations of Nagashima-san's leadership. There was such incredulity over this turn of fortune that even some political and economic writers began wondering aloud whether the fate of the Giants wasn't in some way a foreshadowing of national events. On the final day of the season, Nagashima-san led us from the dugout to stand before our fans and offer them a formal bow of responsibility.

For me, personally, the season was also difficult. I lost a consecutive game streak that year. Over several seasons, well into 1975, I had played in 648 straight games. I had pulled a muscle in my thigh during spring training, and it had never fully healed. Nagashima-san therefore often rested me for parts of games, allowing my streak to continue but conserving my strength at the same time. One day I did not start in a game against the Hanshin Tigers at Osaka. The game progressed and still I did not get in. The game went into extra innings, and at one point Nagashima-san turned to me and said, "Prepare to go in next inning." But there was no next inning. The Tigers won the game then and there with a "sayonara" home run, and my streak was broken. There was gossip afterward that Nagashima-san did this deliberately, but I never took it that way. A manager's job is always to use his players with regard for the team first and individual records second. It would be perversion for it to be otherwise.

But that might well have been a foreshadowing of the season I was to have. For the first time in fourteen years I failed to win the home-run title. It was a very sad time. A boxer is defeated in a single night, but this was a defeat that lasted many months. It was with me every day when I went to the ball park, and there was nothing I could do about it. Koichi Tabuchi of the Tigers won the crown that year with forty-three homers. I finished tied for third with thirty-three.

I certainly did not believe that I was finished as a player, or even that I was really declining. For the first time since I had begun alternating in third and fourth spots in the batting order, there was no "O-N Cannon." I may have been easier to pitch to than in the past. Also, our team was not nearly as intimidating. Davey Johnson, who joined the Giants that year, perhaps suffered more than anyone, because he was expected to fill the void left by Nagashima-san in the lineup. He did not. Many fans rode him with a chant that was a play on his name. ("J-son! J-son!" they called. *Son* in Japanese means loss.) I was reminded all too well of my own early difficulties, but that changed nothing. The year 1975 was just not a good one for the Giants or for me. When it ended, however, I was thirty-three home runs closer to Babe Ruth. I had also closed the distance between myself and Hank Aaron. I trailed him now by seventy-eight home runs. I had an outside chance of catching Ruth the following season, and sometime after that going beyond Aaron.

I worked as hard that winter as I ever had. I was not as concerned about Ruth and Aaron as I was about myself. I had one goal for myself from the moment I lost the home-run title—and that was to get it back. I checked what I did against every memorandum I had ever made on batting. I made sure that my condition the following spring would be excellent. When camp came, my motto was that I would be in better shape than even the hungriest rookie. For the Giants and myself, 1976 would be different.

The Giants, to be sure, did not stand still over the winter. In one of the biggest trades in years, we acquired a top hitter from the Pacific League, Isao Harimoto. Mr. Harimoto, like me, was a left-handed batter. He was more of a line-drive hitter than I was, but he could hit home runs, too. The Giants' hope, soon to be borne out, was that the "O-N Cannon" would now be replaced by an "H-O Cannon."

We won the pennant in 1976, edging out the Tigers by just two games. Even though we lost the Japan Series, which followed, we clearly exhibited good fighting spirit. We lost the first three games of the series to a strong Hankyu Braves team. But then we won two games at Nishinomiya and returned to Tokyo. We took a ten-inning victory in the sixth game, tying the series, but then lost the seventh and final game at home, 4–2.

Isao Harimoto finished second in hitting in the Central League. He hit twenty-two home runs, batting ahead of me, driving in ninety-three runs. He was a strong and helpful teammate. He was also a person with more character than people gave him credit for. He came to the Giants with something of a bad-boy reputation. He was not the most admired of players, though clearly the fact that he held the all-time season record for hitting (.383) gained him respect. It turned out, though, that he and I had a good deal in common.

Like myself, Mr. Harimoto, though born in Japan, held a foreign passport. He had never tried to change his Korean identity. He was the same age as I was, entering professional baseball in 1959, the same year I joined the Giants. He lost a sister in childhood, too. He lived in Hiroshima, and his sister was killed in the atom bombing of 1945. He and his mother happened to be walking on a hill just outside the city when the surprise attack occurred, and she shielded him against herself in the shade of a tree. His brother was a survivor, too, and became something of a surrogate parent, working to allow Mr. Harimoto to pursue a career in professional baseball.

But he impressed me most by who he was and not just by what he had been. When he joined the Giants, his position was particularly difficult, because, like Davey Johnson, he had a specific role to fulfill. Unlike Davey Johnson, he was a star within the Japanese baseball system to begin with. Thus he had the dual problem of accepting both more responsibility and somewhat less status. He told me very early on that he had always regarded me as a rival even though we had played in different leagues. As I had set a standard for myself with Nagashima-san, so he had set one with me. But, he said, he had long since given up trying to chase me. Doubling his own effort was the only reasonable way he had of striving as a professional. He wound up asking me to take him to Arakawa-san's to be taught—which I did. It turned out he had a most humble attitude toward this work, the attitude of a beginner though he was a real star. He was a seven-time batting champion, a master at using all ninety degrees of a baseball field (where I could use only forty-five), but he was genuinely humble, and he became my friend. We could equally share the middle of the Giants' batting order and a good round of sake.

The year 1976 marked my return to form, too. I hit forty-nine home runs, drove in 127 runs, and hit .325, and I won two of the three batting titles. But now, no matter what I did, there was this pursuit not only of Japanese records but of world marks as well. With each passing week of the season, particularly as my home-run production ran far ahead of the previous year's pace, the likelihood grew that this would be the year I reached the 700 mark. There was even the chance, growing stronger through the summer, that I would surpass Babe Ruth.

On July 2 I hit my thirtieth home run of the season. The following day, I hit two more, leaving me one shy of 700 career home runs. Till then I had not felt the pressure of having to produce a "special" home run—for myself or for anyone else. All of a sudden, 700 seemed like a real barrier. I found myself trying, and in trying, trying to stop myself from trying. It was an exasperating and peculiar sensation. Of course I knew I would soon get 700, but one week stretched into three before it finally happened. On July 23, in a game against the Taiyo Whales in Kawasaki, in the same park where I took my first swings as a flamingo hitter, I became the only player in Japanese baseball to reach 700 home runs.

By coincidence, Arakawa-san, who had taken a job as a television commentator, was there covering the game that night. I also think Fortune permits you to play-act a little. In line with his official duties, he formally interviewed me after I hit the home run. We met on the field and very seriously shook hands before the cameras.

"Congratulations, Mr. Oh," Arakawa-san said, most soberly standing straight, with one hand behind his back.

"Thank you very much, Arakawa-san."

"Tell me, Mr. Oh, what kind of pitch did you hit?"

"Well, Arakawa-san, I believe it was . . ."

And so on and so on. Afterward, when the crowds were gone, the last interviews and autographs given, we headed off for a little out-of-the-way restaurant where we had *sushi* and sake. I don't know how long we stayed or how much we drank, but our years together made this private celebration the very best imaginable. I did not have a good game the day following.

Because it had taken longer than expected to reach 700, I was not certain that I would surpass Ruth's record that year. I wanted to. I wanted to get past it and reach Aaron's mark as quickly as possible so that I could get back to playing my own game. I believe that records can help a player set standards for his own individual efforts. But they are individual. When they become a planned part of the season, when managers, for example, are pressured to go out of their way to help them along, then the spirit of professional baseball is violated. A record is between a player and himself and cannot be pursued at the expense of his team.

I found myself too caught up in the records ahead. The pressure this brought upon me and my team—not to mention my family—was most unwelcome. And I did not handle it as well as I might have. Yet I could not blame the fans. Their excitement was natural, and their hopes for my success even became a help when I found that my own efforts, so affected by tension, needed something extra.

I did not do especially well after 700. I hit two more home runs in July and then only three in August and none in the first half of September. Fortunately, we were locked in a close pennant race, thus making it easier for me to concentrate. As we fought off the Tigers down the stretch, I began hitting home runs again. From the fourteenth of the month to the end of September, I hit six home runs in twelve games. With season's end sixteen days away, I stood three homers away from passing Babe Ruth.

On October 10, in our 125th game of the year, I hit home runs 713 and 714. I was one away with five games to play. As we were playing at home and as our opponents were the Hanshin Tigers, the expectation became tremendous. We had a full house the following day, and each time I came to the plate I could feel the excitement and the urging of the fans with me. We took an early lead in the game and held it going into the last of the eighth, 4–1. I came up with two men on base, two out, and worked the count full. I connected solidly on the next pitch.The ball rose on a trajectory toward right field. Straight down the line, however. While I knew instantly that I had enough distance on the ball, I didn't know for sure that the ball would stay fair. I watched it for a second or two. It seemed more like a full minute. The ball seemed to be moving in slow motion as it passed just to the inside of the foul pole.

What I did then—what I had never done as a professional before and have never done after—was to joyously leap into the air with both arms extended wide over my head. There was no planning this.

It happened almost in spite of myself, as though, perhaps, my "other" had taken over. Oh, yes, how happy I was! I was surely happy for the record. And yet, in thinking about it, I was also happy that the ball was fair and that this home run decisively turned a crucial game in our favor. All of it. But I was surprised at myself nonetheless. Reporters had many times asked me why I didn't show more emotion when I hit home runs, and I always answered as frankly as I could that there was never any point in further punishing an opponent. Photographers, who, after all, had a job to do, always wanted something more than a poker-faced trot about the bases, so I had worked out with them that I would make a happy gesture of some sort, briefly lifting my arms out, for example, so they could get better pictures. This time, my own feelings simply had their way.

The person most affected by this home run—really, I think, by my reaction to it—was my brother. He was, as were other members of my family and the Arakawasans, very pleased for me. But, in private, my brother was also very much moved by this reaction of mine. For him it was not a small gesture of triumph but something very different.

"Sada," he told me, "I've been waiting twenty years to say this to you. You remember in high school when I chastised you for being so open about your feelings in the Kanto tournament?"

As if I were likely to forget!

"Well, I've thought about this a great deal, and I must tell you that I was very wrong when I did that."

I, too, was moved when I saw how deeply this affected him and how long he had obviously been living with it.

"I apologize for having done that, Sada! I am deeply sorry. Please, forgive me!"

There was nothing to forgive him for. My brother in recent years had gone from being a kind of elder statesman, with whom only limited confidences could be shared, to being a friend with whom I could share everything. While I surely understood the source of his guilt in this, I wanted to assure him that there really was no need to apologize. If I had had a life not of my own choosing and had so limited my own natural expression, it would have been one thing. But I had spent my life doing what I loved. I certainly envied those who could freely and openly express happy feelings, but I did not really lose because I could not. I gained a peculiar form of self-confidence in the way I limited myself, and I also gained in effectively dealing with opponents. Things are never one-sided, and what is lost in one place is found in another.

Babe Ruth's record, it turned out, was no longer the record by the time I passed it. Ahead was Hank Aaron's. And the end of the 1976 season marked yet an additional milestone along the way. Hank Aaron retired. For the first time, his home-run record was now fixed at a certain number—755. It was immediately apparent to baseball fans, and many, many others in my country, that sometime in the very near future—the following season or, at the very latest, the season after that—I would pass that mark.

I happened to meet Hank that winter in Hawaii. We talked for a while in a hotel room. I was sorry he had retired, because knowing what he did in America kept me sharper in Japan. We talked a lot about hitting styles. It was odd, though. Hank told me that my swing was artistic and beautiful to watch. I, who certainly had been impressed by his batting form for many years, was struck by the look of gentleness and clarity in his eyes. "I'd like to be there when you break my record," he told me. "I remember Stan Musial greeting me at first base when I got my three thousandth hit."

I finished the 1976 season with 716 career home runs. I needed forty home runs to reach a new record. It was far enough away in needed playing time to afford me an interval of ordinary days before the pressure would again build. But in measuring this, perhaps I was also engaging in some wishful thinking. There was to be no letup now in the fever that swept the country. Every day there were requests for interviews and pictures. What was I doing to prepare for 756? Was I in the best condition? Did I have a target date in my own mind for the world record? Even the press beyond Japan began to take an interest now. With Hank Aaron's retirement and my being in such an obvious position to pass his mark, American journalists reported on my doings. The press in Asia, having regularly reported on Japanese baseball, seemed as eager to pursue the story as media people in Japan.

With the coming of the 1977 season, this "Oh fever" actually became a kind of industry. Everywhere, I am told, baseballs with reproductions of my signature were sold as fast as they could reach the stores; companies began producing medals, towels, T-shirts in advance of the commemorative moment; another company manufactured a plate with my portrait as its principal design; restaurants announced incredible bargains on steak dinners to be offered the day following 756 (the cost of a steak dinner is well beyond the reach of most people in Japan); the media even turned up a story about a Mah-Jongg parlor in Yaesu that happened to have the name Oh and that, as a consequence, announced a 40 percent reduction in prices for the day following the big home run. Whether I wished it to be otherwise or not, there was to be no letup in the pressure surrounding me.

In many ways I was lucky to have had the experience of pursuing an earlier "big" record. It was a kind of rehearsal. I learned from it. I had not handled the pressure as well as I might have. I had also found myself resenting the increased public attention. In a way, that was exactly the problem. All the "atmospherics" surrounding my pursuit of the home-run record had interfered with the way I played the game.

As I had on so many other occasions, I returned to Arakawa-san. In June, while the record was still distant, I worked with him every day for a week. We worked from eleven at night until around two in the morning, just as we had in the past. I approached our training sessions as I always had—bowing to my teacher and formally requesting his instruction. We performed the exercises that by now were familiar but that could not be successfully done unless there was absolute concentration.

I approached the problem of excessive public attention in the only way I knew—by disciplined work as a batsman. The way of the flamingo hitter was something I had grown to love. It had yielded its rewards only with persistent effort. Its promise to me had been a kind of proof that effort does effect change. And the change I was looking for was the one I had always been pursuing—oneness with my skill.

What I found in this "interval" between records was something that I was not quite looking for but that was the very thing I needed most. I came to have a changed attitude toward all the attention I was receiving.

I had become quite conscious that the demands placed upon me by the public—for time, autographs, appearances, interviews, and the like—were interfering not only with my play but my life as well. Because crowds had regularly begun to gather outside my house, for example, it was no longer possible for my daughters to go out and play as ordinary children would. My wife could not go to the market, nor could we, if we wanted, go off to a restaurant or have an evening to ourselves. We had to send out for many of our meals, and our children had to accustom themselves to indoor activities, as though imprisoned in their own house.

During my career I had always made it a point to be accessible to fans. This was never something I did reluctantly. I normally enjoyed the relationship I had with them. I have several fan clubs, for instance, and by participating in their events over the years, I have come to meet many interesting people I might otherwise never have known. Mr. Shimei Cho is the best speaker of Japanese among my many Chinese friends. He organized a club after my fifty-five home-run season consisting of Chinese and Japanese members. They hold various events, as does another club organized in Toyama Prefecture by friends of my mother. I attend the annual parties the clubs hold, and they in turn have been very protective and caring toward me. Members send me gifts and cards, which I always respond to in my own hand, and they perform helpful services for which I have been deeply grateful. One member of a fan club regularly visits my twin sister's grave and offers prayers and flowers for me during the regular season when I am not able to attend to this myself.

By midsummer in 1977 two things had become clear. One was that the Giants were not nearly as hard pressed in the pennant race as in the season before. We were well on the way to taking the Central League championship, so the pressure to keep pace, though keen, was not really so draining. The other factor was that I had maintained a steady enough home-run pace to bring Aaron's record within reach by the end of the season. I had twenty-six homers by August 1 and needed fourteen for the record.

On August 4 I got my twenty-seventh home run. I homered again on the sixth, twice more on the ninth, then once again on the tenth, eleventh, and twelfth. With rain-outs and breaks in the schedule, we managed to play only three games between the thirteenth and twenty-third. I hit my thirty-fourth home run of the season on the twenty-third, another the following day, two more the day after that. On August 31 I hit career home run number 755. I was one away from the record.

All the while the uproar around my life grew daily. Each day crowds of people gathered at my house, awaiting my comings and goings. The crowds became so regular that police were assigned to the area to keep order. I had no private life of any kind now. From the moment I got up to the moment I went to bed I was accompanied every step of the way by people who awaited this record with me. When I left my house in the morning, I hoped it would give my family some quiet time. It never did. People simply remained or were joined by others awaiting my return. In traffic, cars, camera crews, motorcycles accompanied me, and at stop signals people waved to me and called out greetings. There were times when I could not move from one place to another without benefit of a police escort. Any time I was on a street anywhere, I was sure, in a matter of seconds, to be engulfed by people.

And yet I did not feel as I had earlier. The people who waited for me at my house—children, families—all wished me well and wanted my home run to come soon. When I came down the steps toward my carport, children would hand me bouquets of flowers, some of them quite carefully and beautifully arranged. They had gifts and mementoes, prayers and little capsule messages of good fortune from local shrines. There is a room in my parents' house where all these keepsakes have been preserved. There was a statue of a dragon, my special protection, rising from a baseball; the Overseas Chinese Club presented me with a figure of Hotei, one of the Seven Gods from Chinese mythology, the one who gives long life and luck; a well-known sculptor did a carving of a fish leaping from the water, this the representation of that in all of us which reaches higher amid the limitations of this world. There were drawings, wood-block prints, dolls, brushwork decorations of every kind. In all of this, instead of resisting a loss of privacy, I took into myself the added strength of these good wishes. I became conscious of how much I was supported in my own efforts.

I had always made it a point to sign autographs. I was never troubled by this, because the time it took cost me so very little. But I had a problem at this time, because the crowds around my house had grown enormously. Over the years I had learned how to sign many autographs in a short while. I could carry on a conversation and sign a baseball or board at the same time. Because it got to the point where I was often faced with many people simultaneously asking for my autograph, I made a study of just how many I could give within a certain period of time. In the past I had not always been able to sign for everyone. It bothered me when this happened, and I did not want it to happen in this special situation at my house.

The best way I could deal with this was to add on an extra fifteen or twenty minutes before I had to leave. I calculated exactly. The greatest number of autographs I could sign in a minute was ten. Before I left the house, I counted the crowd. If there were 150 to 200, I knew that I could sign for everyone within fifteen or twenty minutes. If there were more than 200, then I would sign for no one that day. The point was to sign for all or none. When I got outside, sometimes I would borrow a bullhorn from a policeman and request that people form a line so I could more easily handle their requests for autographs.

There were days when it was impossible to accommodate people. But there were many other days when I could. I was pleased to do this, and in the end I believe it even helped on my way to 756.

On September 1 we finished a series at home against the Taiyo Wahles. The next day we began a three-game set against the Yakult Swallows. I was not able to hit the record home run in the final game against the Whales nor in the first game of the following series. If the home run did not come in the next two days, the chances were it would occur on the road, where we would be playing till the middle of the month.

It was strange waiting for this moment. Really, it was as inevitable as something could be, given the finite and unpredictable character of events. Yet it was like living in the midst of a storm. The storm, of course, would pass. But for me the task was to try to find its center so that I could concentrate on what I had to do. One to go. It was almost as though the only place left in the world where I had room to move my arms freely was the playing field during game time. Reporters, photographers, cameramen were with me now even as I took practice, sometimes getting in the way as I tried to run or throw. I realized how fatigued I had become over these many months. Except for sleeping, I could not remember the last time I had really been alone.

The evening of September 3 was filled with the same expectation as the previous evening. Traffic was brought to a halt as I made my way from my home to the ball park. Swarms of people surrounded me right up to game time. I remember sitting on a metal chair in front of my locker after the press had finally cleared the clubhouse. My teammates were milling around, shortly to take the field. I felt drained of all energy, as though I had not slept for days. Suddenly a door opened. I thought for a moment I was imagining things. It was my mother. No one was allowed in the clubhouse at this point, and she was entering an area that was normally closed to the press. I will forever remember the look on her face, sweet and beckoning. She was dressed very plainly, as though the occasion was an ordinary visit with her son. I rose to greet her. Her eyes spoke so much to me—certainty that I would make it that very night and also that it was even more important that I take care of myself.

My mother is a very small woman. As I leaned over to catch her words, I remember wondering, absurdly, when it was that I first became conscious that my mother only reached the middle of my chest.

She reached out and handed me two parcels, one rather large, the other small.

"I brought some apples for you and your teammates," she said. "Please distribute them. The smaller package is for your daughters."

I began to thank her, but she went right on.

"I brought some *suzumushi* for them. Such crickets are hard to find in the cities these days, aren't they? Take good care of them, and take good care of yourself." She then turned and left, heading back for the grandstand.

I brought the packages back to my locker. What a strange gift at such a time! I held the small package to my ear to see if I could hear the crickets inside. Yes! They were quite alive. Their wings whirred and whirred. I became so caught up in listening to them that the noise of the locker room and the heavy sea tide of the crowd in the stadium completely disappeared. There was only the music of these summertime crickets and the immense silence that their voices invoked.

When I left my locker and headed for the field, I had no feeling of tiredness. I could feel in my bones that this indeed was the night. I came upon the lights and noise of Korakuen almost as if they didn't exist. The quietness my mother had brought me surrounded me like a spell. It was not going to be broken. I hit in the first inning and then in the third. The third inning. One out, no one on base. The pitcher's name, in this twenty-third game of the year against the Swallows, was Kojiro Suzuki. The goal, Arakawa-san had always said, was oneness of mind, body, and skill. You and the opponent together create the moment. The *ma* is the one you create but in which you are not at all separate from your opponent. The pitcher and I, the ball—and the silence my mother gave me—these were all one. In the midst of whatever was going on, there was only this emptiness in which I could do what I wanted to do. The count went full. Mr. Kojiro Suzuki threw a sinker on the outside part of the plate. I followed the ball perfectly. I could almost feel myself waiting for its precise break before I let myself come forward. When I made contact, I felt like I was scooping the ball upward and outward. The ball rose slowly and steadily in the night sky, lit by Korakuen's bright lights. I could follow it all the way, as it lazily reached its height and seemed to linger there in the haze, and then slowly began its descent into the right-field stands.

The crowd erupted, almost as a single voice. A huge banner was suddenly unfurled that read, "Congratulations, World Record!" Everywhere—but on the diamond—people were running and lights were flashing. For me, it was the moment of purest joy I had ever known as a baseball player.

No one can stop a home run. No one can understand what it really is unless you have felt it in your own hands and body. It is different from seeing it or trying to describe it. There is nothing I know quite like meeting a ball in exactly the right spot. As the ball makes its high, long arc beyond the playing field, the diamond and the stands suddenly belong to one man. In that brief, brief time, you are free of all demands and complications. There is no one behind you, no obstruction ahead, as you follow this clear path around all the bases. This is the batsman's center stage, the one time that he may allow himself to freely accept the limelight, to enjoy the sensation of every eye in the stadium fixed on him, waiting for the moment when his foot will touch home plate. In this moment he is free.

Obviously, 756 was special. How could it be otherwise? I know it was not a "world" record (there is no world competition). I don't believe I would have reached 756 if I had played in America. But it was my record and it was baseball's record nevertheless! It was the devotion of a professional's career.

When I reached home plate, all of the noise and excitement I had left behind were there in full force, happy and surging with energy. I don't know where in the midst of all the congratulations that followed it occurred, but someone said to me:

"Your parents, your parents, let your parents come to the field!"

My parents are very shy people, and I was not sure how they would feel in front of so many people. I was uncertain what to do. Also, I did not really want to monopolize things. My home run belonged to many people other than myself. My teammates and my opponents shared in this moment, though no lights found them. I needed no more for myself than my foot touching home plate. But, yes, I did want to share this moment with my parents. If I had planned it exactly, I could not have calculated the depth of thanksgiving and pride I suddenly felt now. By all means, I wanted to stand with them.

Just then a congratulatory message from Hank Aaron flashed on the electronic scoreboard, and, most eerily, his voice boomed out over a loudspeaker as the crowd became hushed. He must have been speaking by telephone hookup.

"Congratulations," his voice resounded. "I had hoped to see you break my record there in Japan, but I haven't been able to make it. . . . Continue slugging for your fans. And again, congratulations."

By now ceremonies were under way. Both teams were lined up in front of their dugouts; a microphone was placed in the center of the diamond. My parents were on the field. They looked so happy and so startled by all the commotion. My mother later told me, contrary to what I saw in her eyes, that she and my father had not really dressed for the occasion because they hadn't expected the home run that night. Just then, my parents impulsively walked over to the players on our team. They bowed to each of them and shook each one's hand, thanking them individually for helping me. It was hard to keep from crying. I was so moved and proud of my parents. I have always believed that success in this life owes to a strong will, and there were no people I knew who were stronger in this way than my mother, who was also tenderhearted, and my father, who had endured so many indignities and who so stubbornly persisted in his dreams anyway. The press made much of how generous I had been to others. In my circumstances, it was easy. My father extended himself when it wasn't so easy. He believed in repaying hatred with virtue not when he was surrounded by an admiring public but when the prejudice of officials and the hands of torturers cut his body and tried his soul. In over seventy years of life he has never once gone back on his deepest belief that the goal of any man's life is to be useful to others.

I was presented with a very large floral award, the official recognition of my achievement. Many cameras were whirring; this was the moment the whole nation had been waiting to celebrate. I could think of nothing more fitting to do then than to bring this award to my parents and offer it to them. I did this. I handed them the award, and I bowed deeply to them—and they to me.

I stood, finally, on the mound with all the lights of the stadium turned off save for a single spot on me. I took my cap off, bowed in four directions, and spoke a few words. I told people that my dream had finally come true, thanks to all those who had given me support. To receive such warm applause and feelings made me a happy man, and I promised to keep playing as long as my body would permit.

Later, I told the press that I was sorry for the pitcher, Suzuki, but that I was relieved to have finally answered the expectations of so many fans. Above all, what I wanted now was to get back to my own style of play. This, however, was still a wish.

There were official parties and functions to attend that night and no end of pursuit by the press. When I got home at two o'clock in the morning, there were over 600 people in front of my house! They greeted me happily and noisily—so much so that my most immediate thought was for the peace and quiet of my neighbors. I had no wish to ruin my fans' happiness either, so rather than have the police ask them to disperse, I signed autographs for them all and to each one said good night.

There was a party in full swing in my house. My parents, my wife, my three daughters, my brother and his family were all there, and so we toasted each other over and over again before we all called it a night.

There was one last matter to attend to. I placed a call to Arakawa-san. He was not with me in the house nor in the entourage that surrounded me before and after the game. I would have liked him to be there, of course, but it was not possible. We might have raised a cup of sake in the midst of all the bedlam, but that would not really have mattered. He knew and I knew—independent of this extraordinary tumult—what we had done together. This night was his, too, and its outcome had been fashioned a long time before.

"Arakawa-san?"

"Yes, it's me."

I said to him what I always said whenever I left one of our training sessions—when I bowed, acknowledging his mastery.

"Domo arigato Gozaimasu."

I thanked him with all my heart, because without him there would have been no record.

POETRY

THIS IS hardly the longest historical piece in this book. In its way, though, it might be the most complete.

From *the wrong season*

JOEL OPPENHEIMER

john g. "scissors"
mcilvain, described by
the sporting news as
remarkable, died
in charleroi, pa.,
recently. he was
88. he pitched for
22 minor league teams
in 15 different leagues
and was still in semi-
pro ball in his seventies.
when he won a 4–3 ball
game at seventy-five he
said: i don't see anything
to get excited about. i
think a person should feel
real good when he does
something unexpected.
i expected this. his
big disappointment was
that he never made the
majors, although he won
26 for chillicothe
one season, and 27 the
next. he was, however,
a bird-dog scout for
the indians for several
years. he had been
deaf since 1912.

EARLIER in these pages Robert Creamer describes the 1916 A's as "majestically inept." And here they are.

The Worst Team of All

JACK ORR

TOM SHEEHAN, the old pitcher who now scouts for the Giants, is making the hegira to California with the team. He was saying goodby to his Philadelphia friends a few weeks ago and boasting that he was on the worst team in the history of modern baseball. The Philadelphia A's of 1916.

"Oh, come now," said a listener, "they couldn't have been worse than the Doc Prothro-Boom Boom Beck Phillies or the Braves of 1935 who won only 38 games or some of those post-war Brownie teams or the Phillies that Fred Fitzsimmons had during the war."

"They were so," Sheehan said. "You could look it up. We lost 117 games, a record. Personally," he said, not without pride, "I had a 1–17 record and my roomie, Johnnie Nabors, won one and lost 20—19 of them in a row."

Study of the records shows that Sheehan had something. Elmer Myers and Bullet Joe Bush, two other pitchers, each lost 24 games. So among four pitchers they lost 85, which some years is almost enough by itself to put you in the cellar. The A's were last by 54½ games.

"You never saw a club like this," Sheehan said. "We lost 20 in a row at one point that summer and I had a haunting feeling we'd never win another.

"We lost 19 straight on the road. In one game our pitchers gave up 18 walks and in another we left 17 men on base, though I don't know how that many guys got on in the first place.

"We had Whitey Witt, an outfielder by trade, at shortstop. He must have made 80 errors that year. [*He made 70—Ed.*] Larry Lajoie was on second, but he was 41 years old, hit .246 and covered as much ground as the waterbucket. He quit after that year.

"Stuffy McInnis (.295) was the first baseman and he was all right, but the third baseman was new every day. Connie Mack must have recruited them from the stands. Some of them didn't stay around long enough to be introduced. (One of them named Charlie Pick made 41 errors.)

"Wally Schang, the old catcher, was in left field, along with a bunch of others. A kid named Eddie King hit .188 in right. Billy Myer (.232) caught half a season until he got an appendicitis attack in July.

" 'Imagine that lucky son-of-a-gun going away for an operation,' we all said.

"After he left, everybody caught. Remember Val Picinich? He was 19, just breaking in. He hit .195. On other days total strangers would catch.

"Once we were playing the Yankees at the Polo Grounds and I'm pitching. Picinich warms me up, but as the first hitter gets in, Val goes back to the bench and takes off the tools.

"Another guy comes out, a guy I've never seen. He comes out to the mound and says, 'My name is Carroll. I'm the catcher. What are your signs?' I tell him not to confuse me and get the heck back there and catch. He stuck around for about a week and nobody ever saw him again. [*The records show a Ralph Carroll caught ten games and hit .091.*]

"We pitchers lost a lot of games, but that collection couldn't have won behind Matty or Grove. Once we go to Boston for a series. I pitch the opener and give up one hit, by Doc Hoblitzel. But it happens to follow a walk and an error by Witt and I lose, 1–0.

"Now Nabors pitches the second game and he is leading, 1–0, going into the ninth. He gets the first man. Witt boots one and the next guy walks. Hooper is up next, I think, and he singles to left and the man on second tries to score.

"Well, Schang has a good arm and he throws one in that has the runner cold by 15 feet. But we have one of those green catchers. (Never forget his name, Mike Murphy.) The ball bounces out of his glove, the run scores, the other runner takes third and it is 1–1.

"Nabors winds up and throws the next pitch 20 feet over the hitter's head into the grandstand, the man on third scores and we lose another, 2–1.

"Later I asked Nabors why he threw that one away.

" 'Look,' he said, 'I knew those guys wouldn't get me another run and if you think I'm going to throw nine more innings on a hot day like this, you're crazy.' "

HISTORY

THE BREAKING of baseball's color line with the signing of Jackie Robinson in 1945 has been a story familiar to fans. Far less familiar are the forces and factors that made integration inevitable.

From *Only the Ball Was White*

ROBERT PETERSON

I am an invisible man. No, I am not a spook like those who haunted Edgar Allan Poe; nor am I one of your Hollywood-movie ectoplasms. I am a man of substance, of flesh and bone, fiber and liquids—and I might even be said to possess a mind. I am invisible, understand, simply because people refuse to see me.

—RALPH ELLISON, *Invisible Man*

THE TWO decades between 1900 and 1920—the period when Negro baseball was growing up—were a time when white America's racial attitudes were hardening. The Black Reconstruction had failed and ebbed into history; Jim Crow was firmly embedded, in fact if not in law, both North and South. Racial tensions exploded in 1906 in Atlanta, where ten Negroes and two whites died in a race riot, and in Springfield, Illinois, two years later when two Negroes and four whites were killed. The Great Migration of Negroes from South to North, beginning in 1915, was accompanied by a crescendo of race fury. During World War I race riots in East St. Louis, Missouri, and Houston, Texas, killed at least thirty-nine Negroes and twenty-five whites. After the Houston uprising, thirteen Negroes were hanged and forty-one imprisoned for life. Immediately after the war, in 1919, there were race riots in twenty-six American cities, the worst in Chicago, where twenty-three Negroes and fifteen whites died.

Riding the tide of race hate, segregation calcified during those two decades. But even during this harsh period for the nation's black men, there was still an occasional white voice raised in organized baseball on behalf of the Negro. In 1915, Walter McCredie, manager of Portland in the Pacific Coast League, tried to provide an opening wedge for Negroes by signing an outfielder of Chinese and Hawaiian parentage. His white players immediately rebelled and McCredie was forced to concede defeat. But, he said, "I don't think the color of the skin ought to be a barrier in baseball. . . . If I had my say the Afro-American would be welcome inside the fold. I would like to have such players as Lloyd and Petway of the Chicago Colored Giants . . ."

Black players also found a champion in *The Sporting News.* In 1923 the baseball weekly (which, when integration finally arrived, was less than enthusiastic) bemoaned the exclusion of Negroes from organized baseball. Calling racial prejudice a "hideous monster," the paper said that it is an "ivory-headed obsession that one man made in God's image is any better than another man made in the same image . . ."

Negro players of that day had little hope that black men would ever play in organized ball. Napoleon Cummings, who began playing with the Bacharach Giants in Atlantic City, N.J., in 1916, remembers, "Yes, we talked about it. We talked about it years back, said there would never be a Negro in the big leagues. But we always used to talk about it among ourselves."

During the late Twenties such talk among players and fans generally receded. Memories that Negroes had once played in organized baseball were dimming, and it seemed more and more the natural order of things that whites played on their teams and Negroes played on theirs. "We never thought much about it," said Bill Yancey, whose career as a professional ballplayer spanned the years from 1923 to 1936. ". . . I remember Rojo [a Cuban-Negro catcher]—he was funny. He didn't speak too much English. He'd see two white kids throwing a baseball and he'd say, 'Bycmby, s'ousands of dollars.' "

Rojo's wistfulness mirrored the belief of Negro players of the 1920s that organized baseball, and particularly the big leagues, were forever beyond their aspirations. That belief was reinforced during the carefree years when America was careening on a headlong course toward the Depression of 1929. Rarely was a white man's voice heard to condemn segregation in baseball. In the early Thirties, when the Depression was at its peak and Americans were blinded to social justice by the pervasive, nagging struggle to put food on their tables, Negro players became even more like Ellison's Invisible Man.

In *An American Dilemma,* Gunnar Myrdal put his finger on the attitude of whites toward blacks during this period:

> The observer finds that in the North there is actually much unawareness on the part of white people to the extent of social discrimination against Negroes. It has been a common experience of this writer to witness how white North-

erners are surprised and shocked when they hear about such things, and how they are moved to feel that something ought to be done to stop it. They often do not understand correctly even the implications of their own behavior and often tell the interviewer that they "have never thought about it in that light." This innocence is, of course, opportunistic in a degree, but it is, nevertheless, real and honest too. It denotes the absence of an explicit theory and an intentional policy. In this situation one of the main difficulties for the Negroes in the North is simply lack of publicity. It is convenient for the Northerners' good conscience to forget about the Negro.

When the question of Negroes playing in the big leagues *was* presented to them, most Northerners did seem to feel that "something ought to be done." In 1928 the New York *Daily News* Inquiring Photographer asked six whites whether they would disapprove of a black player in the big leagues. Four said they would not, and the two who said they would gave as their reason a fear that the fans' race prejudice would inflame the strong feelings aroused by competition on the diamond and possibly lead to riots in the stands. Typical of the favorable replies was this one by a Bronx salesman: "Certainly not. There shouldn't be any race prejudice. It isn't as bitter now as it used to be, and I think prejudice is gradually dying out. Colored men can enter almost any other field (sic). Why not baseball?"

Why not indeed? Years later, after the color line was finally expunged, Judy Johnson became a scout for the Philadelphia Athletics and a good friend of the A's venerable owner, Connie Mack. Johnson recalls, "I asked him one day, I said, 'Mr. Mack, why didn't you ever take any of the colored boys in the big leagues?' He said, 'Well, Judy, if you want to know the truth, there were just too many of you to go in.' As much as to say, it would take too many jobs away from the other boys."

However, the Negroes who played in the Philadelphia area during this time felt that Mack himself was prepared to accept Negroes if his lodge brothers in the league would not protest too much.

Napoleon Cummings remembers talk around Philadelphia in 1929 that Connie Mack wanted to hire a couple of Negro players:

I remember when they played the '29 World Series, they were short of ballplayers, and there was a rumor around here that they wanted to get somebody from around Philadelphia to help them out because they were short. But they wouldn't let Negroes on that ballclub. I remember that, and I was at the World Series. Connie Mack was trying to get Biz Mackey and Santop and all them. No soap.

If Mack did try to hire Negroes for his Athletics, he did not make sufficient fuss about it for the story to break into print. Why didn't he just go ahead and do it? There was no written rule barring Negroes from organized baseball. What stopped him? Presumably the answer lies in the attitudes of the other major-league operators.

The reasons advanced during this period for baseball's color line (on the rare occasions when it was mentioned) were substantially the same as they were in 1946, when it was finally breached. They can be summarized thus:

(1) About a third of all major-league players were Southerners and they would not play with or against Negroes; (2) Negroes could not travel with a big-league club, because hotels would not accommodate them; (3) the clubs trained in the South, where Negroes and whites were forbidden by law to play together; (4) fans might riot in the stands if there was trouble on the field between a white and Negro player; (5) Negroes were not good enough to play in the big leagues anyway.

The first reason given was probably the most serious. It seems likely that some southern players would not have played on the same field with a Negro during the late Twenties and Thirties. But the evidence from the late Forties, when they *were* playing with Negroes, suggests that defections would have been few. Southerners, no less than Northerners, coveted the fame and fortune offered by major-league baseball.

Reasons 2 and 3 were evasions. Plenty of Negro players would have been perfectly willing to be Jim Crowed in hotels for a chance to play in the majors. As for spring training, Cuba and other areas of Latin America provided acceptable facilities, as the Brooklyn Dodgers would demonstrate when the color bar was crumbling.

Reason 4, the danger of racially motivated skirmishes in the stands, was a reasonable concern. But in retrospect it seems probable that if the way had been carefully prepared (as it was in Brooklyn), there would have been little trouble among the fans. In addition, some owners feared they would lose their white fans if they played Negroes. After all, organized baseball is a business; it cannot exist without paying customers.

Concerning Reason 5, the quality of Negro players, the testimony is mixed. Many white ballplayers and respected sportswriters believed that at least a few black players were of major-league calibre. Some baseball men were doubtful. In any case, this was not a very good reason, because, if Negroes were truly not ready for the majors, could they not have been initiated into organized baseball in the minors? (In fact, this turned out to be the way the color line was broken.)

Unspoken, but underlying all the stated objections, was the most compelling reason of all: baseball tradition. Organized baseball was steeped—perhaps a better word would be pickled—in tradition. Among the eternal verities were the sun's rising in the east, the sanctity of motherhood, and baseball's status as the National Pastime; and, since there had not been a Negro in the organized leagues in the memory of most baseball men, it must be part of God's plan that there should be none. Tradition is the father of inertia and the balm of the don't-rock-the-boat school.

By the early Thirties, gentle waves were washing against the stately hull of organized baseball. The Negro press had of course been running a low-keyed but persistent campaign to break down the bars for years, but the first powerful voice to raise the issue in the white press was Westbrook Pegler, who denounced baseball for its apartheid in 1931.

Jimmy Powers of the New York *Daily News* soon took up the cudgels and hammered at the ban for several years. In 1933 he conducted his own poll of the dignitaries at the annual Baseball Writers Association dinner on the question of admitting Negroes to the major leagues. Curiously, the only important baseball man who opposed the idea was John J. McGraw, who had tried in vain to sign Charlie Grant for the Baltimore Orioles more than thirty years earlier. Powers did not explain the basis for McGraw's opposition.

One of the problems in breaking down the color bar was the reluctance of baseball's leaders to admit officially that it even existed. John A. Heydler, president of the National League, could say without blushing in 1933, "Beyond the fundamental requirement that a major-league player must have unique ability and good character and habits, I do not recall one instance where baseball has allowed either race, creed or color to enter into its selection of players."

It was becoming increasingly difficult to sustain this sort of nonsense in the face of the performances against big-leaguers in postseason games by men like Satchel Paige, Josh Gibson, Buck Leonard, Slim Jones, and Cool Papa Bell. In 1938, Clark Griffith became the first member of baseball's official family to admit to the possibility that Negroes might one day be in organized baseball. In an interview with Sam Lacy, an enterprising reporter for the Washington *Tribune,* a Negro weekly, Griffith said:

There are few big-league magnates who are not aware of the fact that the time is not far off when colored players will take their places beside those of other races in the major leagues. However, I'm not sure that time has arrived yet . . .

Griffith predicted:

A lone Negro in the game will face caustic comments. He will be made the target of cruel, filthy epithets. Of course, I know the time will come when the ice will have to be broken. Both by the organized game and by the colored player who is willing to volunteer and thus become a sort of martyr to the cause.

There was no shortage of willing volunteers among the black players. No one, not even Griffith, called for them, but the race question appears to have been on his mind as indicated by his talk with Josh Gibson and Buck Leonard in his office after he had watched the two black men belting the ball.

As the third decade of the century neared its close, powerful voices in the press were calling loudly for an end to baseball's discrimination against Negroes. In New York, Heywood Broun and Jimmy Powers were excoriating the major leagues. Shirley Povich of the Washington *Post* wrote after watching Negro clubs train in Florida:

There's a couple of million dollars' worth of baseball talent on the loose, ready for the big leagues, yet unsigned by any major league. There are pitchers who would win 20 games this season for any big-league club that offered them contracts, and there are outfielders who could hit .350, infielders who could win quick recognition as stars, and there is at least one catcher who at this writing is probably superior to Bill Dickey. [The reference is to John Gibson.]

Only one thing is keeping them out of the big leagues—the pigmentation of their skin. They happen to be colored. That's their crime in the eyes of the big-league club owners. . . . Their talents are being wasted in the rickety parks in the Negro sections of Pittsburgh, Philadelphia, New York, Chicago and four other cities that comprise the major leagues of Negro baseball. They haven't a chance to get into the big leagues of the white folks. It's a tight little boycott that the majors have set up against colored players.

A magazine called *Friday* kept the pot simmering in 1940 by soliciting comments from a number of major-league players and managers on the quality of Negro ballplayers. The response of Gabby Hartnett, manager of the Chicago Cubs, is fairly representative: "I am not interested in the color of a player, just his ability," Hartnett said. "If managers were given permission, there'd be a mad rush to sign up Negroes."

Bill McKechnie, Cincinnati Reds manager, and Leo Durocher, then piloting the Brooklyn Dodgers, replied in a similar vein. Stars like Pepper Martin, Luke Hamlin, Bucky Walters, Johnny Vander Meer, and Carl Hubbell praised Negro players. So did William Benswanger, president of the Pittsburgh Pirates, who declared, "If it came to an issue, I'd vote for Negro players. There's no reason why they should be denied the same chance that Negro fighters and musicians are given."

Benswanger had no appetite for the role of pioneer, however, as he proved in 1942, when the *Daily Worker*, a Communist newspaper published in New York, put pressure on the Pirates. In his autobiography, Roy Campanella tells of being approached by a man from the *Worker* (which he did not know was a Communist paper) who said he had arranged a tryout with the Pirates for Campanella, Dave Barnhill, New York Cubans pitcher, and Sammy Hughes, second baseman for the Baltimore Elite Giants. Long afterward, Campanella got a letter from Benswanger saying that the Pirates would be glad to arrange a tryout, "but it contained so many buts that I was discouraged even before I had finished reading the letter." He replied that all he asked for was a chance. The Pirates did not answer his letter.

The *Worker* quoted Leo Durocher, manager of the Brooklyn Dodgers, as blaming the baseball commissioner's office for the color bar. Commissioner Kenesaw Mountain Landis reacted with stern words.

Negroes are not barred from organized baseball by the commissioner and never have been during the twenty-one years I have served. There is no rule in organized baseball prohibiting their participation and never has been to my knowledge. If Durocher, or any other manager, or all of them, want to sign one, or twenty-five, Negro players, it is all right with me. That is the business of the managers and the club owners. The business of the commissioner is to interpret the rules of baseball and to enforce them.

Negro players were not encouraged by the rising level of discussion about the injustice of the color line. Buck Leonard remembers:

We didn't think anything was going to happen. We thought that they were just going to keep talking about it, that's all. They'd talked about it all those years and there'd been nothing done. We just didn't pay it any attention. We'd say, well, if it comes, we hope to have a chance to play, but we just didn't pay it any mind.

Despite the Negro players' fatalism, the quickening tempo of talk about the color bar was significant; it told of subtle changes in America's racial attitudes. Segregation was still the rule, but it was becoming a shaky bulwark against the steady pricking of white America's conscience by the social and economic changes wrought by Roosevelt's New Deal, the Negro's improving educational and living standards, and perhaps most of all, by World War II. With American black men fighting along with whites in the far corners of the globe, it was no longer quite so convenient for whites at home to forget their black compatriots.

Whitey Gruhler, sports columnist of the Atlantic City *Press-Union* and one of the few white writers who had covered Negro baseball regularly, gave voice to the nation's moral crisis in July 1942, when America had been in the war for seven months. Gruhler had been calling in vain for the entry of Negro players into organized baseball for several years; now, with America fighting for its life, he found himself in the mainstream, articulating a thought that had growing echoes:

We are fighting a war—the most terrible war in all history. We are spending billions of dollars. Our youth is shedding barrels and barrels of blood. Every day is one of heartache and tragedy. And what are we fighting for? Freedom and democracy. But some of us seem to have forgotten that freedom and democracy are the human rights for which we fought the Civil War.

But baseball's conservatives were not yet ready for such a drastic step as removal of the color line. *The Sporting News* argued that Negroes were better off in their own leagues and that they were not ready or even willing to mingle with whites. The paper blamed "agitators" who "have sought to force Negro players on the big leagues, not because it would help the game but because it gives them a chance to thrust themselves into the limelight as great crusaders in the guise of democracy." After noting that some Negro baseball men were lukewarm to the idea of integration, *The Sporting News* concluded:

Of course, there are some colored people who take a different view, and they are entitled to their opinions, but in doing so they are not looking at the question from the broader point of view, or for the ultimate good of either the race or the individuals in it. They ought to concede their own people are now protected and that nothing is served by allowing agitators to make an issue of a question on which both sides prefer to be let alone.

Larry MacPhail, president of the Brooklyn Dodgers, echoed this view. When a Brooklyn priest asked MacPhail whether the Dodgers would be willing to have Negro players, MacPhail replied that black players had their own leagues which would be wrecked if Negroes were in the majors. "Unfortunately," he added, "the discussion of the problem has been contaminated by charges of racial discrimination—most of it vicious propaganda circulated by professional agitators who do not know what they are talking about."

Other baseball executives, although uncertain that the time was yet ripe for introducing black players into organized baseball, saw that it was coming. Among them was William K. Wrigley, Jr., owner of the Chicago Cubs, who said he foresaw the day—"and soon." But, he declared, "there are men in high places who don't want it."

It was becoming apparent that the color question could not be kept submerged indefinitely, and in 1943 it surfaced in two places 3,000 miles apart. In Los Angeles that spring, Clarence (Pants) Rowland, president of the Pacific Coast League Angels, said trials would be given to three Negro players, Chet Brewer, Howard Easterling, and Nate Moreland. Two weeks later he reneged, apparently under pressure from other league operators, but his retreat brought a flurry of protests. The Los Angeles County Board of Supervisors and the huge local of the United Auto Workers union at North American Aircraft went on record opposing discrimination in the Pacific Coast League. The Angels' park was picketed on opening day.

There was trouble in Oakland, too, where Art Cohn, sports editor of the *Tribune,* scored the Oaks for not trying out Negroes. Oakland owner Vince Devincenzi ordered his manager, Johnny Vergez, to give trials to two Negroes, Chet Brewer and Olin Dial, but Vergez refused, despite the fact that most of the good Oakland players were in service.

Meanwhile, at the other end of the nation, Bill Veeck was trying to dig the grave of the color line. Veeck was a master showman and innovator who had been operating the Milwaukee Brewers of the American Association and who, after the war, would bring pennants to the Cleveland Indians and Chicago White Sox (and, incidentally, introduce the first Negroes into the American League). He also suffered the ultimate indignity of presiding over the St. Louis Browns.

Veeck's plan was to buy the sinking Philadelphia Phillies franchise and stock the club with Negro stars for the 1944 season. "With Satchel Paige, Roy Campanella, Luke Easter, Monte Irvin, and countless others in action and available, I had not the slightest doubt that in 1944, a war year, the Phils would have leaped from seventh place to the pennant," Veeck says in his book, *Veeck—as in Wreck.*

Jerry Nugent, president of the Phillies, was willing to sell and Veeck had lined up the necessary financing, but, Veeck says, "I made one bad mistake. Out of long respect for Judge Landis, I felt he was entitled to prior notification of what I intended to do. . . . Judge Landis wasn't exactly shocked but he wasn't exactly overjoyed either. His first reaction, in fact, was that I was kidding him."

The plan foundered soon afterward when Veeck learned that Nugent had turned the team back to the National League, and that Ford Frick, the league president, had arranged its sale to William Cox, a lumber dealer, "for about half what I was willing to pay." So that dream died.

The pressures against baseball's segregation were not building up in a vacuum. In 1941, under the threat of a "March on Washington" by thousands of Negroes, President Franklin D. Roosevelt had issued an executive order establishing a Fair Employment Practices Commission. That first FEPC was not a vigorous enforcement agency, but it did turn the spotlight on discriminatory hiring policies in industry, and it paved the way for state laws barring discrimination in employment.

In 1944 the New York State Legislature began considering the Ives-Quinn Bill to forbid discrimination in hiring on the basis of race, creed, color, or national origin. It was not aimed specifically at baseball's color line, but only the most myopic big-league operator could fail to see that it meant eventual legal challenge to the "gentleman's agreement." Given the increasing awareness of white Americans to the insults and outrages suffered daily by black citizens, there was not much question that it would be passed.

So the stage was being set for the climactic scene in the story of Negro baseball. Appropriately it was to be enacted in New York, the big town, which was represented in the six-club Negro National League in 1944 by the weak sisters of the circuit, the New York Black Yankees and the New York Cubans. If Harlem's fans mourned the lowly status of the Black Yankees and Cubans, it was not for long:

bigger things were in the air than the final standings of the NNL's pennant race.

AUTOBIOGRAPHY

IN AUGUST of 1952, ballplayer Jim Piersall found himself in a mental hospital outside of Boston. Shock treatments had numbed his memory, and it was afterward, in the course of his recovery, that he learned of the wild antics that caused the Boston Red Sox to farm him out to Birmingham . . . where this excerpt from Piersall's book, *Fear Strikes Out,* takes up.

From *Fear Strikes Out*

JIM PIERSALL *and* AL HIRSHBERG

I WAS with the Barons exactly twenty days. During that time, I had countless arguments with the umpires. I was thrown out of half a dozen ball games and suspended four different times. I baffled my teammates, infuriated my manager, insulted the umpires, squabbled with opposing ballplayers and delighted the sports writers and fans. Once I nearly got into an open fist fight. Twice, at my own expense, I flew back to Boston.

At first, the Birmingham baseball people welcomed my clowning. Eddie Glennon, the Barons' general manager, announced a few days after my arrival that I had injected new spirit into the team. "He's the greatest center fielder that I've ever seen," Glennon said. "A one hundred-and-fifty-thousand-dollar ballplayer." I added color to the Barons and made them the talk of the Southern Association—indeed, the talk of baseball. Every unconventional move I made was relayed to the nation's newspapers and splashed all over the sports pages.

But it didn't take long for everyone, including Glennon, to get sick and tired of Piersall. He was funny only as long as he added something refreshing to the ball game. But when he tried to make his antics take the place of the ball game, he was in trouble. His clowning was turning games into travesties. He did stupid little things—anything he could think of—to delay the games, and the angry umpires, anxious to hustle things up, reached a point where they had to banish him in order to get contests completed at all.

Piersall put on one of his most aggravating performances in New Orleans on July 5. Aside from going through the regular routine which had first attracted attention when he was in the majors, Piersall added a whole new bag of tricks, making them up as he went along. When he went up to hit, he stood in the batter's box, dropped his bat and imitated the pitcher as he wound up. Naturally, the umpire had to call time, and the game would be held up while Piersall stooped to pick up his war club. He pulled the stunt two or three times each time he came up.

When Piersall wasn't imitating the pitcher, he was holding up the works while he ran either down the first- or the third-base line to give instructions in a dramatic stage whisper to one of the coaches or to a base runner. Sometimes he rushed back to the dugout to talk to Mathis, who repeatedly ordered him to get back up there and hit.

After Birmingham's turn at bat, Piersall loafed his way out to center field, stopping to talk to infielders on the way, taking his time about picking up his glove, sauntering over near the stands to exchange quips with the crowd and spending so much time reaching his position that the game had to be held up while an umpire came out to hustle him up. Once while New Orleans was at bat, Piersall suddenly ran into the Birmingham dugout from his center-field position and the game had to be stopped. Mathis, who was catching, had to leave his position to come over and tell Piersall to get back on the job.

About halfway through the game, one of the Barons hit what Mathis thought was a home run, and when the umpire called it a foul ball, Red blew his top. He rushed over to George Popp, the plate umpire, yelling and gesticulating—and Piersall rushed right behind him, imitating every move he made. Mathis got so excited that Popp finally threw him out of the game. Piersall didn't stop aping Red until he turned around to go into the locker room.

When Birmingham's half of the inning was over, Piersall went out to the pitcher's mound, picked up the ball, and walked out to the shortstop's position. When Johnny McCall, the Barons' pitcher, came out to warm up, he yelled to Piersall to throw the ball. Piersall wound up and slammed it right at McCall. McCall had to put up his gloved hand fast to keep from getting hit in the face. Boiling mad, McCall threw the ball right back at Piersall, who fell flat on his face, then got up holding his stomach in mock hysterics after the ball had sailed to the outfield.

The crowd laughed, but neither McCall nor Popp thought it was very funny. Popp came halfway out on the diamond and called to Piersall, "Go out and get that ball in here before I throw you out of the game." The ball had stopped in dead center field. Piersall dropped his glove on the ground and kicked it as he went along. Just before he reached the ball, he crouched and crept toward it as though he were a pointer dog and it were his quarry. Then he kicked it a few feet, and kept repeating the performance until the ball and he had reached the scoreboard.

Piersall finally picked it up and threw it to the scoreboard boy, who threw it back. They began playing catch, but that game didn't last long. All of the umpires at once were screaming at Piersall to get out of the ball game. When the scoreboard boy refused to throw the ball back, Piersall walked off the field.

Then, still in uniform, he wandered over to the right-field side of the grandstand, where five hundred boys, guests of Joe L. Brown, the president of the New Orleans club, were chanting, "We want Piersall!" Piersall stood in front of them and led them in the cheers. Somehow they got the game started again on the field, but nobody was watching. Everyone was looking over at Piersall.

Finally, he went down to the Birmingham locker room and changed into street clothes. Then he went back to the stands and sat down in a box occupied by Charles Hurth, the president of the Southern Association. From there, Piersall heckled Popp, as well as Danny Murtaugh, the New Orleans manager, who had been giving him a pretty rough going-over all through the game. For that performance he was suspended.

A few days later, everyone in the league had four days off while the Southern Association all-star game was being played. I hopped a plane and flew back to Boston, wiring Mary ahead of time. I thought that the Red Sox might let me stay with them, once I was in Boston. But when I called Cronin, he told me to go back to the Barons and stick to baseball. I left the next day.

By this time, Glennon was worried about me, too. He persuaded me to let him take me to a doctor in Birmingham, and I was given some pills to calm me down. I behaved all right for a day or so, but then I went off again worse than ever. We were starting a long home stand, and the Birmingham fans and I were enjoying each other hugely. The only trouble was, nobody else was enjoying me.

I became worse and worse. Nobody could keep me under control, including the umpires. One night I stood at the plate and screamed over a called third strike, and when the umpire thumbed me out of the game, I pulled a water pistol out of my pocket, squirted the plate with it and said, "Now maybe you can see it." I drew another suspension for that, my fourth since I had arrived in Birmingham.

It looked as if I were going to be stuck there for the season, so I decided to go back to Boston to get Mary and the children. Up to that point they hadn't moved South because we always had the hope that I'd get back to the Red Sox any day. They kept the house in Newton while I stayed with Garrett Wall in Birmingham.

Garrett had had no more luck trying to settle me down than anyone else did. He was placed in a position similar to that of Ted Lepcio when I was with the Red Sox. Like Mary, they both had to stand by and watch me crack up, doing what they could by talking to me but not daring to go much further, in the desperate hope that I might get straightened out by myself. Every morning when they got up, they were saying to themselves, "This might be the day." And every night they went to bed, thinking, "Maybe tomorrow."

I bought a ticket on a Boston plane that left Birmingham late in the afternoon of July 17. We made several stops on the way, including one at LaGuardia Airport in New York, where Bill Cunningham, the able Boston *Herald* sports columnist, and his secretary, Miss Frances Donovan, got aboard. Apparently, as soon as I saw Cunningham, I rushed over to him and began pouring my troubles into his unwilling ear. Evidently I talked all the way to Boston, where we arrived at one-thirty in the morning. Here, in part, is what he wrote in his column a day or so later.

"I chanced to be on the plane that unexpectedly brought the Red Sox problem child Jimmy Piersall into Boston at one-thirty A.M. From approximately eleven-forty-five P.M. until the ship set down in Boston, I heard little but the machine-gun chatter of this tormented youth who so foolishly is throwing away a promising career . . .

"It's my considered opinion that the less written now the better, and if anybody's really interested in helping the young man, a complete press blackout until he can get his bearings would be the best medicine that could possibly be prescribed.

"I'm no authority on such matters, but my guess is he's heading straight for a nervous breakdown."

Cunningham was an accurate prophet. My breakdown was just around the corner. It happened within forty hours after I arrived in Boston. And, suffering more pangs than I suffered, living more horrible minutes than I lived, fighting more fights than I fought, sinking farther into depths of desperation than I sank, hoping more than I hoped, and praying more than I prayed was Mary. I went through it all under the unhealthy anesthesia of a mental blackout. Mary was fully aware of everything that went on. She carried me through every step of the way without so much as a sleeping pill—and, to this day, she remembers every dreadful minute. She told me all about it during those days when we sat quietly in our rented house and relived the past together.

The house was alive with reporters and photographers the day after I flew into town from Birmingham. All of the papers, the major press services, the radio and television stations—every conceivable dispenser of news—sent out representatives. Everyone interviewed me, and while I reveled in the prospects of so much publicity, I was reasonable and rational in my speech. I told them all the same story—that I was through with clowning, and from that moment on, was going to be no more and no less than a ballplayer. I said that I would go back to Birmingham and do the best I could to help the Barons win the Southern Association pennant, and that my one hope was to get back to the Red Sox as soon as possible. And once with them, I would forget all about these mad antics.

I parried the embarrassing questions—

"Did you spank Stephens' little boy?" . . . Of course not—I just patted him, that's all. . . . "Did you really calm down the way Boudreau told you to?" . . . Certainly. . . . "What about all those stories of your tearing through the Southern Association the way you tore through the American League?" . . . Nothing to them—I've just been sticking to baseball. . . . "Are you really carrying on a running feud with the umpires down there?" . . . Not that I know of—the umpires and me have been getting along fine . . . "Is it true that you mimicked your own manager behind his back while he was protesting a decision?" . . . Absolutely not—my manager is a close friend of mine. . . . "Did you squirt the plate with a water pistol?" . . . Someone dreamed that one up. . . . "And play catch with a scoreboard boy?" . . . I should say not. . . . "Why did you make two trips back to Boston in less than three weeks?" . . . To see my family. . . . "Are you going to take your wife and children back to Birmingham?" . . . As soon as I can get them packed and out of here. . . . "Do you really think McKechnie and not Boudreau is running the Red Sox?" . . . Boudreau is the manager—do you think I'd say anything like that? . . . "Well, did you say it?" . . . I was sore—I didn't know what I was talking about—Bourdeau runs the team, not McKechnie. . . . "And how about Vollmer—did you say he couldn't blow his nose?" . . . A fine ballplayer and a good friend of mine—why should I say anything to hurt him? . . . "Is it true that some of the Red Sox wanted to beat you up on a train and Lepcio stopped them?" . . . I don't know—ask Lepcio. . . .

All day and all evening that sort of thing went on. Questions, questions, questions—one interviewer after another. Sometimes there would be slight variations, but in general the questions were the same. Mary hovered in and out of the living room while I held court. Every so often, she would suggest that I be excused from answering any more questions, but I wouldn't stand for it. I insisted on seeing everyone and answering everything.

Late that afternoon, the Red Sox office called. Cronin wanted to see me. He would expect me in his office at ten o'clock the next morning. I had a long talk with him, then went home and said to Mary, "I'm going to see a doctor. They want you there, too." We drove back to the ball park, where Cronin met us, and then we headed for the doctor's.

Before we sat down, the doctor called in another doctor, and then the five of us—the two doctors, Cronin, Mary and me—went into a long huddle. The conversation was pretty general, as if we were all just passing the time of day, and I took part in it. After a while, one of the doctors suggested, "I think it would be a good idea for Jimmy to go off somewhere for a rest."

GENERAL

GEORGE PLIMPTON is well-known for his book *Paper Lion,* in which he tested personally what it was like to play professional football. A few years before that, though, he had already done the same thing in baseball, and written a book about that too, called *Out of My League*. With *Sports Illustrated* putting up a $1,000 prize to be split among the American or National League team that got the most hits off him, Plimpton set out to pitch once through each batting order just before a post-season All-Star game at Yankee Stadium. Needless to say, he didn't survive the experiment—didn't even get through the National League hitters—and Ernest Hemingway said later, after reading *Out of My League,* "It is the dark side of the moon of Walter Mitty."

From *Out of My League*

GEORGE PLIMPTON

ERNIE BANKS was followed in the batter's box by Frank Thomas, then playing for the Pittsburgh Pirates. He was the only batter I faced who loomed over the plate. Despite a large, homely, friendly face over which his blue plastic helmet perched like a birthday paper hat, Thomas' size made him look dangerous; he had an upright batting stance, which made him easier to pitch to than Banks, but the bat looked small and limber in his hands, and when he swung and missed one of my first pitches to him, I imagined I heard the bat sing in the air like a willow switch. For the first time the batter's box seemed close to, and I could understand why many pitchers manipulate the follow-through of their pitching motion, which brings them in toward the plate by as much as six feet, so that the glove can be flicked up to protect the head in the event of a hard shot toward the mound. You never can tell. In 1947 Schoolboy Rowe threw in a pitch toward Stan Musial and back came the top half of a bat cracked directly in two, whirring at him with the speed and directness of a boomerang, and struck him a brutal blow on the elbow of his upflung arm. Even batters worry about crippling a pitcher over that distance. A hard-hit line drive, after all, will cover those 60 feet 6 inches in one-fifth of a second. Babe Ruth had nightmares of such a thing, and there's a body of thought which believes his fear of smacking down a pitcher was why he changed his batting style (he was originally a line-drive hitter in the early days with Baltimore) and started swinging from the heels of his pipestem legs to get loft and distance.

According to my statistician in the stands, it was the seventh pitch that Thomas whacked in a long high arc, very much like that of a Ruthian home run, deep into the upper deck in left field. The ball looped in at the downward end of its trajectory, and above the swelling roar of the crowd I could hear it smack against the slats of an empty seat. The upper deck was deserted and it was a long time before a scampering boy, leaping the empty rows like a chamois, found the ball and held it aloft, triumphant, the white of it just barely visible at that great distance.

The ball was hit well over 400 feet, and after the roar that had accompanied its flight had died down, you could hear the crowd continue buzzing.

My own reaction, as I stood on the mound, was not one of shame, or outrage. Perhaps it should have been, particularly following my difficulties with Banks, but actually my reaction was one of wonderment at the power necessary to propel a ball out of a major-league park. I could hardly believe a ball could be hit so far.

Later that afternoon in the locker room I asked Billy Pierce, the great White Sox southpaw, about the effect of the home run on the pitcher. He'd been talking about the major-league curve ball, what a marvelous and wicked weapon it was at its best, and the unwelcome shift into the batter's province threw him off. "Home runs?" he said in a high, querulous voice. He shrugged. "Well, the effect of the damn things depends upon their importance in any given game," he said reflectively. "Look at Branca." He thought for a while and then he said, "But when that ball sails out of the park, even if it doesn't mean a damn thing, you just feel awful stupid."

Pierce's mention of Branca, of course, was in reference to Bobby Thomson's home run off the Brooklyn speed pitcher in the Miracle of Coogan's Bluff playoff game in 1951. In the films of that stupendous moment you see Branca wheel to watch the flight of the ball that lost Brooklyn the pennant, then start slowly for the dugout, but almost running finally to get out of that wild public demonstration into privacy where he could project that scene over and over again in his imagination, never quite believing it, puzzled that the script wouldn't change and the ball curve foul or into an outfielder's reach. An enterprising photographer got into the Dodger dressing room—it was barred to the press but he got in somehow—and took a picture of Branca within minutes of his disaster. The photograph, a strange one, shows him face down and prostrate on a flight of cement steps—as if he'd stumbled on the bottom step and fallen face forward, his body absolutely as stiff as cordwood with grief. The effect of that home run finished Branca, practically speaking, as a pitcher. Afterwards he toyed with the idea of changing his uniform number, which was 13, but he never did. Perhaps he knew that nothing would help him.

I found I couldn't explain the effect of Frank Thomas' home run, at least not to Pierce, because in actual fact I felt a certain sense of pride in that home run. Every time I return to Yankee Stadium—to a football game, for example—I automatically look up into the section where the ball hit (it was section 34), remembering then that I felt no sense of stupidity but in fact enjoyed a strong feeling of identification with Thomas' feat—as if I was his partner rather than opposing him, and that between us we'd connived to arrange what had happened. It was as if I'd wheeled to watch the ball climb that long way for the upper deck and called out, "Look, look what I've helped engineer!"

It wasn't a reaction I could have explained to Pierce without being accused of being in sympathy with the enemy. Besides, he was back on pitchers, talking about curve balls, the gloomy consideration of Branca, and the batter and his prowess postponed, laid away in the shadows, as he described a bright and cheerful world full of pitching splendors.

"You've got to see Donovan's curve," he said eagerly. "Can't tell about the curve on TV. Got to catch it, try to catch it, to see what the thing does. It breaks so you can almost hear it."

So we talked comfortably about pitching. I told him that I'd thrown one curve ball that afternoon. "It was the first pitch I threw to Frank Robinson," I said. "It almost ran up the foul screen. It got away from me."

"I see," said Pierce. "So *that's* what it was."

Later that afternoon, Gil Hodges, the Dodger first baseman, complained that I had thrown him a curve ball. He followed Thomas in the lineup, and despite the fact that he hit the curve ball for a sharp single to short center, he spoke to me reproachfully. He told me he didn't think curve balls were allowed.

I was surprised at the high respect major leaguers hold for the curve ball and how they hate to bat against it. If a curve is hit safely, the batter attributes his success less to his own ability than to being given the chance to take advantage of a fault in the curve itself. "That hook hung up there just long enough," he will say later in the dugout, meaning that he was able to get his bat around on the ball before it broke. Any player who professes to prefer taking his swipes against curve balls is looked upon with suspicion. And indeed in the history of the majors only a few players have had the reputation of preferring to see curves thrown at them: Hornsby, for one, Rollie Hemsley, Moose Skowron, Roy Sievers, Ducky Medwick, and Al Simmons, these last two despite both having the fault of stepping away from the pitch with the forward foot, falling away "into the bucket"—supposedly suicidal against the curve. They compensated for their faulty swings with amazing eyes and quick strong wrists. There are others, of course, who do well against curve-ball pitchers, but nonetheless the curve has always been better known for destroying reputations. Jim Thorpe, for example, probably the greatest athlete who ever lived, never stuck in the majors because a curve ball fooled him too often. A rookie's classic letter from the training camp begins: "I'll be home soon, Ma. The pitchers are starting to curve me."

Frankly, I don't remember throwing Hodges a curve ball. But I remember other things about his lengthy tenure at the plate, right from the beginning as he stepped into the batter's box, hitching up his baseball pants, reaching out then and rubbing up the fat part of his bat as he set himself, picking again at those pants as if about to wade into a shallow pond. He has outsized hands which you notice when he stands in at the plate. They span over twelve inches, and Pee Wee Reese, his captain, used to say of him, in connection with those big hands, that he only used a glove for fielding at first base because it was fashionable. They call him Moon, and I remember how he looked, the rather beefy pleasant face under the blue helmet, and the blue piping of the Dodger uniform, and while I don't remember throwing him a curve, I remember the line-drive single he hit, how easy and calculated his swing, and how sharp that hit of his was going out.

FICTION

From *The Chosen*

CHAIM POTOK

DANNY AND I probably would never have met—or we would have met under altogether different circumstances—had it not been for America's entry into the Second World War and the desire this bred on the part of some English teachers in the Jewish parochial schools to show the gentile world that yeshiva students were as physically fit, despite their long hours of study, as any other American student. They went about proving this by organizing the Jewish parochial schools in and around our area into competitive leagues, and once every two weeks the schools would compete against one another in a variety of sports. I became a member of my school's varsity softball team.

On a Sunday afternoon in early June, the fifteen members of my team met with our gym instructor in the play yard of our school. It was a warm day, and the sun was bright on the asphalt floor of the yard. The gym instructor was a short, chunky man in his early thirties who taught in the mornings in a nearby public high school and supplemented his income by teaching in our yeshiva during the afternoons. He wore a white polo shirt, white pants, and white sweater, and from the awkward way the little black skullcap sat perched on his round, balding head, it was clearly apparent that he was not accustomed to wearing it with any sort of regularity. When he talked he frequently thumped his right fist into his left palm to emphasize a point. He walked on the balls of his feet, almost in imitation of a boxer's ring stance, and he was fanatically addicted to professional baseball. He had nursed our softball team along for two years, and by a mixture of patience, luck, shrewd manipulations during some tight ball games, and hard, fist-thumping harangues calculated to shove us into a patriotic awareness of the importance of athletics and physical fitness for the war effort, he was able to mold our original team of fifteen awkward fumblers into the top team of our league. His name was Mr. Galanter, and all of us wondered why he was not off somewhere fighting in the war.

During my two years with the team, I had become quite adept

at second base and had also developed a swift underhand pitch that would tempt a batter into a swing but would drop into a curve at the last moment and slide just below the flaying bat for a strike. Mr. Galanter always began a ball game by putting me at second base and would use me as a pitcher only in very tight moments, because, as he put it once, "My baseball philosophy is grounded on the defensive solidarity of the infield."

That afternoon we were scheduled to play the winning team of another neighborhood league, a team with a reputation for wild, offensive slugging and poor fielding. Mr. Galanter said he was counting upon our infield to act as a solid defensive front. Throughout the warm-up period, with only our team in the yard, he kept thumping his right fist into his left palm and shouting at us to be a solid defensive front.

"No holes," he shouted from near home plate. "No holes, you hear? Goldberg, what kind of solid defensive front is that? Close in. A battleship could get between you and Malter. That's it. Schwartz, what are you doing, looking for paratroops? This is a ball game. The enemy's on the ground. That throw was wide, Goldberg. Throw it like a sharpshooter. Give him the ball again. Throw it. Good. Like a sharpshooter. Very good. Keep the infield solid. No defensive holes in this war."

We batted and threw the ball around, and it was warm and sunny, and there was the smooth, happy feeling of the summer soon to come, and the tight excitement of the ball game. We wanted very much to win, both for ourselves and, more especially, for Mr. Galanter, for we had all come to like his fist-thumping sincerity. To the rabbis who taught in the Jewish parochial schools, baseball was an evil waste of time, a spawn of the potentially assimilationist English portion of the yeshiva day. But to the students of most of the parochial schools, an inter-league baseball victory had come to take on only a shade less significance than a top grade in Talmud, for it was an unquestioned mark of one's Americanism, and to be counted a loyal American had become increasingly important to us during these last years of the war.

So Mr. Galanter stood near home plate, shouting instructions and words of encouragement, and we batted and tossed the ball around. I walked off the field for a moment to set up my eyeglasses for the game. I wore shell-rimmed glasses, and before every game I would bend the earpieces in so the glasses would stay tight on my head and not slip down the bridge of my nose when I began to sweat. I always waited until just before a game to bend down the earpieces, because, bent, they would cut into the skin over my ears, and I did not want to feel the pain a moment longer than I had to. The tops of my ears would be sore for days after every game, but better that, I thought, than the need to keep pushing my glasses up the bridge of my nose or the possibility of having them fall off suddenly during an important play.

Davey Cantor, one of the boys who acted as a replacement if a first-stringer had to leave the game, was standing near the wire screen behind home plate. He was a short boy, with a round face, dark hair, owlish glasses, and a very Semitic nose. He watched me fix my glasses.

"You're looking good out there, Reuven," he told me.

"Thanks," I said.

"Everyone is looking real good."

"It'll be a good game."

He stared at me through his glasses. "You think so?" he asked.

"Sure, why not?"

"You ever see them play, Reuven?"

"No."

"They're murderers."

"Sure," I said.

"No, really. They're wild."

"You saw them play?"

"Twice. They're murderers."

"Everyone plays to win, Davey."

"They don't only play to win. They play like it's the first of the Ten Commandments."

I laughed. "That yeshiva?" I said. "Oh, come on, Davey."

"It's the truth."

"Sure," I said.

"Reb Saunders ordered them never to lose because it would shame their yeshiva or something. I don't know. You'll see."

"Hey, Malter!" Mr. Galanter shouted. "What are you doing, sitting this one out?"

"You'll see," Davey Cantor said.

"Sure," I grinned at him. "A holy war."

He looked at me.

"Are you playing?" I asked him.

"Mr. Galanter said I might take second base if you have to pitch."

"Well, good luck."

"Hey, Malter!" Mr. Galanter shouted. "There's a war on, remember?"

"Yes, sir!" I said, and ran back out to my position at second base.

We threw the ball around a few more minutes, and then I went up to home plate for some batting practice. I hit a long one out to left field, and then a fast one to the shortstop, who fielded it neatly and whipped it to first. I had the bat ready for another swing when someone said, "Here they are," and I rested the bat on my shoulder and saw the team we were going to play turn up our block and come into the yard. I saw Davey Cantor kick nervously at the wire screen behind home plate, then put his hands into the pockets of his dungarees. His eyes were wide and gloomy behind his owlish glasses.

I watched them come into the yard.

There were fifteen of them, and they were dressed alike in white shirts, dark pants, white sweaters, and small black skullcaps. In the fashion of the very Orthodox, their hair was closely cropped, except for the area near their ears from which mushroomed the untouched hair that tumbled down into the long side curls. Some of them had the beginnings of beards, straggly tufts of hair that stood in isolated clumps on their chins, jawbones, and upper lips. They all wore the traditional undergarment beneath their shirts, and the tzitzit, the long fringes appended to the four corners of the garment, came out above their belts and swung against their pants as they walked. These were the very Orthodox, and they obeyed literally the Biblical commandment *And ye shall look upon it,* which pertains to the fringes.

In contrast, our team had no particular uniform, and each of us wore whatever he wished: dungarees, shorts, pants, polo shirts, sweat shirts, even undershirts. Some of us wore the garment, others did not. None of us wore the fringes outside his trousers. The only element of uniform that we had in common was the small, black skullcap which we, too, wore.

They came up to the first-base side of the wire screen behind home plate and stood there in a silent black-and-white mass, holding bats and balls and gloves in their hands. . . .

A man disentangled himself from the black-and-white mass of players and took a step forward. He looked to be in his late twenties and wore a black suit, black shoes, and a black hat. He had a black beard, and he carried a book under one arm. He was obviously a rabbi, and I marveled that the yeshiva had placed a rabbi instead of an athletic coach over its team.

Mr. Galanter came up to him and offered his hand.

"We are ready to play," the rabbi said in Yiddish, shaking Mr. Galanter's hand with obvious uninterest.

"Fine," Mr. Galanter said in English, smiling.

The rabbi looked out at the field. "You played already?" he asked.

"How's that?" Mr. Galanter said.

"You had practice?"

"Well, sure—"

"We want to practice."

"How's that?" Mr. Galanter said again, looking surprised.

"You practiced, now we practice."

"You didn't practice in your own yard?"

"We practiced."

"Well, then—"

"But we have never played in your yard before. We want a few minutes."

"Well, now," Mr. Galanter said, "there isn't much time. The rules are each team practices in its own yard."

"We want five minutes," the rabbi insisted.

"Well—" Mr. Galanter said. He was no longer smiling. He always liked to go right into a game when we played in our own yard. It kept us from cooling off, he said.

"Five minutes," the rabbi said. "Tell your people to leave the field."

"How's that?" Mr. Galanter said.

"We cannot practice with your people on the field. Tell them to leave the field."

"Well, now," Mr. Galanter said, then stopped. He thought for a long moment. The black-and-white mass of players behind the rabbi stood very still, waiting. I saw Davey Cantor kick at the asphalt of the yard. "Well, all right. Five minutes. Just five minutes, now."

"Tell your people to leave the field," the rabbi said.

Mr. Galanter stared gloomily out at the field, looking a little deflated. "Everybody off!" he shouted, not very loudly. "They want a five-minute warm-up. Hustle, hustle. Keep those arms going. Keep it hot. Toss some balls around behind home. Let's go!"

The players scrambled off the field.

The black-and-white mass near the wire screen remained intact. The young rabbi turned and faced his team.

He talked in Yiddish. "We have the field for five minutes," he said."Remember why and for whom we play."

Then he stepped aside, and the black-and-white mass dissolved into fifteen individual players who came quickly onto the field. One of them, a tall boy with sand-colored hair and long arms and legs that semed all bones and angles, stood at home plate and commenced hitting balls out to the players. He hit a few easy grounders and pop-ups, and the fielders shouted encouragement to one another in Yiddish. They handled themselves awkwardly, dropping easy grounders, throwing wild, fumbling fly balls. I looked over at the young rabbi. He had sat down on the bench near the wire screen and was reading his book.

Behind the wire screen was a wide area, and Mr. Galanter kept us busy there throwing balls around.

"Keep those balls going!" he fist-thumped at us. "No one sits out this fire fight! Never underestimate the enemy!"

But there was a broad smile on his face. Now that he was actually seeing the other team, he seemed not at all concerned about the outcome of the game. In the interim between throwing a ball and having it thrown back to me, I told myself that I liked Mr. Galanter, and I wondered about his constant use of war expressions and why he wasn't in the army.

Davey Cantor came past me, chasing a ball that had gone between his legs.

"Some murderers," I grinned at him.

"You'll see," he said as he bent to retrieve the ball.

"Sure," I said.

"Especially the one batting. You'll see."

The ball was coming back to me, and I caught it neatly and flipped it back.

"Who's the one batting?" I asked.

"Danny Saunders."

"Pardon my ignorance, but who is Danny Saunders?"

"Reb Saunders' son," Davey Cantor said, blinking his eyes.

"I'm impressed."

"You'll see," Davey Cantor said, and ran off with his ball.

My father, who had no love at all for Hasidic communities and their rabbinic overlords, had told me about Rabbi Isaac Saunders and the zealousness with which he ruled his people and settled questions of Jewish law.

I saw Mr. Galanter look at his wristwatch, then stare out at the team on the field. The five minutes were apparently over, but the players were making no move to abandon the field. Danny Saunders was now at first base, and I noticed that his long arms and legs were being used to good advantage, for by stretching and jumping he was able to catch most of the wild throws that came his way.

Mr. Galanter went over to the young rabbi who was still sitting on the bench and reading.

"It's five minutes," he said.

The rabbi looked up from his book. "Ah?" he said.

"The five minutes are up," Mr. Galanter said.

The rabbi stared out at the field. "Enough!" he shouted in Yiddish. "It's time to play!" Then he looked down at the book and resumed his reading.

The players threw the ball around for another minute or two, and then slowly came off the field. Danny Saunders walked past me, still wearing his first baseman's glove. He was a good deal taller than I, and in contrast to my somewhat ordinary but decently proportioned features and dark hair, his face seemed to have been cut from stone. His chin, jaw, and cheekbones were made up of jutting hard lines, his nose was straight and pointed, his lips full, rising to a steep angle from the center point beneath his nose and then slanting off to form a too-wide mouth. His eyes were deep blue, and the sparse tufts of hair on his chin, jawbones, and upper lip, the close-cropped hair on his head, and the flow of side curls along his ears were the color of sand. He moved in a loose-jointed, disheveled sort of way, all arms and legs, talking in Yiddish to one of his teammates and ignoring me completely as he passed by. I told myself that I did not like his Hasidic-bred sense of superiority and that it would be a great pleasure to defeat him and his team in this afternoon's game.

The umpire, a gym instructor from a parochial school two blocks away, called the teams together to determine who would bat first. I saw him throw a bat into the air. It was caught and almost dropped by a member of the other team.

During the brief hand-over-hand choosing, Davey Cantor came over and stood next to me.

"What do you think?" he asked.

"They're a snooty bunch," I told him.

"What do you think about their playing?"

"They're lousy."

"They're murderers."

"Oh, come on, Davey."

"You'll see," Davey Cantor said, looking at me gloomily.

"I just did see."

"You didn't see anything."

"Sure," I said. "Elijah the prophet comes in to pitch for them in tight spots."

"I'm not being funny," he said, looking hurt.

"Some murderers," I told him, and laughed. . . .

The umpire, who had taken up his position behind the pitcher, called for the ball and someone tossed it to him. He handed it to the pitcher and shouted, "Here we go! Play ball!" We settled into our positions.

Mr. Galanter shouted, "Goldberg, move in!" and Sidney Goldberg, our shortstop, took two steps forward and moved a little closer to third base. "Okay fine," Mr. Galanter said. "Keep that infield solid!"

A short, thin boy came up to the plate and stood there with his feet together, holding the bat awkwardly over his head. He wore steel-rimmed glasses that gave his face a pinched, old man's look. He swung wildly at the first pitch, and the force of the swing spun him completely around. His earlocks lifted off the sides of his head and followed him around in an almost horizontal circle. Then he steadied himself and resumed his position near the plate, short, thin, his feet together, holding his bat over his head in an awkward grip.

The umpire called the strike in a loud, clear voice, and I saw Sidney Goldberg look over at me and grin broadly.

"If he studies Talmud like that, he's dead," Sidney Goldberg said.

I grinned back at him.

"Keep that infield solid!" Mr. Galanter shouted from third base. "Malter, a little to your left! Good!"

The next pitch was too high, and the boy chopped at it, lost his bat and fell forward on his hands. Sidney Goldberg and I looked at each other again. Sidney was in my class. We were similar in build, thin and lithe, with somewhat spindly arms and legs. He was not a very good student, but he was an excellent shortstop. We lived on the same block and were good but not close friends. He was dressed in an undershirt and dungarees and was not wearing the four-cornered garment. I had on a light-blue shirt and dark-blue work pants, and I wore the four-cornered garment under the shirt.

The short, thin boy was back at the plate, standing with his feet together and holding the bat in his awkward grip. He let the next pitch go by, and the umpire called it a strike. I saw the young rabbi look up a moment from his book, then resume reading.

"Two more just like that!" I shouted encouragingly to the pitcher. "Two more, Schwartzie!" And I thought to myself, Some murderers.

I saw Danny Saunders go over to the boy who had just struck out and talk to him. The boy looked down and seemed to shrivel with hurt. He hung his head and walked away behind the wire screen. Another short, thin boy took his place at the plate. I looked around for Davey Cantor but could not see him.

The boy at bat swung wildly at the first two pitches and missed them both. He swung again at the third pitch, and I heard the loud *thwack* of the bat as it connected with the ball, and saw the ball move in a swift, straight line toward Sidney Goldberg, who caught it, bobbled it for a moment, and finally got it into his glove. He tossed the ball to me, and we threw it around. I saw him take off his glove and shake his left hand.

"That hurt," he said, grinning at me.

"Good catch," I told him.

"That hurt like hell," he said, and put his glove back on his hand.

The batter who stood now at the plate was broad-shouldered and built like a bear. He swung at the first pitch, missed, then swung again at the second pitch and sent the ball in a straight line over the head of the third baseman into left field. I scrambled to second, stood on the base, and shouted for the ball. I saw the left fielder pick it up on the second bounce and relay it to me. It was coming in a little high, and I had my glove raised for it. I felt more than saw the batter charging toward second, and as I was getting my glove on the ball he smashed into me like a truck. The ball went over my head, and I fell forward heavily onto the asphalt floor of the yard, and he passed me, going toward third, his fringes flying out behind him, holding his skullcap to his head with his right hand so it would not fall off. Abe Goodstein, our first baseman, retrieved the ball and whipped it home, and the batter stood at third, a wide grin on his face.

The yeshiva team exploded into wild cheers and shouted loud words of congratulations in Yiddish to the batter.

Sidney Goldberg helped me get to my feet.

"That momzer!" he said. "You weren't in his way!"

"Wow!" I said, taking a few deep breaths. I had scraped the palm of my right hand.

"What a momzer!" Sidney Goldberg said.

I saw Mr. Galanter come storming onto the field to talk to the umpire. "What kind of play was that?" he asked heatedly. "How are you going to rule that?"

"Safe at third," the umpire said. "Your boy was in the way."

Mr. Galanter's mouth fell open. "How's that again?"

"Safe at third," the umpire repeated.

Mr. Galanter looked ready to argue, thought better of it, then stared over at me. "Are you all right, Malter?"

"I'm okay," I said, taking another deep breath.

Mr. Galanter walked angrily off the field.

"Play ball!" the umpire shouted.

The yeshiva team quieted down. I saw that the young rabbi was now looking up from his book and smiling faintly.

A tall, thin player came up to the plate, set his feet in correct position, swung his bat a few times, then crouched into a waiting stance. I saw it was Danny Saunders. I opened and closed my right hand, which was still sore from the fall.

"Move back! Move back!" Mr. Galanter was shouting from alongside third base, and I took two steps back.

I crouched, waiting.

The first pitch was wild, and the yeshiva team burst into loud laughter. The young rabbi was sitting on the bench, watching Danny Saunders intently.

"Take it easy, Schwartzie!" I shouted encouragingly to the pitcher. "There's only one more to go!"

The next pitch was about a foot over Danny Saunders' head, and the yeshiva team howled with laughter. Sidney Goldberg and I looked at each other. I saw Mr. Galanter standing very still alongside third, staring at the pitcher. The rabbi was still watching Danny Saunders.

The next pitch left Schwartzie's hand in a long, slow line, and before it was halfway to the plate I knew Danny Saunders would try for it. I knew it from the way his left foot came forward and the bat snapped back and his long, thin body began its swift pivot. I tensed, waiting for the sound of the bat against the ball, and when it came it sounded like a gunshot. For a wild fraction of a second I lost sight of the ball. Then I saw Schwartzie dive to the ground, and there was the ball coming through the air where his head had been and I tried for it but it was moving too fast, and I barely had my glove raised before it was in center field. It was caught on a bounce and thrown to Sidney Goldberg, but by that time Danny Saunders was standing solidly on my base and the yeshiva team was screaming with joy.

Mr. Galanter called for time and walked over to talk to Schwartzie. Sidney Goldberg nodded to me, and the two of us went over to them.

"That ball could've killed me!" Schwartzie was saying. He was of medium size, with a long face and a bad case of acne. He wiped sweat from his face. "My God, did you see that ball?"

"I saw it," Mr. Galanter said grimly.

"That was too fast to stop, Mr. Galanter," I said in Schwartzie's defense.

"I heard about that Danny Saunders," Sidney Goldberg said. "He always hits to the pitcher."

"You could've told me," Schwartzie lamented. "I could've been ready."

"I only *heard* about it," Sidney Goldberg said. "You always believe everything you hear?"

"God, that ball could've killed me!" Schwartzie said again.

"You want to go on pitching?" Mr. Galanter said. A thin sheen of sweat covered his forehead, and he looked very grim.

"Sure, Mr. Galanter," Schwartzie said. "I'm okay."

"You're sure?"

"Sure I'm sure."

"No heroes in this war, now," Mr. Galanter said. "I want live soldiers, not dead heroes."

"I'm no hero," Schwartzie muttered lamely. "I can still get it over, Mr. Galanter. God, it's only the first inning."

"Okay, soldier," Mr. Galanter said, not very enthusiastically. "Just keep our side of this war fighting."

"I'm trying my best, Mr. Galanter," Schwartzie said.

Mr. Galanter nodded, still looking grim, and started off the field. I saw him take a handkerchief out of his pocket and wipe his forehead.

"Jesus Christ!" Schwartzie said, now that Mr. Galanter was gone. "That bastard aimed right for my head!"

"Oh, come on, Schwartzie," I said. "What is he, Babe Ruth?"

"You heard what Sidney said."

"Stop giving it to them on a silver platter and they won't hit it like that."

"Who's giving it to them on a silver platter?" Schwartzie lamented. "That was a great pitch."

"Sure," I said.

The umpire came over to us. "You boys planning to chat here all afternoon?" he asked. He was a squat man in his late forties, and he looked impatient.

"No, sir," I said very politely, and Sidney and I ran back to our places.

Danny Saunders was standing on my base. His white shirt was pasted to his arms and back with sweat.

"That was a nice shot," I offered.

He looked at me curiously and said nothing.

"You always hit it like that to the pitcher?" I asked.

He smiled faintly. "You're Reuven Malter," he said in perfect English. He had a low, nasal voice.

"That's right," I said, wondering where he had heard my name.

"Your father is David Malter, the one who writes articles on the Talmud?"

"Yes."

"I told my team we're going to kill you apikorsim this afternoon." He said it flatly, without a trace of expression in his voice.

I stared at him and hoped the sudden tight coldness I felt wasn't showing on my face. "Sure," I said. "Rub your tzitzit for good luck."

I walked away from him and took up my position near the base. I looked toward the wire screen and saw Davey Cantor standing there, staring out at the field, his hands in his pockets. I crouched down quickly, because Schwartzie was going into his pitch.

The batter swung wildly at the first two pitches and missed each time. The next one was low, and he let it go by, then hit a grounder to the first baseman, who dropped it, flailed about for it wildly, and recovered in time to see Danny Saunders cross the plate. The first baseman stood there for a moment, drenched in shame, then tossed the ball to Schwartzie. I saw Mr. Galanter standing near third base, wiping his forehead. The yeshiva team had gone wild again, and they were all trying to get to Danny Saunders to shake his hand. I saw the rabbi smile broadly, then look down at his book and resume reading.

Sidney Goldberg came over to me. "What did Saunders tell you?" he asked.

"He said they were going to kill us apikorsim this afternoon." . . .

The next batter hit a long fly ball to right field. It was caught on the run.

"Hooray for us," Sidney Goldberg said grimly as we headed off the field. "Any longer and they'd be asking us to join them for the Mincha Service."

"Not us," I said. "We're not holy enough."

"Where did they learn to hit like that?"

"Who knows?" I said.

We were standing near the wire screen, forming a tight circle around Mr. Galanter.

"Only two runs," Mr. Galanter said, smashing his right fist into his left hand. "And they hit us with all they had. Now we give them *our* heavy artillery. Now *we* barrage *them!*" His skullcap seemed pasted to his head with sweat. "Okay!" he said. "Fire away!"

The circle broke up, and Sidney Goldberg walked to the plate, carrying a bat. I saw the rabbi was still sitting on the bench, reading. I started to walk around behind him to see what book it was, when Davey Cantor came over, his hands in his pockets, his eyes still gloomy.

"Well?" he asked.

"Well what?" I said.

"I told you they could hit."

"So you told me. So what?" I was in no mood for his feelings of doom, and I let my voice show it.

He sensed my annoyance. "I wasn't bragging or anything," he said, looking hurt. "I just wanted to know what you thought."

"They can hit," I said.

"They're murderers," he said.

I watched Sidney Goldberg let a strike go by and said nothing.

"How's your hand?" Davey Cantor asked.

"I scraped it."

"He ran into you real hard."

"Who is he?"

"Dov Shlomowitz," Davey Cantor said. "Like his name, that's what he is," he added in Hebrew. "Dov" is the Hebrew word for bear.

"Was I blocking him?"

Davey Cantor shrugged. "You were and you weren't. The ump could've called it either way."

"He felt like a truck," I said, watching Sidney Goldberg step back from a close pitch.

"You should see his father. He's one of Reb Saunders' shamashim. Some bodyguard he makes."

"Reb Saunders has bodyguards?"

"Sure he has bodyguards," Davey Cantor said. "They protect him from his own popularity. Where've you been living all these years?"

"I don't have anything to do with them."

"You're not missing a thing, Reuven."

"How do you know so much about Reb Saunders?"

"My father gives him contributions."

"Well, good for your father," I said.

"He doesn't pray there or anything. He just gives him contributions."

"You're on the wrong team."

"No, I'm not, Reuven. Don't be like that." He was looking very hurt. "My father isn't a Hasid or anything. He just gives them some money a couple times a year."

"I was only kidding, Davey." I grinned at him. "Don't be so serious about everything."

I saw his face break into a happy smile, and just then Sidney Goldberg hit a fast, low grounder and raced off to first. The ball went right through the legs of the shortstop and into center field.

"Hold it at first!" Mr. Galanter screamed at him, and Sidney stopped at first and stood on the base.

The ball had been tossed quickly to second base. The second baseman looked over toward first, then threw the ball to the pitcher. The rabbi glanced up from the book for a moment, then went back to his reading.

"Malter, coach him at first!" Mr. Galanter shouted, and I ran up the base line.

"They can hit, but they can't field," Sidney Goldberg said, grinning at me as I came to a stop alongside the base.

"Davey Cantor says they're murderers," I said.

"Old gloom-and-doom Davey," Sidney Goldberg said, grinning.

Danny Saunders was standing away from the base, making a point of ignoring us both.

The next batter hit a high fly to the second baseman, who caught it, dropped it, retrieved it, and made a wild attempt at tagging Sidney Goldberg as he raced past him to second.

"Safe all around!" the umpire called, and our team burst out with shouts of joy. Mr. Galanter was smiling. The rabbi continued reading, and I saw he was now slowly moving the upper part of his body back and forth.

"Keep your eyes open, Sidney!" I shouted from alongside first base. I saw Danny Saunders look at me, then look away. Some murderers, I thought. Shleppers is more like it.

"If it's on the ground run like hell," I said to the batter who had just come onto first base, and he nodded at me. He was our third baseman, and he was about my size.

"If they keep fielding like that we'll be here till tomorrow," he said, and I grinned at him.

I saw Mr. Galanter talking to the next batter, who was nodding his head vigorously. He stepped to the plate, hit a hard grounder to the pitcher, who fumbled it for a moment then threw it to first. I saw Danny Saunders stretch for it and stop it.

"Out!" the umpire called. "Safe on second and third!"

As I ran up to the plate to bat, I almost laughed aloud at the pitcher's stupidity. He had thrown it to first rather than third, and now we had Sidney Goldberg on third, and a man on second. I hit a grounder to the shortstop and instead of throwing it to second he threw it to first, wildly, and again Danny Saunders stretched and stopped the ball. But I beat the throw and heard the umpire call out, "Safe all around! One in!" And everyone on our team was patting Sidney Goldberg on the back. Mr. Galanter smiled broadly.

"Hello again," I said to Danny Saunders, who was standing near me, guarding his base. "Been rubbing your tzitzit lately?"

He looked at me, then looked slowly away, his face expressionless.

Schwartzie was at the plate, swinging his bat.

"Keep your eyes open!" I shouted to the runner on third. He looked too eager to head for home. "It's only one out!"

He waved a hand at me.

Schwartzie took two balls and a strike, then I saw him begin to pivot on the fourth pitch. The runner on third started for home. He was almost halfway down the base line when the bat sent the ball in a hard line drive straight to the third baseman, the short, thin boy with the spectacles and the old man's face, who had stood hugging the base and who now caught the ball more with his stomach than with his glove, managed somehow to hold on to it, and stood there, looking bewildered and astonished.

I returned to first and saw our player who had been on third and who was now halfway to home plate turn sharply and start a panicky race back.

"Step on the base!" Danny Saunders screamed in Yiddish across the field, and more out of obedience than awareness the third baseman put a foot on the base.

The yeshiva team howled its happiness and raced off the field. Danny Saunders looked at me, started to say something, stopped, then walked quickly away.

I saw Mr. Galanter going back up the third-base line, his face grim. The rabbi was looking up from his book and smiling.

I took up my position near second base, and Sidney Goldberg came over to me.

"Why'd he have to take off like that?" he asked.

I glared over at our third baseman, who was standing near Mr. Galanter and looking very dejected.

"He was in a hurry to win the war," I said bitterly.

"What a jerk," Sidney Goldberg said.

"Goldberg, get over to your place!" Galanter called out. There was an angry edge to his voice. "Let's keep that infield solid!"

Sidney Goldberg went quickly to his position. I stood still and waited.

It was hot, and I was sweating beneath my clothes. I felt the earpieces of my glasses cutting into the skin over my ears, and I took the glasses off for a moment and ran a finger over the pinched ridges of skin, then put them back on quickly because Schwartzie was going into a windup. I crouched down, waiting, remembering Danny Saunders' promise to his team that they would kill us apikorsim. The word had meant, originally, a Jew educated in Judaism who denied basic tenets of his faith, like the existence of God, the revelation, the resurrection of the dead. To people like Reb Saunders, it also meant any educated Jew who might be reading, say, Darwin, and who was not wearing side curls and fringes outside his trousers. I was an apikoros to Danny Saunders, despite my belief in God and Torah, because I did not have side curls and was attending a parochial school where too many English subjects were offered and where Jewish subjects were taught in Hebrew instead of Yiddish, both unheard-of sins, the former because it took time away from the study of Torah, the latter because Hebrew was the Holy Tongue and to use it in ordinary classroom discourse was a desecration of God's Name. I had never really had any personal contact with this kind of Jew before. My father had told me he didn't mind their beliefs. What annoyed him was their fanatic sense of righteousness, their absolute certainty that they and they alone had God's ear, and every other Jew was wrong, totally wrong, a sinner, a hypocrite, an apikoros, and doomed, therefore, to burn in hell. I found myself wondering again how they had learned to hit a ball like that if time for the study of Torah was so precious to them and why they had sent a rabbi along to waste his time sitting on a bench during a ball game.

Standing on the field and watching the boy at the plate swing at a high ball and miss, I felt myself suddenly very angry, and it was at that point that for me the game stopped being merely a game and became a war. The fun and excitement were out of it now. Somehow the yeshiva team had translated this afternoon's baseball game into a conflict between what they regarded as their righteousness and our sinfulness. I found myself growing more and more angry, and I felt the anger begin to focus itself upon Danny Saunders, and suddenly it was not at all difficult for me to hate him.

Schwartzie let five of their men come up to the plate that half inning and let one of those five score. Sometime during that half inning, one of the members of the yeshiva team had shouted at us in Yiddish, "Burn in hell, you apikorsim!" and by the time that half inning was over and we were standing around Mr. Galanter near the wire screen, all of us knew that this was not just another ball game.

Mr. Galanter was sweating heavily, and his face was grim. All he said was, "We fight it careful from now on. No more mistakes." He said it very quietly, and we were all quiet, too, as the batter stepped up to the plate.

We proceeded to play a slow, careful game, bunting whenever we had to, sacrificing to move runners forward, obeying Mr. Galanter's instructions. I noticed that no matter where the runners were on the bases, the yeshiva team always threw to Danny Saunders, and I realized that they did this because he was the only infielder who could be relied upon to stop their wild throws. Sometime during the inning, I walked over behind the rabbi and looked over his shoulder at the book he was reading. I saw the words were Yiddish. I walked back to the wire screen. Davey Cantor came over and stood next to me, but he remained silent.

We scored only one run that inning, and we walked onto the field for the first half of the third inning with a sense of doom.

Dov Shlomowitz came up to the plate. He stood there like a bear, the bat looking like a matchstick in his beefy hands. Schwartzie pitched, and he sliced one neatly over the head of the third baseman for a single. The yeshiva team howled, and again one of them called out to us in Yiddish, "Burn, you apikorsim!" and Sidney Goldberg and I looked at each other without saying a word.

Mr. Galanter was standing alongside third base, wiping his forehead. The rabbi was sitting quietly, reading his book.

I took off my glasses and rubbed the tops of my ears. I felt a sudden momentary sense of unreality, as if the play yard, with its black asphalt floor and its white base lines, were my entire world now, as if all the previous years of my life had led me somehow to this one ball game, and all the future years of my life would depend upon its outcome. I stood there for a moment, holding the glasses in my hand and feeling frightened. Then I took a deep breath, and the feeling passed. It's only a ball game, I told myself. What's a ball game?

Mr. Galanter was shouting at us to move back. I was standing a few feet to the left of second, and I took two steps back. I saw Danny Saunders walk up to the plate, swinging a bat. The yeshiva team was shouting at him in Yiddish to kill us apikorsim.

Schwartzie turned around to check the field. He looked nervous and was taking his time. Sidney Goldberg was standing up straight, waiting. We looked at each other, then looked away. Mr. Galanter stood very still alongside third base, looking at Schwartzie.

The first pitch was low, and Danny Saunders ignored it. The second one started to come in shoulder-high, and before it was two thirds of the way to the plate, I was already standing on second base. My glove was going up as the bat cracked against the ball, and I saw the ball move in a straight line directly over Schwartzie's head, high over his head, moving so fast he hadn't even had time to regain his balance from the pitch before it went past him. I saw Dov Shlomowitz heading toward me and Danny Saunders racing to first and I heard the yeshiva team shouting and Sidney Goldberg screaming and I jumped, pushing myself upward off the ground with all the strength I had in my legs and stretching my glove hand till I thought it would pull out of my shoulder. The ball hit the pocket of my glove with an impact that numbed my hand and went through me like an electric shock, and I felt the force pull me backward and throw me off balance, and I came down hard on my left hip and elbow. I saw Dov Shlomowitz whirl and start back to first, and I pushed myself up into a sitting position and threw the ball awkwardly to Sidney Goldberg, who caught it and whipped it to first. I heard the umpire scream "Out!" and Sidney Goldberg ran over to help me to my feet, a look of disbelief and ecstatic joy on his face. Mr. Galanter shouted "Time!" and came racing onto the field. Schwartzie was standing in his pitcher's position with his mouth open. Danny Saunders stood on the base line a few feet from first, where he had stopped after I had caught the ball, staring out at me, his face frozen to stone. The rabbi was staring at me, too, and the yeshiva team was deathly silent.

"That was a great catch, Reuven!" Sidney Goldberg said, thumping my back. "That was sensational!"

I saw the rest of our team had suddenly come back to life and was throwing the ball around and talking up the game.

Mr. Galanter came over. "You all right, Malter?" he asked. "Let me see that elbow."

I showed him the elbow. I had scraped it, but the skin had not been broken.

"That was a good play," Mr. Galanter said, beaming at me. I saw his face was still covered with sweat, but he was smiling broadly now.

"Thanks, Mr. Galanter."

"How's the hand?"

"It hurts a little."

"Let me see it."

I took off the glove, and Mr. Galanter poked and bent the wrist and fingers of the hand.

"Does that hurt?" he asked.

"No," I lied.

"You want to go on playing?"

"Sure, Mr. Galanter."

"Okay," he said, smiling at me and patting my back. "We'll put you in for a Purple Heart on that one, Malter."

I grinned at him.

"Okay," Mr. Galanter said. "Let's keep this infield solid!"

He walked away, smiling.

"I can't get over that catch," Sidney Goldberg said.

"You threw it real good to first," I told him.

"Yeah," he said. "While you were sitting on your tail."

We grinned at each other, and went to our positions.

Two more of the yeshiva team got to bat that inning. The first one hit a single, and the second one sent a high fly to short, which Sidney Goldberg caught without having to move a step. We scored two runs that inning and one run the next, and by the top half of the fifth inning we were leading five to three. Four of their men had stood up to bat during the top half of the fourth inning, and they had got only a single on an error to first. When we took to the field in the top half of the fifth inning, Mr. Galanter was walking back and forth alongside third on the balls of his feet, sweating, smiling, grinning, wiping his head nervously; the rabbi was no longer reading; the yeshiva team was silent as death. Davey Cantor was playing second, and I stood in the pitcher's position. Schwartzie had pleaded exhaustion, and since this was the final inning—our parochial school schedules only permitted us time for five-inning games—and the yeshiva team's last chance at bat, Mr. Galanter was taking no chances and told me to pitch. Davey Cantor was a poor fielder, but Mr. Galanter was counting on my pitching to finish off the game. My left hand was still sore from the catch, and the wrist hurt whenever I caught a ball, but the right hand was fine, and the pitches went in fast and dropped into the curve just when I wanted them to. Dov Shlomowitz stood at the plate, swung three times at what looked to him to be perfect pitches, and hit nothing but air. He stood there looking bewildered after the third swing, then slowly walked away. We threw the ball around the infield, and Danny Saunders came up to the plate.

The members of the yeshiva team stood near the wire fence, watching Danny Saunders. They were very quiet. The rabbi was sitting on the bench, his book closed. Mr. Galanter was shouting at everyone to move back. Danny Saunders swung his bat a few times, then fixed himself into position and looked out at me.

Here's a present from an apikoros, I thought, and let go the ball. It went in fast and straight, and I saw Danny Saunders' left foot move out and his bat go up and his body begin to pivot. He swung just as the ball slid into its curve, and the bat cut savagely through empty air, twisting him around and sending him off balance. His black skullcap fell off his head, and he regained his balance and bent quickly to retrieve it. He stood there for a moment, very still, staring out at me. Then he resumed his position at the plate. The ball came back to me from the catcher, and my wrist hurt as I caught it.

The yeshiva team was very quiet, and the rabbi had begun to chew his lip.

I lost control of the next pitch, and it was wide. On the third pitch, I went into a long, elaborate windup and sent him a slow, curving blooper, the kind a batter always wants to hit and always misses. He ignored it completely and the umpire called it a ball.

I felt my left wrist begin to throb as I caught the throw from the catcher. I was hot and sweaty, and the earpieces of my glasses were cutting deeply into the flesh above my ears as a result of the head movements that went with my pitching.

Danny Saunders stood very still at the plate, waiting.

Okay, I thought, hating him bitterly. Here's another present.

The ball went to the plate fast and straight, and dropped just below his swing. He checked himself with difficulty so as not to spin around, but he went off his balance again and took two or three staggering steps forward before he was able to stand up straight.

The catcher threw the ball back, and I winced at the pain in my wrist. I took the ball out of the glove, held it in my right hand, and turned around for a moment to look out at the field and let the pain in my wrist subside. When I turned back I saw that Danny Saunders hadn't moved. He was holding his bat in his left hand, standing very still and staring at me. His eyes were dark, and his lips were parted in a crazy, idiot grin. I heard the umpire yell "Play ball!" but Danny Saunders stood there, staring at me and grinning. I turned and looked out at the field again, and when I turned back he was still standing there, staring at me and grinning. I could see his teeth between his parted lips. I took a deep breath and felt myself wet with sweat. I wiped my right hand on my pants and saw Danny Saunders step slowly to the plate and set his legs in position. He was no longer grinning. He stood looking at me over his left shoulder, waiting.

I wanted to finish it quickly because of the pain in my wrist, and I sent in another fast ball. I watched it head straight for the plate. I saw him go into a sudden crouch, and in the fraction of a second before he hit the ball I realized that he had anticipated the curve and was deliberately swinging low. I was still a little off balance from the pitch, but I managed to bring my glove hand up in front of my face just as he hit the ball. I saw it coming at me, and there was nothing

I could do. It hit the finger section of my glove, deflected off, smashed into the upper rim of the left lens of my glasses, glanced off my forehead, and knocked me down. I scrambled around for it wildly, but by the time I got my hand on it Danny Saunders was standing safely on first.

I heard Mr. Galanter call time, and everyone on the field came racing over to me. My glasses lay shattered on the asphalt floor, and I felt a sharp pain in my left eye when I blinked. My wrist throbbed, and I could feel the bump coming up on my forehead. I looked over at first, but without my glasses Danny Saunders was only a blur. I imagined I could still see him grinning.

I saw Mr. Galanter put his face next to mine. It was sweaty and full of concern. I wondered what all the fuss was about. I had only lost a pair of glasses, and we had at least two more good pitchers on the team.

"Are you all right, boy?" Mr. Galanter was saying. He looked at my face and forehead. "Somebody wet a handkerchief with cold water!" he shouted. I wondered why he was shouting. His voice hurt my head and rang in my ears. I saw Davey Cantor run off, looking frightened. I heard Sidney Goldberg say something, but I couldn't make out his words. Mr. Galanter put his arm around my shoulders and walked me off the field. He sat me down on the bench next to the rabbi. Without my glasses everything more than about ten feet away from me was blurred. I blinked and wondered about the pain in my left eye. I heard voices and shouts, and then Mr. Galanter was putting a wet handkerchief on my head.

"You feel dizzy, boy?" he said.

I shook my head.

"You're sure now?"

"I'm all right," I said, and wondered why my voice sounded husky and why talking hurt my head.

"You sit quiet now," Mr. Galanter said. "You begin to feel dizzy, you let me know right away."

"Yes, sir," I said.

He went away. I sat on the bench next to the rabbi, who looked at me once, then looked away. I heard shouts in Yiddish. The pain in my left eye was so intense I could feel it in the base of my spine. I sat on the bench a long time, long enough to see us lose the game by a score of eight to seven, long enough to hear the yeshiva team shout with joy, long enough to begin to cry at the pain in my left eye, long enough for Mr. Galanter to come over to me at the end of the game, take one look at my face, and go running out of the yard to call a cab.

FICTION

SERGIO RAMIREZ was born in Masatepe, Nicaragua, in 1942. Trained as a lawyer, he served for a time in Costa Rica as the Secretary General of the Council of Central American Universities. From 1973 through 1975 he lived in West Berlin on a writing scholarship and produced the novel *To Bury Our Fathers*, a panoramic story of Nicaraguan history that established him as that country's leading writer of prose.

In 1978 Dr. Ramírez returned home as leader of the "Group of Twelve," a body of influential civilians who gave open support to the Sandinista National Liberation Front against the Somoza dictatorship. After the revolution, he became a civilian member of the governing Sandinista junta, and in 1984 he was elected vice president of Nicaragua.

It is a country with a national passion for baseball, and this is not the only Ramírez story on that subject. But it may be the best. It was written in 1967.

The Centerfielder

SERGIO RAMÍREZ *translated by* NICK CAISTOR

THE FLASHLIGHT picked out one prisoner after another until it came to rest on a bed where a man was asleep, his back to the door. His bare torso glistened with sweat.

"That's him, open up," said the guard, peering through the bars.

The warder's key hung from a length of electric cable he used as a belt. It grated in the rusty lock. Inside, the guards beat their rifle butts on the bedframe until the man struggled to his feet, shielding his eyes from the glare.

"Get up, you're wanted."

He was shivering with cold as he groped for his shirt, even though the heat had been unbearable all night, and the prisoners were sleeping in their underpants or stark naked. The only slit in the wall was so high up that the air never circulated much below the ceiling. He found his shirt, and poked his feet into his laceless shoes.

"Get a move on!" the guard said.

"I'm coming, can't you see?"

"Don't get smart with me, or else . . ."

"Or else what?"

"You know what else!"

The guard stood to one side to let him out of the cell. "Walk, don't talk," he snapped, jabbing him in the ribs with the rifle. The man flinched at the cold metal.

They emerged into the yard. Down by the far wall, the leaves of almond trees glittered in the moonlight. It was midnight, and the slaughtering of animals had begun in the next-door abattoir. The breeze carried a smell of blood and dung.

What a perfect field for baseball! The prisoners must make up teams to play, or take on the off-duty guards. The dugout would be the wall, which left about three hundred and fifty feet from home plate to centerfield. You'd have to field a hit from there running backwards toward the almond trees. When you picked up the ball the diamond would seem far away; the shouts for you to throw would be muffled by the distance; the batter would be rounding second base—and then I'd reach up, catch a branch, and swing myself up. I'd stretch forward, put my hands carefully between the broken bottles on the top of the wall, then edge over with my feet. I'd jump down, ignoring the pain as I crashed into the heap of garbage, bones, bits of horn, broken chairs, tin cans, rags, newspapers, dead vermin. Then I'd run on, tearing myself on thistles, stumbling into a drain of filthy water, but running on and on, as the dry crack of rifles sounded far behind me.

"Halt! Where d'you think you're going?"

"To piss, that's all."

"Scared are you?"

It is almost identical to the square back home, with the rubber trees growing right by the church steps. I was the only one on our team who had a real leather glove: all the others had to catch barehanded. I'd be out there fielding at six in the evening when it was so dark I could hardly see the ball. I could catch them like doves in my hand, just by the sound.

"Here he is, Captain," the guard called, poking his head around a half-open door. From inside came the steady hum of air conditioning.

"Bring him in, then leave us."

He felt immediately trapped in this bare, whitewashed room. Apart from a chair in the center, and the captain's desk up against the far wall, the only adornments were a gilt-framed portrait and a calendar with red and blue numbers. To judge by the fresh plaster, the air conditioning had only recently been installed.

"What time were you picked up?" the captain asked, without looking up.

He stood there at a loss for a reply, wishing with all his heart that the question had been aimed at somebody else—perhaps at someone hiding under the table.

"Are you deaf—I'm talking to you. What time were you taken prisoner?"

"Sometime after six, I reckon," he mumbled, so softly he was convinced the captain hadn't heard him.

"Why do you think it was after six? Can't you tell me the exact time?"

"I don't have a watch, sir, but I'd already eaten, and I always eat at six."

Come and eat, Ma would shout from the sidewalk outside the house. Just one more inning, I'd say, then I'll be there. But son, it's dark already, how can you see to play? I'm coming, there's only one inning left. The violin and the harmonium would be tuning up for Mass in the church as the ball flew safely into my hands for the last out. We'd won yet again.

"What job do you do?"

"I'm a cobbler."

"Do you work in a shop?"

"No, I do repairs at home."

"You used to be a baseball player, didn't you?"

"Yes, once upon a time."

"And you were known as 'Whiplash' Parrales, weren't you?"

"Yes, they called me that because of the way I threw the ball in."

"And you were in the national team that went to Cuba?"

"That's right, twenty years ago. I went as centerfielder."

"But they kicked you out . . ."

"When we got back."

"You made quite a name for yourself with that arm of yours."

The captain's angry stare soon dashed the smile from Parrales' lips.

The best piece of fielding I ever did was at home when I caught a fly ball on the steps of the church itself. I took it with my back to the bases, but fell sprawling on my face and split my tongue. Still, we won the game and the team carried me home in triumph. My mother left her tortilla dough and came to care for my wound. She was sorry and proud at the same time: "Do you have to knock your brains out to prove you're a real sport?"

"Why did they kick you off the team?"

"On account of my dropping a fly and us losing the game."

"In Cuba?"

"We were playing Aruba. I bungled it, they got two runs, and we'd lost."

"Several of you were booted out, weren't you?"

"The fact is, we all drank a lot, and you can't do that in baseball."

"Aha!"

He wanted to ask if he could sit down because his shins were aching so, but didn't dare move an inch. Instead he stood stock still, as though his shoes were glued to the floor.

The captain laboriously wrote out something. He finally lifted his head, and Parrales could see the red imprint of a cap across his forehead.

"Why did they bring you in?"

He shrugged and stared at him blankly.

"Well, why?"

"No," he answered.

"No, what?"

"No, I don't know."

"Aha, so you don't know."

"No."

"I've got your file here," the captain said, flourishing a folder. "Shall I read you a few bits so you can learn about yourself?" He stood up.

From centerfield you can barely hear the ball smack the catcher's mitt. But when the batter connects, the sound travels clearly and all your senses sharpen to follow the ball. As it flies through the distance to my loving hands, I wait patiently, dancing beneath it until finally I clasp it as though I'm making a nest for it.

"At five p.m. on July 28th a green canvas-topped jeep drew up outside your house. Two men got out: one was dark, wore khaki trousers, and sun glasses. The other was fair-skinned, wore bluejeans and a straw hat. The one with dark glasses was carrying a PanAm dufflebag; the other had an army backpack. They went into your house, and didn't come out again until ten o'clock. They didn't have their bags with them."

"The one with the glasses . . . ," nervous, he choked on endless saliva, "he was my son, the one in glasses."

"I know that."

Again there was silence. Parrales' feet were perspiring inside his shoes, making them as wet as if he had just crossed a stream.

"The bag contained ammunition for a fixed machine gun, and the rucksack was full of fuses. When had you last seen your son before that?"

"Not for months," he murmured.

"Speak up, I can't hear you."

"Months—I don't remember how many, but several months. He quit his job at the ropeworks one day, and we didn't see him again after that."

"Weren't you worried about him?"

"Of course—he's my son, after all. We asked, made official enquiries, but got nowhere." Parrales pushed his false teeth back into place, worried in case the plate worked loose.

"Did you know he was in the mountains with the rebels?"

"We did hear rumors."

"So when he turned up in the jeep, what did you think?"

"That he was coming home. But all he did was say hello, then leave again a few hours later."

"And ask you to look after his things?"

"Yes, he said he'd send for them."

"Oh, he did, did he?"

The captain pulled more purple-typed sheets out of the folder. He sifted through them, then laid one out on the desk.

"It says here that for three months you were handling ammunition, firearms, fuses and subversive literature, and that you let enemies of the government sleep in your house."

Parrales said nothing. He took out a handkerchief to blow his nose. He looked gaunt and shrunken in the lamplight, as though already reduced to a skeleton.

"And you weren't aware of a thing, were you?"

"You know what sons are."

"Sons of bitches, you mean."

Parrales stared down at the protruding tongues and mud caking his tattered shoes.

"How long is it since you last saw your son?"

He looked the captain full in the face. "You know he's been killed, so why ask me that?"

The last inning of the game against Aruba, zero to zero, two outs, and the white ball was floating gently home to my hands as I waited, arms outstretched; we were about to meet for ever when the ball clipped the back of my hand, I tried to scoop it up, but it bounced to the ground—far off I could see the batter sliding home, and all was lost. Ma, I needed warm water on my wounds, like you always knew, I was always brave out on the field, even ready to die.

"Sometimes I'd like to be kind, but it's impossible," the captain said, advancing around the desk. He tossed the folder back into the drawer, and turned to switch off the air conditioning. Again the room was plunged into silence. He pulled a towel from a hook and draped it about his shoulders.

"Sergeant!" he shouted.

The sergeant stood to attention in the doorway. He led the prisoner out, then reappeared almost immediately.

"What am I to put in the report?"

"He was a baseball player, so make up anything you like. Say he was playing with the other prisoners, that he was centerfielder and chased a hit down to the wall, then climbed up an almond tree and jumped over the wall. Put down that we shot him as he was escaping across the slaughterhouse yard."

HISTORY

THIS ACCOUNT was done for inclusion in a splendid collection called *The Ultimate Baseball Book*, which was published in 1979.

Up from the Minors in Montreal

MORDECAI RICHLER

PRONOUNCING ON Montreal, my Montreal, Casey Stengel once said, "Well, you see they have these polar bears up there and lots of fellows trip over them trying to run the bases and they're never much good anymore except for hockey or hunting deer."

Alas, we have no polar bears up here, but kids can usually heave snowballs at the outfielders at the opening game of the season, and should the World Series ever dare venture this far north, it is conceivable that a game could be called because of a blizzard. Something else. In April, the loudest cheers in the ball park tend to come when nothing of any consequence seems to have happened on the field, understandably baffling the players on visiting teams. These cheers spring from fans who sit huddled with transistor radios clapped to their ears and signify that something of importance has happened, albeit out of town, where either Guy Lafleur or Pierre Mondou has just scored in a Stanley Cup play-off game.

Baseball remains a popular game here, in spite of the Expos, but hockey is the way of life.

Montreal, it must be understood, is a city unlike any other in Canada. Or, come to think of it, the National League. On the average, eight feet of snow is dumped on us each winter and, whatever the weather, we can usually count on three bank robberies a day here.

This is the city of wonders that gave you Expo in 1967, the baseball Expos a couple of years later and, in 1976, the Olympic Games, its legacy, among other amazing artifacts, a stadium that can seat or intern, as some have it, 60,000 baseball fans. I speak of the monstrous Big O, where our inept Expos disport themselves in summer, their endearing idea of loading the bases being to have two of their runners on second. Hello, hello. Their notion of striking fear into the heart of the opposition being to confront them with muscle, namely one of their pinch-hitting behemoths coming off the bench: group average, .135.

Major league baseball, like the Olympics and the Big O itself, was brought to this long suffering city through the machinations of our very own Artful Dodger, Mayor Jean Drapeau.

Bringing us the Games, he assured Montrealers that it would be as difficult for the Olympics to cost us money as it would be for a man to have a baby. He estimated the total cost of all facilities at $62.2 million but, what with inflation and unfavorable winds, his calculations fell somewhat short of the mark. Counting stationery and long distance calls, the final cost was $1.2 billion. Never mind. To this day our ebullient mayor doesn't allow that the Games were run at a loss. Rather, as he has put it to the rest of us, there has been a gap between costs and revenue. And, considering the spiffy facilities we have been left with, it would be churlish of us to complain.

Ah, the Big O. The largest, coldest slab of poured concrete in Canada. In a city where we endure seven punishing months of winter and spring comes and goes in an afternoon, it is Drapeau's triumph to have provided us with a partially roofed-over $520 million stadium, where the sun never shines on the fans. Tim Burke, one of the liveliest sportswriters in town, once said to me, "You know, there are lots of summer afternoons when I feel like taking in a ball game, but I think, hell, who wants to sit out there in the dark."

"Shivering in the dark" might be more accurate, watching the boys lose line drives in the seams of the artificial turf.

"The outfield," another wag remarked, "looks just like the kind of thing my aunt used to wear."

Furthermore, come cap day or bat night ours is the only park in the National League that fills a social office, letting the poor know where to get off, which is to say, the scruffy kids in the bleachers are beyond the pale. They don't qualify.

It's a shame, because the Expos, admittedly major league in name only, came to a town rich in baseball history and, to begin with, we were all charged with hope. In their opening game, on April 9, 1969, the Expos took the Mets 11–10 at Shea Stadium, collecting three homers and five doubles. Five days later, the 29,184 fans who turned up for the home opener were electrified by an announcement over the public address system. "When the Expos play a doubleheader," we were informed, "the second game will go the full nine innings, not seven."

Those of us old enough to remember baseball's glory here, the Montreal Royals of the old International League, nodded our heads, impressed. This was the big time. "Montreal," said Warren Giles, president of the National League, "is a growing and vibrant city." Yessirree. And we hollered and stamped our feet as our champions took to the field under the grim gaze of manager Gene Mauch, who had the look of a Marine drill sergeant.

I still have that incomparably bubbly opening day program. *Votre première équipe des ligues majeures.* Vol. 1, No. 1. *Publié par Club de Baseball Montreal Ltée.* "The Expos believe they landed a real prize when they snatched Gary Sutherland from the Philadelphia Phillies. Big things are expected from John Bateman, the former Houston Astros' fine receiver. Bob Bailey impressed everybody with his tremendous hustle. Ty Cline is a two-way player. 'In the field,' said Larry Shepard, manager of the Pittsburgh Pirates, 'Don Bosch can be compared with none other than Willie Mays.' Larry Jaster has youth on his side. This may be the year Don Shaw comes into his own. Angel Hermoso is one of the fine young Expo prospects the scouts have hung a 'can't miss' label on. On a given day, Mike Wegener, only 22, can throw with the best. Don Hahn was a standout performer during spring training. Bob Reynolds' main forte is a blistering fastball. Expansion could be 'just what the doctor ordered' for Coco Laboy."

To be fair, the original Expos included Rusty Staub, sweet Mack Jones and Bill Stoneman, a surprisingly effective player who pitched two no-hitters before his arm gave out. Manny Mota, another original draft choice, was one of the first to be sent packing by a management that was to become celebrated for its lame-headed dealings, its most spectacular blunder being a trade that sent Ken Singleton and Mike Torrez to Baltimore for a sore-armed Dave McNally and a totally ineffective Rich Coggins. It should also be noted that the Expos did take their home opener, defeating the Cardinals 8–7, and that tiny Parc Jarry, where they were to play, futile in their fashion, for another eight years, was a charming, intimate stadium with the potential to become another Fenway Park.

Opening day, I recognized many of the plump faces in the box seats on the first-base line. Among them were some of the nervy kids who used to skip school with me on weekday afternoons to sit in the left-field bleachers of Delormier Downs, cheering on the Royals and earning nickels fetching hot dogs for strangers. Gone were the AZA windbreakers, the bubble gum, the scuffed running shoes, the pale wintry faces. These men came bronzed to the ball park from their Florida condominiums. Now they wore foulards and navy blue blazers with brass buttons; they carried Hudson's Bay blankets in plastic cases for their bejeweled wives; and they sucked on Monte Cristos, mindful not to spill ashes on their Gucci sandals. Above all, they radiated pleasure in their own accomplishments and the occasion. And why not? This was an event and there they were, inside, looking out at last, right on the first-base line. Look at me. "Give it some soul, Mack," one of them shouted.

An article in that memorable opening day program noted that while the province of Quebec had never been known as a hotbed of major league talent, we had nevertheless produced a few ballplayers, among them pitchers Claude Raymond and Ron Piché, and that three more native sons, Roland Gladu, Jean-Pierre Roy and Stan Bréard had once played for another ball club here, the Montreal Royals.

O, I remember the Royals, yes indeed, and if they played in a Montreal that was not yet growing and vibrant, it was certainly a place to be cherished.

Betta Dodd, "The Girl in Cellophane," was stripping at the Gayety, supported by 23 Kuddling Kuties. Cantor Moishe Oysher, The Master Singer of his People, was appearing at His Majesty's. The Johnny Holmes Band, playing at Victoria Hall, featured Oscar Peterson; and a sign in the corner cigar-and-soda warned Ziggy Halprin, Yossel Hoffman and me that

LOOSE TALK COSTS LIVES!
Keep It Under
Your
STETSON

I first became aware of the Royals in 1943. Our country was already 76 years old, I was merely 12, and we were both at war.

MAY U BOAT SINKINGS EXCEED REPLACEMENTS;
KING DECORATES 625 CANADIANS ON BIRTHDAY

Many of our older brothers and cousins were serving overseas. Others on the street were delighted to discover they suffered from flat feet or, failing that, arranged to have an eardrum punctured by a specialist in such matters.

R.A.F. HITS HARD AT COLOGNE AND HAMBURG
2,000 Tons of Bombs
Rain on Rhine City

On the home front, sacrifices were called for. On St. Urbain Street, where we served, collecting salvage, we had to give up American comic books for the duration. Good-bye, Superman, so long, Captain Marvel. Instead, we were obliged to make do with shoddy Canadian imitations printed in black and white. And such was the shortage of ballplayers that the one-armed outfielder, Pete Gray, got to play for the Three Rivers club on his way to the Browns and French Canadians, torn from the local sandlots, actually took to the field for our very own Royals: Bréard, Gladu, Roy.

Even in fabled Westmount, where the very rich were rooted, things weren't the same anymore. H.R., emporium to the privileged, enjoined Westmount to "take another step in further aid of the Government's all out effort to defeat aggression!"

HOLT RENFREW ANNOUNCE THAT BEGINNING JUNE FIRST NO DELIVERIES OF MERCHANDISE WILL BE MADE ON WEDNESDAYS

This forethought will help H.R. to save many gallons of gasoline . . . and many a tire . . . for use by the government. Moreover, will it not thrill you to think that the non-delivery of your dress on Wednesday will aid in the delivery of a 'block-buster' over the Ruhr . . . Naples . . . Berlin . . . and many other places of enemy entrenchment?

Our parents feared Hitler and his Panzers, but Ziggy, Yossel and I were in terror of Branch Rickey and his scouts.

Nineteen thirty-nine was not only the date we had gone to war, it was also the year the management of the Royals signed a contract with Mr. Rickey, making them the number one farm club of the Brooklyn Dodgers. This dealt us young players of tremendous promise, but again and again, come the Dodgers' late-summer pennant drive, the best of the bunch were harvested by the parent team. Before we had even reached the age of puberty, Ziggy, Yossel and I had learned to love with caution. If after the first death there is no other, an arguable notion, I do remember that each time one of our heroes abandoned us for Ebbets Field, it stung us badly. We hated Mr. Rickey for his voracious appetite. "There has been no mention officially that the Dodgers will be taking Flowers," Lloyd MacGowan wrote in the *Star* on a typical day, "but Rickey was in Buffalo to watch the team yesterday. The Dodgers can't take Flowers without sending down a flinger, but chances are the replacement for the burly lefty will hardly be adequate."

The International League, as we knew it in the forties, its halcyon years, was Triple A and comprised of eight teams: Montreal, Toronto, Syracuse, Jersey City, Newark, Rochester, Baltimore and Buffalo.

Newark was the number one farm team of the Yankees and Jersey City filled the same office for the Giants. But organized baseball had actually come to Montreal in 1898, the Royals then fielding a team in the old Eastern League, taking the pennant in their inaugural year. In those days the Royals played in Atwater Park, which could seat 12,000, and from all accounts was a fine and intimate stadium, much like Parc Jarry. During the 21 years the Royals played there they offered Montreal, as sportswriter Marc Thibault recently wrote, *"du baseball parfois excitant, plus souvent qu'autrement, assez détestable,"* the problem being the troubled management's need to sell off their most accomplished players for ready cash. Be that as it may, in 1914, long before we were to endure major league baseball in name only here, George Herman Ruth came to Atwater Park to pitch for the Baltimore Orioles. Two years later, the team folded, a casualty of World War I, and another 11 years passed before the Royals were resuscitated.

It was 1928 when George Tweedy "Miracle Man" Stallings bought the then-defunct Syracuse franchise and built Delormier Downs, a stadium with a 22,000 capacity, at the corner of Ontario and Delormier streets. An overflow crowd of 22,500, including Judge Kenesaw Mountain Landis, was at the opening game, which the Royals won, defeating the fearsome Reading Keystones, 7–4. Twelve months later Stallings died. In 1929, not a vintage year for the stock market, the Royals finished fourth. Two years later, Delormier Stadium, like just about everybody, was in deep trouble. There were tax arrears and a heavy bank debt to be settled. The original sponsors resigned.

In the autumn of 1931 a new company was formed by a triumvirate which included a man who had made millions in gas stations, the rambunctious, poker-playing J. Charles-Emile Trudeau, father of our present prime minister. Another associate of the newly-formed club, Frank "Shag" Shaughnessy, cunningly introduced the play-off system in 1933, and two years later became the club's general manager. In 1935, fielding a team that included Fresco Thompson, Jimmy Ripple and Del Bissonette, the Royals won their first pennant since 1898. However, they finished poorly in '37 and '38 and, the following year, Mr. Rickey surfaced, sending in Burleigh Grimes to look after his interests.

Redemption was at hand.

Bruno Betzel came in to manage the team in 1944, the year the nefarious Branch Rickey bought the Royals outright, building it into the most profitable club in all of minor league baseball, its fans loyal but understandably resentful of the head office's appetite, praying that this summer the Dodgers wouldn't falter in the stretch, sending down for fresh bats, strong arms, just when we needed them most.

The Royals finished first in 1945, and in '46 and '48 they won both the pennant and the Little World Series. They were to win the pennant again in '51 and '52, under Clay Hopper, and the Little World Series in '53, when they were managed by Walter Alston. The Royals fielded their greatest team in 1948, the summer young Duke Snider played here, appearing in 77 games before he was snatched by Mr. Rickey. Others on that memorable team included Don Newcombe, Al Gionfriddo, Jimmy Bloodworth, Bobby Morgan and Chuck Connors. The legendary Jackie Robinson and Roy Campanella had already come and gone.

Sam Jethroe was here in 1949 and two years later Junior Gilliam was at third and George Shuba hit 20 home runs. In 1952, our star pitcher was southpaw Tommy Lasorda, the self-styled Bob Feller of the International League. Lasorda pitched his last game for the Royals on July 4, 1960, against Rochester, which seemed to be hitting him at will. Reminiscing recently, Lasorda recalled, "I knew I was in trouble when I saw our manager's foot on the top of the dugout step. If the next guy gets on base, I'm going to be out of there. I turned my back to the hitter and looked up toward the sky. Lord, I said, this is my last game. Get me out of this jam. I make the next pitch and the guy at the plate hits the damnedest line drive you ever saw. Our third baseman, George Risley, gets the tips of his fingers on it but can't hang on. The ball bloops over his hand and our shortstop, Jerry Snyder, grabs it. He fires it to Harry Shewman at second base, who relays it to Jimmy Korada at first. Triple play."

A year later the Royals were dissolved and in 1971 the Delormier Stadium was razed to make way for the Pierre Dupuy School.

On weekday afternoons kids were admitted free into the left-field bleachers and by the third inning the more intrepid had worked their way down as far as the first-base line. Ziggy, Yossel and I would sit out there in the sun, cracking peanuts, nudging each other if a ball struck the Miss Sweet Caporal sign, hitting the young lady you-know-where. Another diversion was a porthole in the outfield wall. If a batter hit a ball through it, he was entitled to a two-year supply of Pal Blades. Heaven.

Sunday afternoons the Royals usually played to capacity crowds, but come the Little World Series fans lined up on the roof of the adjoining Grover Knit-To-Fit Building and temporary stands were set up and roped off in center field. Consequently, as my cousin Seymour who used to sit there liked to boast, "If I get hit on the head, it's a ground rule home run." After the game, we would spill out of the stadium to find streetcars lined up for a half mile, waiting to take us home.

In 1945, the Royals acquired one of ours, their first Jewish player, Kermit Kitman, a William and Mary scholarship boy. Our loyalty to the team was redoubled. Kitman was a centerfielder and an opening day story in *La Presse* declared, *"Trois des meilleurs porte-couleurs du Montréal depuis l'ouverture de la saison ont été ses joueurs de champ: Gladu, Kitman et Yeager. Kitman a exécuté un catch sensationnel encore hier après-midi sur le long coup de Torres à la 8e manche. On les verra tous trois à l'oeuvre cet après-midi contre le Jersey-City lors du programme double de la 'Victoire' au stade de la Rue Delormier."*

In his very first time at bat in that opening game against the Skeeters, Kitman belted a homer, something he would not manage again until August. Alas, in the later innings he also got doubled off second. After the game, when he ventured into a barbershop at the corner of St. Catherine and St. Urbain, a man in another chair studied him intently. "Aren't you Kermit Kitman?" he asked.

"Yeah," he allowed, grinning, remembering his homer.

"You son-of-a-bitch, you got doubled off second, it cost me five hundred bucks."

Lead-off hitter for the Royals, Kitman was entitled to lower berth one on all their road trips. Only 22 years old, but a college boy, he was paid somewhat better than most: $650 monthly for six months of the year. And if the Royals went all the way, winning the Little World Series, he could earn another $1,800. On the road, his hotel bill was paid and he and the other players were each allowed three bucks a day meal money.

There was yet another sea change in the summer of 1946. After scouting what were then called the Negro Leagues for more than a year, Mr. Rickey brought the first black player into organized baseball. So that spring the Royals could not train in the regular park in

Daytona, which was segregated, but had to train in Kelly Field instead.

Actually, Jackie Robinson had been signed on October 23, 1945, in the offices of the Royals at Delormier Stadium, club president Hector Racine saying, "Robinson is a good ball player and comes highly recommended by the Brooklyn Dodgers. We paid him a good bonus to sign with our club."

The bonus was $3,500 and Robinson's salary was $600 monthly.

"One afternoon in Daytona," Kermit Kitman told me, "I was lead-off hitter and quickly singled. Robinson came up next, laying down a sacrifice bunt and running to first. Stanky, covering the sack, tagged him hard and jock-high. Robinson went down, taking a fist in the balls. He was mad as hell, you could see that, but Rickey had warned him, no fights. He got up, dusted himself off and said nothing. After the game, when he was resting, Stanky came over to apologize. He had been testing his temper, under orders from Rickey."

Kitman, a good glove man, was an inadequate hitter. Brooklyn born, he never got to play there. Following the 1946 season he was offered a place on the roster of another team in the Dodger farm system, but elected to quit the game instead.

The 1946 season opened for the Royals on April 18, with a game in Jersey City. The AP dispatch for that day, printed in the Montreal *Gazette,* ran: "The first man of his race to play in modern organized baseball smashed a three-run homer that carried 333 feet and added three singles to the Royals' winning 14–1 margin over Jersey City. Just to make it a full day's work, Robinson stole two bases, scored four times and batted in three runs. He was also charged with an error."

Robinson led the International League in hitting that year with a .349 average. He hit three home runs, batted in 66 runs, stole 40 bases, scored 113 runs and fielded .985 at his second-base position. And, furthermore, Montreal adored him, as no other ballplayer who has been here before or since. No sooner did Robinson reach first base, on a hit or a walk, than the fans roared with joy and hope, our hearts going out to him as he danced up and down the base path, taunting the opposing pitcher with his astonishing speed.

We won the pennant that year and met the Louisville Colonels, another Dodger farm club, in the Little World Series. The series opened in Louisville, where Robinson endured a constant run of racial insults from the Colonels' dugout and was held to a mere single in two games. Montreal evened the series at home and returned to Delormier Downs for the seventh and deciding game. "When they won it," Dick Bacon recently wrote, recalling that game in the 200th anniversary issue of the *Gazette,* "Jackie was accorded an emotional send-off unseen before or since in this city.

"First they serenaded him in true French Canadien spirit with, *'Il a gagné ses Epaulettes,'* and then clamored for his reappearance on the field.

"When he finally came out for a curtain call, the fans mobbed him. They hugged him, kissed him, cried, cheered and pulled and tore at his uniform while parading him around the infield on their shoulders.

"With tears streaming down his face, Robinson finally begged off in order to shower, dress and catch a plane to the States. But the riot of joy wasn't over yet.

"When he emerged from the clubhouse, he had to bull his way through the waiting crowd outside the stadium. The thousands of fans chased him down Ontario Street for several blocks before he was rescued by a passing motorist and driven to his hotel.

"As one southern reporter from Louisville, Kentucky, was to write afterward:

" 'It's probably the first time a white mob of rioters ever chased a Negro down the streets in love rather than hate.' "

That was a long time ago.

I don't know whatever became of Red Durrett. Marvin Rackley, of whom Mr. Rickey once said, "I can see him in a World Series, running and hitting," has also disappeared. Roland Gladu, who got to play 21 games with the old Boston Braves, failed to sign the major league skies with his ability. Robinson died in 1972 and in 1977 a plaque to his memory was installed in the chilly Big O. Jean-Pierre Roy now does the French-language broadcasts for the Expos and a graying but still impressive Duke Snider is also back, doing the color commentary for Expo games on CBC-TV, trying his best to be kind to an uninspired bunch without compromising himself.

The Expos have yet to play .500 ball or, since Mack Jones's brief sojourn here, come up with a player that the fans can warm to. But there is hope. Next year, or maybe five years from now, the Big O will be completed. The retractable roof will be set in place. And, in this city of endless winter and short hot summers, it will be possible to watch baseball played under a roof, on artificial grass, in an air-conditioned, possibly even centrally heated, concrete tomb.

Progress.

ENTERTAINMENT

HERE, from the smash musical *Damn Yankees,* are the lyrics of one of the numbers written by Richard Adler and the late Jerry Ross. "The Game" is not so well-known perhaps as some other pieces from the show, like "Heart" or "Whatever Lola Wants," but it fills beautifully that delightful plateau between the patter song and the chorus number, and is a favorite among those who have seen the show.

The Game

JERRY ROSS *and* RICHARD ADLER

ROCKY:

No drinking, no women—no late hours, no women. (*Music*)
You got to keep your mind on the game.

(*Sings*)

We've got to think about the game!

ALL:

The game, the game!
We've got to think about the game,
The game, the game!
Booze and broads may be great,
Though they're great they'll have to wait,
While we think about the game!

ROCKY:

There was that waitress back in Kansas City
Built for comfort, dumb but pretty!

ALL:

Yeah? Yeah?

ROCKY:

Man, her perfume sure did smell sweet,
Got her up to my hotel suite!

ALL:

Yeah? Yeah?

ROCKY:

She killed a pint of gin more or less,
The lights were low and she slips off her dress!

ALL:

Yeah? Yeah? Yeah? Yeah?

ROCKY:

But then I thought about the game!

ALL:

The game, the game!

ROCKY:

Oh, yes I thought about the game!

ALL:

The game, the game!

ROCKY:

Though I got the lady high,
I just left her high and dry,
'Cause I thought about the game!

ALL:

He thought about the game!

SMOKEY:

There was the Pullman car that I got lost in,
On a sleeper out of Boston!

ALL:

Yeah? Yeah?

SMOKEY:

Compartment doors all look the same there,
Walked in one and there's this dame there!

ALL:

Yeah? Yeah?

SMOKEY:

Blonde, and stacked, and absolutely bare,
And nothin' separatin' us but air!

ALL:

Yeah? Yeah? Yeah? Yeah?

SMOKEY:

But then I thought about the game!

ALL:

The game, the game!

SMOKEY:

Oh, yes I thought about the game!

ALL:

The game, the game!

SMOKEY:

Though my heart said stay for tea,
All I said was pardon me!
'Cause I thought about the game!

ALL:

He thought about the game!

MICKEY:

When a chick gives you the eye, remember—

ALL:

Abstain!

LOWE:

When you're dyin' for some rye, remember—

ALL:

Refrain!

HENRY:

If you're losin' at crap and the clock says it's eleven,
And suddenly each roll you roll—"huh"—comes up a seven,
And you're in the kind of dive where men are men,

ALL:

Be polite, say good night, you should be in bed by ten!

SMOKEY:

When your mother bakes you cakes, remember—

ALL:

Stay thin!

ROCKY:

When you're kissin' till it aches, remember—

ALL:

Don't give in!
Every rule we shall obey to be sure,
Cause to win we've gotta stay good and pure,
Good and pure! Mumm.

SMOKEY:

Hey, Rock, remember those twins we took a ride with,
Operatin' side by side with,

ALL:

Yeah? Yeah?

SMOKEY:

We're out of gas three miles from Philly,

ROCKY:

The night is warm, the sky's a dilly,

ALL:

Yeah? Yeah?

ROCKY:

So I suggest we sleep beneath a tree,

SMOKEY:

No one's there but Rock, the chicks and me.

ALL:

Yeah? Yeah? Yeah? Yeah?

SMOKEY:

So there we are, lyin' side by side under the tree.

ROCKY:

Four minds with a single thought.

SMOKEY:

I look at my girl.

ROCKY:

I look at mine.

SMOKEY:

Then with one fell swoop—
(*Boys clasp hands over* SMOKEY'S *and* ROCKY'S *mouths.*)

ALL:

But then they thought about the game!
The game, the game!

ROCKY *and* SMOKEY:

Oh, yes we thought about the game!

ALL:

The game, the game!
To our women one and all,
We will see you in the fall,
But for now we've got to stall
Every dame!
And think about the game!
Think about the game,
Think about the, think about the, think about the, think about the,
Think about the game!

(*Blackout*)

FICTION

OF BASEBALL and his boyhood, Philip Roth wrote, "I loved the game with all my heart." It was, among other things, the cement that bound a pluralistic society "together in common concerns, loyalties, rituals, enthusiasms, and antagonisms." Is it strange, then, that baseball should find its way so often into Roth's writings, or that he should write an entire book about it and name it *The Great American Novel?*

The answer to that question is no. And neither is it strange that the Ruppert Mundys, losingest team in the Patriot League, here find themselves in the city of Asylum (home of the Keepers, another P. League team), traveling to a real asylum for an exhibition game against the inmates.

From *The Great American Novel*

PHILIP ROTH

ONE SUNNY Saturday morning early in August, the Ruppert Mundys boarded a bus belonging to the mental institution and journeyed from their hotel in downtown Asylum out into the green Ohio countryside to the world-famous hospital for the insane, there to play yet another "away" game—a three-inning exhibition match against a team composed entirely of patients. The August visit to the hospital by a P. League team in town for a series against the Keepers was an annual event of great moment at the institution, and one that was believed to be of considerable therapeutic value to the inmates, particularly the sports-minded among them. Not only was it their chance to make contact, if only for an hour or so, with the real world they had left behind, but it was believed that even so brief a visit by famous big league ballplayers went a long way to assuage the awful sense such people have that they are odious and contemptible to the rest of humankind. Of course, the P. League players (who like all ballplayers despised any exhibition games during the course of the regular season) happened to find playing against the Lunatics, as they called them, a most odious business indeed; but as the General simply would not hear of abandoning a practice that brought public attention to the humane and compassionate side of a league that many still associated with violence and scandal, the tradition was maintained year after year, much to the delight of the insane, and the disgust of the ballplayers themselves.

The chief psychiatrist at the hospital was a Dr. Traum, a heavyset gentleman with a dark chin beard, and a pronounced European accent. Until his arrival in America in the thirties, he had never even heard of baseball, but in that Asylum was the site of a major league ball park, as well as a psychiatric hospital, it was not long before the doctor became something of a student of the game. After all, one whose professional life involved ruminating upon the extremes of human behavior, had certainly to sit up and take notice when a local fan decided to make his home atop a flagpole until the Keepers snapped a losing streak, or when an Asylum man beat his wife to death with a hammer for calling the Keepers "bums" just like himself. If the doctor did not, strictly speaking, become an ardent Keeper fan, he did make it his business to read thoroughly in the literature of the national pastime, with the result that over the years more than one P. League manager had to compliment the bearded Berliner on his use of the hit-and-run, and the uncanny ability he displayed at stealing signals during their annual exhibition game.

Despite the managerial skill that Dr. Traum had developed over the years through his studies, his team proved no match for the Mundys that morning. By August of 1943, the Mundys weren't about to sit back and take it on the chin from a German-born baseball manager and a team of madmen; they had been defeated and disgraced and disgraced and defeated up and down the league since the season had begun back in April, and it was as though on the morning they got out to the insane asylum grounds, all the wrath that had been seething in them for months now burst forth, and nothing, but nothing, could have prevented them from grinding the Lunatics into dust once the possibility for victory presented itself. Suddenly, those '43 flops started looking and sounding like the scrappy, hustling, undefeatable Ruppert teams of Luke Gofannon's day—and this despite the fact that it took nearly an hour to complete a single inning, what with numerous delays and interruptions caused by the Lunatics' style of play. Hardly a moment passed that something did not occur to offend the professional dignity of a big leaguer, and yet, through it all, the Mundys on both offense and defense managed to seize hold of every Lunatic mistake and convert it to their advantage. Admittedly, the big right-hander who started for the institution team was fast and savvy enough to hold the Mundy power in check, but playing just the sort of heads-up, razzle-dazzle baseball that used to characterize the Mundy teams of yore, they were able in their first at bat to put together a scratch hit by Astarte, a bunt by Nickname, a base on balls to Big John, and two Lunatic errors, to score three runs—their biggest inning of the year, and the first Mundy runs to cross the plate in sixty consecutive innings, which was not a record only because they had gone sixty-seven innings without scoring earlier in the season.

When Roland Agni, of all people, took a called third strike to end their half of the inning, the Mundys rushed off the bench like a team that smelled World Series loot. "We was due!" yelped Nickname, taking the peg from Hothead and sweeping his glove over the bag— "Nobody gonna stop us now, babe! We was due! We was *over*due!" Then he winged the ball over to where Deacon Demeter stood on the mound, grinning. "Three big ones for you, Deke!" Old Deacon, the fifty-year-old iron-man starter of the Mundy staff, already a twenty-game loser with two months of the season still to go, shot a string of tobacco juice over his left shoulder to ward off evil spirits, stroked the rabbit's foot that hung on a chain around his neck, closed his eyes to mumble something ending with "Amen," and then stepped up on the rubber to face the first patient. Deacon was a preacher back home, as gentle and kindly a man as you would ever want to bring your problems to, but up on the hill he was all competitor, and had been for thirty years now. "When the game begins," he used to say back in his heydey, "charity ends." And so it was that when he saw the first Lunatic batter digging in as though he owned the batter's box, the Deke decided to take Hothead's advice and stick the first pitch in his ear, just to show the little nut who was boss. The Deacon had taken enough insults that year for a fifty-year-old man of the cloth!

Not only did the Deke's pitch cause the batter to go flying back from the plate to save his skin, but next thing everyone knew the lead-off man was running for the big brick building with the iron bars on its windows. Two of his teammates caught him down the right-field line and with the help of the Lunatic bullpen staff managed to drag him back to home plate. But once there they couldn't get him to take hold of the bat; every time they put it into his hands, he let it fall through to the ground. By the time the game was resumed, with a 1 and 0 count on a new lead-off hitter, one not quite so cocky as the fellow who'd stepped up to bat some ten minutes earlier, there was no doubt in anyone's mind that the Deke was in charge. As it turned out, twice in the inning Mike Rama had to go sailing up into the wall to haul in a long line drive, but as the wall was padded, Mike came away unscathed, and the Deacon was back on the bench with his three-run lead intact.

"We're on our way!" cried Nickname. "We are on our God damn way!"

Hothead too was dancing with excitement; cupping his hands to his mouth, he shouted across to the opposition, "Just watch you bastards go to pieces now!"

And so they did. The Deke's pitching and Mike's fielding seemed to have shaken the confidence of the big Lunatic right-hander whose fastball had reined in the Mundys in the first. To the chagrin of his teammates, he simply would not begin to pitch in the second until the umpire stopped staring at him.

"Oh, come on," said the Lunatic catcher, "he's not staring at *you*. Throw the ball."

"I tell you, he's right behind you and he is too staring. Look you, I see you there behind that mask. What is it you want from me? What is it you think you're looking at, anyway?"

The male nurse, in white half-sleeve shirt and white trousers, who was acting as the plate umpire, called out to the mound, "Play ball now. Enough of that."

"Not until you come out from there."

"Oh, pitch, for Christ sake," said the catcher.

"Not until that person stops staring."

Here Dr. Traum came off the Lunatic bench and started for the field, while down in the Lunatic bullpen a left-hander got up and began to throw. Out on the mound, with his hands clasped behind his back and rocking gently to and fro on his spikes, the doctor conferred with the pitcher. Formal European that he was, he wore, along with his regulation baseball shoes, a dark three-piece business suit, a stiff collar, and a tie.

"What do you think the ol' doc's tellin' that boy?" Bud Parusha asked Jolly Cholly.

"Oh, the usual," the old-timer said. "He's just calmin' him down. He's just askin' if he got any good duck shootin' last season."

It was five full minutes before the conference between the doctor and the pitcher came to an end with the doctor asking the pitcher to hand over the ball. When the pitcher vehemently refused, it was necessary for the doctor to snatch the ball out of his hand; but when he motioned down to the bullpen for the left-hander, the pitcher suddenly reached out and snatched the ball back. Here the doctor turned back to the bullpen and this time motioned for the left-hander *and* a right-hander. Out of the bullpen came two men dressed like the plate umpire in white half-sleeve shirts and white trousers. While they took the long walk to the mound, the doctor made several unsuccessful attempts to talk the pitcher into relinquishing the ball. Finally the two men arrived on the mound and before the pitcher knew what had happened, they had unfurled a straitjacket and wrapped it around him.

"Guess he wanted to stay in," said Jolly Cholly, as the pitcher kicked out at the doctor with his feet.

The hundred Lunatic fans who had gathered to watch the game from the benches back of the foul screen behind home plate, and who looked in their street clothes as sane as any baseball crowd, rose to applaud the pitcher as he left the field, but when he opened his mouth to acknowledge the ovation, the two men assisting him in his departure slipped a gag over his mouth.

Next the shortstop began to act up. In the first inning it was he who had gotten the Lunatics out of trouble with a diving stab of a Bud Parusha liner and a quick underhand toss that had doubled Wayne Heket off third. But now in the top of the second, though he continued to gobble up everything hit to the left of the diamond, as soon as he got his hands on the ball he proceeded to stuff it into his back pocket. Then, assuming a posture of utter nonchalance, he would start whistling between his teeth and scratching himself, as though waiting for the action to *begin.* In that it was already very much underway, the rest of the Lunatic infield would begin screaming at him to take the ball out of his pocket and make the throw to first. "What?" he responded, with an innocent smile. "The ball!" they cried. "Yes, what about it?" "Throw it!" "But I don't have it." "You *do!*" they would scream, converging upon him from all points of the infield, "You do too!" "Hey, leave me alone," the shortstop cried, as they grabbed and pulled at his trousers. "Hey, cut that out—get your hands *out* of there!" And when at last the ball was extracted from where he himself had secreted it, no one could have been more surprised. "Hey, the *ball.* Now who put that there? Well, what's everybody looking at *me* for? Look, this must be some guy's idea of a joke . . . Well, Christ, *I* didn't do it."

Once the Mundys caught on, they were quick to capitalize on this unexpected weakness in the Lunatic defense, pushing two more runs across in the second on two consecutive ground balls to short—both beaten out for hits while the shortstop grappled with the other infielders—a sacrifice by Mike Rama, and a fly to short center that was caught by the fielder who then just stood there holding it in his glove, while Hothead, who was the runner on second, tagged up and hobbled to third, and then, wooden leg and all, broke for home, where he scored with a head-first slide, the only kind he could negotiate. As it turned out, the slide wasn't even necessary, for the center-fielder was standing in the precise spot where he had made the catch—and the ball was still in his glove.

With the bases cleared, Dr. Traum asked for time and walked out to center. He put a hand on the shoulder of the mute and motionless fielder and talked to him in a quiet voice. He talked to him steadily for fifteen minutes, their faces only inches apart. Then he stepped aside, and the center-fielder took the ball from the pocket of his glove and threw a perfect strike to the catcher, on his knees at the plate some two hundred feet away.

"Wow," said Bud Parusha, with ungrudging admiration, "now, that fella has an arm on him."

"Hothead," said Cholly, mildly chiding the catcher, "he woulda had you by a country mile, you know, if only he'd a throwed it."

But Hot, riding high, hollered out, "Woulda don't count, Charles—it's dudda what counts, and I dud it!"

Meanwhile Kid Heket, who before this morning had not been awake for two consecutive innings in over a month, continued to stand with one foot up on the bench, his elbow on his knee and his chin cupped contemplatively in his palm. He had been studying the opposition like this since the game had gotten underway, "You know somethin'," he said, gesturing toward the field, "those fellas ain't thinkin'. No sir, they just ain't usin' their heads."

"We got 'em on the run, Wayne!" cried Nickname. "They don't know *what* hit 'em! Damn, ain't nobody gonna stop us from here on out!"

Deacon was hit hard in the last of the second, but fortunately for the Mundys, in the first two instances the batsman refused to relinquish the bat and move off home plate, and so each was thrown out on what would have been a base hit, right-fielder Parusha to first-baseman Baal; and the last hitter, who drove a tremendous line drive up the alley in left center, ran directly from home to third and was tagged out sitting on the bag with what he took to be a triple, and what would have been one too, had he only run around the bases and gotten to third in the prescribed way.

The quarrel between the Lunatic catcher and the relief pitcher began over what to throw Big John Baal, the lead-off hitter in the top of the third.

"Uh-uh," said the Lunatic pitcher, shaking off the first signal given by his catcher, while in the box, Big John took special pleasure in swishing the bat around menacingly.

"Nope," said the pitcher to the second signal.

His response to the third was an emphatic, "N-O!"

And to the fourth, he said, stamping one foot, "Definitely *not!*"

When he shook off a fifth signal as well, with a caustic, "Are you kidding? Throw him that and it's bye-bye ballgame," the catcher yanked off his mask and cried:

"And I suppose that's what I want, according to you! To lose! To go down in defeat! Oh, sure," the catcher whined, "what I'm doing, you see, is deliberately telling you to throw him the wrong pitch so I can have the wonderful pleasure of being on the losing team again. Oh brother!" His sarcasm spent, he donned his mask, knelt down behind the plate, and tried yet once more.

This time the pitcher had to cross his arms over his chest and look to the heavens for solace. "God give me strength," he sighed.

"In other words," the catcher screamed, "I'm wrong *again.* But then in your eyes I'm *always* wrong. Well, isn't that true? Admit it! Whatever signal I give is *bound* to be wrong. Why? Because *I'm* giving it! I'm daring to give *you* a signal! I'm daring to tell *you* how to pitch! I could kneel here signaling for the rest of my days, and you'd just stand there shaking them off and asking God to give you strength, *because I'm so wrong and so stupid and so hopeless and would rather lose than win!*"

When the relief pitcher, a rather self-possessed fellow from the look of it, though perhaps a touch perverse in his own way, refused to argue, the Lunatic catcher once again assumed his squat behind the plate, and proceeded to offer a seventh signal, an eighth, a ninth, a tenth, each and every one of which the pitcher rejected with a mild, if unmistakably disdainful, remark.

On the sixteenth signal, the pitcher just had to laugh. "Well, that one really takes the cake, doesn't it? That really took brains. Come over here a minute," he said to his infielders. "All right," he called back down to the catcher, "go ahead, show them your new brainstorm." To the four players up on the mound with him, the pitcher whispered, "Catch this," and pointed to the signal that the catcher, in his mortification, was continuing to flash from betweeen his legs.

"Hey," said the Lunatic third-baseman, "that ain't even a finger, is it?"

"No," said the pitcher, "as a matter of fact, it isn't."

"I mean, it ain't got no nail on it, does it?"

"Indeed it has not."

"Why, I'll be darned," said the shortstop, "it's, it's his thingamajig."

"Precisely," said the pitcher.

"But what the hell is that supposed to mean?" asked the first-baseman.

The pitcher had to smile again. "What do you think? Hey, Doc," he called to the Lunatic bench, "I'm afraid my batterymate has misunderstood what's meant by an exhibition game. He's flashing me the signal to meet him later in the shower, if you know what I mean."

The catcher was in tears now. "He made me do it," he said, covering himself with his big glove, and in his shame, dropping all the way to his knees, "everything else I showed him wasn't *good* enough for him—no, he teases me, he taunts me—"

By now the two "coaches" (as they were euphemistically called), who had removed the starting pitcher from the game, descended upon the catcher. With the aid of a fielder's glove, one of them gingerly lifted the catcher's member and placed it back inside his uniform before the opposing players could see what the signal had been, while the other relieved him of his catching equipment. "He provoked me," the catcher said, "he always provokes me—"

The Lunatic fans were on their feet again, applauding, when their catcher was led away from the plate and up to the big brick building, along the path taken earlier by the starting pitcher. "—He won't let me alone, ever. I don't want to do it. I never wanted to do it. I *wouldn't* do it. But then he starts up teasing me and taunting me—"

The Mundys were able to come up with a final run in the top of the third, once they discovered that the second-string Lunatic catcher, for all that he sounded like the real thing—"Chuck to me, babe, no hitter in here, babe—" was a little leery of fielding a bunt dropped out in front of home plate, fearful apparently of what he would find beneath the ball upon picking it up.

When Deacon started out to the mound to pitch the last of the three innings, there wasn't a Mundy who took the field with him, sleepy old Kid Heket included, who didn't realize that the Deke had a shutout working. If he could set the Lunatics down without a run, he could become the first Mundy pitcher to hurl a scoreless game all year, in or out of league competition. Hoping neither to jinx him or unnerve him, the players went through the infield warm-up deliberately keeping the chatter to a minimum, as though in fact it was just another day they were going down to defeat. Nonetheless, the

Deke was already streaming perspiration when the first Lunatic stepped into the box. He rubbed the rabbit's foot, said his prayer, took a swallow of air big enough to fill a gallon jug, and on four straight pitches, walked the center-fielder, who earlier in the game hadn't bothered to return the ball to the infield after catching a fly ball, and now, at the plate, hadn't moved the bat off his shoulder. When he was lifted for a pinch-runner (lifted by the "coaches") the appreciative fans gave him a nice round of applause. "That's lookin' 'em over!" they shouted, as he was carried from the field still in the batting posture, "that's waitin' 'em out! Good eye in there, fella!"

As soon as the pinch-runner took over at first, it became apparent that Dr. Traum had decided to do what he could to save face by spoiling the Deacon's shutout. Five runs down in the last inning and still playing to win, you don't start stealing bases—but that was precisely what this pinch-runner had in mind. And with what daring! First, with an astonishing burst of speed he rushed fifteen feet down the basepath—but then, practically on all fours, he was scrambling back. "No! No!" he cried, as he dove for the bag with his outstretched hand, "I won't! Never mind! Forget it!" But no sooner had he gotten back up on his feet and dusted himself off, than he was running again. "Why not!" he cried, "what the hell!" But having broken fifteen, *twenty*, feet down the basepath, he would come to an abrupt stop, smite himself on his forehead, and charge wildly back to first, crying, "Am I crazy? Am I out of my *mind?*"

In this way did he travel back and forth along the basepath some half-dozen times, before Deacon finally threw the first pitch to the plate. Given all there was to distract him, the pitch was of course a ball, low and in the dirt, but Hothead, having a great day, blocked it beautifully with his wooden leg.

Cholly, managing the club that morning while Mister Fairsmith rested back in Asylum—of the aged Mundy manager's spiritual crisis, more anon—Cholly motioned for Chico to get up and throw a warm-up pitch in the bullpen (one was enough—one was too many, in fact, as far as Chico was concerned) and meanwhile took a stroll out to the hill.

"Startin' to get to you, are they?" asked Cholly.

"It's that goofball on first that's doin' it."

Cholly looked over to where the runner, with time out, was standing up on first engaged in a heated controversy with himself.

"Hell," said Cholly, in his soft and reassuring way, "these boys have been tryin' to rattle us with that there bush league crap all mornin', Deke. I told you fellers comin' out in the bus, you just got to pay no attention to their monkeyshines, because that is their strategy from A to Z. To make you lose your concentration. Otherwise we would be rollin' over them worse than we is. But Deke, you tell me now, if you have had it, if you want for me to bring the Mexican in—"

"With six runs in my hip pocket? And a shutout goin'?"

"Well, I wasn't myself goin' to mention that last that you said."

"Cholly, you and me been in this here game since back in the days they was rubbin' us down with Vaseline and Tabasco sauce. Ain't that right?"

"I know, I know."

"Well," said the Deke, shooting a stream of tobacco juice over his shoulder, "ain't a bunch of screwballs gonna get my goat. Tell Chico to sit down."

Sure enough, the Deacon, old war-horse that he was, got the next two hitters out on long drives to left. "Oh my God!" cried the base runner, each time the Ghost went climbing up the padded wall to snare the ball. "Imagine if I'd broken for second! Imagine what would have happened then! Oh, that'll teach me to take those crazy leads! But then if you don't get a jump on the pitcher, where are you as a pinch-runner? That's the whole idea of a pinch-runner—to break with the pitch, to break *before* the pitch, to score that shutout-breaking run! That's what I'm in here for, that's my entire purpose. The whole thing is on *my* shoulders—so then what am I doing *not* taking a good long lead? But just then, if I'd broken for second, I'd have been doubled off first! For the last out! But then suppose he hadn't made the catch? Suppose he'd dropped it. Then where would I be? Forced out at second? *Out*—and all because I was too cowardly. But then what's the sense of taking an unnecessary risk? What virtue is there in being foolhardy? None! But then what about playing it too safe?"

On the bench, Jolly Cholly winced when he saw that the batter stepping into the box was the opposing team's shortstop. "Uh-oh," he said, "that's the feller what's cost 'em most of the runs to begin with. I'm afraid he is goin' to be lookin' to right his wrongs—and at the expense of Deacon's shutout. Dang!"

From bearing down so hard, the Deacon's uniform showed vast dark continents of perspiration both front and back. There was no doubt that his strength was all but gone, for he was relying now solely on his "junk," that floating stuff that in times gone by used to cause the hitters nearly to break their backs swinging at the air. Twice now those flutter balls of his had damn near been driven out of the institution and Jolly Cholly had all he could do not to cover his eyes with his hand when he saw the Deke release yet another fat pitch in the direction of home plate.

Apparently it was just to the Lunatic shortstop's liking too. He swung from the heels, and with a whoop of joy, was away from the plate and streaking down the basepath. "Run!" he shouted to the fellow on first.

But the pinch-runner was standing up on the bag, scanning the horizon for the ball.

"Two outs!" cried the Lunatic shortstop. "Run, you idiot!"

"But—where is it!" asked the pinch-runner.

The Mundy infielders were looking skywards themselves, wondering where in the hell that ball had been hit to.

"Where *is* it!" screamed the pinch-runner, as the shortstop came charging right up to his face. "I'm not running till I know where the *ball* is!"

"I'm coming into first, you," warned the shortstop.

"But you can't overtake another runner! That's against the law! That's *out!*"

"Then *move!*" screamed the shortstop into the fellow's ear.

"Oh, this *is* crazy. This is exactly what I *didn't* want to do!" But what choice did he have? If he stood his ground, and the shortstop kept coming, that would be the ballgame. It would be all over because he who had been put into the game to run, had simply refused to. Oh, what torment that fellow knew as he rounded the bases with the shortstop right on his tail. "I'm running full speed—and I don't even know where the ball is! I'm running like a chicken with his head cut off! I'm running like a madman, which is just what I don't want to do! Or be! I don't know where I'm going, I don't know what I'm doing, I haven't the foggiest idea of what's happening—and I'm running!"

When, finally, he crossed the plate, he was in such a state, that he fell to his hands and knees, and sobbing with relief, began to kiss the ground. "I'm home! Thank God! I'm safe! I made it! I scored! Oh thank God, thank God!"

And now the shortstop was rounding third—he took a quick glance over his shoulder to see if he could go all the way, and just kept on coming. "Now where's *he* lookin'?" asked Cholly. "What in hell does he see that I can't? Or that Mike don't either?" For out in left, Mike Rama was walking round and round, searching in the grass as though for a dime that might have dropped out of his pocket.

The shortstop was only a few feet from scoring the second run of the inning when Dr. Traum, who all this while had been walking from the Lunatic bench, interposed himself along the foul line between the runner and home plate.

"Doc," screamed the runner, "you're in the way!"

"That's enough now," said Dr. Traum, and he motioned for him to stop in his tracks.

"But I'm only inches from pay dirt! Step aside, Doc—let me score!"

"You just stay vere you are, please."

"Why?"

"You know vy. Stay right vere you are now. And giff me the ball."

"What ball?" asked the shortstop.

"You know vat ball."

"Well, I surely don't have any ball. I'm the *hitter*. I'm about *to score*."

"You are not about to score. You are about to giff me the ball. Come now. Enough foolishness. Giff over the ball."

"But, Doc, I haven't got it. I'm on the offense. It's the *defense* that has the ball—that's the whole idea of the game. No criticism intended, but if you weren't a foreigner, you'd probably understand that better."

"Haf it your vay," said Dr. Traum, and he waved to the bullpen for his two coaches.

"But, Doc," said the shortstop, backpedaling now up the third-base line, "*they're* the ones in the field. *They're* the ones with the gloves—why don't you ask them for the ball? Why me? I'm an innocent base runner, who happens to be rounding third on his way home." But here he saw the coaches coming after him and he turned and broke across the diamond for the big brick building on the hill.

It was only a matter of minutes before one of the coaches returned with the ball and carried it out to where the Mundy infield was now gathered on the mound.

The Deacon turned it over in his hand and said, "Yep, that's it, all right. Ain't it, Hot?"

The Mundy catcher nodded. "How in hell did *he* get it?"

"A hopeless kleptomaniac, that's how," answered the coach.

"He'd steal the bases if they weren't tied down. Here," he said, handing the Deacon a white hand towel bearing the Mundy laundrymark, and the pencil that Jolly Cholly wore behind his ear when he was acting as their manager. "Found this on him too. Looks like he got it when he stumbled into your bench for that pop-up in the first."

The victory celebration began the moment they boarded the asylum bus and lasted nearly all the way back to the city, with Nickname hollering out his window to every passerby, "We beat 'em! We shut 'em out!" and Big John swigging bourbon from his liniment bottle, and then passing it to his happy teammates.

"I'll tell you what did it," cried Nickname, by far the most exuberant of the victors, "it was Deacon throwin' at that first guy's head! Yessir! Now that's my kind of baseball!" said the fourteen-year-old, smacking his thigh. "First man up, give it to 'em right in the noggin'."

"Right!" said Hothead. "Show 'em you ain't takin' no more of their shit no more! Never again!"

"Well," said Deacon, "that is a matter of psychology, Hot, that was somethin' I had to think over real good beforehand. I mean, you try that on the wrong feller and next thing they is all of them layin' it down and then spikin' the dickens out of you when you cover the bag."

"That's so," said Jolly Cholly. "When me and the Deke come up, that was practically a rule in the rule book—feller throws the beanball, the word goes out, 'Drag the ball and spike the pitcher.' Tell you the truth, I was worried we was goin' to see some of that sort of stuff today. They was a desperate bunch. Could tell that right off by their tactics."

"Well," said the Deke, "that was a chance I had to take. But I'll tell you, I couldn't a done it without you fellers behind me. How about Bud out there, throwin' them two runners out at first base? The right-fielder to the first-baseman, *two times in a row*. Buddy," said the Deacon, "that was an exhibition such as I have not seen in all my years in organized ball."

Big Bud flushed, as was his way, and tried to make it sound easy. "Well, a' course, once I seen those guys wasn't runnin', I figured I didn't have no choice. I *had* to play it to first."

Here Mike Rama said, "Only that wasn't what *they* was figurin', Buddy-boy. You got a one-arm outfielder out there, you figure, what the hell, guess I can get on down the base line any old time I feel like it. Guess I can stop off and get me a beer and a sangwich on the way! But old Bud here, guess he showed 'em!"

"You know," said Cholly, philosophically, "I never seen it to fail, the hitters get cocky like them fellers were, and the next thing you know, they're makin' one dumb mistake after another."

"Yep," said Kid Heket, who was still turning the events of the morning over in his head, "no doubt about it, them fellers just was not usin' their heads."

"Well, maybe they wasn't—but *we* was! What about Hot?" said Nickname. "What about a guy with a wooden leg taggin' up from second and scorin' on a fly to center! How's that for heads-up baseball?"

"Well," said Wayne, "I am still puzzlin' that one out myself. What got into that boy in center, that he just sort of stood there after the catch, alookin' the way he did? What in hell did he want to wait fifteen minutes for anyway, before throwin' it? That's a awful long time, don't you think?"

They all looked to Cholly to answer this one. "Well, Wayne," he said, "I believe it is that dang cockiness again. Base runner on second's got a wooden leg, kee-rect? So what does Hot here do—he *goes*. And that swellhead out in center, well, he is so darned stunned by it all, that finally by the time he figures out what hit him, we has got ourselves a gift of a run. Now, if I was managin' that club, I'd bench that there prima donna and slap a fine on him to boot."

"But then how do you figure that shortstop, Cholly?" asked the Kid. "Now, if that ain't the strangest ballplayin' you ever seen, what is? Stickin' the ball in his back pocket like that. And then when he is at bat, with a man on and his team down by six, and it is their last licks 'n all, catchin' a junk pitch like that inside his shirt. Now I cannot figure that out nohow."

"Dang cockiness again!" cried Nickname, looking to Cholly. "He figures, hell, it's only them Mundys out there, I can do any dang thing I please—well, I guess we taught him a thing or two! Right, Cholly?"

"Well, nope, I don't think so, Nickname. I think what we have got there in that shortstop is one of the most tragic cases I have ever seen in my whole life long of all-field-no-hit."

"Kleptomaniac's what the coach there called him," said the Deacon.

"Same thing," said Cholly. "Why, we had a fella down in Class

D when I was just startin' out, fella name a' Mayet. Nothin' got by that boy. Why, Mayet at short wasn't much different than a big pot of glue out there. Fact that's what they called him for short: Glue. Only trouble is, he threw like a girl, and when it come to hittin', well, my pussycat probably do better, if I had one. Well, the same exact thing here, only worse."

"Okay," said Kid Heket, "I see that, sorta. Only how come he run over to field a pop-up and stoled the pencil right off your ear, Cholly? How come he took our towel away, right in the middle of the gosh darn game?"

"Heck, that ain't so hard to figure out. We been havin' such rotten luck this year, you probably forgot just who we all are, anyway. What boy *wouldn't* want a towel from a big league ball club to hang up and frame on the wall? Why, he wanted that thing so bad that when the game was over, I went up to the doc there and I said, 'Doc, no hard feelin's. You did the best you could and six to zip ain't nothin' to be ashamed of against big leaguers.' And then I *give* him the towel to pass on to that there kleptomaniac boy when he seen him again. So as he didn't feel too bad, bein' the last out. And know what else I told him? I give him some advice. I said, 'Doc, if I had a shortstop like that, I'd bat him ninth and play him at first where he don't *have* to make the throw."

"What'd he say?"

"Oh, he laughed at me. He said, 'Ha ha, Jolly Cholly, you haf a good sense of humor. Who efer heard of a first-baseman batting ninth?' So I said, 'Doc, who ever heard of a fifty-year-old preacher hurlin' a shutout with only three days' rest—but he done it, maybe with the help of interference on the last play, but still he done it.' "

"Them's the breaks of the game anyway!" cried Nickname. "About time the breaks started goin' our way. Did you tell him that, Cholly?"

"I told him that, Nickname. I told him more. I said, 'Doc, there is two kinds of baseball played in this country, and maybe somebody ought to tell you, bein' a foreigner and all—there is by the book, the way you do it, the way the Tycoons do it—and I grant, those fellers win their share of pennants doin' it that way. But then there is by hook and crook, by raw guts and all the heart you got, and that is just the way the Mundys done here today.' "

Here the team began whooping and shouting and singing with joy, though Jolly Cholly had momentarily to turn away, to struggle against the tears that were forming in his eyes. In a husky voice he went on—"And then I told him the name for that. I told him the name for wanderin' your ass off all season long, and takin' all the jokes and all the misery they can heap on your head day after day, and then comin' on out for a exhibition game like this one, where another team would just go through the motions and not give two hoots in hell how they played—and instead, instead givin' it everything you got. I told the doc the name for that, fellers. It's called courage."

Only Roland Agni, who had gone down twice, looking, against Lunatic pitching, appeared to be unmoved by Cholly's tribute to the team. Nickname, in fact, touched Jolly Cholly's arm at the conclusion of his speech, and whispered, "Somebody better say somethin' to Rollie. He ain't takin' strikin' out too good, it don't look good."

So Cholly the peacemaker made his way past the boisterous players and down the aisle to where Roland still sat huddled in a rear corner of the bus by himself.

"What's eatin' ya, boy?"

"Nothin'," mumbled Roland.

"Why don'tcha come up front an'—"

"Leave me alone, Tuminikar!"

"Aw, Rollie, come on now," said the sympathetic coach, "even the best of them get caught lookin' once in a while."

"Caught *lookin'?*" cried Agni.

"Hey, Rollie," Hothead shouted, "it's okay, slugger—we won anyway!" And grinning, he waved Big John's liniment bottle in the air to prove it.

"Sure, Rollie," Nickname yelled. "With the Deke on the mound, we didn't need but one run anyway! So what's the difference? Everybody's gotta whiff sometimes! It's the law a' averages!"

But Agni was now standing in the aisle, screaming, "You think I got caught *lookin'?*"

Wayne Heket, whose day had been a puzzle from beginning to end, who just could not really take any more confusion on top of going sleepless all these hours, asked, "Well, wasn't ya?"

"You bunch of morons! You bunch of idiots! Why, you are bigger lunatics even than they are! Those fellers are at least locked up!"

Jolly Cholly, signaling his meaning to the other players with a wink, said, "Seems Roland got somethin' in his eye, boys—seems he couldn't see too good today."

"You're the ones that can't see!" Agni screamed. *"They were madmen! They were low as low can be!"*

"Oh, I don't know, Rollie," said Mike Rama, who'd had his share of scurrying around to do that morning, "they wasn't *that* bad."

"They was *worse!* And you all acted like you was takin' on the Cardinals in the seventh game of the Series!"

"How else you supposed to play, youngster?" asked the Deacon, who was beginning to get a little hot under the collar.

"And you! You're the worst of all! Hangin' in there, like a regular hero! Havin' conferences on the mound about how to pitch to a bunch of hopeless maniacs!"

"Look, son," said Jolly Cholly, "just on account you got caught lookin'—"

"But who got caught lookin'? How could you get caught lookin' against pitchers *that had absolutely nothin' on the ball!"*

"You mean," said Jolly Cholly, incredulous, "you took a *dive?* You mean you throwed it, Roland? *Why?"*

"Why? Oh, please, let me off! Let me off this bus!" he screamed, charging down the aisle toward the door. "I can't take bein' one of you no more!"

As they were all, with the exception of the Deacon, somewhat pie-eyed, it required virtually the entire Mundy team to subdue the boy wonder. Fortunately the driver of the bus, who was an employee of the asylum, carried a straitjacket and a gag under the seat with him at all times, and knew how to use it. "It's from bein' around them nuts all mornin'," he told the Mundys. "Sometimes I ain't always myself either, when I get home at night."

"Oh," said the Mundys, shaking their heads at one another, and though at first it was a relief having a professional explanation for Roland's bizarre behavior, they found that with Roland riding along in the rear seat all bound and gagged, they really could not seem to revive the jubilant mood that had followed upon their first shutout win of the year. In fact, by the time they reached Keeper Park for their regularly scheduled afternoon game, one or two of them were even starting to feel more disheartened about that victory than they had about any of those beatings they had been taking all season long.

SPOT REPORTING

IF YOU THINK of Casey Stengal as a manager but never as a player—if you think of Damon Runyon as an author but never as a reporter—then never must you stand so spectacularly corrected as right now. Read!

1923: New York Giants 5, New York Yankees 4

DAMON RUNYON

THIS IS the way old Casey Stengel ran yesterday afternoon, running his home run home.

This is the way old Casey Stengel ran running his home run to a Giant victory by a score of 5 to 4 in the first game of the World Series of 1923.

This is the way old Casey Stengel ran, running his home run home, when two were out in the ninth inning and the score was tied and the ball was still bounding inside the Yankee yard.

This is the way—

His mouth was open.

His warped old legs bending beneath him at every stride.

His arms flying back and forth like those of a man swimming with a crawl stroke.

His flanks heaving, his breath whistling, his head far back.

Yankee infielders, passed by old Casey Stengel as he was running his home run home, say Casey was muttering to himself, adjuring himself to greater speed as a jockey muttters to his horse in a race, that he was saying: "Go on, Casey! Go on!"

People generally laugh when they see old Casey Stengel run, but they were not laughing while he was running his home run home yesterday afternoon. People—60,000 of 'em, men and women—were standing in the Yankee stands and bleachers up there in the Bronx roaring sympathetically, whether they were for or against the Giants.

"Come on, Casey!"

The warped old legs, twisted and bent by many a year of baseball campaigning, just barely held out under Casey Stengel until he reached the plate, running his home run home.

Then they collapsed.

They gave out just as old Casey slid over the plate in his awkward fashion as Wally Schang made futile efforts to capture the ball which eluded him and rolled toward the dugout. Billy Evans, the American League umpire, poised over him in a set pose, arms spread to indicate that old Casey was safe.

Half a dozen Giants rushed forward to help Casey to his feet, to hammer him on the back, to bawl congratulations in his ears as he limped unsteadily, still panting furiously, to the bench where John J. McGraw, chief of the Giants, relaxed his stern features in a smile for the man who had won the game.

Casey Stengel's warped old legs, one of them broken not so long ago, wouldn't carry him out for the last half of the inning, when the Yankees made a dying effort to undo the damage done by Casey. His place in center field was taken by young Bill Cunningham, whose legs are still unwarped, and Casey sat on the bench with John J. McGraw.

No one expected much of Casey Stengel when he appeared at the plate in the Giants' side of the ninth inning, the score a tie at 4 to 4.

Ross Youngs and Irish Meusel, stout, dependable hitters, had been quickly disposed of by the superb pitching of Bullet Joe Bush.

No one expected Stengel to accomplish anything where they had failed. Bush, pitching as only Bush can pitch in an emergency, soon had two strikes and three balls on Casey.

He was at the plate so long that many of the fans were fidgeting nervously, wondering why he didn't hurry up and get put out, so the game could go on. Casey Stengel is not an imposing figure at bat, not an imposing figure under any circumstances. Those warped old legs have something to do with it. A man with warped legs cannot look very imposing.

People like to laugh at Casey—Casey likes to make people laugh.

A wayfarer of the big leagues—Brooklyn, Pittsburgh, Philadelphia, and finally New York—he has always been regarded by the fans as a great comedian, a funny fellow, a sort of clown.

The baseball land teems with tales of the strange didoes cut by Casey Stengel, whose parents started him out as Charles, with his sayings.

Who knows but that "Bullet Joe" may have been thinking of

Casey Stengel more as a comedian than as a dangerous hitter when he delivered that final pitch yesterday afternoon? Pitchers sometimes let their wits go wool-gathering.

"Bap"—Stengel's bat connected with the last pitch, connected surely, solidly. The ball sailed out over the field, moving high, moving far.

Long Bob Meusel and Whitey Witt, the Yankee outfielders, raced toward each other as they marked the probable point where the ball would alight, and in the meantime Casey Stengel was well advanced on his journey, running his home run home.

As the ball landed between Meusel and Witt it bounded as if possessed toward the left center-field fence. Everybody could see it would be a home run inside the yard, if Casey Stengel's warped old legs could carry him around the bases.

Witt got the ball about the time Stengel hit third, and about that time Stengel was laboring, "all out." Witt threw the ball in to Bob Meusel who had dropped back and let Witt go on. Meusel wheeled and fired for the plate, putting all his strength behind the throw. Few men have ever lived who can throw a baseball as well as Bob Meusel.

Stengel was almost home when Meusel's throw was launched, and sensing the throw Casey called on all that was left in those warped old legs, called no doubt on all the baseball gods to help him—and they helped.

It is something to win a World Series with a home run, and that home run inside the yard.

John J. McGraw perhaps feels that his judgment in taking Stengel on at a time when Casey was a general big-league outcast has been vindicated.

• • •

If you are curious to know the origin of the nickname "Casey," it might be explained that Stengel's home town is Kansas City.

The nickname comes from "K.C." One of these many little coincidences that are always popping out in baseball is the fact that Stengel and Bullet Joe Bush are great pals. They made the baseball tour to Japan last winter as roommates.

Stengel is around thirty-three, if you are seeking more information about the first hero of the World Series of 1923. They call that old in baseball. He has been with the Giants since 1921, from the Philadelphia club. He is all right, Casey Stengel is, and you can prove it by John J. McGraw.

The expected struggle of Mind vs. Matter, or Intelligence against Brute Force, with John J. McGraw representing the one, and Babe Ruth the other, did not materialize.

Both sides began batting the ball so freely that thinking was not necessary.

Ruth got a three-bagger and was cheated out of another hit through an astonishing play by Long George Kelly, perhaps one of the most sensational plays ever seen in a World Series. Kelly got a hit from Ruth's bat with one hand at a seemingly impossible angle and threw a man out at the plate.

Quite as sensational was a play by Frankie Frisch, who backed out into short right field, caught a short fly from Bob Meusel's bat, turned and threw Ruth out at the plate. This was immediately after Ruth's three-bagger. Perhaps if Casey Stengel had not run his home run, Frisch's play would be picked as the feature of the whole afternoon.

The Yanks were three runs ahead of the Giants when McGraw's men caught and passed them, hammering Waite Hoyt for all their runs except Stengel's home run. It was the first real bad inning the one-time Brooklyn schoolboy ever had in a World Series, so say the experts.

Bush took Hoyt's place and pitched marvelous ball. Poor Bush, as usual, suffered from "the breaks," from the bad luck of the game. He has been in a number of World Series, and was always what baseball calls a "tough luck pitcher" in them. He won one game for the Athletics in his first year in the big leagues. Since then he has been a consistent loser.

The Yanks drove Jim Watson, of Louisiana, from the game early. Then Wilfrid Ryan did the pitching for McGraw's men—and did it well. The Yanks outhit the Giants, however, twelve to eight.

It seemed to this writer that the Yanks were very stupid in some of their base running. At least one example probably cost them a run.

However, it was a great game for the spectators. A thrill a minute, finally topped off by the real big thrill of Casey Stengel, running his home run home.

• • •

The umpires, four solemn-looking gentlemen in dark, funeral blue uniforms with little blue caps, held a meeting at the home plate just before game time. They were Billy Evans of the American League, who can wear an umpire's uniform in such fashion that he looks trim and neat, Dick Nallin, of the same league, and Bill Hart, and Hank O'Day, a dour-looking man of the National League.

After the umpires conferred, the Yanks posed in a group at the plate, and Benny Bengough, the Yankee catcher, a young man from Buffalo, was presented with a traveling bag, presumably by his admirers.

Meanwhile, in front of the stand, Waite Hoyt and John Watson were warming up with deliberate motions, to the great surprise of some of the experts who had expected Arthur Nehf and Herb Pennock, left-handers, to start the series.

The breeze died away and the flags were hanging limply on their staffs when Miller Huggins, the little short-legged manager of the Yankees, and Davy Bancroft, captain of the Giants, held their last conference with the umpires and presented their line-ups.

Babe Ruth got the honor of making the first put-out of the game. He easily caught a fly from Beauty Bancroft. Hoyt's first pitch to Bancroft was right over the plate. Bancroft let it go by and Evans called it a strike. The next pitch was a ball, then Bancroft hit the fly to Ruth.

The bandy-legged Groh, waving his bottle-shaped bat, was at the plate but a short time. He hit the first ball thrown by Hoyt for a sharp single across second. The crowd babbled as Groth rushed to first.

Frankie Frisch, slim, graceful—called the "Fordham Flash"—was next to face Hoyt. The first pitch was called a ball, then Hoyt put over a strike. Frisch hit a bounder to Scott, who threw the ball to Ward at second, forcing out Groh.

With Ross Young, the Texan, at bat, Frisch, fastest of the National League base runners, tried to steal second. Schang whipped the ball to Aaron Ward at second, and Ward slapped the ball on Frisch's head as the "Fordham Flash" went sliding in, head foremost, as he always slides, and as few other players slide. That ended the inning.

McGraw was starting his old line of attack early. McGraw is a great believer in speed. He always sends his fast men out to run on the opposing pitcher when they have the opportunity. McGraw argues that a man may as well be thrown out stealing as to have a put-out in some other fashion.

The Yankees quickly set the stage for Babe Ruth in their side of the first inning. That was what perhaps two-thirds of the crowd was waiting for—the appearance of Ruth.

Babe came with Joe Dugan on first base, after Whitey Witt had hit a liner to Bancroft. Whitey was first of the Yankees at bat. Dugan got a base on balls from John Watson. Then "Along came Ruth."

The crowd buzzed as Ruth stood his stalwart frame alongside the plate, his legs slightly spraddled, his long bat waving menacingly at Watson. The first pitch was inside, but over the plate, and Evans motioned a strike. Babe set his feet more firmly. He swung at the next pitch and missed the ball by several inches. The crowd, always buzzing at Ruth's slightest move at bat, now murmured loudly.

The next pitch was a ball far outside the plate. On the following pitch Ruth swung. He drove the ball solidly toward third, directly at Heine Groh. The ball took one fierce bound before reaching Heine. It was going with such force that it bounced off Heine's glove. Then Groh recovered the ball and threw it to Frisch at second for a force play on Dugan.

Now came Long Bob Meusel, brother of the Giants' "Irish," batting one notch ahead of his usual place in the Yankee line-up.

The tall Californian hit the ball a solid smack. As it sailed to center Casey Stengel raced for the spot in which he saw it would land. He got one hand on the ball as it struck the ground, then it twisted away from him elusively.

Meantime, Ruth was thundering around the bases. Stengel threw the ball in the general direction of third, but Ruth was home by that time. Meusel was at second, and the crowd was roaring.

It went as a two-base hit for Meusel. Pipp, the next man up, a tall, raw-boned Michigander, once called "the Pickler," because of his slugging ability, raised a fly to Irish Meusel, leaving brother Bob on second.

Events now began moving with great rapidity. One thrill after another swept the slopes of Islanders.

The Giants were retired without incident in their side of the second. Ward, first of the Yankees up in the last half of the inning, singled to left. Schang followed with a single. Scott bunted to Kelly who tagged him out, but necessarily permitted Ward and Schang to advance.

Hoyt struck out, but Witt banged a single past Frisch and Ward and Schang scored. The Yankees were three runs ahead, as Dugan ended the inning by grounding out to Watson.

It seemed a terrific load to the supporters of the Giants. The fans asked each other why McGraw had not taken Watson out when it was evident that the North Carolina farmer "had nothing."

They were still murmuring their discontent when George Kelly, towering first baseman of the Giants, opened the Giants' third with a single. The murmuring stopped momentarily as Lank Hank Gowdy drew a base on balls. Gowdy, lean backstop of the McGraw club, and once the greatest of heroes of a World Series, was taken out of the game immediately and Maguire, a fleet young Giant recruit, put on first base to run for him. The "Master Mind" on the Giant bench seemed to be working.

Now Watson—John Watson the Third, of North Carolina—also was out of the game. Big Jack Bentley, the left-handed pitcher from Baltimore, who looks something like Babe Ruth, was advancing to the plate to bat in place of Watson. Bentley was accounted a tremendous hitter when he was the star of Jack Dunn's Baltimore Orioles.

Hoyt worked on him with great care, knowing Bentley's reputation, having seen him hit in exhibition games betweeen the Yankees and the Orioles. He soon had two strikes on Bentley, one of them a vicious foul bounder across first which barely missed being safe.

Bentley dropped a looping fly in center field, just outside the clutches of Whitey Witt. It was not far enough out for anyone to score, but it filled the bases.

McGraw, from the Giant bench, called Bentley in and Danny Gearin, a midget recruit pitcher, when to first to run in place of Bentley.

The bases full and no outs. Small wonder the Giant sympathizers were roaring with excitement. Beauty Bancroft drove a slow roller at Everett Scott, and the Yankee shortstop threw the ball to Ward at second, forcing out Gearin. Meantime, Kelly scored and Maguire reached third.

Now the bandy-legged Groh and his bottle-shaped bat were before Hoyt, and the Yankee rooters were squawking nervously "Take him out."

Bancroft suddenly quit first on a pitch to Groh, stealing second well ahead of Schang's throw—so far ahead, in fact, some of the Giant fans laughed derisively.

Now Groh clipped the ball across first, the drive hitting in fair territory, bouncing away past Pipp to right field. Ruth was lumbering in to meet the ball when it struck the screen in right field, and bounded away at a wicked angle. Ruth got his hands on the ball, but the carom deceived him. He could not hold it, and away it went across the grass.

While Ruth was chasing it, two Giants were scoring, the crowd was in a spasm of excitement, and Huggins was raging on the Yankee bench and motioning at Hoyt. Groh reached third before Ruth got the ball. Then Hoyt dejectedly left the field, and out of the flurry of players in front of the Yankee bench came Joe Bush another one-time hero of other World Series.

Bush pitched to Frisch, who singled past Pipp, scoring Groh. Young forced Frisch at second on an infield bounder, and Young himself was an easy out when he tried to steal second.

The Giant rooters fell back limply in their seats, completely exhausted from their vocal efforts during the inning.

Four runs—and the Giants now one run ahead. The Giant rooters felt they had earned their right to demonstration.

Wilfred Ryan—nicknamed "Rosey," for no apparent reason—went in to pitch for the Giants. Nearly all ballplayers have nicknames. Some of them mean much. Some of them mean little, if anything. "Rosey" is one of those names.

Ryan is a Holy Cross man, and a good right-handed pitcher when he is "right," that is to say, when the ball is obeying his muscles as it should.

In the Yankee half of the fifth inning, Ruth, in his fourth trip to the plate, took a shorter grip on his bat than is his habit—"choked up," the ballplayers call it—and swatting a short, sharp smash at the first ball pitched by Ryan drove the ball to deep left. It struck the low concrete in front of the left field pavillion, and bounded away from Irish Meusel.

Ruth was rambling into third when Meusel got the ball and let fly to Groh. The big slugger of the Yankees fairly threw himself at the bag, his long feet reaching for the base as Groh got the ball and plunged at him. It was a close play. Groh thought he had the Babe. He raged for a fleeting instant when Bill Hart waved the runner safe. The scorers called it a three-base hit.

Dugan had gone out just before Ruth went to bat, and now Long Bob Meusel lifted a little fly that rose slowly over the infield and floated on back over short right field, well back of the base line between first and second.

It was a dangerous looking little fly, one of the kind called "Texas Leaguers." Young came racing up from right field and Frisch went running backward, his eye on the ball, his hands waving Young away.

Frisch was twisting and turning with the descending ball; his back was turned from the infield when he caught it. Ruth instantly left third and tore for home. Frisch turned and threw blindly in the direction of the plate, and it happened to be an accurate throw.

The ball bounded in straight and true to huge Frank Snyder, who had taken Gowdy's place behind the plate. As Snyder clasped the ball Ruth came lunging in. The big men collided with terrific force, but Snyder clung to the ball, tagged Ruth with it, and Ruth was out. It was a great play—it was a thrilling play.

Casey Stengel got the first hit off Bush since he relieved Hoyt in the seventh. It was a single. Kelly hit into a double play immediately afterwards.

Bush was given a round of applause when he went to the plate in the Yankees' seventh and Joe, as if by way of acknowledgment, singled to center, his second hit. Witt lifted an easy fly to Meusel in short left field. The Yankee rooters, briefly stirred by hope, sighed dismally and sank back in their seats only to come up shrilling an instant later when Jumping Joe Dugan, third baseman of the Yanks, smashed the ball to the right-field bleacher barrier.

It was a clean, hard drive, well out of reach of Young. Bush raced around the bases, and on across the plate, with Dugan not far behind him. Kelly's throw was right to the mark, and Snyder tagged Dugan a yard from the plate. Bob Meusel ended the inning with a fly to Young, after Ruth had almost been caught napping off first.

"The Giants are getting all the breaks," moaned Yankee sympathizers.

However, it seemed to the ordinary observer that the Yankees made some of the breaks against themselves.

WELL, the Red Sox were in the World Series in 1946, and it went seven games, and they lost it. They were in a one-game pennant playoff with Cleveland in 1948, and they lost it. They closed out their 1949 season with a two-game set against the Yankees, and winning either of those games would have given them the pennant. They lost both. They were in the World Series in 1967, and it went seven games, and they lost it. They were in the World Series in 1975, and it went seven games, and they lost it. They were in a one-game playoff with the Yankees in 1978, and they lost it. They were in the World Series in 1986, and it went seven games, and they lost it. They should have won it in six. They were one strike away, with bases empty and a two-run lead, from winning the Series in the last half of the tenth inning of that sixth game, and they still lost it (Glenn Schwarz, sports editor of the San Francisco *Examiner*, tells how, in the following story).

"One begins to see at last," Roger Angell wrote in *The New Yorker* in the wake of that '86 catastrophe, "that the true function of the Red Sox may be not to win but to provide New England authors with a theme, now that guilt and whaling have gone out of style."

1986: New York Mets 6, Boston Red Sox 5

GLENN SCHWARZ

THE BOSTON Red Sox, one strike away from their first World Series championship in 68 years, lost a game for the ages Saturday night.

The desperate New York Mets pulled off a two-out, three-run rally in the 10th inning to win the sixth game, 6–5, and send the Series to a decisive seventh game Sunday, weather permitting.

"This is not a ballclub that gives up easily," Mets manager Davey Johnson said. "When you're two runs down with two out, and it looks like your season is about to end, that's a huge deficit."

But make no mistake—the Red Sox lost this game more than the Mets won it.

After the Sox scored twice in their half of the 10th, they could've withstood two-out singles by Gary Carter, pinch hitter Kevin Mitchell and Ray Knight off loser Calvin Schiraldi. What the Sox couldn't withstand was Bob Stanley's subsequent 2–2 wild pitch that scored Mitchell with the tying run nor an error by first baseman Bill Buckner that enabled Knight to carry home the winning run from second.

Mookie Wilson's grounder behind the bag skipped under Buckner's glove and through his legs, turning Shea Stadium into an asylum.

"My only thought was to beat the pitcher to first base," Wilson said. "I thought I had a chance to beat it, and I think Buckner saw that too and tried to rush the play a little bit. It wasn't a very well hit ball, but it had the angle and the spin.

"This whole season has been unbelievable. This should really help us tomorrow," Wilson said. "You don't give up with this club. We could have folded, but everybody battled back. It was up to me to do my part, and I did it."

Now the Red Sox know how the California Angels felt.

"I guess I can associate this to what went on in California when they were down to one out and didn't get it," Boston manager John McNamara said. "Yes, it's disappointing . . . I know nothing about history. Don't tell me anything about choking or any of that crap."

In the American League Championship Series, the Angels were one strike away from winning the pennant when Dave Henderson hit a two-run homer off Donnie Moore. The Red Sox went on to win that game and the next two to qualify for the World Series.

Henderson, the unlikeliest of October heroes, was at it again in Game 6. He led off the 10th inning with a home run off Rick Aguilera. The Sox added a run on Wade Boggs' double and Marty Barrett's single, but as it turned out, they needed more.

Schiraldi, the ex-Met, retired Wally Backman and Keith Hernandez before the Mets' three staying-alive singles, and McNamara summoned Stanley. Schiraldi earlier failed to hold a one-run lead for Roger Clemens in the eighth.

Schiraldi's poor throw to second on a bunt by Lenny Dykstra allowed Lee Mazzilli to reach second after his leadoff single. Following Backman's sacrifice and an intentional walk to Hernandez, Carter tied the game with a sacrifice fly.

What had been arguably the least entertaining Series in years finally served up a game with drama, however flawed by both defenses.

The Red Sox scored two quick runs off Mets starter Bobby Ojeda, Dwight Evans doubling home one in the first and the relentless Barrett singling one in the next inning. But Mets fans were at their loudest from the moment parachutist Michael Sergio landed alongside the mound with the Red Sox batting in the first inning.

The crowd retaliated for the Red Sox fans' taunting of Mets right fielder Darryl Strawberry Thursday night, when the Boston audience sing-songed chants of "Dar-ryl, Dar-ryl, Dar-ryl." The Shea gathering started on Evans with "Doo-ey, Doo-ey, Doo-ey." But the repetitive jeering was directed at Clemens—"Ro-ger, Ro-ger, Ro-ger."

It sounded like an English soccer crowd, at least until the Sox took a 3–2 lead in the seventh against Roger McDowell. Barrett's walk, a throwing error by third baseman Knight and rookie shortstop Kevin Elster's botching of a double play—he missed the bag on his pivot—put the Sox ahead briefly.

The Mets didn't show Clemens the utmost respect before the game.

Strawberry, for one, was more impressed by the pitcher who beat the Mets twice.

"I don't think Clemens is a Bruce Hurst," Strawberry said. "Bruce Hurst is a real pitcher. To me, he's their No. 1 . . . There's a lot of guys on this team who hit fastballs."

It took the Mets a spell to hit anything Clemens threw. He struck out six the first three innings and allowed just one base runner before the fifth.

Strawberry was that one, walking with one out in the second and stealing a base to no avail. But Clemens, blowing on his right hand to warm it in the chill, was throwing a lot of pitches. And the expended energy seemed to weaken him in the fifth.

First, critic Strawberry led off with another walk and steal. Then Knight bounced Clemens' first pitch after the stolen base into center for a single, the Mets' first hit driving in their first run.

Wilson followed with a single to right that surprised right fielder Evans. As he reached down, the ball rabbit-hopped into his chest. The error enabled Knight to take third.

By now, the fan noise was as loud as inside an arena. Some were chanting, some sing-songing, some clapping—all were pleading for more.

They got it, though the way the run scored quieted them. Danny Heep, batting for Rafael Santana, grounded into a double play that moved Knight home.

The "Ro-ger, Ro-ger" taunting of Clemens resumed with one out in the seventh. Backman singled despite a diving stop by shortstop Spike Owen and his strong throw from one knee. Then Hernandez, to that point 4-for-20 in the Series, lined a hit-and-run single that shot Backman to third.

Clemens, however, took a deep breath and went to work on cleanup hitter Carter. Three pitches later, The Kid had struck out with the bat on his shoulder. Clemens subsequently silenced Strawberry on a ground ball.

After the Red Sox regained the lead for him, Clemens pitched a clean seventh and was excused for the night.

The night the Red Sox broke New England's heart—again.

POETRY

Baseball Counts

MIKE SHANNON

Because it is so much like life,
Because, in fact, it is life
Baseball counts.
Take the matter of justice for example.
What is just in the hitter
Connecting almost perfectly
Smashing the ball so hard down the line
That it curves wickedly
But right into the path of the waiting
Third baseman who makes the catch in
Self-defense?
Hitters say, "It all evens out."
But does it ever?
Do they really believe the old cliche?
As with the rest of life
Believing that it does makes it
Possible to survive the fact that
It doesn't.

From *Voices of a Summer Day*

IRWIN SHAW

THE RED flag was up when he drove up to the house. He went in. The house was silent. "Peggy," he called. "Peggy!" There was no answer. His wife was not there nor either of his children.

He went out and looked at the ocean. The waves were ten feet high and there was about eight hundred yards of foam ripping between the tide line, marked by seaweed, and the whitecaps of the open Atlantic. The beach was deserted except for a tall girl in a black bathing suit, who was walking along the water's edge with two Siamese cats pacing beside her. The girl had long blond hair that hung down her back and blew in the wind. Her legs and arms were pollen-colored against the sea, and the cats made a small pale jungle at her ankles. The girl was not too far away for him to tell whether she was pretty or not and she didn't look in his direction, but he wished he knew her. He wished he knew her well enough to call out and see her smile and wait for him to join her so that they could walk along the beach together, attended by toy tigers, the noise of the surf beating at them as she told him why a girl like that walked alone on an empty beach on a bright summer afternoon.

He watched her grow smaller and smaller in the distance, the cats, the color of the desert, almost disappearing against the sand. She was outlined for a last moment against the dazzle of the waves and then the beach was empty again.

It was no afternoon for swimming, and the girl was gone, and he didn't feel like hanging around the house alone so he went in and changed his clothes and got into the car and drove into town. On the high school field, there was a pickup game of baseball in progress, boys and young men and several elderly athletes who by Sunday morning would regret having slid into second base on Saturday afternoon.

He saw his son playing center field. He stopped the car and got out and lay back in the sun on the hot planks of the benches along the third-base line, a tall, easy-moving man with a powerful, graying head. He was dressed in slacks and a short-sleeved blue cotton shirt, the costume of a man consciously on holiday. On the long irregular face there were not the unexpected signs of drink and overwork. He was no longer young, and, although at a distance his slimness and way of moving gave a deceptive appearance of youth, close-up age was there, experience was there, above all around the eyes, which were deep black, almost without reflections, hooded by heavy lids and a dark line of thick lashes that suggested secret Mediterranean mourning against the olive tint of the skin stretched tight over jutting cheek bones. He greeted several of the players and spectators, and the impression of melancholy was erased momentarily by the good humor and open friendliness of his voice. The combination of voice and features was that of a man who might be resigned and often cynical, but rarely suspicious. He was a man who permitted himself to be cheated in small matters. Taxi drivers, employees, children, and women took advantage of him. He knew this, each time it happened, and promptly forgot it.

On the field, the batter was crouching and trying to work the pitcher for a walk. The batter was fifteen years old and small for his age. The pitcher was six feet three inches tall and had played for Columbia in 1947.

The third baseman, a boy of eighteen named Andy Roberts, called out, "Do you want to take my place, Mr. Federov? I promised I'd be home by four."

"Thanks, no, Andy," Federov said. "I batted .072 last season and I've hung up my spikes."

The boy laughed. "Maybe you'd have a better season this year if you tried."

"I doubt it," Federov said. "It's very rare that your average goes up after fifty."

The batter got his walk, and while he was throwing his bat away and trotting down to first base Federov waved to his son out in center field. His son waved back. "Andy," Federov said, "how's Mike doing?"

"Good field, ho hit," Andy said.

"Runs in the family," said Federov. "My father never hit a curve ball in his life either."

The next batter sent a line drive out toward right center, and Michael made a nice running catch over his shoulder and pivoted and threw hard and accurately to first base, making the runner scramble back hurriedly to get there before the throw. Michael was left-handed and moved with that peculiar grace that left-handers always seemed to Federov to have in all sports. There had never been a left-hander before in Federov's family, nor in his wife's family that he knew of, and Federov sometimes wondered at this genetic variance and took it as a mark of distinction, a puzzling designation, though whether for good or ill he could not say. Michael's sister, eleven years old and too smart for her age, as Federov sometimes told her, teased Michael about it. "Sinister, sinister," she chanted when she disagreed with her brother's opinions. "Old Pope Sinister the First."

Old Pope Sinister the First popped up to shortstop his next time at bat and then came over to sit beside his father. "Hi, Dad." He touched his father lightly but affectionately on the shoulder. "How're things in the dirty city?"

"Dirty," Federov said. He and his brother ran a building and contracting business together, and while there was a lot of work unfinished on both their desks, the real reason the brothers had stayed in New York on a hot Saturday morning was to try to arrange a settlement with Louis's third wife, whom he wanted to divorce to marry a fourth wife, and who was all for a vengeful and scandalous action in court. Louis was the architect of the firm, and this connection with the arts, plus his quiet good looks, made him a prey for women and a permanent subsidy for the legal profession.

"Where's your mother?" Federov asked his son. "The house was empty when I got in."

"Bridge, hairdresser's, I don't know," Michael said carelessly. "You know—dames. She'll turn up for dinner."

"I'm quite sure she will," Federov said.

Michael's side was retired, and he picked up his glove and started toward his position in the field. "Mike," Federov said, "you swung at a high ball, you know."

"I know," Michael said. "I'm a confirmed sinner."

He was thirteen years old but, like his sister, was a ransacker of libraries and often sounded it.

Five minutes later there was a dispute about a close call at first base, and two or three boys shouted, good-naturedly, "Oh, you bum!" and "Kill the umpire!"

"Stop that!" Federov said sharply. Then he was as surprised as the boys themselves by the harshness of his tone. They kept quiet after that, although they eyed him curiously. Ostentatiously, Federov looked away from them. He had heard the cry thousands of times before, just as the boys had, and he didn't want to explain what was behind his sudden explosion of temper. Ever since the President had been shot, Federov, sometimes consciously, sometimes unconsciously, had refrained from using words like "kill" or "murder" or "shoot" or "gun," and had skipped them, when he could, in the things he read, and moved away from conversations in which the words were likely to come up. He had heard about the mocking black-bordered advertisement in the Dallas newspaper that had greeted the President on his arrival in the city, and he had read about the minister who said that schoolchildren in the city had cheered upon being told of the President's death, and he had heard from a lineman friend of his on the New York Giants football team that, after the game they had played in Dallas ten days after the President was killed, an open car full of high school boys and girls had followed the Giants' bus through downtown Dallas, chanting, "Kennedy gawn, Johnson next. Kennedy gawn, Johnson next."

"Kids," the lineman had said wonderingly, "just kids, like anybody else's kids. You couldn't believe it. And nobody tried to stop them."

Kids, just kids. Like the boys on the field in front of him. Like his own son. In the same blue jeans, going to the same kind of schools, listening to the same awful music on radio and television, playing the same traditional games, loved by their parents as he loved his son and daughter. Kids shouting a tribal chant of hatred for a dead man who had been better than any of them could ever hope to be.

The hell with it, he thought. You can't keep thinking about it forever.

With an effort of will he made himself fall back into lazy afternoon thoughtlessness. Soon, lulled by the slow familiar rhythm of the game, he was watching the field through half-dozing, sun-warmed eyes, lying back and not keeping track of what was happening as boys ran from base to base, stopped grounders, changed sides. He saw his son make two good plays and one mediocre one without pride or anxiety. Michael was tall for his age, and broad, and Federov took what he realized was a normal fatherly pleasure in watching his son's movements as, loose-limbed and browned by the sun, he performed in the wide green spaces of the outfield.

Dozing, almost alone on the rows of benches, one game slid into other games, other generations were at play many years before . . . in Harrison, New Jersey, where he had grown up; on college campuses, where he had never been quite good enough to make the varsity, despite his fleetness of foot and surehandedness in the field. The sounds were the same through the years—the American sounds of summer, the tap of bat against ball, the cries of the infielders, the wooden plump of the ball into catchers' mitts, the umpires calling "Strike three and you're out." The generations circled the bases, the dust rose for forty years as runners slid from third, dead boys hit doubles, famous men made errors at shortstop, forgotten friends tapped the clay from their spikes with their bats as they stepped into the batter's box, coaches' voices warned, across the decades, "Tag up, tag up!" on fly balls. The distant, mortal innings of boyhood and youth . . .

PROFILE

The Man Who Hated Southpaws

COLLIE SMALL

BACK IN BASEBALL'S Pleistocene period, a triangular era bounded on the hypotenuse by John McGraw and on the other sides by Speaker and Cobb, a strange and wondrous outfielder roamed the minor leagues. A giant Texan of prodigious strength and temper, his name was John King, and he raged through a dozen leagues in his time, leaving in his wake a monumental legend of violence and destruction.

Yet, for all his greatness, he never got a tryout in the majors, and you can go a long way without ever finding his name in the newspapers of the period. Old ballplayers and umpires in their dotage tell of John King with an easy and disarming familiarity. But if they would only confess it, many of them are often assailed privately with serious doubts that he ever existed.

More is the pity, for John King, at this very moment, lives in semi-retirement with his wife and son on a ranch near Lubbock, Texas. What is more, he is only about a furlong away from his first $1,000,000, according to the informal estimates of his neighbors, who may or may not be close. In any event, they found oil on his property a few years ago, and he certainly is not wanting.

A heavy-shouldered man with hands like huge bunches of bananas, King moved with an uncommon grace, and no minor leaguer of the day could match his powerful throwing arm. His speed was the talk of baseball—as well as anyone remembers now, he led every league he ever played in in stolen bases. The fame of John King was truly a wonderful thing.

It is therefore painful to relate that John King had a melancholy weakness. He could not, for all his Herculean efforts, hit left-handed pitching. Ultimately, this defection reduced him to a crying impotency, and in time he became so enraged at the mere thought of a left-hander that no portsider could be said to be safe even in the general vicinity. This was the tragedy of John King.

Thus it was, on a sunny afternoon more than thirty years ago, that John King was playing center field for Selma, Alabama, in the Southeastern League, against Pensacola, Florida. Selma was leading, 3–1, in the last half of the ninth inning, but Pensacola had filled the bases with two out, and the count on the batter had gone to three balls and two strikes.

In these historic circumstances, the batter, a left-handed hitter, lofted a lazy fly out to King. King stood patiently, waiting with outstretched glove to make the last put-out.

"Float on down here, little ball," he said. "Old John King is waiting to catch you. Come on down, now."

This the ball did. But to the astonishment of one and all, it popped out of his glove and fell to the ground. The Pensacola runners were already moving. Savagely, King pounced on the ball while his teammates shouted for him to throw it to the plate. Instead, in his consummate rage, he took the ball in his teeth, trying to tear it apart as he would a juicy apple, and the game was lost while John King tried to eat the baseball.

Neither money nor the passing of the years has lessened John King's burning hatred of left-handers. There are some who will tell you that he might have been the greatest ballplayer of all time if it had not been for the southpaws, and though this is an exaggeration, it is true that left-handers wielded a mysterious power over him that robbed him of his great strength when he needed it most and finally reduced him to the stature of ordinary mortals. Now fifty-six and long out of baseball, John King has neither forgotten nor forgiven.

The vast word-of-mouth literature that makes up the legend of John King frequently violates all the laws of credibility. On the other hand, many of the stories, improbably enough, are true. No one can now be found who actually saw John King sitting on the steps of the dugout, malevolently sharpening his spikes with a long file, though this is part of the legend. Yet it is true that he ran the bases as though the devil himself were after him, and many an old ballplayer in the Southwest still carries the mark of John King's spikes.

If the play was close and he was called out, he was infuriated. "Damn it, man!" he would bellow to the umpire. "Old John King *refuses* to be out!"

Once, with Lubbock, in the West Texas League, he was called out at second base on an attempted steal. The injustice of it all outraged him.

Spreading wide his arms, he appealed to the blue sky and cried in an aggrieved voice, "May God strike me dead if I was out!"

Everyone in the park waited tensely for the bolt to strike. When nothing happened, King relaxed. Triumphantly, he turned to the umpire. "See," he said, "he didn't!"

When he was with Cisco, in the same league, he encountered a Fancy-Dan shortstop named Bobby Stow in an exhibition game, and Stow, who had a flair for throwing runners out in the last step, treated the mighty John King with an irreverence that, for one game, threatened his very sanity.

His first time at bat, he hit a sharp bounder down to Stow, who held the throw for a split second and then threw him out by half a step. Disgusted, King returned to the bench, muttering darkly. The next time up, he hit a high hopper over the pitcher's head. With a tremendous burst of speed, Stow crossed over and again nipped King by half a step.

Enraged, King kicked furiously at first base until he had knocked it loose from its buckles. Then he carried it out to right field and hurled it over the fence. Slowly he walked back in and went over to the surprised shortstop.

"Now let's see you throw old John King out," he said.

When with Ardmore, in the Western Association, King taunted a young left-handed pitcher so successfully that the young man imprudently charged our man. It was a one-blow affair. King threw a bucket of water in the pitcher's face, and the latter warily opened his eyes.

"What happened?" he asked.

"Why, son, you just got hit by old John King," King explained kindly.

In another game the same pitcher had two strikes on King when King suddenly stepped out of the batter's box and pointed a finger at him.

"I'm old John King," he announced, somewhat unnecessarily, "and men walk around me like I was a swamp. I'm going to hit your next pitch and drive it into the next state. As I go around the bases, I'm going to undress all the infielders with my spikes. Then, if you're not already running, I'm going to chase you out of the park."

So saying, John King spat in the dust and stepped back into the batter's box. Having no choice, the frightened young southpaw wound up, threw and ducked. And old John King, bless him, struck out, swinging.

All that night he raged at his misfortune to be cast with left-handers. The next morning he was still trumpeting his disgust from the porch of the ramshackle hotel where the team was staying when a string was lowered silently from the manager's third-story window with a piece of paper on the end of it. It was John King's release.

Sadly he went to Fort Smith, Arkansas, the curse of left-handers still weighing heavily on him. Against right-handers he was his usual devastating self. Against southpaws he was more defenseless than ever, and his fury increased. One afternoon in Fort Smith, a whimsical fan brought a beribboned pet pig to the ball game. Poor John was having all sorts of trouble trying to cope with the opposing southpaw, when, late in the game, he popped up for the fourth successive time. Unfortunately, the pig picked that precise moment to run out on the field. With one mighty swipe of his bat, John King killed him.

A few weeks later he was walking down the street with another player when they passed a blind beggar with a violin. King reached into his pocket, drew out a quarter and dropped it into the beggar's cap. In his gratitude, the beggar began to play. Suddenly King wheeled. The blind man was fiddling left-handed. Indignantly, King snatched his quarter out of the cap.

"Damn it," he said to the other player, "I can't seem to get away from 'em."

Even players on his own team steered a careful course around King, particularly left-handers. Once he was playing the sun field when a hitter drove a low line drive at him. Unable to see, he threw up his hands and, by the merest chance, the ball caromed off his glove and rolled insolently to the wall, while the batter galloped happily around the bases for an inside-the-park homer. Considerably chagrined, King retrieved the ball finally and threw it in to the pitcher. Humorlessly, the pitcher, in an ill-considered gesture of contempt, flung it back at him. John King stalked in to the mound, threw one punch and flattened his own pitcher.

It got so that even spectators were in jeopardy. John King did not enjoy being heckled, and there is a story that, in Dallas, where he was the prime target of grandstand jockeys, he once appeared dramatically at the ball park with an armload of dripping meat and bones, which he hurled at the spectators, crying the while, "Here, you wolves, catch this!"

It was, however, the fan in Oklahoma City who asked for it and really got it—with a bottle. It was this particular citizen's dodge to seat himself on a three-legged stool outside the park and yell at King through a knothole. For days the voice tormented King with abuse. Finally, one afternoon while the outfielders were shagging fly balls in a pre-game warm-up, King heard the familiar voice nagging him. "Yah-yah-yah!" it went. "Yah-yah-yah!"

The hairs on the back of John King's neck stood up and a dangerous glint came into his eyes. Quietly he eased away from the other players and stole out of the park. Slipping along the outside of the fence, he came to a corner. There were voices on the other side. Stealthily, King stooped over and picked up an empty bottle. Then he peered around the corner. There, with friends, was his antagonist.

Suddenly the man noticed that King was not on the field with the other players. "I wonder," he mused aloud, "where that no-good King went."

King bellowed like an enraged bull. "Here I am!" he yelled. And with that he let fly.

The bottle, betimes, caught the voice from the knothole squarely between the eyes and tumbled him off his stool while his friends scattered wildly. Hearing the commotion, a policeman rushed up.

"What happened here?" he demanded.

King pointed to the limp figure on the ground. "He attacked me," he said simply.

John King played his first baseball at Polytechnic College in Forth Worth, Texas, circa 1912, doubling in the fall as fullback on the football team. In 1913 he made his debut in the Texas League with Fort

Worth as a pinch hitter, but after twelve games in which he was confronted by what seemed like an entire league full of nothing but left-handers, he slipped quietly into the limbo of the lower leagues, happy to find an occasional right-hander on whom to wreak his vengeance.

The Texas League, where he reappeared briefly on several subsequent occasions, represented the pinnacle of his success. Each time the routine was the same. Word would come from the Central League or the Cotton States League that a brawling young giant named John King was burning up the circuit. Back he would come to the Texas League, only to fail against left-handers again. There was a war, too, and a ruptured appendix, and even John King could not win over it all.

Once it looked as though he might make it. In an exhibition game with the New York Giants, when he was with Oklahoma City, he threw a runner out at the plate with a rifle-like shot from deep left field that made John McGraw's eyes bug. When King trotted in at the end of the inning, McGraw patted him on the shoulder.

"You've got something there," he said. "Keep playing ball like that and you'll be in the major leagues before you know it."

Then McGraw and the Giants found out about John King and the left-handers.

It was always the same. The Boston Braves hinted once that they were interested in King. Several years later he was released by Galveston, in the Texas League, and he decided to advise the Boston club of his availability.

"Am loose and going good," he wired hopefully.

The Braves were unimpressed. "Stay loose and keep going," they answered.

So John King sank even lower into the minors, his greatness wasting. Men still marveled at his great strength, his speed, his throwing arm and his batting prowess against right-handers. But there was also his temper and the mysterious spell cast over him by left-handers. More and more he railed against his plight.

One afternoon a small boy whistled to him in the outfield for help in scaling the fence. King obliged and the youngster clambered over and skipped away toward the bleachers. Unfortunately, he made one fatal mistake. He stopped suddenly, playfully scooped up a pebble from the grass and threw it—with his left hand. John King whirled on him angrily, grabbed him and threw him back over the fence.

"What do you mean," he roared at the shrinking figure, "trying to sneak into this ball game?"

When the war came, John King went to Europe with the army and stayed for part of the occupation. Finally he came home and looked around to see what had changed. Almost immediately he protested.

"Fifty thousand left-handed soldiers went to France," he said, "and all fifty thousand of them came back without a scratch. There is no justice."

Because of the humiliation inflicted on him by southpaws, King began punishing himself for his failures against them. When he was with Longview, in the East Texas League, for example, he struck out one afternoon at a most inopportune moment on a sweeping curve thrown by an enemy portsider. In disgust he broke his bat over the dugout steps and then went to the water pail and drew a dipper of ice water. Holding the dipper high, in the manner of a man proposing a toast, he shouted so that all in the park could hear, "John King, you'd like a drink of water, wouldn't you? Your jaws are dry and there's cotton on your tongue and your taste buds need sprinkling! But, dang your worthless hide, you're not going to get any water! You're not going to drink one swallow until you've got yourself a hit off the cunnythumbed varmint of a pitcher out there!"

With that, he hurled the dipper in the direction of the pitcher, kicked over the water bucket and sat down in the dugout. Fortunately, late in the game, he did indeed scratch one puny infield single off the pitcher, and did therefore permit himself one lovely swallow of ice-cold water.

Fact and legend demonstrate John King was such a man. But, curiously enough, the most widely circulated John King story never happened at all.

Even though it never happened, there is scarcely an old-time Texas ballplayer now alive who does not insist he remembers a singular afternoon at Abilene, Texas, when John King was engaged in a particularly bitter duel with a rookie left-hander. King used all his tricks, but the young pitcher refused to blow up. Finally King laid down a bunt and rocketed down to first base before the pitcher could field the ball.

Puffing mightily, he asked for time out and retired to the dugout, where he filled his mouth with water. Play was duly resumed on his return to first base, and the next hitter responded by driving the ball into center field for a long single. King was off like a shot.

Unfortunately, the umpire was stationed behind the pitcher's mound, according to the vogue of the day, and he was obliged to turn his back to observe the flight of the ball. King thereupon dashed straight across the diamond behind the umpire's back and squirted water in the startled pitcher's face as he raced past. Then, in a great cloud of dust and clods, he slid into third base, got to his feet, and squirted water in the third baseman's face.

The umpire, discovering King on third base, naturally assumed he had arrived there via second base, and was disposed to call him safe when the crowd started to descend menacingly onto the field. Hurriedly he changed his decision, and John King, who might have changed the whole conception of baseball, was ingloriously out.

Since John King denies that the incident ever happened, it is obvious that someone has been tampering with the legend. However, he does concede that he often spit in left-handed pitchers' faces, though never in Abilene.

Actually, it was his custom to fill his mouth with water at third base, and, while the pitcher was winding up, dash out to the mound, squirt the water into his face, and then run back to third base while the pitcher, helpless to stop his windup without committing a balk, pitched the ball and suffered in silence.

"I spit in an awful lot of left-handers' faces that way," King says happily.

It was only a moral victory, however. In 1930 John King had run out his string as a player. Reluctantly he hung up his spikes. The left-handers had triumphed. John King had never reached the major leagues.

Then he did an astonishing thing. He became an umpire. John King umpired in the Texas League for a year before he found out that he had oil on his property. As an ump he was almost as tempestuous as he had been as a player. He once spent most of an afternoon in Galveston arguing with a fan behind first base when he was supposed to be umpiring the bases. The fan was so infuriated that he hunted down King in the umpires' dressing room after the game. King was changing his clothes when the irate spectator, mayhem bent, opened the door. Old John King did not even look up. He simply picked up a broken bat that was standing in the corner, fondled it affectionately in his huge hands, and said quietly, "Stick your head in here and you'll draw back a neck." The fan quickly withdrew.

Ziggy Sears, the erstwhile National League umpire and a graduate of the Texas League, indicated recently that, as he remembered it, King chased the fan clear out of the ball park and into an adjoining parking lot with a .45 in one hand and a gleaming bowie knife in the other. King, who actually did carry a gun frequently, insists, however, that his only weapon on this occasion was a baseball bat and that he wouldn't run that far to catch any fan.

J. Alvin Gardner, president of the Texas League, says that King was an outstanding umpire, but it is doubtful that he was very interested in becoming a great umpire. Most of his pleasure in that capacity came from watching batters knock the ears off left-handed pitchers. It was a soul-satisfying experience to stand behind the plate and watch southpaws suffer.

Toward the end of his one season as an umpire he worked a game in Houston. Shortly before starting time, one of the pitchers, a left-hander, approached him.

"I know you don't like left-handers, Mr. King," he said, "but will you give me a break?"

King looked at him stonily. "Do the best you can," he said. "That's what I'm going to do."

A few minutes later, the other pitcher, also a southpaw, came to him. "Just because I'm a left-handed pitcher doesn't mean you're going to make it tough for me, does it?"

Again King said icily, "Do the best you can. That's what I'm going to do." Then he went behind the plate.

From the outset, both pitchers were in dire straits at the hands of the hitters. Old John King danced in delight as base hits whistled past their ears. Finally he could contain himself no longer. Leaning over the catcher, he asked confidentially, "Did you ever see a left-handed pitcher skipping rope?"

The catcher opined that he had not.

"Well, take a look," John King said happily, as the batter bounced a fast ball through the pitcher's legs. "There is a left-handed pitcher skipping rope."

In 1931 they discovered John King's oil, and he retired from baseball forever. From the proceeds of his holdings, he built a house exactly like Tara in *Gone With the Wind.* Then he and Mrs. King settled down to a life of comparative ease in their mansion on the plains of West Texas.

Still, John is not completely happy. The old bitterness toward left-handers still rankles. When his only son was born, he lived in genuine dread that he would turn out to be a "cunnythumb." At the very beginning, he was shocked speechless when the baby reached for a rattle with his left hand. Frightened, John King called on heaven to witness the cruel injustice. Then, desperately, he stuffed the tiny left hand into a tobacco sack and tied the drawstring around the baby's wrist. There his son's hand stayed until John King was satisfied he was going to be right-handed after all.

During the recent difficulty between the countries he was even under the impression that Hitler was a portsider. "I bought a hundred thousand dollars' worth of War Bonds before I found out he was right-handed," he said solemnly.

A few months ago John King was still endeavoring to explain the mystifying curse of left-handers. "All I know is that I've studied those birds and there is something funny about 'em," he said. "Look around, find a left-hander, watch him. Sooner or later, he'll do one little thing a normal person won't do."

John King shook his head sadly.

"You'll find out," he said. "Just like I did."

SPOT REPORTING

THIS appeared under a Finnish dateline. Does that matter?

Baltic Cooperstown

RED SMITH

THEY PLAYED a ball game here last night, and if there's a stone left upon a stone in Cooperstown today, it's an upset. What the Finns did to the game that Doubleday did not invent shouldn't happen in Brooklyn. Not even under its Finnish name, *pesapallo.*

Although *pesapello* is only about thirty years old, it is a monstrous infant that has grown up to be Finland's national sport. It was invented by Lauri Pihkala, a professor who wears a hearing aid and believes his game was modeled on baseball. Somebody must have described baseball to him when his battery was dead.

"Well," explained a tolerant Finn, "he took baseball and, ah"—he paused to grope for a word meaning "adapted"—"and, ah, mutilated it," he said.

Somebody then performed the same service for the English language while composing program notes to explain *pesapallo* to foreigners.

"The batsman, or striker," wrote this Helsinki Rud Rennie, "must try by power of hit of his own and team-fellows to run from base to base with home-base as final objective. The striker is allowed three serves; i.e., a serve rising at least one-half meter above his head and falling, if not connected by the bat, within base-plate with a diameter of 60 cm."

If that doesn't make you see the game with vivid clarity, there seems little use of further elucidation. Stick around, though, if you've nothing better to do.

Pesapallo hasn't yet achieved Olympic status and was presented merely as an exhibition for about twenty-five thousand spectators in Olympic Stadium. Two nine-man teams came trotting in from the outfield in single file, converged in a V at home plate, and removed caps. Their captains stepped forward and shook hands with the referee, a joker in cinnamon brown carrying a bat, possibly in self-defense. The players wore baseball uniforms, white for one team, malevolent red for the other.

Four other jokers in brown did a lockstep onto the field. These were "assistant controllers" or base umpires. A tasty shortcake in gay peasant costume threw a ball out to the referee and dropped a deep curtsy. The referee fired the ball—which is about the size and weight of a ten-cent "rocket"—to the server and blew a long blast on a police whistle. The game was on.

A *pesapallo* field is a lopsided pentagon 298 feet long and 131 feet wide at its broadest. The pitcher stands across the plate from the batter and tosses the ball straight up like a fungo hitter. Base runners all act like Dodgers gone berserk.

That is, they start for third base and then get lost. First base is just where Phil Rizzuto likes to place his bunts; in Yankee Stadium it would be between third base and the mound. If Finns didn't use chalk lines instead of fences, second base would be against the right-field wall. Third is directly opposite, on the left-field boundary. The route from there home is a dogleg to the left. The plate is a trash-can cover, two feet in diameter.

The pitcher may fling the ball as high as he chooses, but if it doesn't drop on the garbage-can lid it's outside the strike zone. Two successive faulty serves—they must be consecutive—constitute a walk, but the batter goes to first only when there are no runners aboard. Otherwise the runner who has advanced farthest takes one more base.

The batter gets three strikes, but nobody is required to run on a hit except on the third strike. Players are retired only on strikeouts, pick-offs, or throws that beat them to a base. On a fly that is caught, the batter is only "wounded"; he is not out.

A wounded man just stands aside and awaits his next turn at bat. One who has been put out may not bat again in the same inning; if his turn comes around, they skip him. An inning ends after three put-outs or after all nine men have batted without scoring a run. (This can happen if enough men are wounded.)

That's about all, except that over the fence would be a foul ball if there were a fence. Hits must bounce in fair territory. A Ralph Kiner would be a bum in *pesapallo;* a Leo Durocher, whose fungo stick is a squirrel rifle that can brush a fly off an infielder's ear, would be a Finnish Willie Keeler.

This game progressed at bewildering speed, with the ball practically always in motion. There is no balk rule. The server would fake a toss for the batter and whip the ball to a baseman on an attempted pick-off. The baseman would fake a throw back and try the hidden-ball play. Infielders, outfielders, and the pitcher-catcher, they heaved that apple around with the sleight-of-hand of the Harlem Globetrotters.

They played the hit-and-run, with the batter clubbing the ball into the earth like a man beating a snake, then standing still at the plate while the base runners sprinted across the landscape. Everybody showboated frantically. Base umpires lifted cardboard signs to signal "safe" or "out," and the referee announced decisions on his whistle in a sort of Morse code of dots and dashes.

Finally a guy named Eino Kaakkolahti slapped a bounding ball past one infielder, through a second infielder, and past an outfielder, with one runner on base. It was a triple, which counts as a home run in Finland. That was as much as one foreigner could take.

HISTORY

Can You Spare a Dime?

ROBERT SMITH

NINETEEN THIRTY-ONE was the year in which sore-footed young ex-salesmen, unfrocked executives, paper millionaires, businessless businessmen, and laborers with no labor to do found themselves reminded on street radios (with an apologetic semi-laugh for telling an old joke) that "there are no rich people any more" and that, if there was to be an end to the hunger which was lapping so close, they—the dispossessed themselves—must reach down into their empty pockets and "share" what they did not have with the unidentified hordes of pitiful folk who had even less.

Men who were waking in a tremble in the morning, to give a quick thanks that they still had jobs, more often than not rode into the shop or office to hear a solemn talk from a suddenly sober and early-rising executive about the need for a wage cut, a payless payday, and a percentage contribution to the national fund for the unemployed.

But the people were comforted by the fact that the man they had made President on a "four-more-years-of-prosperity" platform was, if not in person, then at least through the medium of his ghostly spokesman, expressing "continuing anxiety for the maintenance of the national standard of living." The standard of living meanwhile was fighting a losing battle without appreciating what great men stood in its corner, or just outside it, urging it on. The United States Steel Company set the style for every other major industry by dealing out a 10-percent pay cut. People who had saved for a rainy day, in the good old American style, were left out in the rain as banks defaulted.

There were, however, at least in the minds of those who ate

regularly, if somewhat less sumptuously than before, greater threats abroad in the land than mere starvation. William Green of the American Federation of Labor, in the face of Lord knows what temptation, refused to surrender the laboring man to the dread languors of the dole—or "unemployment insurance," as those crackpots who favored the scheme persisted in naming it. And leading politicians and newspaper commentators railed against the foolish fear that was keeping people from buying things. Nobody was ever going to be better off, they insisted, unless each one of us went right out and started to buy something—anything—right now, to get the cash to flowing again. One or two, in response to this plea, may have sent a few pennies trickling down the dry stream bed, but they were not enough to unleash the floodwaters nearly everyone had been wallowing in only a few years before.

But at least, in those dreary days, when a man might be asked three times in the same block if he had a dime to spare, and when he had to stare out of car windows at overwhelming posters where big overalled men with their oversize hands in their pockets promised him "I Will Share," there were some mighty good ball games to watch or listen to.

The National League had given up the lively ball, so that in the National League parks the games on exhibition were more in keeping with the times—without inflated batting averages, overlong hits, or bloated scores. And it was in keeping with the times that the baseball hero of 1931 should be a dirty-faced, underpaid, hungry-looking center fielder who had entered baseball on the rods of a freight car. Many a man who had spent the whole morning and part of the afternoon wearily slapping his thinned-out shoe soles against strange pavements, stiffly smiling at erstwhile friends who now wished he would crawl off somewhere and leave them in peace, endlessly listening to his own pallid voice as it tried to recite, without anxiety, its possessor's qualifications for some stingy employment, discovered in the broadcast of the 1931 World's Series a sweeter anodyne than drink. Edging in among the crowd before some enormous bulletin board, he could look a well-fed neighbor in the eye and talk baseball with him as if together they owned the earth. He could yell with the unrestraint of a man whose meals were assured for months uncounted. He could groan and shake his head over strikeouts, errors, and other woes petty enough for the rich to recognize. And when the victory came, he could grasp the arm of the man near him and, in the few last moments before the man became a wary stranger, remind him loudly of the things they had just learned together—how the game was won and lost, how close disaster came, how great, how unbelievably great this little Pepper Martin was!

Pepper in that Series was indeed unbelievably great. Most fans had hardly heard his name in the season before the Series began; and the previous season he had been just a bench rider, an athletic spare tire, kept in case of emergency. In this Series he was the hero three times over. In one game he did enough to enshrine him for a year in the records of the Series. Then in the next game, and in the next, he showed new skill, new daring, new proof that the fellow at the very bottom of the heap was sure to have his day.

Some of the feats he performed were stunts that fans of another day had come to look for in championship baseball—feats which the return of the dead ball had resurrected. Others were mighty deeds with the bat which properly belonged to the modern age.

In the first game, which Philadelphia won, as most fans expected they would, Pepper Martin got three solid hits off Lefty Grove, who was then at the top of his skill and strength. In the second game, which St. Louis won, Martin made two hits, stole two bases, and scored the only two runs. He ran the bases in a manner so heedless of his physical safety that he had the fans screaming with excitement. He slid into bases on his chest, smearing the dirt on himself and his uniform, spurting it high along the base lines, risking a broken nose, a split skull, cracked ribs.

Pepper got on base in the second inning of the second game by lining a single into left field. He rounded first base as Al Simmons rather lazily fielded the ball on the bounce. Simmons slipped to one knee and bobbled the ball a little as if he were trying to find the handle. Pepper kept right on going to second, flinging himself safely into the base with the abandon of a maniac. He took a big lead on second, backing away from the base so that he could keep his eye on both pitcher and second baseman. When big George Earnshaw, the Philadelphia pitcher, started his throw to the plate, Martin broke for third, again landing safely in his breakneck fashion, despite the lightning throw of Mickey Cochrane, who was then supposed to be the best catcher in either league. Wilson, the batter, then drove the ball to deep right center, where Mule Haas caught the ball on the run. Martin scored easily after the catch. He had moved himself into scoring position by his own dash and daring.

In the seventh inning Martin singled again. When he broke for second, he had Mickey Cochrane so nervous that Cochrane heaved the ball almost into the outfield, and Martin again slid safely into the base. Wilson, next at bat, sent an easy roller to the shortstop; but while Wilson was being thrown out at first, Martin charged on to third and stood in scoring position once more. Gabby Street, the St. Louis manager, then put out the sign for the old running squeeze play, which had been laid in mothballs ever since the advent of the lively ball. As soon as George Earnshaw committed himself to the pitch, Martin broke at top speed for home. Gelbert, the St. Louis shortshop, bunted the ball toward the pitcher. Earnshaw was on top of the ball in a flash and flipped it backhanded to Cochrane. It came in just too high, however, and Martin's tough, wiry frame dove under it for the second run.

When the Athletics brought the Series back to their home town and back to the lively ball, experts thought surely their obvious superiority would begin to tell. St. Louis had won one game because a mediocre outfielder had played over his head. Now he had certainly spent his nickel.

But the air in Philadelphia agreed with Pepper Martin, and he liked the lively ball. In the second inning of the third game, Pepper came to bat with one man on base and one out. He swung on Grove's first pitch for a clean single over second base. Bottomley, who had been on first, went all the way to third. Then another relic of old-time "inside" baseball was pulled out of the attic—the hit-and-run play this time. Wilson, the batter, played his part neatly. The ball went right into the hole left by the second baseman. Wilson reached first, Bottomley scored, and Martin arrived safely at third. Gelbert then sent a long hard liner (this American League ball did take a ride!) straight into the hands of the Philadelphia right fielder—but the ball had carried so far that again Martin scored easily after the catch.

In the fourth inning it was Martin again. Chick Hafey opened the St. Louis inning with a single to center field. Then Pepper came up, took a good look at Lefty Grove's famous fireball, and lambasted it from here to Sunday. It rode fast and far toward the right-field scoreboard while the Philadelphia fans, all yelling for Pepper now, stood up and howled: "Home run! Home run!" The ball, however, struck just a foot short of the top and bounced back into play. Hafey was held on third while Martin made two bases. The next two batters went out. Then old Burleigh Grimes (he was thirty-eight) drove out a single that scored both Martin and Hafey. The St. Louis Cardinals won that game 5–2 and were leading the Series two games to one.

The Athletics won the fourth game 3–0, to tie up the Series. But once more Martin blazed into the box score and made sportswriters dream up new adjectives for him. Except for Martin, Earnshaw would have had a no-hit game. Martin made two hits, one a two-bagger, and stole a base. On Pepper's first visit to the plate, Earnshaw had fanned him, and that made Pepper grit his teeth. "I'm going to sock this guy and sock him plenty," he growled to his teammates. He socked him, too; but no one else did. And even though Martin stole a base after his first hit, the Cardinals went scoreless.

The next day, Pepper won the game for St. Louis. He made three hits, one of them a home run, and drove in four of the five St. Louis runs.

In this game, Gabby Street, apparently convinced now that Martin was no flash in the pan, had moved the little center fielder up to fifth place in the batting order. (He had been batting seventh.) In the fourth inning he swung at a ball and missed, stepped out of the batter's box, picked up a handful of gravel and tossed it into the box ahead of him, then stepped back into the box and hit a home run. Frisch was on base at the time, so this meant two runs for St. Louis.

At this point in the game Pepper Martin's wife burst into tears. "He's always been a hero to me," she said. "When we were in grammar school I stood on a soapbox to cheer him. . . . Now when the crowd starts to yell for him my eyes get misty."

In the eighth inning Pepper made his twelfth hit of the Series, tying a major-league record, and sending in still another run. He tried to steal second this time, but Cochrane nailed him with a perfect throw. When Pepper went out to the center field a fan greeted him by flinging a shower of torn-up scorecards over the rail. The tatters fluttered down all over the grass. Pepper, illustrating another superstition, called time and spent five minutes picking up every last scrap of paper. He liked to have the grass all clean behind him.

When the teams returned to St. Louis, and the home-town crowds came out to yell for Pepper, his hitting streak came to an end. St. Louis lost the sixth game 8–1, and Pepper got on base only once, with a base on balls.

In the last game, St. Louis won the World's Championship, but Martin had gone into eclipse. He got a base on balls on the first trip to the plate and immediately stole second base. That seemed to finish him. He went out on a pop fly the next time, grounded out after that, then struck out for his last time at bat. Just to show whose Series it was, in the last half of the ninth inning, with two out and the tying runs on base, Martin ran in from deep center to make a one-handed catch of Max Bishop's high fly, thus ending the game and the Series.

Martin was mobbed when the Series was over. People from all over the country had poured presents upon him: rifles, hunting trophies (Martin's two hobbies were deer hunting and automobile racing), and a big red pepper. Commissioner Landis, his ruddy face made even ruddier by excitement, grabbed Martin's hand and told him fervently, "I wish I could change places with you, Martin."

Martin, having seen too much of the world to lose his balance, replied immediately, "O.K. If you'll swap your fifty thousand a year for my forty-five hundred."

After the Series, Martin started on a vaudeville tour. The Series had paid him an extra $4,500, and his vaudeville contract gave him $1,500 a week. His advisers urged him to cash in while the cashing was good. He might not have so many more years in baseball. . . . Pepper put in four weeks on the stage, then quit with five weeks to go.

"I ain't no actor," he said. "I'm a ballplayer. I'm cheating the public."

Martin, though a conscientious and scrappy ballplayer for several more seasons, never quite attained the same heights again. He was, however, a member of one of the most famous teams of this period—the St. Louis Gashouse Gang of 1934. On this same team were two other men, who, with Lou Gehrig and Joe DiMaggio, became the most widely noted ballplayers of the post-Babe Ruth era. They were Dizzy Dean, whose real name was either Jerome Herman or Jay Hanna, and Leo Durocher, who later became the manager of the other famous team of the time—the Bums of Brooklyn.

Dizzy Dean won his first fame as a pitcher when he was a soldier in the Regular Army, a neurotic, footloose boy, the son of a sharecropper who had been a semipro ballplayer. When, after pitching a number of victories for his Army team, Dean was offered thirty dollars a week to play for a semipro club in San Antonio, his father managed to secure Dizzy's discharge. In 1929 Dean won sixteen straight for the San Antonio club, and in the fall he was picked up by a St. Louis scout and signed to play for the St. Louis farm team in Houston. He was shifted in the spring, however, to another St. Louis farm, St. Joseph, Missouri, where he made an immediate success, not only by his pitching but by his swaggering manner, his willingness to pitch into a fight, his complete good nature, and his public eccentricities—which were still a marketable item in those days.

He went back to Houston before the end of the 1930 season, when he was the idol of all St. Joseph and the despair of the St. Joseph manager, who had had to pick up his IOUs, pay his carelessly contracted hotel bills, and even get him out of jail. With Houston, Dean continued to win (and to cut up) and he was taken up by the parent club in time to pitch a three-hit shutout against the Pittsburgh Pirates just before the season ended. St. Louis won the championship that year, but Dean was not eligible for the World's Series and so missed, by a matter of weeks, his first chance to cash in properly on his really unmatched ability.

The following spring he made a name for himself, in the St. Louis training camp, as a bigmouth with a swelled head, for he talked his own ability up continually and in any company; and he tried, in the matter of keeping hours, to imitate a few of the great stars, whom he knew he could equal. His habit of signing IOUs for the club to pick up was forestalled, and he was taught to limit himself to a dollar a day; but he refused to yield to the type of discipline Manager Gabby Street felt was good for a young recruit and good for the club. He was too damn fine a pitcher for that sort of treatment, Dizzy insisted, and, so insisting, he found himself sent back to Houston for "seasoning."

It is possible that his nature might have made it impossible for him ever to get through a training season with a big-league club, although one look at him was all a man needed in those days to see that he was one of the greatest who had ever played the game. In Texas, however, he married a smart, patient, and devoted girl who gave him the sort of private buildup and sound advice most boys of that type need to keep them even with the world. Dizzy was not, as a few wisecrack specialists of the day propounded, a man who was in love with himself. He was almost typical of the boy who has not quite grown out of an uneasy childhood, where his only hope for matching his fellows is through almost tearful bragging, lying, fighting, inventing of romantic backgrounds and adventures that never took place.

Dean had been a raggedy little cotton picker when he should

have been going to school; and when he should have been living in a secure home, running with playmates he had known since he could talk, he was traveling in a ramshackle car with his father and brothers from one backbreaking job to the next. The Army to him had been a refuge, where a kid could get regular meals, shoes, clean clothes, and a proper bed to sleep on.

His ability with a baseball was the only thing Dean owned, when he was a kid (he was only nineteen when he signed first with Houston), that offered him a chance to vaunt himself on fairly equal terms with boys who had been to school, had known clean clothes, and had taken meals for granted. His boasting, when he was breaking in to baseball, was almost hysterical—fantastic far beyond belief, haphazard to the point of senselessness. He gave himself two different names and three different birthplaces in his eagerness to create a background and a personality that people would want to hear about. He contradicted himself, made promises he sincerely meant to keep, and broke them immediately because he sincerely thought he was doing right to change his mind.

Steering him through this morass of adolescent antics were two people he had been lucky to meet: his wife, who was determined that her Dizzy was going to win the good things he deserved, and a newspaper writer named J. Roy Stockton, who realized how much ability the boy possessed and who owned the patience, the good nature, and the human sympathy to see, through Dizzy's vainglorious babbling, the essential sweetness of the boy's nature.

For Dizzy Dean was not only the finest baseball pitcher of modern times, but an unusually intelligent boy with a great fondness for people, a sharp wit, and, at the bottom of his heart, an honest desire to work his head off for the people who liked him.

In this era, between the end of the Hoover regime and the entry of the United States into the Second World War, there were several distinct types of successful professional ballplayers; and it is well to remember in judging them that practically all of them were still boys, many very poor boys, and that most of them had to grow up in the public prints, with each silly boast, thoughtless threat, and angry recrimination baked into hard type and left for the world to stare at.

Without his fiery speed ball and his sharp-breaking curve, Jerome Herman Dizzy Dean would have been just a goodhearted and unhappy little braggart, cheated by poverty of a chance to develop his better-than-average mind. As he grew older, he became somewhat shrewd about his own eccentricities and saw to it that his priceless publicity did not wither and die. But he learned, too, that just being Dizzy Dean out loud was not what made people love and admire him—that he had to work hard and win ball games. So he worked hard and won ball games; and people bought toothpaste carrying his name, paid money for his pictures, gave their kids clothing with his name inscribed, or fed them the breakfast food that the comic strips said Dizzy Dean consumed.

He was at his most attractive when he talked about his brother Paul (who was called "Daffy" only by the sports writers). Paul, three years younger than Jerome, had a lightning fast ball and excellent control. His three-quarters overhand pitching motion was almost the duplicate of Dizzy's, but he did not have Dizzy's spectacular curve—or Dizzy's penchant for talking loudly, loosely, and endlessly. Without his eccentric brother, he'd have been merely a very good pitcher. But to Dizzy he was "faster than me," "better than I ever was," and compared to Paul, said Dizzy, "I'm just a semipro." He saw to it that Paul got his rights, too. He even threatened a strike unless Paul's salary was increased. And Paul repaid his interest by returning the admiration sevenfold and sticking to Dizzy in whatever tempestuous stunt the older Dean felt he had to turn to.

When Dizzy went on strike against appearing in exhibition games or being shown off like a prize dog, Paul went on strike, too, and acted just as angry. When Dizzy repented and came back to work twice as hard, Paul too bore down and won a row of ball games.

Typical of Dizzy Dean's antics, which won him the dislike of a number of people who were not inclined to make allowances, was his childish lobbing of the ball up to Pittsburgh batters in a game where he thought the rest of the team wasn't trying. One of his most famous stunts—made more famous because he did it all over again in front of a photographer—was his tearing up two uniforms (Paul helped him) when manager Frank Frisch suspended him and his brother after they had refused to take the field unless a fine was rescinded. Frisch kept both Deans out of the game after that, in spite of popular clamor, until Dizzy sought the aid of Landis. Landis, after hearing the story, told the Dean brothers quite frankly what a pair of spoiled kids they looked like. And Dizzy, swallowing his pride and his threats with dignity equal to Babe Ruth's, set to and pitched for Frisch some of the finest games of his career.

Dizzy was a good hitter. He loved baseball enough to play any position, and he knew enough about the game to have been valuable anywhere. But he was most valuable to his club in the pitching box. They got their money's worth from Dizzy, too. Not only did he pull countless customers in at the gate; with the aid of Paul, he pitched the Cardinals into a pennant they had practically abandoned hope of winning. That was the year he and Paul won forty-nine games between them. Toward the end of that season, one Dean or another was pitching almost every day.

To see Paul and Dizzy pitch a doubleheader was like seeing the same man do a perfect job twice. From the center-field bleachers it was not easy to tell them apart. They were built alike and were about the same size. Their motions were nearly identical, both smooth, almost effortless sweeps of the arm halfway between sidearm and overhand. To a batter, there was not much to choose between that streaking fast ball of Paul's and the crackling curve that Dizzy could pour in.

Dizzy shortened his own career by pitching when he had to favor a broken toe. The toe had been hurt when he was pitching his heart out in an All-Star game. When his better nature was appealed to, Dizzy was as generous with his skill and strength as he was with his money. And with money he was another of those who "did not know the value of a dollar"—just as if a kid who had worked from dawn to dark for a grudging fifty cents did not know more about what money was and wasn't worth than any news writer alive.

Dizzy got into many a row, with his own teammates, with opponents, with newspapermen, and with the president of the league. He could take a licking with good grace, and he could dish one out. And when he locked horns with the president of the league, he did not exactly come in second. This last set-to came about because Dizzy, harried by a sudden new ruling which forced him to make a distinct pause after his pre-pitching stretch and before sending the ball to the plate, made extra-long pauses which delayed the game interminably. The umpire penalized him for this; and afterward Dizzy found occasion to declare publicly that umpire George Barr and president Ford Frick were "a pair of crooks." Frick, he went on to say, was "our great little president—but a pain in the neck to me."

For this *lèse-majesté,* Frick suspended Dean and ordered him to New York. Dean denied making the remarks. A newspaper reporter insisted he had. Frick, who, like many other men, thought that a boy becomes a man when he gets a wad of money, insisted on a "written retraction." He wrote it and asked Dean to sign it. But there Dean balked. "I ain't signing nothing," he announced. And he did not sign it, either. Frick lifted the suspension, apparently realizing at last that you could no longer kick a man out of the game just for losing his temper at the boss.

Perhaps not the high point of his career, but certainly the episode that becomes him best, was his fulfillment of a promise to a hospital full of crippled kids to strike out Bill Terry, who was then playing manager of the Giants. The kids had assured Dizzy they would be listening to the radio account of the game, and Dizzy said he would, if possible, fan Terry with the bases full. In the ninth inning of the game next day, with two out and the Cardinals one run ahead, the first two men hit safely. The next man was Critz and after him came Terry. Critz got a base on balls. Dean walked toward Terry and smiled. "I hate to do this, Bill," he said. "But I done promised some kids I'd fan you with the bases full. That's why I walked Critz."

Then Dizzy went back to the mound and poured his fast ball through for two quick strikes. With two strikes on a good hitter, the traditional—and safest—thing to do is to waste a ball; that is, give the batter a chance to hit a bad ball. But Dizzy fogged the next one, waist-high, across the center of the plate, and Terry just stared at it. That was strike three. Dizzy came chuckling in to the bench.

"Bill never figured I'd dare put the last one right through the middle," he explained.

Dizzy, when his arm was gone, managed to keep pitching for a time on his craft. And perhaps he could have held a baseball job for many years more, with his brains and hitting power. He chose, however, to accept an offer to broadcast baseball games over the radio; and his local following, as he flaunted his personality on the air, remained as large as ever. So great was his influence on the small fry of St. Louis that a schoolteacher once gently reproved him for using "ain't" on the air.

"Shucks," said Dizzy. "Everybody knows what 'ain't' means!"

Dean played a little baseball, too, on barnstorming tours with Satchel Paige, the best-loved and best-known Negro star of recent days. In various small towns throughout the West, Dizzy would pitch for one team and Old Satch for the other. Neither one had even a suggestion of his old speed and curves, but they were good enough to throw two or three fairly successful innings against semipros. And Dizzy, grown paunchy from lack of training, loved to knock the ball from here to there. He hit a triple against Satchel once, and arrived at third so out of breath that he could hardly stagger. "I've got to stop hitting that ball so fur!" he laughed.

HISTORY

IN THE FIRST *Fireside Book of Baseball* there appeared an aerodynamic study of a curve ball as tested in the wind tunnel of a modern aircraft company. It had nothing on old Will White, back in 1877, as this excerpt from a classic book by the legendary A. G. Spalding will show. Mr. Spalding's 542-page account of America's National Game (that was its title) was published in 1911 and today is a collector's item.

The Non-Conversion of Colonel Joyce

ALBERT G. SPALDING

ARTHUR CUMMINS of Brooklyn, was the first pitcher of the old school that I ever saw pitch a curved ball. Bobby Matthews soon followed. This was in the early seventies. Both men were very light, spare fellows, with long, sinewy wrists, and having a peculiar wrist-joint motion with a certain way of holding the ball near the fingers' ends that enabled them to impart a rotary motion to the ball, followed by a noticeable outward curve.

In 1874 Tom Bond inaugurated the present style of pitching or, rather, underhand throwing, with its in-curves and out-shoots. This style of delivery was then in violation of the straight-arm pitching rules, but umpires were disposed to let it go, and thus gradually, in spite of legislation, the old style gave way to the new.

In the first year of the existence of the National League several of its pitchers began the delivery of the curved ball, that is, a ball which, after leaving the pitcher's hand, would curve to the right or left, and could be made to deceive the batsman by appearing to come wide of the plate and then suddenly turn in and pass over it; or, appearing to come directly over the plate, to shoot out, missing it entirely.

The result of this work on the part of the pitcher was to make hitting much less frequent and small scores characterized all well-played games. In 1877, as a result of the curved ball, a hot controversy arose into which many scientists were drawn. Distinguished collegians openly declared that the "curved ball" was a myth; that any other deflection of a thrown ball than that caused by the wind or opposing air-currents was impossible. Men high up in the game clung strenuously to the same opinion. Col. J. B. Joyce, who had been a ruling spirit in the old Cincinnati Red Stockings, held to this view. It was absurd, he claimed, to say that any man could throw a ball other than in a straight line. A practical test was made at Cincinnati in the presence of a great crowd to convert the Colonel. A surveyor was employed to set three posts in a row, with the left-hand surface of the two at the ends on a line with the right-hand surface of that in the middle. Then a tight board fence about six feet high was continued from each end post, also bearing on the straight line drawn. Will White, one of the most expert twirlers of the day, was selected to convert Col. Joyce. The test took place in the presence of a big crowd and was a success in everything but the conversion. White stood upon the left of the fence at one end, so that his hand could not possibly pass beyond the straight line, and pitched the ball so that it passed to the right of the middle post. This it did by three or four inches, but curved so much that it passed the third post a half foot to the left. Col. Joyce saw the test successfully performed, but he would not be convinced.

SPOT REPORTING

The 1959 All-Star Game

BOB STEVENS

HANDCUFFED his first three times up, Willie Mays broke loose from his shackles with a triple in the eighth inning today and left the American League for dead.

The incomparable Giant shattered a 4-to-4 tie by ripping into a Yankee Whitey Ford serve and driving it 420 feet into right-center field to score Hank Aaron and do all sorts of other interesting things.

The high hit eluded the desperately clutching glove of Detroit's Harvey Kuenn to give the National Leaguers a 5–4 victory over the Americans in the 26th annual All-Star classic.

It also snapped a two-game winning streak by the Americans, reduced their all-time edge to 15–11, and made it a rather complete day for the San Francisco Giants by sending southpaw Johnny Antonelli into the winners' circle.

The other Giant in this spectacular didn't do so well, however. Orlando Cepeda went four times to the well and got clobbered by the bucket each time. He failed to get the ball past the first line of defense, and totaled five outs as the result of a double play, two pops to shortstop and a foul to first base.

The first six innings were almost completely pitcher-dominated and then the hitters took charge. The Americans snapped a 1–0 drought created by a first-inning home run by Eddie Mathews off Early Wynn with a four-bagger over the wall by Al Kaline off Lew Burdette with two out in the fourth, and it was 1–1.

The Americans tied into Pittsburgh's Roy Face, the 12–0 relief pitching phenom, driving him out of sight with a three-run explosion in the eighth for a 4–3 and then here comes Willie.

Ford, the Yankee southpaw, was greeted by an eighth-inning opening single up the middle by St. Louis' Ken Boyer, and Pittsburgh's Dick Groat successfully sacrificed.

Milwaukee's undeniable Aaron collected his second single, a roaring job over shortstop, to score Boyer for 4–4, and Mays was convoyed to the plate by the throaty roars of 34,763 restless, expectant customers who contributed $104,303.46 to the players' pension fund.

Ford worked carefully but not too well on the unsmiling Willie. With the count two balls and one strike, he got a fast ball high and away and Mays attacked it. Kuenn gave it an honest pursuit, but the only center fielder in baseball who could have caught it just happened to hit it.

As Aaron pounded home, Willie, looking back, loped easily into third and there no longer was a Ford in the future. Whitey went to the garage, and Bud Daley, the Kansas City southpaw with the withered right arm, took the mound. Chicago's Ernie Banks and Cepeda were his easy victims.

Antonelli didn't have to work hard to receive credit for the victory, his first in five All-Star appearances. He came to the rescue of the well-massaged Face in the eighth with three runs across and Americans lurking off second and third bases.

Johnny A. walked Washington's Roy Sievers, then got Chicago's Sherm Lollar to ground into a force at third to end the inning. He was the pitcher of record when the Nationals, with Mays delivering the coup de grace, demolished the Ford in the bottom half of the round.

Willie's rocket was the ninth and last hit by the victors, one more than the power-packed Americans could total during this exciting two-hour-and-30-minute battle. And if you didn't like this one, for the first time in the game's history you can get a shot at an encore when the same casts collide again in the Los Angeles Coliseum on August 3.

Don Drysdale, the great Lost Angeles Dodger side-wheeler, went the first three innings for the Nationals and nailed nine in a row, striking out four with an unforgettable performance.

Wynn, the 39-year-old White Soxer, did almost as well. Matthews, second up, smased a home run deep into the right-field seats, his first All-Star HR in his fourth game. And Banks doubled in the second. Milwaukee's Burdette was fidgeting around the mound when the Americans tied it in the fourth on Kaline's number-two iron-type line-drive home run over the left-field bricks.

Yankee Ryne Duren, the myopic flame-thrower, went the next three innings for the Americans and escaped unscathed, although Mays was lucky to do the same. Duren flattened him in the fourth just before striking him out.

Jim Bunning of Detroit was minding the store when the Nationals broke loose for two runs and a 3–1 lead in the seventh, and in this round Kuenn grew wee little goat's horns.

Banks doubled, barely missing an all-the-wayer as the ball crashed into the light tower just to the right of the scoreboard. Cepeda went out to shortstop, a limp loft, and Wally Moon took a called third strike.

Del Crandall collected his first All-Star hit, a single, and Banks galloped across. Kuenn foolishly tried to throw out Ernie at home, something a rifle couldn't have done, and Del waddled unchallenged down to second.

Crandall scored behind Pittsburgh Bill Mazeroski's ensuing bolt into left field, and it was that giveaway run that prevented this one from going into extra innings.

Face, who has a fabulous 17–0 relief-job record dating back to last year, retired the side in the seventh and had two down in the eighth when he became unglued.

Nellie Fox singled, Kuenn walked, and Cleveland's Vic Power singled to tally the Fox. Ted Williams, making his fifteenth, and probably his last, All-Star appearance, walked as Face seemed quite content to keep all pitches away from the big man from Boston.

Pittsburgh fans, bitter in their disappointment at the failure of their civic and national hero, let out a pitiful groan when San Francisco-born Gus Triandos, the Baltimore backstop, banged a double off the embattled Face to drive ElRoy out of the box and drive across Kuenn with the tying run and Power with the go-ahead tally.

After Willie's game-winning blow, the Americans gave Chicago's Don Elston fits before finally succumbing. Don wiped out Frank Malzone on a pop to Banks and struck out Minnie Minoso of Cleveland.

Then came a little excitement.

Fox missed a ninth-inning right-field home run by inches before singling and going to second on a wild pitch. Kuenn, trying desperately to make up for his throwing goof two innings earlier, crashed one far over the left-field wall, again just barely foul.

Harve then fouled out to third baseman Boyer and pounded his bat savagely into the ground in a fit of monumental frustration as Boyer settled under the ball that ended it all.

POETRY

NOVELIST, critic, short story writer, John Updike is essayist and poet as well, and in those two forms his love of baseball has had extraordinary results. One was his 1960 article in *The New Yorker* about Ted Williams' last game (it was reprinted in *The Third Fireside Book of Baseball* and many other places). Another is this poem, written more than thirty years ago.

Tao in the Yankee Stadium Bleachers

JOHN UPDIKE

Distance brings proportion. From here
the populated tiers
as much as players seem part of the show:
a constructed stage beast, three folds of Dante's rose,
or a Chinese military hat
cunningly chased with bodies.
"Falling from his chariot, a drunk man is unhurt
because his soul is intact. Not knowing his fall,
he is unastonished, he is invulnerable."
So, too, the "pure man"—"pure"
in the sense of undisturbed water.

"It is not necessary to seek out
a wasteland, swamp, or thicket."
The old men who saw Hans Wagner
scoop them up in lobster hands,
the opposing pitcher's pertinent hesitations,
the sky, this meadow, Mantle's thick baked neck,
the old men who in the changing rosters see
a personal mutability,
green slats, wet stone are all to me
as when an emperor commands
a performance with a gesture of his eyes.

"No king on his throne has the joy of the dead,"
the skull told Chuang-tzu.
The thought of death is peppermint to you
when games begin with patriotic song
and a democratic sun beats broadly down.

The Inner Journey seems unjudgeably long
when small boys purchase cups of ice
and, distant as a paradise,
experts, passionate and deft,
wait while Berra flies to left.

GENERAL

WITH the unexpected death of Bart Giamatti barely weeks before what would have been his first World Series as commissioner of baseball, his place was taken by his deputy, Francis T. (Fay) Vincent, Jr., whom many thought of as a more prosaic man. Was he? This piece appeared in the *Washington Post* the following April.

The Real Hero of the 1989 World Series

FAY VINCENT

I INTEND no disrespect to either Dave Stewart or the Oakland A's, but for me the real hero of the 1989 World Series was Commander Isiah Nelson of the San Francisco Police Department. A week ago, Cmdr. Nelson was killed when his motorcycle crashed into a cement barrier on Interstate 280.

The earthquake on Oct. 17, 1989, was a significant disaster. But, like most tragedies, it had its unexpected benefits. I grew to know, respect and admire Commander Nelson.

I met him first at the 1989 All Star Game at Anaheim. I next saw him on the field at Candlestick Park before the earthquake. He was in charge of the police at Candlestick, and cut an impressive figure in his motorcycle uniform. He was trim and ruggedly handsome, and part of his allure, I am sure, was his appearance. As we chatted idly before the game, neither of us could suspect what was about to happen.

And when it happened, Commander Nelson quickly and effectively took charge. My recollections of the moments after the earthquake focus on him. He was calm, fully in charge, crisp and incredibly helpful. He came immediately to my box at the edge of the field to give me the early reports on the damage. As information about the disaster reached us, he was careful to give me what limited facts he had, and to answer my questions clearly and precisely. He knew his job, and he was sensitive to mine.

Our first major problem was that auxiliary generators were not connected to the public address system—an oversight that has since been corrected at every major-league ballpark. One of our principal objectives was, therefore, to get information and instructions to the crowd.

Acting in part on Cmdr. Nelson's advice, I quickly called off the ball game. Just as quickly, he produced a squad car in which he circled the field, and using the car's loudspeaker, told the crowd the game had been called. In clear, but authoritative tones, he directed the fans to leave the ballpark in an orderly fashion and to remain calm. There is no doubt that the remarkable evacuation of the ballpark that night, a thing that brought great credit to the city and its people, was due in large measure to the superb leadership of Cmdr. Nelson.

For the next hour or so, I remained in my box while Commander Nelson, working closely with the Giants' personnel, supervised the fans' departure. Information about the magnitude of the quake continued to reach us, and we became increasingly aware of the size of the disaster. Cmdr. Nelson stayed on the field and remained in touch with police headquarters while continuing to monitor activities in the ballpark and in the parking lots.

When the ballpark was nearly empty, he offered to help me get to the hospitality tent outside the park, and politely suggested that I wait there a few hours until he could figure out how to get me and others in my party back to the hotel. During the next several hours, he periodically appeared with updates on both the situation at the ballpark and within the community.

After a few hours, he told me he was going to move his command center, a huge van full of communications gear, to downtown San Francisco and offered to include my car in the caravan his officers would escort. The ride back to San Francisco that night was eerie. As we proceeded, we could see fires burning in the distance, and the blackened city, unlit and smoking, presented an unforgettable image.

Driving through empty streets, and seeing people standing in shock on corners, made us feel inconsequential and mindful of the awesome power of the earthquake.

After an uneasy night in a hotel without power and water, we convened a conference the next morning attended by representatives of every organization with something to contribute to our decision on the future of "our modest little game." Present was Cmdr. Nelson, looking as alert as if he had experienced a quiet evening in his den.

In the weird press conferences that occurred during the next several days, candle-lit and somber as they were, I regularly asked Cmdr. Nelson to report to the press his predictions on police availability. In those circumstances he was as effective and crisp as he was on the field after the earthquake. This man simply knew what he was doing. He was a professional. All of us quickly learned that he was better at what he did than we could ever be at our duties. And so we admired him—all of us—with the respect that flows to a professional doing his job at the highest levels of proficiency.

And when we returned to Candlestick to resume the World Series on that wonderful Friday night, Cmdr. Nelson and I shared the special satisfaction of having persevered through a difficult time. We had shared the equivalent of a battlefield experience. And in that bonding that occurs under such circumstances, Cmdr. Nelson and I forged a relationship each of us knew was unique.

When we parted after the fourth game, and I tried to thank him for all he had done, he gave me the diffident response that comes naturally to the truly heroic. Guys like Cmdr. Nelson are difficult to praise and more difficult to thank. But I tried, and I think he knew he was special to me. Thus, when I learned of his death, I felt the loss one feels at the death of a dear friend.

I will not forget him.

POETRY

AT ABOUT THE SAME TIME this poem was appearing in *The Atlantic Monthly*, another magazine, *Yankee*, was explaining the obvious baseball connection: "Wiffleball . . . the ball that could curve all by itself was invented by David Mullany, a salesman for an auto polish manufacturer. After watching his son 'tearing his arm out trying to make a ball curve,' he got a dozen plastic globes from a nearby perfume factory where they were used to hold perfume. Then he went to work at his kitchen table cutting slits in them with a razor blade."

Wiffle Ball

RONALD WALLACE

Doing my best to hit
the bat, I serve the pitch up
on a platter.
Limp-wristed and slithery
she spins full around
and falls to the ground
dizzy, a fizzle.
Despair floats out
to the makeshift mound
and I catch it.
So I explain
stance, the snap
of the wrist, the quick
eye and level swing, the love
of the game—
all curve balls
to her blunt stare.
And what do I care
anyway? She's nine, and I
can't make her do
anything she doesn't
want to, so there!
She stumps off adjusting
her mask and pads,
shaking off all my signs.

POETRY

Anthem

WILLIAM (SUGAR) WALLACE

Catfish, Mudcat, Ducky, Coot.
The Babe, The Barber, The Blade, The Brat.
Windy, Dummy, Gabby, Hoot.
Big Train, Big Six, Big Ed, Fat.

Greasy, Sandy, Muddy, Rocky.
Bunions, Twinkletoes, Footsie. The Hat.
Fuzzy, Dizzy, Buddy, Cocky.
The Bull, The Stork, The Weasel, The Cat.
  Schoolboy, Sheriff,
  Rajah, Duke,
  General, Major,
  Spaceman, Spook.

The Georgia Peach, The Fordham Flash,
The Flying Dutchman. Cot.
The People's Cherce, The Blazer. Crash.
The Staten Island Scot.
  Skeeter, Scooter,
  Pepper, Duster,
  Ebba, Bama, Boomer, Buster.

The Little Professor, The Iron Horse. Cap.
Iron Man, Iron Mike, Iron Hands. Hutch.
Jap, The Mad Russian, Irish, Swede. Nap.
Germany, Frenchy, Big Serb, Dutch,
  Turk, Tuck, Tug, Twig.
  Spider, Birdie, Rabbit, Pig.

Fat Jack, Black Jack, Zeke, Zack, Bloop.
Peanuts, Candy, Chewing Gum, Pop.
Chicken, Cracker, Hot Potato, Soup.
  Ding, Bingo.
  Hippity-Hopp.

Three-Finger, No-Neck, The Knuck, The Lip.
Casey, Gavvy, Pumpsie, Zim.
Flit, Bad Henry. Fat Freddie, Flip.

Jolly Cholly, Sunny Jim.
  Shag, Schnozz,
  King Kong, Klu.
  Boog, Buzz,
  Boots, Bump, Boo.

King Carl, The Count, The Tope, The Whip.
Wee Willie, Wild Bill, Gloomy Gus, Cy.
Bobo, Bombo, Bozo, Skip.
Coco, Kiki, Yo-yo, Pie.
  Dinty, Dooley,
  Stuffy, Snuffy,
  Stubby, Dazzy,
  Daffy, Duffy.

Baby Doll, Angel Sleeves, Pep, Sliding Billy,
Buttercup, Bollicky, Boileryard, Juice.
Colby Jack, Dauntless Dave, Cheese,
  Gentle Willie,
Trolley Line, Wagon Tongue, Rough,
  What's the Use.

Ee-yah,
Poosh 'Em Up,
Skoonj, Slats, Ski.
Ding Dong,
Ding-a-Ling,
Dim Dom, Dee.

Famous Amos, Rosy, Rusty.
Handsome Ransom. Home Run, Huck.
Rapid Robert. Cactus, Dusty.
Rowdy Richard. Hot Rod, Truck.
  Jo-Jo, Jumping Joe,
  Little Looie,
  Muggsy, Moe.

Old Folks, Old Pard, Oom Paul, Yaz.
Cowboy, Indian Bob, Chief, Ozark Ike.
Rawhide, Reindeer Bill. Motormouth. Maz.
Pistol Pete, Jungle Jim, Wahoo Sam. Spike.
  The Mad Hungarian.
  Mickey, Minnie.
  Kitten, Bunny.
  Big Dan, Moose.

Jumbo, Pee Wee; Chubby, Skinny.
Little Poison.
Crow, Hawk, Goose.

Marvelous Marv.
Oisk, Oats, Tookie.
Vinegar Bend.
Suds, Hooks, Hug.
Hammerin' Hank.
Cooch, Cod, Cookie.
Harry the Horse.
Speed, Stretch, Slug.

The Splendid Splinter. Pruschka. Sparky.
Chico, Choo Choo, Cha-Cha, Chub.
Dr. Strangeglove. Deacon. Arky.
Abba Dabba, Supersub.
Bubbles, Dimples, Cuddles, Pinky.
Poison Ivy, Vulture, Stinky.
Jigger, Jabbo
Jolting Joe
Blue Moon
Boom Boom
Bubba
Bo

AUTOBIOGRAPHY

OUTFIELDERS Paul and Lloyd Waner were known as "Big Poison" and "Little Poison," and Lee Allen recorded that this was not because of what they meant to enemy pitchers but a corruption of "person." It came into being, Allen wrote, "when a baseball writer overheard an Ebbets Field fan continually say, in Brooklynese, as the Waners came to bat, 'Here comes that big poison' or 'Here comes that little poison.' "

Lawrence Ritter has noted that Paul Waner stood only five feet eight inches tall, and weighed less than 150 pounds, and brother Lloyd was even smaller. *The Baseball Encyclopedia* says Paul was three pounds heavier but half an inch shorter than Lloyd. According to that, we have two little poisons. According to pitchers, they were both big poisons: Paul had 3,152 hits lifetime and Lloyd 2,459—a combined total exceeding, as Ritter points out, the total hits of all three Di-

Maggio brothers by more than 500 and all *five* Delahanty brothers by more than 1,000!

(In this piece, from Ritter's *The Glory of Their Times,* Big Poison does indeed refer to Little Poison as his "little brother.")

"I *Liked* to Be Booed"

PAUL WANER

I COME from a little town right outside of Oklahoma City, a town by the name of Harrah. You can spell that backwards or forwards. From there I went to State Teachers' College at Ada. And you can spell that backwards or forwards, too. Which just naturally explains why I've always been a fuddle-dee-dud!

I went to State Teachers' College at Ada for three years, although I didn't really intend to be a teacher. Maybe for a little while, but not forever. What I wanted to be was a lawyer, and I figured sooner or later I'd go to law school. Eventually I was going to go to Harvard Law School, I reckon. That was my ambition, anyway.

But all at once baseball came up, and that changed everything all around. Of course, I was playing ball on amateur and semipro teams all the while I was in high school and college. In those days, you know, every town that had a thousand people in it had a baseball team. That's not true any more. But in those days there were so many teams along there in the Middle States, and so few scouts, that the chances of a good player being "discovered" and getting a chance to go into organized ball were one in a million. Good young players were a dime a dozen all over the country then.

How did they find me? Well, they found me because a scout went on a drunk. Yes, that's right, because a scout went on a bender. He was a scout for the San Francisco Seals of the Pacific Coast League, and he was in Muskogee looking over a player by the name of Flaskamper that Frisco wanted to buy. He looked him over, and sent in a recommendation—that was late in the summer of 1922—and then he went out on a drunk for about ten days. They never heard a thing from him all this while, didn't know anything about him or where the heck he was.

He finally got in shape to go back to the Coast, but on the way back a train conductor by the name of Burns—you know how they used to stop and talk with you and pass the time of day—found out that this fellow was a baseball scout. Well, it so happened that I went with this conductor's daughter—Lady Burns—at school. So naturally—me going with his daughter and all—what the heck—he couldn't wait to tell this scout how great I was. How I could pitch and hit and run and do just about everything. He was such a convincing talker, and this scout needed an excuse so bad for where he'd been those ten days, that the scout—Dick Williams was his name—decided, "Doggone it, I've got something here."

When he got back to San Francisco, of course they wanted to know where the heck he'd been and what happened. "Well," he said, "I've been looking over a ballplayer at Ada, Oklahoma. His name is Paul Waner and he's only nineteen years old, and I think he's really going to make it big. I've watched him for ten days and I don't see how he can miss."

Then Dick quickly wrote me a letter. He said, "I've just talked to the Frisco ball club about you. I heard about you through this conductor, Burns. I told them that I saw you and all that, and I want you to write me a letter and send it to my home. Don't send it to the ball club, send it to my home. Tell me all about yourself: your height, your weight, whether you're left-handed or right-handed, how fast you can run the hundred, and all that. So I'll know, see, really know."

So I wrote him the letter he wanted, and sent it to his home, not really thinking too much about it at the time. But the next spring, darned if they didn't send me a contract. However, I sent it right back, 'cause my Dad always wanted me to go to school. He didn't want me to quit college. My father was a farmer and he wanted his sons to get a good education.

But they sent the contract right back to me, and even upped the ante some. So I said, "Dad, I'll ask them for $500 a month, and if they give it to me will you let me go?"

He thought about it awhile, and finally said, "Well, if they'll give you $500 a month starting off, and if you'll promise me that if you don't make good you'll come right back and finish college, then it's OK with me."

"Why surely, I'll do that," I said.

So I told the Frisco club about those conditions. But it didn't make any difference to them. Because they could offer you any salary at all and look you over, and if you weren't really good they could just let you go and they'd only be out expenses. They had nothing to lose.

So out I went to San Francisco for spring training. That was in 1923. I was only nineteen years old, almost twenty, just an ol' country boy. I didn't even know, when I got there, that they had a boat going across to San Francisco. My ticket didn't call for any boat trip. But after the train got into Oakland you got on a ferry and went across San Francisco Bay. Boy, as far as I was concerned that was a huge ocean liner!

I had hardly arrived out there before I met Willie Kamm, Lew Fonseca, and Jimmy O'Connell. Those three used to pal around together a lot, because they all came from the Bay Area. I was anxious to be friendly and all, so I said to them, real solicitous-like, "Well, do you fellows think you'll make good up here?" (All the while thinking to myself, you know, "Gee, you sure don't look like it to me.")

How was I to know that all three of them *already* were established Big Leaguers? It turned out that they were just working out with the Frisco club until their own training camps opened. But I didn't know that. That was a big joke they never let me forget—a kid like me asking them did they think they'd make good!

Anyway, there I was, a rookie who'd never played a game in organized ball, at spring training with the San Francisco club in the Coast League, which was the highest minor league classification there was. I was a pitcher then, a left-handed pitcher. At Ada I'd played first base and the outfield when I wasn't pitching, but the Frisco club signed me as a pitcher.

The first or second day of spring training we had a little game, the Regulars against the Yannigans—that's what they called the rookies—and I was pitching for the Yannigans. The umpire was a coach by the name of Spider Baum. Along about the sixth inning my arm started to tighten up, so I shouted in, "Spider, my arm is tying up and getting sore on me."

"Make it or break it!" he says.

They don't say those things to youngsters nowadays. No, sir! And maybe it's just as well they don't, because what happened was that, sure enough, I *broke* it! And the next day, gee, I could hardly lift it.

I figured that was the end of my career, and in a few weeks I'd be back in Ada. I was supposed to be a pitcher, and I couldn't throw the ball ten feet. But just to keep busy, and look like I was doing something, I fooled around in the outfield and shagged balls for the rest of them. I'd toss the ball back underhanded, because I couldn't throw any other way. I did that day after day, but my arm didn't get any better.

After the regular day's practice was over, the three Big Leaguers—Willie Kamm, Lew Fonseca, and Jimmy O'Connell—would stay out an extra hour or so and practice hitting, and I shagged balls for them, too. I figured I'd better make myself useful in any way I could, or I'd be on my way back to Oklahoma.

I don't know which one of them mentioned it to the others, but after about a week or so of this they decided that maybe I'd like a turn at hitting. Especially since if I quit shagging for them, they'd have to go chase all those balls themselves. And they didn't relish the idea of doing that.

So they yelled, "Hey, kid! You want to hit some?"

"Sure I do," I said.

So they threw, and I hit. They just let me hit and hit and hit, and I really belted that ball. There was a carpenter building a house out just beyond the right-field fence, about 360 or 370 feet from home plate. He was pounding shingles on the roof, and he had his back to us. Well, I hit one, and it landed on the roof, pretty close to him. He looked around, wondering what the devil was going on. The first thing you know, I slammed another one out there and it darned near hit him. So he just put his hammer down, and sat there and watched. And I kept right on crashing line drives out there all around where he was sitting. Of course, they were lobbing the ball in just right, and heck—I just swished and away it went.

When we were finished, we went into the clubhouse and nobody said a word to me. Not a word. And there was only dead silence all the while we showered, and got dressed, and walked back to the hotel. We sat down to dinner, and still not a single one of them had said "You looked good," or "You did well," or anything like that.

But when we were almost through eating dinner the manager, Dots Miller, came over to my table. He said, "Okie, tomorrow you fool around in the outfield. Don't throw hard, just toss 'em in underhanded. And you *hit* with the regulars."

Well, boy, that was something! I gulped, and felt like the cat that just ate the canary. And from then on I was with the regulars, and I started playing.

Luckily, my arm came back a month or two later, a few weeks after the season started. We went into Salt Lake City, and was it ever hot. Suddenly, during fielding practice, my arm felt like it stretched out at least a foot longer, and it felt real supple and good. It caught me by surprise, and I was afraid to really throw hard. But I did, a little more each time, and it felt fine!

Duffy Lewis was managing Salt Lake City and he knew about my bad arm, so he'd told his players, "Run on Waner. Anytime the ball goes to him, just duck your head and start running, because he can't throw."

There was a pretty short right-field wall at Salt Lake City, and in the first or second inning one of their players hit one off the wall. I took it on the rebound and threw him out at second by 15 feet. Someone tried to score from second on a single to right, and I threw him out at home. Gee whiz, I could throw all the way from the outfield to home plate! I threw about four men out in nothing flat, and after that they stopped running on me. I never had any trouble with my arm after that. It never bothered me again.

I had a good year in the Coast League that first season; hit about .370. Then the next season I did the same thing, got over 200 hits, and batted in about 100 runs. I was figuring by then that maybe I should be moving up to the Big Leagues. Joe Devine, a Pittsburgh scout, was trying to get the Pirates to buy me, but the San Francisco club wanted $100,000 for me, and the Pittsburgh higher-ups thought that that was a little too much for a small fellow like me. I only weighed 135 pounds then. I never weighed over 148 pounds ever, in all the years I played.

So Joe said to me, "Paul, it looks like you'll have to hit .400 to get up to the majors."

"Well, then," I said, "that's just exactly what I'll do."

I was kidding, you know. But darned if I didn't hit .401 in 1925. I got 280 hits that season, and at the end of the year the Pirates paid the $100,000 for me. San Francisco sold Willie Kamm to the Big Leagues for $100,000 in 1922, and then did the same thing with me three years later.

After I got to Pittsburgh early in 1926, I told Mr. Dreyfuss, the president of the club, that I had a younger brother who was a better ballplayer than I was. So the Pirates signed Lloyd and sent him to Columbia in the Sally League to see how he'd do. Well, Lloyd hit about .350 and was chosen the league's Most Valuable Player.

The Pirates took Lloyd along to spring training in 1927, mostly just to look at him a little closer. They never thought he could possibly make the team, 'cause Lloyd only weighed about 130 pounds then. He was only twenty years old, and was even smaller than me.

Our outfield that season was supposed to be Kiki Cuyler, Clyde Barnhart, and myself. But Barnhart reported that spring weighing about 260 or 270 pounds. He was just a butterball. They took him and did everything they could think of to get his weight down. They gave him steam baths, and exercised him, and ran him, and ran him, and ran him. Well, they got the weight off, all right, but as a result the poor fellow was so weak he could hardly lift a bat.

So on the trip back to Pittsburgh from spring training, Donie Bush came to me and said, "Paul, I'm putting your little brother out there in left field, and he's going to open the season for us."

"Well, you won't regret it," I said. "Lloyd will do the job in first-rate style."

And he did, too, as you know. We won the pennant that year, with Lloyd hitting .355. I hit .380 myself, and between the two of us we got 460 base hits that season: 223 hits for Lloyd and 237 for me. It's an interesting thing that of those 460 hits only 11 were home runs. They were mostly line drives: singles, doubles, and a lot of triples, because both of us were very fast.

Don't get the idea that we won the pennant for Pittsburgh all by ourselves that year, though, because that sure wasn't so. We had Pie Traynor at third base, you know, and Pie hit about .340 that season. Pie was a great ballplayer, I think the greatest third baseman who ever lived. A terrific hitter and a great fielder. Gosh, how he could dive for those line drives down the third base line and knock the ball down and throw the man out at first! It was remarkable. Those two Boyer brothers who are playing now are both great fielding third basemen, but Pie could do all they can and more. In addition to his hitting and fielding, Pie was a good base runner, too. Most people don't remember that.

It's a funny thing, but Pie always said that I was the best first baseman he ever threw to. I played first once in a while, not too much, but every so often. I didn't know very much about how to play first base at the beginning, but one of the greatest fielding first basemen of all time practiced and practiced with me, until I knew my way around the bag well enough to make do. That was Stuffy McInnis, the great first baseman of the Philadelphia Athletics' "$100,000 infield" back in 1911 and 1912 and around there.

When I joined the Pirates in 1926, Stuffy was there as a substitute first baseman. He must have been close to forty at the time, and I think that was his last year in baseball. He'd been in the Big Leagues since 1910 or so. But he could still field that position like nobody's business, and he tried to teach me all he knew. I was his roommate in 1926, before Lloyd came up the next year, and Stuffy would spend hours with me in the room showing me how to play first base, using a pillow as a base. Gee, even at that age he was just a flow of motion out there on the field, just everywhere at once and making everything look so easy.

Actually, I was a little too small to make a good first baseman. On the other hand, I was almost as tall as Stuffy McInnes and George Sisler. Neither of them were six-footers. They were a lot bigger than I was, of course. They must have weighed at least 170 or 180. But neither of them was real tall, like most first basemen are.

They say Hal Chase was the greatest fielding first baseman of all time. I never saw him, so I don't know about that. But I did see Stuffy McInnes and George Sisler, and I don't see how he could have been better than them. They were the best I ever saw. I guess every generation has its own, and it's hard to compare between generations.

Although I did see Honus Wagner play, I really did. Honus came back as a coach with the Pirates during the 'thirties. He must have been sixty years old easy, but goldarned if that old boy didn't get out there at shortstop every once in a while during fielding practice and play that position. When he did that, a hush would come over the whole ball park, and every player on both teams would just stand there, like a bunch of little kids, and watch every move he made. I'll never forget it.

Honus was a wonderful fellow, so good-natured and friendly to everyone. Gee, we loved that guy. And the fans were crazy about him. Yeah, everybody loved that old Dutchman! If anyone told a good joke or a funny story, Honus would slap his knee and let out a loud roar and say, "What about *that!*"

So whenever I'd see him, the first thing I'd say would be, "What about *that,* Honus," and both of us would laugh. I guess there's no doubt at all that Honus was the most popular player who ever put on a Pittsburgh uniform. Those Pittsburgh fans were always fine fans, did you know that? They sure were. And I presume they still are, for that matter.

I remember soon after I came up, Pie Traynor said to me, "Paul, you're going to be a very popular ballplayer. The people like to pull for a little fellow."

And that's the way it turned out. In all the 15 years I played with Pittsburgh, I was never booed at home. Not even once. The same with Lloyd. No matter how bad we were, no booing. We never knew what it was like to be booed at home. I don't imagine it would help a fellow any.

Now on the road, I *liked* to be booed. I really did. Because if they boo you on the road, it's either 'cause you're a sorehead or 'cause you're hurting them. Either one or the other. In my first year in the Big Leagues, the players all told me to watch out for the right-field fans in St. Louis. "That right-field stand is tough," they said. "They ride everybody." And, of course, the fellows didn't know whether I could take a riding in the majors or not.

So the first time we went into St. Louis, I figured if they jumped on me I'd have a little fun. And sure enough, as soon as I showed up in right field they started in and gave me a terrible roasting. I turned around and yelled, "They told me for years about all you fans in St. Louis, that all the drunken bums in the city come here. And now that I'm here, I see it's true." I said it real serious and madlike, you know, never cracked a smile.

Oh, did they scream! Well, such as that went on back and forth between us for two or three months. Then one day in the middle of the summer we were giving them an awful licking. I bounced a triple out to right center and drove in two or three runs, and after the inning was over and I came running out to my position they stood up and gave me the very devil. And then, for the first time, I laughed and waved to them.

It so happened that on the very last out of that game a fly ball was hit out to me. I caught it, and then ran over to the stands and handed it to some old fellow that I'd noticed out there every time we played in St. Louis. Well, by golly, they started to clap, and soon all of them were cheering, and do you know that from then on all of them were for me. And that old fellow, any time I got the last ball after that I'd run over and give it to him.

Anyway, like I was saying, we won the pennant in 1927, the first year Lloyd and I played together in the Pittsburgh outfield. That was a great thrill for us, naturally. We even brought Mother and Dad and our sister to the World Series. But then the Yankees beat us four straight, so we weren't very happy about Mother and Dad seeing *that.*

The one thing I remember best about that Series is that I didn't seem to actually realize I was really playing in a World Series until it was all over. The first time we came to bat in the first game, Lloyd singled and I doubled, and from then on the two of us just kept on hitting like it was an ordinary series during the regular season. Neither of us was a bit nervous.

Finally, we came into the bottom of the ninth of the fourth game, with the score tied, 3–3. We were playing at Yankee Stadium, and the Yankees had already beaten us three times in a row. Before I knew what had happened, the Yankees had loaded the bases: Babe Ruth was on first base, Mark Koenig on second, and Earl Combs on third. And there were none out. But then Johnny Miljus, who was pitching for us, struck out Lou Gehrig and Bob Meusel, and it looked like we'd get out of it. While he was working on Tony Lazzeri, though, Johnny suddenly let loose a wild pitch that sailed over catcher Johnny Gooch's shoulder, and in came Combs with the run that won the game, and the Series, for the Yankees.

Out in right field, I was stunned. And that instant, as the run that beat us crossed the plate, it suddenly struck me that I'd actually played in a World Series. It's an odd thing, isn't it? I didn't think, "It's all over and we lost."

What I thought was, "Gee, I've just played in a World Series!"

And you know, I think that's the first time I really realized it. It's funny how much your frame of mind has to do with your ability to play ball. I guess I forced myself not to think about playing in a World Series, so I wouldn't get nervous.

It's the same way with superstitions. Most ballplayers know that such things are silly. But if it gives you a feeling of confidence in yourself, then it'll work. You figure, "If it helps, why not? What have I got to lose?"

Like the time I got six straight hits in a game. That was in 1926, my first year up. I used six different bats, and swung six different times, and came up with six different hits. You just know there has to be a lot of luck in a thing like that. It so happened that Bill McKechnie, who was our manager that year, changed our batting order a little that day, and I was put hitting second instead of third, where I usually hit. So I was in the corner of the dugout, smoking a cigarette, not figuring it was my turn yet, when somebody yelled, "Hey, Paul, hurry up, you're holding up the parade. Get up to bat."

I hustled out to the plate and just grabbed a bat on the way, any bat, I didn't even look. And I got a hit. So I thought, well, maybe that's not such a bad way to do. The next time up I did the same thing, just grabbed a bat blind, not looking, and off came another hit. So I did that all day. Six bats and six hits. (However, that system stopped working the next day, unfortunately.)

After that disastrous World Series, Mom and Dad and Lloyd and I went back home to Oklahoma, and darned if they didn't have a parade and all for us in our home town. Everybody was so happy that I was hard put to figure it out. After all, we hadn't won the Series, we'd lost it, and in four straight games to boot.

Well, it turned out that there had been a lot of money bet there, but it hadn't been bet on the Pirates against the Yankees. It had been bet on the Waner brothers against Ruth and Gehrig. And our combined batting average for the Series had been .367, against .357 for Ruth and Gehrig. So that's why everybody was so happy.

Well, after that 1927 pennant we never won another one, not one single one, all the years Lloyd and I played in Pittsburgh. Gee, that was tough to take. We ended second about four times, but never could get back on top again. We had good teams, too. You know, Pie, Arky Vaughan, Gus Suhr, Bill Swift, Mace Brown, Ray Kremer, all good boys. But we never quite made it.

It'd just tear you apart. We'd make a good start, but before the season was over they'd always catch up with us. And when you're not in the race any more, it gets to be a long season, really long.

The closest we came was in 1938. God, that was awful! That's the year Gabby Hartnett hit that home run. We thought we had that pennant sewed up. A good lead in the middle of September, it looked like it was ours for sure. Then the Cubs crept up and finally went ahead of us on that home run, and that was it.

It was on September 28, 1938. I remember it like it just happened. We were playing in Chicago, at Wrigley Field, and the score was tied, 5–5, in the bottom of the ninth inning. There were two out, and it was getting dark. If Mace Brown had been able to get Hartnett out, the umpires would have had to call the game on account of darkness, it would have ended in a tie, and we would have kept our one-half-game lead in first place. In fact, Brown had two strikes on Hartnett. All he needed was one more strike.

But he didn't get it. Hartnett swung, and the damn ball landed in the left-field seats. I could hardly believe my eyes. The game was over, and I should have run into the clubhouse. But I didn't. I just stood out there in right field and watched Hartnett circle the bases, and take the lousy pennant with him. I just watched and wondered, sort of objectively, you know, how the devil he could ever get all the way around to touch home plate.

You see, the crowd was in an uproar, absolutely gone wild. They ran onto the field like a bunch of maniacs, and his teammates and the crowd and all were mobbing Hartnett, and piling on top of him, and throwing him up in the air, and everything you could think of. I've never seen anything like it before or since. So I just stood there in the outfield and stared, like I was sort of somebody else, and wondered what the chances were that he could actually make it all the way around the bases.

When I finally did turn and go into the clubhouse, it was just like a funeral. It was terrible. Mace Brown was sitting in front of his locker, crying like a baby. I stayed with him all that night, I was so afraid he was going to commit suicide. I guess technically we still could have won the pennant. There were still a couple of days left to the season. But that home run took all the fight out of us. It broke our hearts.

I still see Mace every once in a while, when he comes down this way on a scouting trip. He's a scout for the Boston Red Sox. Heck of a nice guy, too. He can laugh about it now, practically 30 years later. Well, he can almost laugh about it, anyway. When he stops laughing, he kind of shudders a bit, you know, like it's a bad dream that he can't quite get out of his mind.

Well, there's a lot of happiness and a lot of sadness in playing baseball. The last full season that Lloyd and I played together on the Pirates was 1940. That was my fifteenth year with Pittsburgh, and Lloyd's fourteenth. Heck, I was thirty-seven by then, and Lloyd was thirty-four. Of course, we hung on in the Big Leagues with various teams for about five more years, but that was only on account of the war. With the war and all, they couldn't get young players, so I played until I was forty-two, and then my legs just wouldn't carry me any more.

I remember one day when I was with the Boston Braves in 1942. Casey Stengel was the manager. I was supposed to be just a pinch hitter, but in the middle of the summer, with a whole string of doubleheaders coming up, all the extra outfielders got hurt and I had to go in and play center field every day. Oh, was that ever rough! One doubleheader after the other.

Well, that day—I think we were in Pittsburgh, of all places—in about the middle of the second game, one of the Pittsburgh players hit a long triple to right center. I chased it down, and came back with my tongue hanging out. I hardly got settled before the next guy hit a long triple to left center, and off I went after *it*. Boy, after that I could hardly stand up.

And then the next guy popped a little blooper over second into real short center field. In I went, as fast as my legs would carry me. Which wasn't very fast, I'll tell you. At the last minute I dove for the ball, but I didn't quite make it, and the ball landed about two feet in front of me and just *stuck* in the ground there. And do you know, I just lay there. I *couldn't* get up to reach that ball to save my life! Finally, one of the other outfielders came over and threw it in.

That's like in 1944, when I was playing with the Yankees. I finished up my career with them. Some fan in the bleachers yelled at me, "Hey Paul, how come you're in the outfield for the Yankees?"

"Because," I said, "Joe DiMaggio's in the army."

Of course, in a sense, I've never really left baseball, because I've been a batting coach most of the years since I quit playing. I coached two years with the Phillies, two with the Cardinals, six with Milwaukee, and some with the Red Sox. I took the whole organization, not just the Big League club. When the parent team was at home, I'd usually be there. Then, when they went on the road, I'd start flying to all their minor-league clubs.

Even as a batting coach, you know, my small size has helped me. Because the youngsters figure that, me being small and all, I must know *something* about how to hit. It's obvious I can't strong-back the ball, and yet they know I got over 3,000 hits, over 600 doubles, and all that. So they say to themselves, "Gee, he must know the secret." And they listen.

So that's the way it was. Those 24 years that I played baseball—from 1923 to 1946—somehow, it doesn't seem like I played even a month. It went *so fast*. The first four or five years, I felt like I'd been in baseball a long time. Then, suddenly, I'd been in the Big Leagues for ten years. And then, all at once, it was twenty.

You know . . . sitting here like this . . . it's hard to believe it's more than a quarter of a century since Lloyd and I played together. Somehow . . . I don't know . . . it seems like it all happened only yesterday.

FICTION

Goodwood Comes Back

ROBERT PENN WARREN

LUKE GOODWOOD always could play baseball, but I never could, to speak of. I was little for my age then, but well along in my studies and didn't want to play with the boys my size; I wanted to play with the boys in my class, and if it hadn't been for Luke, I never would have been able to. He was a pitcher then, like he has always been, and so he would say, "Aw, let him field." When he was pitching, it didn't matter much who was fielding, anyway, because there weren't going to be any hits to amount to anything in the first place. I used to play catcher some, too, because I had the best mitt, but he pitched a mighty hard ball and it used to fool the batter all right, but it fooled me too a good part of the time so I didn't hold them so good. Also, I was a little shy about standing close up to the plate on account of the boys flinging the bat the way they did when they started off for first base. Joe Lancaster was the worst for that, and since he almost always played on the other side, being a good hitter to balance off Luke's pitching, I had to come close, nearly getting scared to death of him braining me when he did get a hit. Luke used to yell, "For Christ sake get up to that plate or let somebody else catch for Christ sake that can!"

Joe Lancaster wasn't much bigger than I was, but he was knotty and old-looking, with a white face and hair that was almost white like an old man's, but he wasn't exactly an albino. He was a silent and solemn kind of boy, but he could sure hit; I can remember how he used to give that ball a good solid crack, and start off running the bases with his short legs working fast like a fox terrier's trying to catch up with something, but his face not having any expression and looking like it was dead or was thinking about something else. I've been back home since and seen him in the restaurant where he works behind the counter. I'm bigger than he is now, for he never did grow much. He says hello exactly like a stranger that never saw you before and asks what you want. When he has his sleeves rolled up in the summertime, and puts an order on the counter for you, his arms are small like a boy's, still, with very white skin you can see the veins through.

It was Joe hit me in the head with a bat when I was catching. Luke ran up toward the plate, yelling, "You've killed him!"—for the bat knocked me clean over. It was the last time I played catcher; the next time I came out bringing my mitt, which was a good one, Luke said, "Gimme that mitt." He took it and gave it to another boy, and told me to go play field. That was the only thing I didn't like about Luke, his taking my mitt.

I stayed at the Goodwood house a lot, and liked it, even if it was so different from my own. It was like a farmhouse, outside and inside, but the town was growing out toward it, making it look peculiar set so far back off the street with barns and chicken yards behind it. There was Mr. Goodwood, who had been a sheriff once and who had a bullet in his game leg, they said, a big man one time, but now with his skin too big for him and hanging in folds. His mustache was yellow from the chewing tobacco he used and his eyes were bloodshot; some people said he was drinking himself to death, but I'll say this for him, he drank himself to death upstairs without making any fuss. He had four boys, and drink was their ruination. They was it was likker got Luke out of the big league, and none of the Goodwoods could ever leave the poison alone. Anyway, the Goodwood house was a man's house with six men sitting down to the table, counting the grandfather, and Mrs. Goodwood and her daughter going back and forth to the kitchen with sweat on their faces and their hair damp from the stove. There would be men's coats on the chairs in the living room, sometimes hunting coats with the old blood caked on the khaki, balls of twine and a revolver on the mantelpiece, and shotguns and flyrods lying around, even on the spare bed that was in the living room. And the bird dogs came in the house whenever they got good and ready. At my house everything was different, for men there always seemed to be just visiting.

Luke took me hunting with him or sometimes one of his big brothers took us both, but my mother didn't like for me to go with the grown boys along, because she believed that their morals were not very good. I don't suppose their morals were much worse than ordinary for boys getting their sap up, but hearing them talk was certainly an education for a kid. Luke was as good a shot as you ever hope to see. He hunted a lot by himself, too, for my folks wouldn't let me go just all the time. He would get up before day and eat some cold bread and coffee in the kitchen and then be gone till after dark with his rifle or his shotgun. He never took anything to eat with him, either, for when he was hunting he was like they say the Indians were in that respect. Luke reminded you of an Indian, too, even when he was a boy and even if he was inclined to be a blond and not a brunette; he was long and rangy, had a big fine-cut nose, and looked to be setting his big feet always carefully on the ground, and came up on his toes a little, like a man testing his footing. He walked that way even on a concrete walk, probably from being in the woods so much. It was no wonder with all his hunting he never did study or make any good use and profit of his mind, which was better than most people's, however. The only good grades he made were in penmanship, copybooks still being used then in the grammar-school part of school. He could make his writing look exactly like the writing at the top of the page, a Spencerian hand tilted forward, but not too much like a woman's. He could draw a bird with one line without taking the pencil off the paper once, and he'd draw them all afternoon in school sometimes. The birds all looked alike, all fine and rounded off like his Spencerian writing, their beaks always open, but not looking like any birds God ever made in this world. Sometimes he would put words coming out of a bird's bill, like "You bastard," or worse; then he would scratch it out, for he might just as well have signed his name to it, because the teachers and everybody knew how well he could draw a bird in that way he had.

Luke didn't finish high school. He didn't stop all at once, but just came less and less, coming only on bad days most of the time, for on good days he would be off hunting or fishing. It was so gradual, him not coming, that nobody, maybe not even the teachers, knew when he really stopped for good. In the summer he would lie around the house, sleeping out in the yard on the grass where it was shady, stretched out like a cat, with just a pair of old pants on. Or he would fish or play baseball. It got so he was playing baseball for little town teams around that section, and he picked up some change to buy shells and tackle.

That was the kind of life he was living when I finished school and left town. We had drifted apart, you might say, by that time, for he didn't fool around with the school kids any more. I never found out exactly how he broke into real baseball and got out of what you call the sand lot. My sister wrote me some big man in the business saw Luke pitch some little game somewhere and Luke was gone to pitch for a team up in Indiana somewhere. Then the next year he got on the sport page in the papers. My sister, knowing I would be interested in the boy that was my friend, you might say, used to find out about the write-ups and send me clippings when the home paper would copy stories about Luke from the big papers. She said Luke was making nine thousand dollars playing for the Athletics, which was in Philadelphia. The papers called him the Boy Wizard from Alabama. He must have been making a lot of money that year to judge from the presents he sent home. He sent his mother a five-hundred-dollar radio set and a piano, and I admired him for the way he remembered his mother, who had had a hard time and no doubt about it. I don't know why he sent the piano, because nobody at his house could play one. He also fixed up the house, which was in a bad shape by that time. Mr. Goodwood was still alive, but according to all reports he was spending more time upstairs than ever, and his other three boys never were worth a damn, not even for working in the garden, and didn't have enough git-up-and-git to even go fishing.

The next year Luke pitched in the World Series, for the team that bought him from the Athletics, in Philadelphia, and he got a bonus of three thousand dollars, plus his salary. But he must have hit the skids after that, drink being the reason that was reported to me. When he was home on vacation, my sister said he did some fishing and hunting, but pretty soon he was drunk all the time, and carousing around. The next year he didn't finish the season. My sister sent me a clipping about it, and wrote on the margin, "I'm sure you will be sorry to know this because I know you always liked Luke. I like Luke too." For a matter of fact, I never saw a woman who didn't like Luke, he was so good-looking and he had such a mixture of wildness and a sort of embarrassment around women. You never saw a finer-looking fellow in your life than he was going down the street in summer with nothing on except old khaki pants and underwear tops and his long arms and shoulders near the color of coffee and his blondish hair streaked golden color with sunburn. But he didn't have anything to do with girls, that is, decent girls, probably because he was too impatient. I don't suppose he ever had a regular date in his life.

But the next year he was back in baseball, but not in such a good team, for he had done some training and lived clean for a while before the season opened. He came back with great success, it looked like at first. I was mighty glad when I got a clipping from my sister with the headlines, *Goodwood Comes Back*. He was shutting them out right and left. But it didn't last. The drink got him, and he was out of the big-time game for good and all, clean as a whistle. Then he came back home.

It was on a visit home I saw him after all that time. I was visiting my sister, who was married and lived there, and I had taken a lawn mower down to the blacksmith shop to get it fixed for her. I was waiting out in front of the shop, leaning against one side of the door and looking out on the gravel street, which was sending up heat-dazzles. Two or three old men were sitting there, not even talking; they were the kind of old men you find sitting around town like that, who never did amount to a damn and whose names even people in town can't remember half the time. I saw Luke coming up the road with another boy, who didn't strike me as familiar right off because he was one of those who had grown up in the meantime. I could see they were both nearly drunk, when they got under the shade of the shed; and I noticed Luke's arms had got pretty stringy. I said hello to Luke, and he said, "Well, I'll be damned, how you making it?" I said, "Fine, how's it going?" Then he said, "Fine."

After they stood there a while I could see the other boy wasn't feeling any too good with the combination of whisky and the heat of the day. But Luke kept kidding him and trying to make him go up to the Goodwood house, where he said he had some more whisky. He said he had kept it under a setting hen's nest for two weeks to age, and the other boy said Luke never kept any whisky in his life two days, let alone two weeks, without drinking it up. It was bootleg whisky they were drinking, because Alabama was a dry state then, according to the law, even after repeal; Luke must have been kidding too, because he ought to know if anybody does, whisky don't age in glass whether it's under a setting hen or not. Then he tried to make the boy go up to Tangtown, which is what they call nigger town because of the immoral goings-on up there, where they could get some more whisky, he said, and maybe something else. The other boy said it wasn't decent in the middle of the afternoon. Then he asked me to go, but I said no thanks to the invitation, not ever having approved of that, and Tangtown especially, for it looks like to me a man ought to have more self-respect. The old men sitting there were taking in every word, probably jealous because they weren't good for drinking or anything any more.

Finally Luke and the other boy started up the road in the hot sun, going I don't know where, whether to his house or off to Tangtown in the middle of the afternoon. One of the old men said, "Now, ain't it a shame the way he's throwed away his chances." One of the others said likker always was hard on the Goodwoods. Luke, not being any piece off and having good ears even if he was drinking, must have heard them, for he stooped down and scooped up a rock from the road like a baseball player scooping up an easy grounder, and yelled, "Hey, see that telephone pole?" Then he threw the rock like a bullet and slammed the pole, which was a good way off. He turned around, grinning pretty sour, and yelled, "Still got control, boys!" Then the two of them went off.

It was more than a year before I saw him again, but he had been mentioned in letters from my sister, Mrs. Hargreave, who said that Luke was doing better and that his conduct was not so outrageous, as she put it. His mother's dying that year of cancer may have quieted him down some. And then he didn't have any money to buy whisky with. My sister said he was hunting again and in the summer pitching a little ball for the town team that played on Saturday and Sunday afternoons with the other teams from the towns around there. His pitching probably was still good enough to make the opposition look silly. But maybe not, either, as might be judged from what I heard the next time I saw him. I was sitting on the front porch of my sister's house, which is between the Goodwood house and what might be called the heart of town. It stands close up to the street without much yard like all the houses built since the street got to be a real street and not just a sort of road with a few houses scattered along it. Some men were putting in a concrete culvert just in front of the house, and since it was the middle of the day, they were sitting on the edge of the concrete walk eating their lunch and smoking. When Luke came along, he stopped to see what they were doing and got down in the ditch to inspect it. Although it was getting along in the season, there were still enough leaves on the vine on my sister's porch to hide me from the street, but I could hear every word they said. One of the workmen asked Luke when the next game would be. He said Sunday with Millville. When they asked him if he was going to win, he said he didn't know because Millville had a tough club to beat all right. I noticed on that trip home that the boys talked about their ball club, and not their ball team. It must have been Luke's influence. Then one of the men sitting on the curb said in a tone of voice that sounded righteous and false somehow in its encouragement, "We know you can beat 'em, boy!" For a minute Luke didn't say anything; then he said, "Thanks," pretty short, and turned off down the street, moving in that easy yet fast walk of his that always seemed not to be taking any effort.

It was a couple of days later when I was sitting in my sister's yard trying to cool off, that he came by and saw me there and just turned in at the gate. We said hello, just like we had been seeing each other every day for years, and he sat down in the other chair without waiting to be asked, just like an old friend, which he was. It wasn't long before he got out of the chair, though, and lay on the grass, just like he always used to do, lying relaxed all over just like an animal. I was a little bit embarrassed at first, I reckon, and maybe he was, too, for we hadn't sort of sat down together like that for near fifteen years, and he had been away and been a big-league pitcher, at the top of his profession almost, and here he was back. He must have been thinking along the same lines, for after he had been there on the grass a while he gave a sort of laugh and said, "Well, we sure did have some pretty good times when we were kids going round this country with our guns, didn't we?" I said we sure did. I don't know whether Luke really liked to remember the times we had or whether he was just being polite and trying to get in touch with me again, so to speak.

Then he got to talking about the places he had been and the things he had seen. He said a man took him to a place in some city, Pittsburgh, I believe it was, and showed him the biggest amount of radium there is in the world in one place. His mother having died of cancer not much more than a year before that day we were talking must have made him remember that. He told me how he shot alligators in Florida and went deep-sea fishing. That was the only good time he had away from home, he said, except the first year when the Athletics farmed him out to a smaller team. I was getting embarrassed when he started to talk about baseball, like you will when somebody who has just had a death in the family starts talking natural, like nothing had happened, about the departed one. He said his first year in Pennsylvania he got six hundred dollars a month from the club he was pitching for, plus a little extra. "Being raised in a town like this," he said, "a fellow don't know what to do with real money." So he wrote home for them to crate up his bird dogs and express them to him; which they did. He leased a farm to put his dogs on and hired somebody to take care of them for him, because he couldn't be out there all the time, having his job to attend to. Then he bought some more dogs, for he always was crazy about dogs, and bought some Chinese ring-neck pheasants to put on his farm. He said that was a good time, but it didn't last.

He told me about some other pitchers, too. There was one who used to room with him when the club went on the road. Every time they got to a new city, that pitcher made the rounds of all the stores, then the boxes would begin coming to the hotel room, full of electric trains and mechanical automobiles and boats, and that grown man would sit down and play with them and after the game would hurry back so he could play some more. Luke said his friend liked trains pretty well, but boats best, and used to keep him awake half the night splashing in the bathtub. There was another pitcher up in Indiana who went to a roadhouse with Luke, where they got drunk. They got thrown out of the place because that other pitcher, who was a Polak, kept trying to dance with other people's women. The Polak landed on a rock pile and put his hand down and found all the rocks were just the size of baseballs, and him a pitcher. He started breaking windows, and stood everybody off till the cops came. But Luke was gone by that time; so the police called up the hotel to tell Luke there was a guy needed two thousand dollars to get out of jail. So he and three other players went down and put up five hundred apiece to get the fellow out, who was sobered up by that time and wanted to go to bed and get some rest. Luke didn't know that fellow very well and when the Polak went off with the team to play some little game and Luke didn't go, he figured his five hundred was gone too. The fellow didn't come back with the team, either, for he had slipped off, so he figured he had really kissed his five hundred goodbye. But the night before the trial, about three o'clock in the morning, there was a hammering on the hotel-room door and before Luke could open it, somebody stuck a fist through the panel and opened it. And there was the Polak, wearing a four-bit tuxedo and patent-leather shoes and a derby hat, and his tie under one ear, drunk. He fell flat on the floor, clutching twenty-three hundred dollars' worth of bills in his hands. That Polak had gone back to the mines, having been a miner before he got into baseball, and had gambled for three days, and there he was to pay back the money as soon as he could. Luke said he wouldn't take money from a man who was drunk because the man might not remember and might want to pay him again when he got sober; so he got his the next morning. The fine and expense of fixing up the roadhouse wasn't as much as you'd expect, and the Polak had a good profit, unless a woman who got hit in the head with a rock and sued him got the rest. Luke didn't know how much she got. He said all pitchers are crazy as hell one way or another.

He told me about things that he saw or got mixed up with, but he said he never had a good time after he had to give up the farm where he had the dogs and the Chinese ring-neck pheasants. He said after that it wasn't so good any more, except for a little time in Florida, shooting alligators and fishing. He had been raised in the country, you see, and had the habit of getting up mighty early, with all that time on his hands till the game started or practice. For a while he used to go to the gymnasium in the mornings and take a workout, but the manager caught on and stopped that because he wouldn't be fresh for the game. There wasn't anything to do in the mornings after that, he said, except pound the pavements by himself, everybody else still being asleep, or ride the lobbies, and he didn't have a taste for reading, not ever having cultivated his mind like he should. Most of the boys could sleep late, but he couldn't, being used to getting up before sun to go fishing or hunting or something. He said he could have stood the night drinking all right, it was the morning drinking got him down. Lying there on the grass, all relaxed, it didn't look like he gave a damn either.

He had his plans all worked out. If he could get hold of a few hundred dollars he was going to buy him a little patch of ground back in the country where it was cheap, and just farm a little and hunt and fish. I thought of old Mr. Bullard, an old bachelor who lived off in a cabin on the river and didn't even bother to do any farming any more, they said, or much fishing, either. I used to see him come in town on a Saturday afternoon, walking nine miles in just to sit around in the stores looking at people, but not talking to them, or, if the weather was good, just standing on the street. But Luke probably liked to hunt and fish better than Mr. Bullard ever did in his life, and that was something for a man to hold on to. I told Luke I hoped he got his farm, and that now was the time to buy while the depression was on and land was cheap as dirt. He laughed at that, thinking I was trying to make a joke, which I wasn't, and said, "Hell, a farm ain't nothing but dirt, anyway."

After lying there some more, having about talked himself out, he got up and remarked how he had to be shoving on. We shook hands in a formal way, this time, not like when he came in the yard. I wished him luck, and he said, "The same to you," and when he got outside the gate, he said, "So long, buddy."

About six months later he got married, much to my surprise. My sister wrote me about it and sent a clipping about it. His bride was a girl named Martha Sheppard, who is related to my family in a distant way, though Lord knows my sister wouldn't claim any kin with them. And I reckon they aren't much to brag on. The girl had a half-interest in a piece of land out in the country, in the real hoot-owl sticks, you might say, where she lived with her brother, who had the other half-share. I guessed at the time when I read the letter that Luke just married that girl because it was the only way he could see to get the little piece of ground he spoke of. I never saw the girl to my recollection, and don't know whether she was pretty or not.

I have noticed that people living way back in the country like that are apt to be different from ordinary people who see more varieties and kinds of people every day. That maybe accounts for the stories you read in papers about some farmer way back off the road getting up some morning and murdering his whole family before breakfast. They see the same faces every day till some little something gets to preying on their mind and they can't stand it. And it accounts for the way farmers get to brooding over some little falling-out with a neighbor and start bushwhacking each other with shotguns. After about a year Martha Sheppard's brother shot Luke. My sister wrote me the bad blood developed between them because Luke and his wife didn't get along so well together. I reckon she got to riding him about the way he spent his time, off hunting and all. Whatever it was, her brother shot Luke with Luke's own shotgun, in the kitchen one morning. He shot him three times. The gun was a .12 gauge pump gun, and you know what even one charge of a .12 gauge will do at close range like a kitchen.

SPOT REPORTING

UNTIL HIS DEATH in a railway accident late in 1891, Leonard Dana Washburn covered "Grandpa" Cap Anson's Chicago club for the old Chicago *Inter-Ocean*, and the passage of a full century leaves him dimly remembered, if at all. On that account alone, we are most proud to add his name to the family of *Fireside Baseball* authors. Mr. Washburn's elaborate style was in the mode of the day; but what he did with it, as the following story suggests, stamped him one of the funniest baseball writers of all.

1891: Chicago 4, Pittsburgh 3

LEONARD DANA WASHBURN

YOU CAN WRITE HOME that Grandpa won yesterday.

And say in the postscript that Willie Hutchinson did it. The sweet child stood out in the middle of the big diamond of pompadour grass and slammed balls down the path that looked like the biscuits of a bride. The day was dark, and when Mr. Hutchinson shook out the coils of his right arm, rubbed his left toe meditatively in the soil he loves so well, and let go, there was a blinding streak through the air like the tail of a skyrocket against a black sky. There would follow the ball a hopeless shriek, the shrill, whistling noise of a bat grappling with the wind, and a dull, stifled squash like a portly gentleman sitting down on a ripe tomato.

Then umpire McQuaid would call the attention of a person in a gray uniform to the fact that circumstances rendered it almost imperative for him to go away and give somebody else a chance.

There were ten of the visiting delegation who walked jauntily to the plate and argued with the cold, moist air. Mr. Fields lacerated the ethereal microbes three times out of four opportunities to get solid with the ball, and Brer Lewis Robinson Browning walked away from the plate with a pained expression twice in succession. The Gastown folks found the ball six times. Two of their runs were earned.

Mr. Staley, who pitches for the strangers, did not have speed enough to pass a streetcar going in the opposite direction. His balls wandered down toward the plate like a boy on his way to school. If our zealous and public-spirited townsmen did not baste them all over that voting precinct it was because they grew weary and faint waiting for them to arrive. Dahlen continued his star engagement with the bat, getting a single, a slashing double, and triple that missed being a four-timer only by the skin of its teeth.

Even with all this, it is probable that Pittsburgh would have won the game had it not been for a party named Miller, who played short for the wanderers. He covered about as much ground as a woodshed, and threw to first like a drunkard with a cork leg. By close attention to details Mr. Miller rolled up four errors, and three of them cost three runs.

The town boys won the game in the first and second innings. Ryan hit an easy one to Miller as soon as the procession started. Mr. Miller picked up the ball with great agility and hurled it with wonderful speed at an elderly gentleman on the top row of the bleachers. Then Reilly threw Cooney's effort so that Beckley could easily have landed it had he been eighteen feet tall. Carroll's two-bagger brought both Colts in.

In the second Wilmot removed the ball to the left-field fence. Mr. Browning threw to Miller, who at once fixed his eye on third base and threw the ball with unerring directness at president Hart, who was posing on the roof of the grandstand with a haughty smile. Wilmot scored. And in the seventh Willie Forget-Me-Not Hutchinson hit the ball a lick that brought tears to its eyes. Kittridge, who was just due, got a strong reverse English on the leather and started an artesian well in faraway left. Willie came right home.

Bierbauer's single and a measly throw by Kittridge gave a run to O'Neil's pets in the second. Beckley's beautiful triple and a sacrifice by Carroll fetched another, and in the ninth Reilly hit the ball a welt that caused it to go back out over the north wall. That was all.

Grandpa Anson wasn't feeling real well, and said several saucy things to the umpire out loud. He was on first and Dahlen was on second when Carroll hit down to Bierbauer. That person choked the ball on the ground and thereby removed both the man Anson and the man Dahlen. The former claimed interference and tried to explain things to McQuaid in a voice that could have been heard at the stockyards. McQuaid pulled out his watch and began to study the figures, whereupon the big captain moved grandly to the bench, and the show went on.

PROFILE

THIS PIECE was written in 1978, and one senses that its famous author was as embittered as his famous subject at the absence of an Enos Slaughter plaque in baseball's Hall of Fame. "He can only hope that the Veterans' Committee might choose him," Tom Wicker wrote here. Six years later, the Veterans' Committee did choose him.

Enos Slaughter, on His Toes

TOM WICKER

WHEN BILLY Southworth came to Martinsville, Va., in 1935 to look over St. Louis Cardinals farmhands playing in the Class D Bi-State League, he spotted a stocky young outfielder with one glaring weakness and one promising statistic. The kid was hitting a mediocre .275—but more than a third of his hits were going for extra bases. So he hit with power; but to Southworth's experienced eye, he looked too slow of foot for the major leagues. Southworth took the rookie aside and told him he'd have to learn to run. Get out there in the outfield, he said, demonstrating a proper running stride, and start running on your toes. Get off that flat-footed gait or you're going home to plant some more tobacco.

To Enos Bradsher Slaughter, aged 19 and a short jump away from semi-pro ball and the Cavel Manufacturing Company team in his native Roxboro, N.C., that was a life or death choice. Not that $75 a month was much of a fortune even in Depression days, although room and board in Martinsville came to only five dollars a week. It wasn't even that the big leagues, if he could make it that high, offered something nearer wealth, although it was certainly a better deal than the hardscrabble life on a Person County tobacco farm, like the one on which Slaughter had grown up.

It was rather that baseball *was* life to Enos Slaughter—a fact not particularly unusual in his generation of ballplayers, most of them farm boys or slum kids, at a time when the game was truly the national pastime. It was a leisurely era before technology and affluence pushed American life so near hysteria, in the last years before the old game became modern big business.

To be cut in 1935 would have been worse than merely the end of a professional career, even as bad as that would have been: condemnation to semi-pro, with its cheap uniforms, skinned infields, smelly locker rooms (if any). It would have been worse than that, because making it in baseball in 1935 was not just fun and money in the pocket but living up to a myth.

So young Slaughter took Billy Southworth at his word, went to the outfield and started running on his toes; he ran and then he ran some more. Just four days after Southworth's ultimatum, Enos Slaughter went down the first-base line in *four steps fewer* than he had ever before. If a man worked at it, he observed, he could make himself do more than he had thought he could do; that was baseball, and that was America.

In 1936, the Cards sent the Tar Heel rookie with the newly developed speed to the Columbus, Ga., Redbirds of the Class B Sally League—not a bad jump in one season. At Columbus, the home dugout was set back a long way from the base line. In an early game, Slaughter came running in from the outfield to the line; then he walked to the dugout.

Manager Eddie Dyer met him at the steps. "Son, if you're tired," Dyer said, "we'll try to get you some help."

Enos Slaughter never walked to the bench again—or to his position, or to first base if a pitcher gave him a base on balls, or anywhere else on a baseball field. Dyer later taught him the strike zone and how to throw home on one bounce, but running became Slaughter's obsession, partly to keep his legs in shape, mostly because he believed it was part of the game that was his life. A ballplayer ran, because if he didn't he was out—out at first, out at home, out of the game, out of place in baseball.

So on October 14, 1946, when Enos Slaughter took a steal signal from Eddie Dyer, it was nothing unusual for Slaughter to be off and running; that was his style. But this time he wasn't running in the outfield at Martinsville or across the old ballfield at Columbus; this was Sportsman's Park in St. Louis, the big time—in fact, the eighth inning of the seventh game of the World Series. Enos Slaughter, on first base with a single to center, represented the go-ahead run and perhaps the championship of the world.

The score was tied—the Cards 3, the Boston Red Sox 3—when Slaughter led off the home eighth with his hit. He had watched impatiently from first as Bob Klinger retired Whitey Kurowski and catcher Del Rice, playing for the injured Joe Garagiola. Then, with

Harry Walker at the plate and Klinger concentrating on the third out, Dyer, in the Series in his first year as a big league manager, flashed the steal sign.

Slaughter got his usual jump and was tearing for second at high speed, running on his toes, when the left-handed Walker popped a weak fly into center field. Rounding second, cutting his turn short and charging for third, Slaughter saw from the corner of his eye that Leon Culberson was moving to field the ball and that shortstop Johnny Pesky was already running out for a possible relay. To Slaughter, the ball Walker had hit looked like a "dying seagull"; he saw it was going to fall in front of Culberson and the thought flashed through his mind, *I can score on this guy.*

The inning before, the Red Sox had tied the game when Dominic DiMaggio, with runners on second and third, doubled into right field off relief pitcher Harry Brecheen. But DiMaggio had pulled up lame at second with a torn muscle in his leg; Culberson, his replacement, was no DiMaggio in center field and Slaughter knew Culberson's arm was weak. And now, putting his head down, charging around second and digging hard, Slaughter knew what no one else in Sportsman's Park knew—that he was going all the way home.

Third base coach Mike Gonzalez gave no signal at all ("I think he was flabbergasted," Slaughter says) as the runner began to make the turn toward home with no sign of slowing. Behind him, Culberson fielded Walker's hit and threw to Johnny Pesky, still coming out with his back to the infield. Pesky's play was orthodox; Walker had singled with a man on first, and even with Slaughter's jump on the play, the sensible expectation was that he would pull up at third.

So when Pesky took Culberson's throw, he turned *toward second,* cocking his arm to throw, against the remote possibility that Walker would try to pick up an extra base. By then, the wide sleeves of his old-style baseball shirt flapping like wings, Slaughter was around third—hitting the bag at full speed with his left foot, as he had learned to do long before in the minors—and striding on his toes for home, with 36,143 fans standing and screaming him on.

Just as Pesky set himself for a possible throw to second, he caught sight of Slaughter tearing toward home. He reacted quickly enough, but from a disadvantage. He was set for a throw to second and had to shift quickly to his right to make the throw home, a move that would put any right-hand thrower somewhat off balance. Probably as a result, Pesky's peg was short, and it was late.

Red Sox catcher Roy Partee had to come out into the infield in front of the plate to field the ball. Slaughter, racing down the base line at top speed, could have scored standing up, but he didn't. He slid across the plate, climaxing one of the great individual plays in World Series history not with an unnecessary bit of showboating but with an Enos Slaughter trademark. He *always* slid into every base but first, no matter how badly he had a throw beaten, because Enos Slaughter knew he would never be a better ballplayer than the legs that carried him around the bases and over the outfield, and he had seen too many other players go lame—little Dom DiMaggio just the inning before—by having to pull up sharply, from top speed, in order not to overrun a base. He believed it was safer to slide.

So Slaughter turning third, Pesky's fatal "hesitation" (although Slaughter has always defended the shortstop's turn toward second as the proper play in most circumstances), the hurtling slide home all passed into the bottomless repository of baseball lore. There was more drama to come, as there often is in a World Series game; in the Red Sox ninth, Brecheen gave up singles to Rudy York and Bobby Doerr, then forced three straight batters to hit the ball on the ground for infield outs, no one scoring. The Cat became the ninth pitcher in Series history to win three games (he had won two complete games previously, one of them the day before) and the first since Stan Coveleski of the Indians in 1920.

But with that heat-down, game-winning, 270-foot dash from first to home on a weak single (Walker did go to second and got a soft-hearted scorer's "official" double for his dying seagull), Slaughter became *the* Series star and one of baseball's most memorable heroes—if not quite one of its certified immortals. When all else about the 1946 Series, a cliffhanging upset for the Cards, has been reduced to bloodless statistics, Enos Slaughter's break for home will be remembered, retold, elevated into the kind of myth baseball and America love the most—a story of individual effort, "hustle," playing hard, putting out the extra effort that wins the day.

And if the making of that play actually began far away and 11 years earlier in Martinsville with a desperate rookie trying to teach himself to run on his toes, the play itself was not an isolated moment. However orthodox Pesky's handling of the situation, he should have known by then—as Slaughter had known about Culberson's weak arm—that with Enos Slaughter on base and the game and Series possibly at stake, *something* out of the ordinary was likely to happen.

That could have been learned in the fourth game of that same Series, played in Fenway Park. In the sixth inning of the fourth game, the Cards leading 7 to 1, the Red Sox had loaded the bases with one out and had Cardinal pitcher George Munger (who had got out of the service only in August) on the ropes after a walk and singles by Doerr and Pinky Higgins. Hal Wagner ripped into a Munger pitch and, as Arthur Daley wrote in *The New York Times*, ". . . Rudy York was on third when Hal Wagner's towering smash backed Slaughter to the bullpen. York tagged up and raced home, knowing he couldn't be headed off. A throw was so impossibly far that it wouldn't even be attempted. But Slaughter, who never gave up on anything, threw out York at the plate.

" 'What kind of ball do those fellows play?' asked the flabbergasted Rudy. 'No one else would even have attempted that throw'."

Now that quote from York probably should be taken with a grain of salt, since it doesn't sound like any ballplayer of the day, or any day, let alone Rudy York, and since Arthur Daley just naturally loved Enos Slaughter. Another time, Daley wrote, "On the ballfield he [Slaughter] is perpetual motion itself . . . he would run through a brick wall, if necessary, to make a catch, or slide into a pit of ground glass to score a run." But Slaughter's remarkable throw to take the Red Sox out of a possible big inning can't be questioned; there it is in the box score, under "double plays"—"Slaughter and Garagiola."

Arthur Daley also frequently told a story about the fifth game of that Cards-Sox series. A pitch from Joe Dobson caught Slaughter in the elbow, causing agonizing pain. Slaughter "stoically pattered down to first," Daley recalled in a column nearly 20 years later. Then he attributed to Slaughter a quote that may be as fanciful as the supposed words of Rudy York the day before: " 'I wouldn't give nobody the satisfaction of knowin' I was hurt,' said this Spartan."

Quote or no quote, Enos Slaughter promptly stole second base with his arm still wracked with pain. But the Cards lost that day, to return to St. Louis down three games to two. That night on the train, the Cards' team doctor packed the injured arm in ice and told Slaughter he was through for the Series.

"The fellers need me," Slaughter said, or so Daley reported. "No matter what you say, I'm playin'."

So in the sixth game he singled home a run in the winning rally, and in the seventh he dashed to glory. In neither game did the Red Sox try to run on him—the throw to double York at the plate had convinced them he had a gun for an arm, and he never let on that Dobson's pitch had incapacitated it for the rest of the Series. That year, Enos Slaughter was 30 years old, having lost what probably were his three best years physically to the Army Air Corps: the Cards were paying him less than $25,000.

Enos Slaughter's baseball career was destined to last through 1959, a startling 24 years from its beginning in Martinsville. From 1938 on, he was a big leaguer, playing 19 seasons—he was in the Air Corps in 1943, 1944 and 1945—with the Cards, the Yankees in two different tours, the Kansas City Athletics and the Milwaukee Braves. Slaughter was 43 years old when he ended his last season—typically playing hurt, after hitting a foul ball off his own foot, as Milwaukee finally lost the 1950 National League pennant to Los Angeles in a play-off.

He might have hung on another season or two—into his fourth decade of major league ball—as a pinch hitter, but in 1960 Slaughter took a fling at managing (with Houston, then in the American Association).

He retired with a lifetime batting average of exactly .300 for those 19 big league seasons, and given his total of 2,383 major league hits, it's not inconceivable that if he hadn't lost those three vital years to the Air Corps (when he was 27, 28, 29 years old), he'd have reached the rarefied level of 3,000 hits.

A power hitter, but not a home run-or-strikeout muscle man, Slaughter blasted 148 triples and 413 doubles, as well as 169 home runs, thus maintaining for his career the old Martinsville pace that first caught Billy Southworth's eye—more than a third of his hits were for extra bases. And in almost 8,000 at bats, he struck out only 538 times.

On the pennant-winning Cardinals of 1942 ("by far the best team I ever played on," he says today. "We had everything, we just felt we could beat anybody . . ."), Slaughter led the league in hits with 188, led the club and was second in the league with a .318 average and starred in the World Series the Cards won from the Yankees, hitting a home run in the fifth game.

In the Cards' pennant-winning year 1946, coming out of his three years in service, Slaughter hit .300 and led both leagues in runs batted in with 130. In 10 consecutive All-Star games, Slaughter hit .381 for the National League, and when St. Louis traded him to the Yankees in 1954, of all players then active in both leagues, only Stan Musial had more hits, 2,223 to 2,064, and only Ted Williams of the Red Sox had batted in more runs, 1,298 to 1,148.

When the Yankees traded Slaughter to Kansas City in 1955, he was 39 years old; he hit .315 for the Athletics, playing most of the time, and was voted the team's "most popular" player in a year when he took the field—still running—for his 2,000th game.

The next year, at 40, Slaughter was hitting .279 and had played in 90 games—today's brittle stars, take note—when the Yankees sent cash and Bob Cerv to the Athletics (for delivery in 1957) to get him back a week before the September 1 World Series eligibility deadline. The Yanks released Phil Rizzuto to make room on the roster, whereupon Slaughter played six Series games, hit a game-winning three-run homer in the third game and wound up the Series batting .350, including two of the Yankees' five hits off that other indestructible, Sal Maglie, during Don Larsen's perfect fifth game.

But Slaughter, for all his success on the field, never had any financial luck. That year, for example, the Yankees (who won the Series in seven games) voted Rizzuto a full share of the winners' swag, or $8,714. Slaughter was supposedly due only a half-share, but second baseman Jerry Coleman went to Commissioner Ford Frick and asked on behalf of the other players that Slaughter's cut be raised to a three-quarter share. Frick agreed and Slaughter took down $6,536. Yankee clubhouse steward Pete Sheehy got a three-quarter share, too.

At 41 and 42, Slaughter then put in a couple of solid years with the Yankees—.254 in 96 games in 1957, plus .250 in five World Series games against the Braves; then .304, mostly as a pinch hitter with 138 at bats in 77 games in 1958, with another Yankees-Braves Series following.

Late in 1959, still making a contribution to the Yankees, nearly bald by then but still running on and off the field and weighing only three pounds more than the 188 he had hustled along the Martinsville basepaths 24 years earlier, the 43-year-old Slaughter fouled a pitch off his own foot and was out for a week. Then Casey Stengel asked him how he'd like a shot at his sixth World Series; the Yankees were out of the running in the American League, but over in the National Milwaukee, in a stretch race with the Dodgers, needed a left-handed pinch hitter.

The Yankees hadn't bothered to X-ray Slaughter's injured foot; he recalls that he "hobbled" into general manager George Weiss's office and protested, not the proposed deal, but that his foot might prevent him from helping the Braves. Weiss telephoned John McHale of the Braves with the injury news; but McHale told Slaughter, "If you can swing the bat, we can get a runner for you."

So at an age at which almost all his contemporaries were retired, unable to run in his trademark style, but dead game and still eager to play ball, Enos Slaughter went back to the National League, to his fourth club, to another pennant race, and in his first game delivered a pinch-hit single against Bob Purkey of Cincinnati.

The Braves made it through a last road trip to a dead heat with the Dodgers, but lost the play-offs in two games, and Slaughter finished his playing career on a downbeat. Milwaukee took an 8–4 lead into the home ninth of the second game in the Dodgers' temporary home, the infamous Coliseum, a converted football stadium with a short left-field wall that made Fenway Park look like a pitcher's haven. The Dodgers scored five runs in that ninth inning and it was all over. If some heroics of his could have saved it for Milwaukee, as so often they had for St. Louis, that would have made a better ending; but Enos Slaughter's long day was done at last.

Maybe they still play his kind of tough, shrewd baseball in 1978—Thurman Munson of the Yankees comes to mind, and so does Lou Piniella's smart handling of a crucial hit to right field in that year's Yankee-Red Sox play-off game. Piniella couldn't see the ball in the sun but pretended he was making the catch; that held up baserunner Rick Burleson between second and first long enough so that when the ball dropped, Piniella could grab it and fire to third in time to halt Burleson at second. That could be a story about Slaughter, but few play that hard or smart today, and certainly not for the kind of small change Enos Slaughter was paid throughout his career.

From the start, he had given baseball all he had, but baseball gave him little in return except the fun of the game—admittedly no small reward. Even in the fall of 1934, when on the recommendation of Fred Haney, a baseball writer for the Durham, N.C. *Herald,* the Cardinals invited him to a tryout camp in Greensboro, general manager Branch Rickey made it clear that young Slaughter would have to pay his own expenses if the club didn't sign him.

After his 1937 season in Columbus, Ohio, of the American Association—the highest minor league classification—Slaughter thought his league-leading .382, 27 home runs and 122 runs batted in were worth something more than the $150 a month he'd been paid. Hadn't those statistics made him the MVP? Eddie Dyer was later to recall the heyday of the minor leagues and the farm system as a time when "if you needed help you could reach down to Columbus, Ohio, for a broad-tailed kid named Slaughter who was hitting .382."

So Slaughter went to the top. "Mister Rickey," he asked when the season was over, "how about a bonus?" Forty years later he remembered with a chuckle how Rickey "jumped down my throat and said the older fellows had been talkin' to me, puttin' ideas in my head."

No bonus, naturally. And when Slaughter went up to the Cards in 1938, it was for the munificent sum of $400 a month—not for 12 months, of course, but for the five and a half months of the major league season. The old Gas House Gang was breaking up (Dizzy Dean had just been traded to the Cubs), but some of Slaughter's teammates were legitimate stars—Johnny Mize, Joe Medwick, Pepper Martin, Terry Moore ("the greatest defensive centerfielder I ever played with. . . . I've never been back to the wall at no time that he wasn't there to tell you how much room there was and what base to throw to. . . ."). Catcher Bill DeLancey was a particular hero to Slaughter; after a bad case of tuberculosis, DeLancey played in 1940 with only one lung.

Even now, Slaughter professes not to know what any of these fabled ballplayers were being paid—although on the Cardinals of those years it couldn't have been much ("we didn't make no money with the Cards, they all said we was hungry ballplayers"). Back then, he insists, money wasn't much talked about and "nobody ever talked salary in the clubhouse"—maybe because no one had anything much to brag about. Today, with free agents and million-dollar contracts, the publicized jealousies of such as Billy Martin for the monstrous salaries of such as Reggie Jackson not only dominate the headlines but some clubhouses, too.

Slaughter hit .350 for the first three months of his first big league year, then tailed off to .276, an average that would earn a rookie a fat contract in 1978—and which brought him up to $600 a month for the 1939 season, when Ray Blades's Cards finished second; that year, the young outfielder hit .320 and led the league in doubles. That was worth $750 a month to the Cardinals for 1940, and Slaughter responded with an early-season batting tear.

Then came an Eastern road trip that he recalls as if it were yesterday, but not with pleasure. "I left St. Louis hittin' .371 and came back hittin' .216. I went three for 82, the worst slump I ever had" (perhaps not least because of a personal nemesis, one Jumbo Brown, a 295-pound relief pitcher for the Giants, who knew how to get Slaughter out).

That season the Cards were in the race all the way and once Slaughter shook his slump, he was a leading factor in another second place finish, finally batting .306 for the year. He hit a solid .311 in 1941, and on the great 1942 team could pocket $9,000 for the season, plus a Series winner's share.

Slaughter played that Series as an enlisted man in the Air Corps, having signed up in August, and spent the next three years on what sound like some pretty good service ball clubs at Lackland Air Base, Hickam Field in Hawaii and in the southwest Pacific—where the players often had to build the field before they could play their morale-building exhibitions for the GIs. Birdie Tebbetts, Joe Gordon, Howard Pollet, Taft Wright, Ferris Fain, Tex Hughson—Slaughter remembers playing with or against them all, once on Iwo Jima just after its capture.

He came out of the service to give several great years to the Cardinals and in 1949 he hit .336 and led the league in triples, which earned him a $25,000 contract for 1950—the best he ever had. That season, he batted .290 ("a guy'd own a franchise, he hit that much today") and the niggardly Cardinals proceeded to hand him a 10 percent pay cut.

But baseball was beginning to change and TV was waiting in the wings to wipe out the minors and the farm systems and change the atmosphere and traditions of the game. Night World Series competition in the chill of October, for example, would have been unthinkable before TV; so would players who'd had their basic experience not at Martinsville or Columbus but at Arizona State and Southern Cal. Not far ahead were designated hitters, interchangeable parts for pitching staffs, uniforms gaudy as those of a marching band, rugs for playing surfaces and a time when a hangnail or a wounded ego could become a major factor in a pennant race.

Above all, television put money—big money—in the pockets of owners and players alike, and its largesse ultimately permitted free agentry to make capitalists out of second-string outfielders. But Enos Slaughter, who played his 19 major league seasons without an agent or a holdout, just missed the fat years; as they came in, he was past his prime.

Still, when the Cards traded him to the Yankees in 1954, he wept: *The New York Times* ran a picture of one of baseball's celebrated hard guys with his face in his hands. Even though St. Louis president August Busch blustered that he hated to trade "one of the greatest baseball players in the history" of the Cards, but had to in order to build a younger team, and manager Eddie Stanky mealymouthed that "a champion baseball player is going to a champion baseball club," the truth was apparent. Slaughter spoke it through his tears.

"I've given my life to this organization, and they let you go when you're getting old."

That is also the story of baseball, the dark side of the myth, and in Slaughter's case, even the Russians recognized it. In *Soviet Sport,* the Soviet Union's leading sports magazine, the Slaughter trade was singled out as an example of "flesh-peddling in disregard of the player's wishes and rights . . . a typical example of beer and beizbol. The beizbol bosses care nothing about sport or their athletes but only about profits."

Right on, in 1954, and another of the reasons for free agentry today, as well as the fact that the Slaughter deal could not now be made without his consent. But he might not have vetoed it even if he could have, and not just because it got him away from the one pitcher who seemed to have his number, Carl Erskine of the Dodgers; but because for all his fire and dash on the field, in the clubhouse Enos Slaughter was a company man. He never caused trouble for the club, never groused about his paycheck, never gave anything but his best for whatever he was being paid. And it never occurred to him to do anything else.

So he went to Casey Stengel when he reported to the Yankees during a series in Washington, and told the manager he was ready to give him 100 percent; no doubt Stengel already knew that, but when the 38-year-old Slaughter added that he wanted to play regularly (at a time when the Yankee outfield consisted of Mickey Mantle, Hank Bauer and Irv Noren, with Gene Woodling and Bob Derv in reserve), Stengel told him: "My boy, you play when I tell you to play, and you'll stay up here a long time."

Slaughter did; and Stengel, he says, played him against the "tough clubs" and especially against "the tough lefthanders," because for some reason the left-hand hitting Slaughter feasted on left-hand pitching; over his career, he hit better off lefties than off right-handers. One of his special pleasures is that, at 40, he hit the marvelous Billy Pierce "pretty good," and Herb Score, too. He was playing the outfield for the Yankees the day Gil McDougald's line drive hit Score in the eye and doomed his career—a memory that puts Slaughter in mind of a young pitcher he recalls only as "Slayball" who in the early fifties was hit in the eye by a line drive and injured so badly his eyeball was "hangin' out on his cheek." But, "he pitched the next year in Double-A," which to Enos Slaughter was the natural order of things. ("Slayball" was actually Bobby Slaybaugh, who indeed lost his eye in the accident—and who nonetheless attempted a comeback the following year.)

After his seasons with Kansas City, Slaughter didn't want to come back to the Yankees, where he feared he'd play less, and he was saddened to be the cause of Rizzuto's release; but baseball was still his life and he flew dutifully to Detroit, where at the age of 40 he went five for nine playing both ends of a Sunday doubleheader on his first day back under Stengel's command. In those last seasons, the Yankees paid him $18,000 a year, more or less.

After his last stand with the Braves, he went off to manage at Houston in 1960. His team finished third and Slaughter was released; after he paid his own way to the minor league meetings in 1961, he was signed to manage Raleigh (not far from Roxboro) in the Class B Caroline League. That was a farm club of the embryonic Mets and at the Mobile, Ala., training base, Slaughter looked over his "talent" and bluntly notified the higher-ups: "They ain't even Class D players."

He was told rather indignantly that he had at least 15 major league prospects on the Raleigh roster; as it turned out, he took just one of the 15 back to Raleigh, and that year 52 different Met farmhands, he says, paraded through the Raleigh clubhouse, all going nowhere, like the club itself. At the end of the season, Slaughter was released again.

That was the last of organized ball for one of its most dedicated performers; the myth was finished with him. He was never again offered a job, despite innumerable applications over the next few years. Maybe he was too demanding for today's ballplayers; he wouldn't have understood a player begging off the All-Star game with a sore toe. Or maybe he was too hardbitten for jetset owners and youngsters who hadn't been happy to get $75 a month playing baseball in order to get out of the tobacco fields. Maybe his talent evaluations were too merciless for his bosses.

To an interviewer's suggestion that maybe baseball also feared that a rural Southerner of his generation couldn't deal with blacks, he snorted: "Long as they produce for me I don't care if they're red." He'd had blacks at both Houston and Raleigh, he said, and had no trouble, and he'd managed to bridge baseball's lily-white years and the coming of the blacks in the fifties.

In 1970, Duke University's athletic director, Eddie Cameron, hired Slaughter to coach baseball at a school where it was a secondary sport. He had no scholarships to offer, and often lost his best players to a rule that football scholarship men could play baseball only in conference games. Still, he was 16–15 his first year, and usually won a dozen to 15 games in each of the next six seasons, before he was retired.

Meanwhile, in 1966, when he turned 50 years old, Enos Slaughter applied for the pension organized baseball promises to its players and which TV supposedly had inflated. He drew his first monthly check—for $400, the same as his first major league salary—in July, 1966; it was not until six months later, just too late, that he learned that the complicated pensions rules would have entitled him to $800 a month if he'd waited until 1967 to start taking payments. Years of complaints, to various Commissioners of Baseball and to the Players Association have failed to redress this grievance; in fact, Slaughter says his baseball pension, for some quirky reason, has declined to $379 a month. He had paid into the plan for 20 years.

But there was a final way Slaughter might have been rewarded beyond the fun of the game for his 22 professional seasons of dedicated play, hard running and hard hitting. He had earned little money, been shipped like a chattel among unfeeling teams, found no further place in the game that had been his life, and been shortchanged—at least by his reckoning—on his pension. But the baseball writers, if not baseball's officials, could do something. They had the power to vote him into the Hall of Fame.

That alone, to a man who believed he had given the best of his life to baseball, would have been compensation enough, better than any conceivable perquisite or financial reward, final security within the myth. But the writers have not recognized Enos Slaughter either. In 1978, they chose Eddie Mathews, a home run hitter, with Slaughter coming in second. His last chance was 1979, when the 15 years of eligibility to be voted in came to an end; after that, he can only hope that the Veterans' Committee might choose him—which is less desirable than selection by the writers.

Why the Hall of Fame has eluded a player of Slaughter's caliber and longevity is a mystery. It's true that writers for the West Coast and Canadian teams, Texas, Houston, Atlanta, never saw him play; it's true also that (to Slaughter's undisguised disgust) home run hitting is the name of the game in Cooperstown—"You hit a few home runs, don't matter you got a lifetime average .270, .280, you go in. . . . I got the pinky on that thing."

One outfielder he played against—a home-hitter of brief fame—had an arm so weak, he recalls, "he caught a fly 30 feet behind third base. I'd go home on him." But he's in and Slaughter's not.

Whatever the reason, Slaughter tried to console himself that Red Ruffing and Joe Medwick, "who should have been there earlier," didn't make it until their fifteenth years of eligibility; but an interviewer could sense that he didn't really expect any longer to make it. And he is too honest to act as if he doesn't care.

Exclusion from the Hall of Fame seems to have embittered him far more than the shabby treatment he's had from baseball, which he follows fairly closely. He thinks he could have made more hits in modern ballparks with their symmetrical distances and artificial surfaces, and he thinks that although there are "some great ballplayers today," no team has 25 "top-notch major league players. You hit .275, you're a superstar." He doesn't exactly begrudge today's big salaries but—still the company man who respects the boss—he suggests "they've got out of hand a little bit"; and he sees little of his own hustle and desire in today's players, although he likes to point out that "there's been many a game won by runnin' out a pop fly, 'cause if it falls you're on second base." In 1938, he remembers, he hit a grounder back to Bill Lee, pitching for the Cubs, "and he looked at it a couple of times and when he looked up I was almost on first. He was so surprised he threw it away and I wound up on third. A fly ball got me home and we won the game."

But that's all in the past, however alive that past still seems (Slaughter exemplifies William Faulkner's belief that the past not only isn't dead, "it isn't even past"). Now Enos Slaughter farms six acres of tobacco in Person County, N.C., which, after all, he escaped only temporarily back in 1935. He manages about 2,100 pounds to the acre and brief leaf goes these days for at least $1.50 a pound.

There's plenty of time left over for fishing at Kerr Lake, where over the 1978 Fourth of July weekend he and Max Crowder, the Duke trainer, pulled in 53 stripers in four days; and there's good hunting every day in the autumn deer season.

The night Junior Gilliam died ("hell of a ballplayer. I saw him break in with the Dodgers"), just before the 1978 World Series opened, with Helen Slaughter pottering in the kitchen and their daughter Rhonda watching television, Slaughter—aged 62, up to 208 pounds and more than ever fitting the nickname "Country" that Burt Shotton hung on him 40 years ago—summed up his life in baseball:

"I really enjoyed baseball. It was my livelihood. If they wanted me at the ballpark at eight in the morning, I'd be there. I asked no odds and I give none. A guy got in my way, I run over him. If they knocked me down at the plate, I said nothin'. You can't steal first base but if they hit me, I'm on first. And if you don't get on first, you can't score a run."

In the fading light of the myth Enos Slaughter lived—not just the myth of baseball, but the American myth itself—doesn't that get close to a truth? *If you don't get on first, you can't score a run.* So do anything, accept anything, knock down and be knocked down, to get on first, score a run, win the game.

And then what? Don't they let you go when you're gettin' old? And not even the Hall of Fame will bring back a broad-tailed kid who hit .382 at Columbus and ran on his toes everywhere he went.

GENERAL

Louisville Slugger

GEORGE F. WILL

LOUISVILLE, KY.—I don't want to wax mystical and metaphysical about this, but . . .

Stop. I want to wax. If an American boy can't get all worked up about a genuine "powerized" Louisville Slugger baseball bat, what use is the First Amendment's guarantee of the free exercise of religion?

When Thomas Aquinas was ginning up proofs of God's existence, he neglected to mention the ash tree. It is the source of the Louisville Slugger, and hence is conclusive evidence that a kindly mind superintends the universe.

The Big Bang got the universe rolling and produced among the celestial clutter one planet, Earth, enveloped in an atmosphere that causes rain to patter on Pennsylvania ridgetops where ash trees grow. They grow surrounded by other trees that protect the ash trees from wind-twisting and force them to grow straight toward sunlight. The result is wood with the perfect strength required for the musical "crack" that is the sound the cosmos makes each spring when it clears its throat and says, "We made it."

It is spring and a young man's fancy lightly turns to thoughts of . . . well, to that, too, but also to baseball and its instruments. Baseballs are made in Haiti and many gloves are made in the Orient, but the bats that put people on the path to Cooperstown are made, one at a time, where you would expect, in mid-America.

Wood lathes at Hillerich & Bradsby's "Slugger Park" plant take just eight seconds to make a bat for the masses. But craftsmen—the junior member of the work force has 17 years seniority—take longer to make bats for hitting artists. The makers of bats must take care. Ted Williams once returned a batch of bats because the grips did not feel right. They were found to be 5/1000 of an inch wrong.

Hillerich & Bradsby charges $12 for each major leaguer's bat, and loses about $13 on the deal. They do it for the prestige. They must have been relieved when Orlando Cepeda retired. He used to discard a bat after getting a hit. His reasoning, in which I find no flaw, was that there are only so many hits in a bat, that you can't tell how many there are in a bat and that he did not want to risk using a bat from which all the hits had been taken.

The production of real bats has declined because of a monstrous development—the popularity of aluminum bats. Hillerich & Bradsby makes such ersatz Sluggers, but commits that unnatural act in Southern California, a region of novelties and regrets.

Colleges, those incubators of heresies, use aluminum bats for a grotesque reason: They last longer. But immortality is not a virtue in things that should not exist at all. Because metal bats are livelier than wooden bats, they distort the game. Scoring soars, 200-minute games become common and some teams—yes, teams—have batting averages over .350. Aluminum bats in the big leagues would produce every fan's ultimate nightmare: a blizzard of asterisks in the record book, denoting records set after baseball became subservient to the science of metallurgy.

People who will not recognize tradition as a sufficient argument should bow to aesthetic as well as scientific considerations. Aluminum hitting horsehide makes a sound as grating as fingernails scraping a blackboard. If the sound of the aluminum bat were a food, it would be lima beans. Imagine a balmy summer evening, the portable radio on the front porch emitting the soft sizzle of crowd noise. The announcer says: "Here's the pitch—and the runner is off at the ping of the bat!" "Ping"? The prosecution rests.

A. Ray Smith never rests. Louisville, like Renaissance Florence, is not especially large but is immoderately drenched with the finest art of its century, which in the case of Louisville is baseball. Smith has not gotten the word from French philosophers that angst is the right response to the 20th century. But it is hard to get the hang of existential despair when your Triple-A Louisville Redbirds recently drew 1,062,000 fans, more than five major-league teams.

A few of those fans probably were H&B craftsmen who went to the ballpark to see their handiwork put to work. Imagine, working amidst ash chips, which smell better than bacon in the morning. It is enough to make a boy wax poetical: I think that I shall never see a tree as lovely as what folks here make from some of them.